PS3531.0752 A6 1979
33663001373055
The collected stories of
Katherine Anne Porter.

CYP
Pages Scribbled on in pen T.F. CYP 9/2/08

The Collected Stories of Katherine Anne Porter

P9-CDI-723

Other books by Katherine Anne Porter

Flowering Judas and Other Stories
Pale Horse, Pale Rider
The Leaning Tower and Other Stories
The Days Before
The Old Order
Ship of Fools

The Collected Stories of
Katherine Anne Porter

A Harvest/HBJ Book
Harcourt Brace Jovanovich, Publishers
San Diego   New York   London

Copyright 1930, 1935, 1936, 1937, 1939, 1940, 1941, 1944, © 1960,
1965 by Katherine Anne Porter
Copyright renewed 1958, 1963, 1964, 1965, 1967, 1968 1969,
1972 by Katherine Anne Porter
"Virgin Violeta" copyright 1924 by Century Magazine
Copyright renewed 1951 by Meredith Publishing Co.
"The Martyr" copyright 1923 by Century Magazine
Copyright renewed 1950 by Meredith Publishing Co.
"Hacienda" copyright 1934 by Harrison of Paris

All rights reserved. No part of
this publication may be reproduced or
transmitted in any form or by any means,
electronic or mechanical, including photocopy,
recording, or any information storage and
retrieval system, without permission
in writing from the publisher.

Requests for permission to make copies of any part of the
work should be mailed to: Permissions, Harcourt Brace
Jovanovich, Publishers, Orlando, FL 32887

Library of Congress Cataloging in Publication Data

Porter, Katherine Anne, 1894-1980
The collected stories of Katherine Anne Porter.

(A Harvest/HBJ book)
I. Title.
[PZ3.P8315Cp 1979]   [PS3531.0752]   813'.5'2   79-10398
ISBN 0-15-618876-7

Printed in the United States of America

G H I J

Austin Community College
Learning Resources Center

Go Little Book . . .

This collection of stories has been floating around the world in many editions, countries and languages, in three small volumes, for many years. There are four stories added which have never been collected before, and it is by mere hazard they are here at all. "The Fig Tree," now in its right place in the sequence called *The Old Order,* simply disappeared at the time *The Leaning Tower* was published, in 1944, and reappeared again from a box of otherwise unfinished manuscripts in another house, another city and a different state, in 1961. "Holiday" represents one of my prolonged struggles, not with questions of form or style, but my own moral and emotional collision with a human situation I was too young to cope with at the time it occurred; yet the story haunted me for years and I made three separate versions, with a certain spot in all three where the thing went off track. So I put it away and it disappeared also, and I forgot it. It rose from one of my boxes of papers, after a quarter of a century, and I sat down in great excitement to read all three versions. I saw at once that the first was the right one, and as for the vexing question which had stopped me short long ago, it had in the course of living settled itself so slowly and deeply and secretly I wondered why I had ever been distressed by it. I changed one short paragraph and a line or two at the end and it was done. "María Concepción" was my first published story. It was followed by "Virgin Violeta" and "The Martyr," all stories of Mexico, my much-loved second country, and they were each in turn accepted and published in the old *Century Magazine,* now vanished, by good generous sympathetic Carl Van Doren. He was the first editor—indeed, the first person —to read a story of mine, and I remember how unhesitatingly and warmly he said, "I believe you are a writer!" This was in 1923. Several writers or persons connected with literature in some way or another, from time to time in published reminiscences, have done me the honor to mention that they had, so to speak, "discovered" me.

There is no reason to name them, but I shall only say here and now, to have the business straight, it was Carl Van Doren, gifted writer, editor and resourceful friend to young writers, who just lightly tossed my stories into print and started me on my long career, with such an air of it being all in the day's work, which it was, I went away in a dazzle of joy, not in the least thinking of myself as "discovered"—I had known where I was all along—nor looking towards the future as a "career." What unpleasant words they are in this context. "Virgin Violeta" and "The Martyr" were left out of the first edition, I forget why, possibly oversight. A friend fished them out of the ancient *Century* files, got them re-published, after forty-odd years, and so they join their fellows. Every story I ever finished and published is here. I beg of the reader one gentle favor for which he may be sure of my perpetual gratitude: please do not call my short novels *Novelettes,* or even worse, *Novellas.* Novelette is classical usage for a trivial, dime-novel sort of thing; Novella is a slack, boneless, affected word that we do not need to describe anything. Please call my works by their right names: we have four that cover every division: short stories, long stories, short novels, novels. I now have examples of all four kinds under these headings, and they seem very clear, sufficient, and plain English.

To part is to die a little, it is said (in every language I can read), but my farewell to these stories is a happy one, a renewal of their life, a prolonging of their time under the sun, which is what any artist most longs for—to be read, and remembered.

Go little book. . . .

KATHERINE ANNE PORTER
14 June 1965

Contents

Contents

The Leaning Tower and Other Stories

Flowering Judas and Other Stories

María Concepción

María Concepción walked carefully, keeping to the middle of the white dusty road, where the maguey thorns and the treacherous curved spines of organ cactus had not gathered so profusely. She would have enjoyed resting for a moment in the dark shade by the roadside, but she had no time to waste drawing cactus needles from her feet. Juan and his chief would be waiting for their food in the damp trenches of the buried city.

She carried about a dozen living fowls slung over her right shoulder, their feet fastened together. Half of them fell upon the flat of her back, the balance dangled uneasily over her breast. They wriggled their benumbed and swollen legs against her neck, they twisted their stupefied eyes and peered into her face inquiringly. She did not see them or think of them. Her left arm was tired with the weight of the food basket, and she was hungry after her long morning's work.

Her straight back outlined itself strongly under her clean bright blue cotton rebozo. Instinctive serenity softened her black eyes, shaped like almonds, set far apart, and tilted a bit endwise. She walked with the free, natural, guarded ease of the primitive woman carrying an unborn child. The shape of her body was easy, the swelling life was not a distortion, but the right inevitable proportions of a woman. She was entirely contented. Her husband was at work and she was on her way to market to sell her fowls.

Her small house sat half-way up a shallow hill, under a clump of pepper-trees, a wall of organ cactus enclosing it on the side nearest to the road. Now she came down into the valley, divided by the narrow spring, and crossed a bridge of loose stones near the hut where María Rosa the beekeeper lived with her old godmother, Lupe the medicine woman. María Concepción had no faith in the charred owl bones, the singed rabbit fur, the cat entrails, the messes and ointments sold by Lupe to the ailing of the village. She was a good Christian, and drank simple herb teas for headache and stomachache, or bought her remedies bottled, with printed directions that she could not read, at the drugstore near the city market, where she went almost daily. But she often bought a jar of honey from young María Rosa, a pretty, shy child only fifteen years old.

María Concepción and her husband, Juan Villegas, were each a little past their eighteenth year. She had a good reputation with the neighbors as an energetic religious woman who could drive a bargain to the end. It was commonly known that if she wished to buy a new rebozo for herself or a shirt for Juan, she could bring out a sack of hard silver coins for the purpose.

She had paid for the license, nearly a year ago, the potent bit of stamped paper which permits people to be married in the church. She had given money to the priest before she and Juan walked together up to the altar the Monday after Holy Week. It had been the adventure of the villagers to go, three Sundays one after another, to hear the banns called by the priest for Juan de Dios Villegas and María Concepción Manríquez, who were actually getting married in the church, instead of behind it, which was the usual custom, less expensive, and as binding as any other ceremony. But María Concepción was always as proud as if she owned a hacienda.

She paused on the bridge and dabbled her feet in the water, her eyes resting themselves from the sun-rays in a fixed gaze to the far-off mountains, deeply blue under their hanging drift of clouds. It came to her that she would like a fresh crust of honey. The delicious aroma of bees, their slow thrilling hum, awakened a pleasant desire for a flake of sweetness in her mouth.

"If I do not eat it now, I shall mark my child," she thought, peering through the crevices in the thick hedge of cactus that sheered up nakedly, like bared knife blades set protectingly around the small clearing. The place was so silent she doubted if María Rosa and Lupe were at home.

The leaning jacal of dried rush-withes and corn sheaves, bound to tall saplings thrust into the earth, roofed with yellowed maguey leaves flattened and overlapping like shingles, hunched drowsy and fragrant in the warmth of noonday. The hives, similarly made, were scattered towards the back of the clearing, like small mounds of clean vegetable refuse. Over each mound there hung a dusty golden shimmer of bees.

A light gay scream of laughter rose from behind the hut; a man's short laugh joined in. "Ah, hahahaha!" went the voices together high and low, like a song.

"So María Rosa has a man!" María Concepción stopped short, smiling, shifted her burden slightly, and bent forward shading her eyes to see more clearly through the spaces of the hedge.

María Rosa ran, dodging between beehives, parting two stunted jasmine bushes as she came, lifting her knees in swift leaps, looking over her shoulder and laughing in a quivering, excited way. A heavy jar, swung to her wrist by the handle, knocked against her thighs as she ran. Her toes pushed up sudden spurts of dust, her half-raveled braids showered around her shoulders in long crinkled wisps.

Juan Villegas ran after her, also laughing strangely, his teeth set, both rows gleaming behind the small soft black beard growing sparsely on his lips, his chin, leaving his brown cheeks girl-smooth. When he seized her, he clenched so hard her chemise gave way and ripped from her shoulder. She stopped laughing at this, pushed him away and stood silent, trying to pull up the torn sleeve with one hand. Her pointed chin and dark red mouth moved in an uncertain way, as if she wished to laugh again; her long black lashes flickered with the quick-moving lights in her hidden eyes.

María Concepción did not stir nor breathe for some seconds. Her forehead was cold, and yet boiling water seemed to be pouring slowly along her spine. An unaccountable pain was in her knees, as if they were broken. She was afraid Juan and María Rosa would feel her eyes fixed upon them and would find her there, unable to move, spying upon them. But they did not pass beyond the enclosure, nor even glance towards the gap in the wall opening upon the road.

Juan lifted one of María Rosa's loosened braids and slapped

her neck with it playfully. She smiled softly, consentingly. Together they moved back through the hives of honey-comb. María Rosa balanced her jar on one hip and swung her long full petticoats with every step. Juan flourished his wide hat back and forth, walking proudly as a game-cock.

María Concepción came out of the heavy cloud which enwrapped her head and bound her throat, and found herself walking onward, keeping the road without knowing it, feeling her way delicately, her ears strumming as if all María Rosa's bees had hived in them. Her careful sense of duty kept her moving toward the buried city where Juan's chief, the American archaeologist, was taking his midday rest, waiting for his food.

Juan and María Rosa! She burned all over now, as if a layer of tiny fig-cactus bristles, as cruel as spun glass, had crawled under her skin. She wished to sit down quietly and wait for her death, but not until she had cut the throats of her man and that girl who were laughing and kissing under the cornstalks. Once when she was a young girl she had come back from market to find her jacal burned to a pile of ash and her few silver coins gone. A dark empty feeling had filled her; she kept moving about the place, not believing her eyes, expecting it all to take shape again before her. But it was gone, and though she knew an enemy had done it, she could not find out who it was, and could only curse and threaten the air. Now here was a worse thing, but she knew her enemy. María Rosa, that sinful girl, shameless! She heard herself saying a harsh, true word about María Rosa, saying it aloud as if she expected someone to agree with her: "Yes, she is a whore! She has no right to live."

At this moment the gray untidy head of Givens appeared over the edges of the newest trench he had caused to be dug in his field of excavations. The long deep crevasses, in which a man might stand without being seen, lay crisscrossed like orderly gashes of a giant scalpel. Nearly all of the men of the community worked for Givens, helping him to uncover the lost city of their ancestors. They worked all the year through and prospered, digging every day for those small clay heads and bits of pottery and fragments of painted walls for which there was no good use on earth, being all broken and encrusted with clay. They themselves could make better ones, perfectly stout and new, which they took to town and peddled to foreigners for real money. But the unearthly delight of the chief in finding these worn-out things was an endless puzzle. He would fairly roar for joy at times, waving a shattered pot or a human skull above his head, shouting for his photographer to come and make a picture of this!

Now he emerged, and his young enthusiast's eyes welcomed María Concepción from his old-man face, covered with hard wrinkles and burned to the color of red earth. "I hope you've brought me a nice fat one." He selected a fowl from the bunch dangling nearest him as María Concepción, wordless, leaned over the trench. "Dress it for me, there's a good girl. I'll broil it."

María Concepción took the fowl by the head, and silently, swiftly drew her knife across its throat, twisting the head off with the casual firmness she might use with the top of a beet.

"Good God, woman, you do have nerve," said Givens, watching her. "I can't do that. It gives me the creeps."

"My home country is Guadalajara," explained María Concepción, without bravado, as she picked and gutted the fowl.

She stood and regarded Givens condescendingly, that diverting white man who had no woman of his own to cook for him, and moreover appeared not to feel any loss of dignity in preparing his own food. He squatted now, eyes squinted, nose wrinkled to avoid the smoke, turning the roasting fowl busily on a stick. A mysterious man, undoubtedly rich, and Juan's chief, therefore to be respected, to be placated.

"The tortillas are fresh and hot, señor," she murmured gently. "With your permission I will now go to market."

"Yes, yes, run along; bring me another of these tomorrow." Givens turned his head to look at her again. Her grand manner sometimes reminded him of royalty in exile. He noticed her unnatural paleness. "The sun is too hot, eh?" he asked.

"Yes, sir. Pardon me, but Juan will be here soon?"

"He ought to be here now. Leave his food. The others will eat it."

She moved away; the blue of her rebozo became a dancing spot in the heat waves that rose from the gray-red soil. Givens liked his Indians best when he could feel a fatherly indulgence for their primitive childish ways. He told comic stories of Juan's escapades, of how often he had saved him, in the past five years,

7

from going to jail, and even from being shot, for his varied and always unexpected misdeeds.

"I am never a minute too soon to get him out of one pickle or another," he would say. "Well, he's a good worker, and I know how to manage him."

After Juan was married, he used to twit him, with exactly the right shade of condescension, on his many infidelities to María Concepción. "She'll catch you yet, and God help you!" he was fond of saying, and Juan would laugh with immense pleasure.

It did not occur to María Concepción to tell Juan she had found him out. During the day her anger against him died, and her anger against María Rosa grew. She kept saying to herself, "When I was a young girl like María Rosa, if a man had caught hold of me so, I would have broken my jar over his head." She forgot completely that she had not resisted even so much as María Rosa, on the day that Juan had first taken hold of her. Besides she had married him afterwards in the church, and that was a very different thing.

Juan did not come home that night, but went away to war and María Rosa went with him. Juan had a rifle at his shoulder and two pistols at his belt. María Rosa wore a rifle also, slung on her back along with the blankets and the cooking pots. They joined the nearest detachment of troops in the field, and María Rosa marched ahead with the battalion of experienced women of war, which went over the crops like locusts, gathering provisions for the army. She cooked with them, and ate with them what was left after the men had eaten. After battles she went out on the field with the others to salvage clothing and ammunition and guns from the slain before they should begin to swell in the heat. Sometimes they would encounter the women from the other army, and a second battle as grim as the first would take place.

There was no particular scandal in the village. People shrugged, grinned. It was far better that they were gone. The neighbors went around saying that María Rosa was safer in the army than she would be in the same village with María Concepción.

María Concepción did not weep when Juan left her; and when the baby was born, and died within four days, she did not weep.

"She is mere stone," said old Lupe, who went over and offered charms to preserve the baby.

"May you rot in hell with your charms," said María Concepción.

If she had not gone so regularly to church, lighting candles before the saints, kneeling with her arms spread in the form of a cross for hours at a time, and receiving holy communion every month, there might have been talk of her being devil-possessed, her face was so changed and blind-looking. But this was impossible when, after all, she had been married by the priest. It must be, they reasoned, that she was being punished for her pride. They decided that this was the true cause for everything: she was altogether too proud. So they pitied her.

During the year that Juan and María Rosa were gone María Concepción sold her fowls and looked after her garden and her sack of hard coins grew. Lupe had no talent for bees, and the hives did not prosper. She began to blame María Rosa for running away, and to praise María Concepción for her behavior. She used to see María Concepción at the market or at church, and she always said that no one could tell by looking at her now that she was a woman who had such a heavy grief.

"I pray God everything goes well with María Concepción from this out," she would say, "for she has had her share of trouble."

When some idle person repeated this to the deserted woman, she went down to Lupe's house and stood within the clearing and called to the medicine woman, who sat in her doorway stirring a mess of her infallible cure for sores: "Keep your prayers to yourself, Lupe, or offer them for others who need them. I will ask God for what I want in this world."

"And will you get it, you think, María Concepción?" asked Lupe, tittering cruelly and smelling the wooden mixing spoon. "Did you pray for what you have now?"

Afterward everyone noticed that María Concepción went oftener to church, and even seldomer to the village to talk with the other women as they sat along the curb, nursing their babies and eating fruit, at the end of the market-day.

"She is wrong to take us for enemies," said old Soledad, who was a thinker and a peace-maker. "All women have these troubles. Well, we should suffer together."

9

But María Concepción lived alone. She was gaunt, as if something were gnawing her away inside, her eyes were sunken, and she would not speak a word if she could help it. She worked harder than ever, and her butchering knife was scarcely ever out of her hand.

Juan and María Rosa, disgusted with military life, came home one day without asking permission of anyone. The field of war had unrolled itself, a long scroll of vexations, until the end had frayed out within twenty miles of Juan's village. So he and María Rosa, now lean as a wolf, burdened with a child daily expected, set out with no farewells to the regiment and walked home.

They arrived one morning about daybreak. Juan was picked up on sight by a group of military police from the small barracks on the edge of town, and taken to prison, where the officer in charge told him with impersonal cheerfulness that he would add one to a catch of ten waiting to be shot as deserters the next morning.

María Rosa, screaming and falling on her face in the road, was taken under the armpits by two guards and helped briskly to her jacal, now sadly run down. She was received with professional importance by Lupe, who helped the baby to be born at once.

Limping with foot soreness, a layer of dust concealing his fine new clothes got mysteriously from somewhere, Juan appeared before the captain at the barracks. The captain recognized him as head digger for his good friend Givens, and dispatched a note to Givens saying: "I am holding the person of Juan Villegas awaiting your further disposition."

When Givens showed up Juan was delivered to him with the urgent request that nothing be made public about so humane and sensible an operation on the part of military authority.

Juan walked out of the rather stifling atmosphere of the drumhead court, a definite air of swagger about him. His hat, of unreasonable dimensions and embroidered with silver thread, hung over one eyebrow, secured at the back by a cord of silver dripping with bright blue tassels. His shirt was of a checkerboard pattern in green and black, his white cotton trousers were bound by a belt of yellow leather tooled in red. His feet were bare, full of stone bruises, and sadly ragged as to toenails. He removed his cigarette from the corner of his full-lipped wide mouth. He removed the splendid hat. His black dusty hair, pressed moistly to his forehead, sprang up suddenly in a cloudy thatch on his crown. He bowed to the officer, who appeared to be gazing at a vacuum. He swung his arm wide in a free circle upsoaring towards the prison window, where forlorn heads poked over the window sill, hot eyes following after the lucky departing one. Two or three of the heads nodded, and a half dozen hands were flipped at him in an effort to imitate his own casual and heady manner.

Juan kept up this insufferable pantomime until they rounded the first clump of fig-cactus. Then he seized Givens' hand and burst into oratory. "Blessed be the day your servant Juan Villegas first came under your eyes. From this day my life is yours without condition, ten thousand thanks with all my heart!"

"For God's sake stop playing the fool," said Givens irritably. "Some day I'm going to be five minutes too late."

"Well, it is nothing much to be shot, my chief—certainly you know I was not afraid—but to be shot in a drove of deserters, against a cold wall, just in the moment of my home-coming, by order of that . . ."

Glittering epithets tumbled over one another like explosions of a rocket. All the scandalous analogies from the animal and vegetable worlds were applied in a vivid, unique and personal way to the life, loves, and family history of the officer who had just set him free. When he had quite cursed himself dry, and his nerves were soothed, he added: "With your permission, my chief!"

"What will María Concepción say to all this?" asked Givens. "You are very informal, Juan, for a man who was married in the church."

Juan put on his hat.

"Oh, María Concepción! That's nothing. Look, my chief, to be married in the church is a great misfortune for a man. After that he is not himself any more. How can that woman complain when I do not drink even at fiestas enough to be really drunk? I do not beat her; never, never. We were always at peace. I say to her, Come here, and she comes straight. I say, Go there, and she goes quickly. Yet sometimes I looked at her and thought, Now I am married to that woman in the church, and I felt a sinking inside, as if something were lying heavy on my stomach. With María Rosa it is all different. She is not silent; she talks. When she talks too much, I slap her and say, Silence, thou simpleton! and she weeps. She is just a girl with whom I do as I please. You know how she used to keep those clean little bees in their hives? She is like their honey to me. I swear it. I would not harm María Concepción because I am married to her in the church; but also, my chief, I will not leave María Rosa, because she pleases me more than any other woman."

"Let me tell you, Juan, things haven't been going as well as you think. You be careful. Some day María Concepción will just take your head off with that carving knife of hers. You keep that in mind."

Juan's expression was the proper blend of masculine triumph and sentimental melancholy. It was pleasant to see himself in the rôle of hero to two such desirable women. He had just escaped from the threat of a disagreeable end. His clothes were new and handsome, and they had cost him just nothing. María Rosa had collected them for him here and there after battles. He was walking in the early sunshine, smelling the good smells of ripening cactus-figs, peaches, and melons, of pungent berries dangling from the pepper-trees, and the smoke of his cigarette under his nose. He was on his way to civilian life with his patient chief. His situation was ineffably perfect, and he swallowed it whole.

"My chief," he addressed Givens handsomely, as one man of the world to another, "women are good things, but not at this moment. With your permission, I will now go to the village and eat. My God, *how* I shall eat! Tomorrow morning very early I will come to the buried city and work like seven men. Let us forget María Concepción and María Rosa. Each one in her place. I will manage them when the time comes."

News of Juan's adventure soon got abroad, and Juan found many friends about him during the morning. They frankly commended his way of leaving the army. It was in itself the act of a hero. The new hero ate a great deal and drank somewhat, the occasion being better than a feast-day. It was almost noon before he returned to visit María Rosa.

He found her sitting on a clean straw mat, rubbing fat on her three-hour-old son. Before this felicitous vision Juan's emotions so twisted him that he returned to the village and invited every man in the "Death and Resurrection" pulque shop to drink with him.

Having thus taken leave of his balance, he started back to María Rosa, and found himself unaccountably in his own house, attempting to beat María Concepción by way of reëstablishing himself in his legal household.

María Concepción, knowing all the events of that unhappy day, was not in a yielding mood, and refused to be beaten. She did not scream nor implore; she stood her ground and resisted; she even struck at him. Juan, amazed, hardly knowing what he did, stepped back and gazed at her inquiringly through a leisurely whirling film which seemed to have lodged behind his eyes. Certainly he had not even thought of touching her. Oh, well, no harm done. He gave up, turned away, half-asleep on his feet. He dropped amiably in a shadowed corner and began to snore.

María Concepción, seeing that he was quiet, began to bind the legs of her fowls. It was market-day and she was late. She fumbled and tangled the bits of cord in her haste, and set off across the plowed fields instead of taking the accustomed road. She ran with a crazy panic in her head, her stumbling legs. Now and then she would stop and look about her, trying to place herself, then go on a few steps, until she realized that she was not going towards the market.

At once she came to her senses completely, recognized the thing that troubled her so terribly, was certain of what she wanted. She sat down quietly under a sheltering thorny bush and gave herself over to her long devouring sorrow. The thing which had for so long squeezed her whole body into a tight dumb knot of suffering suddenly broke with shocking violence. She jerked with the involuntary recoil of one who receives a blow, and the sweat poured from her skin as if the wounds of her whole life were shedding their salt ichor. Drawing her rebozo over her head, she bowed her forehead on her updrawn knees, and sat there in deadly silence and immobility. From time to time she lifted her head where the sweat formed steadily and poured down her face, drenching the front of her chemise, and her mouth had the shape of crying, but there were no tears and no sound. All her being was a dark confused memory of grief burning in her at night, of deadly baffled anger eating at her by day, until her very tongue tasted bitter, and her feet were as heavy as if she were mired in the muddy roads during the time of rains.

After a great while she stood up and threw the rebozo off her face, and set out walking again.

Juan awakened slowly, with long yawns and grumblings, alternated with short relapses into sleep full of visions and clamors. A blur of orange light seared his eyeballs when he tried to unseal his lids. There came from somewhere a low voice weeping without tears, saying meaningless phrases over and over. He began to listen. He tugged at the leash of his stupor, he strained to grasp those words which terrified him even though he could not quite hear them. Then he came awake with frightening suddenness, sitting up and staring at the long sharpened streak of light piercing the corn-husk walls from the level disappearing sun.

María Concepción stood in the doorway, looming colossally tall to his betrayed eyes. She was talking quickly, and calling his name. Then he saw her clearly.

"God's name!" said Juan, frozen to the marrow, "here I am facing my death!" for the long knife she wore habitually at her belt was in her hand. But instead, she threw it away, clear from her, and got down on her knees, crawling toward him as he had seen her crawl many times toward the shrine at Guadalupe Villa. He watched her approach with such horror that the hair of his head seemed to be lifting itself away from him. Falling forward upon her face, she huddled over him, lips moving in a ghostly whisper. Her words became clear, and Juan understood them all.

For a second he could not move nor speak. Then he took her head between both his hands, and supported her in this way, saying swiftly, anxiously reassuring, almost in a babble:

"Oh, thou poor creature! Oh, madwoman! Oh, my María Concepción, unfortunate! Listen. . . . Don't be afraid. Listen to me! I will hide thee away, I thy own man will protect thee! Quiet! Not a sound!"

Trying to collect himself, he held her and cursed under his breath for a few moments in the gathering darkness. María Concepción bent over, face almost on the ground, her feet folded under her, as if she would hide behind him. For the first time in his life Juan was aware of danger. This was danger. María Concepción would be dragged away between two gendarmes, with him following helpless and unarmed, to spend the rest of her days in Belén Prison, maybe. Danger! The night swarmed with threats. He stood up and dragged her up with him. She was silent and perfectly rigid, holding to him with resistless strength, her hands stiffened on his arms.

"Get me the knife," he told her in a whisper. She obeyed, her feet slipping along the hard earth floor, her shoulders straight, her arms close to her side. He lighted a candle. María Concepción held the knife out to him. It was stained and dark even to the handle with drying blood.

He frowned at her harshly, noting the same stains on her chemise and hands.

"Take off thy clothes and wash thy hands," he ordered. He washed the knife carefully, and threw the water wide of the doorway. She watched him and did likewise with the bowl in which she had bathed.

"Light the brasero and cook food for me," he told her in the same peremptory tone. He took her garments and went out. When he returned, she was wearing an old soiled dress, and was fanning the fire in the charcoal burner. Seating himself cross-legged near her, he stared at her as at a creature unknown to him, who bewildered him utterly, for whom there was no possible explanation. She did not turn her head, but kept silent and still, except for the movements of her strong hands fanning the blaze which cast sparks and small jets of white smoke, flaring and dying rhythmically with the motion of the fan, lighting her face and darkening it by turns.

Juan's voice barely disturbed the silence: "Listen to me carefully, and tell me the truth, and when the gendarmes come here for us, thou shalt have nothing to fear. But there will be something for us to settle between us afterward."

The light from the charcoal burner shone in her eyes; a yellow phosphorescence glimmered behind the dark iris.

"For me everything is settled now," she answered, in a tone so tender, so grave, so heavy with suffering, that Juan felt his vitals contract. He wished to repent openly, not as a man, but as a very small child. He could not fathom her, nor himself, nor the mysterious fortunes of life grown so instantly confused where all had seemed so gay and simple. He felt too that she had become invaluable, a woman without equal among a million women, and he could not tell why. He drew an enormous sigh that rattled in his chest.

"Yes, yes, it is all settled. I shall not go away again. We must stay here together."

Whispering, he questioned her and she answered whispering, and he instructed her over and over until she had her lesson by heart. The hostile darkness of the night encroached upon them, flowing over the narrow threshold, invading their hearts. It brought with it sighs and murmurs, the pad of secretive feet in the near-by road, the sharp staccato whimper of wind through the cactus leaves. All these familiar, once friendly cadences were now invested with sinister terrors; a dread, formless and uncontrollable, took hold of them both.

"Light another candle," said Juan, loudly, in too resolute, too sharp a tone. "Let us eat now."

They sat facing each other and ate from the same dish, after their old habit. Neither tasted what they ate. With food half-way to his mouth, Juan listened. The sound of voices rose, spread, widened at the turn of the road along the cactus wall. A spray of lantern light shot through the hedge, a single voice slashed the blackness, ripped the fragile layer of silence suspended above the hut.

"Juan Villegas!"

"Pass, friends!" Juan roared back cheerfully.

They stood in the doorway, simple cautious gendarmes from the village, mixed-bloods themselves with Indian sympathies, well known to all the community. They flashed their lanterns almost apologetically upon the pleasant, harmless scene of a man eating supper with his wife.

"Pardon, brother," said the leader. "Someone has killed the woman María Rosa, and we must question her neighbors and friends." He paused, and added with an attempt at severity, "Naturally!"

"Naturally," agreed Juan. "You know that I was a good friend of María Rosa. This is bad news."

They all went away together, the men walking in a group,

María Concepción following a few steps in the rear, near Juan. No one spoke.

The two points of candlelight at María Rosa's head fluttered uneasily; the shadows shifted and dodged on the stained darkened walls. To María Concepción everything in the smothering enclosing room shared an evil restlessness. The watchful faces of those called as witnesses, the faces of old friends, were made alien by the look of speculation in their eyes. The ridges of the rose-colored rebozo thrown over the body varied continually, as though the thing it covered was not perfectly in repose. Her eyes swerved over the body in the open painted coffin, from the candle tips at the head to the feet, jutting up thinly, the small scarred soles protruding, freshly washed, a mass of crooked, half-healed wounds, thornpricks and cuts of sharp stones. Her gaze went back to the candle flame, to Juan's eyes warning her, to the gendarmes talking among themselves. Her eyes would not be controlled.

With a leap that shook her her gaze settled upon the face of María Rosa. Instantly her blood ran smoothly again: there was nothing to fear. Even the restless light could not give a look of life to that fixed countenance. She was dead. María Concepción felt her muscles give way softly; her heart began beating steadily without effort. She knew no more rancor against that pitiable thing, lying indifferently in its blue coffin under the fine silk rebozo. The mouth drooped sharply at the corners in a grimace of weeping arrested half-way. The brows were distressed; the dead flesh could not cast off the shape of its last terror. It was all finished. María Rosa had eaten too much honey and had had too much love. Now she must sit in hell, crying over her sins and her hard death forever and ever.

Old Lupe's cackling voice arose. She had spent the morning helping María Rosa, and it had been hard work. The child had spat blood the moment it was born, a bad sign. She thought then that bad luck would come to the house. Well, about sunset she was in the yard at the back of the house grinding tomatoes and peppers. She had left mother and babe asleep. She heard a strange noise in the house, a choking and smothered calling, like someone wailing in sleep. Well, such a thing is only natural. But there followed a light, quick, thudding sound—

"Like the blows of a fist?" interrupted an officer.

"No, not at all like such a thing."

"How do you know?"

"I am well acquainted with that sound, friends," retorted Lupe. "This was something else." '

She was at a loss to describe it exactly. A moment later, there came the sound of pebbles rolling and slipping under feet; then she knew someone had been there and was running away.

"Why did you wait so long before going to see?"

"I am old and hard in the joints," said Lupe. "I cannot run after people. I walked as fast as I could to the cactus hedge, for it is only by this way that anyone can enter. There was no one in the road, sir, no one. Three cows, with a dog driving them; nothing else. When I got to María Rosa, she was lying all tangled up, and from her neck to her middle she was full of knife-holes. It was a sight to move the Blessed Image Himself! Her eyes were—"

"Never mind. Who came oftenest to her house before she went away? Did you know her enemies?"

Lupe's face congealed, closed. Her spongy skin drew into a network of secretive wrinkles. She turned withdrawn and expressionless eyes upon the gendarmes.

"I am an old woman. I do not see well. I cannot hurry on my feet. I know no enemy of María Rosa. I did not see anyone leave the clearing."

"You did not hear splashing in the spring near the bridge?"

"No, sir."

"Why, then, do our dogs follow a scent there and lose it?"

"God only knows, my friend. I am an old wo—"

"Yes. How did the footfalls sound?"

"Like the tread of an evil spirit!" Lupe broke forth in a swelling oracular tone that startled them. The Indians stirred uneasily, glanced at the dead, then at Lupe. They half expected her to produce the evil spirit among them at once.

The gendarme began to lose his temper.

"No, poor unfortunate; I mean, were they heavy or light? The footsteps of a man or of a woman? Was the person shod or barefoot?"

A glance at the listening circle assured Lupe of their thrilled attention. She enjoyed the dangerous importance of her situation.

She could have ruined that María Concepción with a word, but it was even sweeter to make fools of these gendarmes who went about spying on honest people. She raised her voice again. What she had not seen she could not describe, thank God! No one could harm her because her knees were stiff and she could not run even to seize a murderer. As for knowing the difference between footfalls, shod or bare, man or woman, nay, between devil and human, who ever heard of such madness?

"My eyes are not ears, gentlemen," she ended grandly, "but upon my heart I swear those footsteps fell as the tread of the spirit of evil!"

"Imbecile!" yapped the leader in a shrill voice. "Take her away, one of you! Now, Juan Villegas, tell me—"

Juan told his story patiently, several times over. He had returned to his wife that day. She had gone to market as usual. He had helped her prepare her fowls. She had returned about mid-afternoon, they had talked, she had cooked, they had eaten, nothing was amiss. Then the gendarmes came with the news about María Rosa. That was all. Yes, María Rosa had run away with him, but there had been no bad blood between him and his wife on this account, nor between his wife and María Rosa. Everybody knew that his wife was a quiet woman.

María Concepción heard her own voice answering without a break. It was true at first she was troubled when her husband went away, but after that she had not worried about him. It was the way of men, she believed. She was a church-married woman and knew her place. Well, he had come home at last. She had gone to market, but had come back early, because now she had her man to cook for. That was all.

Other voices broke in. A toothless old man said: "She is a woman of good reputation among us, and María Rosa was not." A smiling young mother, Anita, baby at breast, said: "If no one thinks so, how can you accuse her? It was the loss of her child and not of her husband that changed her so." Another: "María Rosa had a strange life, apart from us. How do we know who might have come from another place to do her evil?" And old Soledad spoke up boldly: "When I saw María Concepción in the market today, I said, 'Good luck to you, María Concepción, this is a happy day for you!' " and she gave María Concepción a long easy stare, and the smile of a born wise-woman.

María Concepción suddenly felt herself guarded, surrounded, upborne by her faithful friends. They were around her, speaking for her, defending her, the forces of life were ranged invincibly with her against the beaten dead. María Rosa had thrown away her share of strength in them, she lay forfeited among them. María Concepción looked from one to the other of the circling, intent faces. Their eyes gave back reassurance, understanding, a secret and mighty sympathy.

The gendarmes were at a loss. They, too, felt that sheltering wall cast impenetrably around her. They were certain she had done it, and yet they could not accuse her. Nobody could be accused; there was not a shred of true evidence. They shrugged their shoulders and snapped their fingers and shuffled their feet. Well, then, good night to everybody. Many pardons for having intruded. Good health!

A small bundle lying against the wall at the head of the coffin squirmed like an eel. A wail, a mere sliver of sound, issued. María Concepción took the son of María Rosa in her arms.

"He is mine," she said clearly, "I will take him with me."

No one assented in words, but an approving nod, a bare breath of complete agreement, stirred among them as they made way for her.

María Concepción, carrying the child, followed Juan from the clearing. The hut was left with its lighted candles and a crowd of old women who would sit up all night, drinking coffee and smoking and telling ghost stories.

Juan's exaltation had burned out. There was not an ember of excitement left in him. He was tired. The perilous adventure was over. María Rosa had vanished, to come no more forever. Their days of marching, of eating, of quarreling and making love between battles, were all over. Tomorrow he would go back to dull and endless labor, he must descend into the trenches of the buried city as María Rosa must go into her grave. He felt his veins fill up with bitterness, with black unendurable melancholy. Oh, Jesus! what bad luck overtakes a man!

Well, there was no way out of it now. For the moment he

craved only to sleep. He was so drowsy he could scarcely guide his feet. The occasional light touch of the woman at his elbow was as unreal, as ghostly as the brushing of a leaf against his face. He did not know why he had fought to save her, and now he forgot her. There was nothing in him except a vast blind hurt like a covered wound.

He entered the jacal, and without waiting to light a candle, threw off his clothing, sitting just within the door. He moved with lagging, half-awake hands, to strip his body of its heavy finery. With a long groaning sigh of relief he fell straight back on the floor, almost instantly asleep, his arms flung up and outward.

María Concepción, a small clay jar in her hand, approached the gentle little mother goat tethered to a sapling, which gave and yielded as she pulled at the rope's end after the farthest reaches of grass about her. The kid, tied up a few feet away, rose bleating, its feathery fleece shivering in the fresh wind. Sitting on her heels, holding his tether, she allowed him to suckle a few moments. Afterward—all her movements very deliberate and even —she drew a supply of milk for the child.

She sat against the wall of her house, near the doorway. The child, fed and asleep, was cradled in the hollow of her crossed legs. The silence overfilled the world, the skies flowed down evenly to the rim of the valley, the stealthy moon crept slantwise to the shelter of the mountains. She felt soft and warm all over; she dreamed that the newly born child was her own, and she was resting deliciously.

María Concepción could hear Juan's breathing. The sound vapored from the low doorway, calmly; the house seemed to be resting after a burdensome day. She breathed, too, very slowly and quietly, each inspiration saturating her with repose. The child's light, faint breath was a mere shadowy moth of sound in the silver air. The night, the earth under her, seemed to swell and recede together with a limitless, unhurried, benign breathing. She drooped and closed her eyes, feeling the slow rise and fall within her own body. She did not know what it was, but it eased her all through. Even as she was falling asleep, head bowed over the child, she was still aware of a strange, wakeful happiness.

New York 1922

Virgin Violeta

Violeta, nearly fifteen years old, sat on a hassock, hugging her knees and watching Carlos, her cousin, and her sister Blanca, who were reading poetry aloud by turns at the long table.

Occasionally she glanced down at her own feet, clad in thick-soled brown sandals, the toes turned in a trifle. Their ugliness distressed her, and she pulled her short skirt over them until the beltline sagged under her loose, dark blue woolen blouse. Then she straightened up, with a full, silent breath, uncovering the sandals again. Each time her eyes moved under shy lids to Carlos, to see if he had noticed; he never did notice. Disappointed, a little troubled, Violeta would sit very still for a while, listening and watching.

> *"'This torment of love which is in my heart:*
> *I know that I suffer it, but I do not know why.'"*

Blanca's voice was thin, with a whisper in it. She seemed anxious to keep the poetry all for Carlos and herself. Her shawl, embroidered in yellow on gray silk, slipped from her shoulders whenever she inclined toward the lamp. Carlos would lift the tassel of fringe nearest him between finger and thumb and toss it deftly into place. Blanca's nod, her smile, were the perfection of amiable indifference. But her voice wavered, caught on the word. She had always to begin again the line she was reading.

Carlos would slant his pale eyes at Blanca; then he would resume his pose, gaze fixed on a small painting on the white-paneled wall over Violeta's head. "Pious Interview between the Most Holy Virgin Queen of Heaven and Her Faithful Servant St. Ignatius

22

Loyola," read the thin metal plate on the carved and gilded frame. The Virgin, with enameled face set in a detached simper, forehead bald of eyebrows, extended one hand remotely over the tonsured head of the saint, who groveled in a wooden posture of ecstasy. Very ugly and old-fashioned, thought Violeta, but a perfectly proper picture; there was nothing to stare at. But Carlos kept squinting his eyelids at it mysteriously, and never moved his eyes from it save to glance at Blanca. His furry, golden eyebrows were knotted sternly, resembling a tangle of crochet wool. He never seemed to be interested except when it was his turn to read. He read in a thrilling voice. Violeta thought his mouth and chin were very beautiful. A tiny spot of light on his slightly moistened under-lip disturbed her, she did not know why.

Blanca stopped reading, bowed her head and sighed lightly, her mouth half open. It was one of her habits. As the sound of voices had lulled Mamacita to sleep beside her sewing basket, now the silence roused her. She looked about her with a vivacious smile on her whole face, except her eyes, which were drowsed and weary.

"Go on with your reading, dear children. I heard every word. Violeta, don't fidget, please, sweet little daughter. Carlos, what is the hour?"

Mamacita liked being chaperon to Blanca. Violeta wondered why Mamacita considered Blanca so very attractive, but she did. She was always saying to Papacito, "Blanquita blooms like a lily!" And Papacito would say, "It is better if she conducts herself like one!" And Mamacita said once to Carlos, "Even if you are my nephew, still you must go home at a reasonable hour!"

"The hour is early, Doña Paz." St. Anthony himself could not have exceeded in respect the pose of Carlos' head toward his aunt. She smiled and relapsed into a shallow nap, as a cat rises from the rug, turns and lies down again.

Violeta did not move, or answer Mamacita. She had the silence and watchfulness of a young wild animal, but no native wisdom. She was at home from the convent in Tacubaya for the first time in almost a year. There they taught her modesty, chastity, silence, obedience, with a little French and music and some arithmetic. She did as she was told, but it was all very confusing, because she could not understand why the things that happen outside of people were so different from what she felt inside of her. Everybody went

about doing the same things every day, precisely as if there were
nothing else going to happen, ever; and all the time she was certain
there was something simply tremendously exciting waiting for her
outside the convent. Life was going to unroll itself like a long, gay
carpet for her to walk upon. She saw herself wearing a long veil,
and it would trail and flutter over this carpet as she came out of
church. There would be six flower girls and two pages, the way
there had been at Cousin Sancha's wedding.

Of course she didn't mean a wedding. Silly! Cousin Sancha had
been quite old, almost twenty-four, and Violeta meant for life to
begin at once—next year, anyway. It would be more like a festival.
She wanted to wear red poppies in her hair and dance. Life would
always be very gay, with no one about telling you that almost
everything you said and did was wrong. She would be free to read
poetry, too, and stories about love, without having to hide them in
her copybooks. Even Carlos did not know that she had learned
nearly all his poems by heart. She had for a year been cutting them
from magazines, keeping them in the pages of her books, in order
to read them during study hours.

Several shorter ones were concealed in her missal, and the thrilling music of strange words drowned the chorus of bell and choir.
There was one about the ghosts of nuns returning to the old square
before their ruined convent, dancing in the moonlight with the
shades of lovers forbidden them in life, treading with bared feet on
broken glass as a penance for their loves. Violeta would shake all
over when she read this, and lift swimming eyes to the delicate
spears of candlelight on the altar.

She was certain she would be like those nuns someday. She
would dance for joy over shards of broken glass. But where begin?
She had sat here in this room, on this very hassock, comfortingly
near Mamacita, through the summer evenings of vacation, ever
since she could remember. Sometimes it was a happiness to be
assured that nothing was expected of her but to follow Mamacita
about and be a good girl. It gave her time to dream about life—
that is, the future. For of course everything beautiful and unexpected would happen later on, when she grew as tall as Blanca and
was allowed to come home from the convent for good and all. She
would then be miraculously lovely—Blanca would look perfectly
dull beside her—and she would dance with fascinating young men

like those who rode by on Sunday mornings, making their horses prance in the bright, shallow street on their way to the *paseo* in Chapultepec Park. She would appear on the balcony above, wearing a blue dress, and everyone would ask who that enchanting girl could be. And Carlos, Carlos! He would understand at last that she had read and loved his poems always.

> *"The nuns are dancing with bare feet*
> *On broken glass in the cobbled street."*

That one above all the rest. She felt it had been written for her. She was even one of the nuns, the youngest and best-loved one, ghostly silent, dancing forever and ever under the moonlight to the shivering tune of old violins.

Mamacita moved her knee uneasily, so that Violeta's head slipped from it, and she almost lost her balance. She sat up, prickling all over with shyness for fear the others would know why she had hidden her face on Mamacita's lap. But no one saw. Mamacita was always lecturing her about things. At such moments it was hard to believe that Blanca was not the favorite child. "You must not run through the house so." "You must brush your hair more smoothly." "And what is this I hear about your using your sister's face powder?"

Blanca, listening, would eye her with superior calm and say nothing. It was really very hard, knowing that Blanca was nicer only because she was allowed to powder and perfume herself and still gave herself such airs about it. Carlos, who used to bring her sugared limes and long strips of dried *membrillo* from the markets, calling her his dear, amusing, modest Violeta, now simply did not know she was present. There were times when Violeta wished to cry, passionately, so everyone could hear her. But what about? And how explain to Mamacita? She would say, "What have you to cry for? And besides, consider the feelings of others in this house and control your moods."

Papacito would say, "What you need is a good renovating." That was his word for a spanking. He would say sternly to Mamacita, "I think her moral nature needs repairment." He and Mamacita seemed to have some mysterious understanding about things. Mamacita's eyes were always perfectly clear when she looked at Papacito, and she would answer: "You are right. I will look after this." Then she would be very severe with Violeta. Papacito always said to the girls: "It is your fault without exception when Mamacita is annoyed with you. So be careful."

But Mamacita never stayed annoyed for long, and afterward it was beautiful to curl up near her, snuggling into her shoulder, and smell the nice, crinkled, perfumed hair at the nape of her neck. But when she was angry her eyes had a considering expression, as if one were a stranger, and she would say, "You are the greatest of my problems." Violeta had often been a problem and it was very humiliating.

¡Ay de mi! Violeta gave a sharp sigh and sat up straight. She wanted to stretch her arms up and yawn, not because she was sleepy but because something inside her felt as if it were enclosed in a cage too small for it, and she could not breathe. Like those poor parrots in the markets, stuffed into tiny wicker cages so that they bulged through the withes, gasping and panting, waiting for someone to come and rescue them.

Church was a terrible, huge cage, but it seemed too small. "Oh, my, I always laugh, to keep from crying!" A silly verse Carlos used to say. Through her eyelashes his face looked suddenly pale and soft, as if he might have tears on his cheeks. Oh, Carlos! But of course he would never cry for anything. She was frightened to find that her own eyes were steeped in tears; they were going to run down her face; she couldn't stop them. Her head bowed over and her chin seemed to be curling up. Where on earth was her handkerchief? A huge, clean, white linen one, almost like a boy's handkerchief. How horrid! The folded corner scratched her eyelids. Sometimes she cried in church when the music wailed terribly and the girls sat in veiled rows, all silent except for the clinking of their beads slipping through their fingers. They were all strangers to her then; what if they knew her thoughts? Suppose she should say aloud, "I love Carlos!" The idea made her blush all over, until her forehead perspired and her hands turned red. She would begin praying frantically, "Oh, Mary! Oh, Mary! Queen Mother of mercy!" while deep underneath her words her thoughts were rushing along in a kind of trance: Oh, dear God, that's my secret; that's a secret between You and me. I should die if anybody knew!

She turned her eyes again to the pair at the long table just in time to see once more the shawl beginning to slip, ever so little, from Blanca's shoulder. A tight shudder of drawn threads played along Violeta's skin, and grew quite intolerable when Carlos reached out to take the fringe in his long fingers. His wrist turned with a delicate toss, the shawl settled into place, Blanca smiled and stammered and bit her lip.

Violeta could not bear to see it. No, no. She wanted to hold her hands over her heart tightly, to quell the slow, burning ache. It felt like a little jar filled with flames, which she could not smother down. It was cruel of Blanca and Carlos to sit there and read and be so pleased with each other without once thinking of her! Yet what could she say if they noticed her? They never did notice.

Blanca rose.

"I am tired of the old poetry. It is all too sad. What else shall we read?"

"Let's have a great deal of gay, modern poetry," suggested Carlos, whose own verses were considered extremely gay and modern. Violeta was always shocked when he called them amusing. He couldn't mean it. It was only his way of pretending he wasn't sad when he wrote them.

"Read me all your new ones again." Blanca was always appreciating Carlos. You could hear it in her voice underneath, like a little trickle of sugar. And Carlos let her do it. He seemed always to be condescending to Blanca a little. But Blanca could never see it, because she really didn't think of anything but the way she had her hair fixed or whether people thought she was pretty. Violeta longed to make a naughty face at Blanca, who posed ridiculously, leaning over the table.

Above the red silk lamp shade her face was not sallow as usual. The thin nose and small lips cast shadows on her cheek. She hated being pale, and had the habit, while reading, of smoothing her cheeks round and round with two fingers, first one cheek and then the other, until deep red spots would burn in them for a long while. Violeta wished to shriek after watching Blanca do this for hours at a time. Why did not Mamacita speak to her about it? It was the worst sort of fidgeting.

"I haven't the new ones with me," said Carlos.

"Then let it be the old ones," agreed Blanca gaily.

She moved to the bookshelves, Carlos beside her. They could not find his book. Their hands touched as fingers sought titles.

Something in the intimate murmur of their voices wounded Violeta acutely. Sharing some delightful secret, they were purposely shutting her out. She spoke.

"If you want your book, Carlos, I can find it." At the sound of her own voice she felt calm and firm and equal to anything. By her tone she tried to shut Blanca out.

They turned and regarded her without interest.

"And where may it be, infant?" Carlos' voice always had that chilling edge on it when he was not reading aloud, and his eyes explored. With a glance he seemed to see all one's faults. Violeta remembered her feet and drew down her skirts. The sight of Blanca's narrow, gray satin slippers was hateful.

"I have it. I have had it for a whole week." She eyed the tip of Blanca's nose, hoping they would understand she wished to say, "You see, I have treasured it!"

She got up, feeling a little clumsy, and walked away with a curious imitation of Blanca's grown-up gait. It made her dreadfully aware of her long, straight legs in their ribbed stockings.

"I will help you search," called Carlos, as if he had thought of something interesting, and he followed. Over his suddenly near shoulder she saw Blanca's face. It looked very vague and faraway, like a distressed doll's. Carlos' eyes were enormous, and he smiled steadily. She wished to run away. He said something in a low voice. She could not understand him at all, and it was impossible to find the lamp cord in the narrow, dark hallway. She was frightened at the soft *pad-pad* of his rubber heels so close behind her as they went without speaking through the chill dining room, full of the odor of fruit that has been all day in a closed place. When they entered the small, open sunroom over the entrance of the patio, the moonlight seemed almost warm, it was so radiant after the shadows of the house. Violeta turned over a huddle of books on the small table, but she did not see them clearly; and her hand shook so, she could not take hold of anything.

Carlos' hand came up in a curve, settled upon hers and held fast. His roundish, smooth cheek and blond eyebrows hovered, swooped. His mouth touched hers and made a tiny smacking sound. She felt herself wrench and twist away as if a hand pushed her violently. And in that second his hand was over her mouth, soft and warm, and his eyes were staring at her, fearfully close. Violeta opened her eyes wide also and peered up at him. She expected to sink into a look warm and gentle, like the touch of his palm. Instead, she felt suddenly, sharply hurt, as if she had collided with a chair in the dark. His eyes were bright and shallow, almost like the eyes of Pepe, the macaw. His pale, fluffy eyebrows were arched; his mouth smiled tightly. A sick thumping began in the pit of her stomach, as it always did when she was called up to explain things to Mother Superior. Something was terribly wrong. Her heart pounded until she seemed about to smother. She was angry with all her might, and turned her head aside in a hard jerk.

"Keep your hand off my mouth!"

"Then be quiet, you silly child!" The words were astounding, but the way he said them was more astounding still, as if they were allies in some shameful secret. Her teeth rattled with chill.

"I will tell my mother! Shame on you for kissing me!"

"I did not kiss you except a little brotherly kiss, Violeta, precisely as I kiss Blanca. Don't be absurd!"

"You do not kiss Blanca. I heard her tell my mother she has never been kissed by a man!"

"But I do kiss her—as a cousin, nothing more. It does not count. We are relatives just the same. What did you think?"

Oh, she had made a hideous mistake. She knew she was blushing until her forehead throbbed. Her breath was gone, but she must explain. "I thought—a kiss—meant—meant—" She could not finish.

"Ah, you're so young, like a little newborn calf," said Carlos. His voice trembled in a strange way. "You smell like a nice baby, freshly washed with white soap! Imagine such a baby being angry at a kiss from her cousin! Shame on you, Violeta!"

He was loathsome. She saw herself before him, almost as if his face were a mirror. Her mouth was too large; her face was simply a moon; her hair was ugly in the tight convent braids.

"Oh, I'm so sorry!" she whispered.

"For what?" His voice had the cutting edge again. "Come, where is the book?"

"I don't know," she said, trying not to cry.

"Well, then, let us go back, or Mamacita will scold you."

"Oh, no, no. I can't go in there. Blanca will see—Mamacita will ask questions. I want to stay here. I want to run away—to kill myself!"

"Nonsense!" said Carlos. "Come with me this minute. What did you expect when you came out here alone with me?"

He turned and started away. She was shamefully, incredibly in the wrong. She had behaved like an immodest girl. It was all bitterly real and unbelievable, like a nightmare that went on and on and no one heard you calling to be waked up. She followed, trying to hold up her head.

Mamacita nodded, shining, crinkled hair stiffly arranged, chin on white collar. Blanca sat like a stone in her deep chair, holding a small gray-and-gold book in her lap. Her angry eyes threw out a look that coiled back upon itself like a whiplash, and the pupils became suddenly blank and bright as Carlos' had.

Violeta folded down on her hassock and gathered up her knees. She stared at the carpet to hide her reddened eyes, for it terrified her to see the way eyes could give away such cruel stories about people.

"I found the book here, where it belonged," said Blanca. "I am tired now. It is very late. We shall not read."

Violeta wished to cry in real earnest now. It was the last blow that Blanca should have found the book. A kiss meant nothing at all, and Carlos had walked away as if he had forgotten her. It was all mixed up with the white rivers of moonlight and the smell of warm fruit and a cold dampness on her lips that made a tiny, smacking sound. She trembled and leaned over until her forehead touched Mamacita's lap. She could not look up, ever, ever again.

The low voices sounded contentious; thin metal wires twanged in the air around them.

"But I do not care to read any more, I tell you."

"Very well, I shall go at once. But I am leaving for Paris on Wednesday, and shall not see you again until the fall."

"It would be like you to go without even stopping in to say good-by."

Even when they were angry they still talked to each other like two grown-up people wrapped together in a secret. The sound of his soft, padding rubber heels came near.

"Good night, my dearest Doña Paz. I have had an enchanting evening."

Mamacita's knees moved; she meant to rise.

"What—asleep, Violeta? Well, let us hear often from you, my dear nephew. Your little cousins and I will miss you greatly."

Mamacita was wide-awake and smiling, holding Carlos' hands. They kissed. Carlos turned to Blanca and bent to kiss her. She swept him into the folds of the gray shawl, but turned her cheek for his salute. Violeta rose, her knees trembling. She turned her head from side to side to close out the sight of the macaw eyes coming closer and closer, the tight, smiling mouth ready to swoop. When he touched her, she wavered for a moment, then slid up and back against the wall. She heard herself screaming uncontrollably.

Mamacita sat upon the side of the bed and patted Violeta's cheek. Her curved hand was warm and gentle and so were her eyes. Violeta choked a little and turned her face away.

"I have explained to Papacito that you quarreled with your cousin Carlos and were very rude to him. Papacito says you need a good renovating." Mamacita's voice was soft and reassuring. Violeta lay without a pillow, the ruffled collar of her nightgown standing up about her chin. She did not answer. Even to whisper hurt her.

"We are going to the country this week and you shall live in the garden all summer. Then you won't be so nervous. You are quite a young lady now, and you must learn to control your nerves."

"Yes, Mamacita." The look on Mamacita's face was very hard to bear. She seemed to be asking questions about very hidden thoughts—those thoughts that were not true at all and could never be talked about with anyone. Everything she could remember in her whole life seemed to have melted together in a confusion and misery that could not be explained because it was all changed and uncertain.

She wanted to sit up, take Mamacita around the neck and say, "Something dreadful happened to me—I don't know what," but her heart closed up hard and aching, and she sighed with all her breath. Even Mamacita's breast had become a cold, strange place. Her blood ran back and forth in her, crying terribly, but when the sound came up to her lips it was only a small whimper, like a puppy's.

"You must not cry any more," said Mamacita after a long pause. Then: "Good night, my poor child. This impression will pass." Mamacita's kiss felt cold on Violeta's cheek.

Whether the impression passed or not, no word of it was spoken again. Violeta and the family spent the summer in the country. She refused to read Carlos' poetry, though Mamacita encouraged her to do so. She would not even listen to his letters from Paris. She quarreled on more equal terms with her sister Blanca, feeling that there was no longer so great a difference of experience to separate them. A painful unhappiness possessed her at times, because she could not settle the questions brooding in her mind. Sometimes she amused herself making ugly caricatures of Carlos.

In the early autumn she returned to school, weeping and complaining to her mother that she hated the convent. There was, she declared as she watched her boxes being tied up, nothing to be learned there.

1923

The Martyr

Rubén, the most illustrious painter in Mexico, was deeply in love with his model Isabel, who was in turn romantically attached to a rival artist whose name is of no importance.

Isabel used to call Rubén her little "Churro," which is a sort of sweet cake, and is, besides, a popular pet name among the Mexicans for small dogs. Rubén thought it a very delightful name, and would say before visitors to the studio, "And now she calls me 'Churro!' Ha! ha!" When he laughed, he shook in the waistcoat, for he was getting fat.

Then Isabel, who was tall and thin, with long, keen fingers, would rip her hands through a bouquet of flowers Rubén had brought her and scatter the petals, or she would cry, "Yah! yah!" derisively, and flick the tip of his nose with paint. She had been observed also to pull his hair and ears without mercy.

When earnest-minded people made pilgrimages down the narrow, cobbled street, picked their way carefully over puddles in the patio, and clattered up the uncertain stairs for a glimpse of the great and yet so simple personage, she would cry, "Here come the pretty sheep!" She enjoyed their gaze of wonder at her daring.

Often she was bored, for sometimes she would stand all day long, braiding and unbraiding her hair while Rubén made sketches of her, and they would forget to eat until late; but there was no place for her to go until her lover, Rubén's rival, should sell a painting, for everyone declared Rubén would kill on sight the man who even attempted to rob him of Isabel. So Isabel stayed, and Rubén made eighteen different drawings of her for his mural, and she cooked for him occasionally, quarreled with him, and put out her long, red tongue at visitors she did not like. Rubén adored her.

He was just beginning the nineteenth drawing of Isabel when his rival sold a very large painting to a rich man whose decorator told him he must have a panel of green and orange on a certain wall of his new house. By a felicitous chance, this painting was prodigiously green and orange. The rich man paid him a huge price, but was happy to do it, he explained, because it would cost six times as much to cover the space with tapestry. The rival was happy, too, though he neglected to explain why. The next day he and Isabel went to Costa Rica, and that is the end of them so far as we are concerned.

Rubén read her farewell note:

"Poor old Churro! It is a pity your life is so very dull, and I cannot live it any longer. I am going away with someone who will never allow me to cook for him, but will make a mural with fifty figures of me in it, instead of only twenty. I am also to have red slippers, and a gay life to my heart's content.
"Your old friend,

"ISABEL."

When Rubén read this, he felt like a man drowning. His breath would not come, and he thrashed his arms about a great deal. Then he drank a large bottle of *tequila,* without lemon or salt to take the edge off, and lay down on the floor with his head in a palette of freshly mixed paint and wept vehemently.

After this, he was altogether a changed man. He could not talk unless he was telling about Isabel, her angelic face, her pretty little tricks and ways: "She used to kick my shins black and blue," he would say, fondly, and the tears would flow into his eyes. He was always eating crisp sweet cakes from a bag near his easel. "See," he would say, holding one up before taking a mouthful, "she used to call me 'Churro,' like this!"

His friends were all pleased to see Isabel go, and said among themselves he was lucky to lose the lean she-devil. They set themselves to help him forget. But Rubén could not be distracted. "There is no other woman like that woman," he would say, shaking his head stubbornly. "When she went, she took my life with her. I have no spirit even for revenge." Then he would add, "I tell you, my poor little angel Isabel is a murderess, for she has broken my heart."

At times he would roam anxiously about the studio, kicking his felt slippers into the shuffles of drawings piled about, gathering dust, or he would grind colors for a few minutes, saying in a dolorous voice: "She once did all this for me. Imagine her goodness!" But always he came back to the window, and ate sweets and fruits and almond cakes from the bag. When his friends took him out for dinner, he would sit quietly and eat huge platefuls of every sort of food, and wash it down with sweet wine. Then he would begin to weep, and talk about Isabel.

His friends agreed it was getting rather stupid. Isabel had been gone for nearly six months, and Rubén refused even to touch the nineteenth figure of her, much less to begin the twentieth, and the mural was getting nowhere.

"Look, my dear friend," said Ramón, who did caricatures, and heads of pretty girls for the magazines, "even I, who am not a great artist, know how women can spoil a man's work for him. Let me tell you, when Trinidad left me, I was good for nothing for a week. Nothing tasted properly, I could not tell one color from another, I positively was tone deaf. That shameless cheat-by-night almost ruined me. But you, *amigo,* rouse yourself, and finish your great mural for the world, for the future, and remember Isabel only when you give thanks to God that she is gone."

Rubén would shake his head as he sat collapsed upon his couch munching sugared almonds, and would cry:

"I have a pain in my heart that will kill me. There is no woman like that one."

His collars suddenly refused to meet under his chin. He loosened his belt three notches, and explained: "I sit still; I cannot move any more. My energy has gone to grief." The layers of fat piled insidiously upon him, he bulged until he became strange even to himself. Ramón, showing his new caricature of Rubén to his friends, declared: "I could as well have drawn it with a compass, I swear. The buttons are bursting from his shirt. It is positively unsafe."

But still Rubén sat, eating moodily in solitude, and weeping over Isabel after his third bottle of sweet wine at night.

His friends talked it over, concluded that the affair was growing desperate; it was high time someone should tell him the true cause of his pain. But everyone wished the other would be the one chosen. And it came out there was not a person in the group, possibly not one in all Mexico, indelicate enough to do such a thing. They decided to shift the responsibility upon a physician from the faculty of the university. In the mind of such a one would be combined a sufficiently refined sentiment with the highest degree of technical knowledge. This was the diplomatic, the discreet, the fastidious thing to do. It was done.

The doctor found Rubén seated before his easel, facing the half-finished nineteenth figure of Isabel. He was weeping, and between sobs he ate spoonfuls of soft Toluca cheese, with spiced mangos. He hung in all directions over his painting-stool, like a mound of kneaded dough. He told the doctor first about Isabel. "I do assure you faithfully, my friend, not even I could capture in paint the line of beauty in her thigh and instep. And, besides, she was an angel for kindness." Later he said the pain in his heart would be the death of him. The doctor was profoundly touched. For a great while he sat offering consolation without courage to prescribe material cures for a man of such delicately adjusted susceptibilities.

"I have only crass and vulgar remedies"—with a graceful gesture he seemed to offer them between thumb and forefinger—"but they are all the world of flesh may contribute toward the healing of the wounded spirit." He named them one at a time. They made a neat, but not impressive, row: a diet, fresh air, long walks, frequent violent exercise, preferably on the cross-bar, ice showers, almost no wine.

Rubén seemed not to hear him. His sustained, oblivious murmur flowed warmly through the doctor's solemnly rounded periods:

"The pains are most unendurable at night, when I lie in my lonely bed and gaze at the empty heavens through my narrow window, and I think to myself, 'Soon my grave shall be narrower than that window, and darker than that firmament,' and my heart gives a writhe. Ah, Isabelita, my executioner!"

The doctor tiptoed out respectfully, and left him sitting there eating cheese and gazing with wet eyes at the nineteenth figure of Isabel.

The friends grew hopelessly bored and left him more and more alone. No one saw him for some weeks except the proprietor of a small café called "The Little Monkeys" where Rubén was accustomed to dine with Isabel and where he now went alone for food.

Here one night quite suddenly Rubén clasped his heart with violence, rose from his chair, and upset the dish of tamales and pepper gravy he had been eating. The proprietor ran to him. Rubén said something in a hurried whisper, made rather an impressive gesture over his head with one arm, and, to say it as gently as possible, died.

His friends hastened the next day to see the proprietor, who gave them a solidly dramatic version of the lamentable episode. Ramón was even then gathering material for an intimate biography of his country's most eminent painter, to be illustrated with large numbers of his own character portraits. Already the dedication was composed to his "Friend and Master, Inspired and Incomparable Genius of Art on the American Continent."

"But what did he say to you," insisted Ramón, "at the final stupendous moment? It is most important. The last words of a great artist, they should be very eloquent. Repeat them precisely, my dear fellow! It will add splendor to the biography, nay, to the very history of art itself, if they are eloquent."

The proprietor nodded his head with the air of a man who understands everything.

"I know, I know. Well, maybe you will not believe me when I tell you that his very last words were a truly sublime message to you, his good and faithful friends, and to the world. He said, gentlemen: 'Tell them I am a martyr to love. I perish in a cause worthy the sacrifice. I die of a broken heart!' and then he said, 'Isabelita, my executioner!' That was all, gentlemen," ended the proprietor, simply and reverently. He bowed his head. They all bowed their heads.

"That was truly magnificent," said Ramón, after the correct interval of silent mourning. "I thank you. It is a superb epitaph. I am most gratified."

"He was also supremely fond of my tamales and pepper gravy," added the proprietor in a modest tone. "They were his final indulgence."

"That shall be mentioned in its place, never fear, my good friend," cried Ramón, his voice crumbling with generous emotion, "with the name of your café, even. It shall be a shrine for artists when this story is known. Trust me faithfully to preserve for the future every smallest detail in the life and character of this great genius. Each episode has its own sacred, its precious and peculiar interest. Yes, truly, I shall mention the tamales."

1923

Magic

And, Madame Blanchard, believe that I am happy to be here with you and your family because it is so serene, everything, and before this I worked for a long time in a fancy house—maybe you don't know what is a fancy house? Naturally . . . everyone must have heard sometime or other. Well, Madame, I work always where there is work to be had, and so in this place I worked very hard all hours, and saw too many things, things you wouldn't believe, and I wouldn't think of telling you, only maybe it will rest you while I brush your hair. You'll excuse me too but I could not help hearing you say to the laundress maybe someone had bewitched your linens, they fall away so fast in the wash. Well, there was a girl there in that house, a poor thing, thin, but well-liked by all the men who called, and you understand she could not get along with the woman who ran the house. They quarreled, the madam cheated her on her checks: you know, the girl got a check, a brass one, every time, and at the week's end she gave those back to the madam, yes, that was the way, and got her percentage, a very small little of her earnings: it is a business, you see, like any other —and the madam used to pretend the girl had given back only so many checks, you see, and really she had given many more, but after they were out of her hands, what could she do? So she would say, I will get out of this place, and curse and cry. Then the madam would hit her over the head. She always hit people over the head with bottles, it was the way she fought. My good heavens, Madame Blanchard, what confusion there would be sometimes with a girl running raving downstairs, and the madam pulling her back by the hair and smashing a bottle on her forehead.

It was nearly always about the money, the girls got in debt so, and if they wished to go they could not without paying every sou marqué. The madam had full understanding with the police; the girls must come back with them or go to the jails. Well, they always came back with the policemen or with another kind of man friend of the madam: she could make men work for her too, but she paid them very well for all, let me tell you: and so the girls stayed on unless they were sick; if so, if they got too sick, she sent them away again.

Madame Blanchard said, "You are pulling a little here," and eased a strand of hair: "and then what?"

Pardon—but this girl, there was a true hatred between her and the madam. She would say many times, I make more money than anybody else in the house, and every week were scenes. So at last she said one morning, Now I will leave this place, and she took out forty dollars from under her pillow and said, Here's your money! The madam began to shout, Where did you get all that, you——? and accused her of robbing the men who came to visit her. The girl said, Keep your hands off or I'll brain you: and at that the madam took hold of her shoulders, and began to lift her knee and kick this girl most terribly in the stomach, and even in her most secret place, Madame Blanchard, and then she beat her in the face with a bottle, and the girl fell back again into her room where I was making clean. I helped her to the bed, and she sat there holding her sides with her head hanging down, and when she got up again there was blood everywhere she had sat. So then the madam came in once more and screamed, Now you can get out, you are no good for me any more: I don't repeat all, you understand it is too much. But she took all the money she could find, and at the door she gave the girl a great push in the back with her knee, so that she fell again in the street, and then got up and went away with the dress barely on her.

After this the men who knew this girl kept saying, Where is Ninette? And they kept asking this in the next days, so that the madam could not say any longer, I put her out because she is a thief. No, she began to see she was wrong to send this Ninette away, and then she said, She will be back in a few days, don't trouble yourself.

And now, Madame Blanchard, if you wish to hear, I come to

the strange part, the thing recalled to me when you said your linens were bewitched. For the cook in that place was a woman, colored like myself, like myself with much French blood just the same, like myself living always among people who worked spells. But she had a very hard heart, she helped the madam in everything, she liked to watch all that happened, and she gave away tales on the girls. The madam trusted her above everything, and she said, Well, where can I find that slut? because she had gone altogether out of Basin Street before the madam began to ask the police to bring her again. Well, the cook said, I know a charm that works here in New Orleans, colored women do it to bring back their men: in seven days they come again very happy to stay and they cannot say why: even your enemy will come back to you believing you are his friend. It is a New Orleans charm for sure, for certain, they say it does not work even across the river. . . . And then they did it just as the cook said. They took the chamber pot of this girl from under her bed, and in it they mixed with water and milk all the relics of her they found there: the hair from her brush, and the face powder from the puff, and even little bits of her nails they found about the edges of the carpet where she sat by habit to cut her finger- and toe-nails; and they dipped the sheets with her blood into the water, and all the time the cook said something over it in a low voice; I could not hear all, but at last she said to the madam, Now spit in it: and the madam spat, and the cook said, When she comes back she will be dirt under your feet.

Madame Blanchard closed her perfume bottle with a thin click: "Yes, and then?"

Then in seven nights the girl came back and she looked very sick, the same clothes and all, but happy to be there. One of the men said, Welcome home, Ninette! and when she started to speak to the madam, the madam said, Shut up and get upstairs and dress yourself. So Ninette, this girl, she said, I'll be down in just a minute. And after that she lived there quietly.

1924

Rope

On the third day after they moved to the country he came walking back from the village carrying a basket of groceries and a twenty-four-yard coil of rope. She came out to meet him, wiping her hands on her green smock. Her hair was tumbled, her nose was scarlet with sunburn; he told her that already she looked like a born country woman. His gray flannel shirt stuck to him, his heavy shoes were dusty. She assured him he looked like a rural character in a play.

Had he brought the coffee? She had been waiting all day long for coffee. They had forgot it when they ordered at the store the first day.

Gosh, no, he hadn't. Lord, now he'd have to go back. Yes, he would if it killed him. He thought, though, he had everything else. She reminded him it was only because he didn't drink coffee himself. If he did he would remember it quick enough. Suppose they ran out of cigarettes? Then she saw the rope. What was that for? Well, he thought it might do to hang clothes on, or something. Naturally she asked him if he thought they were going to run a laundry? They already had a fifty-foot line hanging right before his eyes? Why, hadn't he noticed it, really? It was a blot on the landscape to her.

He thought there were a lot of things a rope might come in handy for. She wanted to know what, for instance. He thought a few seconds, but nothing occurred. They could wait and see, couldn't they? You need all sorts of strange odds and ends around a place in the country. She said, yes, that was so; but she thought just at that time when every penny counted, it seemed funny to buy more rope. That was all. She hadn't meant anything else. She hadn't just seen, not at first, why he felt it was necessary.

Well, thunder, he had bought it because he wanted to, and that was all there was to it. She thought that was reason enough, and couldn't understand why he hadn't said so, at first. Undoubtedly it would be useful, twenty-four yards of rope, there were hundreds of things, she couldn't think of any at the moment, but it would come in. Of course. As he had said, things always did in the country.

But she was a little disappointed about the coffee, and oh, look, look, look at the eggs! Oh, my, they're all running! What had he put on top of them? Hadn't he known eggs mustn't be squeezed? Squeezed, who had squeezed them, he wanted to know. What a silly thing to say. He had simply brought them along in the basket with the other things. If they got broke it was the grocer's fault. He should know better than to put heavy things on top of eggs.

She believed it was the rope. That was the heaviest thing in the pack, she saw him plainly when he came in from the road, the rope was a big package on top of everything. He desired the whole wide world to witness that this was not a fact. He had carried the rope in one hand and the basket in the other, and what was the use of her having eyes if that was the best they could do for her?

Well, anyhow, she could see one thing plain: no eggs for breakfast. They'd have to scramble them now, for supper. It was too damned bad. She had planned to have steak for supper. No ice, meat wouldn't keep. He wanted to know why she couldn't finish breaking the eggs in a bowl and set them in a cool place.

Cool place! if he could find one for her, she'd be glad to set them there. Well, then, it seemed to him they might very well cook the meat at the same time they cooked the eggs and then warm up the meat for tomorrow. The idea simply choked her. Warmed-over meat, when they might as well have had it fresh. Second best and scraps and makeshifts, even to the meat! He rubbed her shoulder a little. It doesn't really matter so much, does it, darling? Sometimes when they were playful, he would rub her shoulder and she would arch and purr. This time she hissed and almost clawed. He was getting ready to say that they could surely manage somehow when she turned on him and said, if he told her they could manage somehow she would certainly slap his face.

He swallowed the words red hot, his face burned. He picked up the rope and started to put it on the top shelf. She would not have it on the top shelf, the jars and tins belonged there; positively she would not have the top shelf cluttered up with a lot of rope. She had borne all the clutter she meant to bear in the flat in town, there was space here at least and she meant to keep things in order.

Well, in that case, he wanted to know what the hammer and nails were doing up there? And why had she put them there when she knew very well he needed that hammer and those nails upstairs to fix the window sashes? She simply slowed down everything and made double work on the place with her insane habit of changing things around and hiding them.

She was sure she begged his pardon, and if she had had any reason to believe he was going to fix the sashes this summer she would have left the hammer and nails right where he put them; in the middle of the bedroom floor where they could step on them in the dark. And now if he didn't clear the whole mess out of there she would throw them down the well.

Oh, all right, all right—could he put them in the closet? Naturally not, there were brooms and mops and dustpans in the closet, and why couldn't he find a place for his rope outside her kitchen? Had he stopped to consider there were seven God-forsaken rooms in the house, and only one kitchen?

He wanted to know what of it? And did she realize she was making a complete fool of herself? And what did she take him for, a three-year-old idiot? The whole trouble with her was she needed something weaker than she was to heckle and tyrannize over. He wished to God now they had a couple of children she could take it out on. Maybe he'd get some rest.

Her face changed at this, she reminded him he had forgot the coffee and had bought a worthless piece of rope. And when she thought of all the things they actually needed to make the place even decently fit to live in, well, she could cry, that was all. She looked so forlorn, so lost and despairing he couldn't believe it was only a piece of rope that was causing all the racket. What *was* the matter, for God's sake?

Oh, would he please hush and go away, and *stay* away, if he could, for five minutes? By all means, yes, he would. He'd stay away indefinitely if she wished. Lord, yes, there was nothing he'd like better than to clear out and never come back. She couldn't for the life of her see what was holding him, then. It was a swell time. Here she was, stuck, miles from a railroad, with a half-empty house on her hands, and not a penny in her pocket, and everything on earth to do; it seemed the God-sent moment for him to get out from under. She was surprised he hadn't stayed in town as it was until she had come out and done the work and got things straightened out. It was his usual trick.

It appeared to him that this was going a little far. Just a touch out of bounds, if she didn't mind his saying so. Why the hell had he stayed in town the summer before? To do a half-dozen extra jobs to get the money he had sent her. That was it. She knew perfectly well they couldn't have done it otherwise. She had agreed with him at the time. And that was the only time so help him he had ever left her to do anything by herself.

Oh, he could tell that to his great-grandmother. She had her notion of what had kept him in town. Considerably more than a notion, if he wanted to know. So, she was going to bring all that up again, was she? Well, she could just think what she pleased. He was tired of explaining. It may have looked funny but he had simply got hooked in, and what could he do? It was impossible to believe that she was going to take it seriously. Yes, yes, she knew how it was with a man: if he was left by himself a minute, some woman was certain to kidnap him. And naturally he couldn't hurt her feelings by refusing!

Well, what was she raving about? Did she forget she had told him those two weeks alone in the country were the happiest she had known for four years? And how long had they been married when she said that? All right, shut up! If she thought that hadn't stuck in his craw.

She hadn't meant she was happy because she was away from him. She meant she was happy getting the devilish house nice and ready for him. That was what she had meant, and now look! Bringing up something she had said a year ago simply to justify himself for forgetting her coffee and breaking the eggs and buying a wretched piece of rope they couldn't afford. She really thought it was time to drop the subject, and now she wanted only two things in the world. She wanted him to get that rope from underfoot, and go back to the village and get her coffee, and if he could remember it, he might bring a metal mitt for the skillets, and two more curtain rods, and if there were any rubber gloves in the village, her hands were simply raw, and a bottle of milk of magnesia from the drugstore.

He looked out at the dark blue afternoon sweltering on the slopes, and mopped his forehead and sighed heavily and said, if only she could wait a minute for *anything*, he was going back. He had said so, hadn't he, the very instant they found he had overlooked it?

Oh, yes, well . . . run along. She was going to wash windows. The country was so beautiful! She doubted they'd have a moment to enjoy it. He meant to go, but he could not until he had said that if she wasn't such a hopeless melancholiac she might see that this was only for a few days. Couldn't she remember anything pleasant about the other summers? Hadn't they ever had any fun? She hadn't time to talk about it, and now would he please not leave that rope lying around for her to trip on? He picked it up, somehow it had toppled off the table, and walked out with it under his arm.

Was he going this minute? He certainly was. She thought so. Sometimes it seemed to her he had second sight about the precisely perfect moment to leave her ditched. She had meant to put the mattresses out to sun, if they put them out this minute they would get at least three hours, he must have heard her say that morning she meant to put them out. So of course he would walk off and leave her to it. She supposed he thought the exercise would do her good.

Well, he was merely going to get her coffee. A four-mile walk for two pounds of coffee was ridiculous, but he was perfectly willing to do it. The habit was making a wreck of her, but if she wanted to wreck herself there was nothing he could do about it. If he thought it was coffee that was making a wreck of her, she congratulated him: he must have a damned easy conscience.

Conscience or no conscience, he didn't see why the mattresses couldn't very well wait until tomorrow. And anyhow, for God's sake, were they living *in* the house, or were they going to let the house ride them to death? She paled at this, her face grew livid about the mouth, she looked quite dangerous, and reminded him that housekeeping was no more her work than it was his: she had other work to do as well, and when did he think she was going to find time to do it at this rate?

Was she going to start on that again? She knew as well as he did that his work brought in the regular money, hers was only occasional, if they depended on what *she* made—and she might as well get straight on this question once for all!

That was positively not the point. The question was, when both of them were working on their own time, was there going to be a division of the housework, or wasn't there? She merely wanted to know, she had to make her plans. Why, he thought that was all arranged. It was understood that he was to help. Hadn't he always, in summers?

Hadn't he, though? Oh, just hadn't he? And when, and where, and doing what? Lord, what an uproarious joke!

It was such a very uproarious joke that her face turned slightly purple, and she screamed with laughter. She laughed so hard she had to sit down, and finally a rush of tears spurted from her eyes and poured down into the lifted corners of her mouth. He dashed towards her and dragged her up to her feet and tried to pour water on her head. The dipper hung by a string on a nail and he broke it loose. Then he tried to pump water with one hand while she struggled in the other. So he gave it up and shook her instead.

She wrenched away, crying out for him to take his rope and go to hell, she had simply given him up: and ran. He heard her high-heeled bedroom slippers clattering and stumbling on the stairs.

He went out around the house and into the lane; he suddenly realized he had a blister on his heel and his shirt felt as if it were on fire. Things broke so suddenly you didn't know where you were. She could work herself into a fury about simply nothing. She was terrible, damn it: not an ounce of reason. You might as well talk to a sieve as that woman when she got going. Damned if he'd spend his life humoring her! Well, what to do now? He would take back the rope and exchange it for something else. Things accumulated, things were mountainous, you couldn't move them or sort them out or get rid of them. They just lay and rotted around. He'd take it back. Hell, why should he? He wanted it. What was it anyhow? A piece of rope. Imagine anybody caring more about a piece of rope than about a man's feelings. What earthly right had she to say a word about it? He remembered all the useless, meaningless things she bought for herself: Why? because I wanted it, that's why! He stopped and selected a large stone by the road. He would put the rope behind it. He would put it in the tool-box when he got back. He'd heard enough about it to last him a life-time.

When he came back she was leaning against the post box beside the road waiting. It was pretty late, the smell of broiled steak floated nose high in the cooling air. Her face was young and smooth and fresh-looking. Her unmanageable funny black hair was all on end. She waved to him from a distance, and he speeded up. She called out that supper was ready and waiting, was he starved?

You bet he was starved. Here was the coffee. He waved it at her. She looked at his other hand. What was that he had there?

Well, it was the rope again. He stopped short. He had meant to exchange it but forgot. She wanted to know why he should exchange it, if it was something he really wanted. Wasn't the air sweet now, and wasn't it fine to be here?

She walked beside him with one hand hooked into his leather belt. She pulled and jostled him a little as he walked, and leaned against him. He put his arm clear around her and patted her stomach. They exchanged wary smiles. Coffee, coffee for the Ootsum-Wootsums! He felt as if he were bringing her a beautiful present.

He was a love, she firmly believed, and if she had had her coffee in the morning, she wouldn't have behaved so funny . . . There was a whippoorwill still coming back, imagine, clear out of season, sitting in the crab-apple tree calling all by himself. Maybe his girl stood him up. Maybe she did. She hoped to hear him once more, she loved whippoorwills . . . He knew how she was, didn't he?

Sure, he knew how she was.

He

Life was very hard for the Whipples. It was hard to feed all the hungry mouths, it was hard to keep the children in flannels during the winter, short as it was: "God knows what would become of us if we lived north," they would say: keeping them decently clean was hard. "It looks like our luck won't never let up on us," said Mr. Whipple, but Mrs. Whipple was all for taking what was sent and calling it good, anyhow when the neighbors were in earshot. "Don't ever let a soul hear us complain," she kept saying to her husband. She couldn't stand to be pitied. "No, not if it comes to it that we have to live in a wagon and pick cotton around the country," she said, "nobody's going to get a chance to look down on us."

Mrs. Whipple loved her second son, the simple-minded one, better than she loved the other two children put together. She was forever saying so, and when she talked with certain of her neighbors, she would even throw in her husband and her mother for good measure.

"You needn't keep on saying it around," said Mr. Whipple, "you'll make people think nobody else has any feelings about Him but you."

"It's natural for a mother," Mrs. Whipple would remind him. "You know yourself it's more natural for a mother to be that way. People don't expect so much of fathers, some way."

This didn't keep the neighbors from talking plainly among themselves. "A Lord's pure mercy if He should die," they said. "It's the sins of the fathers," they agreed among themselves. "There's bad blood and bad doings somewhere, you can bet on that." This behind the Whipples' backs. To their faces everybody said, "He's not so bad off. He'll be all right yet. Look how He grows!"

Mrs. Whipple hated to talk about it, she tried to keep her mind off it, but every time anybody set foot in the house, the subject always came up, and she had to talk about Him first, before she could get on to anything else. It seemed to ease her mind. "I wouldn't have anything happen to Him for all the world, but it just looks like I can't keep Him out of mischief. He's so strong and active, He's always into everything; He was like that since He could walk. It's actually funny sometimes, the way He can do anything; it's laughable to see Him up to His tricks. Emly has more accidents; I'm forever tying up her bruises, and Adna can't fall a foot without cracking a bone. But He can do anything and not get a scratch. The preacher said such a nice thing once when he was here. He said, and I'll remember it to my dying day, 'The innocent walk with God—that's why He don't get hurt.'" Whenever Mrs. Whipple repeated these words, she always felt a warm pool spread in her breast, and the tears would fill her eyes, and then she could talk about something else.

He did grow and He never got hurt. A plank blew off the chicken house and struck Him on the head and He never seemed to know it. He had learned a few words, and after this He forgot them. He didn't whine for food as the other children did, but waited until it was given Him; He ate squatting in the corner, smacking and mumbling. Rolls of fat covered Him like an overcoat, and He could carry twice as much wood and water as Adna. Emly had a cold in the head most of the time—"she takes that after me," said Mrs. Whipple—so in bad weather they gave her the extra blanket off His cot. He never seemed to mind the cold.

Just the same, Mrs. Whipple's life was a torment for fear something might happen to Him. He climbed the peach trees much better than Adna and went skittering along the branches like a monkey, just a regular monkey. "Oh, Mrs. Whipple, you hadn't ought to let Him do that. He'll lose His balance sometime. He can't rightly know what He's doing."

Mrs. Whipple almost screamed out at the neighbor. "He *does* know what He's doing! He's as able as any other child! Come down out of there, you!" When He finally reached the ground she could hardly keep her hands off Him for acting like that before people, a grin all over His face and her worried sick about Him all the time.

"It's the neighbors," said Mrs. Whipple to her husband. "Oh, I do mortally wish they would keep out of our business. I can't afford to let Him do anything for fear they'll come nosing around about it. Look at the bees, now. Adna can't handle them, they sting him up so; I haven't got time to do everything, and now I don't dare let Him. But if He gets a sting He don't really mind."

"It's just because He ain't got sense enough to be scared of anything," said Mr. Whipple.

"You ought to be ashamed of yourself," said Mrs. Whipple, "talking that way about your own child. Who's to take up for Him if we don't, I'd like to know? He sees a lot that goes on, He listens to things all the time. And anything I tell Him to do He does it. Don't never let anybody hear you say such things. They'd think you favored the other children over Him."

"Well, now I don't, and you know it, and what's the use of getting all worked up about it? You always think the worst of everything. Just let Him alone, He'll get along somehow. He gets plenty to eat and wear, don't He?" Mr. Whipple suddenly felt tired out. "Anyhow, it can't be helped now."

Mrs. Whipple felt tired too, she complained in a tired voice. "What's done can't never be undone, I know that as good as anybody; but He's my child, and I'm not going to have people say anything. I get sick of people coming around saying things all the time."

In the early fall Mrs. Whipple got a letter from her brother saying he and his wife and two children were coming over for a little visit next Sunday week. "Put the big pot in the little one," he wrote at the end. Mrs. Whipple read this part out loud twice, she was so pleased. Her brother was a great one for saying funny things. "We'll just show him that's no joke," she said, "we'll just butcher one of the sucking pigs."

"It's a waste and I don't hold with waste the way we are now," said Mr. Whipple. "That pig'll be worth money by Christmas."

"It's a shame and a pity we can't have a decent meal's vittles once in a while when my own family comes to see us," said Mrs.

Whipple. "I'd hate for his wife to go back and say there wasn't a thing in the house to eat. My God, it's better than buying up a great chance of meat in town. There's where you'd spend the money!"

"All right, do it yourself then," said Mr. Whipple. "Christa-mighty, no wonder we can't get ahead!"

The question was how to get the little pig away from his ma, a great fighter, worse than a Jersey cow. Adna wouldn't try it: "That sow'd rip my insides out all over the pen." "All right, old fraidy," said Mrs. Whipple, "*He's* not scared. Watch *Him* do it." And she laughed as though it was all a good joke and gave Him a little push towards the pen. He sneaked up and snatched the pig right away from the teat and galloped back and was over the fence with the sow raging at His heels. The little black squirming thing was screeching like a baby in a tantrum, stiffening its back and stretch-ing its mouth to the ears. Mrs. Whipple took the pig with her face stiff and sliced its throat with one stroke. When He saw the blood He gave a great jolting breath and ran away. "But He'll forget and eat plenty, just the same," thought Mrs. Whipple. Whenever she was thinking, her lips moved making words. "He'd eat it all if I didn't stop Him. He'd eat up every mouthful from the other two if I'd let Him."

She felt badly about it. He was ten years old now and a third again as large as Adna, who was going on fourteen. "It's a shame, a shame," she kept saying under her breath, "and Adna with so much brains!"

She kept on feeling badly about all sorts of things. In the first place it was the man's work to butcher; the sight of the pig scraped pink and naked made her sick. He was too fat and soft and pitiful-looking. It was simply a shame the way things had to happen. By the time she had finished it up, she almost wished her brother would stay at home.

Early Sunday morning Mrs. Whipple dropped everything to get Him all cleaned up. In an hour He was dirty again, with crawling under fences after a possum, and straddling along the rafters of the barn looking for eggs in the hayloft. "My Lord, look at you now after all my trying! And here's Adna and Emily staying so quiet. I get tired trying to keep you decent. Get off that shirt and put on another, people will say I don't half dress you!" And she boxed

Him on the ears, hard. He blinked and blinked and rubbed His head, and His face hurt Mrs. Whipple's feelings. Her knees began to tremble, she had to sit down while she buttoned His shirt. "I'm just all gone before the day starts."

The brother came with his plump healthy wife and two great roaring hungry boys. They had a grand dinner, with the pig roasted to a crackling in the middle of the table, full of dressing, a pickled peach in his mouth and plenty of gravy for the sweet potatoes.

"This looks like prosperity all right," said the brother; "you're going to have to roll me home like I was a barrel when I'm done."

Everybody laughed out loud; it was fine to hear them laughing all at once around the table. Mrs. Whipple felt warm and good about it. "Oh, we've got six more of these; I say it's as little as we can do when you come to see us so seldom."

He wouldn't come into the dining room, and Mrs. Whipple passed it off very well. "He's timider than my other two," she said, "He'll just have to get used to you. There isn't everybody He'll make up with, you know how it is with some children, even cousins." Nobody said anything out of the way.

"Just like my Alfy here," said the brother's wife. "I sometimes got to lick him to make him shake hands with his own grandmammy."

So that was over, and Mrs. Whipple loaded up a big plate for Him first, before everybody. "I always say He ain't to be slighted, no matter who else goes without," she said, and carried it to Him herself.

"He can chin Himself on the top of the door," said Emly, helping along.

"That's fine, He's getting along fine," said the brother.

They went away after supper. Mrs. Whipple rounded up the dishes, and sent the children to bed and sat down and unlaced her shoes. "You see?" she said to Mr. Whipple. "That's the way my whole family is. Nice and considerate about everything. No out-of-the-way remarks—they *have* got refinement. I get awfully sick of people's remarks. Wasn't that pig good?"

Mr. Whipple said, "Yes, we're out three hundred pounds of pork, that's all. It's easy to be polite when you come to eat. Who knows what they had in their minds all along?"

"Yes, that's like you," said Mrs. Whipple. "I don't expect anything else from you. You'll be telling me next that my own brother will be saying around that we made Him eat in the kitchen! Oh, my God!" She rocked her head in her hands, a hard pain started in the very middle of her forehead. "Now it's all spoiled, and everything was so nice and easy. All right, you don't like them and you never did—all right, they'll not come here again soon, never you mind! But they *can't* say He wasn't dressed every lick as good as Adna—oh, honest, sometimes I wish I was dead!"

"I wish you'd let up," said Mr. Whipple. "It's bad enough as it is."

It was a hard winter. It seemed to Mrs. Whipple that they hadn't ever known anything but hard times, and now to cap it all a winter like this. The crops were about half of what they had a right to expect; after the cotton was in it didn't do much more than cover the grocery bill. They swapped off one of the plow horses, and got cheated, for the new one died of the heaves. Mrs. Whipple kept thinking all the time it was terrible to have a man you couldn't depend on not to get cheated. They cut down on everything, but Mrs. Whipple kept saying there are things you can't cut down on, and they cost money. It took a lot of warm clothes for Adna and Emily, who walked four miles to school during the three-months session. "He sets around the fire a lot, He won't need so much," said Mr. Whipple. "That's so," said Mrs. Whipple, "and when He does the outdoor chores He can wear your tarpaullion coat. I can't do no better, that's all."

In February He was taken sick, and lay curled up under His blanket looking very blue in the face and acting as if He would choke. Mr. and Mrs. Whipple did everything they could for Him for two days, and then they were scared and sent for the doctor. The doctor told them they must keep Him warm and give Him plenty of milk and eggs. "He isn't as stout as He looks, I'm afraid," said the doctor. "You've got to watch them when they're like that. You must put more cover onto Him, too."

"I just took off His big blanket to wash," said Mrs. Whipple, ashamed. "I can't stand dirt."

"Well, you'd better put it back on the minute it's dry," said the doctor, "or He'll have pneumonia."

Mr. and Mrs. Whipple took a blanket off their own bed and put His cot in by the fire. "They can't say we didn't do everything for Him," she said, "even to sleeping cold ourselves on His account."

When the winter broke He seemed to be well again, but He walked as if His feet hurt Him. He was able to run a cotton planter during the season.

"I got it all fixed up with Jim Ferguson about breeding the cow next time," said Mr. Whipple. "I'll pasture the bull this summer and give Jim some fodder in the fall. That's better than paying out money when you haven't got it."

"I hope you didn't say such a thing before Jim Ferguson," said Mrs. Whipple. "You oughtn't to let him know we're so down as all that."

"Godamighty, that ain't saying we're down. A man is got to look ahead sometimes. He can lead the bull over today. I need Adna on the place."

At first Mrs. Whipple felt easy in her mind about sending Him for the bull. Adna was too jumpy and couldn't be trusted. You've got to be steady around animals. After He was gone she started thinking, and after a while she could hardly bear it any longer. She stood in the lane and watched for Him. It was nearly three miles to go and a hot day, but He oughtn't to be so long about it. She shaded her eyes and stared until colored bubbles floated in her eyeballs. It was just like everything else in life, she must always worry and never know a moment's peace about anything. After a long time she saw Him turn into the side lane, limping. He came on very slowly, leading the big hulk of an animal by a ring in the nose, twirling a little stick in His hand, never looking back or sideways, but coming on like a sleepwalker with His eyes half shut.

Mrs. Whipple was scared sick of bulls; she had heard awful stories about how they followed on quietly enough, and then suddenly pitched on with a bellow and pawed and gored a body to pieces. Any second now that black monster would come down on Him, my God, He'd never have sense enough to run.

She mustn't make a sound nor a move; she mustn't get the bull started. The bull heaved his head aside and horned the air at a fly. Her voice burst out of her in a shriek, and she screamed at Him to come on, for God's sake. He didn't seem to hear her clamor, but kept on twirling His switch and limping on, and the bull lumbered along behind him as gently as a calf. Mrs. Whipple stopped calling and ran towards the house, praying under her breath: "Lord, don't let anything happen to Him. Lord, you *know* people will say we oughtn't to have sent Him. You *know* they'll say we didn't take care of Him. Oh, get Him home, safe home, safe home, and I'll look out for Him better! Amen."

She watched from the window while He led the beast in, and tied him up in the barn. It was no use trying to keep up, Mrs. Whipple couldn't bear another thing. She sat down and rocked and cried with her apron over her head.

From year to year the Whipples were growing poorer and poorer. The place just seemed to run down of itself, no matter how hard they worked. "We're losing our hold," said Mrs. Whipple. "Why can't we do like other people and watch for our best chances? They'll be calling us poor white trash next."

"When I get to be sixteen I'm going to leave," said Adna. "I'm going to get a job in Powell's grocery store. There's money in that. No more farm for me."

"I'm going to be a schoolteacher," said Emly. "But I've got to finish the eighth grade, anyhow. Then I can live in town. I don't see any chances here."

"Emly takes after my family," said Mrs. Whipple. "Ambitious every last one of them, and they don't take second place for anybody."

When fall came Emly got a chance to wait on table in the railroad eating-house in the town near by, and it seemed such a shame not to take it when the wages were good and she could get her food too, that Mrs. Whipple decided to let her take it, and not bother with school until the next session. "You've got plenty of time," she said. "You're young and smart as a whip."

With Adna gone too, Mr. Whipple tried to run the farm with just Him to help. He seemed to get along fine, doing His work and part of Adna's without noticing it. They did well enough until Christmas time, when one morning He slipped on the ice coming up from the barn. Instead of getting up He thrashed round and round, and when Mr. Whipple got to Him, He was having some sort of fit.

They brought Him inside and tried to make Him sit up, but He blubbered and rolled, so they put Him to bed and Mr. Whipple rode to town for the doctor. All the way there and back he worried about where the money was to come from: it sure did look like he had about all the troubles he could carry.

From then on He stayed in bed. His legs swelled up double their size, and the fits kept coming back. After four months, the doctor said, "It's no use, I think you'd better put Him in the County Home for treatment right away. I'll see about it for you. He'll have good care there and be off your hands."

"We don't begrudge Him any care, and I won't let Him out of my sight," said Mrs. Whipple. "I won't have it said I sent my sick child off among strangers."

"I know how you feel," said the doctor. "You can't tell me anything about that, Mrs. Whipple. I've got a boy of my own. But you'd better listen to me. I can't do anything more for Him, that's the truth."

Mr. and Mrs. Whipple talked it over a long time that night after they went to bed. "It's just charity," said Mrs. Whipple, "that's what we've come to, charity! I certainly never looked for this."

"We pay taxes to help support the place just like everybody else," said Mr. Whipple, "and I don't call that taking charity. I think it would be fine to have Him where He'd get the best of everything . . . and besides, I can't keep up with these doctor bills any longer."

"Maybe that's why the doctor wants us to send Him—he's scared he won't get his money," said Mrs. Whipple.

"Don't talk like that," said Mr. Whipple, feeling pretty sick, "or we won't be able to send Him."

"Oh, but we won't keep Him there long," said Mrs. Whipple. "Soon's He's better, we'll bring Him right back home."

"The doctor has told you and told you time and again He can't ever get better, and you might as well stop talking," said Mr. Whipple.

"Doctors don't know everything," said Mrs. Whipple, feeling almost happy. "But anyhow, in the summer Emly can come home for a vacation, and Adna can get down for Sundays: we'll all work together and get on our feet again, and the children will feel they've got a place to come to."

All at once she saw it full summer again, with the garden going fine, and new white roller shades up all over the house, and Adna and Emly home, so full of life, all of them happy together. Oh, it could happen, things would ease up on them.

They didn't talk before Him much, but they never knew just how much He understood. Finally the doctor set the day and a neighbor who owned a double-seated carryall offered to drive them over. The hospital would have sent an ambulance, but Mrs. Whipple couldn't stand to see Him going away looking so sick as all that. They wrapped Him in blankets, and the neighbor and Mr. Whipple lifted Him into the back seat of the carryall beside Mrs. Whipple, who had on her black shirt waist. She couldn't stand to go looking like charity.

"You'll be all right, I guess I'll stay behind," said Mr. Whipple. "It don't look like everybody ought to leave the place at once."

"Besides, it ain't as if He was going to stay forever," said Mrs. Whipple to the neighbor. "This is only for a little while."

They started away, Mrs. Whipple holding to the edges of the blankets to keep Him from sagging sideways. He sat there blinking and blinking. He worked His hands out and began rubbing His nose with His knuckles, and then with the end of the blanket. Mrs. Whipple couldn't believe what she saw; He was scrubbing away big tears that rolled out of the corners of His eyes. He sniveled and made a gulping noise. Mrs. Whipple kept saying, "Oh, honey, you don't feel so bad, do you? You don't feel so bad, do you?" for He seemed to be accusing her of something. Maybe He remembered that time she boxed His ears, maybe He had been scared that day with the bull, maybe He had slept cold and couldn't tell her about it; maybe He knew they were sending Him away for good and all because they were too poor to keep Him. Whatever it was, Mrs. Whipple couldn't bear to think of it. She began to cry, frightfully, and wrapped her arms tight around Him. His head rolled on her shoulder: she had loved Him as much as she possibly could, there were Adna and Emly who had to be thought of too, there was nothing she could do to make up to Him for His life. Oh, what a mortal pity He was ever born.

They came in sight of the hospital, with the neighbor driving very fast, not daring to look behind him.

Theft

She had the purse in her hand when she came in. Standing in the middle of the floor, holding her bathrobe around her and trailing a damp towel in one hand, she surveyed the immediate past and remembered everything clearly. Yes, she had opened the flap and spread it out on the bench after she had dried the purse with her handkerchief.

She had intended to take the Elevated, and naturally she looked in her purse to make certain she had the fare, and was pleased to find forty cents in the coin envelope. She was going to pay her own fare, too, even if Camilo did have the habit of seeing her up the steps and dropping a nickel in the machine before he gave the turnstile a little push and sent her through it with a bow. Camilo by a series of compromises had managed to make effective a fairly complete set of smaller courtesies, ignoring the larger and more troublesome ones. She had walked with him to the station in a pouring rain, because she knew he was almost as poor as she was, and when he insisted on a taxi, she was firm and said, "You know it simply will not do." He was wearing a new hat of a pretty biscuit shade, for it never occurred to him to buy anything of a practical color; he had put it on for the first time and the rain was spoiling it. She kept thinking, "But this is dreadful, where will he get another?" She compared it with Eddie's hats that always seemed to be precisely seven years old and as if they had been quite purposely left out in the rain, and yet they sat with a careless and incidental rightness on Eddie. But Camilo was far different; if he wore a shabby hat it would be merely shabby on him, and he

59

would lose his spirits over it. If she had not feared Camilo would take it badly, for he insisted on the practice of his little ceremonies up to the point he had fixed for them, she would have said to him as they left Thora's house, "Do go home. I can surely reach the station by myself."

"It is written that we must be rained upon tonight," said Camilo, "so let it be together."

At the foot of the platform stairway she staggered slightly—they were both nicely set up on Thora's cocktails—and said: "At least, Camilo, do me the favor not to climb these stairs in your present state, since for you it is only a matter of coming down again at once, and you'll certainly break your neck."

He made three quick bows, he was Spanish, and leaped off through the rainy darkness. She stood watching him, for he was a very graceful young man, thinking that tomorrow morning he would gaze soberly at his spoiled hat and soggy shoes and possibly associate her with his misery. As she watched, he stopped at the far corner and took off his hat and hid it under his overcoat. She felt she had betrayed him by seeing, because he would have been humiliated if he thought she even suspected him of trying to save his hat.

Roger's voice sounded over her shoulder above the clang of the rain falling on the stairway shed, wanting to know what she was doing out in the rain at this time of night, and did she take herself for a duck? His long, imperturbable face was streaming with water, and he tapped a bulging spot on the breast of his buttoned-up overcoat: "Hat," he said. "Come on, let's take a taxi."

She settled back against Roger's arm which he laid around her shoulders, and with the gesture they exchanged a glance full of long amiable associations, then she looked through the window at the rain changing the shapes of everything, and the colors. The taxi dodged in and out between the pillars of the Elevated, skidding slightly on every curve, and she said: "The more it skids the calmer I feel, so I really must be drunk."

"You must be," said Roger. "This bird is a homicidal maniac, and I could do with a cocktail myself this minute."

They waited on the traffic at Fortieth Street and Sixth Avenue, and three boys walked before the nose of the taxi. Under the globes of light they were cheerful scarecrows, all very thin and all wearing very seedy snappy-cut suits and gay neckties. They were not very sober either, and they stood for a moment wobbling in front of the car, and there was an argument going on among them. They leaned toward each other as if they were getting ready to sing, and the first one said: "When I get married it won't be jus' for getting married, I'm gonna marry for *love,* see?" and the second one said, "Aw, gwan and tell that stuff to *her,* why n't yuh?" and the third one gave a kind of hoot, and said, "Hell, dis guy? Wot the hell's he got?" and the first one said: "Aaah, shurrup yuh mush, I got plenty." Then they all squealed and scrambled across the street beating the first one on the back and pushing him around.

"Nuts," commented Roger, "pure nuts."

Two girls went skittering by in short transparent raincoats, one green, one red, their heads tucked against the drive of the rain. One of them was saying to the other, "Yes, I know all about *that.* But what about me? You're always so sorry for *him . . .*" and they ran on with their little pelican legs flashing back and forth.

The taxi backed up suddenly and leaped forward again, and after a while Roger said: "I had a letter from Stella today, and she'll be home on the twenty-sixth, so I suppose she's made up her mind and it's all settled."

"I had a sort of letter today too," she said, "making up my mind for me. I think it is time for you and Stella to do something definite."

When the taxi stopped on the corner of West Fifty-third Street, Roger said, "I've just enough if you'll add ten cents," so she opened her purse and gave him a dime, and he said, "That's beautiful, that purse."

"It's a birthday present," she told him, "and I like it. How's your show coming?"

"Oh, still hanging on, I guess. I don't go near the place. Nothing sold yet. I mean to keep right on the way I'm going and they can take it or leave it. I'm through with the argument."

"It's absolutely a matter of holding out, isn't it?"

"Holding out's the tough part."

"Good night, Roger."

"Good night, you should take aspirin and push yourself into a tub of hot water, you look as though you're catching cold."

"I will."

With the purse under her arm she went upstairs, and on the first landing Bill heard her step and poked his head out with his hair tumbled and his eyes red, and he said: "For Christ's sake, come in and have a drink with me. I've had some bad news."

"You're perfectly sopping," said Bill, looking at her drenched feet. They had two drinks, while Bill told how the director had thrown his play out after the cast had been picked over twice, and had gone through three rehearsals. "I said to him, 'I didn't say it was a masterpiece, I said it would make a good show.' And he said, 'It just doesn't *play,* do you see? It needs a doctor.' So I'm stuck, absolutely stuck," said Bill, on the edge of weeping again. "I've been crying," he told her, "in my cups." And he went on to ask her if she realized his wife was ruining him with her extravagance. "I send her ten dollars every week of my unhappy life, and I don't really have to. She threatens to jail me if I don't, but she can't do it. God, let her try it after the way she treated me! She's no right to alimony and she knows it. She keeps on saying she's got to have it for the baby and I keep on sending it because I can't bear to see anybody suffer. So I'm way behind on the piano and the victrola, both—"

"Well, this is a pretty rug, anyhow," she said.

Bill stared at it and blew his nose. "I got it at Ricci's for ninety-five dollars," he said. "Ricci told me it once belonged to Marie Dressler, and cost fifteen hundred dollars, but there's a burnt place on it, under the divan. Can you beat that?"

"No," she said. She was thinking about her empty purse and that she could not possibly expect a check for her latest review for another three days, and her arrangement with the basement restaurant could not last much longer if she did not pay something on account. "It's no time to speak of it," she said, "but I've been hoping you would have by now that fifty dollars you promised for my scene in the third act. Even if it doesn't play. You were to pay me for the work anyhow out of your advance."

"Weeping Jesus," said Bill, "you, too?" He gave a loud sob, or hiccough, in his moist handkerchief. "Your stuff was no better than mine, after all. Think of that."

"But you got something for it," she said. "Seven hundred dollars."

Bill said, "Do me a favor, will you? Have another drink and forget about it. I can't, you know I can't, I would if I could, but you know the fix I'm in."

"Let it go, then," she found herself saying almost in spite of herself. She had meant to be quite firm about it. They drank again without speaking, and she went to her apartment on the floor above.

There, she now remembered distinctly, she had taken the letter out of the purse before she spread the purse out to dry.

She had sat down and read the letter over again: but there were phrases that insisted on being read many times, they had a life of their own separate from the others, and when she tried to read past and around them, they moved with the movement of her eyes, and she could not escape them . . . "thinking about you more than I mean to . . . yes, I even talk about you . . . why were you so anxious to destroy . . . even if I could see you now I would not . . . not worth all this abominable . . . the end . . ."

Carefully she tore the letter into narrow strips and touched a lighted match to them in the coal grate.

Early the next morning she was in the bathtub when the janitress knocked and then came in, calling out that she wished to examine the radiators before she started the furnace going for the winter. After moving about the room for a few minutes, the janitress went out, closing the door very sharply.

She came out of the bathroom to get a cigarette from the package in the purse. The purse was gone. She dressed and made coffee, and sat by the window while she drank it. Certainly the janitress had taken the purse, and certainly it would be impossible to get it back without a great deal of ridiculous excitement. Then let it go. With this decision of her mind, there rose coincidentally in her blood a deep almost murderous anger. She set the cup carefully in the center of the table, and walked steadily downstairs, three long flights and a short hall and a steep short flight into the basement, where the janitress, her face streaked with coal dust, was shaking up the furnace. "Will you please give me back my purse? There isn't any money in it. It was a present, and I don't want to lose it."

The janitress turned without straightening up and peered at her with hot flickering eyes, a red light from the furnace reflected in them. "What do you mean, your purse?"

"The gold cloth purse you took from the wooden bench in my room," she said. "I must have it back."

"Before God I never laid eyes on your purse, and that's the holy truth," said the janitress.

"Oh, well then, keep it," she said, but in a very bitter voice; "keep it if you want it so much." And she walked away.

She remembered how she had never locked a door in her life, on some principle of rejection in her that made her uncomfortable in the ownership of things, and her paradoxical boast before the warnings of her friends, that she had never lost a penny by theft; and she had been pleased with the bleak humility of this concrete example designed to illustrate and justify a certain fixed, otherwise baseless and general faith which ordered the movements of her life without regard to her will in the matter.

In this moment she felt that she had been robbed of an enormous number of valuable things, whether material or intangible: things lost or broken by her own fault, things she had forgotten and left in houses when she moved: books borrowed from her and not returned, journeys she had planned and had not made, words she had waited to hear spoken to her and had not heard, and the words she had meant to answer with; bitter alternatives and intolerable substitutes worse than nothing, and yet inescapable: the long patient suffering of dying friendships and the dark inexplicable death of love—all that she had had, and all that she had missed, were lost together, and were twice lost in this landslide of remembered losses.

The janitress was following her upstairs with the purse in her hand and the same deep red fire flickering in her eyes. The janitress thrust the purse towards her while they were still a half dozen steps apart, and said: "Don't never tell on me. I musta been crazy. I get crazy in the head sometimes, I swear I do. My son can tell you."

She took the purse after a moment, and the janitress went on: "I got a niece who is going on seventeen, and she's a nice girl and I thought I'd give it to her. She needs a pretty purse. I musta been crazy; I thought maybe you wouldn't mind, you leave things around and don't seem to notice much."

She said: "I missed this because it was a present to me from someone . . ."

The janitress said: "He'd get you another if you lost this one. My niece is young and needs pretty things, we oughta give the young ones a chance. She's got young men after her maybe will want to marry her. She oughta have nice things. She needs them bad right now. You're a grown woman, you've had your chance, you ought to know how it is!"

She held the purse out to the janitress saying: "You don't know what you're talking about. Here, take it, I've changed my mind. I really don't want it."

The janitress looked up at her with hatred and said: "I don't want it either now. My niece is young and pretty, she don't need fixin' up to be pretty, she's young and pretty anyhow! I guess you need it worse than she does!"

"It wasn't really yours in the first place," she said, turning away. "You mustn't talk as if I had stolen it from you."

"It's not from me, it's from her you're stealing it," said the janitress, and went back downstairs.

She laid the purse on the table and sat down with the cup of chilled coffee, and thought: I was right not to be afraid of any thief but myself, who will end by leaving me nothing.

That Tree

He had really wanted to be a cheerful bum lying under a tree in a good climate, writing poetry. He wrote bushel basketsful of poetry and it was all no good and he knew it, even while he was writing it. Knowing his poetry was no good did not take away much from his pleasure in it. He would have enjoyed just that kind of life: no respectability, no responsibility, no money to speak of, wearing worn-out sandals and a becoming, if probably ragged, blue shirt, lying under a tree writing poetry. That was why he had come to Mexico in the first place. He had felt in his bones that it was the country for him. Long after he had become quite an important journalist, an authority on Latin-American revolutions and a best seller, he confessed to any friends and acquaintances who would listen to him—he enjoyed this confession, it gave him a chance to talk about the thing he believed he loved best, the idle free romantic life of a poet—that the day Miriam kicked him out was the luckiest day of his life. She had left him, really, packing up suddenly in a cold quiet fury, stabbing him with her elbows when he tried to get his arms around her, now and again cutting him to the bone with a short sentence expelled through her clenched teeth; but he felt that he had been, as he always explained, kicked out. She had kicked him out and it had served him right.

The shock had brought him to himself as if he had been surprised out of a long sleep. He had sat quite benumbed in the bare clean room, among the straw mats and the painted Indian chairs Miriam hated, in the sudden cold silence, his head in his hands, nearly all night. It hadn't even occurred to him to lie down. It must have been almost daylight when he got up stiff in every joint from sitting still so long, and though he could not say he had been thinking yet he had formed a new resolution. He had started out, you might almost say that very day, to make a career for himself in journalism. He couldn't say why he had hit on that, except that the word would impress his wife, the work was just intellectual enough to save his self-respect, such as it was, and even to him it seemed a suitable occupation for a man such as he had suddenly become, bent on getting on in the world of affairs. Nothing ever happens suddenly to anyone, he observed, as if the thought had just occurred to him; it had been coming on probably for a long time, sneaking up on him when he wasn't looking. His wife had called him "Parasite!" She had said "Ne'er-do-well!" and as she repeated these things for what proved to be the last time, it struck him she had said them often before, when he had not listened to her with the ear of his mind. He translated these relatively harmless epithets instantly into their proper synonyms of Loafer! and Bum! Miriam had been a schoolteacher, and no matter what her disappointments and provocations may have been, you could not expect her easily to forget such discipline. She had got into a professional habit of primness; besides, she was a properly brought-up girl, not a prissy bore, not at all, but a—well, there you are, a nicely brought-up Middle-Western girl, who took life seriously. And what can you do about that? She was sweet and gay and full of little crazy notions, but she never gave way to them honestly, or at least never at the moment when they might have meant something. She was never able to see the amusing side of a threatening situation which, taken solemnly, would ruin everything. No, her sense of humor never worked for salvation. It was just an extra frill on what would have been a good time anyhow.

He wondered if anybody had ever thought—oh, well, of course everybody else had, he was always making marvelous discoveries that other people had known all along—how impossible it is to explain or to make other eyes see the special qualities in the person you love. There was such a special kind of beauty in Miriam. In certain lights and moods he simply got a clutch in the pit of his stomach when he looked at her. It was something that could happen at any hour of the day, in the midst of the most ordinary occupations. He thought there was something to be said for living with one person day and night the year round. It brings out the worst, but it brings out the best, too, and Miriam's best was pretty damn swell. He couldn't describe it. It was easy to talk about her faults. He remembered all of them, he could add them up against her like rows of figures in a vast unpaid debt. He had lived with her for four years, and even now sometimes he woke out of a sound sleep in a sweating rage with himself, asking himself again why he had ever wasted a minute on her. She wasn't beautiful in his style. He confessed to a weakness for the kind that knocks your eye out. Her notion of daytime dress was a tailored suit with a round-collared blouse and a little felt hat like a bent shovel pulled down over her eyes. In the evening she put on a black dinner dress, positively disappeared into it. But she did her hair well and had the most becoming nightgowns he ever saw. You could have put her mind in a peanut shell. She hadn't temperament of the kind he had got used to in the Mexican girls. She did not approve of his use of the word temperament, either. She thought it was a kind of occupational disease among artists, or a trick they practiced to make themselves interesting. In any case, she distrusted artists and she distrusted temperament. But there was something about her. In cold blood he could size her up to himself, but it made him furious if anyone even hinted a criticism against her. His second wife had made a point of being catty about Miriam. In the end he could almost be willing to say this had led to his second divorce. He could not bear hearing Miriam called a mousy little nit-wit—at least not by *that* woman . . .

They both jumped nervously at an explosion in the street, the backfire of an automobile.

"Another revolution," said the fat scarlet young man in the tight purplish suit, at the next table. He looked like a parboiled sausage ready to burst from its skin. It was the oldest joke since the Mexican Independence, but he was trying to look as if he had invented it. The journalist glanced back at him over a sloping shoulder. "Another of those smart-cracking newspaper guys," he said in a tough voice, too loudly on purpose, "sitting around the Hotel Regis lobby wearing out the spittoons."

The smart-cracker swelled visibly and turned a darker red. "Who do you think you're talking about, you banjo-eyed chinless wonder, you?" he asked explicitly, spreading his chest across the table.

"Somebody way up, no doubt," said the journalist, in his natural voice, "somebody in with the government, I'll bet."

"Dyuhwana fight?" asked the newspaper man, trying to unwedge himself from between the table and his chair, which sat against the wall.

"Oh, I don't mind," said the journalist, "if you don't."

The newspaper man's friends laid soothing paws all over him and held him down. "Don't start anything with that shrimp," said one of them, his wet pink eyes trying to look sober and responsible. "For crisesake, Joe, can't you see he's about half your size and a feeb to boot? You wouldn't hit a feeb, now, Joe, would you?"

"I'll feeb him," said the newspaper man, wiggling faintly under restraint.

"*Señores'n, señores'n,*" urged the little Mexican waiter, "there are respectable ladies and gentlemen present. Please, a little silence and correct behavior, please."

"Who the hell are *you,* anyhow?" the newspaper man asked the journalist, from under his shelter of hands, around the thin form of the waiter.

"Nobody you'd wanta know, Joe," said another of his pawing friends. "Pipe down now before these greasers turn in a general alarm. You know how liable they are to go off when you least expect it. Pipe down, now, Joe, now you just remember what happened the last time, Joe. Whaddayah *care,* anyhow?"

"*Señores'n,*" said the little waiter, working his thin outspread mahogany-colored hands up and down alternately as if they were on sticks, "it is necessary it must cease or the *señores'n* must remove themselves."

It did cease. It seemed to evaporate. The four newspaper men at the next table subsided, cluttered in a circle with their heads together, muttering into their highballs. The journalist turned back, ordered another round of drinks, and went on talking, in a low voice.

He had never liked this café, never had any luck in it. Something always happened here to spoil his evening. If there was one brand of bum on earth he despised, it was a newspaper bum. Or anyhow the drunken illiterates the United Press and Associated Press seemed to think were good enough for Mexico and South America. They were always getting mixed up in affairs that were none of their business, and they spent their time trying to work up trouble somewhere so they could get a story out of it. They were always having to be thrown out on their ears by the government. He just happened to know that the bum at the next table was about due to be deported. It had been pretty safe to make that crack about how he was no doubt way up in Mexican official esteem. . . . He thought that would remind him of something, all right.

One evening he had come here with Miriam for dinner and dancing, and at the very next table sat four fat generals from the North, with oxhorn mustaches and big bellies and big belts full of cartridges and pistols. It was in the old days just after Obregón had taken the city, and the town was crawling with generals. They infested the steam baths, where they took off their soiled campaign harness and sweated away the fumes of tequila and fornication, and they infested the cafés to get drunk again on champagne, and pick up the French whores who had been imported for the festivities of the presidential inauguration. These four were having an argument very quietly, their mean little eyes boring into each other's faces. He and his wife were dancing within arm's length of the table when one of the generals got up suddenly, tugging at his pistol, which stuck, and the other three jumped and grabbed him, all without a word; everybody in the place saw it at once. So far there was nothing unusual. The point was, every right-minded Mexican girl just seized her man firmly by the waist and spun him around until his back was to the generals, holding him before her like a shield, and there the whole roomful had stood frozen for a second, the music dead. His wife Miriam had broken from him and hidden under a table. He had to drag her out by the arm before everybody. "Let's have another drink," he said, and paused, looking around him as if he saw again the place as it had been on that night nearly ten years before. He blinked, and went on. It had been the most utterly humiliating moment of his whole blighted life. He had thought he couldn't survive to pick up their things and get her out of there. The generals had all sat down again and

everybody went on dancing as though nothing had happened.
. . . Indeed, nothing had happened to anyone except himself.

He tried, for hours that night and on and on for nearly a year,
to explain to her how he felt about it. She could not understand at
all. Sometimes she said it was all perfect nonsense. Or she remarked complacently that it had never occurred to her to save her
life at his expense. She thought such tricks were all very well for
the Mexican girls who had only one idea in their heads, and any
excuse would do to hold a man closer than they should, but she
could not, could *not,* see why he should expect her to imitate them.
Besides, she had felt safer under the table. It was her first and only
thought. He told her a bullet might very well have gone through
the wood; a plank was no protection at all, a human torso was as
good as a feather pillow to stop a bullet. She kept saying it simply
had not occurred to her to do anything else, and that it really had
nothing at all to do with him. He could never make her see his
point of view for one moment. It should have had something to do
with him. All those Mexican girls were born knowing what they
should do and they did it instantly, and Miriam had merely proved
once for all that her instincts were out of tune. When she tightened
her mouth to bite her lip and say "Instincts!" she could make it
sound like the most obscene word in any language. It was a shocking word. And she did not stop there. At last she said, she hadn't
the faintest interest in what Mexican girls were born for, but she
had no intention of wasting her life flattering male vanity. "Why
should I trust you in anything?" she asked. "What reason have you
given me to trust you?"

He was surprised at the change in her since he had first met her
in Minneapolis. He chose to believe this change had been caused
by her teaching school. He told her he thought it the most deadly
occupation there was and a law should be passed prohibiting pretty
women under thirty-five years of age from taking it up. She reminded him they were living on the money she had earned at it.
They had been engaged for three years, a chaste long-distance
engagement which he considered morbid and unnatural. Of course
he had to do something to wear away the time, so while she was in
Minneapolis saving her money and filling a huge trunk with household linen, he had been living in Mexico City with an Indian girl
who posed for a set of painters he knew. He had a job teaching

English in one of the technical schools—damned odd, he had been a schoolteacher too, but he never thought of it just that way until this minute—and he lived very comfortably with the Indian girl on his wages, for naturally the painters did not pay her for posing. The Indian girl divided her time cheerfully between the painters, the cooking pot, and his bed, and she managed to have a baby without interrupting any of these occupations for more than a few days. Later on she was taken up by one of the more famous and successful painters, and grew very sophisticated and a "character," but at that time she was still simple and nice. She took, later on, to wearing native art-jewelry and doing native dances in costume, and learned to paint almost as well as a seven-year-old child; "you know," he said, "the primitive style." Well, by that time, he was having troubles of his own. When the time came for Miriam to come out and marry him—the whole delay, he realized afterward, was caused by Miriam's expansive notions of what a bride's outfit should be—the Indian girl had gone away very cheerfully, too cheerfully, in fact, with a new man. She had come back in three days to say she was at last going to get married honestly, and she felt he should give her the furniture for a dowry. He had helped her pile the stuff on the backs of two Indian carriers, and the girl had walked away with the baby's head dangling out of her shawl. For just a moment when he saw the baby's face, he had an odd feeling. "That's mine," he said to himself, and added at once, "perhaps." There was no way of knowing, and it certainly looked like any other little shock-haired Indian baby. Of course the girl had not got married; she had never even thought of it.

When Miriam arrived, the place was almost empty, because he had not been able to save a peso. He had a bed and a stove, and the walls were decorated with drawings and paintings by his Mexican friends, and there was a litter of painted gourds and carved wood and pottery in beautiful colors. It didn't seem so bad to him, but Miriam's face, when she stepped into the first room, was, he had to admit, pretty much of a study. She said very little, but she began to be unhappy about a number of things. She cried intermittently for the first few weeks, for the most mysterious and far-fetched causes. He would wake in the night and find her crying hopelessly. When she sat down to coffee in the morning she would lean her head on her hands and cry. "It's nothing, nothing really," she would tell him. "I don't know what is the matter. I just want to cry." He knew now what was the matter. She had come all that way to marry after three years' planning, and she couldn't see herself going back and facing the music at home. This mood had not lasted, but it made a fairly dreary failure of their honeymoon. She knew nothing about the Indian girl, and believed, or professed to believe, that he was virgin as she was at their marriage. She hadn't much curiosity and her moral standards were severe, so it was impossible for him ever to take her into his confidence about his past. She simply took it for granted in the most irritating way that he hadn't any past worth mentioning except the three years they were engaged, and that, of course, they shared already. He had believed that all virgins, however austere their behavior, were palpitating to learn about life, were you might say hanging on by an eyelash until they arrived safely at initiation within the secure yet libertine advantages of marriage. Miriam upset this theory as in time she upset most of his theories. His intention to play the rôle of a man of the world educating an innocent but interestingly teachable bride was nipped in the bud. She was not at all teachable and she took no trouble to make herself interesting. In their most intimate hours her mind seemed elsewhere, gone into some darkness of its own, as if a prior and greater shock of knowledge had forestalled her attention. She was not to be won, for reasons of her own which she would not or could not give. He could not even play the rôle of a poet. She was not interested in his poetry. She preferred Milton, and she let him know it. She let him know also that she believed their mutual sacrifice of virginity was the most important act of their marriage, and this sacred rite once achieved, the whole affair had descended to a pretty low plane. She had a terrible phrase about "walking the chalk line" which she applied to all sorts of situations. One walked, as never before, the chalk line in marriage; there seemed to be a chalk line drawn between them as they lay together. . . .

The thing that finally got him down was Miriam's devilish inconsistency. She spent three mortal years writing him how dull and dreadful and commonplace her life was, how sick and tired she was of petty little conventions and amusements, how narrow-minded everybody around her was, how she longed to live in a beautiful dangerous place among interesting people who painted and wrote poetry, and how his letters came into her stuffy little world like a breath of free mountain air, and all that. "For God's sake," he said to his guest, "let's have another drink." Well, he had something of a notion he was freeing a sweet bird from a cage. Once freed, she would perch gratefully on his hand. He wrote a poem about a caged bird set free, dedicated it to her and sent her a copy. She forgot to mention it in her next letter. Then she came out with a two-hundred-pound trunk of linen and enough silk underwear to last her a lifetime, you might have supposed, expecting to settle down in a modern steam-heated flat and have nice artistic young couples from the American colony in for dinner Wednesday evenings. No wonder her face had changed at the first glimpse of her new home. His Mexican friends had scattered flowers all over the place, tied bunches of carnations on the door knobs, almost carpeted the floor with red roses, pinned posies of small bright blooms on the sagging cotton curtains, spread a coverlet of gardenias on the lumpy bed, and had disappeared discreetly, leaving gay reassuring messages scribbled here and there, even on the white plastered walls. . . . She had walked through with a vague look of terror in her eyes, pushing back the wilting flowers with her advancing feet. She swept the gardenias aside to sit on the edge of the bed, and she had said not a word. Hail, Hymen! What next?

He had lost his teaching job almost immediately. The Minister of Education, who was a patron of the school superintendent, was put out of office suddenly, and naturally every soul in his party down to the school janitors went out with him, and there you were. After a while you learn to take such things calmly. You wait until your man gets back in the saddle or you work up an alliance with the new one. . . . Whichever . . . Meanwhile the change and movement made such a good show you almost forgot the effect it had on your food supply. Miriam was not interested in politics or the movement of local history. She could see nothing but that he had lost his job. They lived on Miriam's savings eked out with birthday checks and Christmas checks from her father, who threatened constantly to come for a visit, in spite of Miriam's desperate letters warning him that the country was appalling, and the climate would most certainly ruin his health. Miriam went on holding her nose when she went to the markets, trying to cook wholesome civilized American food over a charcoal brasier, and doing the washing in the patio over a stone tub with a cold water tap; and everything that had seemed so jolly and natural and inexpensive with the Indian girl was too damnifying and costly for words with Miriam. Her money melted away and they got nothing for it.

She would not have an Indian servant near her: they were dirty and besides how could she afford it? He could not see why she despised and resented housework so, especially since he offered to help. He had thought it rather a picnic to wash a lot of gayly colored Indian crockery outdoors in the sunshine, with the bougainvillea climbing up the wall and the heaven tree in full bloom. Not Miriam. She despised him for thinking it a picnic. He remembered for the first time his mother doing the housework when he was a child. There were half a dozen assorted children, her work was hard and endless, but she went about it with a quiet certainty, a happy absorbed look on her face, as if her hands were working automatically while her imagination was away playing somewhere. "Ah, your mother," said his wife, without any particular emphasis. He felt horribly injured, as if she were insulting his mother and calling down a curse on her head for bringing such a son into the world. No doubt about it, Miriam had force. She could make her personality, which no one need really respect, felt in a bitter, sinister way. She had a background, and solid earth under her feet, and a point of view and a strong spine: even when she danced with him he could feel her tense controlled hips and her locked knees, which gave her dancing a most attractive strength and lightness without any yielding at all. She had her points, all right, like a good horse, but she had missed being beautiful. It wasn't in her. He began to cringe when she reminded him that if he were an invalid she would cheerfully work for him and take care of him, but he appeared to be in the best of health, he was not even looking for a job, and he was still writing that poetry, which was the last straw. She called him a failure. She called him worthless and shiftless and trifling and faithless. She showed him her ruined hands and asked him what she had to look forward to, and told him again, and again, that she was not used to associating with the simply indescribably savage and awful persons who kept streaming through the place. Moreover, she had no intention of getting used to it. He tried to tell her that these persons were the best painters and poets and what-alls in Mexico, that she should try to appreciate them; these were the artists he had told her about in his letters. She wanted to know why Carlos never changed his shirt. "I told her," said the journalist, "it was because probably he hadn't got any other shirt." And why was Jaime such a glutton, leaning over his plate and wolfing his food? Because he was famished, no doubt. It was precisely that she could not understand. Why didn't they go to work and make a living? It was no good trying to explain to her his Franciscan notions of holy Poverty as being the natural companion for the artist. She said, "So you think they're being poor on purpose? Nobody but you would be such a fool." Really, the things that girl said. And his general impression of her was that she was silent as a cat. He went on in his pawky way trying to make clear to her his mystical faith in these men who went ragged and hungry because they had chosen once for all between what he called in all seriousness their souls, and this world. Miriam knew better. She knew they were looking for the main chance. "She was abominably, obscenely right. How I hate that woman, I hate her as I hate no one else. She assured me they were not so stupid as I thought; and I lived to see Jaime take up with a rich old woman, and Ricardo decide to turn film actor, and Carlos sitting easy with a government job, painting revolutionary frescoes to order, and I asked myself, Why shouldn't a man survive in any way he can?" But some fixed point of feeling in him refused to be convinced, he had a sackful of romantic notions about artists and their destiny and he was left holding it. Miriam had seen through them with half an eye, and how he wished he might have thought of a trick to play on her that would have finished her for life. But he had not. They all in turn ran out on him and in the end he had run out too. "So you see, I don't feel any better about doing what I did finally do, but I can say I am not unusual. That I can say. The trouble was that Miriam was right, damn her. I am not a poet, my poetry is filthy, and I had notions about artists that I must have got out of books. . . . You know, a race apart, dedicated men much superior to common human needs and ambitions. . . . I mean I thought art was a religion. . . . I mean that when Miriam kept saying . . ."

What he meant was that all this conflict began to damage him seriously. Miriam had become an avenging fury, yet he could not condemn her. Hate her, yes, that was almost too simple. His old-fashioned respectable middle-class hard-working American ancestry and training rose up in him and fought on Miriam's side. He felt he had broken about every bone in him to get away from them and live them down, and here he had been overtaken at last and beaten into resignation that had nothing to do with his mind or heart. It was as if his blood stream had betrayed him. The prospect of taking a job and being a decent little clerk with shiny pants and elbows—for he couldn't think of a job in any other terms—seemed like a kind of premature death which would not even compensate him with loss of memory. He didn't do anything about it at all. He did odd jobs and picked up a little money, but never enough. He could see her side of it, at least he tried hard to see it. When it came to a showdown, he hadn't a single argument in favor of his way of life that would hold water. He had been trying to live and think in a way that he hoped would end by making a poet of him, but it hadn't worked. That was the long and short of it. So he might have just gone on to some unimaginably sordid end if Miriam, after four years: four years? yes, good God, four years and one month and eleven days, had not written home for money, packed up what was left of her belongings, called him a few fare-well names, and left. She had been shabby and thin and wild-looking for so long he could not remember ever having seen her any other way, yet all at once her profile in the doorway was unrecognizable to him.

So she went, and she did him a great favor without knowing it. He had fallen into the cowardly habit of thinking their marriage was permanent, no matter how evil it might be, that they loved each other, and so it did not matter what cruelties they committed against each other, and he had developed a real deafness to her words. He was unable, towards the end, either to see her or hear her. He realized this afterward, when remembered phrases and expressions of her eyes and mouth began to eat into his marrow. He was grateful to her. If she had not gone, he might have loitered on, wasting his time trying to write poetry, hanging around dirty picturesque little cafés with a fresh set of clever talkative poverty-stricken young Mexicans who were painting or writing or talking about getting ready to paint or write. His faith had renewed itself; these fellows were pure artists—they would never sell out. They were not bums, either. They worked all the time at something to do with Art. "Sacred Art," he said, "our glasses are empty again."

But try telling anything of the kind to Miriam. Somehow he had never got to that tree he meant to lie down under. If he had, somebody would certainly have come around and collected rent for it, anyhow. He had spent a good deal of time lying under tables at Dinty Moore's or the Black Cat with a gang of Americans like himself who were living a free life and studying the native customs. He was rehearsing, he explained to Miriam, hoping for once she would take a joke, for lying under a tree later on. It didn't go over. She would have died with her boots on before she would have cracked a smile at that. So then . . . He had gone in for a career in the hugest sort of way. It had been easy. He hardly could say now just what his first steps were, but it had been easy. Except for Miriam, he would have been a lousy failure, like those bums at Dinty Moore's, still rolling under the tables, studying the native customs. He had gone in for a career in journalism and he had made a good thing of it. He was a recognized authority on revolutions in twenty-odd Latin-American countries, and his sympathies happened to fall in exactly right with the high-priced magazines of a liberal humanitarian slant which paid him well for telling the world about the oppressed peoples. He could really write, too; if he did say so, he had a prose style of his own. He had made the kind of success you can clip out of newspapers and paste in a book, you can count it and put it in the bank, you can eat and drink and wear it, and you can see it in other people's eyes at tea and dinner parties. Fine, and now what? On the strength of all this he had got married again. Twice, in fact, and divorced twice. That made three times, didn't it? That was plenty. He had spent a good deal of time and energy doing all sorts of things he didn't care for in the least to prove to his first wife, who had been a twenty-three-year-old schoolteacher in Minneapolis, Minnesota, that he was not just merely a bum, fit for nothing but lying under a tree— if he had ever been able to locate that ideal tree he had in his mind's eye—writing poetry and enjoying his life.

Now he had done it. He smoothed out the letter he had been turning in his hands and stroked it as if it were a cat. He said, "I've been working up to the climax all this time. You know, good old surprise technique. Now then, get ready."

Miriam had written to him, after these five years, asking him to take her back. And would you believe it, he was going to break down and do that very thing. Her father was dead, she was terribly lonely, she had had time to think everything over, she believed herself to blame for a great many things, she loved him truly and she always had, truly; she regretted, oh, everything, and hoped it was not too late for them to make a happy life together once more. . . . She had read everything she could find of his in print, and she loved all of it. He had that very morning sent by cable the money for her to travel on, and he was going to take her back. She was going to live again in a Mexican house without any conveniences and she was not going to have a modern flat. She was going to take whatever he chose to hand her, and like it. And he wasn't going to marry her again, either. Not he. If she wanted to live with him on these terms, well and good. If not, she could just go back once more to that school of hers in Minneapolis. If she stayed, she would walk a chalk line, all right, one she hadn't drawn for herself. He picked up a cheese knife and drew a long sharp line in the checkered table-cloth. She would, believe him, walk *that*.

The hands of the clock pointed half past two. The journalist swallowed the last of his drink and went on drawing more cross-hatches on the table-cloth with a relaxed hand. His guest wished to say, "Don't forget to invite me to your wedding," but thought better of it. The journalist raised his twitching lids and swung his half-focused eyes upon the shadow opposite and said, "I suppose you think I don't know—"

His guest moved to the chair edge and watched the orchestra folding up for the night. The café was almost empty. The journalist paused, not for an answer, but to give weight to the important statement he was about to make.

"I don't know what's happening, this time," he said, "don't deceive yourself. This time, I know." He seemed to be admonishing himself before a mirror.

The Jilting of
Granny Weatherall

She flicked her wrist neatly out of Doctor Harry's pudgy careful fingers and pulled the sheet up to her chin. The brat ought to be in knee breeches. Doctoring around the country with spectacles on his nose! "Get along now, take your schoolbooks and go. There's nothing wrong with me."

Doctor Harry spread a warm paw like a cushion on her forehead where the forked green vein danced and made her eyelids twitch. "Now, now, be a good girl, and we'll have you up in no time."

"That's no way to speak to a woman nearly eighty years old just because she's down. I'd have you respect your elders, young man."

"Well, Missy, excuse me." Doctor Harry patted her cheek. "But I've got to warn you, haven't I? You're a marvel, but you must be careful or you're going to be good and sorry."

"Don't tell me what I'm going to be. I'm on my feet now, morally speaking. It's Cornelia. I had to go to bed to get rid of her."

Her bones felt loose, and floated around in her skin, and Doctor Harry floated like a balloon around the foot of the bed. He floated and pulled down his waistcoat and swung his glasses on a cord. "Well, stay where you are, it certainly can't hurt you."

"Get along and doctor your sick," said Granny Weatherall. "Leave a well woman alone. I'll call for you when I want you. . . . Where were you forty years ago when I pulled through milk-leg and double pneumonia? You weren't even born. Don't let Cornelia lead you on," she shouted, because Doctor Harry appeared to float up to the ceiling and out. "I pay my own bills, and I don't throw my money away on nonsense!"

She meant to wave good-by, but it was too much trouble. Her eyes closed of themselves, it was like a dark curtain drawn around the bed. The pillow rose and floated under her, pleasant as a hammock in a light wind. She listened to the leaves rustling outside the window. No, somebody was swishing newspapers: no, Cornelia and Doctor Harry were whispering together. She leaped broad awake, thinking they whispered in her ear.

"She was never like this, *never* like this!" "Well, what can we expect?" "Yes, eighty years old. . . ."

Well, and what if she was? She still had ears. It was like Cornelia to whisper around doors. She always kept things secret in such a public way. She was always being tactful and kind. Cornelia was dutiful; that was the trouble with her. Dutiful and good: "So good and dutiful," said Granny, "that I'd like to spank her." She saw herself spanking Cornelia and making a fine job of it.

"What'd you say, Mother?"

Granny felt her face tying up in hard knots.

"Can't a body think, I'd like to know?"

"I thought you might want something."

"I do. I want a lot of things. First off, go away and don't whisper."

She lay and drowsed, hoping in her sleep that the children would keep out and let her rest a minute. It had been a long day. Not that she was tired. It was always pleasant to snatch a minute now and then. There was always so much to be done, let me see: tomorrow.

Tomorrow was far away and there was nothing to trouble about. Things were finished somehow when the time came; thank God there was always a little margin over for peace: then a person could spread out the plan of life and tuck in the edges orderly. It was good to have everything clean and folded away, with the hair brushes and tonic bottles sitting straight on the white embroidered linen: the day started without fuss and the pantry shelves laid out with rows of jelly glasses and brown jugs and white stone-china jars with blue whirligigs and words painted on them: coffee, tea, sugar, ginger, cinnamon, allspice: and the bronze clock with the lion on top nicely dusted off. The dust that lion could collect in twenty-four hours! The box in the attic with all those letters tied up, well, she'd have to go through that tomorrow. All those letters —George's letters and John's letters and her letters to them both —lying around for the children to find afterwards made her uneasy. Yes, that would be tomorrow's business. No use to let them know how silly she had been once.

While she was rummaging around she found death in her mind and it felt clammy and unfamiliar. She had spent so much time preparing for death there was no need for bringing it up again. Let it take care of itself now. When she was sixty she had felt very old, finished, and went around making farewell trips to see her children and grandchildren, with a secret in her mind: This is the very last of your mother, children! Then she made her will and came down with a long fever. That was all just a notion like a lot of other things, but it was lucky too, for she had once for all got over the idea of dying for a long time. Now she couldn't be worried. She hoped she had better sense now. Her father had lived to be one hundred and two years old and had drunk a noggin of strong hot toddy on his last birthday. He told the reporters it was his daily habit, and he owed his long life to that. He had made quite a scandal and was very pleased about it. She believed she'd just plague Cornelia a little.

"Cornelia! Cornelia!" No footsteps, but a sudden hand on her cheek. "Bless you, where have you been?"

"Here, Mother."

"Well, Cornelia, I want a noggin of hot toddy."

"Are you cold, darling?"

"I'm chilly, Cornelia. Lying in bed stops the circulation. I must have told you that a thousand times."

Well, she could just hear Cornelia telling her husband that Mother was getting a little childish and they'd have to humor her. The thing that most annoyed her was that Cornalia thought she was deaf, dumb, and blind. Little hasty glances and tiny gestures tossed around her and over her head saying, "Don't cross her, let her have her way, she's eighty years old," and she sitting there as if she lived in a thin glass cage. Sometimes Granny almost made up her mind to pack up and move back to her own house where nobody could remind her every minute that she was old. Wait, wait, Cornelia, till your own children whisper behind your back!

In her day she had kept a better house and had got more work done. She wasn't too old yet for Lydia to be driving eighty miles for advice when one of the children jumped the track, and Jimmy still dropped in and talked things over: "Now, Mammy, you've a good business head, I want to know what you think of this? . . ." Old. Cornelia couldn't change the furniture around without asking. Little things, little things! They had been so sweet when they were little. Granny wished the old days were back again with the children young and everything to be done over. It had been a hard pull, but not too much for her. When she thought of all the food she had cooked, and all the clothes she had cut and sewed, and all the gardens she had made—well, the children showed it. There they were, made out of her, and they couldn't get away from that. Sometimes she wanted to see John again and point to them and say, Well, I didn't do so badly, did I? But that would have to wait. That was for tomorrow. She used to think of him as a man, but now all the children were older than their father, and he would be a child beside her if she saw him now. It seemed strange and there was something wrong in the idea. Why, he couldn't possibly recognize her. She had fenced in a hundred acres once, digging the post holes herself and clamping the wires with just a negro boy to help. That changed a woman. John would be looking for a young woman with the peaked Spanish comb in her hair and the painted fan. Digging post holes changed a woman. Riding country roads in the winter when women had their babies was another thing: sitting up nights with sick horses and sick negroes and sick children and hardly ever losing one. John, I hardly ever lost one of them! John would see that in a minute, that would be something he could understand, she wouldn't have to explain anything!

It made her feel like rolling up her sleeves and putting the whole place to rights again. No matter if Cornelia was determined to be everywhere at once, there were a great many things left undone on this place. She would start tomorrow and do them. It was good to be strong enough for everything, even if all you made melted and changed and slipped under your hands, so that by the time you finished you almost forgot what you were working for. What was it I set out to do? she asked herself intently, but she could not remember. A fog rose over the valley, she saw it marching across the creek swallowing the trees and moving up the hill like an army of ghosts. Soon it would be at the near edge of the orchard, and then it was time to go in and light the lamps. Come in, children, don't stay out in the night air.

Lighting the lamps had been beautiful. The children huddled up to her and breathed like little calves waiting at the bars in the twilight. Their eyes followed the match and watched the flame rise and settle in a blue curve, then they moved away from her. The lamp was lit, they didn't have to be scared and hang on to mother any more. Never, never, never more. God, for all my life I thank Thee. Without Thee, my God, I could never have done it. Hail, Mary, full of grace.

I want you to pick all the fruit this year and see that nothing is wasted. There's always someone who can use it. Don't let good things rot for want of using. You waste life when you waste good food. Don't let things get lost. It's bitter to lose things. Now, don't let me get to thinking, not when I am tired and taking a little nap before supper. . . .

The pillow rose about her shoulders and pressed against her heart and the memory was being squeezed out of it: oh, push down the pillow, somebody: it would smother her if she tried to hold it. Such a fresh breeze blowing and such a green day with no threats in it. But he had not come, just the same. What does a woman do when she has put on the white veil and set out the white cake for a man and he doesn't come? She tried to remember. No, I swear he never harmed me but in that. He never harmed me but in that . . . and what if he did? There was the day, the day, but a whirl of dark smoke rose and covered it, crept up and over into the bright field where everything was planted so carefully in orderly rows. That was hell, she knew hell when she saw it. For sixty years she had prayed against remembering him and against losing her soul in the deep pit of hell, and now the two things were mingled in one and the thought of him was a smoky cloud from hell that moved and crept in her head when she had just got rid of Doctor Harry and was trying to rest a minute. Wounded vanity, Ellen, said a sharp voice in the top of her mind. Don't let your wounded vanity get the upper hand of you. Plenty of girls get jilted. You were jilted, weren't you? Then stand up to it. Her eyelids wavered and let in streamers of blue-gray light like tissue paper over her eyes. She must get up and pull the shades down or she'd never sleep. She was in bed again and the shades were not down. How could that happen? Better turn over, hide from the light, sleeping in the light gave you nightmares. "Mother, how do you feel now?" and a stinging wetness on her forehead. But I don't like having my face washed in cold water!

Hapsy? George? Lydia? Jimmy? No, Cornelia, and her features were swollen and full of little puddles. "They're coming, darling, they'll all be here soon." Go wash your face, child, you look funny.

Instead of obeying, Cornelia knelt down and put her head on the pillow. She seemed to be talking but there was no sound. "Well, are you tongue-tied? Whose birthday is it? Are you going to give a party?"

Cornelia's mouth moved urgently in strange shapes. "Don't do that, you bother me, daughter."

"Oh, no, Mother. Oh, no. . . ."

Nonsense. It was strange about children. They disputed your every word. "No what, Cornelia?"

"Here's Doctor Harry."

"I won't see that boy again. He just left five minutes ago."

"That was this morning, Mother. It's night now. Here's the nurse."

"This is Doctor Harry, Mrs. Weatherall. I never saw you look so young and happy!"

"Ah, I'll never be young again—but I'd be happy if they'd let me lie in peace and get rested."

She thought she spoke up loudly, but no one answered. A warm weight on her forehead, a warm bracelet on her wrist, and a breeze went on whispering, trying to tell her something. A shuffle of leaves in the everlasting hand of God, He blew on them and they danced and rattled. "Mother, don't mind, we're going to give you a little hypodermic." "Look here, daughter, how do ants get in this bed? I saw sugar ants yesterday." Did you send for Hapsy too?

It was Hapsy she really wanted. She had to go a long way back through a great many rooms to find Hapsy standing with a baby on her arm. She seemed to herself to be Hapsy also, and the baby on Hapsy's arm was Hapsy and himself and herself, all at once, and there was no surprise in the meeting. Then Hapsy melted from within and turned flimsy as gray gauze and the baby was a gauzy shadow, and Hapsy came up close and said, "I thought you'd never come," and looked at her very searchingly and said, "You haven't changed a bit!" They leaned forward to kiss, when Cornelia began whispering from a long way off, "Oh, is there anything you want to tell me? Is there anything I can do for you?"

Yes, she had changed her mind after sixty years and she would like to see George. I want you to find George. Find him and be sure to tell him I forgot him. I want him to know I had my husband just the same and my children and my house like any other woman. A good house too and a good husband that I loved and fine children out of him. Better than I hoped for even. Tell him I was given back everything he took away and more. Oh, no, oh, God, no, there was something else besides the house and the man and the children. Oh, surely they were not all? What was it? Something not given back. . . . Her breath crowded down under her ribs and grew into a monstrous frightening shape with cutting edges; it bored up into her head, and the agony was unbelievable: Yes, John, get the Doctor now, no more talk, my time has come.

When this one was born it should be the last. The last. It should have been born first, for it was the one she had truly wanted. Everything came in good time. Nothing left out, left over. She was strong, in three days she would be as well as ever. Better. A woman needed milk in her to have her full health.

"Mother, do you hear me?"

"I've been telling you—"

"Mother, Father Connolly's here."

"I went to Holy Communion only last week. Tell him I'm not so sinful as all that."

"Father just wants to speak to you."

He could speak as much as he pleased. It was like him to drop in and inquire about her soul as if it were a teething baby, and then stay on for a cup of tea and a round of cards and gossip. He always had a funny story of some sort, usually about an Irishman who made his little mistakes and confessed them, and the point lay in some absurd thing he would blurt out in the confessional showing his struggles between native piety and original sin. Granny felt easy about her soul. Cornelia, where are your manners? Give Father Connolly a chair. She had her secret comfortable understanding with a few favorite saints who cleared a straight road to God for her. All as surely signed and sealed as the papers for the new

Forty Acres. Forever . . . heirs and assigns forever. Since the day the wedding cake was not cut, but thrown out and wasted. The whole bottom dropped out of the world, and there she was blind and sweating with nothing under her feet and the walls falling away. His hand had caught her under the breast, she had not fallen, there was the freshly polished floor with the green rug on it, just as before. He had cursed like a sailor's parrot and said, "I'll kill him for you." Don't lay a hand on him, for my sake leave something to God. "Now, Ellen, you must believe what I tell you. . . ."

So there was nothing, nothing to worry about any more, except sometimes in the night one of the children screamed in a nightmare, and they both hustled out shaking and hunting for the matches and calling, "There, wait a minute, here we are!" John, get the doctor now, Hapsy's time has come. But there was Hapsy standing by the bed in a white cap. "Cornelia, tell Hapsy to take off her cap. I can't see her plain."

Her eyes opened very wide and the room stood out like a picture she had seen somewhere. Dark colors with the shadows rising towards the ceiling in long angles. The tall black dresser gleamed with nothing on it but John's picture, enlarged from a little one, with John's eyes very black when they should have been blue. You never saw him, so how do you know how he looked? But the man insisted the copy was perfect, it was very rich and handsome. For a picture, yes, but it's not my husband. The table by the bed had a linen cover and a candle and a crucifix. The light was blue from Cornelia's silk lampshades. No sort of light at all, just frippery. You had to live forty years with kerosene lamps to appreciate honest electricity. She felt very strong and she saw Doctor Harry with a rosy nimbus around him.

"You look like a saint, Doctor Harry, and I vow that's as near as you'll ever come to it."

"She's saying something."

"I heard you, Cornelia. What's all this carrying-on?"

"Father Connolly's saying—"

Cornelia's voice staggered and bumped like a cart in a bad road. It rounded corners and turned back again and arrived nowhere. Granny stepped up in the cart very lightly and reached for the reins, but a man sat beside her and she knew him by his hands, driving the cart. She did not look in his face, for she knew without seeing, but looked instead down the road where the trees leaned over and bowed to each other and a thousand birds were singing a Mass. She felt like singing too, but she put her hand in the bosom of her dress and pulled out a rosary, and Father Connolly murmured Latin in a very solemn voice and tickled her feet. My God, will you stop that nonsense? I'm a married woman. What if he did run away and leave me to face the priest by myself? I found another a whole world better. I wouldn't have exchanged my husband for anybody except St. Michael himself, and you may tell him that for me with a thank you in the bargain.

Light flashed on her closed eyelids, and a deep roaring shook her. Cornelia, is that lightning? I hear thunder. There's going to be a storm. Close all the windows. Call the children in. . . . "Mother, here we are, all of us." "Is that you, Hapsy?" "Oh, no, I'm Lydia. We drove as fast as we could." Their faces drifted above her, drifted away. The rosary fell out of her hands and Lydia put it back. Jimmy tried to help, their hands fumbled together, and Granny closed two fingers around Jimmy's thumb. Beads wouldn't do, it must be something alive. She was so amazed her thoughts ran round and round. So, my dear Lord, this is my death and I wasn't even thinking about it. My children have come to see me die. But I can't, it's not time. Oh, I always hated surprises. I wanted to give Cornelia the amethyst set—Cornelia, you're to have the amethyst set, but Hapsy's to wear it when she wants, and, Doctor Harry, do shut up. Nobody sent for you. Oh, my dear Lord, do wait a minute. I meant to do something about the Forty Acres, Jimmy doesn't need it and Lydia will later on, with that worthless husband of hers. I meant to finish the altar cloth and send six bottles of wine to Sister Borgia for her dyspepsia. I want to send six bottles of wine to Sister Borgia, Father Connolly, now don't let me forget.

Cornelia's voice made short turns and tilted over and crashed. "Oh, Mother, oh, Mother, oh, Mother. . . ."

"I'm not going, Cornelia. I'm taken by surprise. I can't go."

You'll see Hapsy again. What about her? "I thought you'd never come." Granny made a long journey outward, looking for Hapsy. What if I don't find her? What then? Her heart sank down and down, there was no bottom to death, she couldn't come to the end of it. The blue light from Cornelia's lampshade drew into a tiny point in the center of her brain, it flickered and winked like an eye, quietly it fluttered and dwindled. Granny lay curled down within herself, amazed and watchful, staring at the point of light that was herself; her body was now only a deeper mass of shadow in an endless darkness and this darkness would curl around the light and swallow it up. God, give a sign!

For the second time there was no sign. Again no bridegroom and the priest in the house. She could not remember any other sorrow because this grief wiped them all away. Oh, no, there's nothing more cruel than this—I'll never forgive it. She stretched herself with a deep breath and blew out the light.

Flowering Judas

Braggioni sits heaped upon the edge of a straight-backed chair much too small for him, and sings to Laura in a furry, mournful voice. Laura has begun to find reasons for avoiding her own house until the latest possible moment, for Braggioni is there almost every night. No matter how late she is, he will be sitting there with a surly, waiting expression, pulling at his kinky yellow hair, thumbing the strings of his guitar, snarling a tune under his breath. Lupe the Indian maid meets Laura at the door, and says with a flicker of a glance towards the upper room, "He waits."

Laura wishes to lie down, she is tired of her hairpins and the feel of her long tight sleeves, but she says to him, "Have you a new song for me this evening?" If he says yes, she asks him to sing it. If he says no, she remembers his favorite one, and asks him to sing it again. Lupe brings her a cup of chocolate and a plate of rice, and Laura eats at the small table under the lamp, first inviting Braggioni, whose answer is always the same: "I have eaten, and besides, chocolate thickens the voice."

Laura says, "Sing, then," and Braggioni heaves himself into song. He scratches the guitar familiarly as though it were a pet animal, and sings passionately off key, taking the high notes in a prolonged painful squeal. Laura, who haunts the markets listening to the ballad singers, and stops every day to hear the blind boy playing his reed-flute in Sixteenth of September Street, listens to Braggioni with pitiless courtesy, because she dares not smile at his miserable performance. Nobody dares to smile at him. Braggioni is cruel to everyone, with a kind of specialized insolence, but he is so vain of his talents, and so sensitive to slights, it would require a cruelty and vanity greater than his own to lay a finger on the vast cureless wound of his self-esteem. It would require courage, too, for it is dangerous to offend him, and nobody has this courage.

Braggioni loves himself with such tenderness and amplitude and eternal charity that his followers—for he is a leader of men, a skilled revolutionist, and his skin has been punctured in honorable warfare—warm themselves in the reflected glow, and say to each other: "He has a real nobility, a love of humanity raised above mere personal affections." The excess of this self-love has flowed out, inconveniently for her, over Laura, who, with so many others, owes her comfortable situation and her salary to him. When he is in a a very good humor, he tells her, "I am tempted to forgive you for being a *gringa. Gringita!*" and Laura, burning, imagines herself leaning forward suddenly, and with a sound back-handed slap wiping the suety smile from his face. If he notices her eyes at these moments he gives no sign.

She knows what Braggioni would offer her, and she must resist tenaciously without appearing to resist, and if she could avoid it she would not admit even to herself the slow drift of his intention. During these long evenings which have spoiled a long month for her, she sits in her deep chair with an open book on her knees, resting her eyes on the consoling rigidity of the printed page when the sight and sound of Braggioni singing threaten to identify themselves with all her remembered afflictions and to add their weight to her uneasy premonitions of the future. The gluttonous bulk of Braggioni has become a symbol of her many disillusions, for a revolutionist should be lean, animated by heroic faith, a vessel of abstract virtues. This is nonsense, she knows it now and is ashamed of it. Revolution must have leaders, and leadership is a career for energetic men. She is, her comrades tell her, full of romantic error, for what she defines as cynicism in them is merely "a developed sense of reality." She is almost too willing to say, "I am wrong, I suppose I don't really understand the principles," and afterward she makes a secret truce with herself, determined not to surrender her will to such expedient logic. But she cannot help feeling that she has been betrayed irreparably by the disunion between her way of living and her feeling of what life should be, and at times she is almost contented to rest in this sense of grievance as a private store of consolation. Sometimes she wishes to run away, but she stays. Now she longs to fly out of this room, down the narrow stairs, and into the street where the houses lean together like conspirators under a single mottled lamp, and leave Braggioni singing to himself.

Instead she looks at Braggioni, frankly and clearly, like a good child who understands the rules of behavior. Her knees cling together under sound blue serge, and her round white collar is not purposely nun-like. She wears the uniform of an idea, and has renounced vanities. She was born Roman Catholic, and in spite of her fear of being seen by someone who might make a scandal of it, she slips now and again into some crumbling little church, kneels on the chilly stone, and says a Hail Mary on the gold rosary she bought in Tehuantepec. It is no good and she ends by examining the altar with its tinsel flowers and ragged brocades, and feels tender about the battered doll-shape of some male saint whose white, lace-trimmed drawers hang limply around his ankles below the hieratic dignity of his velvet robe. She has encased herself in a set of principles derived from her early training, leaving no detail of gesture or of personal taste untouched, and for this reason she will not wear lace made on machines. This is her private heresy, for in her special group the machine is sacred, and will be the salvation of the workers. She loves fine lace, and there is a tiny edge of fluted cobweb on this collar, which is one of twenty precisely alike, folded in blue tissue paper in the upper drawer of her clothes chest.

Braggioni catches her glance solidly as if he had been waiting for it, leans forward, balancing his paunch between his spread knees, and sings with tremendous emphasis, weighing his words. He has, the song relates, no father and no mother, nor even a friend to console him; lonely as a wave of the sea he comes and goes, lonely as a wave. His mouth opens round and yearns sideways, his balloon cheeks grow oily with the labor of song. He bulges marvelously in his expensive garments. Over his lavender collar, crushed upon a purple necktie, held by a diamond hoop: over his ammunition belt of tooled leather worked in silver, buckled cruelly around his gasping middle: over the tops of his glossy yellow shoes Braggioni swells with ominous ripeness, his mauve silk hose stretched taut, his ankles bound with the stout leather thongs of his shoes.

When he stretches his eyelids at Laura she notes again that his eyes are the true tawny yellow cat's eyes. He is rich, not in money, he tells her, but in power, and this power brings with it the blameless ownership of things, and the right to indulge his love of small luxuries. "I have a taste for the elegant refinements," he said once, flourishing a yellow silk handkerchief before her nose. "Smell that? It is Jockey Club, imported from New York." Nonetheless he is wounded by life. He will say so presently. "It is true everything turns to dust in the hand, to gall on the tongue." He sighs and his leather belt creaks like a saddle girth. "I am disappointed in everything as it comes. Everything." He shakes his head. "You, poor thing, you will be disappointed too. You are born for it. We are more alike than you realize in some things. Wait and see. Some day you will remember what I have told you, you will know that Braggioni was your friend."

Laura feels a slow chill, a purely physical sense of danger, a warning in her blood that violence, mutilation, a shocking death, wait for her with lessening patience. She has translated this fear into something homely, immediate, and sometimes hesitates before crossing the street. "My personal fate is nothing, except as the testimony of a mental attitude," she reminds herself, quoting from some forgotten philosophic primer, and is sensible enough to add, "Anyhow, I shall not be killed by an automobile if I can help it."

"It may be true I am as corrupt, in another way, as Braggioni," she thinks in spite of herself, "as callous, as incomplete," and if this is so, any kind of death seems preferable. Still she sits quietly, she does not run. Where could she go? Uninvited she has promised herself to this place; she can no longer imagine herself as living in another country, and there is no pleasure in remembering her life before she came here.

Precisely what is the nature of this devotion, its true motives, and what are its obligations? Laura cannot say. She spends part of her days in Xochimilco, near by, teaching Indian children to say in English, "The cat is on the mat." When she appears in the classroom they crowd about her with smiles on their wise, innocent, clay-colored faces, crying, "Good morning, my titcher!" in immaculate voices, and they make of her desk a fresh garden of flowers every day.

During her leisure she goes to union meetings and listens to busy important voices quarreling over tactics, methods, internal politics. She visits the prisoners of her own political faith in their cells, where they entertain themselves with counting cockroaches, repenting of their indiscretions, composing their memoirs, writing out manifestoes and plans for their comrades who are still walking about free, hands in pockets, sniffing fresh air. Laura brings them food and cigarettes and a little money, and she brings messages disguised in equivocal phrases from the men outside who dare not set foot in the prison for fear of disappearing into the cells kept empty for them. If the prisoners confuse night and day, and complain, "Dear little Laura, time doesn't pass in this infernal hole, and I won't know when it is time to sleep unless I have a reminder," she brings them their favorite narcotics, and says in a tone that does not wound them with pity, "Tonight will really be night for you," and though her Spanish amuses them, they find her comforting, useful. If they lose patience and all faith, and curse the slowness of their friends in coming to their rescue with money and influence, they trust her not to repeat everything, and if she inquires, "Where do you think we can find money, or influence?" they are certain to answer, "Well, there is Braggioni, why doesn't he do something?"

She smuggles letters from headquarters to men hiding from firing squads in back streets in mildewed houses, where they sit in tumbled beds and talk bitterly as if all Mexico were at their heels, when Laura knows positively they might appear at the band concert in the Alameda on Sunday morning, and no one would notice them. But Braggioni says, "Let them sweat a little. The next time they may be careful. It is very restful to have them out of the way for a while." She is not afraid to knock on any door in any street after midnight, and enter in the darkness, and say to one of these men who is really in danger: "They will be looking for you— seriously—tomorrow morning after six. Here is some money from Vicente. Go to Vera Cruz and wait."

She borrows money from the Roumanian agitator to give to his bitter enemy the Polish agitator. The favor of Braggioni is their disputed territory, and Braggioni holds the balance nicely, for he can use them both. The Polish agitator talks love to her over café tables, hoping to exploit what he believes is her secret sentimental preference for him, and he gives her misinformation which he begs her to repeat as the solemn truth to certain persons. The Roumanian is more adroit. He is generous with his money in all good causes, and lies to her with an air of ingenuous candor, as if he were her good friend and confidant. She never repeats anything they may say. Braggioni never asks questions. He has other ways to discover all that he wishes to know about them.

Nobody touches her, but all praise her gray eyes, and the soft, round under lip which promises gayety, yet is always grave, nearly always firmly closed: and they cannot understand why she is in Mexico. She walks back and forth on her errands, with puzzled eyebrows, carrying her little folder of drawings and music and school papers. No dancer dances more beautifully than Laura walks, and she inspires some amusing, unexpected ardors, which cause little gossip, because nothing comes of them. A young captain who had been a soldier in Zapata's army attempted, during a horseback ride near Cuernavaca, to express his desire for her with the noble simplicity befitting a rude folk-hero: but gently, because he was gentle. This gentleness was his defeat, for when he alighted, and removed her foot from the stirrup, and essayed to draw her down into his arms, her horse, ordinarily a tame one, shied fiercely, reared and plunged away. The young hero's horse careered blindly after his stable-mate, and the hero did not return to the hotel until rather late that evening. At breakfast he came to her table in full charro dress, gray buckskin jacket and trousers with strings of silver buttons down the leg, and he was in a humorous, careless mood. "May I sit with you?" and "You are a wonderful rider. I was terrified that you might be thrown and dragged. I should never have forgiven myself. But I cannot admire you enough for your riding!"

"I learned to ride in Arizona," said Laura.

"If you will ride with me again this morning, I promise you a horse that will not shy with you," he said. But Laura remembered that she must return to Mexico City at noon.

Next morning the children made a celebration and spent their playtime writing on the blackboard, "We lov ar ticher," and with tinted chalks they drew wreaths of flowers around the words. The young hero wrote her a letter: "I am a very foolish, wasteful, impulsive man. I should have first said I love you, and then you would not have run away. But you shall see me again." Laura thought, "I must send him a box of colored crayons," but she was trying to forgive herself for having spurred her horse at the wrong moment.

A brown, shock-haired youth came and stood in her patio one night and sang like a lost soul for two hours, but Laura could think of nothing to do about it. The moonlight spread a wash of gauzy silver over the clear spaces of the garden, and the shadows were cobalt blue. The scarlet blossoms of the Judas tree were dull purple, and the names of the colors repeated themselves automatically in her mind, while she watched not the boy, but his shadow, fallen like a dark garment across the fountain rim, trailing in the water. Lupe came silently and whispered expert counsel in her ear: "If you will throw him one little flower, he will sing another song or two and go away." Laura threw the flower, and he sang a last song and went away with the flower tucked in the band of his hat. Lupe said, "He is one of the organizers of the Typographers Union, and before that he sold corridos in the Merced market, and before that, he came from Guanajuato, where I was born. I would not trust any man, but I trust least those from Guanajuato."

She did not tell Laura that he would be back again the next night, and the next, nor that he would follow her at a certain fixed distance around the Merced market, through the Zócolo, up Francisco I. Madero Avenue, and so along the Paseo de la Reforma to Chapultepec Park, and into the Philosopher's Footpath, still with that flower withering in his hat, and an indivisible attention in his eyes.

Now Laura is accustomed to him, it means nothing except that he is nineteen years old and is observing a convention with all propriety, as though it were founded on a law of nature, which in the end it might well prove to be. He is beginning to write poems which he prints on a wooden press, and he leaves them stuck like handbills in her door. She is pleasantly disturbed by the abstract, unhurried watchfulness of his black eyes which will in time turn easily towards another object. She tells herself that throwing the flower was a mistake, for she is twenty-two years old and knows better; but she refuses to regret it, and persuades herself that her negation of all external events as they occur is a sign that she is gradually perfecting herself in the stoicism she strives to cultivate against that disaster she fears, though she cannot name it.

She is not at home in the world. Every day she teaches children who remain strangers to her, though she loves their tender round hands and their charming opportunist savagery. She knocks at unfamiliar doors not knowing whether a friend or a stranger shall answer, and even if a known face emerges from the sour gloom of that unknown interior, still it is the face of a stranger. No matter what this stranger says to her, nor what her message to him, the very cells of her flesh reject knowledge and kinship in one monotonous word. No. No. No. She draws her strength from this one holy talismanic word which does not suffer her to be led into evil. Denying everything, she may walk anywhere in safety, she looks at everything without amazement.

No, repeats this firm unchanging voice of her blood; and she looks at Braggioni without amazement. He is a great man, he wishes to impress this simple girl who covers her great round breasts with thick dark cloth, and who hides long, invaluably beautiful legs under a heavy skirt. She is almost thin except for the incomprehensible fullness of her breasts, like a nursing mother's, and Braggioni, who considers himself a judge of women, speculates again on the puzzle of her notorious virginity, and takes the liberty of speech which she permits without a sign of modesty, indeed, without any sort of sign, which is disconcerting.

"You think you are so cold, *gringita!* Wait and see. You will surprise yourself some day! May I be there to advise you!" He stretches his eyelids at her, and his ill-humored cat's eyes waver in a separate glance for the two points of light marking the opposite ends of a smoothly drawn path between the swollen curve of her breasts. He is not put off by that blue serge, nor by her resolutely fixed gaze. There is all the time in the world. His cheeks are bellying with the wind of song. "O girl with the dark eyes," he sings, and reconsiders. "But yours are not dark. I can change all that. O girl with the green eyes, you have stolen my heart away!" then his mind wanders to the song, and Laura feels the weight of his attention being shifted elsewhere. Singing thus, he seems harmless, he is quite harmless, there is nothing to do but sit patiently and say "No," when the moment comes. She draws a full breath, and her mind wanders also, but not far. She dares not wander too far.

Not for nothing has Braggioni taken pains to be a good revolutionist and a professional lover of humanity. He will never die of it. He has the malice, the cleverness, the wickedness, the sharpness of wit, the hardness of heart, stipulated for loving the world profitably. *He will never die of it.* He will live to see himself kicked out from his feeding trough by other hungry world-saviors. Traditionally he must sing in spite of his life which drives him to bloodshed, he tells Laura, for his father was a Tuscany peasant who drifted to Yucatan and married a Maya woman: a woman of race, an aristocrat. They gave him the love and knowledge of music, thus: and under the rip of his thumbnail, the strings of the instrument complain like exposed nerves.

Once he was called Delgadito by all the girls and married women who ran after him; he was so scrawny all his bones showed under his thin cotton clothing, and he could squeeze his emptiness to the very backbone with his two hands. He was a poet and the revolution was only a dream then; too many women loved him and sapped away his youth, and he could never find enough to eat anywhere, anywhere! Now he is a leader of men, crafty men who whisper in his ear, hungry men who wait for hours outside his office for a word with him, emaciated men with wild faces who waylay him at the street gate with a timid, "Comrade, let me tell you . . ." and they blow the foul breath from their empty stomachs in his face.

He is always sympathetic. He gives them handfuls of small coins from his own pocket, he promises them work, there will be demonstrations, they must join the unions and attend the meetings, above all they must be on the watch for spies. They are closer to him than his own brothers, without them he can do nothing—until tomorrow, comrade!

Until tomorrow. "They are stupid, they are lazy, they are treacherous, they would cut my throat for nothing," he says to Laura. He has good food and abundant drink, he hires an automobile and drives in the Paseo on Sunday morning, and enjoys plenty of sleep in a soft bed beside a wife who dares not disturb him; and he sits pampering his bones in easy billows of fat, singing to Laura, who knows and thinks these things about him. When he was fifteen, he tried to drown himself because he loved a girl, his first love, and she laughed at him. "A thousand women have paid for that," and his tight little mouth turns down at the corners. Now he perfumes his hair with Jockey Club, and confides to Laura: "One woman is really as good as another for me, in the dark. I prefer them all."

His wife organizes unions among the girls in the cigarette factories, and walks in picket lines, and even speaks at meetings in the evening. But she cannot be brought to acknowledge the benefits of true liberty. "I tell her I must have my freedom, net. She does not understand my point of view." Laura has heard this many times. Braggioni scratches the guitar and meditates. "She is an instinctively virtuous woman, pure gold, no doubt of that. If she were not, I should lock her up, and she knows it."

His wife, who works so hard for the good of the factory girls, employs part of her leisure lying on the floor weeping because there are so many women in the world, and only one husband for her, and she never knows where nor when to look for him. He told her: "Unless you can learn to cry when I am not here, I must go away for good." That day he went away and took a room at the Hotel Madrid.

It is this month of separation for the sake of higher principles that has been spoiled not only for Mrs. Braggioni, whose sense of reality is beyond criticism, but for Laura, who feels herself bogged in a nightmare. Tonight Laura envies Mrs. Braggioni, who is alone, and free to weep as much as she pleases about a concrete wrong. Laura has just come from a visit to the prison, and she is waiting for tomorrow with a bitter anxiety as if tomorrow may not come, but time may be caught immovably in this hour, with herself transfixed, Braggioni singing on forever, and Eugenio's body not yet discovered by the guard.

Braggioni says: "Are you going to sleep?" Almost before she can shake her head, he begins telling her about the May-day disturbances coming on in Morelia, for the Catholics hold a festival in honor of the Blessed Virgin, and the Socialists celebrate their martyrs on that day. "There will be two independent processions, starting from either end of town, and they will march until they meet, and the rest depends . . ." He asks her to oil and load his pistols. Standing up, he unbuckles his ammunition belt, and spreads it la-den across her knees. Laura sits with the shells slipping through the cleaning cloth dipped in oil, and he says again he cannot understand why she works so hard for the revolutionary idea unless she loves some man who is in it. "Are you not in love with someone?" "No," says Laura. "And no one is in love with you?" "No." "Then it is your own fault. No woman need go begging. Why, what is the matter with you? The legless beggar woman in the Alameda has a perfectly faithful lover. Did you know that?"

Laura peers down the pistol barrel and says nothing, but a long, slow faintness rises and subsides in her; Braggioni curves his swollen fingers around the throat of the guitar and softly smothers the music out of it, and when she hears him again he seems to have forgotten her, and is speaking in the hypnotic voice he uses when talking in small rooms to a listening, close-gathered crowd. Some day this world, now seemingly so composed and eternal, to the edges of every sea shall be merely a tangle of gaping trenches, of crashing walls and broken bodies. Everything must be torn from its accustomed place where it has rotted for centuries, hurled skyward and distributed, cast down again clean as rain, without separate identity. Nothing shall survive that the stiffened hands of poverty have created for the rich and no one shall be left alive except the elect spirits destined to procreate a new world cleansed of cruelty and injustice, ruled by benevolent anarchy: "Pistols are good, I love them, cannon are even better, but in the end I pin my faith to good dynamite," he concludes, and strokes the pistol lying in her hands. "Once I dreamed of destroying this city, in case it offered resistance to General Ortíz, but it fell into his hands like an overripe pear."

He is made restless by his own words, rises and stands waiting. Laura holds up the belt to him: "Put that on, and go kill somebody in Morelia, and you will be happier," she says softly. The presence of death in the room makes her bold. "Today, I found Eugenio going into a stupor. He refused to allow me to call the prison doctor. He had taken all the tablets I brought him yesterday. He said he took them because he was bored."

"He is a fool, and his death is his own business," says Braggioni, fastening his belt carefully.

"I told him if he had waited only a little while longer, you would have got him set free," says Laura. "He said he did not want to wait."

"He is a fool and we are well rid of him," says Braggioni, reaching for his hat.

He goes away. Laura knows his mood has changed, she will not see him any more for a while. He will send word when he needs her to go on errands into strange streets, to speak to the strange faces that will appear, like clay masks with the power of human speech, to mutter their thanks to Braggioni for his help. Now she is free, and she thinks, I must run while there is time. But she does not go.

Braggioni enters his own house where for a month his wife has spent many hours every night weeping and tangling her hair upon her pillow. She is weeping now, and she weeps more at the sight of him, the cause of all her sorrows. He looks about the room. Nothing is changed, the smells are good and familiar, he is well acquainted with the woman who comes toward him with no reproach except grief on her face. He says to her tenderly: "You are so good, please don't cry any more, you dear good creature." She says, "Are you tired, my angel? Sit here and I will wash your feet." She brings a bowl of water, and kneeling, unlaces his shoes, and when from her knees she raises her sad eyes under her blackened lids, he is sorry for everything, and bursts into tears. "Ah, yes, I am hungry, I am tired, let us eat something together," he says, between sobs. His wife leans her head on his arm and says, "Forgive me!" and this time he is refreshed by the solemn, endless rain of her tears.

Laura takes off her serge dress and puts on a white linen nightgown and goes to bed. She turns her head a little to one side, and lying still, reminds herself that it is time to sleep. Numbers tick in her brain like little clocks, soundless doors close of themselves around her. If you would sleep, you must not remember anything, the children will say tomorrow, good morning, my teacher, the poor prisoners who come every day bringing flowers to their jailor. 1-2-3-4-5—it is monstrous to confuse love with revolution, night with day, life with death—ah, Eugenio!

The tolling of the midnight bell is a signal, but what does it mean? Get up, Laura, and follow me: come out of your sleep, out of your bed, out of this strange house. What are you doing in this house? Without a word, without fear she rose and reached for Eugenio's hand, but he eluded her with a sharp, sly smile and drifted away. This is not all, you shall see—Murderer, he said, follow me, I will show you a new country, but it is far away and we must hurry. No, said Laura, not unless you take my hand, no; and she clung first to the stair rail, and then to the topmost branch of the Judas tree that bent down slowly and set her upon the earth, and then to the rocky ledge of a cliff, and then to the jagged wave of a sea that was not water but a desert of crumbling stone. Where are you taking me, she asked in wonder but without fear. To death, and it is a long way off, and we must hurry, said Eugenio. No, said Laura, not unless you take my hand. Then eat these flowers, poor prisoner, said Eugenio in a voice of pity, take and eat: and from the Judas tree he stripped the warm bleeding flowers, and held them to her lips. She saw that his hand was fleshless, a cluster of small white petrified branches, and his eye sockets were without light, but she ate the flowers greedily for they satisfied both hunger and thirst. Murderer! said Eugenio, and Cannibal! This is my body and my blood. Laura cried No! and at the sound of her own voice, she awoke trembling, and was afraid to sleep again.

The Cracked Looking-Glass

Dennis heard Rosaleen talking in the kitchen and a man's voice answering. He sat with his hands dangling over his knees, and thought for the hundredth time that sometimes Rosaleen's voice was company to him, and other days he wished all day long she didn't have so much to say about everything. More and more the years put a quietus on a man; there was no earthly sense in saying the same things over and over. Even thinking the same thoughts grew tiresome after a while. But Rosaleen was full of talk as ever. If not to him, to whatever passer-by stopped for a minute, and if nobody stopped, she talked to the cats and to herself. If Dennis came near she merely raised her voice and went on with whatever she was saying, so it was nothing for her to shout suddenly, "Come out of that, now—how often have I told ye to keep off the table?" and the cats would scatter in all directions with guilty faces. "It's enough to make a man lep out of his shoes," Dennis would complain. "It's not meant for you, darlin'," Rosaleen would say, as if that cured everything, and if he didn't go away at once, she would start some kind of story. But today she kept shooing him out of the place and hadn't a kind word in her mouth, and Dennis in exile felt that everything and everybody was welcome in the place but himself. For the twentieth time he approached on tiptoe and listened at the parlor keyhole.

Rosaleen was saying: "Maybe his front legs might look a little stuffed for a living cat, but in the picture it's no great matter. I said to Kevin, 'You'll never paint that cat alive,' but Kevin did it, with house paint mixed in a saucer, and a small brush the way he could

103

put in all them fine lines. His legs look like that because I wanted him pictured on the table, but it wasn't so, he was on my lap the whole time. He was a wonder after the mice, a born hunter bringing them in from morning till night—"

Dennis sat on the sofa in the parlor and thought: "There it is. There she goes telling it again." He wondered who the man was, a strange voice, but a loud and ready gabbler as if maybe he was trying to sell something. "It's a fine painting, Miz O'Toole," he said, "and who did you say the artist was?"

"A lad named Kevin, like my own brother he was, who went away to make his fortune," answered Rosaleen. "A house painter by trade."

"The spittin' image of a cat!" roared the voice.

"It is so," said Rosaleen. "The Billy-cat to the life. The Nelly-cat here is own sister to him, and the Jimmy-cat and the Annie-cat and the Mickey-cat is nephews and nieces, and there's a great family look between all of them. It was the strangest thing happened to the Billy-cat, Mr. Pendleton. He sometimes didn't come in for his supper till after dark, he was so taken up with the hunting, and then one night he didn't come at all, nor the next day neither, nor the next, and me with him on my mind so I didn't get a wink of sleep. Then at midnight on the third night I did go to sleep, and the Billy-cat came into my room and lep upon my pillow and said: 'Up beyond the north field there's a maple tree with a great scar where the branch was taken away by the storm, and near to it is a flat stone, and there you'll find me. I was caught in a trap,' he says; 'wasn't set for me,' he says, 'but it got me all the same. And now be easy in your mind about me,' he says, 'for it's all over.' Then he went away, giving me a look over his shoulder like a human creature, and I woke up Dennis and told him. Surely as we live, Mr. Pendleton, it was all true. So Dennis went beyond the north field and brought him home and we buried him in the garden and cried over him." Her voice broke and lowered and Dennis shuddered for fear she was going to shed tears before this stranger.

"For God's *sake*, Miz O'Toole," said the loud-mouthed man, "you can't get around that now, can you? Why, that's the most remarkable thing I ever heard!"

Dennis rose, creaking a little, and hobbled around to the east side of the house in time to see a round man with a flabby red face climbing into a rusty old car with a sign painted on the door. "Always something, now," he commented, putting his head in at the kitchen door. "Always telling a tall tale!"

"Well," said Rosaleen, without the least shame, "he wanted a story so I gave him a good one. That's the Irish in me."

"Always making a thing more than it is," said Dennis. "That's the way it goes."

Rosaleen turned a little edgy. "Out with ye!" she cried, and the cats never budged a whisker. "The kitchen's no place for a man! How often must I tell ye?"

"Well, hand me my hat, will you?" said Dennis, for his hat hung on a nail over the calendar and had hung there within easy reach ever since they had lived in the farmhouse. A few minutes later he wanted his pipe, lying on the lamp shelf where he always kept it. Next he had to have his barn boots at once, though he hadn't seen them for a month. At last he thought of something to say, and opened the door a few inches.

"Wherever have I been sitting unmolested for the past ten years?" he asked, looking at his easy chair with the pillow freshly plumped, sideways to the big table. "And today it's no place for me?"

"If ye grumble ye'll be sorry," said Rosaleen gayly, "and now clear out before I hurl something at ye!"

Dennis put his hat on the parlor table and his boots under the sofa, and sat on the front steps and lit his pipe. It would soon be cold weather, and he wished he had his old leather jacket off the hook on the kitchen door. Whatever was Rosaleen up to now? He decided that Rosaleen was always doing the Irish a great wrong by putting her own faults off on them. To be Irish, he felt, was to be like him, a sober, practical, thinking man, a lover of truth. Rosaleen couldn't see it at all. "It's just your head is like a stone!" she said to him once, pretending she was joking, but she meant it. She had never appreciated him, that was it. And neither had his first wife. Whatever he gave them, they always wanted something else. When he was young and poor his first wife wanted money. And when he was a steady man with money in the bank, his second wife wanted a young man full of life. "They're all born ingrates one way or another," he decided, and felt better at once, as if at last he had something solid to stand on. In September a man could get his death sitting on the steps like this, and little she cared! He clacked his teeth together and felt how they didn't fit any more, and his feet and hands seemed tied on him with strings.

All the while Rosaleen didn't look to be a year older. She might almost be doing it to spite him, except that she wasn't the spiteful kind. He'd be bound to say that for her. But she couldn't forget that her girlhood had been a great triumph in Ireland, and she was forever telling him tales about it, and telling them again. This youth of hers was clearer in his mind than his own. He couldn't remember one thing over another that had happened to him. His past lay like a great lump within him; there it was, he knew it all at once, when he thought of it, like a chest a man has packed away, knowing all that is in it without troubling to name or count the objects. All in a lump it had not been an easy life being named Dennis O'Toole in Bristol, England, where he was brought up and worked sooner than he was able at the first jobs he could find. And his English wife had never forgiven him for pulling her up by the roots and bringing her to New York, where his brothers and sisters were, and a better job. All the long years he had been first a waiter and then head waiter in a New York hotel had telescoped in his mind, somehow. It wasn't the best of hotels, to be sure, but still he was head waiter and there was good money in it, enough to buy this farm in Connecticut and have a little steady money coming in, and what more could Rosaleen ask?

He was not unhappy over his first wife's death a few years after they left England, because they had never really liked each other, and it seemed to him now that even before she was dead he had made up his mind, if she did die, never to marry again. He had held out on this until he was nearly fifty, when he met Rosaleen at a dance in the County Sligo hall far over on East 86th Street. She was a great tall rosy girl, a prize dancer, and the boys were fairly fighting over her. She led him a dance then for two years before she would have him. She said there was nothing against him except he came from Bristol, and the outland Irish had the name of people you couldn't trust. She couldn't say why—it was just a name they had, worse than Dublin people itself. No decent Sligo girl would marry a Dublin man if he was the last man on earth. Dennis didn't believe this, he'd never heard any such thing against the

Dubliners; he thought a country girl would lep at the chance to marry a city man whatever. Rosaleen said, "Maybe," but he'd see whether she would lep to marry Bristol Irish. She was chambermaid in a rich woman's house, a fiend of darkness if there ever was one, said Rosaleen, and at first Dennis had been uneasy about the whole thing, fearing a young girl who had to work so hard might be marrying an older man for his money, but before the two years were up he had got over that notion.

It wasn't long after they were married Dennis began almost to wish sometimes he had let one of those strong-armed boys have her, but he had been fond of her, she was a fine good girl, and after she cooled down a little, he knew he could have never done better. The only thing was, he wished it had been Rosaleen he had married that first time in Bristol, and now they'd be settled together, nearer an age. Thirty years was too much difference altogether. But he never said any such thing to Rosaleen. A man owes something to himself. He knocked out his pipe on the foot scraper and felt a real need to go in the kitchen and find a pipe cleaner.

Rosaleen said, "Come in and welcome!" He stood peering around wondering what she had been making. She warned him: "I'm off to milk now, and mind ye keep your eyes in your pocket. The cow now—the creature! Pretty soon she'll be jumping the stone walls after the apples, and running wild through the fields roaring, and it's all for another calf only, the poor deceived thing!" Dennis said, "I don't see what deceit there is in that." "Oh, don't you now?" said Rosaleen, and gathered up her milk pails.

The kitchen was warm and Dennis felt at home again. The kettle was simmering for tea, the cats lay curled or sprawled as they chose, and Dennis sat within himself smiling a sunken smile, cleaning his pipe. In the barn Rosaleen looped up her purple gingham skirts and sat with her forehead pressed against the warm, calm side of the cow, drawing two thick streams of milk into the pail. She said to the cow: "It's no life, no life at all. A man of his years is no comfort to a woman," and went on with a slow murmur that was not complaining about the things of her life.

She wished sometimes they had never come to Connecticut where there was nobody to talk to but Rooshans and Polacks and Wops no better than Black Protestants when you come right down to it. And the natives were worse even. A picture of her neighbors up the hill came into her mind: a starved-looking woman in a blackish gray dress, and a jaundiced man with red-rimmed eyes, and their mizzle-witted boy. On Sundays they shambled by in their sad old shoes, walking to the meeting-house, but that was all the religion they had, thought Rosaleen, contemptuously. On week days they beat the poor boy and the animals, and fought between themselves. Never a feast-day, nor a bit of bright color in their clothes, nor a Christian look out of their eyes for a living soul. "It's just living in mortal sin from one day to the next," said Rosaleen. But it was Dennis getting old that took the heart out of her. And him with the grandest head of hair she had ever seen on a man. A fine man, oh, a fine man Dennis was in those days! Dennis rose before her eyes in his black suit and white gloves, a knowledgeable man who could tell the richest people the right things to order for a good dinner, such a gentleman in his stiff white shirt front, managing the waiters on the one hand and the customers on the other, and making good money at it. And now. No, she couldn't believe it was Dennis any more. Where was Dennis now? and where was Kevin? She was sorry now she had spited Kevin about his girl. It had been all in fun, really, no harm meant. It was strange if you couldn't speak your heart out to a good friend. Kevin had showed her the picture of his girl, like a clap of thunder it came one day when Rosaleen hadn't even heard there was one. She was a waitress in New York, and if ever Rosaleen had laid eyes on a brassy, bold-faced hussy, the kind the boys make jokes about at home, the kind that comes out to New York and goes wrong, this was the one. "You're never never keeping steady with her, are you?" Rosaleen had cried out and the tears came into her eyes. "And why not?" asked Kevin, his chin square as a box. "We've been great now for three years. Who says a word against her says it against me." And there they were, not exactly quarreling, but not friends for the moment, certainly, with Kevin putting the picture back in his pocket, saying: "There's the last of it between us. I was greatly wrong to tell ye!"

That night he was packing up his clothes before he went to bed, but came down and sat on the steps with them awhile, and they made it up by saying nothing, as if nothing had happened. "A man must do something with his life," Kevin explained. "There's always a place to be made in the world, and I'm off to New York, or Boston, maybe." Rosaleen said, "Write me a letter, don't forget, I'll be waiting." "The very day I know where I'll be," he promised her. They had parted with false wide smiles on their faces, arms around each other to the very gate. There had come a postcard from New York of the Woolworth building, with a word on it: "This is my hotel. Kevin." And never another word for these five years. The wretch, the stump! After he had disappeared down the road with his suitcase strapped on his shoulders, Rosaleen had gone back in the house and had looked at herself in the square looking-glass beside the kitchen window. There was a ripple in the glass and a crack across the middle, and it was like seeing your face in water. "Before God I don't look like that," she said, hanging it on the nail again. "If I did, it's no wonder he was leaving. But I don't." She knew in her heart no good would come of him running off after that common-looking girl; but it was likely he'd find her out soon, and come back, for Kevin was nobody's fool. She waited and watched for Kevin to come back and confess she had been right, and he would say, "I'm sorry I hurt your feelings over some- body not fit to look at you!" But now it was five years. She hung a drapery of crochet lace over the frame on the Billy-cat's picture, and propped it up on a small table in the kitchen, and sometimes it gave her an excuse to mention Kevin's name again, though the sound of it was a crack on the eardrums to Dennis. "Don't speak of him," said Dennis, more than once. "He owed it to send us word. It's ingratitude I can't stand." Whatever was she going to do with Dennis now, she wondered, and sighed heavily into the flank of the cow. It wasn't being a wife at all to wrap a man in flannels like a baby and put hot water bottles to him. She got up sighing and kicked back the stool. "There you are now," she said to the cow.

She couldn't help feeling happy all at once at the sight of the lamp and the fire making everything cozy, and the smell of vanilla reminded her of perfume. She set the table with a white-fringed cloth while Dennis strained the milk.

"Now, Dennis, today's a big day, and we're having a feast for it."

"Is it All-Saints?" asked Dennis, who never looked at a calendar any more. What's a day, more or less?

"It is not," said Rosaleen; "draw up your chair now."

Dennis made another guess it was Christmas, and Rosaleen said it was a better day than Christmas, even.

"I can't think what," said Dennis, looking at the glossy baked goose. "It's nobody's birthday that I mind."

Rosaleen lifted the cake like a mound of new snow blooming with candles. "Count them and see what day is this, will you?" she urged him.

Dennis counted them with a waggling forefinger. "So it is, Rosaleen, so it is."

They went on bandying words. It had slipped his mind entirely. Rosaleen wanted to know when hadn't it slipped his mind? For all he ever thought of it, they might never have had a wedding day at all. "That's not so," said Dennis. "I mind well I married you. It's the date that slips me."

"You might as well be English," said Rosaleen, "you might just as well."

She glanced at the clock, and reminded him it was twenty-five years ago that morning at ten o'clock, and tonight the very hour they had sat down to their first married dinner together. Dennis thought maybe it was telling people what to eat and then watching them eat it all those years that had taken away his wish for food. "You know I can't eat cake," he said. "It upsets my stomach."

Rosaleen felt sure her cake wouldn't upset the stomach of a nursing child. Dennis knew better, any kind of cake sat on him like a stone. While the argument went on, they ate nearly all the goose which fairly melted on the tongue, and finished with wedges of cake and floods of tea, and Dennis had to admit he hadn't felt better in years. He looked at her sitting across the table from him and thought she was a very fine woman, noticed again her red hair and yellow eyelashes and big arms and strong big teeth, and wondered what she thought of him now he was no human good to her. Here he was, all gone, and he had been so for years, and he felt guilt sometimes before Rosaleen, who couldn't always understand how there comes a time when a man is finished, and there is no more to be done that way. Rosaleen poured out two small glasses of home-made cherry brandy.

"I could feel like dancing itself this night, Dennis," she told him. "Do you remember the first time we met in Sligo Hall with the band playing?" She gave him another glass of brandy and took one herself and leaned over with her eyes shining as if she was telling him something he had never heard before.

"I remember a boy in Ireland was a great step-dancer, the best, and he was wild about me and I was a devil to him. Now what makes a girl like that, Dennis? He was a fine match, too, all the girls were glad of a chance with him, but I wasn't. He said to me a thousand times, 'Rosaleen, why won't ye dance with me just once?' And I'd say, 'Ye've plenty to dance with ye without my wasting my time.' And so it went for the summer long with him not dancing at all and everybody plaguing the living life out of him, till in the end I danced with him. Afterwards he walked home with me and a crowd of them, and there was a heaven full of stars and the dogs barking far off. Then I promised to keep steady with him, and was sorry for it the minute I promised. I was like that. We used to be the whole day getting ready for the dances, washing our hair and curling it and trying on our dresses and trimming them, laughing fit to kill about the boys and making up things to say to them. When my sister Honora was married they took me for the bride, Dennis, with my white dress ruffled to the heels and my hair with a wreath. Everybody drank my health for the belle of the ball, and said I would surely be the next bride. Honora said for me to save my blushes or I'd have none left for my own wedding. She was always jealous, Dennis, she's jealous of me to this day, you know that."

"Maybe so," said Dennis.

"There's no maybe about it," said Rosaleen. "But we had grand times together when we was little. I mind the time when my great-grandfather was ninety years old on his deathbed. We watched by turns the night—"

"And he was a weary time on it," said Dennis, to show his interest. He was so sleepy he could hardly hold up his head.

"He was," said Rosaleen, "so this night Honora and me was watching, and we was yawning our hearts out of us, for there had been a great ball the night before. Our mother told us, 'Feel his feet from time to time, and when you feel the chill rising, you'll know he's near the end. He can't last out the night,' she said, 'but stay by him.' So there we was drinking tea and laughing together in whispers to keep awake, and the old man lying there with his chin propped on the quilt. 'Wait a minute,' says Honora, and she felt his feet. 'They're getting cold,' she says, and went on telling me what she had said to Shane at the ball, how he was jealous of Terence and asks her can he trust her out of his sight. And Honora says to Shane, 'No, you cannot,' and oh, but he was roaring mad with anger! Then Honora stuffs her fist in her mouth to keep down the giggles. I felt great-grandfather's feet and legs and they was like clay to the knees, and I says, 'Maybe we'd better call somebody'; but Honora says, 'Oh, there's a power of him left to get cold yet!' So we poured out tea and began to comb and braid each other's hair, and fell to whispering our secrets and laughing more. Then Honora put her hand under the quilt and said, 'Rosaleen, his stomach's cold, it's gone he must be by now.' Then great-grandfather opened the one eye full of rage and says, 'It's nothing of the kind, and to hell with ye!' We let out a great scream, and the others came flying in, and Honora cried out, 'Oh, he's dead and gone surely, God rest him!' And would you believe it, it was so. He was gone. And while the old women were washing him Honora and me sat down laughing and crying in the one breath . . . and it was six months later to the very day great-grandfather came to me in the dream, the way I told you, and he was still after Honora and me for laughing in the watch. 'I've a great mind to thrash ye within an inch of your life,' he told me, 'only I'm wailing in Purgatory this minute for them last words to ye. Go and have an extra Mass said for the repose of me soul because it's by your misconduct I'm here at all,' he says to me. 'Get a move on now,' he said. 'And be damned to ye!' "

"And you woke up in a sweat," said Dennis, "and was off to Mass before daybreak."

Rosaleen nodded her head. "Ah, Dennis, if I'd set my heart on that boy I need never have left Ireland. And when I think how it all came out with him. With me so far away, him struck on the head and left for dead in a ditch."

"You dreamed that," said Dennis.

"Surely I dreamed it, and it is so. When I was crying and crying over him—" Rosaleen was proud of her crying—"I didn't know then what good luck I would find here."

Dennis couldn't think what good luck she was talking about.

"Let it pass, then," said Rosaleen. She went to the corner

shelves again. "The man today was selling pipes," she said, "and I bought the finest he had." It was an imitation meerschaum pipe carved with a crested lion glaring out of a jungle and it was as big as a man's fist.

Dennis said, "You must have paid a pretty penny for that."

"It doesn't concern ye," said Rosaleen. "I wanted to give ye a pipe."

Dennis said, "It's grand carving, I wonder if it'll draw at all." He filled it and lit it and said there wasn't much taste on a new one, for he was tired holding it up.

"It is such a pipe as my father had once," Rosaleen said to encourage him. "And in no time it was fit to knock ye off your feet, he said. So it will be a fine pipe some day."

"And some day I'll be in my tomb," thought Dennis, bitterly, "and she'll find a man can keep her quiet."

When they were in bed Rosaleen took his head on her shoulder. "Dennis, I could cry for the wink of an eyelash. When I think how happy we were that wedding day."

"From the way you carried on," said Dennis, feeling very sly all of a sudden on that brandy, "I thought different."

"Go to sleep," said Rosaleen, prudishly. "That's no way to talk."

Dennis's head fell back like a bag of sand on the pillow. Rosaleen could not sleep, and lay thinking about marriage: not about her own, for once you've given your word there's nothing to think about in it, but all other kinds of marriages, unhappy ones: where the husband drinks, or won't work, or mistreats his wife and the children. Where the wife runs away from home, or spoils the children or neglects them, or turns a perfect strumpet and flirts with other men: where a woman marries a man too young for her, and he feels cheated and strays after other women till it's just a disgrace: or take when a young girl marries an old man, even if he has money she's bound to be disappointed in some way. If Dennis hadn't been such a good man, God knows what might have come out of it. She was lucky. It would break your heart to dwell on it. Her black mood closed down on her and she wanted to walk the floor holding her head and remembering every unhappy thing in the world. She had had nothing but disasters, one after another, and she couldn't get over them, no matter how long ago they happened. Once she had let entirely the wrong man kiss her, she had almost got into bad trouble with him, and even now her heart stopped on her when she thought how near she'd come to being a girl with no character. There was the Billy-cat and his good heart and his sad death, and it was mixed up with the time her father had been knocked down, by a runaway horse, when the drink was in him, and the time when she had to wear mended stockings to a big ball because that sneaky Honora had stolen the only good ones.

She wished now she'd had a dozen children instead of the one that died in two days. This half-forgotten child suddenly lived again in her, she began to weep for him with all the freshness of her first agony; now he would be a fine grown man and the dear love of her heart. The image of him floated before her eyes plain as day, and became Kevin, painting the barn and the pig sty all colors of the rainbow, the brush swinging in his hand like a bell. He would work like a wild man for days and then lie for days under the trees, idle as a tramp. The darling, the darling lad like her own son. A painter by trade was a nice living, but she couldn't bear the thought of him boarding around the country with the heathen Rooshans and Polacks and Wops with their liquor stills and their outlandish lingo. She said as much to Kevin.

"It's not a Christian way to live, and you a good County Sligo boy."

So Kevin started to make jokes at her like any other Sligo boy. "I said to myself, that's a County Mayo woman if ever I clapped eyes on one."

"Hold your tongue," said Rosaleen softly as a dove. "You're talking to a Sligo woman as if you didn't know it!"

"Is it so?" said Kevin in great astonishment. "Well, I'm glad of the mistake. The Mayo people are too proud for me."

"And for me, too," said Rosaleen. "They beat the world for holding up their chins about nothing."

"They do so," said Kevin, "but the Sligo people have a right to be proud."

"And you've a right to live in a good Irish house," said Rosaleen, "so you'd best come with us."

"I'd be proud of that as if I came from Mayo," said Kevin, and he went on slapping paint on Rosaleen's front gate. They stood there smiling at each other, feeling they had agreed enough, it was time to think of how to get the best of each other in the talk from now on. For more than a year they had tried to get the best of each other in the talk, and sometimes it was one and sometimes another, but a gay easy time and such a bubble of joy like a kettle singing. "You've been a sister to me, Rosaleen, I'll not forget ye while I have breath," he had said that the last night.

Dennis muttered and snored a little. Rosaleen wanted to mourn about everything at the top of her voice, but it wouldn't do to wake Dennis. He was sleeping like the dead after all that goose.

Rosaleen said, "Dennis, I dreamed about Kevin in the night. There was a grave, an old one, but with fresh flowers on it, and a name on the headstone cut very clear but as if it was in another language and I couldn't make it out some way. You came up then and I said, 'Dennis, what grave is this?' and you answered me, 'That's Kevin's grave, don't you remember? And you put those flowers there yourself.' Then I said, 'Well, a grave it is then, and let's not think of it any more.' Now isn't it strange to think Kevin's been dead all this time and I didn't know it?"

Dennis said, "He's not fit to mention, going off as he did after all our kindness to him, and not a word from him."

"It was because he hadn't the power any more," said Rosaleen. "And ye mustn't be down on him now. I was wrong to put my judgment on him the way I did. Ah, but to think! Kevin dead and gone, and all these natives and foreigners living on, with the paint still on their barns and houses where Kevin put it! It's very bitter."

Grieving for Kevin, she drifted into thinking of the natives and foreigners who owned farms all around her. She was afraid for her life of them, she said, the way they looked at you out of their heathen faces, the foreigners bold as brass, the natives sly and mean. "The way they do be selling the drink to all, and burning each other in their beds and splitting each other's heads with axes," she complained. "The decent people aren't safe in their houses."

Yesterday she had seen that native Guy Richards going by wild-drunk again, fit to do any crime. He was a great offense to Rosaleen, with his shaggy mustaches and his shirt in rags till the brawny skin showed through; a shame to the world, staring around with his sneering eyes; living by himself in a shack and having his cronies in for drink until you could hear them shouting at all hours and careering round the countryside like the devils from hell. He would pass by the house driving his bony gray horse at top speed, standing up in the rackety buggy singing in a voice like a power of scrap-iron falling, drunk as a lord before breakfast. Once when Rosaleen was standing in her doorway, wearing a green checkerboard dress, he yelled at her: "Hey, Rosie, want to come for a ride?"

"The bold stump!" said Rosaleen to Dennis. "If ever he lays a finger on me I'll shoot him dead."

"If you mind your business by day," said Dennis in a shriveled voice, "and bar the doors well by night, there'll be no call to shoot anybody."

"Little you know!" said Rosaleen. She had a series of visions of Richards laying a finger on her and herself shooting him dead in his tracks. "Whatever would I do without ye, Dennis?" she asked him that night, as they sat on the steps in a soft darkness full of fireflies and the sound of crickets. "When I think of all the kinds of men there are in the world. That Richards!"

"When a man is young he likes his fun," said Dennis, amiably, beginning to yawn.

"Young, is it?" said Rosaleen, warm with anger. "The old crow! Fit to have children grown he is, the same as myself, and I'm a settled woman over her nonsense!"

Dennis almost said, "I'll never call you old," but all at once he was irritable too. "Will you stop your gossiping?" he asked censoriously.

Rosaleen sat silent, without rancor, but there was no denying the old man was getting old, old. He got up as if he gathered his bones in his arms, and carried himself in the house. Somewhere inside of him there must be Dennis, but where? "The world is a wilderness," she informed the crickets and frogs and fireflies.

Richards never had offered to lay a finger on Rosaleen, but now and again he pulled up at the gate when he was not quite drunk, and sat with them afternoons on the doorstep, and there were signs in him of a nice-behaved man before the drink got him down. He would tell them stories of his life, and what a desperate wild fellow he had been, all in all. Not when he was a boy, though. As long as his mother lived he had never done a thing to hurt her feelings. She wasn't what you might call a rugged woman, the least thing made her sick, and she was so religious she prayed all day long under her breath at her work, and even while she ate. He had belonged to a society called The Sons of Temperance, with all the boys in the countryside banded together under a vow never to touch strong drink in any form: "Not even for medicinal purposes," he would quote, raising his right arm and staring solemnly before him. Quite often he would burst into a rousing march tune which he remembered from the weekly singings they had held: "With flags of temperance flying, With banners white as snow," and he could still repeat almost word for word the favorite poem he had been called upon to recite at every meeting: "At midnight, in his guarded tent, The Turk lay dreaming of the hour—"

Rosaleen wanted to interrupt sometimes and tell him that had been no sort of life, he should have been young in Ireland. But she wouldn't say it. She sat stiffly beside Dennis and looked at Richards severely out of the corner of her eye, wondering if he remembered that time he had yelled "Hey, Rosie!" at her. It was enough to make a woman wild not to find a word in her mouth for such boldness. The cheek of him, pretending nothing had happened. One day she was racking her mind for some saying that would put him in his place, while he was telling about the clambakes his gang was always having down by the creek behind the rock pile, with a keg of home-brew beer; and the dances the Railroad Street outfit gave every Saturday night in Winston. "We're always up to some devilment," he said, looking straight at Rosaleen, and before she could say scat, the hellion had winked his near eye at her. She turned away with her mouth down at the corners; after a long minute, she said, "Good day to ye, Mr. Richards," cold as ice, and went in the house. She took down the looking-glass to see what kind of look she had on her, but the wavy place made her eyes broad and blurred as the palm of her hands, and she couldn't tell her nose from her mouth in the cracked seam. . . .

The pipe salesman came back next month and brought a patent cooking pot that cooked vegetables perfectly without any water in them. "It's a lot healthier way of cooking, Miz O'Toole," Dennis heard his mouthy voice going thirteen to the dozen. "I'm telling you as a friend because you're a good customer of mine."

"Is it so?" thought Dennis, and his gall stirred within him.

"You'll find it's going to be a perfect godsend for your husband's health. Old folks need to be mighty careful what they eat, and you know better than I do, Miz O'Toole, that health begins or ends right in the kitchen. Now your husband don't look as stout as he might. It's because, tasty as your cooking is, you've been pouring all the good vitamins, the sunlit life-giving elements, right down the sink. . . . Right down the sink, Miz O'Toole, is where you're pouring your husband's health and your own. And I say it's a shame, a good-looking woman like you wasting your time and strength standing over a cook-stove when all you've got to do from now on is just fill this scientific little contrivance with whatever you've planned for dinner and then go away and read a good book in your parlor while it's cooking—or curl your hair."

"My hair curls by nature," said Rosaleen. Dennis almost groaned aloud from his hiding-place.

"For the love of—why, Miz O'Toole, you don't mean to tell me that! When I first saw that hair, I said to myself, why, it's so perfect it looks to be artificial! I was just getting ready to ask you how you did it so I could tell my wife. Well, if your hair curls like that, without any vitamins at all, I want to come back and have a look at it after you've been cooking in this little pot for two weeks."

Rosaleen said, "Well, it's not my looks I'm thinking about. But my husband isn't up to himself, and that's the truth, Mr. Pendleton. Ah, it would have done your heart good to see that man in his younger days! Strong as an ox he was, the way no man dared to rouse his anger. I've seen my husband, many's the time, swing on a man with his fist and send him sprawling twenty feet, and that for the least thing, mind you! But Dennis could never hold his grudge for long, and the next instant you'd see him picking the man up and dusting him off like a brother and saying, 'Now think no more of that.' He was too forgiving always. It was his great fault."

"And look at him now," said Mr. Pendleton, sadly.

Dennis felt pretty hot around the ears. He stood forward at the corner of the house, listening. He had never weighed more than one hundred thirty pounds at his most, a tall thin man he had been always, a little proud of his elegant shape, and not since he left school in Bristol had he lifted his hand in anger against a creature, brute or human. "He was a fine man a woman could rely on, Mr. Pendleton," said Rosaleen, "and quick as a tiger with his fists."

"I might be dead and moldering away to dust the way she talks," thought Dennis, "and there she is throwing away the money as if she was already a gay widow woman." He tottered out bent on speaking his mind and putting a stop to such foolishness. The salesman turned a floppy smile and shrewd little eyes upon him. "Hello, Mr. O'Toole," he said, with the manly cordiality he used for husbands. "I'm just leaving you a little birthday present with the Missis here."

"It's not my birthday," said Dennis, sour as a lemon.

"That's just a manner of speaking!" interrupted Rosaleen, merrily. "And now many thanks to ye, Mr. Pendleton."

"Many thanks to *you*, Miz O'Toole," answered the salesman, folding away nine dollars of good green money. No more was said except good day, and Rosaleen stood shading her eyes to watch the Ford walloping off down the hummocky lane. "That's a nice, decent family man," she told Dennis, as if rebuking his evil thoughts. "He travels out of New York, and he always has the latest thing and the best. He's full of admiration for ye, too, Dennis. He said he couldn't call to mind another man of your age as sound as you are."

"I heard him," said Dennis. "I know all he said."

"Well, then," said Rosaleen, serenely, "there's no good saying it over." She hurried to wash potatoes to cook in the pot that made the hair curl.

The winter piled in upon them, and the snow was shot through with blizzards. Dennis couldn't bear a breath of cold, and all but sat in the oven, rheumy and grunty, with his muffler on. Rosaleen began to feel as if she couldn't bear her clothes on her in the hot kitchen, and when she did the barn work she had one chill after another. She complained that her hands were gnawed to the bone with the cold. Did Dennis realize that now, or was he going to sit like a log all winter, and where was the lad he had promised her to help with the outside work?

Dennis sat wordless under her unreasonableness, thinking she had very little work for a strong-bodied woman, and the truth was she was blaming him for something he couldn't help. Still she said nothing he could take hold of, only nipping his head off when the kettle dried up or the fire went low. There would come a day when she would say outright, "It's no life here, I won't stay here any longer," and she would drag him back to a flat in New York, or even leave him, maybe. Would she? Would she do such a thing? Such a thought had never occurred to him before. He peered at her as if he watched her through a keyhole. He tried to think of something to ease her mind, but no plan came. She would look at some harmless thing around the house, say—the calendar, and suddenly tear it off the wall and stuff it in the fire. "I hate the very sight of it," she would explain, and she was always hating the very sight of one thing or another, even the cow; almost, but not quite, the cats.

One morning she sat up very tired and forlorn, and began almost before Dennis could get an eye open: "I had a dream in the night that my sister Honora was sick and dying in her bed, and was calling for me." She bowed her head on her hands and breathed brokenly to her very toes, and said, "It's only natural I must go to Boston to find out for myself how it is, isn't it?"

Dennis, pulling on his chest protector she had knitted him for Christmas, said, "I suppose so. It looks that way."

Over the coffee pot she began making her plans. "I could go if only I had a coat. It should be a fur one against this weather. A coat is what I've needed all these years. If I had a coat I'd go this very day."

"You've a greatcoat with fur on it," said Dennis.

"A rag of a coat!" cried Rosaleen. "And I won't have Honora see me in it. She was jealous always, Dennis, she'd be glad to see me without a coat."

"If she's sick and dying maybe she won't notice," said Dennis.

Rosaleen agreed. "And maybe it will be better to buy one there, or in New York—something in the new style."

"It's long out of your way by New York," said Dennis. "There's shorter ways to Boston than that."

"It's by New York I'm going, because the trains are better," said Rosaleen, "and I want to go that way." There was a look on her face as if you could put her on the rack and she wouldn't yield. Dennis kept silence.

When the postman passed she asked him to leave word with the native family up the hill to send their lad down for a few days to help with the chores, at the same pay as before. And tomorrow morning, if it was all the same to him, she'd be driving in with him to the train. All day long, with her hair in curl papers, she worked getting her things together in the lazy old canvas bag. She put a ham on to bake and set bread and filled the closet off the kitchen with firewood. "Maybe there'll come a message saying Honora's better and I sha'n't have to go," she said several times, but her eyes were excited and she walked about so briskly the floor shook.

Late in the afternoon Guy Richards knocked, and floundered in stamping his big boots. He was almost sober, but he wasn't going to be for long. Rosaleen said, "I've sad news about my sister, she's on her deathbed maybe and I'm going to Boston."

"I hope it's nothing serious, Missis O'Toole," said Richards. "Let's drink her health in this," and he took out a bottle half full of desperate-looking drink. Dennis said he didn't mind. Richards said, "Will the lady join us?" and his eyes had the devil in them if Rosaleen had ever seen it.

"I will not," she said. "I've something better to do."

While they drank she sat fixing the hem of her dress, and began to tell again about the persons without number she'd known who came back from the dead to bring word about themselves, and Dennis himself would back her up in it. She told again the story of the Billy-cat, her voice warm and broken with the threat of tears.

Dennis swallowed his drink, leaned over and began to fumble with his shoelace, his face sunken to a handful of wrinkles, and thought right out plainly to himself: "There's not a word of truth in it, not a word. And she'll go on telling it to the world's end for God's truth." He felt helpless, as if he were involved in some disgraceful fraud. He wanted to speak up once for all and say, "It's a lie, Rosaleen, it's something you've made up, and now let's hear no more about it." But Richards, sitting there with his ears lengthened, stopped the words in Dennis's throat. The moment passed. Rosaleen said solemnly, "My dreams never renege on me,

Mr. Richards. They're all I have to go by." "It never happened at all," said Dennis inside himself, stubbornly. "Only the Billy-cat got caught in a trap and I buried him." Could this really have been all? He had a nightmarish feeling that somewhere just out of his reach lay the truth about it, he couldn't swear for certain, yet he was *almost* willing to swear that this had been all. Richards got up saying he had to be getting on to a shindig at Winston. "I'll take you to the train tomorrow, Missus O'Toole," he said. "I love doing a good turn for the ladies."

Rosaleen said very stiffly, "I'll be going in with the letter-carrier, and many thanks just the same."

She tucked Dennis into bed with great tenderness and sat by him a few minutes, putting cold cream on her face. "It won't be for long," she told him, "and you're well taken care of the whole time. Maybe by the grace of God I'll find her recovered."

"Maybe she's not sick at all," Dennis wanted to say, and said instead, "I hope so." It was nothing to him. Everything else aside, it seemed a great fuss to be making over Honora, who might die when she liked for all Dennis would turn a hair.

Dennis hoped until the last minute that Rosaleen would come to her senses and give up the trip, but at the last minute there she was with her hat and the rag of a coat, a streak of pink powder on her chin, pulling on her tan gloves that smelt of naphtha, flourishing a handkerchief that smelt of Azurea, and going every minute to the window, looking for the postman. "In this snow maybe he'll be late," she said in a trembling voice. "What if he didn't come at all?" She took a last glimpse at herself in the mirror. "One thing I must remember, Dennis," she said in another tone. "And that is, to bring back a looking-glass that won't make my face look like a monster's."

"It's a good enough glass," said Dennis, "without throwing away money."

The postman came only a few minutes late. Dennis kissed Rosaleen good-by and shut the kitchen door so he could not see her climbing into the car, but he heard her laughing.

"It's just a born liar she is," Dennis said to himself, sitting by the stove, and at once he felt he had leaped head-first into a very dark pit. His better self tried to argue it out with him. "Have you no shame," said Dennis's better self, "thinking such thoughts about your own wife?" The baser Dennis persisted. "It's not half she deserves," he answered sternly, "leaving me here by my lone, and for what?" That was the great question. Certainly not to run after Honora, living or dying or dead. Where then? For what on earth? Here he stopped thinking altogether. There wasn't a spark in his mind. He had a lump on his chest that could surely be pneumonia if he had a cold, which he hadn't, specially. His feet ached until you'd swear it was rheumatism, only he never had it. Still, he wasn't thinking. He stayed in this condition for two days, and the under-witted lad from the native farm above did all the work, even to washing the dishes. Dennis ate pretty well, considering the grief he was under.

Rosaleen settled back in the plush seat and thought how she had always been a great traveler. A train was like home to her, with all the other people sitting near, and the smell of newspapers and some kind of nice-smelling furniture polish and the perfume from fur collars, and the train dust and something over and above she couldn't place, but it was the smell of travel: fruit, maybe, or was it machinery? She bought chocolate bars, though she wasn't hungry, and a magazine of love stories, though she was never one for reading. She only wished to prove to herself she was once more on a train going somewhere.

She watched the people coming on or leaving at the stations, greeting, or kissing good-by, and it seemed a lucky sign she did not see a sad face anywhere. There was a cold sweet sunshine on the snow, and the city people didn't look all frozen and bundled up. Their faces looked smooth after the gnarled raw frost-bitten country faces. The Grand Central hadn't changed at all, with all the crowds whirling in every direction, and a noise that almost had a tune in it, it was so steady. She held on to her bag the colored men were trying to get away from her, and stood on the sidewalk trying to remember which direction was Broadway where the moving pictures were. She hadn't seen one for five years, it was high time now! She wished she had an hour to visit her old flat in 164th Street—just a turn around the block would be enough, but there wasn't time. An old resentment rose against Honora, who was a born spoil-sport and would spoil this trip for her if she could. She walked on, getting her directions, brooding a little because she had been such a city girl once, thinking only of dress and a good time, and now she hardly knew one street from another. She went into the first moving-picture theater she saw because she liked the name of it. "The Prince of Love," she said to herself. It was about two beautiful young things, a boy with black wavy hair and a girl with curly golden hair, who loved each other and had great troubles, but it all came well in the end, and all the time it was just one fine ballroom or garden after another, and such beautiful clothes! She sniffled a little in the Azurea-smelling handkerchief, and ate her chocolates, and reminded herself these two were really alive and looked just like that, but it was hard to believe living beings could be so beautiful.

After the dancing warm lights of the screen the street was cold and dark and ugly, with the slush and the roar and the millions of people all going somewhere in a great rush, but not one face she knew. She decided to go to Boston by boat the way she used in the old days when she visited Honora. She gazed into the shop windows thinking how the styles in underthings had changed till she could hardly believe her eyes, wondering what Dennis would say if she bought the green glove silk slip with the tea-colored lace. Ah, was he eating his ham now as she told him, and did the boy come to help as he had promised?

She ate ice cream with strawberry preserves on it, and bought a powder puff and decided there was time for another moving-picture. It was called "The Lover King," and it was about a king in a disguise, a lovely young man with black wavy hair and eyes would melt in his head, who married a poor country girl who was more beautiful than all the princesses and ladies in the land. Music came out of the screen, and voices talking, and Rosaleen cried, for the love songs went to her heart like a dagger.

Afterward there was just time to ride in a taxi to Christopher Street and catch the boat. She felt happier the minute she set foot on board, how she always loved a ship! She ate her supper thinking, "That boy didn't have much style to his waiting. Dennis would never have kept him on in the hotel"; and afterward sat in the lounge and listened to the radio until she almost fell asleep there before everybody. She stretched out in her narrow bunk and felt the engine pounding under her, and the grand steady beat shook the very marrow of her bones. The fog horn howled and bellowed through the darkness over the rush of water, and Rosaleen turned on her side. "Howl for me, that's the way I could cry in the night-time in that lost heathen place," for Connecticut seemed a thousand miles and a hundred years away by now. She fell asleep and had no dreams at all.

In the morning she felt this was a lucky sign. At Providence she took the train again, and as the meeting with Honora came nearer, she grew sunken and tired. "Always Honora making trouble," she thought, standing outside the station holding her bag and thinking it strange she hadn't remembered what a dreary ugly place Boston was; she couldn't remember any good times there. Taxicab drivers were yelling in her face. Maybe it would be a good thing to go to a church and light a candle for Honora. The taxi scampered through winding streets to the nearest church, with Rosaleen thinking, what she wouldn't give to be able to ride around all day, and never walk at all!

She knelt near the high altar, and something surged up in her heart and pushed the tears out of her eyes. Prayers began to tumble over each other on her lips. How long it had been since she had seen the church as it should be, dressed for a feast with candles and flowers, smelling of incense and wax. The little doleful church in Winston, now who could really pray in it? "Have mercy on us," said Rosaleen, calling on fifty saints at once; "I confess . . ." she struck her breast three times, then got up suddenly, carrying her bag, and peered into the confessionals hoping she might find a priest in one of them. "It's too early, or it's not the day, but I'll come back," she promised herself with tenderness. She lit the candle for Honora and went away feeling warm and quiet. She was blind and confused, too, and could not make up her mind what to do next. Where ever should she turn? It was a burning sin to spend money on taxicabs when there was always the hungry poor in the world, but she hailed one anyhow, and gave Honora's house number. Yes, there it was, just like in old times.

She read all the names pasted on slips above the bells, all the floors front and back, but Honora's name was not among them. The janitor had never heard of Mrs. Terence Gogarty, nor Mrs. Honora Gogarty, neither. Maybe it would be in the telephone book. There were many Gogartys but no Terence nor Honora. Rosaleen smothered down the impulse to tell the janitor, a good

Irishman, how her dream had gone back on her. "Thank ye kindly, it's no great matter," she said, and stepped out into the street again. The wind hacked at her shoulders through the rag of a coat, the bag was too heavy altogether. Now what kind of nature was in Honora not to drop a line and say she had moved?

Walking about with her mind in a whirl, she came to a small dingy square with iron benches and some naked trees in it. Sitting, she began to shed tears again. When one handkerchief was wet she took out another, and the fresh perfume put new heart in her. She glanced around when a shadow fell on the corner of her eye, and there hunched on the other end of the bench was a scrap of a lad with freckles, his collar turned about his ears, his red hair wilted on his forehead under his bulging cap. He slanted his gooseberry eyes at her and said, "We've all something to cry for in this world, isn't it so?"

Rosaleen said, "I'm crying because I've come a long way for nothing."

The boy said, "I knew you was a County Sligo woman the minute I clapped eyes on ye."

"God bless ye for that," said Rosaleen, "for I am."

"I'm County Sligo myself, long ago, and curse the day I ever thought of leaving it," said the boy, with such anger Rosaleen dried her eyes once for all and turned to have a good look at him.

"Whatever makes ye say that now?" she asked him. "It's a good country, this. There's opportunity for all here."

"So I've heard tell many's the countless times," said the boy. "There's all the opportunity in the wide world to shrivel with the hunger and walk the soles off your boots hunting the work, and there's a great chance of dying in the gutter at last. God forgive me the first thought I had of coming here."

"Ye haven't been out long?" asked Rosaleen.

"Eleven months and five days the day," said the boy. He plunged his hands into his pockets and stared at the freezing mud clotted around his luckless shoes.

"And what might ye do by way of a living?" asked Rosaleen.

"I'm an hostler," he said. "I used to work at the Dublin race tracks, even. No man can tell me about horses," he said proudly. "And it's good work if it's to be found."

Rosaleen looked attentively at his sharp red nose, frozen it was, and the stung look around his eyes, and the sharp bones sticking out at his wrists, and was surprised at herself for thinking, in the first glance, that he had the look of Kevin. She saw different now, but think if it had been Kevin! Better off to be dead and gone. "I'm perishing of hunger and cold," she told him, "and if I knew where there was a place to eat, we'd have some lunch, for it's late."

His eyes looked like he was drowning. "Would ye? I know a place!" and he leaped up as if he meant to run. They did almost run to the edge of the square and the far corner. It was a Coffee Pot and full of the smell of hot cakes. "We'll get our fill here," said Rosaleen, taking off her gloves, "though I'd never call it a grand place."

The boy ate one thing after another as if he could never stop: roast beef and potatoes and spaghetti and custard pie and coffee, and Rosaleen ordered a package of cigarettes. It was like this with her, she was fond of the smell of tobacco, her husband was a famous smoker, never without his pipe. "It's no use keeping it in," said the boy. "I haven't a penny, yesterday and today I didn't eat till now, and I've been fit to hang myself, or go to jail for a place to lay my head."

Rosaleen said, "I'm a woman doesn't have to think of money, I have all my heart desires, and a boy like yourself has a right to think nothing of a little loan will never be missed." She fumbled in her purse and brought out a ten-dollar bill, crumpled it and pushed it under the rim of his saucer so the man behind the counter wouldn't notice. "That's for luck in the new world," she said, smiling at him. "You might be Kevin or my own brother, or my own little lad alone in the world, and it'll surely come back to me if ever I need it."

The boy said, "I never thought to see this day," and put the money in his pocket.

Rosaleen said, "I don't even know your name, think of that!"

"I'm a blight on the name of Sullivan," said he. "Hugh it is—Hugh Sullivan."

"That's a good enough name," said Rosaleen. "I've cousins named Sullivan in Dublin, but I never saw one of them. There was a man named Sullivan married my mother's sister, my aunt Brigid she was, and she went to live in Dublin. You're not related to the Dublin Sullivans, are ye?"

"I never heard of it, but maybe I am."

"Ye have the look of a Sullivan to me," said Rosaleen, "and they're cousins of mine, some of them." She ordered more coffee and he lit another cigarette, and she told him how she had come out more than twenty-five years past, a greenhorn like himself, and everything had turned out well for her and all her family here. Then she told about her husband, how he had been head waiter and a moneyed man, but he was old now; about the farm, if there was someone to help her, they could make a good thing of it; and about Kevin and the way he had gone away and died and sent her news of it in a dream; and this led to the dream about Honora, and here she was, the first time ever a dream had gone back on her. She went on to say there was always room for a strong willing boy in the country if he knew about horses, and how it was a shame for him to be tramping the streets with an empty stomach when there was everything to be had if he only knew which way to look for it. She leaned over and took him by the arm very urgently.

"You've a right to live in a good Irish house," she told him. "Why don't ye come home with me and live there like one of the family in peace and comfort?"

Hugh Sullivan stared at her out of his glazed green eyes down the edge of his sharp nose and a crafty look came over him. " 'Twould be dangerous," he said. "I'd hate to try it."

"Dangerous, is it?" asked Rosaleen. "What danger is there in the peaceful countryside?"

"It's not safe at all," said Hugh. "I was caught at it once in Dublin, and there was a holy row! A fine woman like yourself she was, and her husband peeking through a crack in the wall the whole time. Man, that was a scrape for ye!"

Rosaleen understood in her bones before her mind grasped it. "Whatever—" she began, and the blood boiled up in her face until it was like looking through a red veil. "Ye little whelp," she said, trying to get her breath, "so it's that kind ye are, is it? I might know you're from Dublin! Never in my whole life—" Her rage rose like a bonfire in her, and she stopped. "If I was looking for a man," she said, "I'd choose a *man* and not a half-baked little . . ." She took a deep breath and started again. "The *cheek* of ye," she said, "insulting a woman could be your mother. God keep me from it! It's plain you're just an ignorant greenhorn, doesn't know the ways of decent people, and now be off—" She stood up and motioned to the man behind the counter. "Out of that door now—"

He stood up too, glancing around fearfully with his narrow green eyes, and put out a hand as if he would try to make it up with her. "Not so loud now, woman alive, it's what any man might think the way ye're—"

Rosaleen said, "Hold your tongue or I'll tear it out of your head!" and her right arm went back in a business-like way.

He ducked and shot past her, then collected himself and lounged out of reach. "Farewell to ye, County Sligo woman," he said tauntingly. "I'm from County Cork myself!" and darted through the door.

Rosaleen shook so she could hardly find the money for the bill, and she couldn't see her way before her, but when the cold air struck her, her head cleared, and she could have almost put a curse on Honora for making all this trouble for her. . . .

She took a train the short way home, for the taste of travel had soured on her altogether. She wanted to be home and nowhere else. That shameless boy, whatever was he thinking of? "Boys do be known for having evil minds in them," she told herself, and the blood fairly crinkled in her veins. But he had said, "A fine woman like yourself," and maybe he'd met too many bold ones, and thought they were all alike; maybe she had been too free in her ways because he was Irish and looked so sad and poor. But there it was, he was a mean sort, and he would have made love to her if she hadn't stopped him, maybe. It flashed over her and she saw it clear as day—Kevin had loved her all the time, and she had sent him away to that cheap girl who wasn't half good enough for him! And Kevin a sweet decent boy would have cut off his right hand rather than give her an improper word. Kevin had loved her and she had loved Kevin and, oh, she hadn't known it in time! She bowed herself back into the corner with her elbow on the windowsill, her old fur collar pulled up around her face, and wept long and bitterly for Kevin, who would have stayed if she had said the word—and now he was gone and lost and dead. She would hide herself from the world and never speak to a soul again.

"Safe and sound she is, Dennis," Rosaleen told him. "She's been dangerous, but it's past. I left her in health."

"That's good enough," said Dennis, without enthusiasm. He took off his cap with the ear flaps and ran his fingers through his downy white hair and put the cap on again and stood waiting to hear the wonders of the trip; but Rosaleen had no tales to tell and was full of home-coming.

"This kitchen is a disgrace," she said, putting things to rights. "But not for all the world would I live in the city, Dennis. It's a wild heartless place, full of criminals in every direction as far as the eye can reach. I was scared for my life the whole time. Light the lamp, will you?"

The native boy sat warming his great feet in the oven, and his teeth were chattering with something more than cold. He burst out: "I seed sumpin' comin' up the road whiles ago. Black. Fust it went on all fours like a dawg and then it riz and walked longside of me on its hind legs. I was scairt, I was. I said Shoo! at it, and it went out, like a lamp."

"Maybe it was a dog," said Dennis.

" 'Twarn't a dawg, neither," said the boy.

"Maybe 'twas a cat rising up to climb a fence," said Rosaleen.

" 'Twarn't a cat, neither," said the boy. " 'Twarn't nothin' I ever seed afore, nor *you,* neither."

"Never you mind about that," said Rosaleen. "I have seen it and many times, when I was a girl in Ireland. It's famous there, the way it comes in a black lump and rolls along the path before you, but if you call on the Holy Name and make the sign of the Cross, it flees away. Eat your supper now, and sleep here the night; ye can't go out by your lone and the Evil waiting for ye."

She bedded him down in Kevin's room, and kept Dennis awake all hours telling him about the ghosts she'd seen in Sligo. The trip to Boston seemed to have gone out of her mind entirely.

In the morning, the boy's starveling black dog rose up at the opened kitchen door and stared sorrowfully at his master. The cats streamed out in a body, and silently, intently they chased him far up the road. The boy stood on the doorstep and began to tremble again. "The old woman told me to git back fer supper," he said blankly. "Howma *ever* gointa git back fer supper *now?* The ole man'll skin me alive."

Rosaleen wrapped her green wool shawl around her head and shoulders. "I'll go along with ye and tell what happened," she said.

"They'll never harm ye when they know the straight of it." For he was shaking with fright until his knees buckled under him. "He's away in his mind," she thought, with pity. "Why can't they see it and let him be in peace?"

The steady slope of the lane ran on for nearly a mile, then turned into a bumpy trail leading to a forlorn house with broken-down steps and a litter of rubbish around them. The boy hung back more and more, and stopped short when the haggard, long-toothed woman in the gray dress came out carrying a stick of stove wood. The woman stopped short too when she recognized Rosaleen, and a sly cold look came on her face.

"Good day," said Rosaleen. "Your boy saw a ghost last night, and I didn't have the heart to send him out in the darkness. He slept safe in my house."

The woman gave a sharp dry bark, like a fox. "Ghosts!" she said. "From all I hear, there's more than ghosts around your house nights, Missis O'Toole." She wagged her head and her faded tan hair flew in strings. "A pretty specimen you are, Missis O'Toole, with your old husband and the young boys in your house and the traveling salesmen and the drunkards lolling on your doorstep all hours—"

"Hold your tongue before your lad here," said Rosaleen, the back of her neck beginning to crinkle. She was so taken by surprise she couldn't find a ready answer, but stood in her tracks listening.

"A pretty sight you are, Missis O'Toole," said the woman, raising her thin voice somewhat, but speaking with deadly cold slowness. "With your trips away from your husband and your loud-colored dresses and your dyed hair—"

"May God strike you dead," said Rosaleen, raising her own voice suddenly, "if you say that of my hair! And for the rest may your evil tongue rot in your head with your teeth! I'll not waste words on ye! Here's your poor lad and may God pity him in your house, a blight on it! And if my own house is burnt over my head I'll know who did it!" She turned away and whirled back to call out, "May ye be ten years dying!"

"You can curse and swear, Missis O'Toole, but the whole countryside knows about you!" cried the other, brandishing her stick like a spear.

"Much good they'll get of it!" shouted Rosaleen, striding away in a roaring fury. "Dyed, is it?" She raised her clenched fist and shook it at the world. "Oh, the liar!" and her rage was like a drum beating time for her marching legs. What was happening these days that everybody she met had dirty minds and dirty tongues in their heads? Oh, why wasn't she strong enough to strangle them all at once? Her eyes were so hot she couldn't close her lids over them. She went on staring and walking, until almost before she knew it she came in sight of her own house, sittling like a hen quietly in a nest of snow. She slowed down, her thumping heart eased a little, and she sat on a stone by the roadside to catch her breath and gather her wits before she must see Dennis. As she sat, it came to her that the Evil walking the roads at night in this place was the bitter lies people had been telling about her, who had been a good woman all this time when many another would have gone astray. It was no comfort now to remember all the times she might have done wrong and hadn't. What was the good if she was being scandalized all the same? That lad in Boston now—the little whelp. She spat on the frozen earth and wiped her mouth. Then she put her elbows on her knees and her head in her hands, and thought, "So that's the way it is here, is it? That's what my life has come to, I'm a woman of bad fame with the neighbors."

Dwelling on this strange thought, little by little she began to feel better. Jealousy, of course, that was it. "Ah, what wouldn't that poor thing give to have my hair?" and she patted it tenderly. From the beginning it had been so, the women were jealous, because the men were everywhere after her, as if it was her fault! Well, let them talk. Let them. She knew in her heart what she was, and Dennis knew, and that was enough.

"Life is a dream," she said aloud, in a soft easy melancholy. "It's a mere dream." The thought and the words pleased her, and she gazed with pleasure at the loosened stones of the wall across the road, dark brown, with the thin shining coat of ice on them, in a comfortable daze until her feet began to feel chilled.

"Let me not sit here and take my death at my early time of life," she cautioned herself, getting up and wrapping her shawl carefully around her. She was thinking how this sad countryside needed some young hearts in it, and how she wished Kevin would come back to laugh with her at that woman up the hill; with him, she could just laugh in their faces! That dream about Honora now, it hadn't come true at all. Maybe the dream about Kevin wasn't true either. If one dream failed on you it would be foolish to think another mightn't fail you too: wouldn't it, wouldn't it? She smiled at Dennis sitting by the stove.

"What did the native people have to say this morning?" he asked, trying to pretend it was nothing much to him what they said.

"Oh, we exchanged the compliments of the season," said Rosaleen. "There was no call for more." She went about singing; her heart felt light as a leaf and she couldn't have told why if she died for it. But she was a good woman and she'd show them she was going to be one to her last day. Ah, she'd show them, the low-minded things.

In the evening they settled down by the stove, Dennis cleaning and greasing his boots, Rosaleen with the long tablecloth she'd been working on for fifteen years. Dennis kept wondering what had happened in Boston, or where ever she had been. He knew he would never hear the straight of it, but he wanted Rosaleen's story about it. And there she sat mum, putting a lot of useless stitches in something she would never use, even if she ever finished it, which she would not.

"Dennis," she said after a while, "I don't put the respect on dreams I once did."

"That's maybe a good thing," said Dennis, cautiously. "And why don't you?"

"All day long I've been thinking Kevin isn't dead at all, and we shall see him in this very house before long."

Dennis growled in his throat a little. "That's no sign at all," he said. And to show that he had a grudge against her he laid down his meerschaum pipe, stuffed his old briar and lit it instead. Rosaleen took no notice at all. Her embroidery had fallen on her knees and she was listening to the rattle and clatter of a buggy coming down the road, with Richards's voice roaring a song, "I've been working on the *railroad,* ALL the live-long day!" She stood up, taking hairpins out and putting them back, her hands trembling. Then she ran to the looking-glass and saw her face there, leaping into shapes fit to scare you. "Oh, Dennis," she cried out as if it was that thought had driven her out of her chair. "I forgot to buy a looking-glass, I forgot it altogether!"

"It's a good enough glass," repeated Dennis.

The buggy clattered at the gate, the song halted. Ah, he was coming in, surely! It flashed through her mind a woman would have a ruined life with such a man, it was courting death and danger to let him set foot over the threshold.

She stopped herself from running to the door, hand on the knob even before his knock should sound. Then the wheels creaked and ground again, the song started up; if he thought of stopping he changed his mind and went on, off on his career to the Saturday night dance in Winston, with his rapscallion cronies.

Rosaleen didn't know what to expect, then, and then: surely he couldn't be stopping? Ah, surely he *couldn't* be going on? She sat down again with her heart just nowhere, and took up the table-cloth, but for a long time she couldn't see the stitches. She was wondering what had become of her life; every day she had thought something great was going to happen, and it was all just straying from one terrible disappointment to another. Here in the lamplight sat Dennis and the cats, beyond in the darkness and snow lay Winston and New York and Boston, and beyond that were far off places full of life and gayety she'd never seen nor even heard of, and beyond everything like a green field with morning sun on it lay youth and Ireland as if they were something she had dreamed, or made up in a story. Ah, what was there to remember, or to look forward to now? Without thinking at all, she leaned over and put her head on Dennis's knee. "Whyever," she asked him, in an ordinary voice, "did ye marry a woman like me?"

"Mind you don't tip over in that chair now," said Dennis. "I knew well I could never do better." His bosom began to thaw and simmer. It was going to be all right with everything, he could see that.

She sat up and felt his sleeves carefully. "I want you to wrap up warm this bitter weather, Dennis," she told him. "With two pairs of socks and the chest protector, for if anything happened to you, whatever would become of me in this world?"

"Let's not think of it," said Dennis, shuffling his feet.

"Let's not, then," said Rosaleen. "For I could cry if you crooked a finger at me."

Mexico City–Berlin, 1931

Hacienda

It was worth the price of a ticket to see Kennerly take possession of the railway train among a dark inferior people. Andreyev and I trailed without plan in the wake of his gigantic progress (he was a man of ordinary height merely, physically taller by a head, perhaps, than the nearest Indian; but his moral stature in this moment was beyond calculation) through the second-class coach into which we had climbed, in our haste, by mistake. . . . Now that the true revolution of blessed memory has come and gone in Mexico, the names of many things are changed, nearly always with the view to an appearance of heightened well-being for all creatures. So you cannot ride third-class no matter how poor or humble-spirited or miserly you may be. You may go second in cheerful disorder and sociability, or first in sober ease; or, if you like, you may at great price install yourself in the stately plush of the Pullman, isolated and envied as any successful General from the north. "Ah, it is beautiful as a *pulman!*" says the middle-class Mexican when he wishes truly to praise anything. . . . There was no Pullman with this train or we should most unavoidably have been in it. Kennerly traveled like that. He strode mightily through, waving his free arm, lunging his portfolio and leather bag, stiffening his nostrils as conspicuously as he could against the smell that "poured," he said, "simply poured like mildewed pea soup!" from the teeming clutter of wet infants and draggled turkeys and indignant baby pigs and food baskets and bundles of vegetables and bales and hampers of domestic goods, each little mountain of confusion yet drawn into a unit, from the midst of which its owners glanced up

135

casually from dark pleased faces at the passing strangers. Their pleasure had nothing to do with us. They were pleased because, sitting still, without even the effort of beating a burro, they were on the point of being carried where they wished to go, accomplishing in an hour what would otherwise have been a day's hard journey, with all their households on their backs. . . . Almost nothing can disturb their quiet ecstasy when they are finally settled among their plunder, and the engine, mysteriously and powerfully animated, draws them lightly over the miles they have so often counted step by step. And they are not troubled by the noisy white man because, by now, they are accustomed to him. White men look all much alike to the Indians, and they had seen this maddened fellow with light eyes and leather-colored hair battling his way desperately through their coach many times before. There is always one of him on every train. They watch his performance with as much attention as they can spare from their own always absorbing business; he is a part of the scene of travel.

He turned in the door and motioned wildly at us when we showed signs of stopping where we were. "No, no!" he bellowed. "NO! Not here. This will never do for you," he said, giving me a great look, protecting me, a lady. I followed on, trying to reassure him by noddings and hand-wavings. Andreyev came after, stepping tenderly over large objects and small beings, exchanging quick glances with many pairs of calm, lively dark eyes.

The first-class coach was nicely swept, there were no natives about to speak of, and most of the windows were open. Kennerly hurled bags at the racks, jerked seat-backs about rudely, and spread down topcoats and scarves until, with great clamor, he had built us a nest in which we might curl up facing each other, temporarily secure from the appalling situation of being three quite superior persons of the intellectual caste of the ruling race at large and practically defenseless in what a country! Kennerly almost choked when he tried to talk about it. It was for himself he built the nest, really: he was certain of what he was. Andreyev and I were included by courtesy: Andreyev was a Communist, and I was a writer, or so Kennerly had been told. He had never heard of me until a week before, he had never known anyone who had, and it was really up to Andreyev, who had invited me on this trip, to look out for me. But Andreyev took everything calmly, was not suspicious, never asked questions, and had no sense of social responsibility whatever—not, at least, what Kennerly would ever call by such a name; so it was hopeless to expect anything from him.

I had already proved that I lacked something by arriving at the station first and buying my own ticket, having been warned by Kennerly to meet them at the first-class window, as they were arriving straight from another town. When he discovered this, he managed to fill me with shame and confusion. "You were to have been our guest," he told me bitterly, taking my ticket and handing it to the conductor as if I had appropriated it to my own use from his pocket, stripping me publicly of guesthood once for all, it seemed. Andreyev also rebuked me: "We none of us should throw away our money when Kennerly is so rich and charitable." Kennerly, tucking away his leather billfold, paused, glared blindly at Andreyev for a moment, jumped as if he had discovered that he was stabbed clean through, said, "Rich? Me, rich? What do you mean, rich?" and blustered for a moment, hoping that somehow the proper retort would emerge; but it would not. So he sulked for a moment, got up and shifted his bags, sat down, felt in all his pockets again to make certain of something, sat back and wanted to know if I had noticed that he carried his own bags. It was because he was tired of being gypped by these people. Every time he let a fellow carry his bags, he had a fight to the death in simple self-defense. Literally, in his whole life he had never run into such a set of bandits as these train porters. Besides, think of the risk of infection from their filthy paws on your luggage handles. It was just damned dangerous, if you asked him.

I was thinking that foreigners anywhere traveling were three or four kinds of phonograph records, and of them all I liked Kennerly's kind the least. Andreyev hardly ever looked at him out of his clear, square gray eyes, in which so many different kinds of feeling against Kennerly were mingled, the total expression had become a sort of exasperated patience. Settling back, he drew out a folder of photographs, scenes from the film they had been making all over the country, balanced them on his knees and began where he left off to talk about Russia. . . . Kennerly moved into his corner away from us and turned to the window as if he wished to avoid overhearing a private conversation. The sun was shining when we left Mexico City, but mile by mile through the solemn valley of the pyramids we climbed through the maguey fields towards the thunderous blue cloud banked solidly in the east, until it dissolved and received us gently in a pallid, silent rain. We hung our heads out of the window every time the train paused, raising false hopes in the hearts of the Indian women who ran along beside us, faces thrown back and arms stretching upward even after the train was moving away.

"Fresh pulque!" they urged mournfully, holding up their clay jars filled with thick gray-white liquor. "Fresh maguey worms!" they cried in despair above the clamor of the turning wheels, waving like nosegays the leaf bags, slimy and lumpy with the worms they had gathered one at a time from the cactus whose heart bleeds the honey water for the pulque. They ran along still hoping, their brown fingers holding the bags lightly by the very tips, ready to toss them if the travelers should change their minds and buy, even then, until the engine outran them, their voices floated away and they were left clustered together, a little knot of faded blue skirts and shawls, in the indifferent rain.

Kennerly opened three bottles of luke-warm bitter beer. "The water is filthy!" he said earnestly, taking a ponderous, gargling swig from his bottle. "Isn't it horrible, the things they eat and drink?" he asked, as if, no matter what we might in our madness (for he did not trust either of us) say, he already knew the one possible answer. He shuddered and for a moment could not swallow his lump of sweet American chocolate: "I have just come back," he told me, trying to account for his extreme sensitiveness in these matters, "from God's country," meaning to say California. He ripped open an orange trademarked in purple ink. "I'll simply have to get used to all this all over again. What a relief to eat fruit that isn't full of germs. I brought them all the way back with me." (I could fairly see him legging across the Sonora desert with a knapsack full of oranges.) "Have one. Anyhow it's clean."

Kennerly was very clean, too, a walking reproach to untidiness: washed, shaven, clipped, pressed, polished, smelling of soap, brisk and firm-looking in his hay-colored tweeds. So far as that goes, a fine figure of a man, with the proper thriftiness of a healthy animal. There was no fault to find with him in this. Some day I shall make a poem to kittens washing themselves in the mornings; to Indians scrubbing their clothes to rags and their bodies to sleek-ness, with great slabs of sweet-smelling strong soap and wisps of henequen fiber, in the shade of trees, along river banks at midday; to horses rolling sprawling snorting rubbing themselves against the grass to cleanse their healthy hides; to naked children shouting in pools; to hens singing in their dust baths; to sober fathers of families forgetting themselves in song under the discreet flood of tap-water; to birds on the boughs ruffling and oiling their feathers in delight; to girls and boys arranging themselves like baskets of fruit for each other: to all thriving creatures making themselves cleanly and comely to the greater glory of life. But Kennerly had gone astray somewhere: he had overdone it; he wore the harried air of a man on the edge of bankruptcy, keeping up an expensive establishment because he dared not retrench. His nerves were bundles of dried twigs, they jabbed his insides every time a thought stirred in his head, they kept his blank blue eyes fixed in a white stare. The muscles of his jaw jerked in continual helpless rage. Eight months spent as business manager for three Russian moving-picture men in Mexico had about finished him off, he told me, quite as though Andreyev, one of the three, were not present.

"Ah, he should have business-managed us through China and Mongolia," said Andreyev, to me, as if speaking of an absent Kennerly. "After that, Mexico could never disturb him."

"The altitude!" said Kennerly. "My heart skips every other beat. I can't sleep a wink!"

"There was no altitude at all in Tehuantepec," said Andreyev, with stubborn gayety, "and you should have been there to see him."

Kennerly spewed up his afflictions like a child being sick.

"It's these Mexicans," he said as if it were an outrage to find them in Mexico. "They would drive any man crazy in no time. In Tehuantepec it was frightful." It would take him a week to tell the whole story; and, besides, he was keeping notes and was going to write a book about it some day; but "Just for example, they don't know the meaning of time and they have absolutely no regard for their word." They had to bribe every step of the way. Graft, bribe, graft, bribe it was from morning to night, anything from fifty pesos to the Wise Boys in the municipal councils to a bag of candy for a provincial mayor before they were even allowed to set up their cameras. The mosquitoes ate him alive. And with the bugs and cockroaches and the food and the heat and the water, everybody got sick: Stepanov, the camera-man, was sick; Andreyev was sick . . .

"Not seriously," said Andreyev.

The immortal Uspensky even got sick; and as for himself, Kennerly, he thought more than once he'd never live through it. Amoebic dysentery. You couldn't tell him. Why, it was a miracle they hadn't all died or had their throats cut. Why, it was worse than Africa. . . .

"Were you in Africa, too?" asked Andreyev. "Why do you always choose these inconvenient countries?"

Well, no, he had not been there, but he had friends who made a film among the pygmies and you wouldn't believe what they had gone through. As for him, Kennerly, give him pygmies or headhunters or cannibals outright, every time. At least you knew where you stood with them. Now take for example: they had lost ten thousand dollars flat by obeying the laws of the country—something nobody else does!—by passing their film of the Oaxaca earthquake before the board of censorship in Mexico City. Meanwhile, some unscrupulous native scoundrels who knew the ropes had beaten them to it and sent a complete newsreel to New York. It doesn't pay to have a conscience, but if you've got one what can you do about it? Just throw away your time and your money, that's all. He had written and protested to the censors, charging them with letting the Mexican film company get away with murder, accusing them of favoritism and deliberate malice in holding up the Russian film—everything, in a five-page typewritten letter. They hadn't even answered it. Now what can you do with people like that? Graft, bribe, bribe, graft, that's the way it went. Well, he had been learning, too. "Whatever they ask for, I give 'em half the amount, straight across the board," he said. "I tell 'em, 'Look here, I'll give you just half that amount, and anything more than that is bribery and corruption, d'you understand?' Do they take it? Like a shot. Ha!"

His overwhelming unmodulated voice brayed on agonizingly, his staring eyes accused everything they looked upon. Crickle crackle went the dried twigs of his nerve ends at every slightest jog of memory, every present touch, every cold wing from the future. He talked on. . . . He was afraid of his brother-in-law, a violent prohibitionist who would be furious if he ever heard that Kennerly had gone back to drinking beer openly the minute he got out of California. In a way, his job was at stake, for his brother-in-law had raised most of the money among his friends for this expedition and might just fire him out, though how the fellow expected to get along without him Kennerly could not imagine. He was the best friend his brother-in-law had in the world. If the man could only realize it. Moreover, the friends would be soon, if they were not already, shouting to have some money back on their investment. Nobody but himself ever gave a thought to that side of the business! . . . He glared outright at Andreyev at this point.

Andreyev said: "I did not ask them to invest!"

Beer was the only thing Kennerly could trust—it was food and medicine and a thirst-quencher all in one, and everything else around him, fruit, meat, air, water, bread, were poisoned. . . . The picture was to have been finished in three months and now they'd been there eight months and God knew how much longer they'd have to go. He was afraid the picture would be a failure, now it hadn't been finished on time.

"What time?" asked Andreyev, as if he had made this answer many times before. "When it is finished it is finished."

"Yes, but it isn't merely enough to finish a job just when you please. The public must be prepared for it on the dot." He went on to explain that making good involves all sorts of mysterious interlocking schedules: it must be done by a certain date, it must be art, of course, that's taken for granted, and it must be a hit. Half the chance of making a hit depends upon having your stuff ready to go at the psychological moment. There are thousands of things to be thought of, and if they miss one point, bang goes everything! . . . He sighted along an imaginary rifle, pulled the trigger, and fell back exhausted. His whole life of effort and despair flickered like a film across his relaxed face, a life of putting things over in spite of hell, of keeping up a good front, of lying awake nights fuming with schemes and frothing with beer, rising of mornings gray-faced, stupefied, pushing himself under cold showers and filling himself up on hot coffee and slamming himself into a fight in which there are no rules and no referee and the antagonist is everywhere. "God," he said to me, "you don't know. But I'm going to write a book about it. . . ."

As he sat there, talking about his book, eating American chocolate bars and drinking his third bottle of beer, sleep took him suddenly, upright as he was, in the midst of a sentence. Assertion failed, sleep took him mercifully by the nape and quelled him. His body cradled itself in the tweed, the collar rose above his neck, his closed eyes and limp mouth looked ready to cry.

Andreyev went on showing me pictures from that part of the film they were making at the pulque hacienda. . . . They had chosen it carefully, he said; it was really an old-fashioned feudal estate with the right kind of architecture, no modern improvements to speak of, and with the purest type of peons. Naturally a pulque hacienda would be just such a place. Pulque-making had not changed from the beginning, since the time the first Indian set up a rawidhe vat to ferment the liquor and pierced and hollowed the first gourd to draw with his mouth the juice from the heart of the maguey. Nothing had happened since, nothing could happen. Apparently there was no better way to make pulque. The whole thing, he said, was almost too good to be true. An old Spanish gentleman had revisited the hacienda after an absence of fifty years, and had gone about looking at everything with delight. "Nothing has changed," he said, "nothing at all!"

The camera had seen this unchanged world as a landscape with figures, but figures under a doom imposed by the landscape. The closed dark faces were full of instinctive suffering, without individual memory, or only the kind of memory animals may have, who when they feel the whip know they suffer but do not know why and cannot imagine a remedy. . . . Death in these pictures was a procession with lighted candles, love a matter of vague gravity, of clasped hands and two sculptured figures inclining towards each other. Even the figure of the Indian in his ragged loose white clothing, weathered and molded to his flat-hipped, narrow-waisted body, leaning between the horns of the maguey, his mouth to the gourd, his burro with the casks on either side waiting with hanging head for his load, had this formal traditional tragedy, beautiful and hollow. There were rows of girls, like dark statues walking, their mantles streaming from their smooth brows, water jars on their shoulders; women kneeling at washing stones, their blouses slipping from their shoulders—"so picturesque, all this," said Andreyev, "we shall be accused of dressing them up." The camera had caught and fixed in moments of violence and senseless excitement, of cruel living and tortured death, the almost ecstatic death-expectancy which is in the air of Mexico. The Mexican may know when the danger is real, or may not care whether the thrill is false or true, but strangers feel the acid of death in their bones whether or not any real danger is near them. It was this terror that Kennerly had translated into fear of food, water, and air around him. In the Indian the love of death had become a habit of the spirit. It had smoothed out and polished the faces to a repose so absolute it seemed studied, though studied for so long it was now held without effort; and in them all was a common memory of defeat. The pride of their bodily posture was the mere outward shade of passive, profound resistance; the lifted, arrogant features were a mockery of the servants who lived within.

We looked at many scenes from the life of the master's house, with the characters dressed in the fashion of 1898. They were quite perfect. One girl was especially clever. She was the typical Mexican mixed-blood beauty, her mask-like face powdered white, with a round hard full mouth, and hard slanting dark eyes. Her black waved hair was combed back from a low forehead, and she wore her balloon sleeves and small stiff sailor hat with marvelous elegance.

"But this must be an actress," I said.

"Oh, yes," said Andreyev, "the only one. For that rôle we needed an actress. That is Lolita. We found her at the Jewel Theater."

The story of Lolita and doña Julia was very gay. It had begun by being a very usual story about Lolita and don Genaro, the master of the pulque hacienda. Doña Julia, his wife, was furious with him for bringing a fancy woman into the house. She herself was modern, she said, very modern, she had no old-fashioned ideas at all, but she still considered that she was being insulted. On the contrary, don Genaro was very old-fashioned in his taste for ladies of the theater. He had thought he was being discreet, besides, and was truly apologetic when he was found out. But little doña Julia was fearfully jealous. She screamed and wept and made scenes at night, first. Then she began making don Genaro jealous with other men. So that the men grew very frightened of doña Julia and almost ran when they saw her. Imagine all the things that might happen! There was the picture to think of, after all. . . . And then doña Julia threatened to kill Lolita—to cut her throat, to stab her, to poison her. . . . Don Genaro simply ran away at this, and left everything in the air. He went up to the capital and stayed two days.

When he came back, the first sight that greeted his eyes was his wife and his mistress strolling, arms about each other's waists, on the upper terrace, while a whole scene was being delayed because Lolita would not leave doña Julia and get to work.

Don Genaro, who prided himself on his speed, was thunderstruck by the suddenness of this change. He had borne with his wife's scenes because he really respected her rights and privileges as a wife. A wife's first right is to be jealous and threaten to kill her husband's mistress. Lolita also had her definite prerogatives. Everything, until he left, had gone with automatic precision exactly as it should have. This was thoroughly outrageous. He could not get them separated, either. They continued to walk and talk on the terrace under the trees all morning, affectionately entwined, heads together, one a cinema Chinese—doña Julia loved Chinese dress made by a Hollywood costumer—the other in the stiff elegance of 1898. They remained oblivious to the summons from the embattled males: Uspensky calling for Lolita to get into the scene at once, don Genaro sending messages by an Indian boy that the master had returned and wished to see doña Julia on a matter of the utmost importance. . . .

The women still strolled, or sat on the edge of the fountain, whispering together, arms lying at ease about each other's waists, for all the world to see. When Lolita finally came down the steps and took her place in the scene, doña Julia sat nearby, making up her face by her round mirror in the blinding sunlight, getting in the way, smiling at Lolita whenever their eyes met. When they asked her to sit somewhere else, a little out of camera range, she pouted, moved three feet away, and said, "I want to be in this scene too, with Lolita."

Lolita's deep throaty voice cooed at doña Julia. She tossed strange glances at her from under her heavy eyelids, and when she mounted her horse, she forgot her rôle, and swung her leg over the saddle in a gesture unknown to ladies of 1898. . . . Doña Julia greeted her husband with soft affection, and don Genaro, who had no precedent whatever for a husband's conduct in such a situation, made a terrible scene, and pretended he was jealous of Betancourt, one of the Mexican advisers to Uspensky.

We turned over the pictures again, looked at some of them twice. In the fields, among the maguey, the Indian in his hopeless rags; in the hacienda house, theatrically luxurious persons, posed usually with a large chromo portrait of Porfirio Díaz looming from a gaudy frame on the walls. "That is to show," said Andreyev, "that all this really happened in the time of Díaz, and that all this," he tapped the pictures of the Indians, "has been swept away by the revolution. It was the first requirement of our agreement here." This without cracking a smile or meeting my eye. "We have, in spite of everything, arrived at the third part of our picture."

I wondered how they had managed it. They had arrived from California under a cloud as politically subversive characters. Wild rumor ran before them. It was said they had been invited by the government to make a picture. It was said they had not been so invited, but were being sponsored by Communists and various other shady organizations. The Mexican government was paying them heavily; Moscow was paying Mexico for the privilege of making the film: Uspensky was the most dangerous agent Moscow had ever sent on a mission; Moscow was on the point of repudiating him altogether, it was doubtful he would be allowed to return to Russia. He was not really a Communist at all, but a German spy. American Communists were paying for the film; the Mexican anti-government party was at heart in sympathy with Russia and had paid secretly an enormous sum to the Russians for a picture that would disgrace the present régime. The government officials themselves did not seem to know what was going on. They took all sides at once. A delegation of officials met the Russians at the boat and escorted them to jail. The jail was hot and uncomfortable. Uspensky, Andreyev, and Stepanov worried about their equipment, which was being turned over very thoroughly at the customs: and Kennerly worried about his reputation. Accustomed as he was to the clean, four-square business methods of God's own Hollywood, he trembled to think what he might be getting into. He had, so far as he had been able to see, helped to make all the arrangments before they left California. But he was no longer certain of anything. It was he who started the rumor that Uspensky was not a Party Member, and that one of the three was not even a Russian. He hoped this made the whole business sound more respectable. After a night of confusion another set of officials, more important than the first, arrived, all smiles, explanations and apologies, and set them free. Someone then started a rumor that the whole episode was invented for the sake of publicity.

The government officials still took no chance. They wanted to improve this opportunity to film a glorious history of Mexico, her wrongs and sufferings and her final triumph through the latest revolution; and the Russians found themselves surrounded and insulated from their material by the entire staff of professional propagandists, which had been put at their disposal for the duration of their visit. Dozens of helpful observers, art experts, photographers, literary talents, and travel guides swarmed about them to lead them aright, and to show them all the most beautiful, significant, and characteristic things in the national life and soul: if by chance anything not beautiful got in the way of the camera, there was a very instructed and sharp-eyed committee of censors whose duty it was to see that the scandal went no further than the cutting room.

"It has been astonishing," said Andreyev, "to see how devoted all of them are to art."

Kennerly stirred and muttered; he opened his eyes, closed them again. His head rolled uneasily.

"Wait. He is going to wake up," I whispered.

We sat still watching him.

"Maybe not yet," said Andreyev. "Everything," he added, "is pretty mixed up, and it's going to be worse."

We sat a few moments in silence, Andreyev still watching Kennerly impersonally.

"He would be something nice in a zoo," he said, with no particular malice, "but it is terrible to carry him around this way, all the time, without a cage." After a pause, he went on telling about Russia.

At the last station before we reached the hacienda, the Indian boy who was playing the leading rôle in the film came in looking for us. He entered as if on the stage, followed by several of his hero-worshipers, underfed, shabby youths, living happily in reflected glory. To be an actor in the cinema was enough for him to capture them utterly; but he was already famous in his village, being a pugilist and a good one. Bullfighting is a little out of fashion; pugilism is the newest and smartest thing, and a really ambitious young man of the sporting set will, if God sends him the strength, take to boxing rather than to bulls. Fame added to fame had given this boy a brilliant air of self-confidence and he approached us, brows drawn together, with the easy self-possession of a man of the world accustomed to boarding trains and meeting his friends.

But the pose would not hold. His face, from high cheekbones to square chin, from the full wide-lipped mouth to the low forehead, which had ordinarily the expression of professional-boxer histrionic ferocity, now broke up into a charming open look of simple, smiling excitement. He was happy to see Andreyev again, but there was something more: he had news worth hearing, and would be the first to tell us.

What a to-do there had been at the hacienda that morning! . . . Even while we were shaking hands all around, he broke out with it. "Justino—you remember Justino?—killed his sister. He shot her and ran to the mountains. Vicente—you know which one Vicente is?—chased him on horseback and brought him back." And now they had Justino in jail there in the village we were just leaving.

We were all as astounded and full of curiosity as he had hoped we would be. Yes, it had happened that very morning, at about ten o'clock. . . . No, nothing had gone wrong before that anyone knew about. No, Justino had not quarreled with anybody. No one had seen him do it. He had been in good humor all morning, working, making part of a scene on the set.

Neither Andreyev nor Kennerly spoke Spanish. The boy's words were in a jargon hard for me to understand, but I snatched key words and translated quickly as I could. Kennerly leaped up, white-eyed. . . .

"On the set? My God! We are ruined!"

"But why ruined? Why?"

"Her family will have a damage suit against us!"

The boy wanted to know what this meant.

"The law! the law!" groaned Kennerly. "They can collect money from us for the loss of their daughter. It can be blamed on us."

The boy was fairly baffled by this.

"He says he doesn't understand," I told Kennerly. "He says nobody ever heard of such a thing. He says Justino was in his own house when it happened, and nobody, not even Justino, was to blame."

"Oh," said Kennerly. "Oh, I see. Well, let's hear the rest of it. If he wasn't on the set, it doesn't matter."

He collected himself at once and sat down.

"Yes, do sit down," said Andreyev softly, with a venomous look at Kennerly. The Indian boy seized upon the look, visibly turned it over in his mind, obviously suspected it to refer to him, and stood glancing from one to another, deep frowning eyes instantly on guard.

"Do sit down," said Andreyev, "and don't be giving them all sorts of strange notions not necessary to anybody's peace of mind."

He reached out a free hand and pulled the boy down to sit on the arm of the seat. The other lads had collected near the door.

"Tell us the rest," said Andreyev.

After a small pause, the boy melted and talked. Justino had gone to his hut for the noon meal. His sister was grinding corn for the tortillas, while he stood by waiting, throwing the pistol into the air and catching it. The pistol fired; shot her through here. . . . He touched his ribs level with his heart. . . . She fell forward on her face, over the grinding stone, dead. In no time at all a crowd came running from everywhere. Seeing what he had done, Justino ran, leaping like a crazy man, throwing away the pistol as he went, and struck through the maguey fields toward the mountains. His friend Vicente went after him on horseback, waving a gun and yelling: "Stop or I'll shoot!" and Justino yelled back: "Shoot! I don't care! . . ." But of course Vicente did not: he just galloped up and bashed Justino over the head with the gun butt, threw him across the saddle, and brought him back. Now he was in jail, but don Genaro was already in the village getting him out. Justino did not do it on purpose.

"This is going to hold up everything," said Kennerly. "Everything! It just means more time wasted."

"And that isn't all," said the boy. He smiled ambiguously, lowered his voice a little, put on an air of conspiracy and discretion, and said: "The actress is gone too. She has gone back to the capital. Three days ago."

"A quarrel with doña Julia?" asked Andreyev.

"No," said the boy, "it was with don Genaro she quarreled, after all."

The three of them laughed mightily together, and Andreyev said to me:

"You know that wild girl from the Jewel Theater."

The boy said: "It was because don Genaro was away on other business at a bad moment." He was being more discreet than ever.

Kennerly sat with his chin drawn in severely, almost making faces at Andreyev and the boy in his efforts to hush them. Andreyev stared back at him in hardy innocence. The boy saw the look, again lapsed into perfect silence, and sat very haughtily on the seat arm, clenched fist posed on his thigh, his face turned partly away. As the train slowed down, he rose suddenly and dashed ahead of us.

When we swung down the high narrow steps he was already standing beside the mule car, greeting the two Indians who had come to meet us. His young hangers-on, waving their hats to us, set out to walk a shortcut across the maguey fields.

Kennerly was blustering about, handing bags to the Indians to store away in the small shabby mule car, arranging the party, settling all properly, myself between him and Andreyev, tucking my skirts around my knees with officious hands, to keep a thread of my garments from touching the no doubt infectious foreign things facing us.

The little mule dug its sharp hoof points into the stones and grass of the track, got a tolerable purchase at last on a cross tie, and set off at a finicking steady trot, the bells on its collar jingling like a tambourine.

We jogged away, crowded together facing each other three in a row, with bags under the seats, and the straw falling out of the cushions. The driver, craning around toward the mule now and then, and snapping the reins on its back, added his comments: An unlucky family. This was the second child to be killed by a brother. The mother was half dead with grief and Justino, a good boy, was in jail.

The big man sitting by him in striped riding trousers, his hat bound under his chin with red-tasseled cord, added that Justino was in for it now, God help him. But where did he get the pistol? He borrowed it from the firearms being used in the picture. It was true he was not supposed to touch the pistols, and there was his first mistake. He meant to put it back at once, but you know how a boy of sixteen loves to play with a pistol. Nobody would blame him. . . . The girl was nineteen years old. Her body had been sent already to the village to be buried. There was too much excitement over her; nothing was done so long as she was on the place. Don Genaro had gone, according to custom, to cross her hands, close her eyes, and light a candle beside her. Everything was done in order, they said piously, their eyes dancing with rich, enjoyable feelings. It is always regrettable and exciting when somebody you know gets into such dramatic trouble. Ah, we were alive under that deepening sky, jingling away through the yellow fields of blooming mustard with the pattern of spiked maguey shuttling as we passed, from straight lines to angles, to diamond shapes, and back again, miles and miles of it spreading away to the looming mountains.

"Surely they would not have had loaded pistols among those being used in the picture?" I asked, rather suddenly, of the big man with the red-tasseled cord on his hat.

He opened his mouth to say something and snapped it shut again. There was a pause. Nobody spoke. It was my turn to be uncomfortable under a quick exchange of glances between the others.

There was again the guarded watchful expression on the Indian faces. An awful silence settled over us.

Andreyev, who had been trying his Spanish boldly, said, "If I cannot talk, I can sing," and began in his big gay Russian voice: "Ay, Sandunga, Sandunga, Mamá, por Diós!" All the Indians shouted with joy and delight at the new thing his strange tongue made of the words. Andreyev laughed, too. This laughter was an invitation to their confidence. With a burst of song in Russian, the young pugilist threw himself in turn on the laughter of Andreyev.

Everybody then seized the opportunity to laugh madly in fellowship, even Kennerly. Eyes met eyes through the guard of crinkled lids, and the little mule went without urging into a stiff-legged gallop.

A big rabbit leaped across the track, chased by lean hungry dogs. It was cracking the strings of its heart in flight; its eyes started from its head like crystal bubbles. "Run, rabbit, run!" I cried. "Run, dogs!" shouted the big Indian with the red cords on his hat, his love of a contest instantly aroused. He turned to me with his eyes blazing: "What will you bet, señorita?"

The hacienda lay before us, a monastery, a walled fortress, towered in terra cotta and coral, sheltered against the mountains. An old woman in a shawl opened the heavy double gate and we slid into the main corral. The upper windows in the near end were all alight. Stepanov stood on one balcony; Betancourt, on the next; and for a moment the celebrated Uspensky appeared with waving arms at a third. They called to us, even before they recognized us, glad to see anyone of their party returning from town to relieve the long monotony of the day which had been shattered by the accident and could not be gathered together again. Thin-boned horses with round sleek haunches, long rippling manes and tails were standing under saddle in the patio. Big polite dogs of expensive breeds came out to meet us and walked with dignity beside us up the broad shallow steps.

The room was cold. The round-shaded hanging lamp hardly disturbed the shadows. The doorways, of the style called Porfirian Gothic, in honor of the Díaz period of domestic architecture, soared towards the roof in a cloud of gilded stamped wallpaper, from an undergrowth of purple and red and orange plush arm-chairs fringed and tassled, set on bases with springs. Such spots as this, fitted up for casual visits, interrupted the chill gloom of the rooms marching by tens along the cloisters, now and again casting themselves around patios, gardens, pens for animals. A naked player-piano in light wood occupied one corner. Standing together here, we spoke again of the death of the girl, and Justino's troubles, and all our voices were vague with the vast incurable boredom which hung in the air of the place and settled around our heads clustered together.

Kennerly worried about the possible lawsuit.

"They know nothing about such things," Betancourt assured him. "Besides, it is not our fault."

The Russians were thinking about tomorrow. It was not only a great pity about the poor girl, but both she and her brother were working in the picture; the boy's rôle was important and everything must be halted until he should come back, or if he should never come back everything must be done all over again.

Betancourt, Mexican by birth, French-Spanish by blood, French by education, was completely at the mercy of an ideal of elegance and detachment perpetually at war with a kind of Mexican nationalism which afflicted him like an inherited weakness of the nervous system. Being trustworthy and of cultured taste it was his official duty to see that nothing hurtful to the national dignity got in the way of the foreign cameras. His ambiguous situation seemed to trouble him not at all. He was plainly happy and fulfilled for the first time in years. Beggars, the poor, the deformed, the old and ugly, trust Betancourt to wave them away. "I am sorry for everything," he said, lifting a narrow, pontifical hand, waving away vulgar human pity which always threatened, buzzing like a fly at the edges of his mind. "But when you consider"—he made an almost imperceptible inclination of his entire person in the general direction of the social point of view supposed to be represented by the Russians—"what her life would have been like in this place, it is much better that she is dead. . . ."

He had burning fanatic eyes and a small tremulous mouth. His bones were like reeds.

"It is a tragedy, but it happens too often," he said.

With his easy words the girl was dead indeed, anonymously entombed. . . .

Doña Julia came in silently, walking softly on her tiny feet in embroidered shoes like a Chinese woman's. She was probably twenty years old. Her black hair was sleeked to her round skull, eyes painted, apparently, in the waxed semblance of her face.

"We never really live here," she said, in a gentle smooth voice, glancing vaguely about her strange setting, in which she appeared to be an exotic speaking doll. "It's very ugly, but you must not mind that. It is hopeless to try keeping the place up. The Indians destroy everything with neglect. We stay here now for the excitement about the film. It is thrilling." Then she added, "It is sad about the poor girl. It makes every kind of trouble. It is sad about the poor brother. . . ." As we went towards the dining-room, she murmured along beside me, "It is sad . . . very sad . . . sad. . . ."

Don Genaro's grandfather, who had been described to me as a gentleman of the very oldest school, was absent on a prolonged visit. In no way did he approve of his granddaughter-in-law, who got herself up in a fashion unknown to the ladies of his day, a fashion very upsetting to a man of the world who had always known how to judge, grade, and separate women into their proper categories at a glance. A temporary association with such a young female as this he considered a part of every gentleman's education. Marriage was an altogether different matter. In his day, she would have had at best a career in the theater. He had been silenced but in no wise changed in his conviction by the sudden, astonishing marriage of his grandson, the sole inevitable heir, who was already acting as head of the house, accountable to no one. He did not understand the boy and he did not waste time trying. He had moved his furniture and his keepsakes and his person away, to the very farthest patio in the old garden, above the terraces to the south, where he lived in bleak dignity and loneliness, without hope and without philosophy, perhaps contemptuous of both, joining his family only at mealtimes. His place at the foot of the table was empty, the week-end crowds of sightseers were gone and our party barely occupied part of the upper end.

Uspensky sat in his monkey-suit of striped overalls, his face like a superhumanly enlightened monkey's now well overgrown with a simian beard.

He had a monkey attitude towards life, which amounted almost to a personal philosophy. It saved explanation, and threw off the kind of bores he could least bear with. He amused himself at the low theaters in the capital, flattering the Mexicans by declaring they really were the most obscene he had found in the whole world. He liked staging old Russian country comedies, all the players wearing Mexican dress, on the open roads in the afternoon. He would then shout his lines broadly and be in his best humor, prodding the rear of a patient burro, accustomed to grief and indignity, with a phallus-shaped gourd. "Ah, yes, I remember," he said gallantly, on meeting some southern women, "you are the ladies who are always being raped by those dreadful negroes!" But now he was fevered, restless, altogether silent, and his bawdy humor, which served as cover and disguise for all other moods, was gone.

Stepanov, a champion at tennis and polo, wore flannel tennis slacks and polo shirt. Betancourt wore well-cut riding trousers and puttees, not because he ever mounted a horse if he could avoid it, but he had learned in California, in 1921, that this was the correct costume for a moving-picture director: true, he was not yet a director, but he was assisting somewhat at the making of a film, and when in action, he always added a green-lined cork helmet, which completed some sort of precious illusion he cherished about himself. Andreyev's no-colored wool shirt was elbow to elbow with Kennerly's brash tweeds. I wore a knitted garment of the kind which always appears suitable for any other than the occasion on which it is being worn. Altogether, we provided a staggering contrast for doña Julia at the head of the table, a figure from a Hollywood comedy, in black satin pajamas adorned with rainbow-colored bands of silk, loose sleeves falling over her babyish hands with pointed scarlet finger ends.

"We mustn't wait for my husband," said doña Julia; "he is always so busy and always late."

"Always going at top speed," said Betancourt, pleasantly, "70 kilometers an hour at least, and never on time anywhere." He prided himself on his punctuality, and had theories about speed, its use and abuse. He loved to explain that man, if he had concentrated on his spiritual development, as he should have done, would never have needed to rely on mechanical aids to conquer time and space. In the meantime, he admitted that he himself, who could communicate telepathically with anyone he chose, and who had once levitated himself three feet from the ground by a simple act of the will, found a great deal of pleasurable stimulation in the control of machinery. I knew something about his pleasure in driving an automobile. He had for one thing a habit of stepping on the accelerator and bounding across tracks before approaching trains. Speed, he said, was "modern" and it was everyone's duty to be as modern as one's means allowed. I surmised from Betancourt's talk that don Genaro's wealth allowed him to be at least twice as modern as Betancourt. He could afford high-powered automobiles that simply frightened other drivers off the road before him; he was thinking of an airplane to cut distance between the hacienda and the capital; speed and lightness at great expense was his ideal. Nothing could move too fast for don Genaro, said Betancourt, whether a horse, a dog, a woman or something with metal machinery in it. Doña Julia smiled approvingly at what she considered praise of her husband and, by pleasant inference, of herself.

'There came a violent commotion along the hall, at the door, in the room. The servants separated, fell back, rushed forward, scurried to draw out a chair, and don Genaro entered, wearing Mexican country riding dress, a gray buckskin jacket and tight gray trousers strapped under the boot. He was a tall, hard-bitten, blue-eyed young Spaniard, stringy-muscled, thin-lipped, graceful, and he was in fury. This fury he expected us to sympathize with; he dismissed it long enough to greet everybody all around, then dropped into his chair beside his wife and burst forth, beating his fist on the table.

It seemed that the imbecile village judge refused to let him have Justino. It seemed there was some crazy law about criminal negligence. The law, the judge said, does not recognize accidents in the vulgar sense. There must always be careful inquiry based on suspicion of bad faith in those nearest the victim. Don Genaro gave an imitation of the imbecile judge showing off his legal knowledge. Floods, volcanic eruptions, revolutions, runaway horses, smallpox, train wrecks, street fights, all such things, the judge said, were acts of God. Personal shootings, no. A personal shooting must always be inquired into severely. "All that has nothing to do with this case, I told him," said don Genaro. "I told him, Justino is my peon, his family have lived for three hundred years on our hacienda, this is MY business. I know what happened and all about it, and you don't know anything and all you have to do with this is to let me have Justino back at once. I mean today, tomorrow will not do, I told him." It was no good. The judge wanted two thousand pesos to let Justino go. "Two thousand pesos!" shouted don Genaro, thumping on the table; "try to imagine that!"

"How ridiculous!" said his wife with comradely sympathy and a glittering smile. He glared at her for a second as if he did not recognize her. She gazed back, her eyes flickering, a tiny uncertain smile in the corners of her mouth where the rouge was beginning

to melt. Furiously he ignored her, shook the pause off his shoul
ders and hurried on, turning as he talked, hot and blinded and
baffled, to one and another of his audience. It was not the two
thousand pesos, it was that he was sick of paying here, paying
there, for the most absurd things; every time he turned around
there at his elbow was some thievish politician holding out his
paw. "Well, there's one thing to do. If I pay this judge there'll be
no end to it. He'll go on arresting my peons every time one of
them shows his face in the village. I'll go to Mexico and see Velarde. . . ."

Everybody agreed with him that Velarde was the man to see.
Hè was the most powerful and successful revolutionist in Mexico.
He owned two pulque haciendas which had fallen to his share
when the great repartition of land had taken place. He operated
also the largest dairy farm in the country, furnishing milk and
butter and cheese to every charitable institution, orphans' home,
insane asylum, reform school and workhouse in the country, and
getting just twice the prices for them that any other dairy farm
would have asked. He also owned a great aguacate hacienda; he
controlled the army; he controlled a powerful bank; the president
of the Republic made no appointments to any office without his
advice. He fought counter-revolution and political corruption, daily
upon the front pages of twenty newspapers he had bought for that
very purpose. He employed thousands of peons. As an employer,
he would understand what don Genaro was contending with. As an
honest revolutionist, he would know how to handle that dirty,
bribe-taking little judge. "I'll go to see Velarde," said don Genaro
in a voice gone suddenly flat, as if he despaired or was too bored
with the topic to keep it up any longer. He sat back and looked at
his guests bleakly. Everyone said something, it did not matter
what. The episode of the morning now seemed very far away and
not worth thinking about.

Uspensky sneezed with his hands over his face. He had spent
two early morning hours standing up to his middle in the cold
water of the horse fountain, with Stepanov and the camera balanced on the small stone ledge, directing a scene which he was
convinced could be made from no other angle. He had taken cold;
he now swallowed a mouthful of fried beans, drank half a glass of
beer at one gulp, and slid off the long beach. His too-large striped

overalls disappeared in two jumps through the nearest door, He went as if he were seeking another climate.

"He has a fever," said Andreyev. "If he does not feel better tonight we must send for Doctor Volk."

A large lumpish person in faded blue overalls and a flannel shirt inserted himself into a space near the foot of the table. He nodded to nobody in particular, and Betancourt punctiliously acknowledged the salute.

"You do not even recognize him?" Betancourt asked me in a low voice. "That is Carlos Montaña. You find him changed?"

He seemed anxious that I should find Carlos much changed. I said I supposed we had all changed somewhat after ten years. Besides, Carlos had grown a fine set of whiskers. Betancourt's glance at me plainly admitted that I, like Carlos, had changed and for the worse, but he resisted the notion of change in himself. "Maybe," he said, unwillingly, "but most of us, I think, for the better. It's poor Carlos. It's not only the whiskers, and the fat. He has, you know, become a failure."

"A Puss Moth," said don Genaro to Stepanov. "I flew it half an hour yesterday; awfully *chic*. I may buy it. I need something really fast. Something light, too, but it must be fast. It must be something I can depend upon at any minute." Stepanov was an expert pilot. He excelled in every activity that don Genaro respected. Don Genaro listened attentively while Stepanov gave him some clear sensible advice about airplanes: what kind to buy, how to keep them in order, and what one might expect of airplanes as a usual thing.

"Airplanes!" said Kennerly, listening in. "I wouldn't go up with a Mexican pilot for all the money in—"

"Airplane! At last!" cried doña Julia, like a gently enraptured child. She leaned over the table and called in Spanish softly as if waking someone, "Carlos! Do you hear? Genarito is going to buy me an airplane, after all!"

Don Genaro talked on with Stepanov as if he had not heard.

"And what will you do with it?" asked Carlos, eyes round and amiable from under his bushy brows. Without lifting his head from his hand, he went on eating his fried beans and green chili sauce with a spoon, good Mexican country fashion, and enjoying them.

"I shall turn somersaults in it," said doña Julia.

"A Failure," Betancourt went on, in English, which Carlos

could not understand, "though I must say he looks worse today than usual. He slipped and hurt himself in the bathtub this morning." It was as if this accident were another point against Carlos, symbolic proof of the fatal downward tendency in his character.

"I thought he had composed half the popular songs in Mexico," I said. "I heard nothing but his songs here, ten years ago. What happened?"

"Ah, that was ten years ago, don't forget. He does almost nothing now. He hasn't been director of the Jewel for, oh, ages!"

I observed the Failure. He seemed cheerful enough. He was beating time with the handle of his spoon and humming a song to Andreyev, who listened, nodding his head. "Like that, for two measures," said Carlos in French, "then like this," and he beat time, humming. "Then this for the dance. . . ." Andreyev hummed the tune and tapped on the table with his left forefinger, his right hand waving slightly. Betancourt watched them for a moment. "He feels better just now, poor fellow," he said, "now I have got him this job. It may be a new beginning for him. But he is sometimes tired, he drinks too much, he cannot always do his best."

Carlos had slumped back in his chair, his round shoulders drooped, his swollen lids covered his eyes, he poked fretfully at his plate of enchiladas with sour cream. "You'll see," he said to Andreyev in French, "how Betancourt will not like this idea either. There will be something wrong with it. . . ." He said it not angrily, not timidly, but with an unhappy certainty. "Either it will not be modern enough, or not enough in the old style, or just not Mexican enough. . . . You'll see."

Betancourt had spent his youth unlocking the stubborn secrets of Universal Harmony by means of numerology, astronomy, astrology, a formula of thought-transference and deep breathing, the practice of will-to-power combined with the latest American theories of personality development; certain complicated magical ceremonies; and a careful choice of doctrines from the several schools of Oriental philosophies which are, from time to time, so successfully introduced into California. From this material he had constructed a Way of Life which could be taught to anyone, and once learned led the initiate quietly and surely toward Success: success without pain, almost without effort except of a pleasurable kind, success accompanied by moral and esthetic beauty, as well as the most desirable material reward. Wealth, naturally, could not be an end in itself: alone, it was not Success. But it was the unobtrusive companion of all true Success. . . . From this point of view he was cheerfully explicit about Carlos. Carlos had always been contemptuous of the Eternal Laws. He had always simply written his tunes without giving a thought to the profounder inferences of music, based as it is upon the harmonic system of the spheres. . . . He, Betancourt, had many times warned Carlos. It had done no good at all. Carlos had gone on inviting his own doom.

"I have warned you, too," he said to me kindly. "I have asked myself many times why you will not or cannot accept the Mysteries which would open a whole treasure house for you. . . . All," he said, "is possible through scientific intuition. If you depend on mere intellect, you must fail."

"You must fail," he had been saying all this time to poor simple Carlos. "He has failed," he said of him to others. He now looked almost fondly upon his handiwork, who sat there, somewhat grubby and gloomy, a man who had done a good day's work in his time, and was not altogether finished yet. The neat light figure beside me posed gracefully upon its slender spine, the too-beautiful slender hands waved rhythmically upon insubstantial wrists. I remembered all that Carlos had done for Betancourt in other days; he had, in his thoughtless hopelessly human way, piled upon these thin shoulders a greater burden of gratitude than they could support. Betancourt had set in motion all the machinery of the laws of Universal Harmony he could command to help him revenge himself on Carlos. It was slow work, but he never tired.

"I don't, of course, understand just what you mean by failure, or by success either," I told him at last. "You know, I never could understand."

"It is true, you could not," he said, "that was the great trouble."

"As for Carlos," I said, "you should forgive him. . . ."

Betancourt said with perfect sincerity, "You know I never blame anyone for anything at all."

Carlos came round and shook hands with me as everybody pushed back his chair and began drifting out by the several doorways. He was full of humanity and good humor about Justino and his troubles. "These family love affairs," he said, "what can you expect?"

"Oh, no, now," said Betancourt, uneasily. He laughed his twanging tremulous little laugh.

"Oh, yes, now," said Carlos, walking beside me. "I shall make a *corrido* about Justino and his sister." He began to sing almost in a whisper, imitating the voice and gestures of a singer peddling broadsides in the market. . . .

> *Ah, poor little Rosalita*
> *Took herself a new lover,*
> *Thus betraying the heart's core*
> *Of her impassioned brother . . .*
>
> *Now she lies dead, poor Rosalita,*
> *With two bullets in her heart. . . .*
> *Take warning, my young sisters,*
> *Who would from your brothers part.*

"One bullet," said Betancourt, wagging a long finger at Carlos. "One bullet!"

Carlos laughed. "Very well, one bullet! Such a precisionist! Good night," he said.

Kennerly and Carlos disappeared early. Don Genaro spent the evening playing billiards with Stepanov, who won always. Don Genaro was very good at billiards, but Stepanov was a champion, with all sorts of trophies to show, so it was no humiliation to be defeated by him.

In the drafty upper-hall room fitted up as a parlor, Andreyev turned off the mechanical attachment of the piano and sang Russian songs, running his hands over the keys while he waited to remember yet other songs. Doña Julia and I sat listening. He sang for us, but for himself mostly, in the same kind of voluntary forgetfulness of his surroundings, the same self-induced absence of mind that had kept him talking about Russia in the afternoon.

We sat until very late. Doña Julia smiled steadily every time she caught the glance of Andreyev or myself, yawning now and then under her hand, her Pekinese sprawling and snoring on her lap. "You're not tired?" I asked her. "You wouldn't let us stay up too late?"

"Oh, no, let's go on with the music. I love sitting up all night. I never go to bed if I can possibly sit up. Don't go yet."

At half-past one Uspensky sent for Andreyev, for Stepanov. He was restless, in a fever, he wished to talk. Andreyev said, "I have already sent for Doctor Volk. It is better not to delay."

Doña Julia and I looked on in the billiard room downstairs, where Stepanov and don Genaro were settling the score. Several Indians leaned in at the windows, their vast straw hats tilted forward, watching in silence. Doña Julia asked her husband, "Then you're not going to Mexico tonight?"

"Why should I?" he inquired suddenly without looking at her.

"I thought you might," said Doña Julia. "Good night, Stepanov," she said, her black eyes shining under her long lids painted silver blue.

"Good night, Julita," said Stepanov, his frank Northern smile meaning anything or nothing at all. When he was not smiling, his face was severe, expressive, and intensely alive. His smile was misleadingly simple, like a very young boy's. He was anything but simple; he smiled now like a merry open book upon the absurd little figure strayed out of a marionette theater. Turning away, Doña Julia slanted at him the glittering eye of a femme fatale in any Hollywood film. He examined the end of his cue as if he looked through a microscope. Don Genaro said violently, "Good night!" and disappeared violently through the door leading to the corral.

Doña Julia and I passed through her apartment, a long shallow room between the billiard and the vat-room. It was puffy with silk and down, glossy with bright new polished wood and wide mirrors, restless with small ornaments, boxes of sweets, French dolls in ruffled skirts and white wigs. The air was thick with perfume which fought with another heavier smell. From the vat-room came a continual muffled shouting, the rumble of barrels as they rolled down the wooden trestles to the flat mule-car standing on the tracks running past the wide doorway. The smell had not been out of my nostrils since I came, but here it rose in a thick vapor through the heavy drone of flies, sour, stale, like rotting milk and blood; this sound and this smell belonged together, and both belonged to the intermittent rumble of barrels and the long chanting cry of the Indians. On the narrow stairs I glanced back at doña

Julia. She was looking up, wrinkling her little nose, her Pekinese with his wrinkled nose of perpetual disgust held close to her face. "Pulque!" she said. "Isn't it horrid? But I hope the noise will not keep you awake."

On my balcony there was no longer any perfume to disturb the keen fine wind from the mountains, or the smell from the vat-room. "Twenty-one!" sang the Indians in a long, melodious chorus of weariness and excitement, and the twenty-first barrel of fresh pulque rolled down the slide, was seized by two men and loaded on the flat-car under my window.

From the window next to mine, the three Russian voices murmured along quietly. Pigs grunted and rooted in the soft wallow near the washing fountain, where the women were still kneeling in the darkness, thumping wet cloth on the stones, chattering, laughing. All the women seemed to be laughing that night: long after midnight, the high bright sound sparkled again and again from the long row of peon quarters along the corral. Burros sobbed and mourned to each other, there was everywhere the drowsy wakefulness of creatures, stamping hoofs, breathing and snorting. Below in the vat-room a single voice sang suddenly a dozen notes of some rowdy song; and the women at the washing fountain were silenced for a moment, then tittered among themselves. There occurred a light flurry at the arch of the gate leading into the inner patio: one of the polite, expensive dogs had lost his dignity and was chasing, with snarls of real annoyance, a little fat-bottomed soldier back to his proper place, the barracks by the wall opposite the Indian huts. The soldier scrambled and stumbled silently away, without resistance, his dim lantern agitated violently. At a certain point, as if here was the invisible boundary line, the dog stopped, watched while the soldier ran on, then returned to his post under the archway. The soldiers, sent by the government as a guard against the Agrarians, sprawled in idleness eating their beans at don Genaro's expense. He tolerated and resented them, and so did the dogs.

I fell asleep to the long chanting of the Indians, counting their barrels in the vat-room, and woke again at sunrise, summer sunrise, to their long doleful morning song, the clatter of metal and hard leather, and the stamping of mules as they were being harnessed to the flat-cars. . . . The drivers swung their whips and shouted, the loaded cars creaked and slid away in a procession, off to meet the pulque train for Mexico City. The field workers were leaving for the maguey fields, driving their donkeys. They shouted, too, and whacked the donkeys with sticks, but no one was really hurrying, nor really excited. It was just another day's work, another day's weariness. A three-year-old man-child ran beside his father; he drove a weanling donkey carrying two miniature casks on its furry back. The two small creatures imitated each in his own kind perfectly the gestures of their elders. The baby whacked and shouted, the donkey trudged and flapped his ears at each blow.

"My God!" said Kennerly over coffee an hour later. "Do you remember—" he beat off a cloud of flies and filled his cup with a wobbling hand—"I thought of it all night and couldn't sleep— *don't* you remember," he implored Stepanov, who held one palm over his coffee cup while he finished a cigarette, "those scenes we shot only two weeks ago, when Justino played the part of a boy who killed a girl by accident, tried to escape, and Vicente was one of the men who ran him down on horseback? Well, the same thing has happened to the same people in *reality!* And—" he turned to me, "the strangest thing is, we have to make that scene again, it didn't turn out so well, and look, my God, we had it happening really, and nobody thought of it then! Then was the time. We could have got a close-up of the girl, really dead, and real blood running down Justino's face where Vicente hit him, and my God! we never even thought of it. That kind of thing," he said, bitterly, "has been happening ever since we got here. Just happens over and over. . . . Now, what was the matter, I wonder?"

He stared at Stepanov full of accusation. Stepanov lifted his palm from his cup, and beating off flies, drank. "Light no good, probably," he said. His eyes flickered open, clicked shut in Kennerly's direction, as if they had taken a snapshot of something and that episode was finished.

"If you want to look at it that way," said Kennerly, with resentment, "but after all, there it was, it had happened, it wasn't our fault, and we might as well have had it."

"We can always do it again," said Stepanov. "When Justino comes back, and the light is better. The light," he said to me, "it is always our enemy. Here we have one good day in five, or less."

"Imagine," said Kennerly, pouncing, "just try to imagine that—

when that poor boy comes back he'll have to go through the same scene he has gone through twice before, once in play and once in reality. *Reality!*" He licked his chops. "Think how he'll feel. Why, it ought to drive him crazy."

"If he comes back," said Stepanov, "we must think of that."

In the patio half a dozen Indian boys, their ragged white clothes exposing their tawny smooth skin, were flinging over the sleek-backed horses great saddles of deerskin encrusted with silver embroidery and mother-of-pearl. The women were returning to the washing fountain. The pigs were out rooting in their favorite wallows, and in the vat-room, silently, the day-workers were already filling the bullhide vats with freshly drawn pulque juice. Carlos Montaña was out early too, enjoying himself in the fresh morning air, watching three dogs chase a long-legged pig from wallow to barn. The pig, screaming steadily, galloped like a rocking horse towards the known safety of his pen, the dogs nipping at his heels just enough to keep him up to his best speed. Carlos roared with joy, holding his ribs, and the Indian boys laughed with him.

The Spanish overseer, who had been cast for the rôle of villain —one of them—in the film, came out wearing a new pair of tight riding trousers, of deerskin and silver embroidery, like the saddles, and sat slouched on the long bench near the arch, facing the great corral where the Indians and soldiers were. There he sat nearly all day, as he had sat for years and might sit for years more. His long wry North-Spanish face was dead with boredom. He slouched, with his English cap pulled over his close-set eyes, and did not even glance to see what Carlos was laughing at. Andreyev and I waved to Carlos and he came over at once. He was still laughing. It seemed he had forgotten the pig and was laughing at the overseer, who had already forty pairs of fancy charro trousers, but had thought none of them quite good enough for the film and had caused to be made, at great expense, the pair he was now wearing, which were entirely too tight. He hoped by wearing them every day to stretch them. He was miserable, entirely, for his trousers were all he had to live for, anyhow. "All he can do with his life," said Andreyev, "is to put on a different pair of fancy trousers every day, and sit on that bench hoping that something, anything, may happen."

I said I should have thought there had been enough happening for the past few weeks . . . or at any rate the past few days.

"Oh, no," said Carlos, "nothing that lasts long enough. I mean real excitement like the last Agrarian raid. . . . There were machine guns on the towers, and every man on the place had a rifle and a pistol. They had the time of their lives. They drove the raiders off, and then they fired the rest of their ammunition in the air by way of celebration; and the next day they were bored. They wanted to have the whole show over again. It was very hard to explain to them that the fiesta was ended."

"They do really hate the Agrarians, then?" I asked.

"No, they love excitement," said Carlos.

We walked through the vat-room, picking our way through the puddles of sap sinking into the mud floor, idly stopping to watch, without comment, the flies drowning in the stinking liquor which seeped over the hairy bullhides sagging between the wooden frames. María Santísima stood primly in her blue painted niche in a frame of fly-brown paper flowers, with a perpetual light at her feet. The walls were covered with a faded fresco relating the legend of pulque; how a young Indian girl discovered this divine liquor, and brought it to the emperor, who rewarded her well; and after her death she became a half-goddess. An old legend: maybe the oldest: something to do with man's confused veneration for, and terror of, the fertility of women and vegetation. . . .

Betancourt stood in the door sniffing the air bravely. He glanced around the walls with the eye of an expert. "This is a very good example," he said, smiling at the fresco, "the perfect example, really. . . . The older ones are always the best, of course. It is a fact," he said, "that the Spaniards found wall paintings in the pre-Conquest pulquerías . . . always telling this legend. So it goes on. Nothing ever ends," he waved his long beautiful hand, "it goes on being and becomes little by little something else."

"I'd call that an end, of a kind," said Carlos.

"Oh, well, *you*," said Betancourt, smiling with immense indulgence upon his old friend, who was becoming gradually something else.

At ten o'clock don Genaro emerged on his way to visit the village judge once more. Doña Julia, Andreyev, Stepanov, Carlos, and I were walking on the roofs in the intermittent sun-and-cloud light, looking out over the immense landscape of patterned field and mountain. Stepanov carried his small camera and took snapshots of us, with the dogs. We had already had our pictures taken on the steps with a nursling burro, with Indian babies; at the fountain on the long upper terrace to the south, where the grandfather lived; before the closed chapel door (with Carlos being a fat pious priest); in the patio still farther back with the ruins of the old monastery stone bath; and in the pulquería.

So we were tired of snapshots, and leaned in a row over the roof to watch don Genaro take his leave. . . . He leaped down the shallow steps with half a dozen Indian boys standing back for him to pass, hurled himself at the saddle of his Arab mare, his man let go the bridle instantly and leaped to his own horse, and don Genaro rode hell-for-leather out of the corral with his mounted man pounding twenty feet behind him. Dogs, pigs, burros, women, babies, boys, chickens, scattered and fled before him, little soldiers hurled back the great outer gates at his approach, and the two went through at a dead run, disappearing into the hollow of the road. . . .

"That judge will never let Justino go without the money, I know that, and everybody knows it. Genaro knows it. Yet he will still go and fight and fight," said doña Julia in her toneless soft voice, without rebuke.

"Oh, it is barely possible he may," said Carlos. "If Velarde sends word, you'll see—Justino will pop out! like that!" He shot an imaginary pea between forefinger and thumb.

"Yes, but think how Genaro will have to pay Velarde!" said doña Julia. "It's too tiresome, just when the film was going so well." She looked at Stepanov.

He said, "Stay just that way one little second," raised his camera and pressed the lever; then turned, gazed through the lens at a figure standing in the lower patio. Foreshortened, dirty gray-white against dirty yellow-gray wall, hat pulled down over his eyes, arms folded, Vicente stood without moving. He had been standing there for some time, staring. At last he did move; walked away suddenly with some decision, almost to the gate; then stood again staring, framed in the archway. Stepanov took another picture of him.

I said, to Andreyev, walking a little apart, "I wonder why he did not let his friend Justino escape, or at least give him his chance to try. . . . Why did he go after him, I wonder?"

"Revenge," said Andreyev. "Imagine a man's friend betraying him so, and with a woman, and a sister! He was furious. He did not know what he was doing, maybe. . . . Now I imagine he is regretting it."

In two hours don Genaro and his servant were back; they approached the hacienda at a reasonable pace, but once fairly in sight they whipped up their horses and charged into the corral in the same style as when they left it. The servants, suddenly awake, ran back and forth, up and down steps, round and round; the animals scurried for refuge as before. Three Indian boys flew to the mare's bridle, but Vicente was first. He leaped and danced as the mare plunged and fought for her head, his eyes fixed on don Genaro, who flung himself to the ground, landed lightly as an acrobat, and strode away with a perfectly expressionless face.

Nothing had happened. The judge still wanted two thousand pesos to let Justino go. This may have been the answer Vicente expected. He sat against the wall all afternoon, knees drawn up to his chin, hat over his eyes, his feet in their ragged sandals fallen limp on their sides. In half an hour the evil news was known even to the farthest man in the maguey fields. At the table, don Genaro ate and drank in silent haste, like a man who must catch the last train for a journey on which his life depends. "No, I won't have this," he broke out, hammering the table beside his plate. "Do you know what that imbecile judge said to me? He asked me why I worried so much over one peon. I told him it was my business what I chose to worry about. He said he had heard we were making a picture over here with men shooting each other in it. He said he had a jailful of men waiting to be shot, and he'd be glad to send them over for us to shoot in the picture. He couldn't see why, he said, we were pretending to kill people when we could have all we needed to kill really. He thinks Justino should be shot, too. Let him try it! But never in this world will I give him two thousand pesos!"

At sunset the men driving the burros came in from the maguey fields. The workers in the vat-room began to empty the fermented pulque into barrels, and to pour the fresh maguey water into the reeking bullhide vats. The chanting and counting and the rolling of barrels down the incline began again for the night. The white flood of pulque flowed without pause; all over Mexico the Indians would drink the corpse-white liquor, swallow forgetfulness and ease by the riverful, and the money would flow silver-white into the government treasury; don Genaro and his fellow-hacendados would fret and curse, the Agrarians would raid, and ambitious politicians in the capital would be stealing right and left enough to buy such haciendas for themselves. It was all arranged.

We spent the evening in the billiard room. Doctor Volk had arrived, had passed an hour with Uspensky, who had a simple sore throat and a threat of tonsilitis. Doctor Volk would cure him. Meantime he played a round of billiards with Stepanov and don Genaro. He was a splendid, conscientious, hard-working doctor, a Russian, and he could not conceal his delight at being once more with Russians, having a little holiday with a patient who was not very sick, after all, and a chance to play billiards, which he loved. When it was his turn, he climbed, smiling, on the edge of the table, leaned halfway down the green baize, closed one eye, balanced his cue and sighted and balanced again. Without taking his shot, he rolled off the table, smiling, placed himself at another angle, sighted again, leaned over almost flat, sighted, took his shot, and missed, smiling. Then it was Stepanov's turn. "I simply cannot understand it," said Doctor Volk, shaking his head, watching Stepanov with such an intensity of admiration that his eyes watered.

Andreyev sat on a low stool playing the guitar and singing Russian songs in a continuous murmur. Doña Julia curled up on the divan near him, in her black pajamas, with her Pekinese slung around her neck like a scarf. The beast snuffled and groaned and rolled his eyes in a swoon of flabby enjoyment. The big dogs sniffed around him with pained knotted foreheads. He yammered and snapped and whimpered at them. "They cannot believe he is really a dog," said doña Julia in delight. Carlos and Betancourt sat at a small table with music and costume designs spread before them. They were talking as if they were going over again a subject which wearied them both. . . .

I was learning a new card game with a thin dark youth who was some sort of assistant to Betancourt. He was very sleek and slim-waisted and devoted, he said, to fresco painting, "only modern," he told me, "like Rivera's, the method, but not old-fashioned style like his. I am decorating a house in Cuernavaca, come and look at it. You will see what I mean. You should not have played the dagger," he added; "now I shall play the crown, and there you are, defeated." He gathered up the cards and shuffled them. "When Justino was here," he said, "the director was always having trouble with him in the serious scenes, because Justino thought everything was a joke. In the death scenes, he smiled all over his face and ruined a great deal of film. Now they are saying that when Justino comes back no one will ever have to say again to him, 'Don't laugh, Justino, this is death, this is not funny.' "

Doña Julia turned her Pekinese over and rolled him back and forth on her lap. "He will forget everything, the minute it is over . . . his sister, everything," she said, gently, looking at me with soft empty eyes. "They are animals. Nothing means anything to them. And," she added, "it is quite possible he may not come back."

A silence like a light trance fell over the whole room in which all these chance-gathered people who had nothing to say to each other were for the moment imprisoned. Action was their defense against the predicament they were in, all together, and for the moment nothing was happening. The suspense in the air seemed ready to explode when Kennerly came in almost on tiptoe, like a man entering church. Everybody turned toward him as if he were in himself a whole rescue party. He announced his bad news loudly: "I've got to go back to Mexico City tonight. There's all sorts of trouble there. About the film. I better get back there and have it out with the censors. I just talked over the telephone there and he says there is some talk about cutting out a whole reel . . . you know, that scene with the beggars at the fiesta."

Don Genaro laid down his cue. "I'm going back tonight," he said; "you can go with me."

"Tonight?" doña Julia turned her face towards him, her eyes down. "What for?"

"Lolita," he said briefly and angrily. "She must come back. They have to make three or four scenes over again."

"Ah, that's lovely!" said doña Julia. She buried her face in the fur of her little dog. "Ah, lovely! Lolita back again! Do go for her —I can't wait!"

Stepanov spoke over his shoulder to Kennerly with no attempt to conceal his impatience—"I shouldn't worry about the censors—let them have their way."

Kennerly's jaw jerked and his voice trembled: "My God! I've *got* to worry and *somebody* has got to think of the future around here!"

Ten minutes later don Genaro's powerful car roared past the billiard room and fled down the wild dark road towards the capital.

In the morning there began a gradual drift back to town, by train, by automobile. "Stay here," each said to me in turn, "we are coming back tomorrow, Uspensky will be feeling better the work will begin again." Doña Julia was stopping in bed. I said good-by to her in the afternoon. She was sleepy and downy, curled up with her Pekinese on her shoulder. "Tomorrow," she said, "Lolita will be here, and there will be great excitement. They are going to do some of the best scenes over again." I could not wait for tomorrow in this deathly air. "If you should come back in about ten days," said the Indian driver, "you would see a different place. It is very sad-here now. But then the green corn will be ready, and ah, there will be enough to eat again!"

Pale Horse, Pale Rider

Three Short Novels

Old Mortality

She was a spirited-looking young woman, with dark curly hair cropped and parted on the side, a short oval face with straight eyebrows, and a large curved mouth. A round white collar rose from the neck of her tightly buttoned black basque, and round white cuffs set off lazy hands with dimples in them, lying at ease in the folds of her flounced skirt which gathered around to a bustle. She sat thus, forever in the pose of being photographed, a motionless image in her dark walnut frame with silver oak leaves in the corners, her smiling gray eyes following one about the room. It was a reckless indifferent smile, rather disturbing to her nieces Maria and Miranda. Quite often they wondered why every older person who looked at the picture said, "How lovely"; and why everyone who had known her thought her so beautiful and charming.

There was a kind of faded merriment in the background, with its vase of flowers and draped velvet curtains, the kind of vase and the kind of curtains no one would have any more. The clothes were not even romantic looking, but merely most terribly out of fashion, and the whole affair was associated, in the minds of the little girls, with dead things: the smell of Grandmother's medicated cigarettes and her furniture that smelled of beeswax, and her old-fashioned perfume, Orange Flower. The woman in the picture had been Aunt Amy, but she was only a ghost in a frame, and a sad, pretty story from old times. She had been beautiful, much loved, unhappy, and she had died young.

Maria and Miranda, aged twelve and eight years, knew they were young, though they felt they had lived a long time. They had lived not only their own years; but their memories, it seemed to them, began years before they were born, in the lives of the grown-ups around them, old people above forty, most of them, who had a way of insisting that they too had been young once. It was hard to believe.

Their father was Aunt Amy's brother Harry. She had been his favorite sister. He sometimes glanced at the photograph and said, "It's not very good. Her hair and her smile were her chief beauties, and they aren't shown at all. She was much slimmer than that, too. There were never any fat women in the family, thank God."

When they heard their father say things like that, Maria and Miranda simply wondered, without criticism, what he meant. Their grandmother was thin as a match; the pictures of their mother, long since dead, proved her to have been a candle-wick, almost. Dashing young ladies, who turned out to be, to Miranda's astonishment, merely more of Grandmother's grandchildren, like herself, came visiting from school for the holidays, boasting of their eighteen-inch waists. But how did their father account for great-aunt Eliza, who quite squeezed herself through doors, and who, when seated, was one solid pyramidal monument from floor to neck? What about great-aunt Keziah, in Kentucky? Her husband, great-uncle John Jacob, had refused to allow her to ride his good horses after she had achieved two hundred and twenty pounds. "No," said great-uncle John Jacob, "my sentiments of chivalry are not dead in my bosom; but neither is my common sense, to say nothing of charity to our faithful dumb friends. And the greatest of these is charity." It was suggested to great-uncle John Jacob that charity should forbid him to wound great-aunt Keziah's female vanity by such a comment on her figure. "Female vanity will recover," said great-uncle John Jacob, callously, "but what about my horses' backs? And if she had the proper female vanity in the first place, she would never have got into such shape." Well, great-aunt Keziah was famous for her heft, and wasn't she in the family? But something seemed to happen to their father's memory when he thought of the girls he had known in the family of his youth, and he declared steadfastly they had all been, in every generation without exception, as slim as reeds and graceful as sylphs.

This loyalty of their father's in the face of evidence contrary to his ideal had its springs in family feeling, and a love of legend that he shared with the others. They loved to tell stories, romantic and poetic, or comic with a romantic humor; they did not gild the outward circumstance, it was the feeling that mattered. Their hearts and imaginations were captivated by their past, a past in which worldly considerations had played a very minor role. Their stories were almost always love stories against a bright blank heavenly blue sky.

Photographs, portraits by inept painters who meant earnestly to flatter, and the festival garments folded away in dried herbs and camphor were disappointing when the little girls tried to fit them to the living beings created in their minds by the breathing words of their elders. Grandmother, twice a year compelled in her blood by the change of seasons, would sit nearly all of one day beside old trunks and boxes in the lumber room, unfolding layers of garments and small keepsakes; she spread them out on sheets on the floor around her, crying over certain things, nearly always the same things, looking again at pictures in velvet cases, unwrapping locks of hair and dried flowers, crying gently and easily as if tears were the only pleasure she had left.

If Maria and Miranda were very quiet, and touched nothing until it was offered, they might sit by her at these times, or come and go. There was a tacit understanding that her grief was strictly her own, and must not be noticed or mentioned. The little girls examined the objects, one by one, and did not find them, in themselves, impressive. Such dowdy little wreaths and necklaces, some of them made of pearly shells; such moth-eaten bunches of pink ostrich feathers for the hair; such clumsy big breast pins and bracelets of gold and colored enamel; such silly-looking combs, standing up on tall teeth capped with seed pearls and French paste. Miranda, without knowing why, felt melancholy. It seemed such a pity that these faded things, these yellowed long gloves and misshapen satin slippers, these broad ribbons cracking where they were folded, should have been all those vanished girls had to decorate themselves with. And where were they now, those girls, and the boys in the odd-looking collars? The young men seemed even more unreal than the girls, with their high-buttoned coats, their puffy neckties, their waxed mustaches, their waving thick hair combed carefully over their foreheads. Who could have taken them seriously, looking like that?

No, Maria and Miranda found it impossible to sympathize with those young persons, sitting rather stiffly before the camera, hopelessly out of fashion; but they were drawn and held by the mysterious love of the living, who remembered and cherished these dead. The visible remains were nothing; they were dust, perishable as the flesh; the features stamped on paper and metal were nothing, but their living memory enchanted the little girls. They listened, all ears and eager minds, picking here and there among the floating ends of narrative, patching together as well as they could fragments of tales that were like bits of poetry or music, indeed were associated with the poetry they had heard or read, with music, with the theater.

"Tell me again how Aunt Amy went away when she was married." "She ran into the gray cold and stepped into the carriage and turned and smiled with her face as pale as death, and called out 'Good-by, good-by,' and refused her cloak, and said, 'Give me a glass of wine.' And none of us saw her alive again." "Why wouldn't she wear her cloak, Cousin Cora?" "Because she was not in love, my dear." Ruin hath taught me thus to ruminate, that time will come and take my love away. "Was she really beautiful, Uncle Bill?" "As an angel, my child." There were golden-haired angels with long blue pleated skirts dancing around the throne of the Blessed Virgin. None of them resembled Aunt Amy in the least, nor the kind of beauty they had been brought up to admire. There were points of beauty by which one was judged severely. First, a beauty must be tall; whatever color the eyes, the hair must be dark, the darker the better; the skin must be pale and smooth. Lightness and swiftness of movement were important points. A beauty must be a good dancer, superb on horseback, with a serene manner, an amiable gaiety tempered with dignity at all hours. Beautiful teeth and hands, of course, and over and above all this, some mysterious crown of enchantment that attracted and held the heart. It was all very exciting and discouraging.

Miranda persisted through her childhood in believing, in spite of her smallness, thinness, her little snubby nose saddled with freckles, her speckled gray eyes and habitual tantrums, that by some miracle she would grow into a tall, cream-colored brunette, like cousin Isabel; she decided always to wear a trailing white satin gown. Maria, born sensible, had no such illusions. "We are going to take after Mamma's family," she said. "It's no use, we are. We'll never be beautiful, we'll always have freckles. And *you*," she told Miranda, "haven't even a good disposition."

Miranda admitted both truth and justice in this unkindness, but still secretly believed that she would one day suddenly receive beauty, as by inheritance, riches laid suddenly in her hands through no deserts of her own. She believed for quite a while that she would one day be like Aunt Amy, not as she appeared in the photograph, but as she was remembered by those who had seen her.

When Cousin Isabel came out in her tight black riding habit, surrounded by young men, and mounted gracefully, drawing her horse up and around so that he pranced learnedly on one spot while the other riders sprang to their saddles in the same sedate flurry, Miranda's heart would close with such a keen dart of admiration, envy, vicarious pride it was almost painful; but there would always be an elder present to lay a cooling hand upon her emotions. "She rides almost as well as Amy, doesn't she? But Amy had the pure Spanish style, she could bring out paces in a horse no one else knew he had." Young namesake Amy, on her way to a dance, would swish through the hall in ruffled white taffeta, glimmering like a moth in the lamplight, carrying her elbows pointed backward stiffly as wings, sliding along as if she were on rollers, in the fashionable walk of her day. She was considered the best dancer at any party, and Maria, sniffing the wave of perfume that followed Amy, would clasp her hands and say, "Oh, I can't *wait* to be grown up." But the elders would agree that the first Amy had been lighter, more smooth and delicate in her waltzing; young Amy would never equal her. Cousin Molly Parrington, far past her youth, indeed she belonged to the generation before Aunt Amy, was a noted charmer. Men who had known her all her life still gathered about her; now that she was happily widowed for the second time there was no doubt that she would yet marry again. But Amy, said the elders, had the same high spirits and wit without boldness, and you really could not say that Molly had ever been discreet. She dyed her hair, and made jokes about it. She had a way of collecting the men around her in a corner, where she told them stories. She was an unnatural mother to her ugly daughter Eva, an old maid past forty while her mother was still the belle of the ball. "Born when I was fifteen, you remember," Molly would say shamelessly, looking an old beau straight in the eye, both of them remembering that he had been best man at her first wedding when she was past twenty-one. "Everyone said I was like a little girl with her doll."

Eva, shy and chinless, straining her upper lip over two enormous teeth, would sit in corners watching her mother. She looked hungry, her eyes were strained and tired. She wore her mother's old clothes, made over, and taught Latin in a Female Seminary. She believed in votes for women, and had traveled about, making speeches. When her mother was not present, Eva bloomed out a little, danced prettily, smiled, showing all her teeth, and was like a dry little plant set out in a gentle rain. Molly was merry about her ugly duckling. "It's lucky for me my daughter is an old maid. She's not so apt," said Molly naughtily, "to make a grandmother of me." Eve would blush as if she had been slapped.

Eva was a blot, no doubt about it, but the little girls felt she belonged to their everyday world of dull lessons to be learned, stiff shoes to be limbered up, scratchy flannels to be endured in cold weather, measles and disappointed expectations. Their Aunt Amy belonged to the world of poetry. The romance of Uncle Gabriel's long, unrewarded love for her, her early death, was such a story as one found in old books: unworldly books, but true, such as the Vita Nuova, the Sonnets of Shakespeare and the Wedding Song of Spenser; and poems by Edgar Allan Poe. "Her tantalized spirit now blandly reposes, Forgetting or never regretting its roses. . . ." Their father read that to them, and said, "He was our greatest poet," and they knew that "our" meant he was Southern. Aunt Amy was real as the pictures in the old Holbein and Dürer books were real. The little girls lay flat on their stomachs and peered into a world of wonder, turning the shabby leaves that fell apart easily, not surprised at the sight of the Mother of God sitting on a hollow log nursing her Child; not doubting either Death or the Devil riding at the stirrups of the grim knight; not questioning the propriety of the stiffly dressed ladies of Sir Thomas More's household, seated in dignity on the floor, or seeming to be. They missed all the dog and pony shows, and lantern-slide entertainments, but their father took them to see "Hamlet," and "The Taming of the Shrew," and "Richard the Third," and a long sad play with Mary, Queen of Scots, in it. Miranda thought the magnificent lady in black velvet was truly the Queen of Scots, and was pained to learn that the real Queen had died long ago, and not at all on the night she, Miranda, had been present.

The little girls loved the theater, that world of personages taller than human beings, who swept upon the scene and invested it with their presences, their more than human voices, their gestures of gods and goddesses ruling a universe. But there was always a voice recalling other and greater occasions. Grandmother in her youth had heard Jenny Lind, and thought that Nellie Melba was much overrated. Father had seen Bernhardt, and Madame Modjeska was no sort of rival. When Paderewski played for the first time in their city, cousins came from all over the state and went from the grandmother's house to hear him. The little girls were left out of this great occasion. They shared the excitement of the going away, and shared the beautiful moment of return, when cousins stood about in groups, with coffee cups and glasses in their hands, talking in low voices, awed and happy. The little girls, struck with the sense of a great event, hung about in their nightgowns and listened, until someone noticed and hustled them away from the sweet nimbus of all that glory. One old gentleman, however, had heard Rubinstein frequently. He could not but feel that Rubinstein had reached the final height of musical interpretation, and, for him, Paderewski had been something of an anticlimax. The little girls heard him muttering on, holding up one hand, patting the air as if he were calling for silence. The others looked at him, and listened, without any disturbance of their grave tender mood. They had never heard Rubinstein; they had, one hour since, heard Paderewski, and why should anyone need to recall the past? Miranda, dragged away, half understanding the old gentleman, hated him. She felt that she too had heard Paderewski.

There was then a life beyond a life in this world, as well as in the next; such episodes confirmed for the little girls the nobility of human feeling, the divinity of man's vision of the unseen, the importance of life and death, the depths of the human heart, the romantic value of tragedy. Cousin Eva, on a certain visit, trying to interest them in the study of Latin, told them the story of John

Wilkes Booth, who, handsomely garbed in a long black cloak, had leaped to the stage after assassinating President Lincoln. "Sic semper tyrannis," he had shouted superbly, in spite of his broken leg. The little girls never doubted that it had happened in just that way, and the moral seemed to be that one should always have Latin, or at least a good classical poetry quotation, to depend upon in great or desperate moments. Cousin Eva reminded them that no one, not even a good Southerner, could possibly approve of John Wilkes Booth's deed. It was murder, after all. They were to remember that. But Miranda, used to tragedy in books and in family legends—two great-uncles had committed suicide and a remote ancestress had gone mad for love—decided that, without the murder, there would have been no point to dressing up and leaping to the stage shouting in Latin. So how could she disapprove of the deed? It was a fine story. She knew a distantly related old gentleman who had been devoted to the art of Booth, had seen him in a great many plays, but not, alas, at his greatest moment. Miranda regretted this; it would have been so pleasant to have the assassination of Lincoln in the family.

Uncle Gabriel, who had loved Aunt Amy so desperately, still lived somewhere, though Miranda and Maria had never seen him. He had gone away, far away, after her death. He still owned racehorses, and ran them at famous tracks all over the country, and Miranda believed there could not possibly be a more brilliant career. He had married again, quite soon, and had written to Grandmother, asking her to accept his new wife as a daughter in place of Amy. Grandmother had written coldly, accepting, inviting them for a visit, but Uncle Gabriel had somehow never brought his bride home. Harry had visited them in New Orleans, and reported that the second wife was a very good-looking well-bred blonde girl who would undoubtedly be a good wife for Gabriel. Still, Uncle Gabriel's heart was broken. Faithfully once a year he wrote a letter to someone of the family, sending money for a wreath for Amy's grave. He had written a poem for her gravestone, and had come home, leaving his second wife in Atlanta, to see that it was carved properly. He could never account for having written this poem; he had certainly never tried to write a single rhyme since leaving school. Yet one day when he had been thinking about Amy, the verse occurred to him, out of the air. Maria and Miranda had seen it, printed in gold on a mourning card. Uncle Gabriel had sent a great number of them to be handed around among the family.

> *"She lives again who suffered life,*
> *Then suffered death, and now set free*
> *A singing angel, she forgets*
> *The griefs of old mortality."*

"Did she really sing?" Maria asked her father.

"Now what has that to do with it?" he asked. "It's a poem."

"I think it's very pretty," said Miranda, impressed. Uncle Gabriel was second cousin to her father and Aunt Amy. It brought poetry very near.

"Not so bad for tombstone poetry," said their father, "but it should be better."

Uncle Gabriel had waited five years to marry Aunt Amy. She had been ill, her chest was weak; she was engaged twice to other young men and broke her engagements for no reason; and she laughed at the advice of older and kinder-hearted persons who thought it very capricious of her not to return the devotion of such a handsome and romantic young man as Gabriel, her second cousin, too; it was not as if she would be marrying a stranger. Her coldness was said to have driven Gabriel to a wild life and even to drinking. His grandfather was rich and Gabriel was his favorite; they had quarreled over the race horses, and Gabriel had shouted, "By God, I must have *something*." As if he had not everything already: youth, health, good looks, the prospect of riches, and a devoted family circle. His grandfather pointed out to him that he was little better than an ingrate, and showed signs of being a wastrel as well. Gabriel said, "You had racehorses, and made a good thing of them." "I never depended upon them for a livelihood, sir," said his grandfather.

Gabriel wrote letters about this and many other things to Amy from Saratoga and from Kentucky and from New Orleans, sending her presents, and flowers packed in ice, and telegrams. The presents were amusing, such as a huge cage full of small green lovebirds; or, as an ornament for her hair, a full-petaled enameled rose with paste dewdrops, with an enameled butterfly in brilliant colors suspended quivering on a gold wire above it; but the telegrams always frightened her mother, and the flowers, after a journey by train and then by stage into the country, were much the worse for wear. He would send roses when the rose garden at home was in full bloom. Amy could not help smiling over it, though her mother insisted it 'was touching and sweet of Gabriel. It must prove to Amy that she was always in his thoughts.

"That's no place for me," said Amy, but she had a way of speaking, a tone of voice, which made it impossible to discover what she meant by what she said. It was possible always that she might be serious. And she would not answer questions.

"Amy's wedding dress," said the grandmother, unfurling an immense cloak of dove-colored cut velvet, spreading beside it a silvery-gray watered-silk frock, and a small gray velvet toque with a dark red breast of feathers. Cousin Isabel, the beauty, sat with her. They talked to each other, and Miranda could listen if she chose.

"She would not wear white, nor a veil," said Grandmother. "I couldn't oppose her, for I had said my daughters should each have exactly the wedding dress they wanted. But Amy surprised me. 'Now what would I look like in white satin?' she asked. It's true she was pale, but she would have been angelic in it, and all of us told her so. 'I shall wear mourning if I like,' she said, 'it is *my* funeral, you know.' I reminded her that Lou and your mother had worn white with veils and it would please me to have my daughters all alike in that. Amy said, 'Lou and Isabel are not like me,' but I could not persuade her to explain what she meant. One day when she was ill she said, 'Mammy, I'm not long for this world,' but not as if she meant it. I told her, 'You might live as long as anyone, if only you will be sensible.' 'That's the whole trouble,' said Amy. 'I feel sorry for Gabriel,' she told me. He doesn't know what he's asking for.'

"I tried to tell her once more," said the grandmother, "that marriage and children would cure her of everything. 'All women of our family are delicate when they are young,' I said. 'Why, when I was your age no one expected me to live a year. It was called greensickness, and everybody knew there was only one cure.' 'If I live for a hundred years and turn green as grass,' said Amy, 'I still shan't want to marry Gabriel.' So I told her very seriously that if she truly felt that way she must never do it, and Gabriel must be told once for all, and sent away. He would get over it. 'I have told him, and I have sent him away,' said Amy. 'He just doesn't listen.' We both laughed at that, and I told her young girls found a hundred ways to deny they wished to be married, and a thousand more to test their power over men, but that she had more than enough of that, and now it was time for her to be entirely sincere and make her decision. As for me," said the grandmother, "I wished with all my heart to marry your grandfather, and if he had not asked me, I should have asked him most certainly. Amy insisted that she could not imagine wanting to marry anybody. She would be, she said, a nice old maid like Eva Parrington. For even then it was pretty plain that Eva was an old maid, born. Harry said, 'Oh, Eva—Eva has no chin, that's her trouble. If you had no chin, Amy, you'd be in the same fix as Eva, no doubt.' Your Uncle Bill would say, 'When women haven't anything else, they'll take a vote for consolation. A pretty thin bed-fellow,' said your Uncle Bill. 'What I really need is a good dancing partner to guide me through life,' said Amy, 'that's the match I'm looking for.' It was no good trying to talk to her."

Her brothers remembered her tenderly as a sensible girl. After listening to their comments on her character and ways, Maria decided that they considered her sensible because she asked their advice about her appearance when she was going out to dance. If they found fault in any way, she would change her dress or her hair until they were pleased, and say, "You are an angel not to let your poor sister go out looking like a freak." But she would not listen to her father, nor to Gabriel. If Gabriel praised the frock she was wearing, she was apt to disappear and come back in another. He loved her long black hair, and once, lifting it up from her pillow when she was ill, said, "I love your hair, Amy, the most beautiful hair in the world." When he returned on his next visit, he found her with her hair cropped and curled close to her head. He was horrified, as if she had willfully mutilated herself. She would not let it grow again, not even to please her brothers. The photograph hanging on the wall was one she had made at that time to send to Gabriel, who sent it back without a word. This pleased her, and she framed the photograph. There was a thin inky scrawl low in one corner, "To dear brother Harry, who likes my hair cut."

This was a mischievous reference to a very grave scandal. The little girls used to look at their father, and wonder what would have happened if he had really hit the young man he shot at. The young man was believed to have kissed Aunt Amy, when she was not in the least engaged to him. Uncle Gabriel was supposed to have had a duel with the young man, but Father had got there first. He was a pleasant, everyday sort of father, who held his daughters on his knee if they were prettily dressed and well behaved, and pushed them away if they had not freshly combed hair and nicely scrubbed fingernails. "Go away, you're disgusting," he would say, in a matter-of-fact voice. He noticed if their stocking seams were crooked. He caused them to brush their teeth with a revolting mixture of prepared chalk, powdered charcoal and salt. When they behaved stupidly he could not endure the sight of them. They understood dimly that all this was for their own future good; and when they were snivelly with colds, he prescribed delicious hot toddy for them, and saw that it was given them. He was always hoping they might not grow up to be so silly as they seemed to him at any given moment, and he had a disconcerting way of inquiring, "How do you *know?*" when they forgot and made dogmatic statements in his presence. It always came out embarrassingly that they did not know at all, but were repeating something they had heard. This made conversation with him difficult, for he laid traps and they fell into them, but it became important to them that their father should not believe them to be fools. Well, this very father had gone to Mexico once and stayed there for nearly a year, because he had shot at a man with whom Aunt Amy had flirted at a dance. It had been very wrong of him, because he should have challenged the man to a duel, as Uncle Gabriel had done. Instead, he just took a shot at him, and this was the lowest sort of manners. It had caused great disturbance in the whole community and had almost broken up the affair between Aunt Amy and Uncle Gabriel for good. Uncle Gabriel insisted that the young man had kissed Aunt Amy, and Aunt Amy insisted that the young man had merely paid her a compliment on her hair.

During the Mardi Gras holidays there was to be a big gay fancy-dress ball. Harry was going as a bull-fighter because his sweetheart, Mariana, had a new black lace mantilla and high comb from Mexico. Maria and Miranda had seen a photograph of their mother in this dress, her lovely face without a trace of coquetry

looking gravely out from under a tremendous fall of lace from the
peak of the comb, a rose tucked firmly over her ear. Amy copied
her costume from a small Dresden-china shepherdess which stood
on the mantelpiece in the parlor; a careful copy with ribboned hat,
gilded crook, very low-laced bodice, short basket skirts, green slippers and all. She wore it with a black half-mask, but it was no
disguise. "You would have known it was Amy at any distance,"
said Father. Gabriel, six feet three in height as he was, had got
himself up to match, and a spectacle he provided in pale blue satin
knee breeches and a blond curled wig with a hair ribbon. "He felt
a fool, and he looked like one," said Uncle Bill, "and he behaved
like one before the evening was over."

Everything went beautifully until the party gathered downstairs
to leave for the ball. Amy's father—he must have been born a
grandfather, thought Miranda—gave one glance at his daughter,
her white ankles shining, bosom deeply exposed, two round spots
of paint on her cheeks, and fell into a frenzy of outraged propriety.
"It's disgraceful," he pronounced, loudly. "No daughter of mine is
going go show herself in such a rig-out. It's bawdy," he thundered.
"Bawdy!"

Amy had taken off her mask to smile at him. "Why, Papa," she
said very sweetly, "what's wrong with it? Look on the mantelpiece.
She's been there all along, and you were never shocked before."

"There's all the difference in the world," said her father, "all the
difference, young lady, and you know it. You go upstairs this minute and pin up that waist in front and let down those skirts to a
decent length before you leave this house. *And wash your face!*"

"I see nothing wrong with it," said Amy's mother, firmly, "and
you shouldn't use such language before innocent young girls." She
and Amy sat down with several females of the household to help,
and they made short work of the business. In ten minutes Amy
returned, face clean, bodice filled in with lace, shepherdess skirt
modestly sweeping the carpet behind her.

When Amy appeared from the dressing room for her first dance
with Gabriel, the lace was gone from her bodice, her skirts were
tucked up more daringly than before, and the spots on her cheeks
were like pomegranates. "Now Gabriel, tell me truly, wouldn't it
have been a pity to spoil my costume?" Gabriel, delighted that she
had asked his opinion, declared it was perfect. They agreed with

kindly tolerance that old people were often tiresome, but one need not upset them by open disobedience: their youth was gone, what had they to live for?

Harry, dancing with Mariana who swung a heavy train around her expertly at every turn of the waltz, began to be uneasy about his sister Amy. She was entirely too popular. He saw young men make beelines across the floor, eyes fixed on those white silk ankles. Some of the young men he did not know at all, others he knew too well and could not approve of for his sister Amy. Gabriel, unhappy in his lyric satin and wig, stood about holding his ribboned crook as though it had sprouted thorns. He hardly danced at all with Amy, he did not enjoy dancing with anyone else, and he was having a thoroughly wretched time of it.

There appeared late, alone, got up as Jean Lafitte, a young Creole gentleman who had, two years before, been for a time engaged to Amy. He came straight to her, with the manner of a happy lover, and said, clearly enough for everyone near by to hear him, "I only came because I knew you were to be here. I only want to dance with you and I shall go again." Amy, with a face of delight, cried out, "Raymond!" as if to a lover. She had danced with him four times, and had then disappeared from the floor on his arm.

Harry and Mariana, in conventional disguise of romance, irreproachably betrothed, safe in their happiness, were waltzing slowly to their favorite song, the melancholy farewell of the Moorish King on leaving Granada. They sang in whispers to each other, in their uncertain Spanish, a song of love and parting and that sword's point of grief that makes the heart tender towards all other lost and disinherited creatures: Oh, mansion of love, my earthly paradise . . . that I shall see no more . . . whither flies the poor swallow, weary and homeless, seeking for shelter where no shelter is? I too am far from home without the power to fly. . . . Come to my heart, sweet bird, beloved pilgrim, build your nest near my bed, let me listen to your song, and weep for my lost land of joy. . . .

Into this bliss broke Gabriel. He had thrown away his shepherd's crook and he was carrying his wig. He wanted to speak to Harry at once, and before Mariana knew what was happening she was sitting beside her mother and the two excited young men were gone. Waiting, disturbed and displeased, she smiled at Amy who waltzed past with a young man in Devil costume, including ill-fitting scarlet cloven hoofs. Almost at once, Harry and Gabriel came back, with serious faces, and Harry darted on the dance floor, returning with Amy. The girls and the chaperones were asked to come at once, they must be taken home. It was all mysterious and sudden, and Harry said to Mariana, "I will tell you what is happening, but not now——"

The grandmother remembered of this disgraceful affair only that Gabriel brought Amy home alone and that Harry came in somewhat later. The other members of the party straggled in at various hours, and the story came out piecemeal. Amy was silent and, her mother discovered later, burning with fever. "I saw at once that something was very wrong. 'What has happened, Amy?' 'Oh, Harry goes about shooting at people at a party,' she said, sitting down as if she were exhausted. 'It was on your account, Amy,' said Gabriel. 'Oh, no, it was not,' said Amy. 'Don't believe him, Mammy.' So I said, 'Now enough of this. Tell me what happened, Amy.' And Amy said, 'Mammy, this is it. Raymond came in, and you know I like Raymond, and he is a good dancer. So we danced together, too much, maybe. We went on the gallery for a breath of air, and stood there. He said, "How well your hair looks. I like this new shingled style."' She glanced at Gabriel. 'And then another young man came out and said, "I've been looking everywhere. This is our dance, isn't it?" And I went in to dance. And now it seems that Gabriel went out at once and challenged Raymond to a duel about something or other, but Harry doesn't wait for that. Raymond had already gone out to have his horse brought, I suppose one doesn't duel in fancy dress,' she said, looking at Gabriel, who fairly shriveled in his blue satin shepherd's costume, 'and Harry simply went out and shot at him. I don't think that was fair,' said Amy."

Her mother agreed that indeed it was not fair; it was not even decent, and she could not imagine what her son Harry thought he was doing. "It isn't much of a way to defend your sister's honor," she said to him afterward. "I didn't want Gabriel to go fighting duels," said Harry. "That wouldn't have helped much, either."

Gabriel had stood before Amy, leaning over, asking once more the question he had apparently been asking her all the way home. "Did he kiss you, Amy?"

Amy took off her shepherdess hat and pushed her hair back. "Maybe he did," she answered, "and maybe I wished him to."

"Amy, you must not say such things," said her mother. "Answer Gabriel's question."

"He hasn't the right to ask it," said Amy, but without anger.

"Do you love him, Amy?" asked Gabriel, the sweat standing out on his forehead.

"It doesn't matter," answered Amy, leaning back in her chair.

"Oh, it does matter; it matters terribly," said Gabriel. "You must answer me now." He took both of her hands and tried to hold them. She drew her hands away firmly and steadily so that he had to let go.

"Let her alone, Gabriel," said Amy's mother. "You'd better go now. We are all tired. Let's talk about it tomorrow."

She helped Amy to undress, noticing the changed bodice and the shortened skirt. "You shouldn't have done that, Amy. That was not wise of you. It was better the other way."

Amy said, "Mammy, I'm sick of this world. I don't like anything in it. It's so *dull*," she said, and for a moment she looked as if she might weep. She had never been tearful, even as a child, and her mother was alarmed. It was then she discovered that Amy had fever.

"Gabriel is dull, Mother—he sulks," she said. "I could see him sulking every time I passed. It spoils things," she said. "Oh, I want to go to sleep."

Her mother sat looking at her and wondering how it had happened she had brought such a beautiful child into the world. "Her face," said her mother, "was angelic in sleep."

Some time during that fevered night, the projected duel between Gabriel and Raymond was halted by the offices of friends on both sides. There remained the open question of Harry's impulsive shot, which was not so easily settled. Raymond seemed vindictive about that, it was possible he might choose to make trouble. Harry, taking the advice of Gabriel, his brothers and friends, decided that the best way to avoid further scandal was for him to disappear for a while. This being decided upon, the young men returned about daybreak, saddled Harry's best horse and helped him pack a few things; accompanied by Gabriel and Bill, Harry set out for the border, feeling rather gay and adventurous.

Amy, being wakened by the stirring in the house, found out the plan. Five minutes after they were gone, she came down in her riding dress, had her own horse saddled, and struck out after them. She rode almost every morning; before her parents had time to be uneasy over her prolonged absence, they found her note.

What had threatened to be a tragedy became a rowdy lark. Amy rode to the border, kissed her brother Harry good-by, and rode back again with Bill and Gabriel. It was a three days' journey, and when they arrived Amy had to be lifted from the saddle. She was really ill by now, but in the gayest of humors. Her mother and father had been prepared to be severe with her, but, at sight of her, their feelings changed. They turned on Bill and Gabriel. "Why did you let her do this?" they asked.

"You know we could not stop her," said Gabriel helplessly, "and she did enjoy herself so much!"

Amy laughed. "Mammy, it was splendid, the most delightful trip I ever had. And if I am to be the heroine of this novel, why shouldn't I make the most of it?"

The scandal, Maria and Miranda gathered, had been pretty terrible. Amy simply took to bed and stayed there, and Harry had skipped out blithely to wait until the little affair blew over. The rest of the family had to receive visitors, write letters, go to church, return calls, and bear the whole brunt, as they expressed it. They sat in the twilight of scandal in their little world, holding themselves very rigidly, in a shared tension as if all their nerves began at a common center. This center had received a blow, and family nerves shuddered, even into the farthest reaches of Kentucky. From whence in due time great-great-aunt Sally Rhea addressed a letter to *Mifs Amy Rhea*. In deep brown ink like dried blood, in a spidery hand adept at archaic symbols and abbreviations, great-great-aunt Sally informed Amy that she was fairly convinced that this calamity was only the forerunner of a series shortly to be visited by the Almighty God upon a race already condemned through its own wickedness, a warning that man's time was short, and that they must all prepare for the end of the world. For herself, she had long expected it, she was entirely resigned to the prospect of meeting her Maker; and Amy, no less than her wicked brother Harry, must likewise place herself in God's hands and prepare for the worst. *"Oh, my dear unfortunate young relative,"* twittered great-great-aunt Sally, *"we must in our Extremty join hands and appr before ye Dread Throne of Jdgmnt a United Fmly, if One is Mssg from ye Flock, what will Jesus say?"*

Great-great-aunt Sally's religious career had become comic legend. She had forsaken her Catholic rearing for a young man whose family were Cumberland Presbyterians. Unable to accept their opinions, however, she was converted to the Hard-Shell Baptists, a sect as loathsome to her husband's family as the Catholic could possibly be. She had spent a life of vicious self-indulgent martyrdom to her faith; as Harry commented: "Religion put claws on Aunt Sally and gave her a post to whet them on." She had out-argued, out-fought, and out-lived her entire generation, but she did not miss them. She bedeviled the second generation without ceasing, and was beginning hungrily on the third.

Amy, reading this letter, broke into her gay full laugh that always caused everyone around her to laugh too, even before they knew why, and her small green lovebirds in their cage turned and eyed her solemnly. "Imagine drawing a pew in heaven beside Aunt Sally," she said. "What a prospect."

"Don't laugh too soon," said her father. "Heaven was made to order for Aunt Sally. She'll be on her own territory there."

"For my sins," said Amy, "I must go to heaven with Aunt Sally."

During the uncomfortable time of Harry's absence, Amy went on refusing to marry Gabriel. Her mother could hear their voices going on in their endless colloquy, during many long days. One afternoon Gabriel came out, looking very sober and discouraged. He stood looking down at Amy's mother as she sat sewing, and said, "I think it is all over, I believe now that Amy will never have me." The grandmother always said afterward, "Never have I pitied anyone as I did poor Gabriel at that moment. But I told him, very firmly, 'Let her alone, then, she is ill.' " So Gabriel left, and Amy had no word from him for more than a month.

The day after Gabriel was gone, Amy rose looking extremely well, went hunting with her brothers Bill and Stephen, bought a velvet wrap, had her hair shingled and curled again, and wrote long letters to Harry, who was having a most enjoyable exile in Mexico City.

After dancing all night three times in one week, she woke one morning in a hemorrhage. She seemed frightened and asked for the doctor, promising to do whatever he advised. She was quiet for a few days, reading. She asked for Gabriel. No one knew where he was. "You should write him a letter; his mother will send it on." "Oh, no," she said. "I miss him coming in with his sour face. Letters are no good."

Gabriel did come in, only a few days later, with a very sour face and unpleasant news. His grandfather had died, after a day's illness. On his death bed, in the name of God, being of a sound and disposing mind, he had cut off his favorite grandchild Gabriel with one dollar. "In the name of God, Amy," said Gabriel, "the old devil has ruined me in one sentence."

It was the conduct of his immediate family in the matter that had embittered him, he said. They could hardly conceal their satisfaction. They had known and envied Gabriel's quite just, well-founded expectations. Not one of them offered to make any private settlement. No one even thought of repairing this last-minute act of senile vengeance. Privately they blessed their luck. "I have been cut off with a dollar," said Gabriel, "and they are all glad of it. I think they feel somehow that this justifies every criticism they ever made against me. They were right about me all along. I am a worthless poor relation," said Gabriel. "My God, I wish you could see them."

Amy said, "I wonder how you will ever support a wife, now."

Gabriel said, "Oh, it isn't so bad as that. If you would, Amy—"

Amy said, "Gabriel, if we get married now there'll be just time to be in New Orleans for Mardi Gras. If we wait until after Lent, it may be too late."

"Why, Amy," said Gabriel, "how could it ever be too late?"

"You might change your mind," said Amy. "You know how fickle you are."

There were two letters in the grandmother's many packets of letters that Maria and Miranda read after they were grown. One of them was from Amy. It was dated ten days after her marriage.

"Dear Mammy, New Orleans hasn't changed as much as I have

since we saw each other last. I am now a staid old married woman, and Gabriel is very devoted and kind. Footlights won a race for us yesterday, she was the favorite, and it was wonderful. I go to the races every day, and our horses are doing splendidly; I had my choice of Erin Go Bragh or Miss Lucy, and I chose Miss Lucy. She is mine now, she runs like a streak. Gabriel says I made a mistake, Erin Go Bragh will stay better. I think Miss Lucy will stay my time.

"We are having a lovely visit. I'm going to put on a domino and take to the streets with Gabriel sometime during Mardi Gras. I'm tired of watching the show from a balcony. Gabriel says it isn't safe. He says he'll take me if I insist, but I doubt it. Mammy, he's very nice. Don't worry about me. I have a beautiful black-and-rose-colored velvet gown for the Proteus Ball. Madame, my new mother-in-law, wanted to know if it wasn't a little dashing. I told her I hoped so or I had been cheated. It is fitted perfectly smooth in the bodice, very low in the shoulders—Papa would not approve —and the skirt is looped with wide silver ribbons between the waist and knees in front, and then it surges around and is looped enormously in the back, with a train just one yard long. I now have an eighteen-inch waist, thanks to Madame Duré. I expect to be so dashing that my mother-in-law will have an attack. She has them quite often. Gabriel sends love. Please take good care of Graylie and Fiddler. I want to ride them again when I come home. We're going to Saratoga, I don't know just when. Give everybody my dear dear love. It rains all the time here, of course. . . .

"P.S. Mammy, as soon as I get a minute to myself, I'm going to be terribly homesick. Good-by, my darling Mammy."

The other was from Amy's nurse, dated six weeks after Amy's marriage.

"I cut off the lock of hair because I was sure you would like to have it. And I do not want you to think I was careless, leaving her medicine where she could get it, the doctor has written and explained. It would not have done her any harm except that her heart was weak. She did not know how much she was taking, often she said to me, one more of those little capsules wouldn't do any harm, and so I told her to be careful and not take anything except what I gave her. She begged me for them sometimes but I would not give her more than the doctor said. I slept during the night because she did not seem to be so sick **as all that** and the doctor did not order me to sit up with her. Please accept my regrets for your great loss and please do not think that anybody was careless with your dear daughter. She suffered a great deal and now she is at rest. She could not get well but she might have lived longer. Yours respectfully. . . ."

The letters and all the strange keepsakes were packed away and forgotten for a great many years. They seemed to have no place in the world.

PART II: 1904

During vacation on their grandmother's farm, Maria and Miranda, who read as naturally and constantly as ponies crop grass, and with much the same kind of pleasure, had by some happy chance laid hold of some forbidden reading matter, brought in and left there with missionary intent, no doubt, by some Protestant cousin. It fell into the right hands if enjoyment had been its end. The reading matter was printed in poor type on spongy paper, and was ornamented with smudgy illustrations all the more exciting to the little girls because they could not make head or tail of them. The stories were about beautiful but unlucky maidens, who for mysterious reasons had been trapped by nuns and priests in dire collusion; they were then "immured" in convents, where they were forced to take the veil—an appalling rite during which the victims shrieked dreadfully—and condemned forever after to most uncomfortable and disorderly existences. They seemed to divide their time between lying chained in dark cells and assisting other nuns to bury throttled infants under stones in moldering rat-infested dungeons.

Immured! It was the word Maria and Miranda had been needing all along to describe their condition at the Convent of the Child Jesus, in New Orleans, where they spent the long winters trying to avoid an education. There were no dungeons at the Child Jesus, and this was only one of numerous marked differences between convent life as Maria and Miranda knew it and the thrilling paper-backed version. It was no good at all trying to fit the stories to life, and they did not even try. They had long since learned to draw the lines between life, which was real and earnest, and the grave was not its goal; poetry, which was true but not real; and stories, or forbidden reading matter, in which things happened as nowhere else, with the most sublime irrelevance and unlikelihood, and one need not turn a hair, because there was not a word of truth in them.

It was true the little girls were hedged and confined, but in a large garden with trees and a grotto; they were locked at night into a long cold dormitory, with all the windows open, and a sister sleeping at either end. Their beds were curtained with muslin, and small night-lamps were so arranged that the sisters could see through the curtains, but the children could not see the sisters. Miranda wondered if they ever slept, or did they sit there all night quietly watching the sleepers through the muslin? She tried to work up a little sinister thrill about this, but she found it impossible to care much what either of the sisters did. They were very dull good-natured women who managed to make the whole dormitory seem dull. All days and all things in the Convent of the Child Jesus were dull, in fact, and Maria and Miranda lived for Saturdays.

No one had even hinted that they should become nuns. On the contrary Miranda felt that the discouraging attitude of Sister Claude and Sister Austin and Sister Ursula towards her expressed ambition to be a nun barely veiled a deeply critical knowledge of her spiritual deficiencies. Still Maria and Miranda had got a fine new word out of their summer reading, and they referred to themselves as "immured." It gave a romantic glint to what was otherwise a very dull life for them, except for blessed Saturday afternoons during the racing season.

If the nuns were able to assure the family that the deportment and scholastic achievements of Maria and Miranda were at least passable, some cousin or other always showed up smiling, in holiday mood, to take them to the races, where they were given a dollar each to bet on any horse they chose. There were black Saturdays now and then, when Maria and Miranda sat ready, hats in hand, curly hair plastered down and slicked behind their ears, their stiffly pleated navy-blue skirts spread out around them, waiting with their hearts going down slowly into their high-topped laced-up black shoes. They never put on their hats until the last minute, for somehow it would have been too horrible to have their hats on, when, after all, Cousin Henry and Cousin Isabel, or Uncle George and Aunt Polly, were not coming to take them to the races. When no one appeared, and Saturday came and went a sickening waste, they were then given to understand that it was a punishment for bad marks during the week. They never knew until it was too late to avoid the disappointment. It was very wearing.

One Saturday they were sent down to wait in the visitors' parlor, and there was their father. He had come all the way from Texas to see them. They leaped at sight of him, and then stopped short, suspiciously. Was he going to take them to the races? If so, they were happy to see him.

"Hello," said father, kissing their cheeks. "Have you been good girls? Your Uncle Gabriel is running a mare at the Crescent City today, so we'll all go and bet on her. Would you like that?"

Maria put on her hat without a word, but Miranda stood and addressed her father sternly. She had suffered many doubts about this day. "*Why* didn't you send word yesterday? I could have been looking forward all this time."

"We didn't know," said father, in his easiest paternal manner, "that you were going to deserve it. Remember Saturday before last?"

Miranda hung her head and put on her hat, with the round elastic under the chin. She remembered too well. She had, in midweek, given way to despair over her arithmetic and had fallen flat on her face on the classroom floor, refusing to rise until she was carried out. The rest of the week had been a series of novel deprivations, and Saturday a day of mourning; secret mourning, for if one mourned too noisily, it simply meant another bad mark against deportment.

"Never mind," said father, as if it were the smallest possible matter, "today you're going. Come along now. We've barely time."

These expeditions were all joy, every time, from the moment they stepped into a closed one-horse cab, a treat in itself with its dark, thick upholstery, soaked with strange perfumes and tobacco smoke, until the thrilling moment when they walked into a restaurant under big lights and were given dinner with things to eat they never had at home, much less at the convent. They felt worldly and grown up, each with her glass of water colored pink with claret.

The great crowd was always exciting as if they had never seen it before, with the beautiful, incredibly dressed ladies, all plumes and flowers and paint, and the elegant gentlemen with yellow gloves. The bands played in turn with thundering drums and brasses, and now and then a wild beautiful horse would career around the track with a tiny, monkey-shaped boy on his back, limbering up for his race.

Miranda had a secret personal interest in all this which she knew better than to confide to anyone, even Maria. Least of all to Maria. In ten minutes the whole family would have known. She had lately decided to be a jockey when she grew up. Her father had said one day that she was going to be a little thing all her life, she would never be tall; and this meant, of course, that she would never be a beauty like Aunt Amy, or Cousin Isabel. Her hope of being a beauty died hard, until the notion of being a jockey came suddenly and filled all her thoughts. Quietly, blissfully, at night before she slept, and too often in the daytime when she should have been studying, she planned her career as a jocky. It was dim in detail, but brilliant at the right distance. It seemed too silly to be worried about arithmetic at all, when what she needed for her future was to ride better—much better. "You ought to be ashamed of yourself," said father, after watching her gallop full tilt down the lane at the farm, on Trixie, the mustang mare. "I can see the sun, moon and stars between you and the saddle every jump." Spanish style meant that one sat close to the saddle, and did all kinds of things with the knees and reins. Jockeys bounced lightly, their knees almost level with the horse's back, rising and falling like a rubber ball. Miranda felt she could do that easily. Yes, she would be a jockey, like Tod Sloan, winning every other race at least. Meantime, while she was training, she would keep it a secret, and one day she would ride out, bouncing lightly, with the other jockeys, and win a great race, and surprise everybody, her family most of all.

On that particular Saturday, her idol, the great Tod Sloan, was riding, and he won two races. Miranda longed to bet her dollar on Tod Sloan, but father said, "Not now, honey. Today you must bet on Uncle Gabriel's horse. Save your dollar for the fourth race, and put it on Miss Lucy. You've got a hundred to one shot. Think if she wins."

Miranda knew well enough that a hundred to one shot was no bet at all. She sulked, the crumpled dollar in her hand grew damp and warm. She could have won three dollars already on Tod Sloan. Maria said virtuously, "It wouldn't be nice not to bet on Uncle Gabriel. That way, we keep the money in the family." Miranda put out her under lip at her sister. Maria was too prissy for words. She wrinkled her nose back at Miranda.

They had just turned their dollar over to the bookmaker for the fourth race when a vast bulging man with a red face and immense tan ragged mustaches fading into gray hailed them from a lower level of the grandstand, over the heads of the crowd, "Hey, there, Harry?" Father said, "Bless my soul, there's Gabriel." He motioned to the man, who came pushing his way heavily up the shallow steps. Maria and Miranda stared, first at him, then at each other. "Can that be our Uncle Gabriel?" their eyes asked. "Is that Aunt Amy's handsome romantic beau? Is that the man who wrote the poem about our Aunt Amy?" Oh, what did grown-up people *mean* when they talked, anyway?

He was a shabby fat man with bloodshot blue eyes, sad beaten eyes, and a big melancholy laugh, like a groan. He towered over them shouting to their father, "Well, for God's sake, Harry, it's been a coon's age. You ought to come out and look 'em over. You look just like yourself, Harry, how are you?"

The band struck up "Over the River" and Uncle Gabriel shouted louder. "Come on, let's get out of this. What are you doing up here with the pikers?"

"Can't," shouted Father. "Brought my little girls. Here they are."

Uncle Gabriel's bleared eyes beamed blindly upon them. "Fine looking set, Harry," he bellowed, "pretty as pictures, how old are they?"

"Ten and fourteen now," said Father; "awkward ages. Nest of vipers," he boasted, "perfect batch of serpent's teeth. Can't do a thing with 'em." He fluffed up Miranda's hair, pretending to tousle it.

"Pretty as pictures," bawled Uncle Gabriel, "but rolled into one they don't come up to Amy, do they?"

"No, they don't," admitted their father at the top of his voice, "but they're only half-baked." *Over the river, over the river,* moaned the band, *my sweetheart's waiting for me.*

"I've got to get back now," yelled Uncle Gabriel. The little girls felt quite deaf and confused. "Got the God-damnedest jockey in the world, Harry, just my luck. Ought to tie him on. Fell off Fiddler yesterday, just plain fell off on his tail— Remember Amy's mare, Miss Lucy? Well, this is her namesake, Miss Lucy IV. None of 'em ever came up to the first one, though. Stay right where you are, I'll be back."

Maria spoke up boldly. "Uncle Gabriel, tell Miss Lucy we're betting on her." Uncle Gabriel bent down and it looked as if there were tears in his swollen eyes. "God bless your sweet heart," he bellowed, "I'll tell her." He plunged down through the crowd again, his fat back bowed slightly in his loose clothes, his thick neck rolling over his collar.

Miranda and Maria, disheartened by the odds, by their first sight of their romantic Uncle Gabriel, whose language was so coarse, sat listlessly without watching, their chances missed, their dollars gone, their hearts sore. They didn't even move until their father leaned over and hauled them up. "Watch your horse," he said, in a quick warning voice, "watch Miss Lucy come home."

They stood up, scrambled to their feet on the bench, every vein in them suddenly beating so violently they could hardly focus their eyes, and saw a thin little mahogany-colored streak flash by the judges' stand, only a neck ahead, but their Miss Lucy, oh, their darling, their lovely—oh, Miss Lucy, their Uncle Gabriel's Miss Lucy, had won, had won. They leaped up and down screaming and clapping their hands, their hats falling back on their shoulders, their hair flying wild. *Whoa, you heifer,* squalled the band with snorting brasses, and the crowd broke into a long roar like the falling of the walls of Jericho.

The little girls sat down, feeling quite dizzy, while their father tried to pull their hats straight, and taking out his handkerchief held it to Miranda's face, saying very gently, "Here, blow your nose," and he dried her eyes while he was about it. He stood up then and shook them out of their daze. He was smiling with deep laughing wrinkles around his eyes, and spoke to them as if they were grown young ladies he was squiring around.

"Let's go out and pay our respects to Miss Lucy," he said. "She's the star of the day."

The horses were coming in, looking as if their hides had been drenched and rubbed with soap, their ribs heaving, their nostrils flaring and closing. The jockeys sat bowed and relaxed, their faces calm, moving a little at the waist with the movement of their horses. Miranda noted this for future use; that was the way you came in from a race, easy and quiet, whether you had won or lost. Miss Lucy came last, and a little handful of winners applauded her and cheered the jockey. He smiled and lifted his whip, his eyes and shriveled brown face perfectly serene. Miss Lucy was bleeding at the nose, two thick red rivulets were stiffening her tender mouth and chin, the round velvet chin that Miranda thought the nicest kind of chin in the world. Her eyes were wild and her knees were trembling, and she snored when she drew her breath.

Miranda stood staring. That was winning, too. Her heart clinched tight; that was winning, for Miss Lucy. So instantly and completely did her heart reject that victory, she did not know when it happened, but she hated it, and was ashamed that she had screamed and shed tears for joy when Miss Lucy, with her blood-ied nose and bursting heart had gone past the judges' stand a neck ahead. She felt empty and sick and held to her father's hand so hard that he shook her off a little impatiently and said, "What is the matter with you? Don't be so fidgety."

Uncle Gabriel was standing there waiting, and he was completely drunk. He watched the mare go in, then leaned against the fence with its white-washed posts and sobbed openly. "She's got the nosebleed, Harry," he said. "Had it since yesterday. We thought we had her all fixed up. But she did it, all right. She's got a heart like a lion. I'm going to breed her, Harry. Her heart's worth a million dollars, by itself, God bless her." Tears ran over his brick-colored face and into his straggling mustaches. "If anything happens to her now I'll blow my brains out. She's my last hope. She saved my life. I've had a run," he said, groaning into a large handkerchief and mopping his face all over, "I've had a run of luck that would break a brass billy goat. God, Harry, let's go some-where and have a drink."

"I must get the children back to school first, Gabriel," said their father, taking each by a hand.

"No, no, don't go yet," said Uncle Gabriel desperately. "Wait here a minute, I want to see the vet and take a look at Miss Lucy, and I'll be right back. Don't go, Harry, for God's sake. I want to talk to you a few minutes."

Maria and Miranda, watching Uncle Gabriel's lumbering, unsteady back, were thinking that this was the first time they had ever seen a man that they knew to be drunk. They had seen pictures and read descriptions, and had heard descriptions, so they recognized the symptoms at once. Miranda felt it was an important moment in a great many ways.

"Uncle Gabriel's a drunkard, isn't he?" she asked her father, rather proudly.

"Hush, don't say such things," said father, with a heavy frown, "or I'll never bring you here again." He looked worried and unhappy, and, above all, undecided. The little girls stood stiff with resentment against such obvious injustice. They loosed their hands from his and moved away coldly, standing together in silence. Their father did not notice, watching the place where Uncle Gabriel had disappeared. In a few minutes he came back, still wiping his face, as if there were cobwebs on it, carrying his big black hat. He waved at them from a short distance, calling out in a cheerful way, "She's going to be all right, Harry. It's stopped now. Lord, this will be good news for Miss Honey. Come on, Harry, let's all go home and tell Miss Honey. She deserves some good news."

Father said, "I'd better take the children back to school first, then we'll go."

"No, no," said Uncle Gabriel, fondly. "I want her to see the girls. She'll be tickled pink to see them, Harry. Bring 'em along."

"Is it another race horse we're going to see?" whispered Miranda in her sister's ear.

"Don't be silly," said Maria. "It's Uncle Gabriel's second wife."

"Let's find a cab, Harry," said Uncle Gabriel, "and take your little girls out to cheer up Miss Honey. Both of 'em rolled into one look a lot like Amy, I swear they do. I want Miss Honey to see them. She's always liked our family, Harry, though of course she's not what you'd call an expansive kind of woman."

Maria and Miranda sat facing the driver, and Uncle Gabriel squeezed himself in facing them beside their father. The air became at once bitter and sour with his breathing. He looked sad and poor. His necktie was on crooked and his shirt was rumpled. Father said, "You're going to see Uncle Gabriel's second wife, children," exactly if they had not heard everything; and to Gabriel, "How *is* your wife nowadays? It must be twenty years since I saw her last."

"She's pretty gloomy, and that's a fact," said Uncle Gabriel. "She's been pretty gloomy for years now, and nothing seems to shake her out of it. She never did care for horses, Harry, if you remember; she hasn't been near the track three times since we were married. When I think how Amy wouldn't have missed a race for anything . . . She's very different from Amy, Harry, a very different kind of woman. As fine a woman as ever lived in her own way, but she hates change and moving around, and she just lives in the boy."

"Where is Gabe now?" asked father.

"Finishing college," said Uncle Gabriel; "a smart boy, but awfully like his mother. Awfully like," he said, in a melancholy way. "She hates being away from him. Just wants to sit down in the same town and wait for him to get through with his education. Well, I'm sorry it can't be done if that's what she wants, but God Almighty— And this last run of luck has about got her down. I hope you'll be able to cheer her up a little, Harry, she needs it."

The little girls sat watching the streets grow duller and dingier and narrower, and at last the shabbier and shabbier white people gave way to dressed-up Negroes, and then to shabby Negroes, and after a long way the cab stopped before a desolate-looking little hotel in Elysian Fields. Their father helped Maria and Miranda out, told the cabman to wait, and they followed Uncle Gabriel through a dirty damp-smelling patio, down a long gas-lighted hall full of a terrible smell, Miranda couldn't decide what it was made of but it had a bitter taste even, and up a long staircase with a ragged carpet. Uncle Gabriel pushed open a door without warning, saying, "Come in, here we are."

A tall pale-faced woman with faded straw-colored hair and pink-rimmed eyelids rose suddenly from a squeaking rocking chair. She wore a stiff blue-and-white-striped shirtwaist and a stiff black skirt of some hard shiny material. Her large knuckled hands rose to her round, neat pompadour at sight of her visitors.

"Honey," said Uncle Gabriel, with large false heartiness, "you'll never guess who's come to see you." He gave her a clumsy hug. Her face did not change and her eyes rested steadily on the three strangers. "Amy's brother Harry, Honey, you remember, don't you?"

"Of course," said Miss Honey, putting out her hand straight as a paddle, "of course I remember you, Harry." She did not smile.

"And Amy's two little nieces," went on Uncle Gabriel, bringing them forward. They put out their hands limply, and Miss Honey gave each one a slight flip and dropped it. "And we've got good news for you," went on Uncle Gabriel, trying to bolster up the painful situation. "Miss Lucy stepped out and showed 'em today, Honey. We're rich again, old girl, cheer up."

Miss Honey turned her long, despairing face towards her visitors. "Sit down," she said with a heavy sigh, seating herself and motioning towards various rickety chairs. There was a big lumpy bed, with a grayish-white counterpane on it, a marble-topped washstand, grayish coarse lace curtains on strings at the two small windows, a small closed fireplace with a hole in it for a stovepipe, and two trunks, standing at odds as if somebody were just moving in, or just moving out. Everything was dingy and soiled and neat and bare; not a pin out of place.

"We'll move to the St. Charles tomorrow," said Uncle Gabriel, as much to Harry as to his wife. "Get your best dresses together, Honey, the long dry spell is over."

Miss Honey's nostrils pinched together and she rocked slightly, with her arms folded. "I've lived in the St. Charles before, and I've lived here before," she said, in a tight deliberate voice, "and this time I'll just stay where I am, thank you. I prefer it to moving back here in three months. I'm settled now, I feel at home here," she told him, glancing at Harry, her pale eyes kindling with blue fire, a stiff white line around her mouth.

The little girls sat trying not to stare, miserably ill at ease. Their grandmother had pronounced Harry's children to be the most unteachable she had ever seen in her long experience with the young; but they had learned by indirection one thing well—nice people did not carry on quarrels before outsiders. Family quarrels were sacred, to be waged privately in fierce hissing whispers, low choked mutters and growls. If they did yell and stamp, it must be behind closed doors and windows. Uncle Gabriel's second wife was hop-

ping mad and she looked ready to fly out at Uncle Gabriel any
second, with him sitting there like a hound when someone shakes a
whip at him.

"She loathes and despises everybody in this room," thought Miranda, coolly, "and she's afraid we won't know it. She needn't
worry, we knew it when we came in." With all her heart she
wanted to go, but her father, though his face was a study, made no
move. He seemed to be trying to think of something pleasant to
say. Maria, feeling guilty, though she couldn't think why, was calculating rapidly, "Why, she's only Uncle Gabriel's second wife, and
Uncle Gabriel was only married before to Aunt Amy, why, she's
no kin at all, and I'm glad of it." Sitting back easily, she let her
hands fall open in her lap; they would be going in a few minutes,
undoubtedly, and they need never come back.

Then father said, "We mustn't be keeping you, we just dropped
in for a few minutes. We wanted to see how you are."

Miss Honey said nothing, but she made a little gesture with her
hands, from the wrist, as if to say, "Well, you see how I am, and
now what next?"

"I must take these young ones back to school," said father, and
Uncle Gabriel said stupidly, "Look, Honey, don't you think they
resemble Amy a little? Especially around the eyes, especially
Maria, don't you think, Harry?"

Their father glanced at them in turn. "I really couldn't say," he
decided, and the little girls saw he was more monstrously embarrassed than ever. He turned to Miss Honey, "I hadn't seen Gabriel
for so many years," he said, "we thought of getting out for a talk
about old times together. You know how it is."

"Yes, I know," said Miss Honey, rocking a little, and all that
she knew gleamed forth in a pallid, unquenchable hatred and bitterness that seemed enough to bring her long body straight up out of
the chair in a fury, "I know," and she sat staring at the floor. Her
mouth shook and straightened. There was a terrible silence, which
was broken when the little girls saw their father rise. They got up,
too, and it was all they could do to keep from making a dash for
the door.

"I must get the young ones back," said their father. "They've
had enough excitement for one day. They each won a hundred
dollars on Miss Lucy. It was a good race," he said, in complete

wretchedness, as if he simply could not extricate himself from the situation. "Wasn't it, Gabriel?"

"It was a grand race," said Gabriel, brokenly, "a grand race."

Miss Honey stood up and moved a step towards the door. "Do you take them to the races, actually?" she asked, and her lids flickered towards them as if they were loathsome insects, Maria felt.

"If I feel they deserve a little treat, yes," said their father, in an easy tone but with wrinkled brow.

"I had rather, much rather," said Miss Honey clearly, "see my son dead at my feet than hanging around a race track."

The next few moments were rather a blank, but at last they were out of it, going down the stairs, across the patio, with Uncle Gabriel seeing them back into the cab. His face was sagging, the features had fallen as if the flesh had slipped from the bones, and his eyelids were puffed and blue. "Good-by, Harry," he said soberly. "How long you expect to be here?"

"Starting back tomorrow," said Harry. "Just dropped in on a little business and to see how the girls were getting along."

"Well," said Uncle Gabriel, "I may be dropping into your part of the country one of these days. Good-by, children," he said, taking their hands one after the other in his big warm paws. "They're nice children, Harry. I'm glad you won on Miss Lucy," he said to the little girls, tenderly. "Don't spend your money foolishly, now. Well, so long, Harry." As the cab jolted away he stood there fat and sagging, holding up his arm and wagging his hand at them.

"Goodness," said Maria, in her most grown-up manner, taking her hat off and hanging it over her knee, "I'm glad that's over."

"What I want to know is," said Miranda, "*is* Uncle Gabriel a real drunkard?"

"Oh, hush," said their father, sharply, "I've got the heartburn."

There was a respectful pause, as before a public monument. When their father had the heartburn it was time to lay low. The cab rumbled on, back to clean gay streets, with the lights coming on in the early February darkness, past shimmering shop windows, smooth pavements, on and on, past beautiful old houses set in deep gardens, on, on back to the dark walls with the heavy-topped trees hanging over them. Miranda sat thinking so hard she forgot and spoke out in her thoughtless way: "I've decided I'm not going to be a jockey, after all." She could as usual have bitten her tongue, but as usual it was too late.

Father cheered up and twinkled at her knowingly, as if that didn't surprise him in the least. "Well, well," said he, "so you aren't going to be a jockey! That's very sensible of you. I think she ought to be a lion-tamer, don't you, Maria? That's a nice, womanly profession."

Miranda, seeing Maria from the height of her fourteen years suddenly joining with their father to laugh at her, made an instant decision and laughed with them at herself. That was better. Everybody laughed and it was such a relief.

"Where's my hundred dollars?" asked Maria, anxiously.

"It's going in the bank," said their father, "and yours too," he told Miranda. "That is your nest-egg."

"Just so they don't buy my stockings with it," said Miranda, who had long resented the use of her Christmas money by their grandmother. "I've got enough stockings to last me a year."

"I'd like to buy a racehorse," said Maria, "but I know it's not enough." The limitations of wealth oppressed her. "*What* could you buy with a hundred dollars?" she asked fretfully.

"Nothing, nothing at all," said their father, "a hundred dollars is just something you put in the bank."

Maria and Miranda lost interest. They had won a hundred dollars on a horse race once. It was already in the far past. They began to chatter about something else.

The lay sister opened the door on a long cord, from behind the grille; Maria and Miranda walked in silently to their familiar world of shining bare floors and insipid wholesome food and cold-water washing and regular prayers; their world of poverty, chastity and obedience, of early to bed and early to rise, of sharp little rules and tittle-tattle. Resignation was in their childish faces as they held them up to be kissed.

"Be good girls," said their father, in the strange serious, rather helpless way he always had when he told them good-by. "Write to your daddy, now, nice long letters," he said, holding their arms firmly for a moment before letting go for good. Then he disappeared, and the sister swung the door closed after him.

Maria and Miranda went upstairs to the dormitory to wash their faces and hands and slick down their hair again before supper.

Miranda was hungry. "We didn't have a thing to eat, after all," she grumbled. "Not even a chocolate nut bar. I think that's mean. We didn't even get a quarter to spend," she said.

"Not a living bite," said Maria. "Not a nickel." She poured out cold water into the bowl and rolled up her sleeves.

Another girl about her own age came in and went to a washbowl near another bed. "Where have you been?" she asked. "Did you have a good time?"

"We went to the races, with our father," said Maria, soaping her hands.

"Our uncle's horse won," said Miranda.

"My goodness," said the other girl, vaguely, "that must have been grand."

Maria looked at Miranda, who was rolling up her own sleeves. She tried to feel martyred, but it wouldn't go. "Immured for another week," she said, her eyes sparkling over the edge of her towel.

PART III: 1912

Miranda followed the porter down the stuffy aisle of the sleeping-car, where the berths were nearly all made down and the dusty green curtains buttoned, to a seat at the further end. "Now yo' berth's ready any time, Miss," said the porter.

"But I want to sit up a while," said Miranda. A very thin old lady raised choleric black eyes and fixed upon her a regard of unmixed disapproval. She had two immense front teeth and a receding chin, but she did not lack character. She had piled her luggage around her like a barricade, and she glared at the porter when he picked some of it up to make room for his new passenger. Miranda sat, saying mechanically, "May I?"

"You may, indeed," said the old lady, for she seemed old in spite of a certain brisk, rustling energy. Her taffeta petticoats creaked like hinges every time she stirred. With ferocious sarcasm, after a half second's pause, she added, "You may be so good as to get off my hat!"

Miranda rose instantly in horror, and handed to the old lady a wilted contrivance of black horsehair braid and shattered white poppies. "I'm dreadfully sorry," she stammered, for she had been brought up to treat ferocious old ladies respectfully, and this one seemed capable of spanking her, then and there. "I didn't dream it was your hat."

"And whose hat did you dream it might be?" inquired the old lady, baring her teeth and twirling the hat on a forefinger to restore it.

"I didn't think it was a hat at all," said Miranda with a touch of hysteria.

"Oh, you didn't think it was a hat? Where on earth are your eyes, child?" and she proved the nature and function of the object by placing it on her head at a somewhat tipsy angle, though still it did not much resemble a hat. "Now can you see what it is?"

"Yes, oh, yes," said Miranda, with a meekness she hoped was disarming. She ventured to sit again after a careful inspection of the narrow space she was to occupy.

"Well, well," said the old lady, "let's have the porter remove some of these encumbrances," and she stabbed the bell with a lean sharp forefinger. There followed a flurry of rearrangements, during which they both stood in the aisle, the old lady giving a series of impossible directions to the Negro which he bore philosophically while he disposed of the luggage exactly as he had meant to do. Seated again, the old lady asked in a kindly, authoritative tone, "And what might your name be, child?"

At Miranda's answer, she blinked somewhat, unfolded her spectacles, straddled them across her high nose competently, and took a good long look at the face beside her.

"If I'd had my spectacles on," she said, in an astonishingly changed voice, "I might have known. I'm Cousin Eva Parrington," she said, "Cousin Molly Parrington's daughter, remember? I knew you when you were a little girl. You were a lively little girl," she added as if to console her, "and very opinionated. The last thing I heard about you, you were planning to be a tight-rope walker. You were going to play the violin and walk the tight rope at the same time."

207

"I must have seen it at the vaudeville show," said Miranda. "I couldn't have invented it. Now I'd like to be an air pilot!"

"I used to go to dances with your father," said Cousin Eva, busy with her own thoughts, "and to big holiday parties at your grandmother's house, long before you were born. Oh, indeed, yes, a long time before."

Miranda remembered several things at once. Aunt Amy had threatened to be an old maid like Eva. Oh, Eva, the trouble with her is she has no chin. Eva has given up, and is teaching Latin in a Female Seminary. Eva's gone out for votes for women, God help her. The nice thing about an ugly daughter is, she's not apt to make me a grandmother. . . . "They didn't do you much good, those parties, dear Cousin Eva," thought Miranda.

"They didn't do me much good, those parties," said Cousin Eva aloud as if she were a mind-reader, and Miranda's head swam for a moment with fear that she had herself spoken aloud. "Or at least, they didn't serve their purpose, for I never got married; but I enjoyed them, just the same. I had a good time at those parties, even if I wasn't a belle. And so you are Harry's child, and here I was quarreling with you. You do remember me, don't you?"

"Yes," said Miranda, and thinking that even if Cousin Eva had been really an old maid ten years before, still she couldn't be much past fifty now, and she looked so withered and tired, so famished and sunken in the cheeks, so *old,* somehow. Across the abyss separating Cousin Eva from her own youth, Miranda looked with painful premonition. "Oh, must I ever be like that?" She said aloud, "Yes, you used to read Latin to me, and tell me not to bother about the sense, to get the sound in my mind, and it would come easier later."

"Ah, so I did," said Cousin Eva, delighted. "So I did. You don't happen to remember that I once had a beautiful sapphire velvet dress with a train on it?"

"No, I don't remember that dress," said Miranda.

"It was an old dress of my mother's made over and cut down to fit," said Eva, "and it wasn't in the least becoming to me, but it was the only really good dress I ever had, and I remember it as if it were yesterday. Blue was never my color." She sighed with a humorous bitterness. The humor seemed momentary, but the bitterness was a constant state of mind.

Miranda, trying to offer the sympathy of fellow suffering, said, "I know. I've had Maria's dresses made over for me, and they were never right. It was dreadful."

"Well," said Cousin Eva, in the tone of one who did not wish to share her unique disappointments. "How is your father? I always liked him. He was one of the finest-looking young men I ever saw. Vain, too, like all his family. He wouldn't ride any but the best horses he could buy, and I used to say he made them prance and then watched his own shadow. I used to tell this on him at dinner parties, and he hated me for it. I feel pretty certain he hated me." An overtone of complacency in Cousin Eva's voice explained better than words that she had her own method of commanding attention and arousing emotion. "How *is* your father, I asked you, my dear?"

"I haven't seen him for nearly a year," answered Miranda, quickly, before Cousin Eva could get ahead again. "I'm going home now to Uncle Gabriel's funeral; you know, Uncle Gabriel died in Lexington and they have brought him back to be buried beside Aunt Amy."

"So that's how we meet," said Cousin Eva. "Yes, Gabriel drank himself to death at last. I'm going to the funeral, too. I haven't been home since I went to Mother's funeral, it must be, let's see, yes, it will be nine years next July. I'm going to Gabriel's funeral, though. I wouldn't miss that. Poor fellow, what a life he had. Pretty soon, they'll all be gone."

Miranda said, "We're left, Cousin Eva," meaning those of her own generation, the young, and Cousin Eva said, "Pshaw, you'll live forever, and you won't bother to come to our funerals." She didn't seem to think this was a misfortune, but flung the remark from her like a woman accustomed to saying what she thought.

Miranda sat thinking, "Still, I suppose it would be pleasant if I could say something to make her believe that she and all of them would be lamented, but—but—" With a smile which she hoped would be her denial of Cousin Eva's cynicism about the younger generation, she said, "You were right about the Latin, Cousin Eva, your reading did help when I began with it. I still study," she said. "Latin, too."

"And why shouldn't you?" asked Cousin Eva, sharply, adding at once mildly, "I'm glad you are going to use your mind a little.

child. Don't let yourself rust away. Your mind outwears all sorts of things you may set your heart upon; you can enjoy it when all other things are taken away." Miranda was chilled by her melancholy. Cousin Eva went on: "In our part of the country, in my time, we were so provincial—a woman didn't dare to think or act for herself. The whole world was a little that way," she said, "but we were the worst, I believe. I suppose you must know how I fought for votes for women when it almost made a pariah of me— I was turned out of my chair at the Seminary, but I'm glad I did it and I would do it again. You young things don't realize. You'll live in a better world because we worked for it."

Miranda knew something of Cousin Eva's career. She said sincerely, "I think it was brave of you, and I'm glad you did it, too. I loved your courage."

"It wasn't just showing off, mind you," said Cousin Eva, rejecting praise, fretfully. "Any fool can be brave. We were working for something we knew was right, and it turned out that we needed a lot of courage for it. That was all. I didn't expect to go to jail, but I went three times, and I'd go three times three more if it were necessary. We aren't voting yet," she said, "but we will be."

Miranda did not venture any answer, but she felt convinced that indeed women would be voting soon if nothing fatal happened to Cousin Eva. There was something in her manner which said such things could be left safely to her. Miranda was dimly fired for the cause herself; it seemed heroic and worth suffering for, but discouraging, too, to those who came after: Cousin Eva so plainly had swept the field clear of opportunity.

They were silent for a few minutes, while Cousin Eva rummaged in her handbag, bringing up odds and ends: peppermint drops, eye drops, a packet of needles, three handkerchiefs, a little bottle of violet perfume, a book of addresses, two buttons, one black, one white, and, finally, a packet of headache powders.

"Bring me a glass of water, will you, my dear?" she asked Miranda. She poured the headache powder on her tongue, swallowed the water, and put two peppermints in her mouth.

"So now they're going to bury Gabriel near Amy," she said after a while, as if her eased headache had started her on a new train of thought. "Miss Honey would like that, poor dear, if she could know. After listening to stories about Amy for twenty-five years, she must lie alone in her grave in Lexington while Gabriel sneaks off to Texas to make his bed with Amy again. It was a kind of life-long infidelity, Miranda, and now an eternal infidelity on top of that. He ought to be ashamed of himself."

"It was Aunt Amy he loved," said Miranda, wondering what Miss Honey could have been like before her long troubles with Uncle Gabriel. "First, anyway."

"Oh, that Amy," said Cousin Eva, her eyes glittering. "Your Aunt Amy was a devil and a mischief-maker, but I loved her dearly. I used to stand up for Amy when her reputation wasn't worth that." Her fingers snapped like castanets. "She used to say to me, in that gay soft way she had, 'Now, Eva, don't go talking votes for women when the lads ask you to dance. Don't recite Latin poems to 'em,' she would say, 'they got sick of that in school. Dance and say nothing, Eva,' she would say, her eyes perfectly devilish, 'and hold your chin up, Eva.' My chin was my weak point, you see. 'You'll never catch a husband if you don't look out,' she would say. Then she would laugh and fly away, and where did she fly to?" demanded Cousin Eva, her sharp eyes pinning Miranda down to the bitter facts of the case. "To scandal and to death, nowhere else."

"She was joking, Cousin Eva," said Miranda, innocently, "and everybody loved her."

"Not everybody, by a long shot," said Cousin Eva in triumph. "She had enemies. If she knew, she pretended she didn't. If she cared, she never said. You couldn't make her quarrel. She was sweet as a honeycomb to everybody. *Everybody*," she added, "that was the trouble. She went through life like a spoiled darling, doing as she pleased and letting other people suffer for it, and pick up the pieces after her. I never believed for one moment," said Cousin Eva, putting her mouth close to Miranda's ear and breathing peppermint hotly into it, "that Amy was an impure woman. Never! But let me tell you, there were plenty who did believe it. There were plenty to pity poor Gabriel for being so completely blinded by her. A great many persons were not surprised when they heard that Gabriel was perfectly miserable all the time, on their honeymoon, in New Orleans. Jealousy. And why not? But I used to say to such persons that, no matter what the appearances were, I had faith in Amy's virtue. Wild, I said, indiscreet, I said, heartless, I said, but *virtuous,* I feel certain. But you could hardly blame any-one for being mystified. The way she rose up suddenly from death's door to marry Gabriel Breaux, after refusing him and treat-ing him like a dog for years, looked odd, to say the least. To say the very least," she added, after a moment, "odd is a mild word for it. And there was something very mysterious about her death, only six weeks after marriage."

Miranda roused herself. She felt she knew this part of the story and could set Cousin Eva right about one thing. "She died of a hemorrhage from the lungs," said Miranda. "She had been ill for five years, don't you remember?"

Cousin Eva was ready for that. "Ha, that was the story, indeed. The official account, you might say. Oh, yes, I heard that often enough. But did you ever hear about that fellow Raymond some-body-or-other from Calcasieu Parish, almost a stranger, who per-suaded Amy to elope with him from a dance one night, and she just ran out into the darkness without even stopping for her cloak, and your poor dear nice father Harry—you weren't even thought of then—had to run him down to earth and shoot him?"

Miranda leaned back from the advancing flood of speech. "Cousin Eva, my father shot *at* him, don't you remember? He didn't hit him. . . ."

"Well, that's a pity."

". . . and they had only gone out for a breath of air between dances. It was Uncle Gabriel's jealousy. And my father shot at the man because he thought that was better than letting Uncle Gabriel fight a duel about Aunt Amy. There was *nothing* in the whole affair except Uncle Gabriel's jealousy."

"You poor baby," said Cousin Eva, and pity gave a light like daggers to her eyes, "you dear innocent, you—do you believe that? How old are you, anyway?"

"Just past eighteen," said Miranda.

"If you don't understand what I tell you," said Cousin Eva por-tentously, "you will later. Knowledge can't hurt you. You mustn't live in a romantic haze about life. You'll understand when you're married, at any rate."

"I'm married now, Cousin Eva," said Miranda, feeling for al-most the first time that it might be an advantage, "nearly a year. I eloped from school." It seemed very unreal even as she said it, and seemed to have nothing at all to do with the future; still, it was important, it must be declared, it was a situation in life which people seemed to be most exacting about, and the only feeling she could rouse in herself about it was an immense weariness as if it were an illness that she might one day hope to recover from.

"Shameful, shameful," cried Cousin Eva, genuinely repelled. "If you had been my child I should have brought you home and spanked you."

Miranda laughed out. Cousin Eva seemed to believe things could be arranged like that. She was so solemn and fierce, so comic and baffled.

"And you must know I should have just gone straight out again, through the nearest window," she taunted her. "If I went the first time, why not the second?"

"Yes, I suppose so," said Cousin Eva. "I hope you married rich."

"Not so very," said Miranda. "Enough." As if anyone could have stopped to think of such a thing!

Cousin Eva adjusted her spectacles and sized up Miranda's dress, her luggage, examined her engagement ring and wedding ring, with her nostrils fairly quivering as if she might smell out wealth on her.

"Well, that's better than nothing," said Cousin Eva. "I thank God every day of my life that I have a small income. It's a Rock of Ages. What would have become of me if I hadn't a cent of my own? Well, you'll be able now to do something for your family."

Miranda remembered what she had always heard about the Parringtons. They were money-hungry, they loved money and nothing else, and when they had got some they kept it. Blood was thinner than water between the Parringtons where money was concerned.

"We're pretty poor," said Miranda, stubbornly allying herself with her father's family instead of her husband's, "but a rich marriage is no way out," she said, with the snobbishness of poverty. She was thinking, "You don't know my branch of the family, dear Cousin Eva, if you think it is."

"Your branch of the family," said Cousin Eva, with that terrifying habit she had of lifting phrases out of one's mind, "has no more practical sense than so many children. Everything for love," she said, with a face of positive nausea, "that was it. Gabriel would have been rich if his grandfather had not disinherited him, but would Amy be sensible and marry him and make him settle down so the old man would have been pleased with him? No. And what could Gabriel do without money? I wish you could have seen the life he led Miss Honey, one day buying her Paris gowns and the next day pawning her earrings. It just depended on how the horses ran, and they ran worse and worse, and Gabriel drank more and more."

Miranda did not say, "I saw a little of it." She was trying to imagine Miss Honey in a Paris gown. She said, "But Uncle Gabriel was so mad about Aunt Amy, there was no question of her not marrying him at last, money or no money."

Cousin Eva strained her lips tightly over her teeth, let them fly again and leaned over, gripping Miranda's arm. "What I ask myself, what I ask myself over and over again," she whispered, "is, what connection did this man Raymond from Calcasieu have with Amy's sudden marriage to Gabriel, and *what* did Amy do to make away with herself so soon afterward? For mark my words, child, Amy wasn't so ill as all that. She'd been flying around for years after the doctors said her lungs were weak. Amy did away with herself to escape some disgrace, some exposure that she faced."

The beady black eyes glinted; Cousin Eva's face was quite frightening, so near and so intent. Miranda wanted to say, "Stop. Let her rest. What harm did she ever do you?" but she was timid and unnerved, and deep in her was a horrid fascination with the terrors and the darkness Cousin Eva had conjured up. What was the end of this story?

"She was a bad, wild girl, but I was fond of her to the last," said Cousin Eva. "She got into trouble somehow, and she couldn't get out again, and I have every reason to believe she killed herself with the drug they gave her to keep her quiet after a hemorrhage. If she didn't, what happened, what happened?"

"I don't know," said Miranda. "How should I know? She was very beautiful," she said, as if this explained everything. "Everybody said she was very beautiful."

"Not everybody," said Cousin Eva, firmly, shaking her head. "I for one never thought so. They made entirely too much fuss over her. She was good-looking enough, but why did they think she was beautiful? I cannot understand it. She was too thin when she was young, and later I always thought she was too fat, and again in her last year she was altogether too thin. She always got herself up to be looked at, and so people looked, of course. She rode too hard, and she danced too freely, and she talked too much, and you'd have to be blind, deaf and dumb not to notice her. I don't mean she was loud or vulgar, she wasn't, but she was *too free*," said Cousin Eva. She stopped for breath and put a peppermint in her mouth. Miranda could see Cousin Eva on the platform, making her speeches, stopping to take a peppermint. But why did she hate Aunt Amy so, when Aunt Amy was dead and she alive? Wasn't being alive enough?

"And her illness wasn't romantic either," said Cousin Eva, "though to hear them tell it she faded like a lily. Well, she coughed blood, if that's romantic. If they had made her take proper care of herself, if she had been nursed sensibly, she might have been alive today. But no, nothing of the kind. She lay wrapped in beautiful shawls on a sofa with flowers around her, eating as she liked or not eating, getting up after a hemorrhage and going out to ride or dance, sleeping with the windows closed; with crowds coming in and out laughing and talking at all hours, and Amy sitting up so her hair wouldn't get out of curl. And why wouldn't that sort of thing kill a well person in time? I have almost died twice in my life," said Cousin Eva, "and both times I was sent to a hospital where I belonged and left there until I came out. And I came out," she said, her voice deepening to a bugle note, "and I went to work again."

"Beauty goes, character stays," said the small voice of axiomatic morality in Miranda's ear. It was a dreary prospect; why was a strong character so deforming? Miranda felt she truly wanted to be strong, but how could she face it, seeing what it did to one?

"She had a lovely complexion," said Cousin Eva, "perfectly transparent with a flush on each cheekbone. But it was tuberculosis, and is disease beautiful? And she brought it on herself by drinking lemon and salt to stop her periods when she wanted to go to dances. There was a superstition among young girls about that. They fancied that young men could tell what ailed them by touching their hands, or even by looking at them. As if it mattered? But they were terribly self-conscious and they had immense respect for man's worldly wisdom in those days. My own notion is that a man couldn't—but anyway, the whole thing was stupid."

"I should have thought they'd have stayed at home if they couldn't manage better than that," said Miranda, feeling very knowledgeable and modern.

"They didn't dare. Those parties and dances were their market, a girl couldn't afford to miss out, there were always rivals waiting to cut the ground from under her. The rivalry—" said Cousin Eva, and her head lifted, she arched like a cavalry horse getting a whiff of the battlefield—"you can't imagine what the rivalry was like. The way those girls treated each other—nothing was too mean, nothing too false—"

Cousin Eva wrung her hands. "It was just sex," she said in despair; "their minds dwelt on nothing else. They didn't call it that, it was all smothered under pretty names, but that's all it was, sex." She looked out of the window into the darkness, her sunken cheek near Miranda flushed deeply. She turned back. "I took to the soap box and the platform when I was called upon," she said proudly, "and I went to jail when it was necessary, and my condition didn't make any difference. I was booed and jeered and shoved around just as if I had been in perfect health. But it was part of our philosophy not to let our physical handicaps make any difference to our work. You know what I mean," she said, as if until now it was all mystery. "Well, Amy carried herself with more spirit than the others, and she didn't seem to be making any sort of fight, but she was simply sex-ridden, like the rest. She behaved as if she hadn't a rival on earth, and she pretended not to know what marriage was about, but I know better. None of them had, and they didn't want to have, anything else to think about, and they didn't really know anything about that, so they simply festered inside—they festered—"

Miranda found herself deliberately watching a long procession of living corpses, festering women stepping gaily towards the charnel house, their corruption concealed under laces and flowers, their dead faces lifted smiling, and thought quite coldly, "Of course it was not like that. This is no more true than what I was told before, it's every bit as romantic," and she realized that she was tired of her intense Cousin Eva, she wanted to go to sleep, she wanted to be at home, she wished it were tomorrow and she could see her father and her sister, who were so alive and solid; who would mention her freckles and ask her if she wanted something to eat.

"My mother was not like that," she said, childishly. "My mother was a perfectly natural woman who liked to cook. I have seen some of her sewing," she said. "I have read her diary."

"Your mother was a saint," said Cousin Eva, automatically.

Miranda sat silent, outraged. "My mother was nothing of the sort," she wanted to fling in Cousin Eva's big front teeth. But Cousin Eva had been gathering bitterness until more speech came of it.

" 'Hold your chin up, Eva,' Amy used to tell me," she began, doubling up both her fists and shaking them a little. "All my life the whole family bedeviled me about my chin. My entire girlhood was spoiled by it. Can you imagine," she asked, with a ferocity that seemed much too deep for this one cause, "people who call themselves civilized spoiling life for a young girl because she had one unlucky feature? Of course, you understand perfectly it was all in the very best humor, everybody was very amusing about it, no harm meant—oh, no, no harm at all. That is the hellish thing about it. It is that I can't forgive," she cried out, and she twisted her hands together as if they were rags. "Ah, the family," she said, releasing her breath and sitting back quietly, "the whole hideous institution should be wiped from the face of the earth. It is the root of all human wrongs," she ended, and relaxed, and her face became calm. She was trembling. Miranda reached out and took Cousin Eva's hand and held it. The hand fluttered and lay still, and Cousin Eva said, "You've not the faintest idea what some of us went through, but I wanted you to hear the other side of the story. And I'm keeping you up when you need your beauty sleep," she said grimly, stirring herself with an immense rustle of petticoats.

Miranda pulled herself together, feeling limp, and stood up. Cousin Eva put out her hand again, and drew Miranda down to her. "Good night, you dear child," she said, "to think you're grown up." Miranda hesitated, then quite suddenly kissed her Cousin Eva on the cheek. The black eyes shone brightly through water for an instant, and Cousin Eva said with a warm note in her sharp clear orator's voice, "Tomorrow we'll be at home again. I'm looking forward to it, aren't you? Good night."

Miranda fell asleep while she was getting off her clothes. Instantly it was morning again. She was still trying to close her suit-case when the train pulled into the small station, and there on the platform she saw her father, looking tired and anxious, his hat pulled over his eyes. She rapped on the window to catch his atten-tion, then ran out and threw herself upon him. He said, "Well, here's my big girl," as if she were still seven, but his hands on her arms held her off, the tone was forced. There was no welcome for her, and there had not been since she had run away. She could not persuade herself to remember how it would be; between one home-coming and the next her mind refused to accept its own knowledge. Her father looked over her head and said, without surprise, "Why, hello, Eva, I'm glad somebody sent you a telegram." Miranda, rebuffed again, let her arms fall away again, with the same painful dull jerk of the heart.

"No one in my family," said Eva, her face framed in the thin black veil she reserved, evidently, for family funerals, "ever sent me a telegram in my life. I had the news from young Keziah who had it from young Gabriel. I suppose Gabe is here?"

"Everybody seems to be here," said Father. "The house is get-ting full."

"I'll go to the hotel if you like," said Cousin Eva.

"Damnation, no," said Father. "I didn't mean that. You'll come with us where you belong."

Skid, the handy man, grabbed the suitcases and started down the rocky village street. "We've got the car," said Father. He took Miranda by the hand, then dropped it again, and reached for Cousin Eva's elbow.

"I'm perfectly able, thank you," said Cousin Eva, shying away.

"If you're so independent now," said Father, "God help us when you get that vote."

Cousin Eva pushed back her veil. She was smiling merrily. She liked Harry, she always had liked him, he could tease as much as he liked. She slipped her arm through his. "So it's all over with poor Gabriel, isn't it?"

"Oh, yes," said Father, "it's all over, all right. They're pegging out pretty regularly now. It will be our turn next, Eva?"

"I don't know, and I don't care," said Eva, recklessly. "It's good to be back now and then, Harry, even if it is only for funerals. I feel sinfully cheerful."

"Oh, Gabriel wouldn't mind, he'd like seeing you cheerful. Gabriel was the cheerfullest cuss I ever saw, when we were young. Life for Gabriel," said Father, "was just one perpetual picnic."

"Poor fellow," said Cousin Eva.

"Poor old Gabriel," said Father, heavily.

Miranda walked along beside her father, feeling homeless, but not sorry for it. He had not forgiven her, she knew that. When would he? She could not guess, but she felt it would come of itself, without words and without acknowledgment on either side, for by the time it arrived neither of them would need to remember what had caused their division, nor why it had seemed so important. Surely old people cannot hold their grudges forever because the young want to live, too, she thought, in her arrogance, her pride. I will make my own mistakes, not yours; I cannot depend upon you beyond a certain point, why depend at all? There was something more beyond, but this was a first step to take, and she took it, walking in silence beside her elders who were no longer Cousin Eva and Father, since they had forgotten her presence, but had become Eva and Harry, who knew each other well, who were comfortable with each other, being contemporaries on equal terms, who occupied by right their place in this world, at the time of life to which they had arrived by paths familiar to them both. They need not play their roles of daughter, of son, to aged persons who did not understand them; nor of father and elderly female cousin to young persons whom they did not understand. They were precisely themselves; their eyes cleared, their voices relaxed into perfect naturalness, they need not weigh their words or calculate the effect of their manner. "It is I who have no place," thought Miranda. "Where are my own people and my own time?" She resented, slowly and deeply and in profound silence, the presence of these aliens who lectured and admonished her, who loved her with bitterness and denied her the right to look at the world with her own eyes, who demanded that she accept their version of life and yet could not tell her the truth, not in the smallest thing. "I hate them both," her most inner and secret mind said plainly, *"I will be free of them, I shall not even remember them."*

She sat in the front seat with Skid, the Negro boy. "Come back with us, Miranda," said Cousin Eva, with the sharp little note of elderly command, "there is plenty of room."

"No, thank you," said Miranda, in a firm cold voice. "I'm quite comfortable. Don't disturb yourself."

Neither of them noticed her voice or her manner. They sat back and went on talking steadily in their friendly family voices, talking about their dead, their living, their affairs, their prospects, their common memories, interrupting each other, catching each other up on small points of dispute, with a gaiety and freshness which Miranda had not known they were capable of, going over old memories and finding new points of interest in them.

Miranda could not hear the stories above the noisy motor, but she felt she knew them well, or stories like them. She knew too many stories like them, she wanted something new of her own. The language was familiar to them, but not to her, not any more. The house, her father had said, was full. It would be full of cousins, many of them strangers. Would there be any young cousins there, to whom she could talk about things they both knew? She felt a vague distaste for seeing cousins. There were too many of them and her blood rebelled against the ties of blood. She was sick to death of cousins. She did not want any more ties with this house, she was going to leave it, and she was not going back to her husband's family either. She would have no more bonds that smothered her in love and hatred. She knew now why she had run away to marriage, and she knew that she was going to run away from marriage, and she was not going to stay in any place, with anyone, that threatened to forbid her making her own discoveries, that said "No" to her. She hoped no one had taken her old room, she would like to sleep there once more, she would say good-by there where she had loved sleeping once, sleeping and waking and waiting to be grown, to begin to live. Oh, what is life, she asked herself in desperate seriousness, in those childish unanswerable words, and what shall I do with it? It is something of my own, she thought in a fury of jealous possessiveness, what shall I make of it? She did not know that she asked herself this because all her earliest training had argued that life was a substance, a material to be used, it took shape and direction and meaning only as the possessor guided and worked it; living was a progress of continuous and varied acts of the will directed towards a definite end. She had been assured that there were good and evil ends, one must make a choice. But what was good, and what was evil? I hate love, she thought, as if this were the answer, I hate loving and being loved, I hate it. And her disturbed and seething mind received a shock of comfort from this sudden collapse of an old painful structure of distorted images and misconceptions. "You don't know anything about it," said Miranda to herself, with extraordinary clearness as if she were an elder admonishing some younger misguided creature. "You have to find out about it." But nothing in her prompted her to decide, "I will now do this, I will be that, I will go yonder, I will take a certain road to a certain end." There are questions to be asked first, she thought, but who will answer them? No one, or there will be too many answers, none of them right. What is the truth, she asked herself as intently as if the question had never been asked, the truth, even about the smallest, the least important of all the things I must find out? and where shall I begin to look for it? Her mind closed stubbornly against remembering, not the past but the legend of the past, other people's memory of the past, at which she had spent her life peering in wonder like a child at a magic-lantern show. Ah, but there is my own life to come yet, she thought, my own life now and beyond. I don't want any promises, I won't have false hopes, I won't be romantic about myself. I can't live in their world any longer, she told herself, listening to the voices back of her. Let them tell their stories to each other. Let them go on explaining how things happened. I don't care. At least I can know the truth about what happens to me, she assured herself silently, making a promise to herself, in her hopefulness, her ignorance.

Noon Wine

TIME: *1896–1905*
PLACE: *Small South Texas Farm*

The two grubby small boys with tow-colored hair who were digging among the ragweed in the front yard sat back on their heels and said, "Hello," when the tall bony man with straw-colored hair turned in at their gate. He did not pause at the gate; it had swung back, conveniently half open, long ago, and was now sunk so firmly on its broken hinges no one thought of trying to close it. He did not even glance at the small boys, much less give them good-day. He just clumped down his big square dusty shoes one after the other steadily, like a man following a plow, as if he knew the place well and knew where he was going and what he would find there. Rounding the right-hand corner of the house under the row of chinaberry trees, he walked up to the side porch where Mr. Thompson was pushing a big swing churn back and forth.

Mr. Thompson was a tough weather-beaten man with stiff black hair and a week's growth of black whiskers. He was a noisy proud man who held his neck so straight his whole face stood level with his Adam's apple, and the whiskers continued down his neck and disappeared into a black thatch under his open collar. The churn rumbled and swished like the belly of a trotting horse, and Mr. Thompson seemed somehow to be driving a horse with one hand, reining it in and urging it forward; and every now and then he turned halfway around and squirted a tremendous spit of tobacco juice out over the steps. The door stones were brown and gleaming with fresh tobacco juice. Mr. Thompson had been churning quite a while and he was tired of it. He was just fetching a mouthful of juice to squirt again when the stranger came around the corner and stopped. Mr. Thompson saw a narrow-chested man with blue eyes so pale they were almost white, looking and not looking at him from a long gaunt face, under white eyebrows. Mr. Thompson judged him to be another of these Irishmen, by his long upper lip.

"Howdy do, sir," said Mr. Thompson politely, swinging his churn.

"I need work," said the man, clearly enough but with some kind of foreign accent Mr. Thompson couldn't place. It wasn't Cajun and it wasn't Nigger and it wasn't Dutch, so it had him stumped. "You need a man here?"

Mr. Thompson gave the churn a great shove and it swung back and forth several times on its own momentum. He sat on the steps, shot his quid into the grass, and said, "Set down. Maybe we can make a deal. I been kinda lookin' round for somebody. I had two niggers but they got into a cutting scrape up the creek last week, one of 'em dead now and the other in the hoosegow at Cold Springs. Neither one of 'em worth killing, come right down to it. So it looks like I'd better get somebody. Where'd you work last?"

"North Dakota," said the man, folding himself down on the other end of the steps, but not as if he were tired. He folded up and settled down as if it would be a long time before he got up again. He never had looked at Mr. Thompson, but there wasn't anything sneaking in his eye, either. He didn't seem to be looking anywhere else. His eyes sat in his head and let things pass by them. They didn't seem to be expecting to see anything worth looking at. Mr. Thompson waited a long time for the man to say something more, but he had gone into a brown study.

"North Dakota," said Mr. Thompson, trying to remember where that was. "That's a right smart distance off, seems to me."

"I can do everything on farm," said the man; "cheap. I need work."

Mr. Thompson settled himself to get down to business. "My name's Thompson, Mr. Royal Earle Thompson," he said.

"I'm Mr. Helton," said the man, "Mr. Olaf Helton." He did not move.

"Well, now," said Mr. Thompson in his most carrying voice, "I guess we'd better talk turkey."

When Mr. Thompson expected to drive a bargain he always grew very hearty and jovial. There was nothing wrong with him except that he hated like the devil to pay wages. He said so himself. "You furnish grub and a shack," he said, "and then you got to pay 'em besides. It ain't right. Besides the wear and tear on your implements," he said, "they just let everything go to rack and ruin." So he began to laugh and shout his way through the deal.

"Now, what I want to know is, how much you fixing to gouge outa me?" he brayed, slapping his knee. After he had kept it up as long as he could, he quieted down, feeling a little sheepish, and cut himself a chew. Mr. Helton was staring out somewhere between the barn and the orchard, and seemed to be sleeping with his eyes open.

"I'm good worker," said Mr. Helton as from the tomb. "I get dollar a day."

Mr. Thompson was so shocked he forgot to start laughing again at the top of his voice until it was nearly too late to do any good. "Haw, haw," he bawled. "Why, for a dollar a day I'd hire out myself. What kinda work is it where they pay you a dollar a day?"

"Wheatfields, North Dakota," said Mr. Helton, not even smiling.

Mr. Thompson stopped laughing. "Well, this ain't any wheatfield by a long shot. This is more of a dairy farm," he said, feeling apologetic. "My wife, she was set on a dairy, she seemed to like working around with cows and calves, so I humored her. But it was a mistake," he said. "I got nearly everything to do, anyhow. My wife ain't very strong. She's sick today, that's a fact. She's been porely for the last few days. We plant a little feed, and a corn patch, and there's the orchard, and a few pigs and chickens, but our main hold is the cows. Now just speakin' as one man to another, there ain't any money in it. Now I can't give you no dollar a day because ackshally I don't make that much out of it. No, sir, we get along on a lot less than a dollar a day, I'd say, if we figger up everything in the long run. Now, I paid seven dollars a month to the two niggers, three-fifty each, and grub, but what I say is, one middlin'-good white man ekals a whole passel of niggers any day in the week, so I'll give you seven dollars and you eat at the table with us, and you'll be treated like a white man, as the feller says—"

"That's all right," said Mr. Helton. "I take it."

"Well, now I guess we'll call it a deal, hey?" Mr. Thompson

jumped up as if he had remembered important business. "Now, you just take hold of that churn and give it a few swings, will you, while I ride to town on a coupla little errands. I ain't been able to leave the place all week. I guess you know what to do with butter after you get it, don't you?"

"I know," said Mr. Helton without turning his head. "I know butter business." He had a strange drawling voice, and even when he spoke only two words his voice waved slowly up and down and the emphasis was in the wrong place. Mr. Thompson wondered what kind of foreigner Mr. Helton could be.

"Now just where did you say you worked last?" he asked, as if he expected Mr. Helton to contradict himself.

"North Dakota," said Mr. Helton.

"Well, one place is good as another once you get used to it," said Mr. Thompson, amply. "You're a forriner, ain't you?"

"I'm a Swede." said Mr. Helton, beginning to swing the churn.

Mr. Thompson let forth a booming laugh, as if this was the best joke on somebody he'd ever heard. "Well, I'll be damned," he said at the top of his voice. "A Swede: well, now, I'm afraid you'll get pretty lonesome around here. I never seen any Swedes in this neck of the woods."

"That's all right," said Mr. Helton. He went on swinging the churn as if he had been working on the place for years.

"In fact, I might as well tell you, you're practically the first Swede I ever laid eyes on."

"That's all right," said Mr. Helton.

Mr. Thompson went into the front room where Mrs. Thompson was lying down, with the green shades drawn. She had a bowl of water by her on the table and a wet cloth over her eyes. She took the cloth off at the sound of Mr. Thompson's boots and said, "What's all the noise out there? Who is it?"

"Got a feller out there says he's a Swede, Ellie," said Mr Thompson; "says he knows how to make butter."

"I hope it turns out to be the truth," said Mrs. Thompson. "Looks like my head never will get any better."

"Don't you worry," said Mr. Thompson. "You fret too much. Now I'm gointa ride into town and get a little order of groceries."

"Don't you linger, now, Mr. Thompson," said Mrs. Thompson.

"Don't go to the hotel." She meant the saloon; the proprietor also had rooms for rent upstairs.

"Just a coupla little toddies," said Mr. Thompson, laughing loudly, "never hurt anybody."

"I never took a dram in my life," said Mrs. Thompson, "and what's more I never will."

"I wasn't talking about the womenfolks," said Mr. Thompson.

The sound of the swinging churn rocked Mrs. Thompson first into a gentle doze, then a deep drowse from which she waked suddenly knowing that the swinging had stopped a good while ago. She sat up shading her weak eyes from the flat strips of late summer sunlight between the sill and the lowered shades. There she was, thank God, still alive, with supper to cook but no churning on hand, and her head still bewildered, but easy. Slowly she realized she had been hearing a new sound even in her sleep. Somebody was playing a tune on the harmonica, not merely shrilling up and down making a sickening noise, but really playing a pretty tune, merry and sad.

She went out through the kitchen, stepped off the porch, and stood facing the east, shading her eyes. When her vision cleared and settled, she saw a long, pale-haired man in blue jeans sitting in the doorway of the hired man's shack, tilted back in a kitchen chair, blowing away at the harmonica with his eyes shut. Mrs. Thompson's heart fluttered and sank. Heavens, he looked lazy and worthless, he did, now. First a lot of no-count fiddling darkies and then a no-count white man. It was just like Mr. Thompson to take on that kind. She did wish he would be more considerate, and take a little trouble with his business. She wanted to believe in her husband, and there were too many times when she couldn't. She wanted to believe that tomorrow, or at least the day after, life, such a battle at best, was going to be better.

She walked past the shack without glancing aside, stepping carefully, bent at the waist because of the nagging pain in her side, and went to the springhouse, trying to harden her mind to speak very plainly to that new hired man if he had not done his work.

The milk house was only another shack of weather-beaten boards nailed together hastily years before because they needed a milk house; it was meant to be temporary, and it was; already shapeless, leaning this way and that over a perpetual cool trickle of water that fell from a little grot, almost choked with pallid ferns. No one else in the whole countryside had such a spring on his land. Mr. and Mrs. Thompson felt they had a fortune in that spring, if ever they get around to doing anything with it.

Rickety wooden shelves clung at hazard in the square around the small pool where the larger pails of milk and butter stood, fresh and sweet in the cold water. One hand supporting her flat, pained side, the other shading her eyes, Mrs. Thompson leaned over and peered into the pails. The cream had been skimmed and set aside, there was a rich roll of butter, the wooden molds and shallow pans had been scrubbed and scalded for the first time in who knows when, the barrel was full of buttermilk ready for the pigs and the weanling calves, the hard packed-dirt floor had been swept smooth. Mrs. Thompson straightened up again, smiling tenderly. She had been ready to scold him, a poor man who needed a job, who had just come there and who might not have been expected to do things properly at first. There was nothing she could do to make up for the injustice she had done him in her thoughts but to tell him how she appreciated his good clean work, finished already, in no time at all. She ventured near the door of the shack with her careful steps; Mr. Helton opened his eyes, stopped playing, and brought his chair down straight, but did not look at her, or get up. She was a little frail woman with long thick brown hair in a braid, a suffering patient mouth and diseased eyes which cried easily. She wove her fingers into an eyeshade, thumbs on temples, and, winking her tearful lids, said with a polite little manner, "Howdy do, sir. I'm Miz Thompson, and I wanted to tell you I think you did real well in the milk house. It's always been a hard place to keep."

He said, "That's all right," in a slow voice, without moving.

Mrs. Thompson waited a moment. "That's a pretty tune you're playing. Most folks don't seem to get much music out of a harmonica."

Mr. Helton sat humped over, long legs sprawling, his spine in a bow, running his thumb over the square mouth-stops; except for his moving hand he might have been asleep. The harmonica was a big shiny new one, and Mrs. Thompson, her gaze wandering about, counted five others, all good and expensive, standing in a row on the shelf beside his cot. "He must carry them around in his jumper pocket," she thought, and noted there was not a sign of any other possession lying about. "I see you're mighty fond of music," she said. "We used to have an old accordion, and Mr. Thompson could play it right smart, but the little boys broke it up."

Mr. Helton stood up rather suddenly, the chair clattered under him, his knees straightened though his shoulders did not, and he looked at the floor as if he were listening carefully. "You know how little boys are," said Mrs. Thompson. "You'd better set them harmonicas on a high shelf or they'll be after them. They're great hands for getting into things. I try to learn 'em, but it don't do much good."

Mr. Helton, in one wide gesture of his long arms, swept his harmonicas up against his chest, and from there transferred them in a row to the ledge where the roof joined to the wall. He pushed them back almost out of sight.

"That'll do, maybe," said Mrs. Thompson. "Now I wonder," she said, turning and closing her eyes helplessly against the stronger western light, "I wonder what became of them little tads. I can't keep up with them." She had a way of speaking about her children as if they were rather troublesome nephews on a prolonged visit.

"Down by the creek," said Mr. Helton, in his hollow voice. Mrs. Thompson, pausing confusedly, decided he had answered her question. He stood in silent patience, not exactly waiting for her to go, perhaps, but pretty plainly not waiting for anything else. Mrs. Thompson was perfectly accustomed to all kinds of men full of all kinds of cranky ways. The point was, to find out just how Mr. Helton's crankiness was different from any other man's, and then get used to it, and let him feel at home. Her father had been cranky, her brothers and uncles had all been set in their ways and none of them alike; and every hired man she'd ever seen had quirks and crotchets of his own. Now here was Mr. Helton, who was a Swede, who wouldn't talk, and who played the harmonica besides.

"They'll be needing something to eat," said Mrs. Thompson in a vague friendly way, "pretty soon. Now I wonder what I ought to be thinking about for supper? Now what do you like to eat, Mr. Helton? We always have plenty of good butter and milk and cream, that's a blessing. Mr. Thompson says we ought to sell all of it, but I say my family comes first." Her little face went all out of shape in a pained blind smile.

"I eat anything," said Mr. Helton, his words wandering up and down.

He *can't* talk, for one thing, thought Mrs. Thompson; it's a shame to keep at him when he don't know the language good. She took a slow step away from the shack, looking back over her shoulder. "We usually have cornbread except on Sundays," she told him. "I suppose in your part of the country you don't get much good cornbread."

Not a word from Mr. Helton. She saw from her eye-corner that he had sat down again, looking at his harmonica, chair tilted. She hoped he would remember it was getting near milking time. As she moved away, he started playing again, the same tune.

Milking time came and went. Mrs. Thompson saw Mr. Helton going back and forth between the cow barn and the milk house. He swung along in an easy lope, shoulders bent, head hanging, the big buckets balancing like a pair of scales at the ends of his bony arms. Mr. Thompson rode in from town sitting straighter than usual, chin in, a towsack full of supplies swung behind the saddle. After a trip to the barn, he came into the kitchen full of good will, and gave Mrs. Thompson a hearty smack on the cheek after dusting her face off with his tough whiskers. He had been to the hotel, that was plain. "Took a look around the premises, Ellie," he shouted. "That Swede sure is grinding out the labor. But he is the closest mouthed feller I ever met up with in all my days. Looks like he's scared he'll crack his jaw if he opens his front teeth."

Mrs. Thompson was stirring up a big bowl of buttermilk cornbread. "You smell like a toper, Mr. Thompson," she said with perfect dignity. "I wish you'd get one of the little boys to bring me in an extra load of firewood. I'm thinking about baking a batch of cookies tomorrow."

Mr. Thompson, all at once smelling the liquor on his own breath, sneaked out, justly rebuked, and brought in the firewood himself. Arthur and Herbert, grubby from thatched head to toes, from skin to shirt, came stamping in yelling for supper. "Go wash your faces and comb your hair," said Mrs. Thompson, automatically. They retired to the porch. Each one put his hand under the pump and wet his forelock, combed it down with his fingers, and returned at once to the kitchen, where all the fair prospects of life were centered. Mrs. Thompson set an extra plate and commanded Arthur, the eldest, eight years old, to call Mr. Helton for supper.

Arthur, without moving from the spot, bawled like a bull calf, "Saaaaaay, Hellllllton, suuuuuupper's ready!" and added in a lower voice, "You big Swede!"

"Listen to me," said Mrs. Thompson, "that's no way to act. Now you go out there and ask him decent, or I'll get your daddy to give you a good licking."

Mr. Helton loomed, long and gloomy, in the doorway. "Sit right there," boomed Mr. Thompson, waving his arm. Mr. Helton swung his square shoes across the kitchen in two steps, slumped onto the bench and sat. Mr. Thompson occupied his chair at the head of the table, the two boys scrambled into place opposite Mr. Helton, and Mrs. Thompson sat at the end nearest the stove. Mrs. Thompson clasped her hands, bowed her head and said aloud hastily, "Lord, for all these and Thy other blessings we thank Thee in Jesus' name, amen," trying to finish before Herbert's rusty little paw reached the nearest dish. Otherwise she would be duty-bound to send him away from the table, and growing children need their meals. Mr. Thompson and Arthur always waited, but Herbert, aged six, was too young to take training yet.

Mr. and Mrs. Thompson tried to engage Mr. Helton in conversation, but it was a failure. They tried first the weather, and then the crops, and then the cows, but Mr. Helton simply did not reply. Mr. Thompson then told something funny he had seen in town. It was about some of the other old grangers at the hotel, friends of his, giving beer to a goat, and the goat's subsequent behavior. Mr. Helton did not seem to hear. Mrs. Thompson laughed dutifully, but she didn't think it was very funny. She had heard it often before, though Mr. Thompson, each time he told it, pretended it had happened that self-same day. It must have happened years ago if it ever happened at all, and it had never been a story that Mrs. Thompson thought suitable for mixed company. The whole thing came of Mr. Thompson's weakness for a dram too much now and then, though he voted for local option at every election. She passed the food to Mr. Helton, who took a helping of everything, but not much, not enough to keep him up to his full powers if he expected to go on working the way he had started.

At last, he took a fair-sized piece of cornbread, wiped his plate up as clean as if it had been licked by a hound dog, stuffed his mouth full, and, still chewing, slid off the bench and started for the door.

"Good night, Mr. Helton," said Mrs. Thompson, and the other Thompsons took it up in a scattered chorus. "Good night, Mr. Helton!"

"Good night," said Mr. Helton's wavering voice grudgingly from the darkness.

"Gude not," said Arthur, imitating Mr. Helton.

"Gude not," said Herbert, the copy-cat.

"You don't do it right," said Arthur. "Now listen to me. Guuuuuude naht," and he ran a hollow scale in a luxury of successful impersonation. Herbert almost went into a fit with joy.

"Now you *stop* that," said Mrs. Thompson. "He can't help the way he talks. You ought to be ashamed of yourselves, both of you, making fun of a poor stranger like that. How'd you like to be a stranger in a strange land?"

"I'd like it," said Arthur. "I think it would be fun."

"They're both regular heathens, Ellie," said Mr. Thompson. "Just plain ignoramuses." He turned the face of awful fatherhood upon his young. "You're both going to get sent to school next year, and that'll knock some sense into you."

"I'm going to git sent to the 'formatory when I'm old enough," piped up Herbert. "That's where I'm goin'."

"Oh, you are, are you?" asked Mr. Thompson. "Who says so?"

"The Sunday School Supintendant," said Herbert, a bright boy showing off.

"You see?" said Mr. Thompson, staring at his wife. "What did I tell you?" He became a hurricane of wrath. "Get to bed, you two," he roared until his Adam's apple shuddered. "Get now before I take the hide off you!" They got, and shortly from their attic bedroom the sounds of scuffling and snorting and giggling and growling filled the house and shook the kitchen ceiling.

Mrs. Thompson held her head and said in a small uncertain

voice, "It's no use picking on them when they're so young and tender. I can't stand it."

"My goodness, Ellie," said Mr. Thompson, "we've got to raise 'em. We can't just let 'em grow up hog wild."

She went on in another tone. "That Mr. Helton seems all right, even if he can't be made to talk. Wonder how he comes to be so far from home."

"Like I said, he isn't no whamper-jaw," said Mr. Thompson, "but he sure knows how to lay out the work. I guess that's the main thing around here. Country's full of fellers trampin' round looking for work."

Mrs. Thompson was gathering up the dishes. She now gathered up Mr. Thompson's plate from under his chin. "To tell you the honest truth," she remarked, "I think it's a mighty good change to have a man round the place who knows how to work and keep his mouth shut. Means he'll keep out of our business. Not that we've got anything to hide, but it's convenient."

"That's a fact," said Mr. Thompson. "Haw, haw," he shouted suddenly. "Means you can do all the talking, huh?"

"The only thing," went on Mrs. Thompson, "is this: he don't eat hearty enough to suit me. I like to see a man set down and relish a good meal. My granma used to say it was no use putting dependence on a man who won't set down and make out his dinner. I hope it won't be that way this time."

"Tell *you* the truth, Ellie," said Mr. Thompson, picking his teeth with a fork and leaning back in the best of good humors, "I always thought your granma was a ter'ble ole fool. She'd just say the first thing that popped into her head and call it God's wisdom."

"My granma wasn't anybody's fool. Nine times out of ten she knew what she was talking about. I always say, the first thing you think is the best thing you can say."

"Well," said Mr. Thompson, going into another shout, "You're so reefined about that goat story, you just try speaking out in mixed comp'ny sometime! You just try it. S'pose you happened to be thinking about a hen and a rooster, hey? I reckon you'd shock the Babtist preacher!" He gave her a good pinch on her thin little rump. "No more meat on you than a rabbit," he said, fondly. "Now I like 'em cornfed."

Mrs. Thompson looked at him open-eyed and blushed. She

could see better by lamplight. "Why, Mr. Thompson, sometimes I think you're the evilest-minded man that ever lived." She took a handful of hair on the crown of his head and gave it a good, slow pull. "That's to show you how it feels, pinching so hard when you're supposed to be playing," she said, gently.

In spite of his situation in life, Mr. Thompson had never been able to outgrow his deep conviction that running a dairy and chasing after chickens was woman's work. He was fond of saying that he could plow a furrow, cut sorghum, shuck corn, handle a team, build a corn crib, as well as any man. Buying and selling, too, were man's work. Twice a week he drove the spring wagon to market with the fresh butter, a few eggs, fruits in their proper season, sold them, pocketed the change, and spent it as seemed best, being careful not to dig into Mrs. Thompson's pin money.

But from the first the cows worried him, coming up regularly twice a day to be milked, standing there reproaching him with their smug female faces. Calves worried him, fighting the rope and strangling themselves until their eyes bulged, trying to get at the teat. Wrestling with a calf unmanned him, like having to change a baby's diaper. Milk worried him, coming bitter sometimes, drying up, turning sour. Hens worried him, cackling, clucking, hatching out when you least expected it and leading their broods into the barnyard where the horses could step on them; dying of roup and wryneck and getting plagues of chicken lice; laying eggs all over God's creation so that half of them were spoiled before a man could find them, in spite of a rack of nests Mrs. Thompson had set out for them in the feed room. Hens were a blasted nuisance.

Slopping hogs was hired man's work, in Mr. Thompson's opinion. Killing hogs was a job for the boss, but scraping them and cutting them up was for the hired man again; and again woman's proper work was dressing meat, smoking, pickling, and making lard and sausage. All his carefully limited fields of activity were related somehow to Mr. Thompson's feeling for the appearance of things, his own appearance in the sight of God and man. "It don't *look* right," was his final reason for not doing anything he did not wish to do.

It was his dignity and his reputation that he cared about, and there were only a few kinds of work manly enough for Mr. Thompson to undertake with his own hands. Mrs. Thompson, to whom so many forms of work would have been becoming, had simply gone down on him early. He saw, after a while, how short-sighted it had been of him to expect much from Mrs. Thompson; he had fallen in love with her delicate waist and lace-trimmed petticoats and big blue eyes, and, though all those charms had disappeared, she had in the meantime become Ellie to him, not at all the same person as Miss Ellen Bridges, popular Sunday School teacher in the Mountain City First Baptist Church, but his dear wife, Ellie, who was not strong. Deprived as he was, however, of the main support in life which a man might expect in marriage, he had almost without knowing it resigned himself to failure. Head erect, a prompt payer of taxes, yearly subscriber to the preacher's salary, land owner and father of a family, employer, a hearty good fellow among men, Mr. Thompson knew, without putting it into words, that he had been going steadily down hill. God amighty, it did look like somebody around the place might take a rake in hand now and then and clear up the clutter around the barn and the kitchen steps. The wagon shed was so full of broken-down machinery and ragged harness and old wagon wheels and battered milk pails and rotting lumber you could hardly drive in there any more. Not a soul on the place would raise a hand to it, and as for him, he had all he could do with his regular work. He would sometimes in the slack season sit for hours worrying about it, squirting tobacco on the ragweeds growing in a thicket against the wood pile, wondering what a fellow could do, handicapped as he was. He looked forward to the boys growing up soon; he was going to put them through the mill just as his own father had done with him when he was a boy; they were going to learn how to take hold and run the place right. He wasn't going to overdo it, but those two boys were going to earn their salt, or he'd know why. Great big lubbers sitting around whittling! Mr. Thompson sometimes grew quite enraged with them, when imagining their possible future, big lubbers sitting around whittling or thinking about fishing trips. Well, he'd put a stop to that, mighty damn quick.

As the seasons passed, and Mr. Helton took hold more and more, Mr. Thompson began to relax in his mind a little. There seemed to be nothing the fellow couldn't do, all in the day's work and as a matter of course. He got up at five o'clock in the morning, boiled his own coffee and fried his own bacon and was out in the cow lot before Mr. Thompson had even begun to yawn, stretch, groan, roar and thump around looking for his jeans. He milked the cows, kept the milk house, and churned the butter; rounded the hens up and somehow persuaded them to lay in the nests, not under the house and behind the haystacks; he fed them regularly and they hatched out until you couldn't set a foot down for them. Little by little the piles of trash around the barns and house disappeared. He carried buttermilk and corn to the hogs, and curried cockleburs out of the horses' manes. He was gentle with the calves, if a little grim with the cows and hens; judging by his conduct, Mr. Helton had never heard of the difference between man's and woman's work on a farm.

In the second year, he showed Mr. Thompson the picture of a cheese press in a mail order catalogue, and said, "This is a good thing. You buy this, I make cheese." The press was bought and Mr. Helton did make cheese, and it was sold, along with the increased butter and the crates of eggs. Sometimes Mr. Thompson felt a little contemptuous of Mr. Helton's ways. It did seem kind of picayune for a man to go around picking up half a dozen ears of corn that had fallen off the wagon on the way from the field, gathering up fallen fruit to feed to the pigs, storing up old nails and stray parts of machinery, spending good time stamping a fancy pattern on the butter before it went to market. Mr. Thompson, sitting up high on the spring-wagon seat, with the decorated butter in a five-gallon lard can wrapped in wet towsack, driving to town, chirruping to the horses and snapping the reins over their backs, sometimes thought that Mr. Helton was a pretty meeching sort of fellow; but he never gave way to these feelings, he knew a good thing when he had it. It was a fact the hogs were in better shape and sold for more money. It was a fact that Mr. Thompson stopped buying feed, Mr. Helton managed the crops so well. When beef- and hog-slaughtering time came, Mr. Helton knew how to save the scraps that Mr. Thompson had thrown away, and wasn't above scraping guts and filling them with sausages that he made by his own methods. In all, Mr. Thompson had no grounds for complaint. In the third year, he raised Mr. Helton's wages, though Mr. Helton had not asked for a raise. The fourth year, when Mr. Thompson was not only out of debt but had a little cash in the bank, he raised Mr. Helton's wages again, two dollars and a half a month each time.

"The man's worth it, Ellie," said Mr. Thompson, in a glow of self-justification for his extravagance. "He's made this place pay, and I want him to know I appreciate it."

Mr. Helton's silence, the pallor of his eyebrows and hair, his long, glum jaw and eyes that refused to see anything, even the work under his hands, had grown perfectly familiar to the Thompsons. At first, Mrs. Thompson complained a little. "It's like sitting down at the table with a disembodied spirit," she said. "You'd think he'd find something to say, sooner or later."

"Let him alone," said Mr. Thompson. "When he gets ready to talk, he'll talk."

The years passed, and Mr. Helton never got ready to talk. After his work was finished for the day, he would come up from the barn or the milk house or the chicken house, swinging his lantern, his big shoes clumping like pony hoofs on the hard path. They, sitting in the kitchen in the winter, or on the back porch in summer, would hear him drag out his wooden chair, hear the creak of it tilted back, and then for a little while he would play his single tune on one or another of his harmonicas. The harmonicas were in different keys, some lower and sweeter than the others, but the same changeless tune went on, a strange tune, with sudden turns in it, night after night, and sometimes even in the afternoons when Mr. Helton sat down to catch his breath. At first the Thompsons liked it very much, and always stopped to listen. Later there came a time when they were fairly sick of it, and began to wish to each other that he would learn a new one. At last they did not hear it any more, it was as natural as the sound of the wind rising in the evenings, or the cows lowing, or their own voices.

Mrs. Thompson pondered now and then over Mr. Helton's soul. He didn't seem to be a church-goer, and worked straight through Sunday as if it were any common day of the week. "I think we ought to invite him to go to hear Dr. Martin," she told Mr. Thompson. "It isn't very Christian of us not to ask him. He's not a forward kind of man. He'd wait to be asked."

"Let him alone," said Mr. Thompson. "The way I look at it, his religion is every man's own business. Besides, he ain't got any Sunday clothes. He wouldn't want to go to church in them jeans and jumpers of his. I don't know what he does with his money. He certainly don't spend it foolishly."

Still, once the notion got into her head, Mrs. Thompson could not rest until she invited Mr. Helton to go to church with the family next Sunday. He was pitching hay into neat little piles in the field back of the orchard. Mrs. Thompson put on smoked glasses and a sunbonnet and walked all the way down there to speak to him. He stopped and leaned on his pitchfork, listening, and for a moment Mrs. Thompson was almost frightened at his face. The pale eyes seemed to glare past her, the eyebrows frowned, the long jaw hardened. "I got work," he said bluntly, and lifting his pitchfork he turned from her and began to toss the hay. Mrs. Thompson, her feelings hurt, walked back thinking that by now she should be used to Mr. Helton's ways, but it did seem like a man, even a foreigner, could be just a little polite when you gave him a Christian invitation. "He's not polite, that's the only thing I've got against him," she said to Mr. Thompson. "He just can't seem to behave like other people. You'd think he had a grudge against the world," she said. "I sometimes don't know what to make of it."

In the second year something had happened that made Mrs. Thompson uneasy, the kind of thing she could not put into words, hardly into thoughts, and if she had tried to explain to Mr. Thompson it would have sounded worse than it was, or not bad enough. It was that kind of queer thing that seems to be giving a warning, and yet, nearly always nothing comes of it. It was on a hot, still spring day, and Mrs. Thompson had been down to the garden patch to pull some new carrots and green onions and string beans for dinner. As she worked, sunbonnet low over her eyes, putting each kind of vegetable in a pile by itself in her basket, she noticed how neatly Mr. Helton weeded, and how rich the soil was. He had spread it all over with manure from the barns, and worked it in, in the fall, and the vegetables were coming up fine and full. She walked back under the nubbly little fig trees where the unpruned branches leaned almost to the ground, and the thick leaves made a cool screen. Mrs. Thompson was always looking for shade to save her eyes. So she, looking idly about, saw through the screen a sight that struck her as very strange. If it had been a noisy spectacle, it would have been quite natural. It was the silence that struck her. Mr. Helton was shaking Arthur by the shoulders, ferociously, his face most terribly fixed and pale. Arthur's head snapped back and forth and he had not stiffened in resistance, as he did when Mrs. Thompson tried to shake him. His eyes were rather frightened, but surprised, too, probably more surprised than anything else. Herbert stood by meekly, watching. Mr. Helton dropped Arthur, and seized Herbert, and shook him with the same methodical ferocity, the same face of hatred. Herbert's mouth crumpled as if he would cry, but he made no sound. Mr. Helton let him go, turned and strode into the shack, and the little boys ran, as if for their lives, without a word. They disappeared around the corner to the front of the house.

Mrs. Thompson took time to set her basket on the kitchen table, to push her sunbonnet back on her head and draw it forward again, to look in the stove and make certain the fire was going, before she followed the boys. They were sitting huddled together under a clump of chinaberry trees in plain sight of her bedroom window, as if it were a safe place they had discovered.

"What are you doing?" asked Mrs. Thompson.

They looked hang-dog from under their foreheads and Arthur mumbled, "Nothin'."

"Nothing *now,* you mean," said Mrs. Thompson, severely. "Well, I have plenty for you to do. Come right in here this minute and help me fix vegetables. This minute."

They scrambled up very eagerly and followed her close. Mrs. Thompson tried to imagine what they had been up to; she did not like the notion of Mr. Helton taking it on himself to correct her little boys, but she was afraid to ask them for reasons. They might tell her a lie, and she would have to overtake them in it, and whip them. Or she would have to pretend to believe them, and they would get in the habit of lying. Or they might tell her the truth, and it would be something she would have to whip them for. The very thought of it gave her a headache. She supposed she might ask Mr. Helton, but it was not her place to ask. She would wait and tell Mr. Thompson, and let him get at the bottom of it. While her mind ran on, she kept the little boys hopping. "Cut those carrot tops closer, Herbert, you're just being careless. Arthur, stop breaking up the beans so little. They're little enough already. Herbert, you go get an armload of wood. Arthur, you take these onions and wash them under the pump. Herbert, as soon as you're done here, you get a broom and sweep out this kitchen. Arthur, you get a shovel and take up the ashes. Stop picking your nose, Herbert. How often must I tell you? Arthur, you go look in the top drawer of my bureau, left-hand side, and bring me the vaseline for Herbert's nose. Herbert, come here to me. . . ."

They galloped through their chores, their animal spirits rose with activity, and shortly they were out in the front yard again, engaged in a wrestling match. They sprawled and fought, scrambled, clutched, rose and fell shouting, as aimlessly, noisily, monotonously as two puppies. They imitated various animals, not a human sound from them, and their dirty faces were streaked with sweat. Mrs. Thompson, sitting at her window, watched them with baffled pride and tenderness, they were so sturdy and healthy and growing so fast; but uneasily, too, with her pained little smile and the tears rolling from her eyelids that clinched themselves against the sunlight. They were so idle and careless, as if they had no future in this world, and no immortal souls to save, and oh, what had they been up to that Mr. Helton had shaken them, with his face positively dangerous?

In the evening before supper, without a word to Mr. Thompson of the curious fear the sight had caused her, she told him that Mr. Helton had shaken the little boys for some reason. He stepped out to the shack and spoke to Mr. Helton. In five minutes he was back, glaring at his young. "He says them brats been fooling with his harmonicas, Ellie, blowing in them and getting them all dirty and full of spit and they don't play good."

"Did he say all that?" asked Mrs. Thompson. "It doesn't seem possible."

"Well, that's what he meant, anyhow," said Mr. Thompson. "He didn't say it just that way. But he acted pretty worked up about it."

"That's a shame," said Mrs. Thompson, "a perfect shame. Now we've got to do something so they'll remember they mustn't go into Mr. Helton's things."

"I'll tan their hides for them," said Mr. Thompson. "I'll take a calf rope to them if they don't look out."

"Maybe you'd better leave the whipping to me," said Mrs. Thompson. "You haven't got a light enough hand for children."

"That's just what's the matter with them now," shouted Mr.

Thompson, "rotten spoiled and they'll wind up in the penitentiary. You don't half whip 'em. Just little love taps. My pa used to knock me down with a stick of stove wood or anything else that came handy."

"Well, that's not saying it's right," said Mrs. Thompson. "I don't hold with that way of raising children. It makes them run away from home. I've seen too much of it."

"I'll break every bone in 'em," said Mr. Thompson, simmering down, "if they don't mind you better and stop being so bull-headed."

"Leave the table and wash your face and hands," Mrs. Thompson commanded the boys, suddenly. They slunk out and dabbled at the pump and slunk in again, trying to make themselves small. They had learned long ago that their mother always made them wash when there was trouble ahead. They looked at their plates. Mr. Thompson opened up on them.

"Well, now, what you got to say for yourselves about going into Mr. Helton's shack and ruining his harmonicas?"

The two little boys wilted, their faces drooped into the grieved hopeless lines of children's faces when they are brought to the terrible bar of blind adult justice; their eyes telegraphed each other in panic, "Now we're really going to catch a licking"; in despair, they dropped their buttered cornbread on their plates, their hands lagged on the edge of the table.

"I ought to break your ribs," said Mr. Thompson, "and I'm a good mind to do it."

"Yes, sir," whispered Arthur, faintly.

"Yes, sir," said Herbert, his lip trembling.

"Now, papa," said Mrs. Thompson in a warning tone. The children did not glance at her. They had no faith in her good will. She had betrayed them in the first place. There was no trusting her. Now she might save them and she might not. No use depending on her.

"Well, you ought to get a good thrashing. You deserve it, don't you, Arthur?"

Arthur hung his head. "Yes, sir."

"And the next time I catch either of you hanging around Mr. Helton's shack, I'm going to take the hide off *both* of you, you hear me, Herbert?"

Herbert mumbled and choked, scattering his cornbread. "Yes, sir."

"Well, now sit up and eat your supper and not another word out of you," said Mr. Thompson, beginning on his own food. The little boys perked up somewhat and started chewing, but every time they looked around they met their parents' eyes, regarding them steadily. There was no telling when they would think of something new. The boys ate warily, trying not to be seen or heard, the cornbread sticking, the buttermilk gurgling, as it went down their gullets.

"And something else, Mr. Thompson," said Mrs. Thompson after a pause. "Tell Mr. Helton he's to come straight to us when they bother him, and not to trouble shaking them himself. Tell him we'll look after that."

"They're so mean," answered Mr. Thompson, staring at them. "It's a wonder he don't just kill 'em off and be done with it." But there was something in the tone that told Arthur and Herbert that nothing more worth worrying about was going to happen this time. Heaving deep sighs, they sat up, reaching for the food nearest them.

"Listen," said Mrs. Thompson, suddenly. The little boys stopped eating. "Mr. Helton hasn't come for his supper. Arthur, go and tell Mr. Helton he's late for supper. Tell him nice, now."

Arthur, miserably depressed, slid out of his place and made for the door, without a word.

There were no miracles of fortune to be brought to pass on a small dairy farm. The Thompsons did not grow rich, but they kept out of the poor house, as Mr. Thompson was fond of saying, meaning he had got a little foothold in spite of Ellie's poor health, and unexpected weather, and strange declines in market prices, and his own mysterious handicaps which weighed him down. Mr. Helton was the hope and the prop of the family, and all the Thompsons became fond of him, or at any rate they ceased to regard him as in any way peculiar, and looked upon him, from a distance they did not know how to bridge, as a good man and a good friend. Mr. Helton went his way, worked, played his tune. Nine years passed. The boys grew up and learned to work. They could not remember the time when Ole Helton hadn't been there: a grouchy cuss,

Brother Bones; Mr. Helton, the dairymaid; that Big Swede. If he had heard them, he might have been annoyed at some of the names they called him. But he did not hear them, and besides they meant no harm—or at least such harm as existed was all there, in the names; the boys referred to their father as the Old Man, or the Old Geezer, but not to his face. They lived through by main strength all the grimy, secret, oblique phases of growing up and got past the crisis safely if anyone does. Their parents could see they were good solid boys with hearts of gold in spite of their rough ways. Mr. Thompson was relieved to find that, without knowing how he had done it, he had succeeded in raising a set of boys who were not trifling whittlers. They were such good boys Mr. Thompson began to believe they were born that way, and that he had never spoken a harsh word to them in their lives, much less thrashed them. Herbert and Arthur never disputed his word.

Mr. Helton, his hair wet with sweat, plastered to his dripping forehead, his jumper streaked dark and light blue and clinging to his ribs, was chopping a little firewood. He chopped slowly, struck the ax into the end of the chopping log, and piled the wood up neatly. He then disappeared round the house into his shack, which shared with the wood pile a good shade from a row of mulberry trees. Mr. Thompson was lolling in a swing chair on the front porch, a place he had never liked. The chair was new, and Mrs. Thompson had wanted it on the front porch, though the side porch was the place for it, being cooler; and Mr. Thompson wanted to sit in the chair, so there he was. As soon as the new wore off of it, and Ellie's pride in it was exhausted, he would move it round to the side porch. Meantime the August heat was almost unbearable, the air so thick you could poke a hole in it. The dust was inches thick on everything, though Mr. Helton sprinkled the whole yard regularly every night. He even shot the hose upward and washed the tree tops and the roof of the house. They had laid waterpipes to the kitchen and an outside faucet. Mr. Thompson must have dozed, for he opened his eyes and shut his mouth just in time to save his face before a stranger who had driven up to the front gate. Mr. Thompson stood up, put on his hat, pulled up his jeans, and watched while the stranger tied his team, attached to a light spring wagon, to the hitching post. Mr. Thompson recognized the team and wagon. They were from a livery stable in Buda. While the stranger was opening the gate, a strong gate that Mr. Helton had built and set firmly on its hinges several years back, Mr. Thompson strolled down the path to greet him and find out what in God's world a man's business might be that would bring him out at this time of day, in all this dust and welter.

He wasn't exactly a fat man. He was more like a man who had been fat recently. His skin was baggy and his clothes were too big for him, and he somehow looked like a man who should be fat, ordinarily, but who might have just got over a spell of sickness. Mr. Thompson didn't take to his looks at all, he couldn't say why.

The stranger took off his hat. He said in a loud hearty voice, "Is this Mr. Thompson, Mr. Royal Earle Thompson?"

"That's my name," said Mr. Thompson, almost quietly, he was so taken aback by the free manner of the stranger.

"My name is Hatch," said the stranger, "Mr. Homer T. Hatch, and I've come to see you about buying a horse."

"I expect you've been misdirected," said Mr. Thompson. "I haven't got a horse for sale. Usually if I've got anything like that to sell," he said, "I tell the neighbors and tack up a little sign on the gate."

The fat man opened his mouth and roared with joy, showing rabbit teeth brown as shoeleather. Mr. Thompson saw nothing to laugh at, for once. The stranger shouted, "That's just an old joke of mine." He caught one of his hands in the other and shook hands with himself heartily. "I always say something like that when I'm calling on a stranger, because I've noticed that when a feller says he's come to buy something nobody takes him for a suspicious character. You see? Haw, haw, haw."

His joviality made Mr. Thompson nervous, because the expression in the man's eyes didn't match the sounds he was making. "Haw, haw," laughed Mr. Thompson obligingly, still not seeing the joke. "Well, that's all wasted on me because I never take any man for a suspicious character 'til he shows hisself to be one. Says or does something," he explained. "Until that happens, one man's as good as another, so far's *I'm* concerned."

"Well," said the stranger, suddenly very sober and sensible, "I ain't come neither to buy nor sell. Fact is, I want to see you about something that's of interest to us both. Yes, sir, I'd like to have a little talk with you, and it won't cost you a cent."

"I guess that's fair enough," said Mr. Thompson, reluctantly. "Come on around the house where there's a little shade."

They went round and seated themselves on two stumps under a chinaberry tree.

"Yes, sir, Homer T. Hatch is my name and America is my nation," said the stranger. "I reckon you must know the name? I used to have a cousin named Jameson Hatch lived up the country a ways."

"Don't think I know the name," said Mr. Thompson. "There's some Hatchers settled somewhere around Mountain City."

"Don't know the old Hatch family," cried the man in deep concern. He seemed to be pitying Mr. Thompson's ignorance. "Why, we came over from Georgia fifty years ago. Been here long yourself?"

"Just all my whole life," said Mr. Thompson, beginning to feel peevish. "And my pa and my grampap before me. Yes, sir, we've been right here all along. Anybody wants to find a Thompson knows where to look for him. My grampap immigrated in 1836."

"From Ireland, I reckon?" said the stranger.

"From Pennsylvania," said Mr. Thompson. "Now what makes you think we came from Ireland?"

The stranger opened his mouth and began to shout with merriment, and he shook hands with himself as if he hadn't met himself for a long time. "Well, what I always says is, a feller's got to come from *somewhere,* ain't he?"

While they were talking, Mr. Thompson kept glancing at the face near him. He certainly did remind Mr. Thompson of somebody, or maybe he really had seen the man himself somewhere. He couldn't just place the features. Mr. Thompson finally decided it was just that all rabbit-teethed men looked alike.

"That's right," acknowledged Mr. Thompson, rather sourly, "but what I always say is, Thompsons have been settled here for so long it don't make much difference any more *where* they come from. Now a course, this is the slack season, and we're all just laying round a little, but nevertheless we've all got our chores to do, and I don't want to hurry you, and so if you've come to see me on business maybe we'd better get down to it."

"As I said, it's not in a way, and again in a way it is," said the fat man. "Now I'm looking for a man named Helton, Mr. Olaf Eric Helton, from North Dakota, and I was told up around the country a ways that I might find him here, and I wouldn't mind having a little talk with him. No, siree, I sure wouldn't mind, if it's all the same to you."

"I never knew his middle name," said Mr. Thompson, "but Mr. Helton is right here, and been here now for going on nine years. He's a mighty steady man, and you can tell anybody I said so."

"I'm glad to hear that," said Mr. Homer T. Hatch. "I like to hear of a feller mending his ways and settling down. Now when I knew Mr. Helton he was pretty wild, yes, sir, wild is what he was, he didn't know his own mind atall. Well, now, it's going to be a great pleasure to me to meet up with an old friend and find him all settled down and doing well by hisself."

"We've all got to be young once," said Mr. Thompson. "It's like the measles, it breaks out all over you, and you're a nuisance to yourself and everybody else, but it don't last, and it usually don't leave no ill effects." He was so pleased with this notion he forgot and broke into a guffaw. The stranger folded his arms over his stomach and went into a kind of fit, roaring until he had tears in his eyes. Mr. Thompson stopped shouting and eyed the stranger uneasily. Now he liked a good laugh as well as any man, but there ought to be a little moderation. Now this feller laughed like a perfect lunatic, that was a fact. And he wasn't laughing because he really thought things were funny, either. He was laughing for reasons of his own. Mr. Thompson fell into a moody silence, and waited until Mr. Hatch settled down a little.

Mr. Hatch got out a very dirty blue cotton bandanna and wiped his eyes. "That joke just about caught me where I live," he said, almost apologetically. "Now I wish I could think up things as funny as that to say. It's a gift. It's . . ."

"If you want to speak to Mr. Helton, I'll go and round him up," said Mr. Thompson, making motions as if he might get up. "He may be in the milk house and he may be setting in his shack this time of day." It was drawing towards five o'clock. "It's right around the corner," he said.

"Oh, well, there ain't no special hurry," said Mr. Hatch. "I've been wanting to speak to him for a good long spell now and I guess a few minutes more won't make no difference. I just more wanted to locate him, like. That's all."

Mr. Thompson stopped beginning to stand up, and unbuttoned one more button of his shirt, and said, "Well, he's here, and he's this kind of man, that if he had any business with you he'd like to get it over. He don't dawdle, that's one thing you can say for him."

Mr. Hatch appeared to sulk a little at these words. He wiped his face with the bandanna and opened his mouth to speak, when round the house there came the music of Mr. Helton's harmonica. Mr. Thompson raised a finger. "There he is," said Mr. Thompson. "Now's your time."

Mr. Hatch cocked an ear towards the east side of the house and listened for a few seconds, a very strange expression on his face.

"I know that tune like I know the palm of my own hand," said Mr. Thompson, "but I never heard Mr. Helton say what it was."

"That's a kind of Scandahoovian song," said Mr. Hatch. "Where I come from they sing it a lot. In North Dakota, they sing it. It says something about starting out in the morning feeling so good you can't hardly stand it, so you drink up all your likker before noon. All the likker, y' understand, that you was saving for the noon lay-off. The words ain't much, but it's a pretty tune. It's a kind of drinking song." He sat there drooping a little, and Mr. Thompson didn't like his expression. It was a satisfied expression, but it was more like the cat that et the canary.

"So far as I know," said Mr. Thompson, "he ain't touched a drop since he's been on the place, and that's nine years this coming September. Yes, sir, nine years, so far as I know, he ain't wetted his whistle once. And that's more than I can say for myself," he said, meekly proud.

"Yes, that's a drinking song," said Mr. Hatch. "I used to play 'Little Brown Jug' on the fiddle when I was younger than I am now," he went on, "but this Helton, he just keeps it up. He just sits and plays it by himself."

"He's been playing it off and on for nine years right here on the place," said Mr. Thompson, feeling a little proprietary.

"And he was certainly singing it as well, fifteen years before that, in North Dakota," said Mr. Hatch. "He used to sit up in a straitjacket, practically, when he was in the asylum—"

"What's that you say?" said Mr. Thompson. "What's that?"

"Shucks, I didn't mean to tell you," said Mr. Hatch, a faint leer of regret in his drooping eyelids. "Shucks, that just slipped out. Funny, now I'd made up my mind I wouldn' say a word, because it would just make a lot of excitement, and what I say is, if a man has lived harmless and quiet for nine years it don't matter if he *is* loony, does it? So long's he keeps quiet and don't do nobody harm."

"You mean they had him in a straitjacket?" asked Mr. Thompson, uneasily. "In a lunatic asylum?"

"They sure did," said Mr. Hatch. "That's right where they had him, from time to time."

"They put my Aunt Ida in one of them things in the State asylum," said Mr. Thompson. "She got vi'lent, and they put her in one of these jackets with long sleeves and tied her to an iron ring in the wall, and Aunt Ida got so wild she broke a blood vessel and when they went to look after her she was dead. I'd think one of them things was dangerous."

"Mr. Helton used to sing his drinking song when he was in a straitjacket," said Mr. Hatch. "Nothing ever bothered him, except if you tried to make him talk. That bothered him, and he'd get vi'lent, like your Aunt Ida. He'd get vi'lent and then they'd put him in the jacket and go off and leave him, and he'd lay there perfickly contented, so fars you could see, singing his song. Then one night he just disappeared. Left, you might say, just went, and nobody ever saw hide or hair of him again. And then I come along and find him here," said Mr. Hatch, "all settled down and playing the same song."

"He never acted crazy to me," said Mr. Thompson. "He always acted like a sensible man, to me. He never got married, for one thing, and he works like a horse, and I bet he's got the first cent I paid him when he landed here, and he don't drink, an he never says a word, much less swear, and he don't waste time runnin' around Saturday nights, and if he's crazy," said Mr. Thompson, "why, I think I'll go crazy myself for a change."

"Haw, ha," said Mr. Hatch, "heh, he, that's good! Ha, ha, ha, I hadn't thought of it jes like that. Yeah, that's right! Let's all go crazy and get rid of our wives and save our money, hey?" He smiled unpleasantly, showing his little rabbit teeth.

Mr. Thompson felt he was being misunderstood. He turned

around and motioned toward the open window back of the honeysuckle trellis. "Let's move off down here a little," he said. "I
oughta thought of that before." His visitor bothered Mr. Thompson. He had a way of taking the words out of Mr. Thompson's
mouth, turning them around and mixing them up until Mr. Thompson didn't know himself what he had said. "My wife's not very
strong," said Mr. Thompson. "She's been kind of invalid now goin'
on fourteen years. It's mighty tough on a poor man, havin' sickness
in the family. She had four operations," he said proudly, "one right
after the other, but they didn't do any good. For five years hand-
runnin', I just turned every nickel I made over to the doctors.
Upshot is, she's a mighty delicate woman."

"My old woman," said Mr. Homer T. Hatch, "had a back like a
mule, yes, sir. That woman could have moved the barn with her
bare hands if she'd ever took the notion. I used to say, it was a
good thing she didn't know her own stren'th. She's dead now,
though. That kind wear out quicker than the puny ones. I never
had much use for a woman always complainin'. I'd get rid of her
mighty quick, yes, sir, mighty quick. It's just as you say: a dead
loss, keepin' one of 'em up."

This was not at all what Mr. Thompson had heard himself say;
he had been trying to explain that a wife as expensive as his was a
credit to a man. "She's a mighty reasonable woman," said Mr.
Thompson, feeling baffled, "but I wouldn't answer for what she'd
say or do if she found out we'd had a lunatic on the place all this
time." They had moved away from the window; Mr. Thompson
took Mr. Hatch the front way, because if he went the back way
they would have to pass Mr. Helton's shack. For some reason he
didn't want the stranger to see or talk to Mr. Helton. It was
strange, but that was the way Mr. Thompson felt.

Mr. Thompson sat down again, on the chopping log, offering his
guest another tree stump. "Now, I mighta got upset myself at such
a thing, once," said Mr. Thompson, "but now I *deefy* anything to
get me lathered up." He cut himself an enormous plug of tobacco
with his horn-handled pocketknife, and offered it to Mr. Hatch,
who then produced his own plug and, opening a huge bowie knife
with a long blade sharply whetted, cut off a large wad and put it in
his mouth. They then compared plugs and both of them were aston-

ished to see how different men's ideas of good chewing tobacco were.

"Now, for instance," said Mr. Hatch, "mine is lighter colored. That's because, for one thing, there ain't any sweetenin' in this plug. I like it dry, natural leaf, medium strong."

"A little sweetenin' don't do no harm so far as I'm concerned," said Mr. Thompson, "but it's got to be mighty little. But with me, now, I want a strong leaf, I want it heavy-cured, as the feller says. There's a man near here, named Williams, Mr. John Morgan Williams, who chews a plug—well, sir, it's black as your hat and soft as melted tar. It fairly drips with molasses, jus' plain molasses, and it chews like licorice. Now, I don't call that a good chew."

"One man's meat," said Mr. Hatch, "is another man's poison. Now, such a chew would simply gag me. I couldn't begin to put it in my mouth."

"Well," said Mr. Thompson, a tinge of apology in his voice, "I jus' barely tasted it myself, you might say. Just took a little piece in my mouth and spit it out again."

"I'm dead sure I couldn't even get that far," said Mr. Hatch. "I like a dry natural chew without any artificial flavorin' of any kind."

Mr. Thompson began to feel that Mr. Hatch was trying to make out he had the best judgment in tobacco, and was going to keep up the argument until he proved it. He began to feel seriously annoyed with the fat man. After all, who was he and where did he come from? Who was he to go around telling other people what kind of tobacco to chew?

"Artificial flavorin'," Mr. Hatch went on, doggedly, "is jes put in to cover up a cheap leaf and make a man think he's gettin' somethin' more than he *is* gettin'. Even a little sweetenin' is a sign of a cheap leaf, you can mark my words."

"I've always paid a fair price for my plug," said Mr. Thompson, stiffly. "I'm not a rich man and I don't go round settin' myself up for one, but I'll say this, when it comes to such things as tobacco, I buy the best on the market."

"Sweetenin', even a little," began Mr. Hatch, shifting his plug and squirting tobacco juice at a dry-looking little rose bush that was having a hard enough time as it was, standing all day in the blazing sun, its roots clenched in the baked earth, "is the sign of—"

"About this Mr. Helton, now," said Mr. Thompson, determinedly, "I don't see no reason to hold it against a man because he went loony once or twice in his lifetime and so I don't expect to take no steps about it. Not a step. I've got nothin' against the man, he's always treated me fair. They's things and people," he went on, " 'nough to drive any man loony. The wonder to me is, more men don't wind up in straitjackets, the way things are going these days and times."

"That's right," said Mr. Hatch, promptly, entirely too promptly, as if he were turning Mr. Thompson's meaning back on him. "You took the words right out of my mouth. There ain't every man in a straitjacket that ought to be there. Ha, ha, you're right all right. You got the idea."

Mr. Thompson sat silent and chewed steadily and stared at a spot on the ground about six feet away and felt a slow muffled resentment climbing from somewhere deep down in him, climbing and spreading all through him. What was this fellow driving at? What was he trying to say? It wasn't so much his words, but his looks and his way of talking: that droopy look in the eye, that tone of voice, as if he was trying to mortify Mr. Thompson about something. Mr. Thompson didn't like it, but he couldn't get hold of it either. He wanted to turn around and shove the fellow off the stump, but it wouldn't look reasonable. Suppose something happened to the fellow when he fell off the stump, just for instance, if he fell on the ax and cut himself, and then someone should ask Mr. Thompson why he shoved him, and what could a man say? It would look mighty funny, it would sound mighty strange to say, Well him and me fell out over a plug of tobacco. He might just shove him anyhow and then tell people he was a fat man not used to the heat and while he was talking he got dizzy and fell off by himself, or something like that, and it wouldn't be the truth either, because it wasn't the heat and it wasn't the tobacco. Mr. Thompson made up his mind to get the fellow off the place pretty quick, without seeming to be anxious, and watch him sharp till he was out of sight. It doesn't pay to be friendly with strangers from another part of the country. They're always up to something, or they'd stay at home where they belong.

"And they's some people," said Mr. Hatch, "would jus' as soon have a loonatic around their house as not, they can't see no difference between them and anybody else. I always say, if that's the way a man feels, don't care who he associates with, why, why, that's his business, not mine. I don't wanta have a thing to do with it. Now back home in North Dakota, we don't feel that way. I'd like to a seen anybody hiring a loonatic there, aspecially after what he done."

"I didn't understand your home was North Dakota," said Mr. Thompson. "I thought you said Georgia."

"I've got a married sister in North Dakota," said Mr. Hatch, "married a Swede, but a white man if ever I saw one. So I say *we* because we got into a little business together out that way. And it seems like home, kind of."

"What did he do?" asked Mr. Thompson, feeling very uneasy again.

"Oh, nothin' to speak of," said Mr. Hatch, jovially, "jus' went loony one day in the hayfield and shoved a pitchfork right square through his brother, when they was makin' hay. They was goin' to execute him, but they found out he had went crazy with the heat, as the feller says, and so they put him in the asylum. That's all he done. Nothin' to get lathered up about, ha, ha, ha!" he said, and taking out his sharp knife he began to slice off a chew as carefully as if he were cutting cake.

"Well," said Mr. Thompson, "I don't deny that's news. Yes, sir, news. But I still say somethin' must have drove him to it. Some men make you feel like giving 'em a good killing just by lookin' at you. His brother may a been a mean ornery cuss."

"Brother was going to get married," said Mr. Hatch; "used to go courtin' his girl nights. Borrowed Mr. Helton's harmonica to give her a serenade one evenin', and lost it. Brand new harmonica."

"He thinks a heap of his harmonicas," said Mr. Thompson. "Only money he ever spends, now and then he buys hisself a new one. Must have a dozen in that shack, all kinds and sizes."

"Brother wouldn't buy him a new one," said Mr. Hatch, "so Mr. Helton just ups, as I says, and runs his pitchfork through his brother. Now you know he musta been crazy to get all worked up over a little thing like that."

"Sounds like it," said Mr. Thompson, reluctant to agree in anything with this intrusive and disagreeable fellow. He kept thinking he couldn't remember when he had taken such a dislike to a man on first sight.

"Seems to me you'd get pretty sick of hearin' the same tune year in, year out," said Mr. Hatch.

"Well, sometimes I think it wouldn't do no harm if he learned a new one," said Mr. Thompson, "but he don't, so there's nothin' to be done about it. It's a pretty good tune, though."

"One of the Scandahoovians told me what it meant, that's how I come to know," said Mr. Hatch. "Especially that part about getting so gay you jus' go ahead and drink up all the likker you got on hand before noon. It seems like up in them Swede countries a man carries a bottle of wine around with him as a matter of course, at least that's the way I understood it. Those fellers will tell you anything, though—" He broke off and spat.

The idea of drinking any kind of liquor in this heat made Mr. Thompson dizzy. The idea of anybody feeling good on a day like this, for instance, made him tired. He felt he was really suffering from the heat. The fat man looked as if he had grown to the stump; he slumped there in his damp, dark clothes too big for him, his belly slack in his pants, his wide black felt hat pushed off his narrow forehead red with prickly heat. A bottle of good cold beer, now, would be a help, thought Mr. Thompson, remembering the four bottles sitting deep in the pool at the springhouse, and his dry tongue squirmed in his mouth. He wasn't going to offer this man anything, though, not even a drop of water. He wasn't even going to chew any more tobacco with him. He shot out his quid suddenly, and wiped his mouth on the back of his hand, and studied the head near him attentively. The man was no good, and he was there for no good, but what was he up to? Mr. Thompson made up his mind he'd give him a little more time to get his business, whatever it was, with Mr. Helton over, and then if he didn't get off the place he'd kick him off.

Mr. Hatch, as if he suspected Mr. Thompson's thoughts, turned his eyes, wicked and pig-like, on Mr. Thompson. "Fact is," he said, as if he had made up his mind about something, "I might need your help in the little matter I've got on hand, but it won't cost you any trouble. Now, this Mr. Helton here, like I tell you, he's a dangerous escaped loonatic, you might say. Now fact is, in the last twelve years or so I musta rounded up twenty-odd escaped loonatics, besides a couple of escaped convicts that I just run into by accident, like. I don't make a business of it, but if there's a reward, and there usually is a reward, of course, I get it. It amounts to a tidy little sum in the long run, but that ain't the main question. Fact is, I'm for law and order, I don't like to see law-breakers and loonatics at large. It ain't the place for them. Now I reckon you're bound to agree with me on that, aren't you?"

Mr. Thompson said, "Well, circumstances alters cases, as the feller says. Now, what I know of Mr. Helton, he ain't danger-ous, as I told you." Something serious was going to happen, Mr. Thompson could see that. He stopped thinking about it. He'd just let this fellow shoot off his head and then see what could be done about it. Without thinking he got out his knife and plug and started to cut a chew, then remembered himself and put them back in his pocket.

"The law," said Mr. Hatch, "is solidly behind me. Now this Mr. Helton, he's been one of my toughest cases. He's kept my record from being practically one hundred per cent. I knew him before he went loony, and I know the fam'ly, so I undertook to help out rounding him up. Well, sir, he was gone slick as a whistle, for all we knew the man was as good as dead long while ago. Now we never might have caught up with him, but do you know what he did? Well, sir, about two weeks ago his old mother gets a letter from him, and in that letter, what do you reckon she found? Well, it was a check on that little bank in town for eight hundred and fifty dollars, just like that; the letter wasn't nothing much, just said he was sending her a few little savings, she might need something, but there it was, name, postmark, date, everything. The old woman practically lost her mind with joy. She's gettin' childish, and it looked like she kinda forgot that her only living son killed his brother and went loony. Mr. Helton said he was getting along all right, and for her not to tell nobody. Well, natchally, she couldn't keep it to herself, with that check to cash and everything. So that's how I come to know." His feelings got the better of him. "You coulda knocked me down with a feather." He shook hands with himself and rocked, wagging his head, going "Heh, heh," in his throat. Mr. Thompson felt the corners of his mouth turning down. Why, the dirty low-down hound, sneaking around spying into other people's business like that. Collecting blood money, that's what it was! Let him talk!

"Yea, well, that musta been a surprise all right," he said, trying to hold his voice even. "I'd say a surprise."

"Well, siree," said Mr. Hatch, "the more I got to thinking about it, the more I just come to the conclusion that I'd better look into the matter a little, and so I talked to the old woman. She's pretty decrepid, now, half blind and all, but she was all for taking the first train out and going to see her son. I put it up to her square—how she was too feeble for the trip, and all. So, just as a favor to her, I told her for my expenses I'd come down and see Mr. Helton and bring her back all the news about him. She gave me a new shirt she made herself by hand, and a big Swedish kind of cake to bring to him, but I musta mislaid them along the road somewhere. It don't reely matter, though, he prob'ly ain't in any state of mind to appreciate 'em."

Mr. Thompson sat up and turning round on the log looked at Mr. Hatch and asked as quietly as he could, "And now what are you aiming to do? That's the question."

Mr. Hatch slouched up to his feet and shook himself. "Well, I come all prepared for a little scuffle," he said. "I got the handcuffs," he said, "but I don't want no violence if I can help it. I didn't want to say nothing around the countryside, making an uproar. I figured the two of us could overpower him." He reached into his big inside pocket and pulled them out. Handcuffs, for God's sake, thought Mr. Thompson. Coming round on a peaceable afternoon worrying a man, and making trouble, and fishing handcuffs out of his pocket on a decent family homestead, as if it was all in the day's work.

Mr. Thompson, his head buzzing, got up too. "Well," he said, roundly, "I want to tell you I think you've got a mighty sorry job on hand, you sure must be hard up for something to do, and now I want to give you a good piece of advice. You just drop the idea that you're going to come here and make trouble for Mr. Helton, and the quicker you drive that hired rig away from my front gate the better I'll be satisfied."

Mr. Hatch put one handcuff in his outside pocket, the other dangling down. He pulled his hat down over his eyes, and re- minded Mr. Thompson of a sheriff, somehow. He didn't seem in the least nervous, and didn't take up Mr. Thompson's words. He said, "Now listen just a minute, it ain't reasonable to suppose that a man like yourself is going to stand in the way of getting an escaped loonatic back to the asylum where he belongs. Now I know it's enough to throw you off, coming sudden like this, but fact is I counted on your being a respectable man and helping me out to see that justice is done. Now a course, if you won't help, I'll have to look around for help somewheres else. It won't look very good to your neighbors that you was harbring an escaped loonatic who killed his own brother, and then you refused to give him up. It will look mighty funny."

Mr. Thompson knew almost before he heard the words that it would look funny. It would put him in a mighty awkward position. He said, "But I've been trying to tell you all along that the man ain't loony now. He's been perfectly harmless for nine years. He's —he's—"

Mr. Thompson couldn't think how to describe how it was with Mr. Helton. "Why, he's been like one of the family," he said, "the best standby a man ever had." Mr. Thompson tried to see his way out. It was a fact Mr. Helton might go loony again any minute, and now this fellow talking around the country would put Mr. Thompson in a fix. It was a terrible position. He couldn't think of any way out. "You're crazy," Mr. Thompson roared suddenly, "you're the crazy one around here, you're crazier than he ever was! You get off this place or I'll handcuff you and turn you over to the law. You're trespassing," shouted Mr. Thompson. "Get out of here before I knock you down!"

He took a step towards the fat man, who backed off, shrinking, "Try it, try it, go ahead!" and then something happened that Mr. Thompson tried hard afterwards to piece together in his mind, and in fact it never did come straight. He saw the fat man with his long bowie knife in his hand, he saw Mr. Helton come round the corner on the run, his long jaw dropped, his arms swinging, his eyes wild. Mr. Helton came in between them, fists doubled up, then stopped short, glaring at the fat man, his big frame seemed to collapse, he trembled like a shied horse; and then the fat man drove at him, knife in one hand, handcuffs in the other. Mr. Thompson saw it coming, he saw the blade going into Mr. Helton's stomach, he knew he had the ax out of the log in his own hands, felt his arms go up over his head and bring the ax down on Mr. Hatch's head as if he were stunning a beef.

Mrs. Thompson had been listening uneasily for some time to the voices going on, one of them strange to her, but she was too tired at first to get up and come out to see what was going on. The confused shouting that rose so suddenly brought her up to her feet and out across the front porch without her slippers, hair half-braided. Shading her eyes, she saw first Mr. Helton, running all stooped over through the orchard, running like a man with dogs after him; and Mr. Thompson supporting himself on the ax handle was leaning over shaking by the shoulder a man Mrs. Thompson had never seen, who lay doubled up with the top of his head smashed and the blood running away in a greasy-looking puddle. Mr. Thompson without taking his hand from the man's shoulder, said in a thick voice, "He killed Mr. Helton, he killed him, I saw him do it. I had to knock him out," he called loudly, "but he won't come to."

Mrs. Thompson said in a faint scream, "Why, yonder goes Mr. Helton," and she pointed. Mr. Thompson pulled himself up and looked where she pointed. Mrs. Thompson sat down slowly against the side of the house and began to slide forward on her face; she felt as if she were drowning, she couldn't rise to the top somehow, and her only thought was she was glad the boys were not there, they were out, fishing at Halifax, oh, God, she was glad the boys were not there.

Mr. and Mrs. Thompson drove up to their barn about sunset. Mr. Thompson handed the reins to his wife, got out to open the big door, and Mrs. Thompson guided old Jim in under the roof. The buggy was gray with dust and age, Mrs. Thompson's face was gray with dust and weariness, and Mr. Thompson's face, as he stood at the horse's head and began unhitching, was gray except for the dark blue of his freshly shaven jaws and chin, gray and blue and caved in, but patient, like a dead man's face.

Mrs. Thompson stepped down to the hard packed manure of the barn floor, and shook out her light flower-sprigged dress. She wore her smoked glasses, and her wide shady leghorn hat with the wreath of exhausted pink and blue forget-me-nots hid her forehead, fixed in a knot of distress.

The horse hung his head, raised a huge sigh and flexed his stiffened legs. Mr. Thompson's words came up muffled and hollow. "Poor ole Jim," he said, clearing his throat, "he looks pretty sunk in the ribs. I guess he's had a hard week." He lifted the harness up in one piece, slid it off and Jim walked out of the shafts halting a little. "Well, this is the last time," Mr. Thompson said, still talking to Jim. "Now you can get a good rest."

Mrs. Thompson closed her eyes behind her smoked glasses. The last time, and high time, and they should never have gone at all. She did not need her glasses any more, now the good darkness was coming down again, but her eyes ran full of tears steadily, though she was not crying, and she felt better with the glasses, safer, hidden away behind them. She took out her handkerchief with her hands shaking as they had been shaking ever since *that day,* and blew her nose. She said, "I see the boys have lighted the lamps. I hope they've started the stove going."

She stepped along the rough path holding her thin dress and starched petticoats around her, feeling her way between the sharp small stones, leaving the barn because she could hardly bear to be near Mr. Thompson, advancing slowly towards the house because she dreaded going there. Life was all one dread, the faces of her neighbors, of her boys, of her husband, the face of the whole world, the shape of her own house in the darkness, the very smell of the grass and the trees were horrible to her. There was no place to go, only one thing to do, bear it somehow—but how? She asked herself that question often. How was she going to keep on living now? Why had she lived at all? She wished now she had died one of those times when she had been so sick, instead of living on for this.

The boys were in the kitchen; Herbert was looking at the funny pictures from last Sunday's newspapers, the Katzenjammer Kids and Happy Hooligan. His chin was in his hands and his elbows on the table, and he was really reading and looking at the pictures, but his face was unhappy. Arthur was building the fire, adding kindling a stick at a time, watching it catch and blaze. His face was heavier and darker than Herbert's, but he was a little sullen by nature; Mrs. Thompson thought, he takes things harder, too. Arthur said, "Hello, Momma," and went on with his work. Herbert swept the papers together and moved over on the bench. They were big boys—fifteen and seventeen, and Arthur as tall as his father. Mrs. Thompson sat down beside Herbert, taking off her hat. She said, "I guess you're hungry. We were late today. We went the Log Hollow road, it's rougher than ever." Her pale mouth drooped with a sad fold on either side.

"I guess you saw the Mannings, then," said Herbert.

"Yes, and the Fergusons, and the Allbrights, and that new family McClellan."

"Anybody say anything?" asked Herbert.

"Nothing much, you know how it's been all along, some of them keeps saying, yes, they know it was a clear case and a fair trial and they say how glad they are your papa came out so well, and all that, some of 'em do, anyhow, but it looks like they don't really take sides with him. I'm about wore out," she said, the tears rolling again from under her dark glasses. "I don't know what good it does, but your papa can't seem to rest unless he's telling how it happened. I don't know."

"I don't think it does any good, not a speck," said Arthur, moving away from the stove. "It just keeps the whole question stirred up in people's minds. Everybody will go round telling what he heard, and the whole thing is going to get worse mixed up than ever. It just makes matters worse. I wish you could get Papa to stop driving round the country talking like that."

"Your papa knows best," said Mrs. Thompson. "You oughtn't to criticize him. He's got enough to put up with without that."

Arthur said nothing, his jaw stubborn. Mr. Thompson came in, his eyes hollowed out and dead-looking, his thick hands gray white and seamed from washing them clean every day before he started out to see the neighbors to tell them his side of the story. He was wearing his Sunday clothes, a thick pepper-and-salt-colored suit with a black string tie.

Mrs. Thompson stood up, her head swimming. "Now you-all get out of the kitchen, it's too hot in here and I need room. I'll get us a little bite of supper, if you'll just get out and give me some room."

They went as if they were glad to go, the boys outside, Mr. Thompson into his bedroom. She heard him groaning to himself as he took off his shoes, and heard the bed creak as he lay down. Mrs. Thompson opened the icebox and felt the sweet coldness flow out of it; she had never expected to have an icebox, much less did she hope to afford to keep it filled with ice. It still seemed like a miracle, after two or three years. There was the food, cold and clean, all ready to be warmed over. She would never have had that icebox if Mr. Helton hadn't happened along one day, just by the strangest luck; so saving, and so managing, so good, thought Mrs. Thompson, her heart swelling until she feared she would faint again, standing there with the door open and leaning her head upon it. She simply could not bear to remember Mr. Helton, with his long sad face and silent ways, who had always been so quiet and harmless, who had worked so hard and helped Mr. Thompson so much, running through the hot fields and woods, being hunted like a mad dog, everybody turning out with ropes and guns and sticks to catch and tie him. Oh, God, said Mrs. Thompson in a long dry moan, kneeling before the icebox and fumbling inside for the dishes, even if they did pile mattresses all over the jail floor and against the walls, and five men there to hold him to keep him from hurting himself any more, he was already hurt too badly, he couldn't have lived anyway. Mr. Barbee, the sheriff, told her about it. He said, well, they didn't aim to harm him but they had to catch him, he was crazy as a loon; he picked up rocks and tried to brain every man that got near him. He had two harmonicas in his jumper pocket, said the sheriff, but they fell out in the scuffle, and Mr. Helton tried to pick 'em up again, and that's when they finally got him. "They *had* to be rough, Miz Thompson, he fought like a wildcat." Yes, thought Mrs. Thompson again with the same bitterness, of course, they had to be rough. They always have to be rough. Mr. Thompson can't argue with a man and get him off the place peaceably; no, she thought, standing up and shutting the icebox, he has to kill somebody, he has to be a murderer and ruin his boys' lives and cause Mr. Helton to be killed like a mad dog.

Her thoughts stopped with a little soundless explosion, cleared and began again. The rest of Mr. Helton's harmonicas were still in the shack, his tune ran in Mrs. Thompson's head at certain times of the day. She missed it in the evenings. It seemed so strange she had never known the name of that song, nor what it meant, until after Mr. Helton was gone. Mrs. Thompson, trembling in the knees, took a drink of water at the sink and poured the red beans into the baking dish, and began to roll the pieces of chicken in flour to fry them. There was a time, she said to herself, when I thought I had neighbors and friends, there was a time when we could hold up our heads, there was a time when my husband hadn't killed a man and I could tell the truth to anybody about anything.

Mr. Thompson, turning on his bed, figured that he had done all he could, he'd just try to let the matter rest from now on. His lawyer, Mr. Burleigh, had told him right at the beginning, "Now you keep calm and collected. You've got a fine case, even if you haven't got witnesses. Your wife must sit in court, she'll be a powerful argument with the jury. You just plead not guilty and I'll do the rest. The trial is going to be a mere formality, you haven't got a thing to worry about. You'll be clean out of this before you know it." And to make talk Mr. Burleigh had got to telling about all the men he knew around the country who for one reason or another had been forced to kill somebody, always in self-defense, and there just wasn't anything to it at all. He even told about how his own father in the old days had shot and killed a man just for setting foot inside his gate when he told him not to. "Sure, I shot the scoundrel," said Mr. Burleigh's father, "in self-defense; I *told* him I'd shoot him if he set his foot in my yard, and he did, and I did." There had been bad blood between them for years, Mr. Burleigh said, and his father had waited a long time to catch the other fellow in the wrong, and when he did he certainly made the most of his opportunity.

"But Mr. Hatch, as I told you," Mr. Thompson had said, "made a pass at Mr. Helton with his bowie knife. That's why I took a hand."

"All the better," said Mr. Burleigh. "That stranger hadn't any right coming to your house on such an errand. Why, hell," said Mr. Burleigh, "that wasn't even manslaughter you committed. So now you just hold your horses and keep your shirt on. And don't say one word without I tell you."

Wasn't even manslaughter. Mr. Thompson had to cover Mr. Hatch with a piece of wagon canvas and ride to town to tell the sheriff. It had been hard on Ellie. When they got back, the sheriff and the coroner and two deputies, they found her sitting beside the road, on a low bridge over a gulley, about half a mile from the place. He had taken her up behind his saddle and got her back to the house. He had already told the sheriff that his wife had witnessed the whole business, and now he had time, getting her to her room and in bed, to tell her what to say if they asked anything. He had left out the part about Mr. Helton being crazy all along, but it came out at the trial. By Mr. Burleigh's advice Mr. Thompson had pretended to be perfectly ignorant; Mr. Hatch hadn't said a word about that. Mr. Thompson pretended to believe that Mr. Hatch had just come looking for Mr. Helton to settle old scores, and the two members of Mr. Hatch's family who had come down to try to get Mr. Thompson convicted didn't get anywhere at all. It hadn't been much of a trial, Mr. Burleigh saw to that. He had charged a reasonable fee, and Mr. Thompson had paid him and felt grateful, but after it was over Mr. Burleigh didn't seem pleased to see him when he got to dropping into the office to talk it over, telling him things that had slipped his mind at first: trying to explain what an ornery low hound Mr. Hatch had been, anyhow. Mr. Burleigh seemed to have lost his interest; he looked sour and upset when he saw Mr. Thompson at the door. Mr. Thompson kept saying to himself that he'd got off, all right, just as Mr. Burleigh had predicted, but, but—and it was right there that Mr. Thompson's mind stuck, squirming like an angleworm on a fishhook: he had killed Mr. Hatch, and he was a murderer. That was the truth about himself that Mr. Thompson couldn't grasp, even when he said the word to himself. Why, he had not even once *thought* of killing anybody, much less Mr. Hatch, and if Mr. Helton hadn't come out so unexpectedly, hearing the row, why, then—but then, Mr. Helton had come on the run that way to help him. What he couldn't understand was what happened next. He had seen Mr. Hatch go after Mr. Helton with the knife, he had seen the point, blade up, go into Mr. Helton's stomach and slice up like you slice a hog, but when they finally caught Mr. Helton there wasn't a knife scratch on him. Mr. Thompson knew he had the ax in his own hands and felt himself lifting it, but he couldn't remember hitting Mr. Hatch. He couldn't remember it. He couldn't. He remembered only that he had been determined to stop Mr. Hatch from cutting Mr. Helton. If he was given a chance he could explain the whole matter. At the trial they hadn't let him talk. They just asked questions and he answered yes or no, and they never did get to the core of the matter. Since the trial, now, every day for a week he had washed

and shaved and put on his best clothes and had taken Ellie with
him to tell every neighbor he had that he never killed Mr. Hatch
on purpose, and what good did it do? Nobody believed him. Even
when he turned to Ellie and said, "You was there, you saw it,
didn't you?" and Ellie spoke up, saying, "Yes, that's the truth. Mr.
Thompson was trying to save Mr. Helton's life," and he added, "If
you don't believe me, you can believe my wife. She won't lie," Mr.
Thompson saw something in all their faces that disheartened him,
made him feel empty and tired out. They didn't believe he was not
a murderer.

Even Ellie never said anything to comfort him. He hoped she
would say finally, "I remember now, Mr. Thompson, I really did
come round the corner in time to see everything. It's not a lie, Mr.
Thompson. Don't you worry." But as they drove together in silence, with the days still hot and dry, shortening for fall, day after
day, the buggy jolting in the ruts, she said nothing; they grew to
dread the sight of another house, and the people in it: all houses
looked alike now, and the people—old neighbors or new—had
the same expression when Mr. Thompson told them why he had
come and began his story. Their eyes looked as if someone had
pinched the eyeball at the back; they shriveled and the light went
out of them. Some of them sat with fixed tight smiles trying to be
friendly. "Yes, Mr. Thompson, we know how you must feel. It
must be terrible for you, Mrs. Thompson. Yes, you know, I've
about come to the point where I believe in such a thing as killing
in self-defense. Why, certainly, we believe you, Mr. Thompson,
why shouldn't we believe you? Didn't you have a perfectly fair and
above-board trial? Well, now, natchally, Mr. Thompson, we think
you done right."

Mr. Thompson was satisfied they didn't think so. Sometimes the
air around him was so thick with their blame he fought and pushed
with his fists, and the sweat broke out all over him, he shouted his
story in a dust-choked voice, he would fairly bellow at last: "My
wife, here, you know her, she was there, she saw and heard it all, if
you don't believe me, ask her, she won't lie!" and Mrs. Thompson,
with her hands knotted together, aching, her chin trembling, would
never fail to say: "Yes, that's right, that's the truth—"

The last straw had been laid on today, Mr. Thompson decided.
Tom Allbright, an old beau of Ellie's, why, he had squired Ellie

around a whole summer, had come out to meet them when they drove up, and standing there bareheaded had stopped them from getting out. He had looked past them with an embarrassed frown on his face, telling them his wife's sister was there with a raft of young ones, and the house was pretty full and everything upset, or he'd ask them to come in. "We've been thinking of trying to get up to your place one of these days," said Mr. Allbright, moving away trying to look busy, "we've been mighty occupied up here of late." So they had to say. "Well, we just happened to be driving this way," and go on. "The Allbrights," said Mrs. Thompson, "always was fair-weather friends." "They look out for number one, that's a fact," said Mr. Thompson. But it was cold comfort to them both.

Finally Mrs. Thompson had given up. "Let's go home," she said. "Old Jim's tired and thirsty, and we've gone far enough."

Mr. Thompson said, "Well, while we're out this way, we might as well stop at the McClellans'." They drove in, and asked a little cotton-haired boy if his mamma and papa were at home. Mr. Thompson wanted to see them. The little boy stood gazing with his mouth open, then galloped into the house shouting, "Mommer, Popper, come out hyah. That man that kilt Mr. Hatch has come ter see yer!"

The man came out in his sock feet, with one gallus up, the other broken and dangling, and said, "Light down, Mr. Thompson, and come in. The ole woman's washing, but she'll git here." Mrs. Thompson, feeling her way, stepped down and sat in a broken rocking-chair on the porch that sagged under her feet. The woman of the house, barefooted, in a calico wrapper, sat on the edge of the porch, her fat sallow face full of curiosity. Mr. Thompson began, "Well, as I reckon you happen to know, I've had some strange troubles lately, and, as the feller says, it's not the kind of trouble that happens to a man every day in the year, and there's some things I don't want no misunderstanding about in the neighbors' minds, so—" He halted and stumbled forward, and the two listening faces took on a mean look, a greedy, despising look, a look that said plain as day, "My, you must be a purty sorry feller to come round worrying about what *we* think, *we* know you wouldn't be here if you had anybody else to turn to—my, I wouldn't lower myself that much, myself." Mr. Thompson was ashamed of himself, he was suddenly in a rage, he'd like to knock their dirty skunk heads together, the low-down white trash—but he held himself down and went on to the end. "My wife will tell you," he said, and this was the hardest place, because Ellie always without moving a muscle seemed to stiffen as if somebody had threatened to hit her; "ask my wife, she won't lie."

"It's true, I saw it—"

"Well, now," said the man, drily, scratching his ribs inside his shirt, "that sholy is too bad. Well, now, I kaint see what we've got to do with all this here, however. I kaint see no good reason for us to git mixed up in these murder matters, I shore kaint. Whichever way you look at it, it ain't none of my business. However, it's mighty nice of you-all to come around and give us the straight of it, fur we've heerd some mighty queer yarns about it, mighty queer, I golly you couldn't hardly make head ner tail of it."

"Evvybody goin' round shootin' they heads off," said the woman. "Now we don't hold with killin'; the Bible says—"

"Shet yer trap," said the man, "and keep it shet 'r I'll shet it fer yer. Now it shore looks like to me—"

"We mustn't linger," said Mrs. Thompson, unclasping her hands. "We've lingered too long now. It's getting late, and we've far to go." Mr. Thompson took the hint and followed her. The man and the woman lolled against their rickety porch poles and watched them go.

Now lying on his bed, Mr. Thompson knew the end had come. Now, this minute, lying in the bed where he had slept with Ellie for eighteen years; under this roof where he had laid the shingles when he was waiting to get married; there as he was with his whiskers already sprouting since his shave that morning; with his fingers feeling his bony chin, Mr. Thompson felt he was a dead man. He was dead to his other life, he had got to the end of something without knowing why, and he had to make a fresh start, he did not know how. Something different was going to begin, he didn't know what. It was in some way not his business. He didn't feel he was going to have much to do with it. He got up, aching, hollow, and went out to the kitchen where Mrs. Thompson was just taking up the supper.

"Call the boys," said Mrs. Thompson. They had been down to the barn, and Arthur put out the lantern before hanging it on a nail near the door. Mr. Thompson didn't like their silence. They had hardly said a word about anything to him since that day. They seemed to avoid him, they ran the place together as if he wasn't there, and attended to everything without asking him for any advice. "What you boys been up to?" he asked, trying to be hearty. "Finishing your chores?"

"No, sir," said Arthur, "there ain't much to do. Just greasing some axles." Herbert said nothing. Mrs. Thompson bowed her head: "For these and all Thy blessings. . . . Amen," she whispered weakly, and the Thompsons sat there with their eyes down and their faces sorrowful, as if they were at a funeral.

Every time he shut his eyes, trying to sleep, Mr. Thompson's mind started up and began to run like a rabbit. It jumped from one thing to another, trying to pick up a trail here or there that would straighten out what had happened that day he killed Mr. Hatch. Try as he might, Mr. Thompson's mind would not go anywhere that it had not already been, he could not see anything but what he had seen once, and he knew that was not right. If he had not seen straight that first time, then everything about his killing Mr. Hatch was wrong from start to finish, and there was nothing more to be done about it, he might just as well give up. It still seemed to him that he had done, maybe not the right thing, but the only thing he could do, that day, but had he? *Did he have to kill Mr. Hatch?* He had never seen a man he hated more, the minute he laid eyes on him. He knew in his bones the fellow was there for trouble. What seemed so funny now was this: Why hadn't he just told Mr. Hatch to get out before he ever even got in?

Mrs. Thompson, her arms crossed on her breast, was lying beside him, perfectly still, but she seemed awake, somehow. "Asleep, Ellie?"

After all, he might have got rid of him peaceably, or maybe he might have had to overpower him and put those handcuffs on him and turn him over to the sheriff for disturbing the peace. The most they could have done was to lock Mr. Hatch up while he cooled off for a few days, or fine him a little something. He would try to think of things he might have said to Mr. Hatch. Why, let's see, I could just have said, Now look here, Mr. Hatch, I want to talk to you as man to man. But his brain would go empty. What could he have said or done? But if he *could* have done anything else almost except kill Mr. Hatch, then nothing would have happened to Mr. Helton. Mr. Thompson hardly ever thought of Mr. Helton. His mind just skipped over him and went on. If he stopped to think about Mr. Helton he'd never in God's world get anywhere. He tried to imagine how it might all have been, this very night even, if Mr. Helton were still safe and sound out in his shack playing his tune about feeling so good in the morning, drinking up all the wine so you'd feel even better; and Mr. Hatch safe in jail somewhere, mad as hops, maybe, but out of harm's way and ready to listen to reason and to repent of his meanness, the dirty, yellow-livered hound coming around persecuting an innocent man and ruining a whole family that never harmed him! Mr. Thompson felt the veins of his forehead start up, his fists clutched as if they seized an ax handle, the sweat broke out on him, he bounded up from the bed with a yell smothered in his throat, and Ellie started up after him, crying out, "Oh, oh, don't! Don't! Don't!" as if she were having a nightmare. He stood shaking until his bones rattled in him, crying hoarsely, "Light the lamp, light the lamp, Ellie."

Instead, Mrs. Thompson gave a shrill weak scream, almost the same scream he had heard on that day she came around the house when he was standing there with the ax in his hand. He could not see her in the dark, but she was on the bed, rolling violently. He felt for her in horror, and his groping hands found her arms, up, and her own hands pulling her hair straight out from her head, her neck strained back, and the tight screams strangling her. He shouted out for Arthur, for Herbert. "Your mother!" he bawled, his voice cracking. As he held Mrs. Thompson's arms, the boys came tumbling in, Arthur with the lamp above his head. By this light Mr. Thompson saw Mrs. Thompson's eyes, wide open, staring dreadfully at him, the tears pouring. She sat up at sight of the boys, and held out one arm towards them, the hand wagging in a crazy circle, then dropped on her back again, and suddenly went limp. Arthur set the lamp on the table and turned on Mr. Thompson. "She's scared," he said, "she's scared to death." His face was in a knot of rage, his fists were doubled up, he faced his father as if he meant to strike him. Mr. Thompson's jaw fell, he was so surprised he stepped back from the bed. Herbert went to the other side. They stood on each side of Mrs. Thompson and watched Mr. Thompson as if he were a dangerous wild beast. "What did you do

to her?" shouted Arthur, in a grown man's voice. "You touch her
again and I'll blow your heart out!" Herbert was pale and his
cheek twitched, but he was on Arthur's side; he would do what he
could to help Arthur.

Mr. Thompson had no fight left in him. His knees bent as he
stood, his chest collapsed. "Why, Arthur," he said, his words crumbling and his breath coming short. "She's fainted again. Get the
ammonia." Arthur did not move. Herbert brought the bottle, and
handed it, shrinking, to his father.

Mr. Thompson held it under Mrs. Thompson's nose. He poured
a little in the palm of his hand and rubbed it on her forehead. She
gasped and opened her eyes and turned her head away from him.
Herbert began a doleful hopeless sniffling. "Mamma," he kept
saying, "Mamma, don't die."

"I'm all right," Mrs. Thompson said. "Now don't you worry
around. Now Herbert, you mustn't do that. I'm all right." She
closed her eyes. Mr. Thompson began pulling on his best pants; he
put on his socks and shoes. The boys sat on each side of the bed,
watching Mrs. Thompson's face. Mr. Thompson put on his shirt
and coat. He said, "I reckon I'll ride over and get the doctor.
Don't look like all this fainting is a good sign. Now you just keep
watch until I get back." They listened, but said nothing. He said,
"Don't you get any notions in your head. I never did your mother
any harm in my life, on purpose." He went out, and, looking back,
saw Herbert staring at him from under his brows, like a stranger.
"You'll know how to look after her," said Mr. Thompson.

Mr. Thompson went through the kitchen. There he lighted the
lantern, took a thin pad of scratch paper and a stub pencil from
the shelf where the boys kept their schoolbooks. He swung the
lantern on his arm and reached into the cupboard where he kept
the guns. The shotgun was there to his hand, primed and ready, a
man never knows when he may need a shotgun. He went out of
the house without looking around, or looking back when he had
left it, passed his barn without seeing it, and struck out to the
farthest end of his fields, which ran for half a mile to the east. So
many blows had been struck at Mr. Thompson and from so many
directions he couldn't stop any more to find out where he was hit.
He walked on, over plowed ground and over meadow, going
through barbed wire fences cautiously, putting his gun through

first; he could almost see in the dark, now his eyes were used to it. Finally he came to the last fence; here he sat down, back against a post, lantern at his side, and, with the pad on his knee, moistened the stub pencil and began to write:

"Before Almighty God, the great judge of all before who I am about to appear, I do hereby solemnly swear that I did not take the life of Mr. Homer T. Hatch on purpose. It was done in defense of Mr. Helton. I did not aim to hit him with the ax but only to keep him off Mr. Helton. He aimed a blow at Mr. Helton who was not looking for it. It was my belief at the time that Mr. Hatch would of taken the life of Mr. Helton if I did not interfere. I have told all this to the judge and the jury and they let me off but nobody believes it. This is the only way I can prove I am not a cold blooded murderer like everybody seems to think. If I had been in Mr. Helton's place he would of done the same for me. I still think I done the only thing there was to do. My wife—"

Mr. Thompson stopped here to think a while. He wet the pencil point with the tip of his tongue and marked out the last two words. He sat a while blacking out the words until he had made a neat oblong patch where they had been, and started again:

"It was Mr. Homer T. Hatch who came to do wrong to a harmless man. He caused all this trouble and he deserved to die but I am sorry it was me who had to kill him."

He licked the point of his pencil again, and signed his full name carefully, folded the paper and put it in his outside pocket. Taking off his right shoe and sock, he set the butt of the shotgun along the ground with the twin barrels pointed towards his head. It was very awkward. He thought about this a little, leaning his head against the gun mouth. He was trembling and his head was drumming until he was deaf and blind, but he lay down flat on the earth on his side, drew the barrel under his chin and fumbled for the trigger with his great toe. That way he could work it.

Pale Horse, Pale Rider

In sleep she knew she was in her bed, but not the bed she had lain down in a few hours since, and the room was not the same but it was a room she had known somewhere. Her heart was a stone lying upon her breast outside of her; her pulses lagged and paused, and she knew that something strange was going to happen, even as the early morning winds were cool through the lattice, the streaks of light were dark blue and the whole house was snoring in its sleep.

Now I must get up and go while they are all quiet. Where are my things? Things have a will of their own in this place and hide where they like. Daylight will strike a sudden blow on the roof startling them all up to their feet; faces will beam asking, Where are you going, What are you doing, What are you thinking, How do you feel, Why do you say such things, What do you mean? No more sleep. Where are my boots and what horse shall I ride? Fiddler or Graylie or Miss Lucy with the long nose and the wicked eye? How I have loved this house in the morning before we are all awake and tangled together like badly cast fishing lines. Too many people have been born here, and have wept too much here, and have laughed too much, and have been too angry and outrageous with each other here. Too many have died in this bed already, there are far too many ancestral bones propped up on the mantelpieces, there have been too damned many antimacassars in this house, she said loudly, and oh, what accumulation of storied dust never allowed to settle in peace for one moment.

And the stranger? Where is that lank greenish stranger I remember hanging about the place, welcomed by my grandfather, my great-aunt, my five times removed cousin, my decrepit hound and my silver kitten? Why did they take to him, I wonder? And where are they now? Yet I saw him pass the window in the evening. What else besides them did I have in the world? Nothing. Nothing is mine, I have only nothing but it is enough, it is beautiful and it is all mine. Do I even walk about in my own skin or is it something I have borrowed to spare my modesty? Now what horse shall I borrow for this journey I do not mean to take, Graylie or Miss Lucy or Fiddler who can jump ditches in the dark and knows how to get the bit between his teeth? Early morning is best for me because trees are trees in one stroke, stones are stones set in shades known to be grass, there are no false shapes or surmises, the road is still asleep with the crust of dew unbroken. I'll take Graylie because he is not afraid of bridges.

Come now, Graylie, she said, taking his bridle, we must outrun Death and the Devil. You are no good for it, she told the other horses standing saddled before the stable gate, among them the horse of the stranger, gray also, with tarnished nose and ears. The stranger swung into his saddle beside her, leaned far towards her and regarded her without meaning, the blank still stare of mindless malice that makes no threats and can bide its time. She drew Graylie around sharply, urged him to run. He leaped the low rose hedge and the narrow ditch beyond, and the dust of the lane flew heavily under his beating hoofs. The stranger rode beside her, easily, lightly, his reins loose in his half-closed hand, straight and elegant in dark shabby garments that flapped upon his bones; his pale face smiled in an evil trance, he did not glance at her. Ah, I have seen this fellow before, I know this man if I could place him. He is no stranger to me.

She pulled Graylie up, rose in her stirrups and shouted, I'm not going with you this time—ride on! Without pausing or turning his head the stranger rode on. Graylie's ribs heaved under her, her own ribs rose and fell, Oh, why am I so tired, I must wake up. "But let me get a fine yawn first," she said, opening her eyes and stretching, "a slap of cold water in my face, for I've been talking in my sleep again, I heard myself but what was I saying?"

Slowly, unwillingly, Miranda drew herself up inch by inch out of the pit of sleep, waited in a daze for life to begin again. A single word struck in her mind, a gong of warning, reminding her for the day long what she forgot happily in sleep, and only in sleep. The war, said the gong, and she shook her head. Dangling her feet idly with their slippers hanging, she was reminded of the way all sorts of persons sat upon her desk at the newspaper office. Every day she found someone there, sitting upon her desk instead of the chair provided, dangling his legs, eyes roving, full of his important affairs, waiting to pounce about something or other. "*Why* won't they sit in the chair? Should I put a sign on it, saying, 'For God's sake, sit here'?"

Far from putting up a sign, she did not even frown at her visitors. Usually she did not notice them at all until their determination to be seen was greater than her determination not to see them. Saturday, she thought, lying comfortably in her tub of hot water, will be pay day, as always. Or I hope always. Her thoughts roved hazily in a continual effort to bring together and unite firmly the disturbing oppositions in her day-to-day existence, where survival, she could see clearly, had become a series of feats of sleight of hand. I owe—let me see, I wish I had pencil and paper—well, suppose I *did* pay five dollars now on a Liberty Bond, I couldn't possibly keep it up. Or maybe. Eighteen dollars a week. So much for rent, so much for food, and I mean to have a few things besides. About five dollars' worth. Will leave me twenty-seven cents. I suppose I can make it. I suppose I should be worried. I am worried. Very well, now I am worried and what next? Twenty-seven cents. That's not so bad. Pure profit, really. Imagine if they should suddenly raise me to twenty I should then have two dollars and twenty-seven cents left over. But they aren't going to raise me to twenty. They are in fact going to throw me out if I don't buy a Liberty Bond. I hardly believe that. I'll ask Bill. (Bill was the city editor.) I wonder if a threat like that isn't a kind of blackmail. I don't believe even a Lusk Committeeman can get away with that.

Yesterday there had been two pairs of legs dangling, on either side of her typewriter, both pairs stuffed thickly into funnels of dark expensive-looking material. She noticed at a distance that one of them was oldish and one was youngish, and they both of them had a stale air of borrowed importance which apparently they had got from the same source. They were both much too well nourished and the younger one wore a square little mustache. Being what they were, no matter what their business was it would be something unpleasant. Miranda had nodded at them, pulled out her chair and without removing her cap or gloves had reached into a pile of letters and sheets from the copy desk as if she had not a moment to spare. They did not move, or take off their hats. At last she had said "Good morning" to them, and asked if they were, perhaps, waiting for her?

The two men slid off the desk, leaving some of her papers rumpled, and the oldish man had inquired why she had not bought a Liberty Bond. Miranda had looked at him then, and got a poor impression. He was a pursy-faced man, gross-mouthed, with little lightless eyes, and Miranda wondered why nearly all of those selected to do the war work at home were of his sort. He might be anything at all, she thought; advance agent for a road show, promoter of a wildcat oil company, a former saloon keeper announcing the opening of a new cabaret, an automobile salesman—any follower of any one of the crafty, haphazard callings. But he was now all Patriot, working for the government. "Look here," he asked her, "do you know there's a war, or don't you?"

Did he expect an answer to that? Be quiet, Miranda told herself, this was bound to happen. Sooner or later it happens. Keep your head. The man wagged his finger at her, "Do you?" he persisted, as if he were prompting an obstinate child.

"Oh, the war," Miranda had echoed on a rising note and she almost smiled at him. It was habitual, automatic, to give that solemn, mystically uplifted grin when you spoke the words or heard them spoken. *"C'est la guerre,"* whether you could pronounce it or not, was even better, and always, always, you shrugged.

"Yeah," said the younger man in a nasty way, "the war." Miranda, startled by the tone, met his eye; his stare was really stony, really viciously cold, the kind of thing you might expect to meet behind a pistol on a deserted corner. This expression gave temporary meaning to a set of features otherwise nondescript, the face of those men who have no business of their own. "We're having a war, and some people are buying Liberty Bonds and others just don't seem to get around to it," he said. "That's what we mean."

Miranda frowned with nervousness, the sharp beginnings of

fear. "Are you selling them?" she asked, taking the cover off her typewriter and putting it back again.

"No, we're not selling them," said the older man. "We're just asking you why you haven't bought one." The voice was persuasive and ominous.

Miranda began to explain that she had no money, and did not know where to find any, when the older man interrupted: "That's no excuse, no excuse at all, and you know it, with the Huns overrunning martyred Belgium."

"With our American boys fighting and dying in Belleau Wood," said the younger man, "anybody can raise fifty dollars to help beat the Boche."

Miranda said hastily, "I have eighteen dollars a week and not another cent in the world. I simply cannot buy anything."

"You can pay for it five dollars a week," said the older man (they had stood there cawing back and forth over her head), "like a lot of other people in this office, and a lot of other offices besides are doing."

Miranda, desperately silent, had thought, "Suppose I were not a coward, but said what I really thought? Suppose I said to hell with this filthy war? Suppose I asked that little thug, What's the matter with you, why aren't you rotting in Belleau Wood? I wish you were . . ."

She began to arrange her letters and notes, her fingers refusing to pick up things properly. The older man went on making his little set speech. It was hard, of course. Everybody was suffering, naturally. Everybody had to do his share. But as to that, a Liberty Bond was the safest investment you could make. It was just like having the money in the bank. Of course. The government was back of it and where better could you invest?

"I agree with you about that," said Miranda, "but I haven't any money to invest."

And of course, the man had gone on, it wasn't so much her fifty dollars that was going to make any difference. It was just a pledge of good faith on her part. A pledge of good faith that she was a loyal American doing her duty. And the thing was safe as a church. Why, if he had a million dollars he'd be glad to put every last cent of it in these Bonds. . . . "You can't lose by it," he said, almost benevolently, "and you can lose a lot if you don't. Think it over. You're the only one in this whole newspaper office that hasn't come in. And every firm in this city has come in one hundred per cent. Over at the *Daily Clarion* nobody had to be asked twice."

"They pay better over there," said Miranda. "But next week, if I can. Not now, next week."

"See that you do," said the younger man. "This ain't any laughing matter."

They lolled away, past the Society Editor's desk, past Bill the City Editor's desk, past the long copy desk where old man Gibbons sat all night shouting at intervals, "Jarge! Jarge!" and the copy boy would come flying. "Never say *people* when you mean *persons*," old man Gibbons had instructed Miranda, "and never say *practically,* say *virtually,* and don't for God's sake ever so long as I am at this desk use the barbarism *inasmuch* under any circumstances whatsoever. Now you're educated, you may go." At the head of the stairs her inquisitors had stopped in their fussy pride and vainglory, lighting cigars and wedging their hats more firmly over their eyes.

Miranda turned over in the soothing water, and wished she might fall asleep there, to wake up only when it was time to sleep again. She had a burning slow headache, and noticed it now, remembering she had waked up with it and it had in fact begun the evening before. While she dressed she tried to trace the insidious career of her headache, and it seemed reasonable to suppose it had started with the war. "It's been a headache, all right, but not quite like this." After the Committeemen had left, yesterday, she had gone to the cloakroom and had found Mary Townsend, the Society Editor, quietly hysterical about something. She was perched on the edge of the shabby wicker couch with ridges down the center, knitting on something rose-colored. Now and then she would put down her knitting, seize her head with both hands and rock, saying, "My *God,*" in a surprised, inquiring voice. Her column was called Ye Towne Gossyp, so of course everybody called her Towney. Miranda and Towney had a great deal in common, and liked each other. They had both been real reporters once, and had been sent together to "cover" a scandalous elopement, in which no marriage had taken place, after all, and the recaptured girl, her face swollen, had sat with her mother, who was moaning steadily under a mound of blankets. They had both wept painfully and implored the young reporters to suppress the worst of the story. They had suppressed it, and the rival newspaper printed it all the next day. Miranda and Towney had then taken their punishment together, and had been degraded publicly to routine female jobs, one to the theaters, the other to society. They had this in common, that neither of them could see what else they could possibly have done, and they knew they were considered fools by the rest of the staff— nice girls, but fools. At sight of Miranda, Towney had broken out in a rage. "I can't do it, I'll never be able to raise the money, I told them, I can't, I can't, but they wouldn't listen."

Miranda said, "I knew I wasn't the only person in this office who couldn't raise five dollars. I told them I couldn't, too, and I can't."

"My *God*," said Towney, in the same voice, "they told me I'd lose my job—"

"I'm going to ask Bill," Miranda said; "I don't believe Bill would do that."

"It's not up to Bill," said Towney. "He'd have to if they got after him. Do you suppose they could put us in jail?"

"I don't know," said Miranda. "If they do, we won't be lonesome." She sat down beside Towney and held her own head. "What kind of soldier are you knitting that for? It's a sprightly color, it ought to cheer him up."

"Like hell," said Towney, her needles going again. "I'm making this for myself. That's that."

"Well," said Miranda, "we won't be lonesome and we'll catch up on our sleep." She washed her face and put on fresh make-up. Taking clean gray gloves out of her pocket she went out to join a group of young women fresh from the country club dances, the morning bridge, the charity bazaar, the Red Cross workrooms, who were wallowing in good works. They gave tea dances and raised money, and with the money they bought quantities of sweets, fruit, cigarettes, and magazines for the men in the cantonment hospitals. With this loot they were now setting out, a gay procession of high-powered cars and brightly tinted faces to cheer the brave boys who already, you might very well say, had fallen in defense of their country. It must be frightfully hard on them, the dears, to be floored like this when they're all crazy to get overseas and into the trenches as quickly as possible. Yes, and some of them are the cutest things you ever saw, I didn't know there were so many good-looking men in this country, good heavens, I said, where do they come from? Well, my dear, you may ask yourself that question, who knows where they did come from? You're quite right, the way I feel about it is this, we must do everything we can to make them contented, but I draw the line at talking to them. I told the chaperons at those dances for enlisted men, I'll dance with them, every dumbbell who asks me, but I will NOT talk to them, I said, even if there is a war. So I danced hundreds of miles without opening my mouth except to say, Please keep your knees to yourself. I'm glad we gave those dances up. Yes, and the men stopped coming, anyway. But listen, I've heard that a great many of the enlisted men come from very good families; I'm not good at catching names, and those I did catch I'd never heard before, so I don't know . . . but it seems to me if they were from good families, you'd know it, wouldn't you? I mean, if a man is well bred he doesn't step on your feet, does he? At least not that. I used to have a pair of sandals ruined at every one of those dances. Well, I think any kind of social life is in very poor taste just now, I think we should all put on our Red Cross head dresses and wear them for the duration of the war—

Miranda, carrying her basket and her flowers, moved in among the young women, who scattered out and rushed upon the ward uttering girlish laughter meant to be refreshingly gay, but there was a grim determined clang in it calculated to freeze the blood. Miserably embarrassed at the idiocy of her errand, she walked rapidly between the long rows of high beds, set foot to foot with a narrow aisle between. The men, a selected presentable lot, sheets drawn up to their chins, not seriously ill, were bored and restless, most of them willing to be amused at anything. They were for the most part picturesquely bandaged as to arm or head, and those who were not visibly wounded invariably replied "Rheumatism" if some tactless girl, who had been solemnly warned never to ask this question, still forgot and asked a man what his illness was. The good-natured, eager ones, laughing and calling out from their hard narrow beds, were soon surrounded. Miranda, with her wilting bouquet and her basket of sweets and cigarettes, looking about, caught the unfriendly bitter eye of a young fellow lying on his back, his right leg in a cast and pulley. She stopped at the foot of his bed and continued to look at him, and he looked back with an unchanged, hostile face. Not having any, thank you and be damned to the whole business, his eyes said plainly to her, and will you be so good as to take your trash off my bed? For Miranda had set it down, leaning over to place it where he might be able to reach it if he would. Having set it down, she was incapable of taking it up again, but hurried away, her face burning, down the long aisle and out into the cool October sunshine, where the dreary raw barracks swarmed and worked with an aimless life of scurrying, dun-colored insects; and going around to a window near where he lay, she looked in, spying upon her soldier. He was lying with his eyes closed, his eyebrows in a sad bitter frown. She could not place him at all, she could not imagine where he came from nor what sort of being he might have been "in life," she said to herself. His face was young and the features sharp and plain, the hands were not laborer's hands but not well-cared-for hands either. They were good useful properly shaped hands, lying there on the coverlet. It occurred to her that it would be her luck to find him, instead of a jolly hungry puppy glad of a bite to eat and a little chatter. It is like turning a corner absorbed in your painful thoughts and meeting your state of mind embodied, face to face, she said. "My own feelings about this whole thing, made flesh. Never again will I come here, this is no sort of thing to be doing. This is disgusting," she told herself plainly. "Of course I would pick him out," she thought, getting into the back seat of the car she came in, "serves me right, I know better."

Another girl came out looking very tired and climbed in beside her. After a short silence, the girl said in a puzzled way, "I don't know what good it does, really. Some of them wouldn't take anything at all. I don't like this, do you?"

"I hate it," said Miranda.

"I suppose it's all right, though," said the girl, cautiously.

"Perhaps," said Miranda, turning cautious also.

That was for yesterday. At this point Miranda decided there was no good in thinking of yesterday, except for the hour after midnight she had spent dancing with Adam. He was in her mind so much, she hardly knew when she was thinking about him directly.

His image was simply always present in more or less degree, he was sometimes nearer the surface of her thoughts, the pleasantest, the only really pleasant thought she had. She examined her face in the mirror between the windows and decided that her uneasiness was not all imagination. For three days at least she had felt odd and her expression was unfamiliar. She would have to raise that fifty dollars somehow, she supposed, or who knows what can happen? She was hardened to stories of personal disaster, of outrageous accusations and extraordinarily bitter penalties that had grown monstrously out of incidents very little more important than her failure—her refusal—to buy a Bond. No, she did not find herself a pleasing sight, flushed and shiny, and even her hair felt as if it had decided to grow in the other direction. I must do something about this, I can't let Adam see me like this, she told herself, knowing that even now at that moment he was listening for the turn of her door knob, and he would be in the hallway, or on the porch when she came out, as if by sheerest coincidence. The noon sunlight cast cold slanting shadows in the room where, she said, I suppose I live, and this day is beginning badly, but they all do now, for one reason or another. In a drowse, she sprayed perfume on her hair, put on her moleskin cap and jacket, now in their second winter, but still good, still nice to wear, again being glad she had paid a frightening price for them. She had enjoyed them all this time, and in no case would she have had the money now. Maybe she could manage for that Bond. She could not find the lock without leaning to search for it, then stood undecided a moment possessed by the notion that she had forgotten something she would miss seriously later on.

Adam was in the hallway, a step outside his own door; he swung about as if quite startled to see her, and said, "Hello. I don't have to go back to camp today after all—isn't that luck?"

Miranda smiled at him gaily because she was always delighted at the sight of him. He was wearing his new uniform, and he was all olive and tan and tawny, hay colored and sand colored from hair to boots. She half noticed again that he always began by smiling at her; that his smile faded gradually; that his eyes became fixed and thoughtful as if he were reading in a poor light.

They walked out together into the fine fall day, scuffling bright ragged leaves under their feet, turning their faces up to a generous sky really blue and spotless. At the first corner they waited for a funeral to pass, the mourners seated straight and firm as if proud in their sorrow.

"I imagine I'm late," said Miranda, "as usual. What time is it?"

"Nearly half past one," he said, slipping back his sleeve with an exaggerated thrust of his arm upward. The young soldiers were still self-conscious about their wrist watches. Such of them as Miranda knew were boys from southern and southwestern towns, far off the Atlantic seaboard, and they had always believed that only sissies wore wrist watches. "I'll slap you on the wrist watch," one vaudeville comedian would simper to another, and it was always a good joke, never stale.

"I think it's a most sensible way to carry a watch," said Miranda. "You needn't blush."

"I'm nearly used to it," said Adam, who was from Texas. "We've been told time and again how all the he-manly regular army men wear them. It's the horrors of war," he said; "are we downhearted? I'll say we are."

It was the kind of patter going the rounds. "You look it," said Miranda.

He was tall and heavily muscled in the shoulders, narrow in the waist and flanks, and he was infinitely buttoned, strapped, harnessed into a uniform as tough and unyielding in cut as a strait jacket, though the cloth was fine and supple. He had his uniforms made by the best tailor he could find, he confided to Miranda one day when she told him how squish he was looking in his new soldier suit. "Hard enough to make anything of the outfit, anyhow," he told her. "It's the least I can do for my beloved country, not to go around looking like a tramp." He was twenty-four years old and a Second Lieutenant in an Engineers Corps, on leave because his outfit expected to be sent over shortly. "Came in to make my will," he told Miranda, "and get a supply of toothbrushes and razor blades. By what gorgeous luck do you suppose," he asked her, "I happened to pick on your rooming house? How did I know you were there?"

Strolling, keeping step, his stout polished well-made boots setting themselves down firmly beside her thin-soled black suède, they put off as long as they could the end of their moment together, and kept up as well as they could their small talk that flew back and forth over little grooves worn in the thin upper surface of the brain, things you could say and hear clink reassuringly at once without disturbing the radiance which played and darted about the simple and lovely miracle of being two persons named Adam and Miranda, twenty-four years old each, alive and on the earth at the same moment: "Are you in the mood for dancing, Miranda?" and "I'm always in the mood for dancing, Adam!" but there were things in the way, the day that ended with dancing was a long way to go.

He really did look, Miranda thought, like a fine healthy apple this morning. One time or another in their talking, he had boasted that he had never had a pain in his life that he could remember. Instead of being horrified at this monster, she approved his monstrous uniqueness. As for herself, she had had too many pains to mention, so she did not mention them. After working for three years on a morning newspaper she had an illusion of maturity and experience; but it was fatigue merely, she decided, from keeping what she had been brought up to believe were unnatural hours, eating casually at dirty little restaurants, drinking bad coffee all night, and smoking too much. When she said something of her way of living to Adam, he studied her face a few seconds as if he had never seen it before, and said in a forthright way, "Why, it hasn't hurt you a bit, I think you're beautiful," and left her dangling there, wondering if he had thought she wished to be praised. She did wish to be praised, but not at that moment. Adam kept unwholesome hours too, or had in the ten days they had known each other, staying awake until one o'clock to take her out for supper; he smoked also continually, though if she did not stop him he was apt to explain to her exactly what smoking did to the lungs. "But," he said, "does it matter so much if you're going to war, anyway?"

"No," said Miranda, "and it matters even less if you're staying at home knitting socks. Give me a cigarette, will you?" They paused at another corner, under a half-foliaged maple, and hardly glanced at a funeral procession approaching. His eyes were pale tan with orange flecks in them, and his hair was the color of a haystack when you turn the weathered top back to the clear straw beneath. He fished out his cigarette case and snapped his silver lighter at her, snapped it several times in his own face, and they moved on, smoking.

"I can see you knitting socks," he said. "That would be just your speed. You know perfectly well you can't knit."

"I do worse," she said, soberly; "I write pieces advising other young women to knit and roll bandages and do without sugar and help win the war."

"Oh, well," said Adam, with the easy masculine morals in such questions, "that's merely your job, that doesn't count."

"I wonder," said Miranda. "How did you manage to get an extension of leave?"

"They just gave it," said Adam, "for no reason. The men are dying like flies out there, anyway. This funny new disease. Simply knocks you into a cocked hat."

"It seems to be a plague," said Miranda, "something out of the Middle Ages. Did you ever see so many funerals, ever?"

"Never did. Well, let's be strong minded and not have any of it. I've got four days more straight from the blue and not a blade of grass must grow under our feet. What about tonight?"

"Same thing," she told him, "but make it about half past one. I've got a special job beside my usual run of the mill."

"What a job you've got," said Adam, "nothing to do but run from one dizzy amusement to another and then write a piece about it."

"Yes, it's too dizzy for words," said Miranda. They stood while a funeral passed, and this time they watched it in silence. Miranda pulled her cap to an angle and winked in the sunlight, her head swimming slowly "like goldfish," she told Adam, "my head swims. I'm only half awake, I must have some coffee."

They lounged on their elbows over the counter of a drug store. "No more cream for the stay-at-homes," she said, "and only one lump of sugar. I'll have two or none; that's the kind of martyr I'm being. I mean to live on boiled cabbage and wear shoddy from now on and get in good shape for the next round. No war is going to sneak up on me again."

"Oh, there won't be any more wars, don't you read the newspapers?" asked Adam. "We're going to mop 'em up this time, and they're going to stay mopped, and this is going to be all."

"So they told me," said Miranda, tasting her bitter lukewarm brew and making a rueful face. Their smiles approved of each other, they felt they had got the right tone, they were taking the war properly. Above all, thought Miranda, no tooth-gnashing, no hair-tearing, it's noisy and unbecoming and it doesn't get you anywhere.

"Swill," said Adam rudely, pushing back his cup. "Is that all you're having for breakfast?"

"It's more than I want," said Miranda.

"I had buckwheat cakes, with sausage and maple syrup, and two bananas, and two cups of coffee, at eight o'clock, and right now, again, I feel like a famished orphan left in the ashcan. I'm all set," said Adam, "for broiled steak and fried potatoes and—"

"Don't go on with it," said Miranda, "it sounds delirious to me. Do all that after I'm gone." She slipped from the high seat, leaned against it slightly, glanced at her face in her round mirror, rubbed rouge on her lips and decided that she was past praying for.

"There's something terribly wrong," she told Adam. "I feel too rotten. It can't just be the weather, and the war."

"The weather is perfect," said Adam, "and the war is simply too good to be true. But since when? You were all right yesterday."

"I don't know," she said slowly, her voice sounding small and thin. They stopped as always at the open door before the flight of littered steps leading up to the newspaper loft. Miranda listened for a moment to the rattle of typewriters above, the steady rumble of presses below. "I wish we were going to spend the whole afternoon on a park bench," she said, "or drive to the mountains."

"I do too," he said; "let's do that tomorrow."

"Yes, tomorrow, unless something else happens. I'd like to run away," she told him; "let's both."

"Me?" said Adam. "Where I'm going there's no running to speak of. You mostly crawl about on your stomach here and there among the debris. You know, barbed wire and such stuff. It's going to be the kind of thing that happens once in a lifetime." He reflected a moment, and went on, "I don't know a darned thing about it, really, but they make it sound awfully messy. I've heard so much about it I feel as if I had been there and back. It's going to be an anticlimax," he said, "like seeing the pictures of a place so often you can't see it at all when you actually get there. Seems to me I've been in the army all my life."

Six months, he meant. Eternity. He looked so clear and fresh, and he had never had a pain in his life. She had seen them when they had been there and back and they never looked like this again. "Already the returned hero," she said, "and don't I wish you were."

"When I learned the use of the bayonet in my first training camp," said Adam, "I gouged the vitals out of more sandbags and sacks of hay than I could keep track of. They kept bawling at us, 'Get him, get that Boche, stick him before he sticks you'—and we'd go for those sandbags like wildfire, and honestly, sometimes I felt a perfect fool for getting so worked up when I saw the sand trickling out. I used to wake up in the night sometimes feeling silly about it."

"I can imagine," said Miranda. "It's perfect nonsense." They lingered, unwilling to say good-by. After a little pause, Adam, as if keeping up the conversation, asked, "Do you know what the average life expectation of a sapping party is after it hits the job?"

"Something speedy, I suppose."

"Just nine minutes," said Adam; "I read that in your own newspaper not a week ago."

"Make it ten and I'll come along," said Miranda.

"Not another second," said Adam, "exactly nine minutes, take it or leave it."

"Stop bragging," said Miranda. "Who figured that out?"

"A noncombatant," said Adam, "a fellow with rickets."

This seemed very comic, they laughed and leaned towards each other and Miranda heard herself being a little shrill. She wiped the tears from her eyes. "My, it's a funny war," she said; "isn't it? I laugh every time I think about it."

Adam took her hand in both of his and pulled a little at the tips of her gloves and sniffed them. "What nice perfume you have," he said, "and such a lot of it, too. I like a lot of perfume on gloves and hair," he said, sniffing again.

"I've got probably too much," she said. "I can't smell or see or hear today. I must have a fearful cold."

"Don't catch cold," said Adam; "my leave is nearly up and it will be the last, the very last." She moved her fingers in her gloves as he pulled at the fingers and turned her hands as if they were something new and curious and of great value, and she turned shy and quiet. She liked him, she liked him, and there was more than this but it was no good even imagining, because he was not for her nor for any woman, being beyond experience already, committed without any knowledge or act of his own to death. She took back her hands. "Good-by," she said finally, "until tonight."

She ran upstairs and looked back from the top. He was still watching her, and raised his hand without smiling. Miranda hardly ever saw anyone look back after he had said good-by. She could not help turning sometimes for one glimpse more of the person she had been talking with, as if that would save too rude and too sudden a snapping of even the lightest bond. But people hurried away, their faces already changed, fixed, in their straining towards their next stopping place, already absorbed in planning their next act or encounter. Adam was waiting as if he expected her to turn, and under his brows fixed in a strained frown, his eyes were very black.

At her desk she sat without taking off jacket or cap, slitting envelopes and pretending to read the letters. Only Chuck Rouncivale, the sports reporter, and Ye Towne Gossyp were sitting on her desk today, and them she liked having there. She sat on theirs when she pleased. Towney and Chuck were talking and they went on with it.

"They say," said Towney, "that it is really caused by germs brought by a German ship to Boston, a camouflaged ship, naturally, it didn't come in under its own colors. Isn't that ridiculous?"

"Maybe it was a submarine," said Chuck, "sneaking in from the bottom of the sea in the dead of night. Now that sounds better."

"Yes, it does," said Towney; "they always slip up somewhere in these details . . . and they think the germs were sprayed over the city—it started in Boston, you know—and somebody reported seeing a strange, thick, greasy-looking cloud float up out of Boston Harbor and spread slowly all over that end of town. I think it was an old woman who saw it."

"Should have been," said Chuck.

"I read it in a New York newspaper," said Towney; "so it's bound to be true."

Chuck and Miranda laughed so loudly at this that Bill stood up and glared at them. "Towney still reads the newspapers," explained Chuck.

"Well, what's funny about that?" asked Bill, sitting down again and frowning into the clutter before him.

"It was a noncombatant saw that cloud," said Miranda.

"Naturally," said Towney.

"Member of the Lusk Committee, maybe," said Miranda.

"The Angel of Mons," said Chuck, "or a dollar-a-year man."

Miranda wished to stop hearing, and talking, she wished to think for just five minutes of her own about Adam, really to think about him, but there was no time. She had seen him first ten days ago, and since then they had been crossing streets together, darting between trucks and limousines and pushcarts and farm wagons; he had waited for her in doorways and in little restaurants that smelled of stale frying fat; they had eaten and danced to the urgent whine and bray of jazz orchestras, they had sat in dull theaters because Miranda was there to write a piece about the play. Once they had gone to the mountains and, leaving the car, had climbed a stony trail, and had come out on a ledge upon a flat stone, where they sat and watched the lights change on a valley landscape that was, no doubt, Miranda said, quite apocryphal—"We need not believe it, but it is fine poetry," she told him; they had leaned their shoulders together there, and had sat quite still, watching. On two Sundays they had gone to the geological museum, and had pored in shared fascination over bits of meteors, rock formations, fossilized tusks and trees, Indian arrows, grottoes from the silver and gold lodes. "Think of those old miners washing out their fortunes in little pans beside the streams," said Adam, "and inside the earth there was this—" and he had told her he liked better those things that took long to make; he loved airplanes too, all sorts of machinery, things carved out of wood or stone. He knew nothing much about them, but he recognized them when he saw them. He had confessed that he simply could not get through a book, any kind of book except textbooks on engineering; reading bored him to crumbs; he regretted now he hadn't brought his roadster, but he hadn't thought he would need a car; he loved driving, he wouldn't expect her to believe how many hundreds of miles he could get over in a day . . . he had showed her snapshots of himself at the wheel of his roadster; of himself sailing a boat, looking very free and windblown, all angles, hauling on the ropes; he would have joined the air force, but his mother had hysterics every time he mentioned it. She didn't seem to realize that dog fighting in the air was a good deal safer than sapping parties on the ground at night.

But he hadn't argued, because of course she did not realize about sapping parties. And here he was, stuck, on a plateau a mile high with no water for a boat and his car at home, otherwise they could really have had a good time. Miranda knew he was trying to tell her what kind of person he was when he had his machinery with him. She felt she knew pretty well what kind of person he was, and would have liked to tell him that if he thought he had left himself at home in a boat or an automobile, he was much mistaken. The telephones were ringing, Bill was shouting at somebody who kept saying, "Well, but listen, well, but listen—" but nobody was going to listen, of course, nobody. Old man Gibbons bellowed in despair, "Jarge, Jarge—"

"Just the same," Towney was saying in her most complacent patriotic voice. "Hut Service is a fine idea, and we should all volunteer even if they don't want us." Towney does well at this, thought Miranda, look at her; remembering the rose-colored sweater and the tight rebellious face in the cloakroom. Towney was now all open-faced glory and goodness, willing to sacrifice herself for her country. "After all," said Towney, "I *can* sing and dance well enough for the Little Theater, and I could write their letters for them, and at a pinch I might drive an ambulance. I have driven a Ford for years."

Miranda joined in: "Well, I can sing and dance too, but who's going to do the bed-making and the scrubbing up? Those huts are hard to keep, and it would be a dirty job and we'd be perfectly miserable; and as I've got a hard dirty job and am perfectly miserable, I'm going to stay at home."

"I think the women should keep out of it," said Chuck Rouncivale. "They just add skirts to the horrors of war." Chuck had bad lungs and fretted a good deal about missing the show. "I could have been there and back with a leg off by now; it would have served the old man right. Then he'd either have to buy his own hooch or sober up."

Miranda had seen Chuck on pay day giving the old man money for hooch. He was a good-humored ingratiating old scoundrel, too, that was the worst of him. He slapped his son on the back and beamed upon him with the bleared eye of paternal affection while he took his last nickel.

"It was Florence Nightingale ruined wars," Chuck went on.

"What's the idea of petting soldiers and binding up their wounds and soothing their fevered brows? That's not war. Let 'em perish where they fall. That's what they're there for."

"You can talk," said Towney, with a slantwise glint at him.

"What's the idea?" asked Chuck, flushing and hunching his shoulders. "You know I've got this lung, or maybe half of it anyway by now."

"You're much too sensitive," said Towney. "I didn't mean a thing."

Bill had been raging about, chewing his half-smoked cigar, his hair standing up in a brush, his eyes soft and lambent but wild, like a stag's. He would never, thought Miranda, be more than fourteen years old if he lived for a century, which he would not, at the rate he was going. He behaved exactly like city editors in the moving pictures, even to the chewed cigar. Had he formed his style on the films, or had scenario writers seized once for all on the type Bill in its inarguable purity? Bill was shouting to Chuck: *"And if he comes back here take him up the alley and saw his head off by hand!"*

Chuck said, "He'll be back, don't worry." Bill said mildly, already off on another track, "Well, saw him off." Towney went to her own desk, but Chuck sat waiting amiably to be taken to the new vaudeville show. Miranda, with two tickets, always invited one of the reporters to go with her on Monday. Chuck was lavishly hardboiled and professional in his sports writing, but he had told Miranda that he didn't give a damn about sports, really; the job kept him out in the open, and paid him enough to buy the old man's hooch. He preferred shows and didn't see why women always had the job.

"Who does Bill want sawed today?" asked Miranda.

"That hoofer you panned in this morning's," said Chuck. "He was up here bright and early asking for the guy that writes up show business. He said he was going to take the goof who wrote that piece up the alley and bop him in the nose. He said . . ."

"I hope he's gone," said Miranda; "I do hope he had to catch a train."

Chuck stood up and arranged his maroon-colored turtle-necked sweater, glanced down at the peasoup tweed plus fours and the hobnailed tan boots which he hoped would help to disguise the fact that he had a bad lung and didn't care for sports, and said, "He's long gone by now, don't worry. Let's get going; you're late as usual."

Miranda, facing about, almost stepped on the toes of a little drab man in a derby hat. He might have been a pretty fellow once, but now his mouth drooped where he had lost his side teeth, and his sad red-rimmed eyes had given up coquetry. A thin brown wave of hair was combed out with brilliantine and curled against the rim of the derby. He didn't move his feet, but stood planted with a kind of inert resistance, and asked Miranda: "Are you the so-called dramatic critic on this hick newspaper?"

"I'm afraid I am," said Miranda.

"Well," said the little man, "I'm just asking for one minute of your valuable time." His underlip shot out, he began with shaking hands to fish about in his waistcoat pocket. "I just hate to let you get away with it, that's all." He riffled through a collection of shabby newspaper clippings. "Just give these the once-over, will you? And then let me ask you if you think I'm gonna stand for being knocked by a tanktown critic," he said, in a toneless voice; "look here, here's Buffalo, Chicago, Saint Looey, Philadelphia, Frisco, besides New York. Here's the best publications in the business, *Variety,* the *Billboard,* they all broke down and admitted that Danny Dickerson knows his stuff. So you don't think so, hey? That's all I wanta ask you."

"No, I don't," said Miranda, as bluntly as she could, "and I can't stop to talk about it."

The little man leaned nearer, his voice shook as if he had been nervous for a long time. "Look here, what was there you didn't like about me? Tell me that."

Miranda said, "You shouldn't pay any attention at all. What does it matter what I think?"

"I don't care what you think, it ain't that," said the little man, "but these things get round and booking agencies back East don't know how it is out here. We get panned in the sticks and they think it's the same as getting panned in Chicago, see? They don't know the difference. They don't know that the more high class an act is the more the hick critics pan it. But I've been called the best in the business by the best in the business and I wanta know what you think is wrong with me."

Chuck said, "Come on, Miranda, curtain's going up." Miranda handed the little man his clippings, they were mostly ten years old, and tried to edge past him. He stepped before her again and said without much conviction, "If you was a man I'd knock your block off." Chuck got up at that and lounged over, taking his hands out of his pockets, and said, "Now you've done your song and dance you'd better get out. Get the hell out now before I throw you downstairs."

The little man pulled at the top of his tie, a small blue tie with red polka dots, slightly frayed at the knot. He pulled it straight and repeated as if he had rehearsed it, "Come out in the alley." The tears filled his thickened red lids. Chuck said, "Ah, shut up," and followed Miranda, who was running towards the stairs. He overtook her on the sidewalk. "I left him sniveling and shuffling his publicity trying to find the joker," said Chuck, "the poor old heel."

Miranda said, "There's too much of everything in this world just now. I'd like to sit down here on the curb, Chuck, and die, and never again see—I wish I could lose my memory and forget my own name . . . I wish—"

Chuck said, "Toughen up, Miranda. This is no time to cave in. Forget that fellow. For every hundred people in show business, there are ninety-nine like him. But you don't manage right, anyway. You bring it on yourself. All you have to do is play up the headliners, and you needn't even mention the also-rans. Try to keep in mind that Rypinsky has got show business cornered in this town; please Rypinsky and you'll please the advertising department, please them and you'll get a raise. Hand-in-glove, my poor dumb child, will you never learn?"

"I seem to keep learning all the wrong things," said Miranda, hopelessly.

"You do for a fact," Chuck told her cheerfully. "You are as good at it as I ever saw. Now do you feel better?"

"This is a rotten show you've invited me to," said Chuck. "Now what are you going to do about it? If I were writing it up, I'd—"

"Do write it up," said Miranda. "You write it up this time. I'm getting ready to leave, anyway, but don't tell anybody yet."

"You mean it? All my life," said Chuck, "I've yearned to be a so-called dramatic critic on a hick newspaper, and this is positively my first chance."

"Better take it," Miranda told him. "It may be your last." She thought, This is the beginning of the end of something. Something terrible is going to happen to me. I shan't need bread and butter where I'm going. I'll will it to Chuck, he has a venerable father to buy hooch for. I hope they let him have it. Oh, Adam, I hope I see you once more before I go under with whatever is the matter with me. "I wish the war were over," she said to Chuck, as if they had been talking about that. "I wish it were over and I wish it had never begun."

Chuck had got out his pad and pencil and was already writing his review. What she had said seemed safe enough but how would he take it? "I don't care how it started or when it ends," said Chuck, scribbling away, "I'm not going to be there."

All the rejected men talked like that, thought Miranda. War was the one thing they wanted, now they couldn't have it. Maybe they had wanted badly to go, some of them. All of them had a sidelong eye for the women they talked with about it, a guarded resentment which said, "Don't pin a white feather on me, you bloodthirsty female. I've offered my meat to the crows and they won't have it." The worst thing about war for the stay-at-homes is there isn't anyone to talk to any more. The Lusk Committee will get you if you don't watch out. Bread will win the war. Work will win, sugar will win, peach pits will win the war. Nonsense. *Not* nonsense, I tell you, there's some kind of valuable high explosive to be got out of peach pits. So all the happy housewives hurry during the canning season to lay their baskets of peach pits on the altar of their country. It keeps them busy and makes them feel useful, and all these women running wild with the men away are dangerous, if they aren't given something to keep their little minds out of mischief. So rows of young girls, the intact cradles of the future, with their pure serious faces framed becomingly in Red Cross wimples, roll cock-eyed bandages that will never reach a base hospital, and knit sweaters that will never warm a manly chest, their minds dwelling lovingly on all the blood and mud and the next dance at the Acanthus Club for the officers of the flying corps. Keeping still and quiet will win the war.

"I'm simply not going to be there," said Chuck, absorbed in his review. No, Adam will be there, thought Miranda. She slipped down in the chair and leaned her head against the dusty plush, closed her eyes and faced for one instant that was a lifetime the certain, the overwhelming and awful knowledge that there was nothing at all ahead for Adam and for her. Nothing. She opened her eyes and held her hands together palms up, gazing at them and trying to understand oblivion.

"Now look at this," said Chuck, for the lights had come on and the audience was rustling and talking again. "I've got it all done, even before the headliner comes on. It's old Stella Mayhew, and she's always good, she's been good for forty years, and she's going to sing 'O the blues ain't nothin' but the easy-going heart disease.' That's all you need to know about her. Now just glance over this. Would you be willing to sign it?"

Miranda took the pages and stared at them conscientiously, turning them over, she hoped, at the right moment, and gave them back. "Yes, Chuck, yes, I'd sign that. But I won't. We must tell Bill you wrote it, because it's your start, maybe."

"You don't half appreciate it," said Chuck. "You read it too fast. Here, listen to this—" and he began to mutter excitedly. While he was reading she watched his face. It was a pleasant face with some kind of spark of life in it, and a good severity in the modeling of the brow above the nose. For the first time since she had known him she wondered what Chuck was thinking about. He looked preoccupied and unhappy, he wasn't so frivolous as he sounded. The people were crowding into the aisle, bringing out their cigarette cases ready to strike a match the instant they reached the lobby; women with waved hair clutched at their wraps, men stretched their chins to ease them of their stiff collars, and Chuck said, "We might as well go now." Miranda, buttoning her jacket, stepped into the moving crowd, thinking, What did I ever know about them? There must be a great many of them here who think as I do, and we dare not say a word to each other of our desperation, we are speechless animals letting ourselves be destroyed, and why? Does anybody here believe the things we say to each other?

Stretched in unease on the ridge of the wicker couch in the cloakroom, Miranda waited for time to pass and leave Adam with her.

Time seemed to proceed with more than usual eccentricity, leaving twilight gaps in her mind for thirty minutes which seemed like a second, and then hard flashes of light that shone clearly on her watch proving that three minutes is an intolerable stretch of waiting, as if she were hanging by her thumbs. At last it was reasonable to imagine Adam stepping out of the house in the early darkness into the blue mist that might soon be rain, he would be on the way, and there was nothing to think about him, after all. There was only the wish to see him and the fear, the present threat, of not seeing him again; for every step they took towards each other seemed perilous, drawing them apart instead of together, as a swimmer in spite of his most determined strokes is yet drawn slowly backward by the tide. "I don't want to love," she would think in spite of herself, "not Adam, there is no time and we are not ready for it and yet this is all we have—"

And there he was on the sidewalk, with his foot on the first step, and Miranda almost ran down to meet him. Adam, holding her hands, asked, "Do you feel well now? Are you hungry? Are you tired? Will you feel like dancing after the show?"

"Yes to everything," said Miranda, "yes, yes. . . ." Her head was like a feather, and she steadied herself on his arm. The mist was still mist that might be rain later, and though the air was sharp and clean in her mouth, it did not, she decided, make breathing any easier. "I hope the show is good, or at least funny," she told him, "but I promise nothing."

It was a long, dreary play, but Adam and Miranda sat very quietly together waiting patiently for it to be over. Adam carefully and seriously pulled off her glove and held her hand as if he were accustomed to holding her hand in theaters. Once they turned and their eyes met, but only once, and the two pairs of eyes were equally steady and noncommittal. A deep tremor set up in Miranda, and she set about resisting herself methodically as if she were closing windows and doors and fastening down curtains against a rising storm. Adam sat watching the monotonous play with a strange shining excitement, his face quite fixed and still.

When the curtain rose for the third act, the third act did not take place at once. There was instead disclosed a backdrop almost covered with an American flag improperly and disrespectfully exposed, nailed at each upper corner, gathered in the middle and nailed again, sagging dustily. Before it posed a local dollar-a-year man, now doing his bit as a Liberty Bond salesman. He was an ordinary man past middle life, with a neat little melon buttoned into his trousers and waistcoat, an opinionated tight mouth, a face and figure in which nothing could be read save the inept sensual record of fifty years. But for once in his life he was an important fellow in an impressive situation, and he reveled, rolling his words in an actorish tone.

"Looks like a penguin," said Adam. They moved, smiled at each other, Miranda reclaimed her hand, Adam folded his together and they prepared to wear their way again through the same old moldy speech with the same old dusty backdrop. Miranda tried not to listen, but she heard. These vile Huns—glorious Belleau Wood —our keyword is Sacrifice—Martyred Belgium—give till it hurts —our noble boys Over There—Big Berthas—the death of civilization—the Boche—

"My head aches," whispered Miranda. "Oh, why won't he hush?"

"He won't," whispered Adam. "I'll get you some aspirin."

"In Flanders Field the poppies grow, Between the crosses row on row"—"He's getting into the home stretch," whispered Adam —atrocities, innocent babes hoisted on Boche bayonets—your child and my child—if our children are spared these things, then let us say with all reverence that these dead have not died in vain —the war, the *war,* the WAR to end WAR, war for Democracy, for humanity, a safe world forever and ever—and to prove our faith in Democracy to each other, and to the world, let everybody get together and buy Liberty Bonds and do without sugar and wool socks—was that it? Miranda asked herself, Say that over, I didn't catch the last line. Did you mention Adam? If you didn't I'm not interested. What about Adam, you little pig? And what are we going to sing this time, "Tipperary" or "There's a Long, Long Trail"? Oh, please do let the show go on and get over with. I must write a piece about it before I can go dancing with Adam and we have no time. Coal, oil, iron, gold, international finance, why don't you tell us about them, you little liar?

The audience rose and sang, "There's a Long, Long Trail A-winding," their opened mouths black and faces pallid in the reflected footlights; some of the faces grimaced and wept and had shining streaks like snail's tracks on them. Adam and Miranda joined in at the tops of their voices, grinning shamefacedly at each other once or twice.

In the street, they lit their cigarettes and walked slowly as always. "Just another nasty old man who would like to see the young ones killed," said Miranda in a low voice; "the tom-cats try to eat the little tom-kittens, you know. They don't fool you really, do they, Adam?"

The young people were talking like that about the business by then. They felt they were seeing pretty clearly through that game. She went on, "I hate these potbellied baldheads, too fat, too old, too cowardly, to go to war themselves, they know they're safe; it's you they are sending instead—"

Adam turned eyes of genuine surprise upon her. "Oh, *that* one," he said. "Now what could the poor sap do if they did take him? It's not his fault," he explained, "he can't do anything but talk." His pride in his youth, his forbearance and tolerance and contempt for that unlucky being breathed out of his very pores as he strolled, straight and relaxed in his strength. "What *could* you expect of him, Miranda?"

She spoke his name often, and he spoke hers rarely. The little shock of pleasure the sound of her name in his mouth gave her stopped her answer. For a moment she hesitated, and began at another point of attack. "Adam," she said, "the worst of war is the fear and suspicion and the awful expression in all the eyes you meet . . . as if they had pulled down the shutters over their minds and their hearts and were peering out at you, ready to leap if you make one gesture or say one word they do not understand instantly. It frightens me; I live in fear too, and no one should have to live in fear. It's the skulking about, and the lying. It's what war does to the mind and the heart, Adam, and you can't separate these two—what it does to them is worse than what it can do to the body."

Adam said soberly, after a moment, "Oh, yes, but suppose one comes back whole? The mind and the heart sometimes get another chance, but if anything happens to the poor old human frame, why, it's just out of luck, that's all."

"Oh, yes," mimicked Miranda. "It's just ouf of luck, that's all."

"If I didn't go," said Adam, in a matter-of-fact voice, "I couldn't look myself in the face."

So that's all settled. With her fingers flattened on his arm, Miranda was silent, thinking about Adam. No, there was no resentment or revolt in him. Pure, she thought, all the way through, flawless, complete, as the sacrificial lamb must be. The sacrificial lamb strode along casually, accommodating his long pace to hers, keeping her on the inside of the walk in the good American style, helping her across street corners as if she were a cripple—"I hope we don't come to a mud puddle, he'll carry me over it"—giving off whiffs of tobacco smoke, a manly smell of scentless soap, freshly cleaned leather and freshly washed skin, breathing through his nose and carrying his chest easily. He threw back his head and smiled into the sky which still misted, promising rain. "Oh, boy," he said, "what a night. Can't you hurry that review of yours so we can get started?"

He waited for her before a cup of coffee in the restaurant next to the pressroom, nicknamed The Greasy Spoon. When she came down at last, freshly washed and combed and powdered, she saw Adam first, sitting near the dingy big window, face turned to the street, but looking down. It was an extraordinary face, smooth and fine and golden in the shabby light, but now set in a blind melancholy, a look of pained suspense and disillusion. For just one split second she got a glimpse of Adam when he would have been older, the face of the man he would not live to be. He saw her then, rose, and the bright glow was there.

Adam pulled their chairs together at their table; they drank hot tea and listened to the orchestra jazzing "Pack Up Your Troubles."

"In an old kit bag, and smoil, smoil, smoil," shouted half a dozen boys under the draft age, gathered around a table near the orchestra. They yelled incoherently, laughed in great hysterical bursts of something that appeared to be merriment, and passed around under the tablecloth flat bottles containing a clear liquid—for in this western city founded and built by roaring drunken miners, no one was allowed to take his alcohol openly—splashed it into their tumblers of ginger ale, and went on singing, "It's a Long Way to Tipperary." When the tune changed to "Madelon," Adam said, "Let's dance." It was a tawdry little place, crowded and hot and full of smoke, but there was nothing better. The music was gay; and life is completely crazy anyway, thought Miranda, so what does it matter? This is what we have, Adam and I, this is all we're going to get, this is the way it is with us. She wanted to say, "Adam, come out of your dream and listen to me. I have pains in my chest and my head and my heart and they're real. I am in pain all over, and you are in such danger as I can't bear to think about, and why can we not save each other?" When her hand tightened on his shoulder his arm tightened about her waist instantly, and stayed there, holding firmly. They said nothing but smiled continually at each other, odd changing smiles as though they had found a new language. Miranda, her face near Adam's shoulder, noticed a dark young pair sitting at a corner table, each with an arm around the waist of the other, their heads together, their eyes staring at the same thing, whatever it was, that hovered in space before them. Her right hand lay on the table, his hand over it, and her face was a blur with weeping. Now and then he raised her hand and kissed it, and set it down and held it, and her eyes would fill again. They were not shameless, they had merely forgotten where they were, or they had no other place to go, perhaps. They said not a word, and the small pantomime repeated itself, like a melancholy short film running monotonously over and over again. Miranda envied them. She envied that girl. At least she can weep if that helps, and he does not even have to ask, What is the matter? Tell me. They had cups of coffee before them, and after a long while—Miranda and Adam had danced and sat down again twice —when the coffee was quite cold, they drank it suddenly, then embraced as before, without a word and scarcely a glance at each other. Something was done and settled between them, at least; it was enviable, enviable, that they could sit quietly together and have the same expression on their faces while they looked into the hell they shared, no matter what kind of hell, it was theirs, they were together.

At the table nearest Adam and Miranda a young woman was leaning on her elbow, telling her young man a story. "And I don't like him because he's too fresh. He kept on asking me to take a drink and I kept telling him, I don't drink and he said, Now look here, I want a drink the worst way and I think it's mean of you not to drink with me, I can't sit up here and drink by myself, he said. I told him, You're not by yourself in the first place; I like that, I said, and if you want a drink go ahead and have it, I told him, why drag *me* in? So he called the waiter and ordered ginger ale and two glasses and I drank straight ginger ale like I always do but he poured a shot of hooch in his. He was awfully proud of that hooch, said he made it himself out of potatoes. Nice homemade likker, warm from the pipe, he told me, three drops of this and your ginger ale will taste like Mumm's Extry. But I said, No, and I mean no, can't you get that through your bean? He took another drink and said, Ah, come on, honey, don't be so stubborn, this'll make your shimmy shake. So I just got tired of the argument, and I said, I don't need to drink, to shake my shimmy, I can strut my stuff on tea, I said. Well, why don't you then, he wanted to know, and I just told him—"

She knew she had been asleep for a long time when all at once without even a warning footstep or creak of the door hinge, Adam was in the room turning on the light, and she knew it was he, though at first she was blinded and turned her head away. He came over at once and sat on the side of the bed and began to talk as if he were going on with something they had been talking about before. He crumpled a square of paper and tossed it in the fireplace.

"You didn't get my note," he said. "I left it under the door. I was called back suddenly to camp for a lot of inoculations. They kept me longer than I expected, I was late. I called the office and they told me you were not coming in today. I called Miss Hobbe here and she said you were in bed and couldn't come to the telephone. Did she give you my message?"

"No," said Miranda drowsily, "but I think I have been asleep all day. Oh, I do remember. There was a doctor here. Bill sent him. I was at the telephone once, for Bill told me he would send an ambulance and have me taken to the hospital. The doctor tapped my chest and left a prescription and said he would be back, but he hasn't come."

"Where is it, the prescription?" asked Adam.

"I don't know. He left it, though, I saw him."

Adam moved about searching the tables and the mantelpiece.

"Here it is," he said. "I'll be back in a few minutes. I must look for an all-night drug store. It's after one o'clock. Good-by."

Good-by, good-by. Miranda watched the door where he had disappeared for quite a while, then closed her eyes, and thought, When I am not here I cannot remember anything about this room where I have lived for nearly a year, except that the curtains are too thin and there was never any way of shutting out the morning light. Miss Hobbe had promised heavier curtains, but they had never appeared. When Miranda in her dressing gown had been at the telephone that morning, Miss Hobbe had passed through, carrying a tray. She was a little red-haired nervously friendly creature, and her manner said all too plainly that the place was not paying and she was on the ragged edge.

"My dear *child,*" she said sharply, with a glance at Miranda's attire, "what is the matter?"

Miranda, with the receiver to her ear, said, "Influenza, I think."

"*Horrors,*" said Miss Hobbe, in a whisper, and the tray wavered in her hands. "Go back to bed at once . . . go at *once!*"

"I must talk to Bill first," Miranda had told her, and Miss Hobbe had hurried on and had not returned. Bill had shouted directions at her, promising everything, doctor, nurse, ambulance, hospital, her check every week as usual, everything, but she was to get back to bed and stay there. She dropped into bed, thinking that Bill was the only person she had ever seen who actually tore his own hair when he was excited enough . . . I suppose I should ask to be sent home, she thought, it's a respectable old custom to inflict your death on the family if you can manage it. No, I'll stay here, this is my business, but not in this room, I hope . . . I wish I were in the cold mountains in the snow, that's what I should like best; and all about her rose the measured ranges of the Rockies wearing their perpetual snow, their majestic blue laurels of cloud, chilling her to the bone with their sharp breath. Oh, no, I must have warmth—and her memory turned and roved after another place she had known first and loved best, that now she could see only in drifting fragments of palm and cedar, dark shadows and a sky that warmed without dazzling, as this strange sky had dazzled without warming her; there was the long slow wavering of gray moss in the drowsy oak shade, the spacious hovering of buzzards overhead, the smell of crushed water herbs along a bank, and without warning a broad tranquil river into which flowed all the rivers she had known. The walls shelved away in one deliberate silent movement on either side, and a tall sailing ship was moored near by, with a gangplank weathered to blackness touching the foot of her bed. Back of the ship was jungle, and even as it appeared before her, she knew it was all she had ever read or had been told or felt or thought about jungles; a writhing terribly alive and secret place of death, creeping with tangles of spotted serpents, rainbow-colored birds with malign eyes, leopards with humanly wise faces and extravagantly crested lions; screaming long-armed monkeys tumbling among broad fleshy leaves that glowed with sulphur-colored light and exuded the ichor of death, and rotting trunks of unfamiliar trees sprawled in crawling slime. Without surprise, watching from her pillow, she saw herself run swiftly down this gangplank to the slanting deck, and standing there, she leaned on the rail and waved gaily to herself in bed, and the slender ship spread its wings and sailed away into the jungle. The air trembled with the shattering scream and the hoarse bellow of voices all crying together, rolling and colliding above her like ragged storm-clouds, and the words became two words only rising and falling and clamoring about her head. Danger, danger, danger, the voices said, and War, war, war. There was her door half open, Adam standing with his hand on the knob, and Miss Hobbe with her face all out of shape with terror was crying shrilly, "I tell you, they must come for her *now*, or I'll put her on the sidewalk . . . I tell you, this is a plague, a plague, my God, and I've got a houseful of people to think about!"

Adam said, "I know that. They'll come for her tomorrow morning."

"Tomorrow morning, my God, they'd better come now!"

"They can't get an ambulance," said Adam, "and there aren't any beds. And we can't find a doctor or a nurse. They're all busy. That's all there is to it. You stay out of the room, and I'll look after her."

"Yes, you'll look after her, I can see that," said Miss Hobbe, in a particularly unpleasant tone.

"Yes, that's what I said," answered Adam, drily, "and you keep out."

He closed the door carefully. He was carrying an assortment of misshapen packages, and his face was astonishingly impassive.

"Did you hear that?" he asked, leaning over and speaking very quietly.

"Most of it," said Miranda, "it's a nice prospect, isn't it?"

"I've got your medicine," said Adam, "and you're to begin with it this minute. She can't put you out."

"So it's really as bad as that," said Miranda.

"It's as bad as anything can be," said Adam, "all the theaters and nearly all the shops and restaurants are closed, and the streets have been full of funerals all day and ambulances all night—"

"But not one for me," said Miranda, feeling hilarious and light-headed. She sat up and beat her pillow into shape and reached for her robe. "I'm glad you're here, I've been having a nightmare. Give me a cigarette, will you, and light one for yourself and open all the windows and sit near one of them. You're running a risk," she told him, "don't you know that? Why do you do it?"

"Never mind," said Adam, "take your medicine," and offered her two large cherry-colored pills. She swallowed them promptly and instantly vomited them up. "*Do* excuse me," she said, beginning to laugh. "I'm so sorry." Adam without a word and with a very concerned expression washed her face with a wet towel, gave her some cracked ice from one of the packages, and firmly offered her two more pills. "That's what they always did at home," she explained to him, "and it worked." Crushed with humiliation, she put her hands over her face and laughed again, painfully.

"There are two more kinds yet," said Adam, pulling her hands from her face and lifting her chin. "You've hardly begun. And I've got other things, like orange juice and ice cream—they told me to feed you ice cream—and coffee in a thermos bottle, and a thermometer. You have to work through the whole lot so you'd better take it easy."

"This time last night we were dancing," said Miranda, and drank something from a spoon. Her eyes followed him about the room, as he did things for her with an absent-minded face, like a man alone; now and again he would come back, and slipping his hand under her head, would hold a cup or a tumbler to her mouth, and she drank, and followed him with her eyes again, without a clear notion of what was happening.

"Adam," she said, "I've just thought of something. Maybe they forgot St. Luke's Hospital. Call the sisters there and ask them not to be so selfish with their silly old rooms. Tell them I only want a very small dark ugly one for three days, or less. Do try them, Adam."

He believed, apparently, that she was still more or less in her right mind, for she heard him at the telephone explaining in his deliberate voice. He was back again almost at once, saying, "This seems to be my day for getting mixed up with peevish old maids. The sister said that even if they had a room you couldn't have it without doctor's orders. But they didn't have one, anyway. She was pretty sour about it."

"Well," said Miranda in a thick voice, "I think that's abominably rude and mean, don't you?" She sat up with a wild gesture of both arms, and began to retch again, violently.

"Hold it, as you were," called Adam, fetching the basin. He held her head, washed her face and hands with ice water, put her head straight on the pillow, and went over and looked out of the window. "Well," he said at last, sitting beside her again, "they haven't got a room. They haven't got a bed. They haven't even got a baby crib, the way she talked. So I think that's straight enough, and we may as well dig in."

"Isn't the ambulance coming?"

"Tomorrow, maybe."

He took off his tunic and hung it on the back of a chair. Kneeling before the fireplace, he began carefully to set kindling sticks in the shape of an Indian tepee, with a little paper in the center for them to lean upon. He lighted this and placed other sticks upon them, and larger bits of wood. When they were going nicely he added still heavier wood, and coal a few lumps at a time, until there was a good blaze, and a fire that would not need rekindling. He rose and dusted his hands together, the fire illuminated him from the back and his hair shone.

"Adam," said Miranda, "I think you're very beautiful." He laughed out at this, and shook his head at her. "What a hell of a word," he said, "for me." "It was the first that occurred to me," she said, drawing up on her elbow to catch the warmth of the blaze. "That's a good job, that fire."

He sat on the bed again, dragging up a chair and putting his feet on the rungs. They smiled at each other for the first time since he had come in that night. "How do you feel now?" he asked.

"Better, much better," she told him. "Let's talk. Let's tell each other what we meant to do."

"You tell me first," said Adam. "I want to know about you."

"You'd get the notion I had a very sad life," she said, "and perhaps it was, but I'd be glad enough to have it now. If I could have it back, it would be easy to be happy about almost anything at all. That's not true, but that's the way I feel now." After a pause, she said, "There's nothing to tell, after all, if it ends now, for all this time I was getting ready for something that was going to happen later, when the time came. So now it's nothing much."

"But it must have been worth having until now, wasn't it?" he asked seriously as if it were something important to know.

"Not if this is all," she repeated obstinately.

"Weren't you ever—happy?" asked Adam, and he was plainly afraid of the word; he was shy of it as he was of the word *love,* he seemed never to have spoken it before, and was uncertain of its sound or meaning.

"I don't know," she said, "I just lived and never thought about it. I remember things I liked, though, and things I hoped for."

"I was going to be an electrical engineer," said Adam. He stopped short. "And I shall finish up when I get back," he added, after a moment.

"Don't you love being alive?" asked Miranda. "Don't you love weather and the colors at different times of the day, and all the sounds and noises like children screaming in the next lot, and automobile horns and little bands playing in the street and the smell of food cooking?"

"I love to swim, too," said Adam.

"So do I," said Miranda; "we never did swim together."

"Do you remember any prayers?" she asked him suddenly. "Did you ever learn anything at Sunday School?"

"Not much," confessed Adam without contrition. "Well, the Lord's Prayer."

"Yes, and there's Hail Mary," she said, "and the really useful one beginning, I confess to Almighty God and to blessed Mary ever virgin and to the holy Apostles Peter and Paul—"

"Catholic," he commented.

"Prayers just the same, you big Methodist. I'll bet you *are* a Methodist."

"No, Presbyterian."

"Well, what others do you remember?"

"Now I lay me down to sleep——" said Adam.

"Yes, that one, and Blessed Jesus meek and mild—you see that my religious education wasn't neglected either. I even know a prayer beginning O Apollo. Want to hear it?"

"No," said Adam, "you're making fun."

"I'm not," said Miranda, "I'm trying to keep from going to sleep. I'm afraid to go to sleep, I may not wake up. Don't let me go to sleep, Adam. Do you know Matthew, Mark, Luke and John? Bless the bed I lie upon?"

"If I should die before I wake, I pray the Lord my soul to take. Is that it?" asked Adam. "It doesn't sound right, somehow."

"Light me a cigarette, please, and move over and sit near the window. We keep forgetting about fresh air. You must have it." He lighted the cigarette and held it to her lips. She took it between her fingers and dropped it under the edge of her pillow. He found it and crushed it out in the saucer under the water tumbler. Her head swam in darkness for an instant, cleared, and she sat up in panic, throwing off the covers and breaking into a sweat. Adam leaped up with an alarmed face, and almost at once was holding a cup of hot coffee to her mouth.

"You must have some too," she told him, quiet again, and they sat huddled together on the edge of the bed, drinking coffee in silence.

Adam said, "You must lie down again. You're awake now."

"Let's sing," said Miranda. "I know an old spiritual, I can remember some of the words." She spoke in a natural voice. "I'm fine now." She began in a hoarse whisper, " 'Pale horse, pale rider, done taken my lover away . . .' Do you know that song?"

"Yes," said Adam, "I heard Negroes in Texas sing it, in an oil field."

"I heard them sing it in a cotton field," she said; "it's a good song."

They sang that line together. "But I can't remember what comes next," said Adam.

" 'Pale horse, pale rider,' " said Miranda, "(We really need a good banjo) 'done taken my lover away—' " Her voice cleared and she said, "But we ought to get on with it. What's the next line?"

"There's a lot more to it than that," said Adam, "about forty verses, the rider done taken away mammy, pappy, brother, sister, the whole family besides the lover—"

"But not the singer, not yet," said Miranda. "Death always leaves one singer to mourn. 'Death,' " she sang, " 'oh, leave one singer to mourn—' "

" 'Pale horse, pale rider,' " chanted Adam, coming in on the beat, " 'done taken my lover away!' (I think we're good, I think we ought to get up an act—)"

"Go in Hut Service," said Miranda, "entertain the poor defenseless heroes Over There."

"We'll play banjos," said Adam; "I always wanted to play the banjo."

Miranda sighed, and lay back on the pillow and thought, I must give up, I can't hold out any longer. There was only that pain, only that room, and only Adam. There were no longer any multiple planes of living, no tough filaments of memory and hope pulling taut backwards and forwards holding her upright between them. There was only this one moment and it was a dream of time, and Adam's face, very near hers, eyes still and intent, was a shadow, and there was to be nothing more. . . .

"Adam," she said out of the heavy soft darkness that drew her down, down, "I love you, and I was hoping you would say that to me, too."

He lay down beside her with his arm under her shoulder, and pressed his smooth face against hers, his mouth moved towards her mouth and stopped. "Can you hear what I am saying? . . . What do you think I have been trying to tell you all this time?"

She turned towards him, the cloud cleared and she saw his face for an instant. He pulled the covers about her and held her, and said, "Go to sleep, darling, darling, if you will go to sleep now for one hour I will wake you up and bring you hot coffee and tomorrow we will find somebody to help. I love you, go to sleep—"

Almost with no warning at all, she floated into the darkness, holding his hand, in sleep that was not sleep but clear evening light in a small green wood, an angry dangerous wood full of inhuman concealed voices singing sharply like the whine of arrows and she saw Adam transfixed by a flight of these singing arrows that struck him in the heart and passed shrilly cutting their path through the leaves. Adam fell straight back before her eyes, and rose again unwounded and alive; another flight of arrows loosed from the invisible bow struck him again and he fell, and yet he was there before her untouched in a perpetual death and resurrection. She threw herself before him, angrily and selfishly she interposed between him and the track of the arrow, crying, No, no, like a child cheated in a game, It's my turn now, why must you always be the one to die? and the arrows struck her cleanly through the heart and through his body and he lay dead, and she still lived, and the wood whistled and sang and shouted, every branch and leaf and blade of grass had its own terrible accusing voice. She ran then, and Adam caught her in the middle of the room, running, and said, "Darling, I must have been asleep too. What happened, you screamed terribly?"

After he had helped her to settle again, she sat with her knees drawn up under her chin, resting her head on her folded arms and began carefully searching for her words because it was important to explain clearly. "It was a very odd sort of dream, I don't know why it could have frightened me. There was something about an old-fashioned valentine. There were two hearts carved on a tree, pierced by the same arrow—you know, Adam—"

"Yes, I know, honey," he said in the gentlest sort of way, and sat kissing her on the cheek and forehead with a kind of accustomedness, as if he had been kissing her for years, "one of those lace paper things."

"Yes, and yet they were alive, and were us, you understand—this doesn't seem to be quite the way it was, but it was something like that. It was in a wood—"

"Yes," said Adam. He got up and put on his tunic and gathered up the thermos bottle. "I'm going back to that little stand and get us some ice cream and hot coffee," he told her, "and I'll be back in five minutes, and you keep quiet. Good-by for five minutes," he said, holding her chin in the palm of his hand and trying to catch her eye, "and you be very quiet."

"Good-by," she said. "I'm awake again." But she was not, and the two alert young internes from the County hospital who had arrived, after frantic urgings from the noisy city editor of the Blue Mountain *News,* to carry her away in a police ambulance, decided that they had better go down and get the stretcher. Their voices roused her, she sat up, got out of bed at once and stood glancing about brightly. "Why, you're all right," said the darker and stouter of the two young men, both extremely fit and competent-looking in their white clothes, each with a flower in his buttonhole. "I'll just carry you." He unfolded a white blanket and wrapped it around her. She gathered up the folds and asked, "But where is Adam?" taking hold of the doctor's arm. He laid a hand on her drenched forehead, shook his head, and gave her a shrewd look. "Adam?"

"Yes," Miranda told him, lowering her voice confidentially, "he was here and now he is gone."

"Oh, he'll be back," the interne told her easily, "he's just gone round the block to get cigarettes. Don't worry about Adam. He's the least of your troubles."

"Will he know where to find me?" she asked, still holding back.

"We'll leave him a note," said the interne. "Come now, it's time we got out of here."

He lifted and swung her up to his shoulder. "I feel very badly," she told him; "I don't know why."

"I'll bet you do," said he, stepping out carefully, the other doctor going before them, and feeling for the first step of the stairs. "Put your arms around my neck," he instructed her. "It won't do you any harm and it's a great help to me."

"What's your name?" Miranda asked as the other doctor opened the front door and they stepped out into the frosty sweet air.

"Hildesheim," he said, in the tone of one humoring a child.

"Well, Dr. Hildesheim, aren't we in a pretty mess?"

"We certainly are," said Dr. Hildesheim.

The second young interne, still quite fresh and dapper in his white coat, though his carnation was withering at the edges, was leaning over listening to her breathing through a stethoscope, whistling thinly, "There's a Long, Long Trail—" From time to time he tapped her ribs smartly with two fingers, whistling. Miranda observed him for a few moments until she fixed his bright busy hazel eye not four inches from hers. "I'm not unconscious," she explained, "I know what I want to say." Then to her horror she heard herself babbling nonsense, knowing it was nonsense though she could not hear what she was saying. The flicker of attention in the eye near her vanished, the second interne went on tapping and listening, hissing softly under his breath.

"I wish you'd stop whistling," she said clearly. The sound stopped. "It's a beastly tune," she added. Anything, anything at all to keep her small hold on the life of human beings, a clear line of communication, no matter what, between her and the receding world. "Please let me see Dr. Hildesheim," she said, "I have something important to say to him. I must say it now." The second interne vanished. He did not walk away, he fled into the air without a sound, and Dr. Hildesheim's face appeared in his stead.

"Dr. Hildesheim, I want to ask you about Adam."

"That young man? He's been here, and left you a note, and has gone again," said Dr. Hildesheim, "and he'll be back tomorrow and the day after." His tone was altogether too merry and flippant.

"I don't believe you," said Miranda, bitterly, closing her lips and eyes and hoping she might not weep.

"Miss Tanner," called the doctor, "have you got that note?"

Miss Tanner appeared beside her, handed her an unsealed envelope, took it back, unfolded the note and gave it to her.

"I can't see it," said Miranda, after a pained search of the page full of hasty scratches in black ink.

"Here, I'll read it," said Miss Tanner. "It says, 'They came and took you while I was away and now they will not let me see you. Maybe tomorrow they will, with my love, Adam,' " read Miss Tanner in a firm dry voice, pronouncing the words distinctly. "Now, do you see?" she asked soothingly.

Miranda, hearing the words one by one, forgot them one by one. "Oh, read it again, what does it say?" she called out over the silence that pressed upon her, reaching towards the dancing words that just escaped as she almost touched them. "That will do," said Dr. Hildesheim, calmly authoritarian. "Where is that bed?"

"There is no bed yet," said Miss Tanner, as if she said, We are short of oranges. Dr. Hildesheim said, "Well, we'll manage something," and Miss Tanner drew the narrow trestle with bright crossed metal supports and small rubbery wheels into a deep jut of the corridor, out of the way of the swift white figures darting about, whirling and skimming like water flies all in silence. The white walls rose sheer as cliffs, a dozen frosted moons followed each other in perfect self-possession down a white lane and dropped mutely one by one into a snowy abyss.

What is this whiteness and silence but the absence of pain? Miranda lay lifting the nap of her white blanket softly between eased fingers, watching a dance of tall deliberate shadows moving behind a wide screen of sheets spread upon a frame. It was there, near her, on her side of the wall where she could see it clearly and enjoy it, and it was so beautiful she had no curiosity as to its meaning. Two dark figures nodded, bent, curtsied to each other, retreated and bowed again, lifted long arms and spread great hands against the white shadow of the screen; then with a single round movement, the sheets were folded back, disclosing two speechless men in white, standing, and another speechless man in white, lying on the bare springs of a white iron bed. The man on the springs was swathed smoothly from head to foot in white, with folded bands across the face, and a large stiff bow like merry rabbit ears dangled at the crown of his head.

The two living men lifted a mattress standing hunched against the wall, spread it tenderly and exactly over the dead man. Wordless and white they vanished down the corridor, pushing the wheeled bed before them. It had been an entrancing and leisurely spectacle, but now it was over. A pallid white fog rose in their wake insinuatingly and floated before Miranda's eyes, a fog in which was concealed all terror and all weariness, all the wrung faces and twisted backs and broken feet of abused, outraged living things, all the shapes of their confused pain and their estranged hearts; the fog might part at any moment and loose the horde of human torments. She put up her hands and said, Not yet, not yet, but it was too late. The fog parted and two executioners, white clad, moved towards her pushing between them with marvelously deft and practiced hands the misshapen figure of an old man in filthy rags whose scanty beard waggled under his opened mouth as he bowed his back and braced his feet to resist and delay the fate they had prepared for him. In a high weeping **voice** he was trying to explain to them that the crime of which he was accused did not merit the punishment he was about to receive; and except for this whining cry there was silence as they advanced. The soiled cracked bowls of the old man's hands were held before him beseechingly as a beggar's as he said, "Before God I am not guilty," but they held his arms and drew him onward, passed, and were gone.

The road to death is a long march beset with all evils, and the heart fails little by little at each new terror, the bones rebel at each step, the mind sets up its own bitter resistance and to what end? The barriers sink one by one, and no covering of the eyes shuts out the landscape of disaster, nor the sight of crimes committed there. Across the field came Dr. Hildesheim, his face a skull beneath his German helmet, carrying a naked infant writhing on the point of his bayonet, and a huge stone pot marked Poison in Gothic letters. He stopped before the well that Miranda remembered in a pasture on her father's farm, a well once dry but now bubbling with living water, and into its pure depths he threw the child and the poison, and the violated water sank back soundlessly into the earth. Miranda, screaming, ran with her arms above her head; her voice echoed and came back to her like a wolf's howl, Hildesheim is a Boche, a spy, a Hun, kill him, kill him before he kills you. . . . She woke howling, she heard the foul words accusing Dr. Hildesheim tumbling from her mouth; opened her eyes and knew she was in a bed in a small white room, with Dr. Hildesheim sitting beside her, two firm fingers on her pulse. His hair was brushed sleekly and his buttonhole flower was fresh. Stars gleamed through the window, and Dr. Hildesheim seemed to be gazing at them with no particular expression, his stethoscope dangling around his neck. Miss Tanner stood at the foot of the bed writing something on a chart.

"Hello," said Dr. Hildesheim, "at least you take it out in shouting. You don't try to get out of bed and go running around." Miranda held her eyes open with a terrible effort, saw his rather heavy, patient face clearly even as her mind tottered and slithered again, broke from its foundation and spun like a cast wheel in a ditch. "I didn't mean it, I never believed it, Dr. Hildesheim, you musn't remember it—" and was gone again, not being able to wait for an answer.

The wrong she had done followed her and haunted her dream: this wrong took vague shapes of horror she could not recognize or name, though her heart cringed at sight of them. Her mind, split in two, acknowledged and denied what she saw in the one instant, for across an abyss of complaining darkness her reasoning coherent self watched the strange frenzy of the other coldly, reluctant to admit the truth of its visions, its tenacious remorses and despairs.

"I know those are your hands," she told Miss Tanner, "I know it, but to me they are white tarantulas, don't touch me."

"Shut your eyes," said Miss Tanner.

"Oh, no," said Miranda, "for then I see worse things," but her eyes closed in spite of her will, and the midnight of her internal torment closed about her.

Oblivion, thought Miranda, her mind feeling among her memories of words she had been taught to describe the unseen, the unknowable, is a whirlpool of gray water turning upon itself for all eternity . . . eternity is perhaps more than the distance to the farthest star. She lay on a narrow ledge over a pit that she knew to be bottomless, though she could not comprehend it; the ledge was her childhood dream of danger, and she strained back against a reassuring wall of granite at her shoulders, staring into the pit, thinking, There it is, there it is at last, it is very simple; and soft carefully shaped words like oblivion and eternity are curtains hung before nothing at all. I shall not know when it happens, I shall not feel or remember, why can't I consent now, I am lost, there is no hope for me. Look, she told herself, there it is, that is death and there is nothing to fear. But she could not consent, still shrinking stiffly against the granite wall that was her childhood dream of safety, breathing slowly for fear of squandering breath, saying desperately, Look, don't be afraid, it is nothing, it is only eternity.

Granite walls, whirlpools, stars are things. None of them is death, nor the image of it. Death is death, said Miranda, and for the dead it has no attributes. Silenced she sank easily through deeps under deeps of darkness until she lay like a stone at the farthest bottom of life, knowing herself to be blind, deaf, speechless, no longer aware of the members of her own body, entirely withdrawn from all human concerns, yet alive with a peculiar lucidity and coherence; all notions of the mind, the reasonable inquiries of doubt, all ties of blood and the desires of the heart, dissolved and fell away from her, and there remained of her only a minute fiercely burning particle of being that knew itself alone, that relied upon nothing beyond itself for its strength; not susceptible to any appeal or inducement, being itself composed entirely of one single motive, the stubborn will to live. This fiery motionless particle set itself unaided to resist destruction, to survive and to be in its own madness of being, motiveless and planless beyond that one essential end. Trust me, the hard unwinking angry point of light said. Trust me. I stay.

At once it grew, flattened, thinned to a fine radiance, spread like a great fan and curved out into a rainbow through which Miranda, enchanted, altogether believing, looked upon a deep clear landscape of sea and sand, of soft meadow and sky, freshly washed and glistening with transparencies of blue. Why, of course, of course, said Miranda, without surprise but with serene rapture as if some promise made to her had been kept long after she had ceased to hope for it. She rose from her narrow ledge and ran lightly through the tall portals of the great bow that arched in its splendor over the burning blue of the sea and the cool green of the meadow on either hand.

The small waves rolled in and over unhurriedly, lapped upon the sand in silence and retreated; the grasses flurried before a breeze that made no sound. Moving towards her leisurely as clouds through the shimmering air came a great company of human beings, and Miranda saw in an amazement of joy that they were all the living she had known. Their faces were transfigured, each in its own beauty, beyond what she remembered of them, their eyes were clear and untroubled as good weather, and they cast no shadows. They were pure identities and she knew them every one without calling their names or remembering what relation she bore to them. They surrounded her smoothly on silent feet, then turned their entranced faces again towards the sea, and she moved among them easily as a wave among waves. The drifting circle widened, separated, and each figure was alone but not solitary; Miranda, alone too, questioning nothing, desiring nothing, in the quietude of her ecstasy, stayed where she was, eyes fixed on the overwhelming deep sky where it was always morning.

Lying at ease, arms under her head, in the prodigal warmth which flowed evenly from sea and sky and meadow, within touch but not touching the serenely smiling familiar beings about her, Miranda felt without warning a vague tremor of apprehension, some small flick of distrust in her joy; a thin frost touched the edges of this confident tranquillity; something, somebody, was missing, she had lost something, she had left something valuable in another country, oh, what could it be? There are no trees, no trees here, she said in fright, I have left something unfinished. A thought struggled at the back of her mind, came clearly as a voice in her ear. Where are the dead? We have forgotten the dead, oh, the dead, where are they? At once as if a curtain had fallen, the bright landscape faded, she was alone in a strange stony place of bitter cold, picking her way along a steep path of slippery snow, calling out, Oh, I must go back! But in what direction? Pain returned, a terrible compelling pain running through her veins like heavy fire, the stench of corruption filled her nostrils, the sweetish sickening smell of rotting flesh and pus; she opened her eyes and saw pale light through a coarse white cloth over her face, knew that the smell of death was in her own body, and struggled to lift her hand. The cloth was drawn away; she saw Miss Tanner filling a hypodermic needle in her methodical expert way, and heard Dr. Hildesheim saying, "I think that will do the trick. Try another." Miss Tanner plucked firmly at Miranda's arm near the shoulder, and the unbelievable current of agony ran burning through her veins again. She struggled to cry out, saying, Let me go, let me go; but heard only incoherent sounds of animal suffering. She saw doctor and nurse glance at each other with the glance of initiates at a mystery, nodding in silence, their eyes alive with knowledgeable pride. They looked briefly at their handiwork and hurried away.

Bells screamed all off key, wrangling together as they collided in mid air, horns and whistles mingled shrilly with cries of human distress; sulphur colored light exploded through the black window pane and flashed away in darkness. Miranda waking from a dreamless sleep asked without expecting an answer, "What is happening?" for there was a bustle of voices and footsteps in the corridor, and a sharpness in the air; the far clamor went on, a furious exasperated shrieking like a mob in revolt.

The light came on, and Miss Tanner said in a furry voice, "Hear that? They're celebrating. It's the Armistice. The war is over, my dear." Her hands trembled. She rattled a spoon in a cup, stopped to listen, held the cup out to Miranda. From the ward for old bedridden women down the hall floated a ragged chorus of cracked voices singing, "My country, 'tis of thee . . ."

Sweet land . . . oh, terrible land of this bitter world where the sound of rejoicing was a clamor of pain, where ragged tuneless old women, sitting up waiting for their evening bowl of cocoa, were singing, "Sweet land of Liberty—"

"Oh, say, can you see?" their hopeless voices were asking next, the hammer strokes of metal tongues drowning them out. "The war is over," said Miss Tanner, her underlip held firmly, her eyes blurred. Miranda said, "Please open the window, please, I smell death in here."

Now if real daylight such as I remember having seen in this world would only come again, but it is always twilight or just before morning, a promise of day that is never kept. What has become of the sun? That was the longest and loneliest night and yet it will not end and let the day come. Shall I ever see light again?

Sitting in a long chair, near a window, it was in itself a melancholy wonder to see the colorless sunlight slanting on the snow, under a sky drained of its blue. "Can this be my face?" Miranda asked her mirror. "Are these my own hands?" she asked Miss Tanner, holding them up to show the yellow tint like melted wax glimmering between the closed fingers. The body is a curious monster, no place to live in, how could anyone feel at home there? Is it possible I can ever accustom myself to this place? she asked herself. The human faces around her seemed dulled and tired, with no radiance of skin and eyes as Miranda remembered radiance; the once white walls of her room were now a soiled gray. Breathing slowly, falling asleep and waking again, feeling the splash of water on her flesh, taking food, talking in bare phrases with Dr. Hildesheim and Miss Tanner, Miranda looked about her with the covertly hostile eyes of an alien who does not like the country in which he finds himself, does not understand the language nor wish to learn it, does not mean to live there and yet is helpless, unable to leave it at his will.

"It is morning," Miss Tanner would say, with a sigh, for she had grown old and weary once for all in the past month, "morning again, my dear," showing Miranda the same monotonous landscape of dulled evergreens and leaden snow. She would rustle about in her starched skirts, her face bravely powdered, her spirit unbreakable as good steel, saying, "Look, my dear, what a heavenly morning, like a crystal," for she had an affection for the salvaged creature before her, the silent ungrateful human being whom she, Cornelia Tanner, a nurse who knew her business, had snatched back from death with her own hands. "Nursing is nine-tenths, just the same," Miss Tanner would tell the other nurses; "keep that in mind." Even the sunshine was Miss Tanner's own prescription for the further recovery of Miranda, this patient the doctors had given up for lost, and who yet sat here, visible proof of Miss Tanner's theory. She said, "Look at the sunshine, now," as she might be saying, "I ordered this for you, my dear, do sit up and take it."

"It's beautiful," Miranda would answer, even turning her head to look, thanking Miss Tanner for her goodness, most of all her goodness about the weather, "beautiful, I always loved it." And I might love it again if I saw it, she thought, but truth was, she could not see it. There was no light, there might never be light again, compared as it must always be with the light she had seen beside the blue sea that lay so tranquilly along the shore of her paradise. That was a child's dream of the heavenly meadow, the vision of repose that comes to a tired body in sleep, she thought, but I have seen it when I did not know it was a dream. Closing her eyes she would rest for a moment remembering that bliss which had repaid all the pain of the journey to reach it; opening them again she saw with a new anguish the dull world to which she was condemned, where the light seemed filmed over with cobwebs, all the bright surfaces corroded, the sharp planes melted and formless, all objects and beings meaningless, ah, dead and withered things that believed themselves alive!

At night, after the long effort of lying in her chair, in her extremity of grief for what she had so briefly won, she folded her painful body together and wept silently, shamelessly, in pity for herself and her lost rapture. There was no escape. Dr. Hildesheim, Miss Tanner, the nurses in the diet kitchen, the chemist, the surgeon, the precise machine of the hospital, the whole humane conviction and custom of society, conspired to pull her inseparable rack of bones and wasted flesh to its feet, to put in order her disordered mind, and to set her once more safely in the road that would lead her again to death.

Chuck Rouncivale and Mary Townsend came to see her, bringing her a bundle of letters they had guarded for her. They brought

314

a basket of delicate small hothouse flowers, lilies of the valley with sweet peas and feathery fern, and above these blooms their faces were merry and haggard.

Mary said, "You *have* had a tussle, haven't you?" and Chuck said, "Well, you made it back, didn't you?" Then after an uneasy pause, they told her that everybody was waiting to see her again at her desk. "They've put me back on sports already, Miranda," said Chuck. For ten minutes Miranda smiled and told them how gay and what a pleasant surprise it was to find herself alive. For it will not do to betray the conspiracy and tamper with the courage of the living; there is nothing better than to be alive, everyone has agreed on that; it is past argument, and who attempts to deny it is justly outlawed. "I'll be back in no time at all," she said; "this is almost over."

Her letters lay in a heap in her lap and beside her chair. Now and then she turned one over to read the inscription, recognized this handwriting or that, examined the blotted stamps and the postmarks, and let them drop again. For two or three days they lay upon the table beside her, and she continued to shrink from them. "They will all be telling me again how good it is to be alive, they will say again they love me, they are glad I am living too, and what can I answer to that?" and her hardened, indifferent heart shuddered in despair at itself, because before it had been tender and capable of love.

Dr. Hildesheim said, "What, all these letters not opened yet?" and Miss Tanner said, "Read your letters, my dear, I'll open them for you." Standing beside the bed, she slit them cleanly with a paper knife. Miranda, cornered, picked and chose until she found a thin one in an unfamiliar handwriting. "Oh, no, now," said Miss Tanner, "take them as they come. Here, I'll hand them to you." She sat down, prepared to be helpful to the end.

What a victory, what triumph, what happiness to be alive, sang the letters in a chorus. The names were signed with flourishes like the circles in air of bugle notes, and they were the names of those she had loved best; some of those she had known well and pleasantly; and a few who meant nothing to her, then or now. The thin letter in the unfamiliar handwriting was from a strange man at the camp where Adam had been, telling her that Adam had died of

influenza in the camp hospital. Adam had asked him, in case anything happened, to be sure to let her know.

If anything happened. To be sure to let her know. If anything
happened. "Your friend, Adam Barclay," wrote the strange man.
It had happened—she looked at the date—more than a month
ago.

"I've been here a long time, haven't I?" she asked Miss Tanner,
who was folding letters and putting them back in their proper envelopes.

"Oh, quite a while," said Miss Tanner, "but you'll be ready to
go soon now. But you must be careful of yourself and not overdo,
and you should come back now and then and let us look at you,
because sometimes the aftereffects are very—"

Miranda, sitting up before the mirror, wrote carefully: "One
lipstick, medium, one ounce flask Bois d'Hiver perfume, one pair
of gray suède gauntlets without straps, two pairs gray sheer stockings without clocks—"

Towney, reading after her, said, "Everything without something
so that it will be almost impossible to get?"

"Try it, though," said Miranda, "they're nicer without. One
walking stick of silvery wood with a silver knob."

"That's going to be expensive," warned Towney. "Walking is
hardly worth it."

"You're right," said Miranda, and wrote in the margin, "a nice
one to match my other things. Ask Chuck to look for this, Mary.
Good looking and not too heavy." Lazarus, come forth. Not unless
you bring me my top hat and stick. Stay where you are then, you
snob. Not at all. I'm coming forth. "A jar of cold cream," wrote
Miranda, "a box of apricot powder—and, Mary, I don't need eye
shadow, do I?" She glanced at her face in the mirror and away
again. "Still, no one need pity this corpse if we look properly to
the art of the thing."

Mary Townsend said, "You won't recognize yourself in a
week."

"Do you suppose, Mary," asked Miranda, "I could have my old
room back again?"

"That should be easy," said Mary. "We stored away all your
things there with Miss Hobbe." Miranda wondered again at the
time and trouble the living took to be helpful to the dead. But not

quite dead now, she reassured herself, one foot in either world now; soon I shall cross back and be at home again. The light will seem real and I shall be glad when I hear that someone I know has escaped from death. I shall visit the escaped ones and help them dress and tell them how lucky they are, and how lucky I am still to have them. Mary will be back soon with my gloves and my walking stick, I must go now, I must begin saying good-by to Miss Tanner and Dr. Hildesheim. Adam, she said, now you need not die again, but still I wish you were here; I wish you had come back, what do you think I came back for, Adam, to be deceived like this?

At once he was there beside her, invisible but urgently present, a ghost but more alive than she was, the last intolerable cheat of her heart; for knowing it was false she still clung to the lie, the unpardonable lie of her bitter desire. She said, "I love you," and stood up trembling, trying by the mere act of her will to bring him to sight before her. If I could call you up from the grave I would, she said, if I could see your ghost I would say, I believe . . . "I believe," she said aloud. "Oh, let me see you once more." The room was silent, empty, the shade was gone from it, struck away by the sudden violence of her rising and speaking aloud. She came to herself as if out of sleep. Oh, no, that is not the way, I must never do that, she warned herself. Miss Tanner said, "Your taxicab is waiting, my dear," and there was Mary. Ready to go.

No more war, no more plague, only the dazed silence that follows the ceasing of the heavy guns; noiseless houses with the shades drawn, empty streets, the dead cold light of tomorrow. Now there would be time for everything.

The Leaning Tower and Other Stories

The Old Order

THE SOURCE

Once a year, in early summer, after school was closed and the children were to be sent to the farm, the Grandmother began to long for the country. With an air of tenderness, as if she enquired after a favorite child, she would ask questions about the crops, wonder what kind of gardens the Negroes were making, how the animals were faring. She would remark now and then, "I begin to feel the need of a little change and relaxation, too," in a vague tone of reassurance, as if to say this did not mean that she intended for a moment really to relax her firm hold on family affairs. It was her favorite theory that change of occupation was one way, probably the best way, of resting. The three grandchildren would begin to feel the faint sure stirrings of departure in the house; her son, their father, would assume the air of careful patience which imperfectly masked his annoyance at the coming upsets and inconveniences to be endured at the farm. "Now, Harry, now, Harry!" his mother would warn him, for she was never deceived by his manner; indeed, he never meant her to be; and she would begin trying to placate him by wondering falsely if she could possibly get away, after all, with so much yet to be done where she was. She looked forward with pleasure to a breath of country air. She always imagined herself as walking at leisure in the shade of the orchards watching the peaches ripen; she spoke with longing of clipping the rosebushes, or of tying up the trellised honeysuckle with her own hands. She would pack up her summer-weight black

321

skirts, her thin black-and-white basques, and would get out a broad-brimmed, rather battered straw shepherdess hat she had woven for herself just after the war. Trying it on, turning her head critically this way and that before the mirror, she would decide that it might do nicely for the sun and she always took it along, but never wore it. She wore instead a stiffly starched white chambray bonnet, with a round crown buttoned on a narrow brim; it sat pertly on the top of her head with a fly-away look, the long strings hanging stiffly. Underneath this headdress, her pale, tightly drawn, very old face looked out with stately calm.

In the early spring, when the Indian cling peach-tree against the wall of the town house began to bloom, she would say, "I have planted five orchards in three States, and now I see only one tree in bloom." A soft, enjoyable melancholy would come over her; she would stand quite still for a moment looking at the single tree, representing all her beloved trees still blooming, flourishing, and preparing to bring forth fruit in their separate places.

Leaving Aunt Nannie, who had been nurse to her children, in charge of the town house, she set out on her journey.

If departure was a delightful adventure for the children, arriving at the farm was an event for Grandmother. Hinry came running to open the gate, his coal-black face burst into a grin, his voice flying before him: "Howdy-do, Miss Sophia Jane!", simply not noticing that the carry-all was spilling over with other members of the family. The horses jogged in, their bellies jolting and churning, and Grandmother, calling out greetings in her feast-day voice, alighted, surrounded by her people, with the same flurry of travel that marked her journeys by train; but now with an indefinable sense of homecoming, not to the house but to the black, rich soft land and the human beings living on it. Without removing her long veiled widow's bonnet, she would walk straight through the house, observing instantly that everything was out of order; pass out into the yards and gardens, silently glancing, making instant plans for changes; down the narrow path past the barns, with a glance into and around them as she went, a glance of firm and purposeful censure; and on past the canebrake to the left, the hayfields to the right, until she arrived at the row of Negro huts that ran along the bois d'arc hedge.

Stepping up with a pleasant greeting to all, which in no way promised exemption from the wrath to come, she went into their kitchens, glanced into their meal barrels, their ovens, their cupboard shelves, into every smallest crevice and corner, with Littie and Dicey and Hinry and Bumper and Keg following, trying to explain that things was just a little out of shape right now because they'd had so much outside work they hadn't just been able to straighten out the way they meant to; but they were going to get at it right away.

Indeed they were, as Grandmother well knew. Within an hour someone would have driven away in the buckboard with an order for such lime for whitewash, so many gallons of kerosene oil, and so much carbolic acid and insect powder. Home-made lye soap would be produced from the washhouse, and the frenzy would begin. Every mattress cover was emptied of its corn husks and boiled, every little Negro on the place was set to work picking a fresh supply of husks, every hut was thickly whitewashed, bins and cupboards were scrubbed, every chair and bedstead was varnished, every filthy quilt was brought to light, boiled in a great iron washpot and stretched in the sun; and the uproar had all the special character of any annual occasion. The Negro women were put at making a fresh supply of shirts for the men and children, cotton dresses and aprons for themselves. Whoever wished to complain now seized his opportunity. Mister Harry had clean forgot to buy shoes for Hinry, look at Hinry: Hinry had been just like that, barefooted the live-long winter. Mister Miller (a red-whiskered man who occupied a dubious situation somewhere between overseer when Mister Harry was absent, and plain hired hand when he was present) had skimped them last winter on everything you could think of—not enough cornmeal, not half enough bacon, not enough wood, not enough of anything. Littie had needed a little sugar for her cawfy and do you think Mister Miller would let her have it? No. Mister Miller had said nobody needed sugar in their cawfy. Hinry said Mister Miller didn't even take sugar in his own cawfy because he was just too stingy. Boosker, the three-year-old baby, had earache in January and Miz Carleton had come down and put lodnum in it and Boosker was acting like she was deef ever since. The black horse Mister Harry bought last fall had gone clean wild and jumped a barbed wire fence and tore his chest almost off and hadn't been any good from that time on.

All these annoyances and dozens like them had to be soothed at once, then Grandmother's attention was turned to the main house, which must be overhauled completely. The big secretaries were opened and shabby old sets of Dickens, Scott, Thackeray, Dr. Johnson's dictionary, the volumes of Pope and Milton and Dante and Shakespeare were dusted off and closed up carefully again. Curtains came down in dingy heaps and went up again stiff and sweet-smelling; rugs were heaved forth in dusty confusion and returned flat and gay with flowers once more; the kitchen was no longer dingy and desolate but a place of heavenly order where it was tempting to linger.

Next the barns and smokehouses and the potato cellar, the gardens and every tree or vine or bush must have that restoring touch upon it. For two weeks this would go on, with the Grandmother a tireless, just and efficient slave driver of every creature on the place. The children ran wild outside, but not as they did when she was not there. The hour came in each day when they were rounded up, captured, washed, dressed properly, made to eat what was set before them without giving battle, put to bed when the time came and no nonsense . . . They loved their Grandmother; she was the only reality to them in a world that seemed otherwise without fixed authority or refuge, since their mother had died so early that only the eldest girl remembered her vaguely: just the same they felt that Grandmother was tyrant, and they wished to be free of her; so they were always pleased when, on a certain day, as a sign that her visit was drawing to an end, she would go out to the pasture and call her old saddle horse, Fiddler.

He had been a fine, thorough-paced horse once, but he was now a weary, disheartened old hero, gray-haired on his jaw and chin, who spent his life nuzzling with pendulous lips for tender bits of grass or accepting sugar cautiously between his shaken teeth. He paid no attention to anyone but the Grandmother. Every summer when she went to his field and called him, he came doddering up with almost a gleam in his filmy eyes. The two old creatures would greet each other fondly. The Grandmother always treated her animal friends as if they were human beings temporarily metamorphosed, but not by this accident dispensed from those duties suitable to their condition. She would have Fiddler brought around under her old side-saddle—her little granddaughters rode astride and she saw no harm in it, for them—and mount with her foot in Uncle Jimbilly's curved hand. Fiddler would remember his youth and break into a stiff-legged gallop, and off she would go with her crepe bands and her old-fashioned riding skirt flying. They always returned at a walk, the Grandmother sitting straight as a sword, smiling, triumphant. Dismounting at the horse-block by herself, she would stroke Fiddler on the neck before turning him over to Uncle Jimbilly, and walk away carrying her train grandly over her arm.

This yearly gallop with Fiddler was important to her; it proved her strength, her unabated energy. Any time now Fiddler might drop in his tracks, but she would not. She would say, "He's getting stiff in the knees," or "He's pretty short-winded this year," but she herself walked lightly and breathed as easily as ever, or so she chose to believe.

That same afternoon or the next day, she would take her long-promised easy stroll in the orchards with nothing to do, her Grandchildren running before her and running back to her side: with nothing at all to do, her hands folded, her skirts trailing and picking up twigs, turning over little stones, sweeping a faint path behind her, her white bonnet askew over one eye, an absorbed fixed smile on her lips, her eyes missing nothing. This walk would usually end with Hinry or Jimbilly being dispatched to the orchards at once to make some trifling but indispensable improvement.

It would then come over her powerfully that she was staying on idling when there was so much to be done at home . . . There would be a last look at everything, instructions, advices, good-bys, blessings. She would set out with that strange look of leaving forever, and arrive at the place in town with the same air of homecoming she had worn on her arrival in the country, in a gentle flurry of greeting and felicitations, as if she had been gone for half a year. At once she set to work restoring to order the place which no doubt had gone somewhat astray in her absence.

THE JOURNEY

In their later years, the Grandmother and old Nannie used to sit together for some hours every day over their sewing. They shared a passion for cutting scraps of the family finery, hoarded for fifty years, into strips and triangles, and fitting them together again in a carefully disordered patchwork, outlining each bit of velvet or satin or taffeta with a running briar stitch in clear lemon-colored silk floss. They had contrived enough bed and couch covers, table spreads, dressing table scarfs, to have furnished forth several households. Each piece as it was finished was lined with yellow silk, folded, and laid away in a chest, never again to see the light of day. The Grandmother was the great-granddaughter of Kentucky's most famous pioneer: he had, while he was surveying Kentucky, hewed out rather competently a rolling pin for his wife. This rolling pin was the Grandmother's irreplaceable treasure. She covered it with an extraordinarily complicated bit of patchwork, added golden tassels to the handles, and hung it in a conspicuous place in her room. She was the daughter of a notably heroic captain in the War of 1812. She had his razors in a shagreen case and a particularly severe-looking daguerreotype taken in his old age, with his chin in a tall stock and his black satin waistcoat smoothed over a still-handsome military chest. So she fitted a patchwork case over the shagreen and made a sort of envelope of cut velvet and violet satin, held together with briar stitching, to contain the portrait. The rest of her handiwork she put away, to the relief of her grandchildren, who had arrived at the awkward age when Grandmother's quaint old-fashioned ways caused them acute discomfort.

In the summer the women sat under the mingled trees of the side garden, which commanded a view of the east wing, the front and back porches, a good part of the front garden and a corner of the small fig grove. Their choice of this location was a part of their domestic strategy. Very little escaped them: a glance now and then would serve to keep them fairly well informed as to what was going on in the whole place. It is true they had not seen Miranda the day she pulled up the whole mint bed to give to a pleasant strange young woman who stopped and asked her for a sprig of fresh mint. They had never found out who stole the giant pomegranates growing too near the fence: they had not been in time to stop Paul from setting himself on fire while experimenting with a miniature blowtorch, but they had been on the scene to extinguish him with rugs, to pour oil on him, and lecture him. They never saw Maria climbing trees, a mania she had to indulge or pine away, for she chose tall ones on the opposite side of the house. But such casualties were so minor a part of the perpetual round of events that they did not feel defeated nor that their strategy was a failure. Summer, in many ways so desirable a season, had its drawbacks. The children were everywhere at once and the Negroes loved lying under the hackberry grove back of the barns playing seven-up, and eating watermelons. The summer house was in a small town a few miles from the farm, a compromise between the rigorously ordered house in the city and the sprawling old farmhouse which Grandmother had built with such pride and pains. It had, she often said, none of the advantages of either country or city, and all the discomforts of both. But the children loved it.

During the winters in the city, they sat in Grandmother's room, a large squarish place with a small coal grate. All the sounds of life in the household seemed to converge there, echo, retreat, and return. Grandmother and Aunt Nannie knew the whole complicated code of sounds, could interpret and comment on them by an exchange of glances, a lifted eyebrow, or a tiny pause in their talk.

They talked about the past, really—always about the past. Even the future seemed like something gone and done with when they spoke of it. It did not seem an extension of their past, but a repetition of it. They would agree that nothing remained of life as they had known it, the world was changing swiftly, but by the mysterious logic of hope they insisted that each change was probably the last; or if not, a series of changes might bring them, blessedly, back full-circle to the old ways they had known. Who knows why they loved their past? It had been bitter for them both, they had questioned the burdensome rule they lived by every day of their lives, but without rebellion and without expecting an answer. This unbroken thread of inquiry in their minds contained no doubt as to the utter rightness and justice of the basic laws of human existence, founded as they were on God's plan; but they wondered perpetually, with only a hint now and then to each other of the uneasiness of their hearts, how so much suffering and confusion could have been built up and maintained on such a foundation. The Grandmother's rôle was authority, she knew that; it was her duty to portion out activities, to urge or restrain where necessary, to teach morals, manners, and religion, to punish and reward her own household according to a fixed code. Her own doubts and hesitations she concealed, also, she reminded herself, as a matter of duty. Old Nannie had no ideas at all as to her place in the world. It had been assigned to her before birth, and for her daily rule she had all her life obeyed the authority nearest to her.

So they talked about God, about heaven, about planting a new hedge of rose bushes, about the new ways of preserving fruit and vegetables, about eternity and their mutual hope that they might pass it happily together, and often a scrap of silk under their hands would start them on long trains of family reminiscences. They were always amused to notice again how the working of their memories differed in such important ways. Nannie could recall names to perfection; she could always say what the weather had been like on all important occasions, what certain ladies had worn, how handsome certain gentlemen had been, what there had been to eat and drink. Grandmother had masses of dates in her mind, and no memories attached to them: her memories of events seemed detached and floating beyond time. For example, the 26th of August, 1871, had been some sort of red-letter day for her. She had said to herself then that never would she forget that date; and indeed, she remembered it well, but she no longer had the faintest notion what had happened to stamp it on her memory. Nannie was no help in the matter; she had nothing to do with dates. She did not know the year of her birth, and would never have had a birthday to celebrate if Grandmother had not, when she was still Miss Sophia Jane, aged ten, opened a calendar at random, closed her eyes, and marked a date unseen with a pen. So it turned out that Nannie's birthday thereafter fell on June 11, and the year, Miss Sophia Jane decided, should be 1827, her own birth-year, making Nannie just three months younger than her mistress. Sophia Jane then made an entry of Nannie's birth-date in the family Bible, inserting it just below her own. "Nannie Gay," she wrote, in stiff careful letters, "(black)," and though there was some uproar when this was discovered, the ink was long since sunk deeply into the paper, and besides no one was really upset enough to have it scratched out. There it remained, one of their pleasantest points of reference.

They talked about religion, and the slack way the world was going nowadays, the decay of behavior, and about the younger children, whom these topics always brought at once to mind. On these subjects they were firm, critical, and unbewildered. They had received educations which furnished them an assured habit of mind about all the important appearances of life, and especially about the rearing of young. They relied with perfect acquiescence on the dogma that children were conceived in sin and brought forth in iniquity. Childhood was a long state of instruction and probation for adult life, which was in turn a long, severe, undeviating devotion to duty, the largest part of which consisted in bringing up children. The young were difficult, disobedient, and tireless in wrongdoing, apt to turn unkind and undutiful when they grew up, in spite of all one had done for them, or had tried to do: for small painful doubts rose in them now and again when they looked at their completed works. Nannie couldn't abide her new-fangled grandchildren. "Wuthless, shiftless lot, jes plain scum, Miss Sophia Jane; I cain't undahstand it aftah all the raisin' dey had."

The Grandmother defended them, and dispraised her own second generation—heartily, too, for she sincerely found grave faults in them—which Nannie defended in turn. "When they are little, they trample on your feet, and when they grow up they trample on your heart." This was about all there was to say about children in any generation, but the fascination of the theme was endless. They said it thoroughly over and over with thousands of small variations, with always an example among their own friends or family connections to prove it. They had enough material of their own. Grandmother had borne eleven children, Nannie thirteen. They boasted of it. Grandmother would say, "I am the mother of eleven children," in a faintly amazed tone, as if she hardly expected to be believed, or could even quite believe it herself. But she could still point to nine of them. Nannie had lost ten of hers. They were all buried in Kentucky. Nannie never doubted or expected anyone else to doubt she had children. Her boasting was of another order. "Thirteen of 'em," she would say, in an appalled voice, "yas, my Lawd and my Redeemah, thirteen!"

The friendship between the two old women had begun in early childhood, and was based on what seemed even to them almost mythical events. Miss Sophia Jane, a prissy, spoiled five-year-old, with tight black ringlets which were curled every day on a stick, with her stiffly pleated lawn pantalettes and tight bodice, had run to meet her returning father, who had been away buying horses and Negroes. Sitting on his arm, clasping him around the neck, she had watched the wagons filing past on the way to the barns and quarters. On the floor of the first wagon sat two blacks, male and female, holding between them a scrawny, half-naked black child, with a round nubbly head and fixed bright monkey eyes. The baby Negro had a potbelly and her arms were like sticks from wrist to shoulder. She clung with narrow, withered, black leather fingers to her parents, a hand on each.

"I want the little monkey," said Sophia Jane to her father, nuzzling his cheek and pointing. "I want that one to play with."

Behind each wagon came two horses in lead, but in the second wagon there was a small shaggy pony with a thatch of mane over his eyes, a long tail like a brush, a round, hard barrel of a body. He was standing in straw to the knees, braced firmly in a padded stall with a Negro holding his bridle. "Do you see that?" asked her father. "That's for you. High time you learned to ride."

Sophia Jane almost leaped from his arm for joy. She hardly recognized her pony or her monkey the next day, the one clipped and sleek, the other clean in new blue cotton. For a while she could not decide which she loved more, Nannie or Fiddler. But Fiddler did not wear well. She outgrew him in a year, saw him pass without regret to a small brother, though she refused to allow him to be called Fiddler any longer. That name she reserved for a long series of saddle horses. She had named the first in honor of Fiddler Gay, an old Negro who made the music for dances and parties. There was only one Nannie and she outwore Sophia Jane. During all their lives together it was not so much a question of affection between them as a simple matter of being unable to imagine getting on without each other.

Nannie remembered well being on a shallow platform out in

front of a great building in a large busy place, the first town she
had ever seen. Her father and mother were with her, and there was
a thick crowd around them. There were several other small groups
of Negroes huddled together with white men bustling them about
now and then. She had never seen any of these faces before, and
she never saw but one of them again. She remembered it must
have been summer, because she was not shivering with cold in her
cotton shift. For one thing, her bottom was still burning from a
spanking someone (it might have been her mother) had given her
just before they got on the platform, to remind her to keep still.
Her mother and father were field hands, and had never lived in
white folks' houses. A tall gentleman with a long narrow face and
very high curved nose, wearing a great-collared blue coat and im-
mensely long light-colored trousers (Nannie could close her eyes
and see him again, clearly, as he looked that day) stepped up near
them suddenly, while a great hubbub rose. The red-faced man
standing on a stump beside them shouted and droned, waving his
arms and pointing at Nannie's father and mother. Now and then
the tall gentleman raised a finger, without looking at the black
people on the platform. Suddenly the shouting died down, the tall
gentleman walked over and said to Nannie's father and mother,
"Well, Eph! Well, Steeny! Mister Jimmerson comin' to get you in a
minute." He poked Nannie in the stomach with a thickly gloved
forefinger. "Regular crowbait," he said to the auctioneer. "I should
have had lagniappe with this one."

"A pretty worthless article right now, sir, I agree with you," said
the auctioneer, "but it'll grow out of it. As for the team, you won't
find a better, I swear."

"I've had an eye on 'em for years," said the tall gentleman, and
walked away, motioning as he went to a fat man sitting on a
wagon tongue, spitting quantities of tobacco juice. The fat man
rose and came over to Nannie and her parents.

Nannie had been sold for twenty dollars: a gift, you might say,
hardly sold at all. She learned that a really choice slave sometimes
cost more than a thousand dollars. She lived to hear slaves brag
about how much they had cost. She had not known how little she
fetched on the block until her own mother taunted her with it. This
was after Nannie had gone to live for good at the big house, and
her mother and father were still in the fields. They lived and

331

worked and died there. A good worming had cured Nannie's pot-belly, she thrived on plentiful food and a species of kindness not so indulgent, maybe, as that given to the puppies; still it more than fulfilled her notions of good fortune.

The old women often talked about how strangely things come out in this life. The first owner of Nannie and her parents had gone, Sophia Jane's father said, hog-wild about Texas. It was a new Land of Promise, in 1832. He had sold out his farm and four slaves in Kentucky to raise the money to take a great twenty-mile stretch of land in southwest Texas. He had taken his wife and two young children and set out, and there had been no more news of him for many years. When Grandmother arrived in Texas forty years later, she found him a prosperous ranchman and district judge. Much later, her youngest son met his granddaughter, fell in love with her, and married her—all in three months.

The judge, by then eighty-five years old, was uproarious and festive at the wedding. He reeked of corn liquor, swore by God every other breath, and was rearing to talk about the good old times in Kentucky. The Grandmother showed Nannie to him. "Would you recognize her?" "For God Almighty's sake!" bawled the judge, "is that the strip of crowbait I sold to your father for twenty dollars? Twenty dollars seemed like a fortune to me in those days!"

While they were jolting home down the steep rocky road on the long journey from San Marcos to Austin, Nannie finally spoke out about her grievance. "Look lak a jedge might had better raisin'," she said, gloomily, "look lak he didn't keer how much he hurt a body's feelins."

The Grandmother, muffled down in the back seat in the corner of the old carryall, in her worn sealskin pelisse, showing coffee-brown at the edges, her eyes closed, her hands wrung together, had been occupied once more in reconciling herself to losing a son, and, as ever, to a girl and a family of which she could not alto-gether approve. It was not that there was anything seriously damag-ing to be said against any of them; only—well, she wondered at her sons' tastes. What had each of them in turn found in the wife he had chosen? The Grandmother had always had in mind the kind of wife each of her sons needed; she had tried to bring about better marriages for them than they had made for themselves. They had merely resented her interference in what they considered strictly their personal affairs. She did not realize that she had spoiled and pampered her youngest son until he was in all probability unfit to be any kind of a husband, much less a good one. And there was something about her new daughter-in-law, a tall, handsome, firm-looking young woman, with a direct way of speaking, walking, talking, that seemed to promise that the spoiled Baby's days of clover were ended. The Grandmother was annoyed deeply at seeing how self-possessed the bride had been, how she had had her way about the wedding arrangements down to the last detail, how she glanced now and then at her new husband with calm, humorous, level eyes, as if she had already got him sized up. She had even suggested at the wedding dinner that her idea of a honeymoon would be to follow the chuck-wagon on the round-up, and help in the cattle-branding on her father's ranch. Of course she may have been joking. But she was altogether too Western, too modern, something like the "new" woman who was beginning to run wild, asking for the vote, leaving her home and going out in the world to earn her own living . . .

The Grandmother's narrow body shuddered to the bone at the thought of women so unsexing themselves; she emerged with a start from the dark reverie of foreboding thoughts which left a bitter taste in her throat. "Never mind, Nannie. The judge just wasn't thinking. He's very fond of his good cheer."

Nannie had slept in a bed and had been playmate and workfellow with her mistress; they fought on almost equal terms, Sophia Jane defending Nannie fiercely against any discipline but her own. When they were both seventeen years old, Miss Sophia Jane was married off in a very gay wedding. The house was jammed to the roof and everybody present was at least fourth cousin to everybody else. There were forty carriages and more than two hundred horses to look after for two days. When the last wheel disappeared down the lane (a number of the guests lingered on for two weeks), the larders and bins were half empty and the place looked as if a troop of cavalry had been over it. A few days later Nannie was married off to a boy she had known ever since she came to the family, and they were given as a wedding present to Miss Sophia Jane.

Miss Sophia Jane and Nannie had then started their grim and terrible race of procreation, a child every sixteen months or so, with Nannie nursing both, and Sophia Jane, in dreadful discomfort, suppressing her milk with bandages and spirits of wine. When they each had produced their fourth child, Nannie almost died of puerperal fever. Sophia Jane nursed both children. She named the black baby Charlie, and her own child Stephen, and she fed them justly turn about, not favoring the white over the black, as Nannie felt obliged to do. Her husband was shocked, tried to forbid her; her mother came to see her and reasoned with her. They found her very difficult and quite stubborn. She had already begun to develop her implicit character, which was altogether just, humane, proud, and simple. She had many small vanities and weaknesses on the surface: a love of luxury and a tendency to resent criticism. This tendency was based on her feeling of superiority in judgment and sensibility to almost everyone around her. It made her very hard to manage. She had a quiet way of holding her ground which convinced her antagonist that she would really die, not just threaten to, rather than give way. She had learned now that she was badly cheated in giving her children to another woman to feed; she resolved never again to be cheated in just that way. She sat nursing her child and her foster child, with a sensual warm pleasure she had not dreamed of, translating her natural physical relief into something holy, God-sent, amends from heaven for what she had suffered in childbed. Yes, and for what she missed in the marriage bed, for there also something had failed. She said to Nannie quite calmly, "From now on, you will nurse your children and I will nurse mine," and it was so. Charlie remained her special favorite among the Negro children. "I understand now," she said to her older sister Keziah, "why the black mammies love their foster children. I love mine." So Charlie was brought up in the house as playmate for her son Stephen, and exempted from hard work all his life.

Sophia Jane had been wooed at arm's length by a mysteriously attractive young man whom she remembered well as rather a snubby little boy with curls like her own, but shorter, a frilled white blouse and kilts of the Macdonald tartan. He was her second cousin and resembled her so closely they had been mistaken for brother and sister. Their grandparents had been first cousins, and sometimes Sophia Jane saw in him, years after they were married, all the faults she had most abhorred in her elder brother: lack of aim, failure to act at crises, a philosophic detachment from practical affairs, a tendency to set projects on foot and then leave them to perish or to be finished by someone else; and a profound conviction that everyone around him should be happy to wait upon him hand and foot. She had fought these fatal tendencies in her brother, within the bounds of wifely prudence she fought them in her husband, she was long after to fight them again in two of her sons and in several of her grandchildren. She gained no victory in any case, the selfish, careless, unloving creatures lived and ended as they had begun. But the Grandmother developed a character truly portentous under the discipline of trying to change the characters of others. Her husband shared with her the family sharpness of eye. He disliked and feared her deadly willfulness, her certainty that her ways were not only right but beyond criticism, that her feelings were important, even in the lightest matter, and must not be tampered with or treated casually. He had disappeared at the critical moment when they were growing up, had gone to college and then for travel; she forgot him for a long time, and when she saw him again forgot him as he had been once for all. She was gay and sweet and decorous, full of vanity and incredibly exalted daydreams which threatened now and again to cast her over the edge of some mysterious forbidden frenzy. She dreamed recurrently that she had lost her virginity (her virtue, she called it), her sole claim to regard, consideration, even to existence, and after frightful moral suffering which masked altogether her physical experience she would wake in a cold sweat, disordered and terrified. She had heard that her cousin Stephen was a little "wild," but that was to be expected. He was leading, no doubt, a dashing life full of manly indulgences, the sweet dark life of the knowledge of evil which caused her hair to crinkle on her scalp when she thought of it. Ah, the delicious, the free, the wonderful, the mysterious and terrible life of men! She thought about it a great deal. "Little day-dreamer," her mother or father would say to her, surprising her in a brown study, eyes moist, lips smiling vaguely over her embroidery or her book, or with hands fallen on her lap, her face turned away to a blank wall. She memorized and saved for these moments scraps of high-minded poetry, which she instantly quoted at them when they offered her a penny for her thoughts; or she broke into a melancholy little song of some kind, a song she knew they liked. She would run to the piano and tinkle the tune out with one hand, saying, "I love this part best," leaving no doubt in their minds as to what her own had been occupied with. She lived her whole youth so, without once giving herself away; not until she was in middle age, her husband dead, her property dispersed, and she found herself with a houseful of children, making a new life for them in another place, with all the responsibilities of a man but with none of the privileges, did she finally emerge into something like an honest life: and yet, she was passionately honest. She had never been anything else.

Sitting under the trees with Nannie, both of them old and their long battle with life almost finished, she said, fingering a scrap of satin, "It was not fair that Sister Keziah should have had this ivory brocade for her wedding dress, and I had only dotted swiss . . ."

"Times was harder when you got married, Missy," said Nannie. "Dat was de yeah all de crops failed."

"And they failed ever afterward, it seems to me," said Grandmother.

"Seems to me like," said Nannie, "dotted swiss was all the style when you got married."

"I never cared for it," said Grandmother.

Nannie, born in slavery, was pleased to think she would not die in it. She was wounded not so much by her state of being as by the word describing it. Emancipation was a sweet word to her. It had not changed her way of living in a single particular, but she was proud of having been able to say to her mistress, "I aim to stay wid you as long as you'll have me." Still, Emancipation had seemed to set right a wrong that stuck in her heart like a thorn. She could not understand why God, Whom she loved, had seen fit to be so hard on a whole race because they had got a certain kind of skin. She talked it over with Miss Sophia Jane. Many times. Miss Sophia Jane was always brisk and opinionated about it: "Nonsense! I tell you, God does not know whether a skin is black or white. He sees only souls. Don't be getting notions, Nannie—of course you're going to Heaven."

Nannie showed the rudiments of logic in a mind altogether untutored. She wondered, simply and without resentment, whether God, Who had been so cruel to black people on earth, might not continue His severity in the next world. Miss Sophia Jane took pleasure in reassuring her; as if she, who had been responsible for Nannie, body and soul in this life, might also be her sponsor before the judgment seat.

Miss Sophia Jane had taken upon herself all the responsibilities of her tangled world, half white, half black, mingling steadily and the confusion growing ever deeper. There were so many young men about the place, always, younger brothers-in-law, first cousins, second cousins, nephews. They came visiting and they stayed, and there was no accounting for them nor any way of controlling their quietly headstrong habits. She learned early to keep silent and give no sign of uneasiness, but whenever a child was born in the Negro quarters, pink, worm-like, she held her breath for three days, she told her eldest granddaughter, years later, to see whether the newly born would turn black after the proper interval . . . It was a strain that told on her, and ended by giving her a deeply grounded contempt for men. She could not help it, she despised men. She despised them and was ruled by them. Her husband threw away her dowry and her property in wild investments in strange territories: Louisiana, Texas; and without protest she watched him play away her substance like a gambler. She felt that she could have managed her affairs profitably. But her natural activities lay elsewhere, it was the business of a man to make all decisions and dispose of all financial matters. Yet when she got the reins in her hands, her sons could persuade her to this and that enterprise or investment; against her will and judgment she accepted their advice, and among them they managed to break up once more the stronghold she had built for the future of her family. They got from her their own start in life, came back for fresh help when they needed it, and were divided against each other. She saw it as her natural duty to provide for her household, after her husband had fought stubbornly through the War, along with every other man of military age in the connection; had been wounded, had lingered helpless, and had died of his wound long after the great fervor and excitement had faded in hopeless defeat, when to be a man wounded and ruined in the War was merely to have proved oneself, perhaps, more heroic than wise. Left so, she drew her family together and set out for Louisiana, where her husband, with her money, had bought a sugar refinery. There was going to be a fortune in sugar, he said; not in raising the raw material, but in manufacturing it. He had schemes in his head for operating cotton gins, flour mills, refineries. Had he lived . . . but he did not live, and Sophia Jane had hardly repaired the house she bought and got the orchard planted when she saw that, in her hands, the sugar refinery was going to be a failure.

She sold out at a loss, and went on to Texas, where her husband had bought cheaply, some years before, a large tract of fertile black land in an almost unsettled part of the country. She had with her nine children, the youngest about two, the eldest about seventeen years old; Nannie and her three sons, Uncle Jimbilly, and two other Negroes, all in good health, full of hope and greatly desiring to live. Her husband's ghost persisted in her, she was bitterly outraged by his death almost as if he had willfully deserted her. She mourned for him at first with dry eyes, angrily. Twenty years later, seeing after a long absence the eldest son of her favorite daughter, who had died early, she recognized the very features and look of the husband of her youth, and she wept.

During the terrible second year in Texas, two of her younger sons, Harry and Robert, suddenly ran away. They chose good weather for it, in mid-May, and they were almost seven miles from home when a neighboring farmer saw them, wondered and asked questions, and ended by persuading them into his gig, and so brought them back.

Miss Sophia Jane went through the dreary ritual of discipline she thought appropriate to the occasion. She whipped them with her riding whip. Then she made them kneel down with her while she prayed for them, asking God to help them mend their ways and not be undutiful to their mother; her duty performed, she broke down and wept with her arms around them. They had endured their punishment stoically, because it would have been disgraceful to cry when a woman hit them, and besides, she did not hit very hard; they had knelt with her in a shamefaced gloom, because religious feeling was a female mystery which embarrassed them, but when they saw her tears they burst into loud bellows of repentance. They were only nine and eleven years old. She said in a voice of mourning, so despairing it frightened them: "Why did you run away from me? What do you think I brought you here for?" as if they were grown men who could realize how terrible the situation was. All the answer they could make, as they wept too, was that they had wanted to go back to Louisiana to eat sugar cane. They had been thinking about sugar cane all winter . . . Their mother was stunned. She had built a house large enough to shelter them all, of hand-sawed lumber dragged by ox-cart for forty miles, she had got the fields fenced in and the crops planted, she had, she believed, fed and clothed her children; and now she realized they were hungry. These two had worked like men; she felt their growing bones through their thin flesh, and remembered how mercilessly she had driven them, as she had driven herself, as she had driven the Negroes and the horses, because there was no choice in the matter. They must labor beyond their strength or perish. Sitting there with her arms around them, she felt her heart break in her breast. She had thought it was a silly phrase. It happened to her. It was not that she was incapable of feeling afterward, for in a way she was more emotional, more quick, but griefs never again lasted with her so long as they had before. This day was the beginning of her spoiling her children and being afraid of them. She said to them after a long dazed silence, when they began to grow restless under her arms: "We'll grow fine ribbon cane here. The soil is perfect for it. We'll have all the sugar we want. But we must be patient."

By the time her children began to marry, she was able to give them each a good strip of land and a little money, she was able to help them buy more land in places they preferred by selling her own, tract by tract, and she saw them all begin well, though not all of them ended so. They went about their own affairs, scattering out and seeming to lose all that sense of family unity so precious to the Grandmother. They bore with her infrequent visits and her advice and her tremendous rightness, and they were impatient of her tenderness. When Harry's wife died—she had never approved of Harry's wife, who was delicate and hopelessly inadequate at housekeeping, and who could not even bear children successfully, since she died when her third was born—the Grandmother took the children and began life again, with almost the same zest, and with more indulgence. She had just got them brought up to the point

where she felt she could begin to work the faults out of them—
faults inherited, she admitted fairly, from both sides of the house—
when she died. It happened quite suddenly one afternoon in early
October, after a day spent in helping the Mexican gardener of her
third daughter-in-law to put the garden to rights. She was on a visit
in far western Texas and enjoying it. The daughter-in-law was exasperated but apparently so docile, the Grandmother, who looked
upon her as a child, did not notice her little moods at all. The son
had long ago learned not to oppose his mother. She wore him
down with patient, just, and reasonable argument. She was careful
never to venture to command him in anything. He consoled his
wife by saying that everything Mother was doing could be changed
back after she was gone. As this change included moving a fifty-
foot adobe wall, the wife was not much consoled. The Grandmother came into the house quite flushed and exhilarated, saying
how well she felt in the bracing mountain air—and dropped dead
over the doorsill.

THE WITNESS

Uncle Jimbilly was so old and had spent so many years bowed
over things, putting them together and taking them apart, making
them over and making them do, he was bent almost double. His
hands were closed and stiff from gripping objects tightly, while he
worked at them, and they could not open altogether even if a child
took the thick black fingers and tried to turn them back. He hobbled on a stick; his purplish skull showed through patches in his
wool, which had turned greenish gray and looked as if the moths
had got at it.

He mended harness and put half soles on the other Negroes'
shoes, he built fences and chicken coops and barn doors; he
stretched wires and put in new window panes and fixed sagging
hinges and patched up roofs; he repaired carriage tops and cranky
plows. Also he had a gift for carving miniature tombstones out of
blocks of wood; give him almost any kind of piece of wood and he
could turn out a tombstone, shaped very like the real ones, with

carving, and a name and date on it if they were needed. They were often needed, for some small beast or bird was always dying and having to be buried with proper ceremonies: the cart draped as a hearse, a shoe-box coffin with a pall over it, a profuse floral outlay, and, of course, a tombstone. As he worked, turning the long blade of his bowie knife deftly in circles to cut a flower, whittling and smoothing the back and sides, stopping now and then to hold it at arm's length and examine it with one eye closed, Uncle Jimbilly would talk in a low, broken, abstracted murmur, as if to himself; but he was really saying something he meant one to hear. Sometimes it would be an incomprehensible ghost story; listen ever so carefully, at the end it was impossible to decide whether Uncle Jimbilly himself had seen the ghost, whether it was a real ghost at all, or only another man dressed like one; and he dwelt much on the horrors of slave times.

"Dey used to take 'em out and tie 'em down and whup 'em," he muttered, "wid gret big leather strops inch thick long as yo' ahm, wid round holes bored in 'em so's evey time dey hit 'em de hide and de meat done come off dey bones in little round chunks. And wen dey had whupped 'em wid de strop till dey backs was all raw and bloody, dey spread dry cawnshucks on dey backs and set 'em afire and pahched 'em, and den dey poured vinega all ovah 'em . . . Yassuh. And den, the ve'y nex day dey'd got to git back to work in the fiels or dey'd do the same thing right ovah agin. Yassah. Dat was it. If dey didn't git back to work dey got it all right ovah agin."

The children—three of them: a serious, prissy older girl of ten, a thoughtful sad looking boy of eight, and a quick flighty little girl of six—sat disposed around Uncle Jimbilly and listened with faint tinglings of embarrassment. They knew, of course, that once upon a time Negroes had been slaves; but they had all been freed long ago and were now only servants. It was hard to realize that Uncle Jimbilly had been born in slavery, as the Negroes were always saying. The children thought that Uncle Jimbilly had got over his slavery very well. Since they had known him, he had never done a single thing that anyone told him to do. He did his work just as he pleased and when he pleased. If you wanted a tombstone, you had to be very careful about the way you asked for it. Nothing could have been more impersonal and faraway than his tone and manner of talking about slavery, but they wriggled a little and felt guilty. Paul would have changed the subject, but Miranda, the little quick one, wanted to know the worst. "Did they act like that to you, Uncle Jimbilly?" she asked.

"No, *mam*," said Uncle Jimbilly. "Now whut name you want on dis one? Dey nevah did. Dey done 'em dat way in the rice swamps. I always worked right here close to the house or in town with Miss Sophia. Down in the swamps . . ."

"Didn't they ever die, Uncle Jimbilly?" asked Paul.

"Cose dey died," said Uncle Jimbilly, "cose dey died—dey died," he went on, pursing his mouth gloomily, "by de thousands and tens upon thousands."

"Can you carve 'Safe in Heaven' on that, Uncle Jimbilly?" asked Maria in her pleasant, mincing voice.

"To put over a tame jackrabbit, Missy?" asked Uncle Jimbilly indignantly. He was very religious. "A heathen like dat? No, *mam*. In de swamps dey used to stake 'em out all day and all night, and all day and all night and all day wid dey hans and feet tied so dey couldn't scretch and let de muskeeters eat 'em alive. De muskeeters 'ud bite 'em tell dey was all swole up like a balloon all over, and you could heah 'em howlin and prayin all ovah the swamp. Yassuh. Dat was it. And nary a drop of watah noh a moufful of braid . . . Yassuh, dat's it. Lawd, dey done it. Hosanna! Now take dis yere tombstone and don' bother me no more . . . or I'll . . ."

Uncle Jimbilly was apt to be suddenly annoyed and you never knew why. He was easily put out about things, but his threats were always so exorbitant that not even the most credulous child could be terrified by them. He was always going to do something quite horrible to somebody and then he was going to dispose of the remains in a revolting manner. He was going to skin somebody alive and nail the hide on the barn door, or he was just getting ready to cut off somebody's ears with a hatchet and pin them on Bongo, the crop-eared brindle dog. He was often all prepared in his mind to pull somebody's teeth and make a set of false teeth for Ole Man Ronk . . . Ole Man Ronk was a tramp who had been living all summer in the little cabin behind the smokehouse. He got his rations along with the Negroes and sat all day mumbling his naked gums. He had skimpy black whiskers which appeared to be set in wax, and angry red eyelids. He took morphine, it was said; but what morphine might be, or how he took it, or why, no one seemed to know . . . Nothing could have been more unpleasant than the notion that one's teeth might be given to Ole Man Ronk.

The reason why Uncle Jimbilly never did any of these things he threatened was, he said, because he never could get round to them. He always had so much other work on hand he never seemed to get caught up on it. But some day, somebody was going to get a mighty big surprise, and meanwhile everybody had better look out.

THE CIRCUS

The long planks set on trestles rose one above the other to a monstrous height and stretched dizzyingly in a wide oval ring. They were packed with people—"lak fleas on a dog's ear," said Dicey, holding Miranda's hand firmly and looking about her with disapproval. The white billows of enormous canvas sagged overhead, held up by three poles set evenly apart down the center. The family, when seated, occupied almost a whole section on one level.

On one side of them in a long row sat Father, sister Maria, brother Paul, Grandmother; great-aunt Keziah, cousin Keziah, and second-cousin Keziah, who had just come down from Kentucky on a visit; uncle Charles Breaux, cousin Charles Breaux, and aunt Marie-Anne Breaux. On the other side sat small cousin Lucie Breaux, big cousin Paul Gay, great-aunt Sally Gay (who took snuff and was therefore a disgrace to the family); two strange, extremely handsome young men who might be cousins but who were certainly in love with cousin Miranda Gay; and cousin Miranda Gay herself, a most dashing young lady with crisp silk skirts, a half dozen of them at once, a lovely perfume and wonderful black curly hair above enormous wild gray eyes, "like a colt's," Father said. Miranda hoped to be exactly like her when she grew up. Hanging to Dicey's arm she leaned out and waved to cousin Miranda, who waved back smiling, and the strange young men waved to her also. Miranda was most fearfully excited. It was her first circus; it might also be her last because the whole family had combined to persuade Grandmother to allow her to come with them. "Very well, this once," Grandmother said, "since it's a family reunion."

This once! This once! She could not look hard enough at everything. She even peeped down between the wide crevices of the piled-up plank seats, where she was astonished to see odd-looking, roughly dressed little boys peeping up from the dust below. They were squatted in little heaps, staring up quietly. She looked squarely into the eyes of one, who returned her a look so peculiar she gazed and gazed, trying to understand it. It was a bold grinning stare without any kind of friendliness in it. He was a thin, dirty little boy with a floppy old checkerboard cap pulled over crumpled red ears and dust-colored hair. As she gazed he nudged the little boy next to him, whispered, and the second little boy caught her eye. This was too much. Miranda pulled Dicey's sleeve. "Dicey, what are those little boys doing down there?" "Down where?" asked Dicey, but she seemed to know already, for she bent over and looked through the crevice, drew her knees together and her skirts around her, and said severely: "You jus mind yo' own business and stop throwin' yo' legs around that way. Don't you pay any mind. Plenty o' monkeys right here in the show widout you studyin dat kind."

An enormous brass band seemed to explode right at Miranda's ear. She jumped, quivered, thrilled blindly and almost forgot to breathe as sound and color and smell rushed together and poured through her skin and hair and beat in her head and hands and feet and pit of her stomach. "Oh," she called out in her panic, closing her eyes and seizing Dicey's hand hard. The flaring lights burned through her lids, a roar of laughter like rage drowned out the steady raging of the drums and horns. She opened her eyes . . . A creature in a blousy white overall with ruffles at the neck and ankles, with bone-white skull and chalk-white face, with tufted eyebrows far apart in the middle of his forehead, the lids in a black sharp angle, a long scarlet mouth stretching back into sunken cheeks, turned up at the corners in a perpetual bitter grimace of pain, astonishment, not smiling, pranced along a wire stretched down the center of the ring, balancing a long thin pole with little wheels at either end. Miranda thought at first he was walking on air, or flying, and this did not surprise her; but when she saw the wire, she was terrified. High above their heads the inhuman figure pranced, spinning the little wheels. He paused, slipped, the flapping white leg waved in space; he staggered, wobbled, slipped sidewise, plunged, and caught the wire with frantic knee, hanging there upside down, the other leg waving like a feeler above his head; slipped once more, caught by one frenzied heel, and swung back and forth like a scarf . . . The crowd roared with savage delight, shrieks of dreadful laughter like devils in delicious torment . . . Miranda shrieked too, with real pain, clutching at her stomach with her knees drawn up . . . The man on the wire, hanging by his foot, turned his head like a seal from side to side and blew sneering kisses from his cruel mouth. Then Miranda covered her eyes and screamed, the tears pouring over her cheeks and chin.

"Take her home," said her father, "get her out of here at once," but the laughter was not wiped from his face. He merely glanced at her and back to the ring. "Take her away, Dicey," called the Grandmother, from under her half-raised crepe veil. Dicey, rebelliously, very slowly, without taking her gaze from the white figure swaying on the wire, rose, seized the limp, suffering bundle, prodded and lumped her way over knees and feet, through the crowd, down the levels of the scaffolding, across a space of sandy tanbark, out through a flap in the tent. Miranda was crying steadily with an occasional hiccough. A dwarf was standing in the entrance, wearing a little woolly beard, a pointed cap, tight red breeches, long shoes with turned-up toes. He carried a thin white wand. Miranda almost touched him before she saw him, her distorted face with its open mouth and glistening tears almost level with his. He leaned forward and peered at her with kind, not-human golden eyes, like a near-sighted dog: then made a horrid grimace at her, imitating her own face. Miranda struck at him in sheer ill temper, screaming. Dicey drew her away quickly, but not before Miranda had seen in his face, suddenly, a look of haughty, remote displeasure, a true grown-up look. She knew it well. It chilled her with a new kind of fear: she had not believed he was really human.

"Raincheck, get your raincheck!" said a very disagreeable looking fellow as they passed. Dicey turned toward him almost in tears herself. "Mister, caint you see I won't be able to git back? I got this young un to see to . . . What good dat lil piece of paper goin to do *me*?" All the way home she was cross, and grumbled under her breath: little ole meany . . . little ole scare-cat . . . gret big

baby . . . never go nowhere . . . never see nothin . . . come
on here now, hurry up—always ruinin everything for othah folks
. . . won't let anybody rest a minute, won't let anybody have
any good times . . . come on here now, you wanted to go home
and you're going there . . . snatching Miranda along, vicious but
cautious, careful not to cross the line where Miranda could say
outright: "Dicey did this or said this to me . . ." Dicey was allowed a certain freedom up to a point.

The family trooped into the house just before dark and scattered
out all over it. From every room came the sound of chatter and
laughter. The other children told Miranda what she had missed:
wonderful little ponies with plumes and bells on their bridles, rid-
den by darling little monkeys in velvet jackets and peaked hats
. . . trained white goats that danced . . . a baby elephant that
crossed his front feet and leaned against his cage and opened his
mouth to be fed, *such* a baby! . . . more clowns, funnier than the
first one even . . . beautiful ladies with bright yellow hair, wearing white silk tights with red satin sashes had performed on white
trapezes; they also had hung by their toes, but how gracefully, like
flying birds! Huge white horses had lolloped around and round the
ring with men and women dancing on their backs! One man had
swung by his teeth from the top of the tent and another had put his
head in a lion's mouth. Ah, what she had not missed! Everybody
had been enjoying themselves while she was missing her first big
circus and spoiling the day for Dicey. Poor Dicey. Poor dear
Dicey. The other children who hadn't thought of Dicey until that
moment, mourned over her with sad mouths, their malicious eyes
watching Miranda squirm. Dicey had been looking forward for
weeks this day! And then Miranda must get scared—"Can you
imagine being afraid of that funny old clown?" each one asked the
other, and then they smiled pityingly on Miranda . . .

Then too, it had been a very important occasion in another
way: it was the first time Grandmother had ever allowed herself to
be persuaded to go to the circus. One could not gather, from her
rather generalized opinions, whether there had been no circuses
when she was young, or there had been and it was not proper to
see them. At any rate for her usual sound reasons, Grandmother
had never approved of circuses, and though she would not deny
she had been amused somewhat, still there had been sights and

sounds in this one which she maintained were, to say the least, not particularly edifying to the young. Her son Harry, who came in while the children made an early supper, looked at their illuminated faces, all the brothers and sisters and visiting cousins, and said, "This basket of young doesn't seem to be much damaged." His mother said, "The fruits of their present are in a future so far off, neither of us may live to know whether harm has been done or not. That is the trouble," and she went on ladling out hot milk to pour over their buttered toast. Miranda was sitting silent, her underlip drooping. Her father smiled at her. "You missed it, Baby," he said softly, "and what good did that do you?"

Miranda burst again into tears: had to be taken away at last, and her supper was brought up to her. Dicey was exasperated and silent. Miranda could not eat. She tried, as if she were really remembering them, to think of the beautiful wild beings in white satin and spangles and red sashes who danced and frolicked on the trapezes; of the sweet little furry ponies and the lovely pet monkeys in their comical clothes. She fell asleep, and her invented memories gave way before her real ones, the bitter terrified face of the man in blowsy white falling to his death—ah, the cruel joke! —and the terrible grimace of the unsmiling dwarf. She screamed in her sleep and sat up crying for deliverance from her torments.

Dicey came, her cross, sleepy eyes half-closed, her big dark mouth pouted, thumping the floor with her thick bare feet. "I *swear*," she said, in a violent hoarse whisper. "What the matter with you? You need a good spankin, I *swear!* Wakin everybody up like this . . ."

Miranda was completely subjugated by her fears. She had a way of answering Dicey back. She would say, "Oh, hush up, Dicey." Or she would say, "I don't have to mind *you*. I don't have to mind anybody but my grandmother," which was provokingly true. And she would say, "You don't know what you're talking about." The day just past had changed that. Miranda sincerely did not want anybody, not even Dicey, to be cross with her. Ordinarily she did not care how cross she made the harassed adults around her. Now if Dicey must be cross, she still did not really care, if only Dicey might not turn out the lights and leave her to the fathomless terrors of the darkness where sleep could overtake her once more.

She hugged Dicey with both arms, crying, "Don't, don't leave me. *Don't* be so angry! I c-c-can't b-bear it!"

Dicey lay down beside her with a long moaning sigh, which meant that she was collecting her patience and making up her mind to remember that she was a Christian and must bear her cross. "Now you go to sleep," she said, in her usual warm being-good voice. "Now you jes shut yo eyes and go to sleep. I ain't going to leave you. Dicey ain't mad at nobody . . . *no*body in the whole worl' . . ."

THE LAST LEAF

Old Nannie sat hunched upon herself expecting her own death momentarily. The Grandmother had said to her at parting, with the easy prophecy of the aged, that this might be their last farewell on earth; they embraced and kissed each other on the cheeks, and once more promised to meet each other in heaven. Nannie was prepared to start her journey at once. The children gathered around her: "Aunt Nannie, never you mind! We love you!" She paid no attention; she did not care whether they loved her or not. Years afterward, Maria, the elder girl, thought with a pang, they had not really been so very nice to Aunt Nannie. They went on depending upon her as they always had, letting her assume more burdens and more, allowing her to work harder than she should have. The old woman grew silent, hunched over more deeply—she was thin and tall also, with a nobly modeled Negro face, worn to the bone and a thick fine sooty black, no mixed blood in Nannie —and her spine seemed suddenly to have given way. They could hear her groaning at night on her knees beside her bed, asking God to let her rest.

When a black family moved out of a little cabin across the narrow creek, the first cabin empty for years, Nannie went down to look at it. She came back and asked Mister Harry, "Whut you aim to do wid dat cabin?" Mister Harry said, "Nothing," he supposed; and Nannie asked for it. She wanted a house of her own, she said; in her whole life she never had a place of her very own. Mister

Harry said, of course she could have it. But the whole family was surprised, a little wounded. "Lemme go there and pass my last days in peace, chil'ren," she said. They had the place scrubbed and whitewashed, shelves put in and the chimney cleaned, they fixed Nannie up with a good bed and a fairly good carpet and allowed her to take all sorts of odds and ends from the house. It was astonishing to discover that Nannie had always liked and hoped to own certain things, she had seemed so contented and wantless. She moved away, and as the children said afterwards to each other, it was almost funny and certainly very sweet to see how she tried not to be too happy the day she left, but they felt rather put upon, just the same.

Thereafter she sat in the serene idleness of making patchwork and braiding woolen rugs. Her grandchildren and her white family visited her, and all kinds of white persons who had never owned a soul related to Nannie, went to see her, to buy her rugs or leave little presents with her.

She had always worn black wool dresses, or black and white figured calico with starchy white aprons and a white ruffled mobcap, or a black taffety cap for Sundays. She had been finicking precise and neat in her ways, and she still was. But she was no more the faithful old servant Nannie, a freed slave: she was an aged Bantu woman of independent means, sitting on the steps, breathing the free air. She began wearing a blue bandanna wrapped around her head, and at the age of eighty-five she took to smoking a corncob pipe. The black iris of the deep, withdrawn old eyes turned a chocolate brown and seemed to spread over the whole surface of the eyeball. As her sight failed, the eyelids crinkled and drew in, so that her face was like an eyeless mask.

The children, brought up in an out-of-date sentimental way of thinking, had always complacently believed that Nannie was a real member of the family, perfectly happy with them, and this rebuke, so quietly and firmly administered, chastened them somewhat. The lesson sank in as the years went on and Nannie continued to sit on the doorstep of her cabin. They were growing up, times were changing, the old world was sliding from under their feet, they had not yet laid hold of the new one. They missed Nannie every day. As their fortunes went down, and they had very few servants, they needed her terribly. They realized how much the old woman had done for them, simply by seeing how, almost immediately after she went, everything slackened, lost tone, went off edge. Work did not accomplish itself as it once had. They had not learned how to work for themselves, they were all lazy and incapable of sustained effort or planning. They had not been taught and they had not yet educated themselves. Now and then Nannie would come back up the hill for a visit. She worked then almost as she had before, with a kind of satisfaction in proving to them that she had been almost indispensable. They would miss her more than ever when she went away. To show their gratitude, and their hope that she would come again, they would heap upon her baskets and bales of the precious rubbish she loved, and one of her great grandsons Skid or Hasty would push them away beside her on a wheelbarrow. She would again for a moment be the amiable, dependent, like-one-of-the-family old servant: "I know my chil'ren won't let me go away empty-handed."

Uncle Jimbilly still pottered around, mending harness, currying horses, patching fences, now and then setting out a few plants or loosening the earth around shrubs in the spring. He muttered perpetually to himself, his blue mouth always moving in an endless disjointed comment on things past and present, and even to come, no doubt, though there was nothing about him that suggested any connection with even the nearest future . . . Maria had not realized until after her grandmother's death that Uncle Jimbilly and Aunt Nannie were husband and wife . . . That marriage of convenience, in which they had been mated with truly royal policy, with an eye to the blood and family stability, had dissolved of itself between them when the reasons for its being had likewise dissolved . . . They took no notice whatever of each other's existence, they seemed to forget they had children together (each spoke of "my children"), they had stored up no common memories that either wished to keep. Aunt Nannie moved away into her own house without even a glance or thought for Uncle Jimbilly, and he did not seem to notice that she was gone . . . He slept in a little attic over the smoke-house, and ate in the kitchen at odd hours, and did as he pleased, lonely as a wandering spirit and almost as invisible . . . But one day he passed by the little house and saw

Aunt Nannie sitting on her steps with her pipe. He sat down awhile, groaning a little as he bent himself into angles, and sunned himself like a weary old dog. He would have stayed on from that minute, but Nannie would not have him. "Whut you doin with all this big house to yoself?" he wanted to know. " 'Tain't no more than just enough fo' me," she told him pointedly; "I don' aim to pass my las' days waitin on no man," she added, "I've served my time, I've done my do, and dat's all." So Uncle Jimbilly crept back up the hill and into his smoke-house attic, and never went near her again . . .

On summer evenings she sat by herself long after dark, smoking to keep away the mosquitoes, until she was ready to sleep. She said she wasn't afraid of anything: never had been, never expected to be. She had long ago got in the way of thinking that night was a blessing, it brought the time when she didn't have to work any more until tomorrow. Even after she stopped working for good and all, she still looked forward with longing to the night, as if all the accumulated fatigues of her life, lying now embedded in her bones, still begged for easement. But when night came, she remembered that she didn't have to get up in the morning until she was ready. So she would sit in the luxury of having at her disposal all of God's good time there was in this world.

When Mister Harry, in the old days, had stood out against her word in some petty dispute, she could always get the better of him by slapping her slatty old chest with the flat of her long hand and crying out: "Why, Mister Harry, you, ain't you shamed to talk lak dat to me? I nuhsed you at dis bosom!"

Harry knew this was not literally true. She had nursed three of his elder brothers; but he always said at once, "All right, Mammy, all right, for God's sake!"—precisely as he said it to his own mother, exploding in his natural irascibility as if he hoped to clear the air somewhat of the smothering matriarchal tyranny to which he had been delivered by the death of his father. Still he submitted, being of that latest generation of sons who acknowledged, however reluctantly, however bitterly, their mystical never to be forgiven debt to the womb that bore them, and the breast that suckled them.

351

THE FIG TREE

Old Aunt Nannie had a habit of gripping with her knees to hold Miranda while she brushed her hair or buttoned her dress down the back. When Miranda wriggled, Aunt Nannie squeezed still harder, and Miranda wriggled more, but never enough to get away. Aunt Nannie gathered up Miranda's scalp lock firmly, snapped a rubber band around it, jammed a freshly starched white chambray bonnet over her ears and forehead, fastened the crown to the lock with a large safety pin, and said: "Got to hold you still someways. Here now, don't you take this off your head till the sun go down."

"I didn't want a bonnet, it's too hot, I wanted a hat," said Miranda.

"You not goin' to get a hat, you goin' to get just what you got," said Aunt Nannie in the bossy voice she used for washing and dressing time, "and mo'over some of these days I'm goin' to *sew* this bonnet to your topknot. Your daddy says if you get freckles he blame me. Now, you're all ready to set out."

"Where are we going, Aunty?" Miranda could never find out about anything until the last minute. She was always being surprised. Once she went to sleep in her bed with her kitten curled on the pillow purring, and woke up in a stuffy tight bed in a train, hugging a hot-water bottle; and there was Grandmother stretched out beside her in her McLeod tartan dressing-gown, her eyes wide open. Miranda thought something wonderful had happened. "My goodness, Grandmother, where are we going?" And it was only for another trip to El Paso to see Uncle Bill.

Now Tom and Dick were hitched to the carry-all standing outside the gate with boxes and baskets tied on everywhere. Grandmother was walking alone through the house very slowly, taking a last look at everything. Now and then she put something else in the big leather portmoney on her arm until it was pretty bulgy. She carried a long black mohair skirt on her other arm, the one she put on over her other skirt when she rode horseback. Her son Harry, Miranda's father, followed her saying: "I can't see the sense in rushing off to Halifax on five minutes' notice."

Grandmother said, walking on: "It's five hours exactly." Halifax wasn't the name of Grandmother's farm at all, it was Cedar Grove, but Father always called it Halifax. "Hot as Halifax," he would say when he wanted to describe something very hot. Cedar Grove was very hot, but they went there every summer because Grandmother loved it. "I went to Cedar Grove for fifty summers before you were born," she told Miranda, who remembered last summer very well, and the summer before a little. Miranda liked it for watermelons and grasshoppers and the long rows of blooming chinaberry trees where the hounds flattened themselves out and slept. They whined and winked their eyelids and worked their feet and barked faintly in their sleep, and Uncle Jimbilly said it was because dogs always dreamed they were chasing something. In the middle of the day when Miranda looked down over the thick green fields towards the spring she could simply see it being hot: everything blue and sleepy and the mourning doves calling.

"Are we going to Halifax, Aunty?"

"Now just ask your dad if you wanta know so much."

"Are we going to Halifax, Dad?"

Her father twitched her bonnet straight and pulled her hair forward so it would show. "You mustn't get sunburned. No, let it alone. Show the pretty curls. You'll be wading in Whirlpool before supper this evening."

Grandmother said, "Don't say Halifax, child, say Cedar Grove. Call things by their right names."

"Yes, ma'am," said Miranda. Grandmother said again, to her son, "It's five hours, exactly, and your Aunt Eliza has had plenty of time to pack up her telescope, and take my saddle horse. She's been there three hours by now. I imagine she's got the telescope already set up on the hen-house roof. I hope nothing happens."

"You worry too much, Mammy," said her son, trying to conceal his impatience.

"I am not worrying," said Grandmother, shifting her riding skirt to the arm carrying the portmoney. "It will scarcely be any good taking this," she said; "I might in fact as well throw it away for this summer."

"Never mind, Mammy, we'll send to the Black Farm for Pompey, he's a good easy saddler."

"You may ride him yourself," said Grandmother. "I'll never

mount Pompey while Fiddler is alive. Fiddler is my horse, and I hate having his mouth spoiled by a careless rider. Eliza never could ride, and she never will. . . ."

Miranda gave a little skip and ran away. So they were going to Cedar Grove. Miranda never got over being surprised at the way grown-up people simply did not seem able to give anyone a straight answer to any question, unless the answer was "No." Then it popped out with no trouble at all. At a little distance, she heard her grandmother say, "Harry, have you seen my riding crop lately?" and her father answered, at least maybe he thought it was an answer, "Now, Mammy, for God's sake let's get this thing over with." That was it, exactly.

Another strange way her father had of talking was calling Grandmother "Mammy." Aunt Jane was Mammy. Sometimes he called Grandmother "Mama," but she wasn't Mama either, she was really Grandmother. Mama was dead. Dead meant gone away forever. Dying was something that happened all the time, to people and everything else. Somebody died, and there was a long string of carriages going at a slow walk over the rocky ridge of the hill towards the river while the bell tolled and tolled, and that person was never seen again by anybody. Kittens and chickens and specially little turkeys died much oftener, and sometimes calves, but hardly ever cows or horses. Lizards on rocks turned into shells, with no lizard inside at all. If caterpillars all curled up and furry didn't move when you poked them with a stick, that meant they were dead—it was a sure sign.

When Miranda found any creature that didn't move or make a noise, or looked somehow different from the live ones, she always buried it in a little grave with flowers on top and a smooth stone at the head. Even grasshoppers. Everything dead had to be treated this way. "This way and no other!" Grandmother always said when she was laying down the law about all kinds of things. "It must be done *this* way, and no other!"

Miranda went down the crooked flat-stone walk hopping zigzag between the grass tufts. First there were pomegranate and cape jessamine bushes mixed together; then it got very dark and shady and that was the fig grove. She went to her favorite fig tree where the deep branches bowed down level with her chin, and she could gather figs without having to climb and skin her knees. Grandmother hadn't remembered to take any figs to the country the last time, she said there were plenty of them at Cedar Grove. But the ones at Cedar Grove were big soft greenish white ones, and these at home were black and sugary. It was strange that Grandmother did not seem to notice the difference. The air was sweet among the fig trees, and chickens were always getting out of the run and rushing there to eat the figs off the ground. One mother hen was scurrying around scratching and clucking. She would scratch around a fig lying there in plain sight and cluck to her children as if it was a worm and she had dug it up for them.

"Old smarty," said Miranda, "you're just pretending."

When the little chickens all ran to their mother under Miranda's fig tree, one little chicken did not move. He was spread out on his side with his eyes shut and his mouth open. He was yellow fur in spots and pinfeathers in spots, and the rest of him was naked and sunburned. "Lazy," said Miranda, poking him with her toe. Then she saw that he was dead.

Oh, and in no time at all they'd be setting out for Halifax. Grandmother never went away, she always set out for somewhere. She'd have to hurry like anything to get him buried properly. Back into the house she went on tiptoe hoping not to be seen, for Grandmother always asked: "Where are you going, child? What are you doing? What is that you're carrying? Where did you get it? Who gave you permission?" and after Miranda had explained all that, even if there turned out not to be anything wrong in it, nothing ever seemed so nice any more. Besides it took forever to get away.

Miranda slid open her bureau drawer, third down, left-hand side where her new shoes were still wrapped in tissue paper in a nice white box the right size for a chicken with pinfeathers. She pushed the rustling white folded things and the lavender bags out of the way and trembled a little. Down in front the carry-all wheels screeched and crunched on the gravel, with Old Uncle Jimbilly yelling like a foghorn, "Hiyi, thar, back up, you steeds! Back up thar, you!" and of course, that meant he was turning Tom and Dick around so they would be pointing towards Halifax. They'd be after her, calling and hurrying her, and she wouldn't have time for anything and they wouldn't listen to a word.

*

It wasn't hard work digging a hole with her little spade in the loose dry soil. Miranda wrapped the slimpsy chicken in tissue paper, trying to make it look pretty, laid it in the box carefully, and covered it up with a nice mound, just like people's. She had hardly got it piled up grave shape, kneeling and leaning to smooth it over, when a strange sound came from somewhere, a very sad little crying sound. It said Weep, weep, weep, three times like that slowly, and it seemed to come from the mound of dirt. "My goodness," Miranda asked herself aloud, "what's that?" She pushed her bonnet off her ears and listened hard. "Weep, weep," said the tiny sad voice. And People began calling and urging her, their voices coming nearer. She began to clamor, too.

"Yes, Aunty, wait a minute, Aunty!"

"You come right on here this minute, we're goin'!"

"You *have* to wait, Aunty!"

Her father was coming along the edge of the fig trees. "Hurry up, Baby, you'll get left!"

Miranda felt she couldn't bear to be left. She ran all shaking with fright. Her father gave her the annoyed look he always gave her when he said something to upset her and then saw that she was upset. His words were kind but his voice scolded: "Stop getting so excited, Baby, you know we wouldn't leave you for anything." Miranda wanted to talk back: "Then why did you say so?" but she was still listening for that tiny sound: "Weep, weep." She lagged and pulled backward, looking over her shoulder, but her father hurried her towards the carry-all. But things didn't make sounds if they were dead. They couldn't. That was one of the signs. Oh, but she had heard it.

Her father sat in front and drove, and old Uncle Jimbilly didn't do anything but get down and open gates. Grandmother and Aunt Nannie sat in the back seat, with Miranda between them. She loved setting out somewhere, with everybody smiling and settling down and looking up at the weather, with the horses bouncing and pulling on the reins, the springs jolting and swaying with a creaky noise that made you feel sure you were traveling. That evening she would go wading with Maria and Paul and Uncle Jimbilly, and that very night she would lie out on the grass in her nightgown to cool off, and they would all drink lemonade before going to bed. Sister Maria and Brother Paul would already be burned like muffins because they were sent on ahead the minute school was out. Sister Maria had got freckled and Father was furious. "Keep your bonnet on," he said to Miranda, sternly. "Now remember. I'm not going to have that face ruined, too." But oh, what had made that funny sound? Miranda's ears buzzed and she had a dull round pain in her just under her front ribs. She had to go back and let him out. He'd never get out by himself, all tangled up in tissue paper and that shoebox. He'd never get out without her.

"Grandmother, I've got to go back. Oh, I've *got* to go back!"

Grandmother turned Miranda's face around by the chin and looked at her closely, the way grown folks did. Grandmother's eyes were always the same. They never looked kind or sad or angry or tired or anything. They just looked, blue and still. "What is the matter with you, Miranda, what happened?"

"Oh, I've got to go back—I forg-got something important."

"Stop that silly crying and tell me what you want."

Miranda couldn't stop. Her father looked very anxious. "Mammy, maybe the Baby's sick." He reached out his handkerchief to her face. "What's the matter with my honey? Did you eat something?"

Miranda had to stand up to cry as hard as she wanted to. The wheels went grinding round in the road, the carry-all wobbled so that Grandmother had to take her by one arm, and her father by the other. They stared at each other over Miranda's head with a moveless gaze that Miranda had seen often, and their eyes looked exactly alike. Miranda blinked up at them, waiting to see who would win. Then Grandmother's hand fell away, and Miranda was handed over to her father. He gave the reins to Uncle Jimbilly, and lifted her over the top of the seat. She sprawled against his chest and knees as if he were an armchair and stopped crying at once. "We can't go back just for notions," he told her in the reasoning tone he always talked in when Grandmother scolded, and held the muffly handkerchief for her. "Now, blow hard. What did you forget, honey? We'll find another. Was it your doll?"

Miranda hated dolls. She never played with them. She always pulled the wigs off and tied them on the kittens, like hats. The kittens pulled them off instantly. It was fun. She put the doll clothes on the kittens and it took any one of them just half a minute to get them all off again. Kittens had sense. Miranda wailed suddenly, "Oh, I want my doll!" and cried again, trying to drown out the strange little sound, "Weep, weep"—

"Well now, if that's all," said her father comfortably, "there's a raft of dolls at Cedar Grove, and about forty fresh kittens. How'd you like that?"

"Forty?" asked Miranda.

"About," said Father.

Old Aunt Nannie leaned and held out her hand. "Look, honey, I toted you some nice black figs."

Her face was wrinkled and black and it looked like a fig upside down with a white ruffled cap. Miranda clenched her eyes tight and shook her head.

"Is that a pretty way to behave when Aunt Nannie offers you something nice?" asked Grandmother in her gentle reminding tone of voice.

"No, ma'am," said Miranda meekly. "Thank you, Aunt Nannie." But she did not accept the figs.

Great-Aunt Eliza, half way up a stepladder pitched against the flat-roofed chicken house, was telling Hinry just how to set up her telescope. "For a fellow who never saw or heard of a telescope," Great-Aunt Eliza said to Grandmother, who was really her sister Sophia Jane, "he doesn't do so badly so long as I tell him."

"I do wish you'd stop clambering up stepladders, Eliza," said Grandmother, "at your time of life."

"You're nothing but a nervous wreck, Sophia, I declare. When did you ever know me to get hurt?"

"Even so," said Grandmother tartly, "there is such a thing as appropriate behavior at your time of . . ."

Great-Aunt Eliza seized a fold of her heavy brown pleated skirt with one hand, with the other she grasped the ladder one rung higher and ascended another step. "Now Hinry," she called, "just swing it around facing west and leave it level. I'll fix it the way I want when I'm ready. You can come on down now." She came down then herself, and said to her sister: "So long as you can go bouncing off on that horse of yours, Sophia Jane, I s'pose I can climb ladders. I'm three years younger than you, and *at your time of life* that makes all the difference!"

Grandmother turned pink as the inside of a seashell, the one on her sewing table that had the sound of the sea in it; Miranda knew that she had always been the pretty one, and she was pretty still, but Great-Aunt Eliza was not pretty now and never had been. Miranda, watching and listening—for everything in the world was strange to her and something she had to know about—saw two old women, who were proud of being grandmothers, who spoke to children always as if they knew best about everything and children knew nothing, and they told children all day long to come here, go there, do this, do not do that, and they were always right and children never were except when they did anything they were told right away without a word. And here they were bickering like two little girls at school, or even the way Miranda and her sister Maria bickered and nagged and picked on each other and said things on purpose to hurt each other's feelings. Miranda felt sad and strange and a little frightened. She began edging away.

"Where are you going, Miranda?" asked Grandmother in her everyday voice.

"Just to the house," said Miranda, her heart sinking.

"Wait and walk with us," said Grandmother. She was very thin and pale and had white hair. Beside her, Great-Aunt Eliza loomed like a mountain with her grizzled iron-colored hair like a curly wig, her steel-rimmed spectacles over her snuff-colored eyes, and snuff-colored woollen skirts billowing about her, and her smell of snuff. When she came through the door she quite filled it up. When she sat down the chair disappeared under her, and she seemed to be sitting solidly on herself from her waistband to the floor.

Now with Grandmother sitting across the room rummaging in her work basket and pretending not to see anything, Great-Aunt Eliza took a small brown bottle out of her pocket, opened it, took a pinch of snuff in each nostril, sneezed loudly, wiped her nose with a big white starchy-looking handkerchief, pushed her spectacles up on her forehead, took a little twig chewed into a brush at one end, dipped and twisted it around in the little bottle, and placed it firmly between her teeth. Miranda had heard of this shameful habit in women of the lower classes, but no lady had been known to "dip snuff," and surely not in the family. Yet here was Great-Aunt Eliza, a lady even if not a very pretty one, dipping snuff. Miranda knew how her grandmother felt about it; she stared

fascinated at Great-Aunt Eliza until her eyes watered. Great-Aunt
Eliza stared back in turn.

"Look here, young one, d'ye s'pose if I gave you a gumdrop
you'd get out from underfoot?"

She reached in the other pocket and took out a roundish, rather
crushed-looking pink gumdrop with the sugar coating pretty badly
crackled. "Now take this, and don't let me lay eyes on you any
more today."

Miranda hurried away, clenching the gumdrop in her palm.
When she reached the kitchen it was oozing through her fingers.
She went to the tap and held her hand under the water and tried to
wash off the snuffy smell. After this crime she did not really dare
go near Great-Aunt Eliza again soon. "What did you do with that
gumdrop so quickly, child?" she could almost hear her asking.

Yet Miranda almost forgot her usual interests, such as kittens
and other little animals on the place, pigs, chickens, rabbits, anything at all so it was a baby and would let her pet and feed it,
for Great-Aunt Eliza's ways and habits kept Miranda following her
about, gazing, or sitting across the dining-table, gazing, for when
Great-Aunt Eliza was not on the roof before her telescope, always
just before daylight or just after dark, she was walking about with
a microscope and a burning glass, peering closely at something she
saw on a tree trunk, something she found in the grass; now and
then she collected fragments that looked like dried leaves or bits of
bark, brought them in the house, spread them out on a sheet of
white paper, and sat there, poring, as still as if she were saying her
prayers. At table she would dissect a scrap of potato peeling or
anything else she might be eating, and sit there, bowed over,
saying, "Hum," from time to time. Grandmother, who did not
allow the children to bring anything to the table to play with and
who forbade them to do anything but eat while they were there,
ignored her sister's manners as long as she could, then remarked
one day, when Great-Aunt Eliza was humming like a bee to herself
over what her microscope had found in a raisin, "Eliza, if it is
interesting save it for me to look at after dinner. Or tell me what it
is."

"You wouldn't know if I told you," said Great-Aunt Eliza,
coolly, putting her microscope away and finishing off her pudding.

When at last, just before they were all going back to town again, Great-Aunt Eliza invited the children to climb the ladder with her and see the stars through her telescope, they were so awed they looked at each other like strangers, and did not exchange a word. Miranda saw only a great pale flaring disk of cold light, but she knew it was the moon and called out in pure rapture, "Oh, it's like another world!"

"Why, of course, child," said Great-Aunt Eliza, in her growling voice, but kindly, "other worlds, a million other worlds."

"Like this one?" asked Miranda, timidly.

"Nobody knows, child. . . ."

"Nobody knows, nobody knows," Miranda sang to a tune in her head, and when the others walked on, she was so dazzled with joy she fell back by herself, walking a little distance behind Great-Aunt Eliza's swinging lantern and her wide-swinging skirts. They took the dewy path through the fig grove, much like the one in town, with the early dew bringing out the sweet smell of the milky leaves. They passed a fig tree with low hanging branches, and Miranda reached up by habit and touched it with her fingers for luck. From the earth beneath her feet came a terrible, faint troubled sound. "Weep weep, weep weep . . ." murmured a little crying voice from the smothering earth, the grave.

Miranda bounded like a startled pony against the back of Great-Aunt Eliza's knees, crying out, "Oh, oh, oh, wait . . ."

"What on earth's the matter, child?"

Miranda seized the warm snuffy hand held out to her and hung on hard. "Oh, there's something saying 'weep weep' out of the ground!"

Great-Aunt Eliza stooped, put her arm around Miranda and listened carefully, for a moment. "Hear them?" she said. "They're not in the ground at all. They are the first tree frogs, means it's going to rain," she said, "weep weep—hear them?"

Miranda took a deep trembling breath and heard them. They were in the trees. They walked on again, Miranda holding Great-Aunt Eliza's hand.

"Just think," said Great-Aunt Eliza, in her most scientific voice, "when tree frogs shed their skins, they pull them off over their heads like little shirts, and they eat them. Can you imagine? They have the prettiest little shapes you ever saw—I'll show you one some time under the microscope."

"Thank you, ma'am," Miranda remembered finally to say through her fog of bliss at hearing the tree frogs sing, "Weep weep . . ."

THE GRAVE

The grandfather, dead for more than thirty years, had been twice disturbed in his long repose by the constancy and possessiveness of his widow. She removed his bones first to Louisiana and then to Texas as if she had set out to find her own burial place, knowing well she would never return to the places she had left. In Texas she set up a small cemetery in a corner of her first farm, and as the family connection grew, and oddments of relations came over from Kentucky to settle, it contained at last about twenty graves. After the grandmother's death, part of her land was to be sold for the benefit of certain of her children, and the cemetery happened to lie in the part set aside for sale. It was necessary to take up the bodies and bury them again in the family plot in the big new public cemetery, where the grandmother had been buried. At last her husband was to lie beside her for eternity, as she had planned.

The family cemetery had been a pleasant small neglected garden of tangled rose bushes and ragged cedar trees and cypress, the simple flat stones rising out of uncropped sweet-smelling wild grass. The graves were lying open and empty one burning day when Miranda and her brother Paul, who often went together to hunt rabbits and doves, propped their twenty-two Winchester rifles carefully against the rail fence, climbed over and explored among the graves. She was nine years old and he was twelve.

They peered into the pits all shaped alike with such purposeful accuracy, and looking at each other with pleased adventurous eyes, they said in solemn tones: "These were graves!" trying by words to shape a special, suitable emotion in their minds, but they felt nothing except an agreeable thrill of wonder: they were seeing a new sight, doing something they had not done before. In them both there was also a small disappointment at the entire commonplaceness of the actual spectacle. Even if it had once contained a coffin for years upon years, when the coffin was gone a grave was just a hole in the ground. Miranda leaped into the pit that had held her grandfather's bones. Scratching around aimlessly and pleasurably as any young animal, she scooped up a lump of earth and weighed it in her palm. It had a pleasantly sweet, corrupt smell, being mixed with cedar needles and small leaves, and as the crumbs fell apart, she saw a silver dove no larger than a hazel nut, with spread wings and a neat fan-shaped tail. The breast had a deep round hollow in it. Turning it up to the fierce sunlight, she saw that the inside of the hollow was cut in little whorls. She scrambled out, over the pile of loose earth that had fallen back into one end of the grave, calling to Paul that she had found something, he must guess what . . . His head appeared smiling over the rim of another grave. He waved a closed hand at her. "I've got something too!" They ran to compare treasures, making a game of it, so many guesses each, all wrong, and a final showdown with opened palms. Paul had found a thin wide gold ring carved with intricate flowers and leaves. Miranda was smitten at sight of the ring and wished to have it. Paul seemed more impressed by the dove. They made a trade, with some little bickering. After he had got the dove in his hand, Paul said, "Don't you know what this is? This is a screw head for a *coffin!* . . . I'll bet nobody else in the world has one like this!"

Miranda glanced at it without covetousness. She had the gold ring on her thumb; it fitted perfectly. "Maybe we ought to go now," she said, "maybe one of the niggers 'll see us and tell somebody." They knew the land had been sold, the cemetery was no longer theirs, and they felt like trespassers. They climbed back over the fence, slung their rifles loosely under their arms—they had been shooting at targets with various kinds of firearms since they were seven years old—and set out to look for the rabbits and doves or whatever small game might happen along. On these expeditions Miranda always followed at Paul's heels along the path, obeying instructions about handling her gun when going through fences; learning how to stand it up properly so it would not slip and fire unexpectedly; how to wait her time for a shot and not just bang away in the air without looking, spoiling shots for Paul, who really could hit things if given a chance. Now and then, in her excitement at seeing birds whizz up suddenly before her face, or a rabbit leap across her very toes, she lost her head, and almost without sighting she flung her rifle up and pulled the trigger. She hardly ever hit any sort of mark. She had no proper sense of hunting at all. Her brother would be often completely disgusted with her. "You don't care whether you get your bird or not," he said. "That's no way to hunt." Miranda could not understand his indignation. She had seen him smash his hat and yell with fury when he had missed his aim. "What I like about shooting," said Miranda, with exasperating inconsequence, "is pulling the trigger and hearing the noise."

"Then, by golly," said Paul, "whyn't you go back to the range and shoot at bulls-eyes?"

"I'd just as soon," said Miranda, "only like this, we walk around more."

"Well, you just stay behind and stop spoiling my shots," said Paul, who, when he made a kill, wanted to be certain he had made it. Miranda, who alone brought down a bird once in twenty rounds, always claimed as her own any game they got when they fired at the same moment. It was tiresome and unfair and her brother was sick of it.

"Now, the first dove we see, or the first rabbit, is mine," he told her. "And the next will be yours. Remember that and don't get smarty."

"What about snakes?" asked Miranda idly. "Can I have the first snake?"

Waving her thumb gently and watching her gold ring glitter, Miranda lost interest in shooting. She was wearing her summer roughing outfit: dark blue overalls, a light blue shirt, a hired-man's straw hat, and thick brown sandals. Her brother had the same outfit except his was a sober hickory-nut color. Ordinarily Miranda preferred her overalls to any other dress, though it was making rather a scandal in the countryside, for the year was 1903, and in the back country the law of female decorum had teeth in it. Her father had been criticized for letting his girls dress like boys and go careering around astride barebacked horses. Big sister Maria, the really independent and fearless one, in spite of her rather affected ways, rode at a dead run with only a rope knotted around her horse's nose. It was said the motherless family was running down, with the Grandmother no longer there to hold it together. It was known that she had discriminated against her son Harry in her will, and that he was in straits about money. Some of his old neighbors reflected with vicious satisfaction that now he would probably not be so stiffnecked, nor have any more high-stepping horses either. Miranda knew this, though she could not say how. She had met along the road old women of the kind who smoked corn-cob pipes, who had treated her grandmother with most sincere respect. They slanted their gummy old eyes side-ways at the grand-daughter and said, "Ain't you ashamed of yoself, Missy? It's aginst the Scriptures to dress like that. Whut yo Pappy thinkin about?" Miranda, with her powerful social sense, which was like a fine set of antennae radiating from every pore of her skin, would feel ashamed because she knew well it was rude and ill-bred to shock anybody, even bad-tempered old crones, though she had faith in her father's judgment and was perfectly comfortable in the clothes. Her father had said, "They're just what you need, and they'll save your dresses for school . . ." This sounded quite simple and natural to her. She had been brought up in rigorous economy. Wastefulness was vulgar. It was also a sin. These were truths; she had heard them repeated many times and never once disputed.

Now the ring, shining with the serene purity of fine gold on her rather grubby thumb, turned her feelings against her overalls and sockless feet, toes sticking through the thick brown leather straps. She wanted to go back to the farmhouse, take a good cold bath, dust herself with plenty of Maria's violet talcum powder—provided Maria was not present to object, of course—put on the thinnest, most becoming dress she owned, with a big sash, and sit in a wicker chair under the trees . . . These things were not all she wanted, of course; she had vague stirrings of desire for luxury and a grand way of living which could not take precise form in her imagination but were founded on family legend of past wealth and leisure. These immediate comforts were what she could have, and she wanted them at once. She lagged rather far behind Paul, and once she thought of just turning back without a word and going home. She stopped, thinking that Paul would never do that to her, and so she would have to tell him. When a rabbit leaped, she let Paul have it without dispute. He killed it with one shot.

When she came up with him, he was already kneeling, examining the wound, the rabbit trailing from his hands. "Right through the head," he said complacently, as if he had aimed for it. He took out his sharp, competent bowie knife and started to skin the body. He did it very cleanly and quickly. Uncle Jimbilly knew how to prepare the skins so that Miranda always had fur coats for her dolls, for though she never cared much for her dolls she liked seeing them in fur coats. The children knelt facing each other over the dead animal. Miranda watched admiringly while her brother stripped the skin away as if he were taking off a glove. The flayed flesh emerged dark scarlet, sleek, firm; Miranda with thumb and finger felt the long fine muscles with the silvery flat strips binding them to the joints. Brother lifted the oddly bloated belly. "Look," he said, in a low amazed voice. "It was going to have young ones."

Very carefully he slit the thin flesh from the center ribs to the flanks, and a scarlet bag appeared. He slit again and pulled the bag open, and there lay a bundle of tiny rabbits, each wrapped in a thin scarlet veil. The brother pulled these off and there they were, dark gray, their sleek wet down lying in minute even ripples, like a baby's head just washed, their unbelievably small delicate ears folded close, their little blind faces almost featureless.

Miranda said, "Oh, I want to *see*," under her breath. She looked and looked—excited but not frightened, for she was accustomed to the sight of animals killed in hunting—filled with pity and astonishment and a kind of shocked delight in the wonderful little creatures for their own sakes, they were so pretty. She touched one of them ever so carefully, "Ah, there's blood running over them," she said and began to tremble without knowing why. Yet she wanted most deeply to see and to know. Having seen, she felt at once as if she had known all along. The very memory of her former ignorance faded, she had always known just this. No one had ever told her anything outright, she had been rather unobservant of the animal life around her because she was so accustomed to animals. They seemed simply disorderly and unaccountably rude in their habits, but altogether natural and not very interesting. Her brother had spoken as if he had known about everything all along. He may have seen all this before. He had never said a word to her, but she knew now a part at least of what he knew. She understood a little of the secret, formless intuitions in her own mind and body, which had been clearing up, taking form, so gradually and so steadily she had not realized that she was learning what she had to know. Paul said cautiously, as if he were talking about something forbidden: "They were just about ready to be born." His voice dropped on the last word. "I know," said Miranda, "like kittens. I know, like babies." She was quietly and terribly agitated, standing again with her rifle under her arm, looking down at the bloody heap. "I don't want the skin," she said, "I won't have it." Paul buried the young rabbits again in their mother's body, wrapped the skin around her, carried her to a clump of sage bushes, and hid her away. He came out again at once and said to Miranda, with an eager friendliness, a confidential tone quite unusual in him, as if he were taking her into an important secret on equal terms: "Listen now. Now you listen to me, and don't ever forget. Don't you ever tell a living soul that you saw this. Don't tell a soul. Don't tell Dad because I'll get into trouble. He'll say I'm leading you into things you ought not to do. He's always saying that. So now don't you go and forget and blab out sometime the way you're always doing . . . Now, that's a secret. Don't you tell."

Miranda never told, she did not even wish to tell anybody. She thought about the whole worrisome affair with confused unhappiness for a few days. Then it sank quietly into her mind and was heaped over by accumulated thousands of impressions, for nearly twenty years. One day she was picking her path among the puddles and crushed refuse of a market street in a strange city of a strange country, when without warning, plain and clear in its true colors as if she looked through a frame upon a scene that had not stirred nor changed since the moment it happened, the episode of that far-off day leaped from its burial place before her mind's eye. She was so reasonlessly horrified she halted suddenly staring, the scene before her eyes dimmed by the vision back of them. An Indian vendor had held up before her a tray of dyed sugar sweets, in the shapes of all kinds of small creatures: birds, baby chicks, baby rabbits, lambs, baby pigs. They were in gay colors and smelled of vanilla, maybe. . . . It was a very hot day and the smell in the market, with its piles of raw flesh and wilting flowers, was like the mingled sweetness and corruption she had smelled that other day in the empty cemetery at home: the day she had remembered always until now vaguely as the time she and her brother had found treasure in the opened graves. Instantly upon this thought the dreadful vision faded, and she saw clearly her brother, whose childhood face she had forgotten, standing again in the blazing sunshine, again twelve years old, a pleased sober smile in his eyes, turning the silver dove over and over in his hands.

The Downward
Path to Wisdom

In the square bedroom with the big window Mama and Papa were lolling back on their pillows handing each other things from the wide black tray on the small table with crossed legs. They were smiling and they smiled even more when the little boy, with the feeling of sleep still in his skin and hair, came in and walked up to the bed. Leaning against it, his bare toes wriggling in the white fur rug, he went on eating peanuts which he took from his pajama pocket. He was four years old.

"Here's my baby," said Mama. "Lift him up, will you?"

He went limp as a rag for Papa to take him under the arms and swing him up over a broad, tough chest. He sank between his parents like a bear cub in a warm litter, and lay there comfortably. He took another peanut between his teeth, cracked the shell, picked out the nut whole and ate it.

"Running around without his slippers again," said Mama. "His feet are like icicles."

"He crunches like a horse," said Papa. "Eating peanuts before breakfast will ruin his stomach. Where did he get them?"

"You brought them yesterday," said Mama, with exact memory, "in a grisly little cellophane sack. I have asked you dozens of times not to bring him things to eat. Put him out, will you? He's spilling shells all over me."

Almost at once the little boy found himself on the floor again. He moved around to Mama's side of the bed and leaned confidingly near her and began another peanut. As he chewed he gazed solemnly in her eyes.

"Bright-looking specimen, isn't he?" asked Papa, stretching his long legs and reaching for his bathrobe. "I suppose you'll say it's my fault he's dumb as an ox."

"He's my little baby, my only baby," said Mama richly, hugging him, "and he's a dear lamb." His neck and shoulders were quite boneless in her firm embrace. He stopped chewing long enough to receive a kiss on his crumby chin. "He's sweet as clover," said Mama. The baby went on chewing.

"Look at him staring like an owl," said Papa.

Mama said, "He's an angel and I'll never get used to having him."

"We'd be better off if we never *had* had him," said Papa. He was walking about the room and his back was turned when he said that. There was silence for a moment. The little boy stopped eating, and stared deeply at his Mama. She was looking at the back of Papa's head, and her eyes were almost black. "You're going to say that just once too often," she told him in a low voice. "I hate you when you say that."

Papa said, "You spoil him to death. You never correct him for anything. And you don't take care of him. You let him run around eating peanuts before breakfast."

"You gave him the peanuts, remember that," said Mama. She sat up and hugged her only baby once more. He nuzzled softly in the pit of her arm. "Run along, my darling," she told him in her gentlest voice, smiling at him straight in the eyes. "Run along," she said, her arms falling away from him. "Get your breakfast."

The little boy had to pass his father on the way to the door. He shrank into himself when he saw the big hand raised above him. "Yes, get out of here and stay out," said Papa, giving him a little shove toward the door. It was not a hard shove, but it hurt the little boy. He slunk out, and trotted down the hall trying not to look back. He was afraid something was coming after him, he could not imagine what. Something hurt him all over, he did not know why.

He did not want his breakfast; he would not have it. He sat and stirred it round in the yellow bowl, letting it stream off the spoon and spill on the table, on his front, on the chair. He liked seeing it spill. It was hateful stuff, but it looked funny running in white rivulets down his pajamas.

"Now look what you're doing, dirty boy," said Marjory. "You dirty little old boy."

The little boy opened his mouth to speak for the first time. "You're dirty yourself," he told her.

"That's right," said Marjory, leaning over him and speaking so her voice would not carry. "That's right, just like your papa. Mean," she whispered, "mean."

The little boy took up his yellow bowl full of cream and oatmeal and sugar with both hands and brought it down with a crash on the table. It burst and some of the wreck lay in chunks and some of it ran all over everything. He felt better.

"You see?" said Marjory, dragging him out of the chair and scrubbing him with a napkin. She scrubbed him as roughly as she dared until he cried out. "That's just what I said. That's exactly it." Through his tears he saw her face terribly near, red and frowning under a stiff white band, looking like the face of somebody who came at night and stood over him and scolded him when he could not move or get away. "Just like your papa, *mean*."

The little boy went out into the garden and sat on a green bench dangling his legs. He was clean. His hair was wet and his blue woolly pull-over made his nose itch. His face felt stiff from the soap. He saw Marjory going past a window with the black tray. The curtains were still closed at the window he knew opened into Mama's room. Papa's room. Mommanpoppasroom, the word was pleasant, it made a mumbling snapping noise between his lips; it ran in his mind while his eyes wandered about looking for something to do, something to play with.

Mommanpoppas' voices kept attracting his attention. Mama was being cross with Papa again. He could tell by the sound. That was what Marjory always said when their voices rose and fell and shot up to a point and crashed and rolled like the two tomcats who fought at night. Papa was being cross, too, much crosser than Mama this time. He grew cold and disturbed and sat very still, wanting to go to the bathroom, but it was just next to Mommanpoppasroom; he didn't dare think of it. As the voices grew louder he could hardly hear them any more, he wanted so badly to go to the bathroom. The kitchen door opened suddenly and Marjory ran out, making the motion with her hand that meant he was to come to her. He didn't move. She came to him, her face still red and frowning, but she was not angry; she was scared just as he was. She said, "Come on, honey, we've got to go to your gran'ma's again." She took his hand and pulled him. "Come on quick, your gran'ma is waiting for you." He slid off the bench. His mother's voice rose in a terrible scream, screaming something he could not understand, but she was furious; he had seen her clenching her fists and stamping in one spot, screaming with her eyes shut; he knew how she looked. She was screaming in a tantrum, just as he remembered having heard himself. He stood still, doubled over, and all his body seemed to dissolve, sickly, from the pit of his stomach.

"Oh, my God," said Marjory. "Oh, my God. Now look at you. Oh, my God. I can't stop to clean you up."

He did not know how he got to his grandma's house, but he was there at last, wet and soiled, being handled with disgust in the big bathtub. His grandma was there in long black skirts saying, "Maybe he's sick; maybe we should send for the doctor."

"I don't think so, m'am," said Marjory. "He hasn't et anything; he's just scared."

The little boy couldn't raise his eyes, he was so heavy with shame. "Take this note to his mother," said Grandma.

She sat in a wide chair and ran her hands over his head, combing his hair with her fingers; she lifted his chin and kissed him. "Poor little fellow," she said. "Never you mind. You always have a good time at your grandma's, don't you? You're going to have a nice little visit, just like the last time."

The little boy leaned against the stiff, dry-smelling clothes and felt horribly grieved about something. He began to whimper and said, "I'm hungry. I want something to eat." This reminded him. He began to bellow at the top of his voice; he threw himself upon the carpet and rubbed his nose in a dusty woolly bouquet of roses. "I want my peanuts," he howled. "Somebody took my peanuts."

His grandma knelt beside him and gathered him up so tightly he could hardly move. She called in a calm voice above his howls to Old Janet in the doorway, "Bring me some bread and butter with strawberry jam."

"I want peanuts," yelled the little boy desperately.

"No, you don't, darling," said his grandma. "You don't want horrid old peanuts to make you sick. You're going to have some of grandma's nice fresh bread with good strawberries on it. That's what you're going to have." He sat afterward very quietly and ate and ate. His grandma sat near him and Old Janet stood by, near a tray with a loaf and a glass bowl of jam upon the table at the window. Outside there was a trellis with tube-shaped red flowers clinging all over it, and brown bees singing.

"I hardly know what to do," said Grandma, "it's very . . ."

"Yes, m'am," said Old Janet, "it certainly is . . ."

Grandma said, "I can't possibly see the end of it. It's a terrible . . ."

"It certainly is bad," said Old Janet, "all this upset all the time and him such a baby."

Their voices ran on soothingly. The little boy ate and forgot to listen. He did not know these women, except by name. He could not understand what they were talking about; their hands and their clothes and their voices were dry and far away; they examined him with crinkled eyes without any expression that he could see. He sat there waiting for whatever they would do next with him. He hoped they would let him go out and play in the yard. The room was full of flowers and dark red curtains and big soft chairs, and the windows were open, but it was still dark in there somehow; dark, and a place he did not know, or trust.

"Now drink your milk," said Old Janet, holding out a silver cup.

"I don't want any milk," he said, turning his head away.

"Very well, Janet, he doesn't have to drink it," said Grandma quickly. "Now run out in the garden and play, darling. Janet, get his hoop."

A big strange man came home in the evenings who treated the little boy very confusingly. "Say 'please,' and 'thank you,' young man," he would roar, terrifyingly, when he gave any smallest object to the little boy. "Well, fellow, are you ready for a fight?" he would say, again, doubling up huge, hairy fists and making passes at him. "Come on now, you must learn to box." After the first few times this was fun.

"Don't teach him to be rough," said Grandma. "Time enough for all that."

"Now, Mother, we don't want him to be a sissy," said the big man. "He's got to toughen up early. Come on now, fellow, put up your mitts." The little boy liked this new word for hands. He learned to throw himself upon the strange big man, whose name was Uncle David, and hit him on the chest as hard as he could; the big man would laugh and hit him back with his huge, loose fists. Sometimes, but not often, Uncle David came home in the middle of the day. The little boy missed him on the other days, and would hang on the gate looking down the street for him. One evening he brought a large square package under his arm.

"Come over here, fellow, and see what I've got," he said, pulling off quantities of green paper and string from the box which was full of flat, folded colors. He put something in the little boy's hand. It was limp and silky and bright green with a tube on the end. "Thank you," said the little boy nicely, but not knowing what to do with it.

"Balloons," said Uncle David in triumph. "Now just put your mouth here and blow hard." The little boy blew hard and the green thing began to grow round and thin and silvery.

"Good for your chest," said Uncle David. "Blow some more." The little boy went on blowing and the balloon swelled steadily.

"Stop," said Uncle David, "that's enough." He twisted the tube to keep the air in. "That's the way," he said. "Now I'll blow one, and you blow one, and let's see who can blow up a big balloon the fastest."

They blew and blew, especially Uncle David. He puffed and panted and blew with all his might, but the little boy won. His balloon was perfectly round before Uncle David could even get started. The little boy was so proud he began to dance and shout, "I beat, I beat," and blew in his balloon again. It burst in his face and frightened him so he felt sick. "Ha ha, ho ho ho," whooped Uncle David. "That's the boy. I bet I can't do that. Now let's see." He blew until the beautiful bubble grew and wavered and burst into thin air, and there was only a small colored rag in his hand. This was a fine game. They went on with it until Grandma came in and said, "Time for supper now. No, you can't blow balloons at the table. Tomorrow maybe." And it was all over.

The next day, instead of being given balloons, he was hustled out of bed early, bathed in warm soapy water and given a big breakfast of soft-boiled eggs with toast and jam and milk. His grandma came in to kiss him good morning. "And I hope you'll be a good boy and obey your teacher," she told him.

"What's teacher?" asked the little boy.

"Teacher is at school," said Grandma. "She'll tell you all sorts of things and you must do as she says."

Mama and Papa had talked a great deal about School, and how they must send him there. They had told him it was a fine place with all kinds of toys and other children to play with. He felt he knew about School. "I didn't know it was time, Grandma," he said. "Is it today?"

"It's this very minute," said Grandma. "I told you a week ago."

Old Janet came in with her bonnet on. It was a prickly looking bundle held with a black rubber band under her back hair. "Come on," she said. "This is my busy day." She wore a dead cat slung around her neck, its sharp ears bent over under her baggy chin.

The little boy was excited and wanted to run ahead. "Hold to my hand like I told you," said Old Janet. "Don't go running off like that and get yourself killed."

"I'm going to get killed, I'm going to get killed," sang the little boy, making a tune of his own.

"Don't say that, you give me the creeps," said Old Janet. "Hold to my hand now." She bent over and looked at him, not at his face but at something on his clothes. His eyes followed hers.

"I declare," said Old Janet, "I did forget. I was going to sew it up. I might have known. I *told* your grandma it would be that way from now on."

"What?" asked the little boy.

"Just look at yourself," said Old Janet crossly. He looked at himself. There was a little end of him showing through the slit in his short blue flannel trousers. The trousers came halfway to his knees above, and his socks came halfway to his knees below, and all winter long his knees were cold. He remembered now how cold his knees were in cold weather. And how sometimes he would have to put the part of him that came through the slit back again, because he was cold there too. He saw at once what was wrong, and tried to arrange himself, but his mittens got in the way. Janet said, "Stop that, you bad boy," and with a firm thumb she set him in order, at the same time reaching under his belt to pull down and fold his knit undershirt over his front.

"There now," she said, "try not to disgrace yourself today." He felt guilty and red all over, because he had something that showed when he was dressed that was not supposed to show then. The different women who bathed him always wrapped him quickly in towels and hurried him into his clothes, because they saw something about him he could not see for himself. They hurried him so he never had a chance to see whatever it was they saw, and though he looked at himself when his clothes were off, he could not find out what was wrong with him. Outside, in his clothes, he knew he looked like everybody else, but inside his clothes there was something bad the matter with him. It worried him and confused him and he wondered about it. The only people who never seemed to notice there was something wrong with him were Mommanpoppa. They never called him a bad boy, and all summer long they had taken all his clothes off and let him run in the sand beside a big ocean.

"Look at him, isn't he a love?" Mama would say and Papa would look, and say, "He's got a back like a prize fighter." Uncle David was a prize fighter when he doubled up his mitts and said, "Come on, fellow."

Old Janet held him firmly and took long steps under her big rustling skirts. He did not like Old Janet's smell. It made him a little quivery in the stomach; it was just like wet chicken feathers.

School was easy. Teacher was a square-shaped woman with square short hair and short skirts. She got in the way sometimes, but not often. The people around him were his size; he didn't have always to be stretching his neck up to faces bent over him, and he could sit on the chairs without having to climb. All the children had names, like Frances and Evelyn and Agatha and Edward and Martin, and his own name was Stephen. He was not Mama's "Baby," nor Papa's "Old Man"; he was not Uncle David's "Fellow," or Grandma's "Darling," or even Old Janet's "Bad Boy." He was Stephen. He was learning to read, and to sing a tune to some strange-looking letters or marks written in chalk on a blackboard. You talked one kind of lettering, and you sang another. All the children talked and sang in turn, and then all together. Stephen thought it a fine game. He felt awake and happy. They had soft clay and paper and wires and squares of colors in tin boxes to play with, colored blocks to build houses with. Afterward they all danced in a big ring, and then they danced in pairs, boys with girls. Stephen danced with Frances, and Frances kept saying, "Now you just follow me." She was a little taller than he was, and her hair stood up in short, shiny curls, the color of an ash tray on Papa's desk. She would say, "You can't dance." "I can dance too," said Stephen, jumping around holding her hands, "I can, too, dance." He was certain of it. "*You* can't dance," he told Frances, "you can't dance at all."

Then they had to change partners, and when they came round again, Frances said, "I don't *like* the way you dance." This was different. He felt uneasy about it. He didn't jump quite so high when the phonograph record started going dumdiddy dumdiddy again. "Go ahead, Stephen, you're doing fine," said Teacher, waving her hands together very fast. The dance ended, and they all played "relaxing" for five minutes. They relaxed by swinging their arms back and forth, then rolling their heads round and round. When Old Janet came for him he didn't want to go home. At lunch his grandma told him twice to keep his face out of his plate. "Is that what they teach you at school?" she asked. Uncle David was at home. "Here you are, fellow," he said and gave Stephen two balloons. "Thank you," said Stephen. He put the balloons in his pocket and forgot about them. "I told you that boy could learn something," said Uncle David to Grandma. "Hear him say 'thank you'?"

In the afternoon at school Teacher handed out big wads of clay and told the children to make something out of it. Anything they liked. Stephen decided to make a cat, like Mama's Meeow at home. He did not like Meeow, but he thought it would be easy to make a cat. He could not get the clay to work at all. It simply fell into one lump after another. So he stopped, wiped his hands on his pull-over, remembered his balloons and began blowing one.

"Look at Stephen's horse," said Frances. "Just look at it."

"It's not a horse, it's a cat," said Stephen. The other children gathered around. "It looks like a horse, a little," said Martin.

"It is a cat," said Stephen, stamping his foot, feeling his face turning hot. The other children all laughed and exclaimed over Stephen's cat that looked like a horse. Teacher came down among them. She sat usually at the top of the room before a big table covered with papers and playthings. She picked up Stephen's lump of clay and turned it round and examined it with her kind eyes. "Now, children," she said, "everybody has the right to make anything the way he pleases. If Stephen says this is a cat, it *is* a cat. Maybe you were thinking about a horse, Stephen?"

"It's a *cat*," said Stephen. He was aching all over. He knew then he should have said at first, "Yes, it's a horse." Then they would have let him alone. They would never have known he was trying to make a cat. "It's Meeow," he said in a trembling voice, "but I forgot how she looks."

His balloon was perfectly flat. He started blowing it up again, trying not to cry. Then it was time to go home, and Old Janet came looking for him. While Teacher was talking to other grown-up people who came to take other children home, Frances said, "Give me your balloon; I haven't got a balloon." Stephen handed it to her. He was happy to give it. He reached in his pocket and took out the other. Happily, he gave her that one too. Frances took it, then handed it back. "Now you blow up one and I'll blow up the other, and let's have a race," she said. When their balloons were only half filled Old Janet took Stephen by the arm and said, "Come on here, this is my busy day."

Frances ran after them, calling, "Stephen, you give me back my balloon," and snatched it away. Stephen did not know whether he was surprised to find himself going away with Frances' balloon, or whether he was surprised to see her snatching it as if it really belonged to her. He was badly mixed up in his mind, and Old Janet was hauling him along. One thing he knew, he liked Frances, he was going to see her again tomorrow, and he was going to bring her more balloons.

That evening Stephen boxed awhile with his uncle David, and Uncle David gave him a beautiful orange. "Eat that," he said, "it's good for your health."

"Uncle David, may I have some more balloons?" asked Stephen.

"Well, what do you say first?" asked Uncle David, reaching for the box on the top bookshelf.

"Please," said Stephen.

"That's the word," said Uncle David. He brought out two balloons, a red and a yellow one. Stephen noticed for the first time they had letters on them, very small letters that grew taller and wider as the balloon grew rounder. "Now that's all, fellow," said Uncle David. "Don't ask for any more because that's all." He put the box back on the bookshelf, but not before Stephen had seen that the box was almost full of balloons. He didn't say a word, but went on blowing, and Uncle David blew also. Stephen thought it was the nicest game he had ever known.

He had only one left, the next day, but he took it to school and gave it to Frances. "There are a lot," he said, feeling very proud and warm; "I'll bring you a lot of them."

Frances blew it up until it made a beautiful bubble, and said, "Look, I want to show you something." She took a sharp-pointed stick they used in working the clay; she poked the balloon, and it exploded. "Look at that," she said.

"That's nothing," said Stephen, "I'll bring you some more."

After school, before Uncle David came home, while Grandma was resting, when Old Janet had given him his milk and told him to run away and not bother her, Stephen dragged a chair to the bookshelf, stood upon it and reached into the box. He did not take three or four as he believed he intended; once his hands were upon them he seized what they could hold and jumped off the chair, hugging them to him. He stuffed them into his reefer pocket where they folded down and hardly made a lump.

He gave them all to Frances. There were so many, Frances gave most of them away to the other children. Stephen, flushed with his new joy, the lavish pleasure of giving presents, found almost at once still another happiness. Suddenly he was popular among the children; they invited him specially to join whatever games were up; they fell in at once with his own notions for play, and asked him what he would like to do next. They had festivals of blowing up the beautiful globes, fuller and rounder and thinner, changing as they went from deep color to lighter, paler tones, growing glassy thin, bubbly thin, then bursting with a thrilling loud noise like a toy pistol.

For the first time in his life Stephen had almost too much of something he wanted, and his head was so turned he forgot how this fullness came about, and no longer thought of it as a secret. The next day was Saturday, and Frances came to visit him with her nurse. The nurse and Old Janet sat in Old Janet's room drinking coffee and gossiping, and the children sat on the side porch blowing balloons. Stephen chose an apple-colored one and Frances a pale green one. Between them on the bench lay a tumbled heap of delights still to come.

"I once had a silver balloon," said Frances, "a beyootiful silver one, not round like these; it was a long one. But these are even nicer, I think," she added quickly, for she did want to be polite.

"When you get through with that one," said Stephen, gazing at her with the pure bliss of giving added to loving, "you can blow up a blue one and then a pink one and a yellow one and a purple one." He pushed the heap of limp objects toward her. Her clear-looking eyes, with fine little rays of brown in them like the spokes of a wheel, were full of approval for Stephen. "I wouldn't want to be greedy, though, and blow up all your balloons."

"There'll be plenty more left," said Stephen, and his heart rose under his thin ribs. He felt his ribs with his fingers and discovered with some surprise that they stopped somewhere in front, while Frances sat blowing balloons rather halfheartedly. The truth was, she was tired of balloons. After you blow six or seven your chest gets hollow and your lips feel puckery. She had been blowing balloons steadily for three days now. She had begun to hope they were giving out. "There's boxes and boxes more of them, Frances," said Stephen happily. "Millions more. I guess they'd last and last if we didn't blow too many every day."

Frances said somewhat timidly, "I tell you what. Let's rest awhile and fix some liquish water. Do you like liquish?"

"Yes, I do," said Stephen, "but I haven't got any."

"Couldn't we buy some?" asked Frances. "It's only a cent a stick, the nice rubbery, twisty kind. We can put it in a bottle with some water, and shake it and shake it, and it makes foam on top like soda pop and we can drink it. I'm kind of thirsty," she said in a small, weak voice. "Blowing balloons all the time makes you thirsty, I think."

Stephen, in silence, realized a dreadful truth and a numb feeling crept over him. He did not have a cent to buy licorice for Frances and she was tired of his balloons. This was the first real dismay of his whole life, and he aged at least a year in the next minute, huddled, with his deep, serious blue eyes focused down his nose in intense speculation. What could he do to please Frances that would not cost money? Only yesterday Uncle David had given him a nickel, and he had thrown it away on gumdrops. He regretted that nickel so bitterly his neck and forehead were damp. He was thirsty too.

"I tell you what," he said, brightening with a splendid idea, lamely trailing off on second thought, "I know something we can do, I'll—I . . ."

"I *am* thirsty," said Frances with gentle persistence. "I think I'm so thirsty maybe I'll have to go home." She did not leave the bench, though, but sat, turning her grieved mouth toward Stephen.

Stephen quivered with the terrors of the adventure before him, but he said boldly, "I'll make some lemonade. I'll get sugar and lemon and some ice and we'll have lemonade."

"Oh, I love lemonade," cried Frances. "I'd rather have lemonade than liquish."

"You stay right here," said Stephen, "and I'll get everything."

He ran around the house, and under Old Janet's window he heard the dry, chattering voices of the two old women whom he must outwit. He sneaked on tiptoe to the pantry, took a lemon lying there by itself, a handful of lump sugar and a china teapot, smooth, round, with flowers and leaves all over it. These he left on the kitchen table while he broke a piece of ice with a sharp metal pick he had been forbidden to touch. He put the ice in the pot, cut the lemon and squeezed it as well as he could—a lemon was tougher and more slippery than he had thought—and mixed sugar and water. He decided there was not enough sugar so he sneaked back and took another handful. He was back on the porch in an astonishingly short time, his face tight, his knees trembling, carrying iced lemonade to thirsty Frances with both his devoted hands.

A pace distant from her he stopped, literally stabbed through with a thought. Here he stood in broad daylight carrying a teapot with lemonade in it, and his grandma or Old Janet might walk through the door at any moment.

"Come on, Frances," he whispered loudly. "Let's go round to the back behind the rose bushes where it's shady." Frances leaped up and ran like a deer beside him, her face wise with knowledge of why they ran; Stephen ran stiffly, cherishing his teapot with clenched hands.

It was shady behind the rose bushes, and much safer. They sat side by side on the dampish ground, legs doubled under, drinking in turn from the splender spout. Stephen took his just share in large, cool, delicious swallows. When Frances drank she set her round pink mouth daintily to the spout and her throat beat steadily as a heart. Stephen was thinking he had really done something pretty nice for Frances. He did not know where his own happiness was; it was mixed with the sweet-sour taste in his mouth and a cool feeling in his bosom because Frances was there drinking his lemonade which he had got for her with great danger.

Frances said, "My, what big swallows you take," when his turn came next.

"No bigger than yours," he told her downrightly. "You take awfully big swallows."

"Well," said Frances, turning this criticism into an argument for her rightness about things, "that's the way to drink lemonade anyway." She peered into the teapot. There was quite a lot of lemonade left and she was beginning to feel she had enough. "Let's make up a game and see who can take the biggest swallows."

This was such a wonderful notion they grew reckless, tipping the spout into their opened mouths above their heads until lemonade welled up and ran over their chins in rills down their fronts. When they tired of this there was still lemonade left in the pot. They played first at giving the rosebush a drink and ended by baptizing it. "Name father son holygoat," shouted Stephen, pouring. At this sound Old Janet's face appeared over the low hedge, with the tan, disgusted-looking face of Frances' nurse hanging over her shoulder.

"Well, just as I thought," said Old Janet. "Just as I expected." The bag under her chin waggled.

"We were thirsty," he said; "we were awfully thirsty." Frances said nothing, but she gazed steadily at the toes of her shoes.

"Give me that teapot," said Old Janet, taking it with a rude snatch. "Just because you're thirsty is no reason," said Old Janet. "You can ask for things. You don't have to steal."

"We didn't steal," cried Frances suddenly. "We didn't. We didn't!"

"That's enough from you, missy," said her nurse. "Come straight out of there. You have nothing to do with this."

"Oh, I don't know," said Old Janet with a hard stare at Frances' nurse. "*He* never did such a thing before, by himself."

"Come on," said the nurse to Frances, "this is no place for

you." She held Frances by the wrist and started walking away so fast Frances had to run to keep up. "Nobody can call *us* thieves and get away with it."

"You don't have to steal, even if others do," said Old Janet to Stephen, in a high carrying voice. "If you so much as pick up a lemon in somebody else's house you're a little thief." She lowered her voice then and said, "Now I'm going to tell your grandma and you'll see what you get."

"He went in the icebox and left it open," Janet told Grandma, "and he got into the lump sugar and spilt it all over the floor. Lumps everywhere underfoot. He dribbled water all over the clean kitchen floor, and he baptized the rose bush, blaspheming. And he took your Spode teapot."

"I didn't either," said Stephen loudly, trying to free his hand from Old Janet's big hard fist.

"Don't tell fibs," said Old Janet; "that's the last straw."

"Oh, dear," said Grandma. "He's not a baby any more." She shut the book she was reading and pulled the wet front of his pullover toward her. "What's this sticky stuff on him?" she asked and straightened her glasses.

"Lemonade," said Old Janet. "He took the last lemon."

They were in the big dark room with the red curtains. Uncle David walked in from the room with the bookcases, holding a box in his uplifted hand. "Look here," he said to Stephen. "What's become of all my balloons?"

Stephen knew well that Uncle David was not really asking a question.

Stephen, sitting on a footstool at his grandma's knee, felt sleepy. He leaned heavily and wished he could put his head on her lap, but he might go to sleep, and it would be wrong to go to sleep while Uncle David was still talking. Uncle David walked about the room with his hands in his pockets, talking to Grandma. Now and then he would walk over to a lamp and, leaning, peer into the top of the shade, winking in the light, as if he expected to find something there.

"It's simply in the blood, I told her," said Uncle David. "I told her she would simply have to come and get him, and keep him. She asked me if I meant to call him a thief and I said if she could think of a more exact word I'd be glad to hear it."

"You shouldn't have said that," commented Grandma calmly.

"Why not? She might as well know the facts. . . . I suppose he can't help it," said Uncle David, stopping now in front of Stephen and dropping his chin into his collar, "I shouldn't expect too much of him, but you can't begin too early—"

"The trouble is," said Grandma, and while she spoke she took Stephen by the chin and held it up so that he had to meet her eye; she talked steadily in a mournful tone, but Stephen could not understand. She ended, "It's not just about the balloons, of course."

"It *is* about the balloons," said Uncle David angrily, "because balloons now mean something worse later. But what can you expect? His father—well, it's in the blood. He—"

"That's your sister's husband you're talking about," said Grandma, "and there is no use making things worse. Besides, you don't really *know*."

"I *do* know," said Uncle David. And he talked again very fast, walking up and down. Stephen tried to understand, but the sounds were strange and floating just over his head. They were talking about his father, and they did not like him. Uncle David came over and stood above Stephen and Grandma. He hunched over them with a frowning face, a long, crooked shadow from him falling across them to the wall. To Stephen he looked like his father, and he shrank against his grandma's skirts.

"The question is, what to do with him now?" asked Uncle David. "If we keep him here, he'd just be a—I won't be bothered with him. Why can't they take care of their own child? That house is crazy. Too far gone already, I'm afraid. No training. No example."

"You're right, they must take him and keep him," said Grandma. She ran her hands over Stephen's head; tenderly she pinched the nape of his neck between thumb and forefinger. "You're your Grandma's darling," she told him, "and you've had a nice long visit, and now you're going home. Mama is coming for you in a few minutes. Won't that be nice?"

"I want my mama," said Stephen, whimpering, for his grandma's face frightened him. There was something wrong with her smile.

Uncle David sat down. "Come over here, fellow," he said, wagging a forefinger at Stephen. Stephen went over slowly, and Uncle

David drew him between his wide knees in their loose, rough clothes. "You ought to be ashamed of yourself," he said, "stealing Uncle David's balloons when he had already given you so many."

"It wasn't that," said Grandma quickly. "Don't say that. It will make an impression—"

"I hope it does," said Uncle David in a louder voice; "I hope he remembers it all his life. If he belonged to me I'd give him a good thrashing."

Stephen felt his mouth, his chin, his whole face jerking. He opened his mouth to take a breath, and tears and noise burst from him. "Stop that, fellow, stop that," said Uncle David, shaking him gently by the shoulders, but Stephen could not stop. He drew his breath again and it came back in a howl. Old Janet came to the door.

"Bring me some cold water," called Grandma. There was a flurry, a commotion, a breath of cool air from the hall, the door slammed, and Stephen heard his mother's voice. His howl died away, his breath sobbed and fluttered, he turned his dimmed eyes and saw her standing there. His heart turned over within him and he bleated like a lamb, "Maaaaama," running toward her. Uncle David stood back as Mama swooped in and fell on her knees beside Stephen. She gathered him to her and stood up with him in her arms.

"What are you doing to my baby?" she asked Uncle David in a thickened voice. "I should never have let him come here. I should have known better—"

"You always should know better," said Uncle David, "and you never do. And you never will. You haven't got it here," he told her, tapping his forehead.

"David," said Grandma, "that's your—"

"Yes, I know, she's my sister," said Uncle David. "I know it. But if she must run away and marry a—"

"Shut up," said Mama.

"And bring more like him into the world, let her keep them at home. I say let her keep—"

Mama set Stephen on the floor and, holding him by the hand, she said to Grandma all in a rush as if she were reading something, "Good-by, Mother. This is the last time, really the last. I can't bear it any longer. Say good-by to Stephen; you'll never see him again.

You let this happen. It's your fault. You know David was a coward and a bully and a self-righteous little beast all his life and you never crossed him in anything. You let him bully me all my life and you let him slander my husband and call my baby a thief, and now this is the end. . . . He calls my baby a thief over a few horrible little ballons because he doesn't like my husband. . . ."

She was panting and staring about from one to the other. They were all standing. Now Grandma said, "Go home, daughter. Go away, David. I'm sick of your quarreling. I've never had a day's peace or comfort from either of you. I'm sick of you both. Now let me alone and stop this noise. Go away," said Grandma in a wavering voice. She took out her handkerchief and wiped first one eye and then the other and said, "All this hate, hate—what is it for? . . . So this is the way it turns out. Well, let me alone."

"You and your little advertising balloons," said Mama to Uncle David. "The big honest businessman advertises with balloons and if he loses one he'll be ruined. And your beastly little moral notions . . ."

Grandma went to the door to meet Old Janet, who handed her a glass of water. Grandma drank it all, standing there.

"Is your husband coming for you, or are you going home by yourself?" she asked Mama.

"I'm driving myself," said Mama in a far-away voice as if her mind had wandered. "You know he wouldn't set foot in this house."

"I should think not," said Uncle David.

"Come on, Stephen darling," said Mama. "It's far past his bedtime," she said, to no one in particular. "Imagine keeping a baby up to torture him about a few miserable little bits of colored rubber." She smiled at Uncle David with both rows of teeth as she passed him on the way to the door, keeping between him and Stephen. "Ah, where would we be without high moral standards," she said, and then to Grandma, "Good night, Mother," in quite her usual voice. "I'll see you in a day or so."

"Yes, indeed," said Grandma cheerfully, coming out into the hall with Stephen and Mama. "Let me hear from you. Ring me up tomorrow. I hope you'll be feeling better."

"I feel very well now," said Mama brightly, laughing. She bent down and kissed Stephen. "Sleepy, darling? Papa's waiting to see you. Don't go to sleep until you've kissed your papa good night."

Stephen woke with a sharp jerk. He raised his head and put out his chin a little. "I don't want to go home," he said; "I want to go to school. I don't want to see Papa, I don't like him."

Mama laid her palm over his mouth softly. "Darling, don't."

Uncle David put his head out with a kind of snort. "There you are," he said. "There you've got a statement from headquarters."

Mama opened the door and ran, almost carrying Stephen. She ran across the sidewalk, jerking open the car door and dragging Stephen in after her. She spun the car around and dashed forward so sharply Stephen was almost flung out of the seat. He sat braced then with all his might, hands digging into the cushions. The car speeded up and the trees and houses whizzed by all flattened out. Stephen began suddenly to sing to himself, a quiet, inside song so Mama would not hear. He sang his new secret; it was a comfortable, sleepy song: "I hate Papa, I hate Mama, I hate Grandma, I hate Uncle David, I hate Old Janet, I hate Marjory, I hate Papa, I hate Mama . . ."

His head bobbed, leaned, came to rest on Mama's knee, eyes closed. Mama drew him closer and slowed down, driving with one hand.

A Day's Work

The dull scrambling like a giant rat in the wall meant the dumb-waiter was on its way up, the janitress below hauling on the cable. Mrs. Halloran paused, thumped her iron on the board, and said, "There it is. Late. You could have put on your shoes and gone around the corner and brought the things an hour ago. I can't do everything."

Mr. Halloran pulled himself out of the chair, clutching the arms and heaving to his feet slowly, looking around as if he hoped to find crutches standing near. "Wearing out your socks, too," added Mrs. Halloran. "You ought either go barefoot outright or wear your shoes over your socks as God intended," she said. "Sock feet. What's the good of it, I'd like to know? Neither one thing nor the other."

She unrolled a salmon-colored chiffon nightgown with cream-colored lace and broad ribbons on it, gave it a light flirt in the air, and spread it on the board. "God's mercy, look at that indecent thing," she said. She thumped the iron again and pushed it back and forth over the rumpled cloth. "You might just set the things in the cupboard," she said, "and not leave them around on the floor. You might just."

Mr. Halloran took a sack of potatoes from the dumb-waiter and started for the cupboard in the corner next the icebox. "You might as well take a load," said Mrs. Halloran. "There's no need on earth making a half-dozen trips back and forth. I'd think the poorest sort of man could well carry more than five pounds of potatoes at one time. But maybe not."

Her voice tapped on Mr. Halloran's ears like wood on wood. "Mind your business, will you?" he asked, not speaking to her directly. He carried on the argument with himself. "Oh, I couldn't do that, Mister Honey," he answered in a dull falsetto. "Don't ever ask me to think of such a thing, even. It wouldn't be right," he said, standing still with his knees bent, glaring bitterly over the potato sack at the scrawny strange woman he had never liked, that one standing there ironing clothes with a dirty look on her whole face like a suffering saint. "I may not be much good any more," he told her in his own voice, "but I still have got wits enough to take groceries off a dumb-waiter, mind you."

"That's a miracle," said Mrs. Halloran. "I'm thankful for that much."

"There's the telephone," said Mr. Halloran, sitting in the armchair again and taking his pipe out of his shirt pocket.

"I heard it as well," said Mrs. Halloran, sliding the iron up and down over the salmon-colored chiffon.

"It's for you, I've no further business in this world," said Mr. Halloran. His little greenish eyes glittered; he exposed his two sharp dogteeth in a grin.

"You could answer it. It could be the wrong number again or for somebody downstairs," said Mrs. Halloran, her flat voice going flatter, even.

"Let it go in any case," decided Mr. Halloran, "for my own part, that is." He struck a match on the arm of his chair, touched off his pipe, and drew in his first puff while the telephone went on with its nagging.

"It might be Maggie again," said Mrs. Halloran.

"Let her ring, then," said Mr. Halloran, settling back and crossing his legs.

"God help a man who won't answer the telephone when his own daughter calls up for a word," commented Mrs. Halloran to the ceiling. "And she in deep trouble, too, with her husband treating her like a dog about the money, and sitting out late nights in saloons with that crowd from the Little Tammany Association. He's getting into politics now with the McCorkery gang. No good will come of it, and I told her as much."

"She's no troubles at all, her man's a sharp fellow who will get ahead if she'll let him alone," said Mr. Halloran. "She's nothing to complain of, I could tell her. But what's a father?" Mr. Halloran cocked his head toward the window that opened on the brick-paved areaway and crowed like a rooster, "What's a father these days and who would heed his advice?"

"You needn't tell the neighbors, there's disgrace enough already," said Mrs. Halloran. She set the iron back on the gas ring and stepped out to the telephone on the first stair landing. Mr. Halloran leaned forward, his thin, red-haired hands hanging loosely between his knees, his warm pipe sending up its good decent smell right into his nose. The woman hated the pipe and the smell; she was a woman born to make any man miserable. Before the depression, while he still had a good job and prospects of a raise, before he went on relief, before she took in fancy washing and ironing, in the Good Days Before, God's pity, she didn't exactly keep her mouth shut, there wasn't a word known to man she couldn't find an answer for, but she knew which side her bread was buttered on, and put up with it. Now she was, you might say, buttering her own bread and she never forgot it for a minute. And it's her own fault we're not riding round today in a limousine with ash trays and a speaking tube and a cut-glass vase for flowers in it. It's what a man gets for marrying one of these holy women. Gerald McCorkery had told him as much, in the beginning.

"There's a girl will spend her time holding you down," Gerald had told him. "You're putting your head in a noose will strangle the life out of you. Heed the advice of one who wishes you well," said Gerald McCorkery. This was after he had barely set eyes on Lacey Mahaffy one Sunday morning in Coney Island. It was like McCorkery to see that in a flash, born judge of human nature that he was. He could look a man over, size him up, and there was an end to it. And if the man didn't pass muster, McCorkery could ease him out in a way that man would never know how it happened. It was the secret of McCorkery's success in the world.

"This is Rosie, herself," said Gerald that Sunday in Coney Island. "Meet the future Mrs. Gerald J. McCorkery." Lacey Mahaffy's narrow face had gone sour as whey under her big straw hat. She barely nodded to Rosie, who gave Mr. Halloran a look that fairly undressed him right there. Mr. Halloran had thought, too, that McCorkery was picking a strange one; she was good-looking all right, but she had the smell of a regular little Fourteenth

Street hustler if Halloran knew anything about women. "Come on," said McCorkery, his arm around Rosie's waist, "let's all go on the roller coaster." But Lacey would not. She said, "No, thank you. We didn't plan to stay, and we must go now." On the way home Mr. Halloran said, "Lacey, you judge too harshly. Maybe that's a nice girl at heart; hasn't had your opportunities." Lacey had turned upon him a face ugly as an angry cat's, and said, "She's a loose, low woman, and 'twas an insult to introduce her to me." It was a good while before the pretty fresh face that Mr. Halloran had fallen in love with returned to her.

Next day in Billy's Place, after three drinks each, McCorkery said, "Watch your step, Halloran; think of your future. There's a straight good girl I don't doubt, but she's no sort of mixer. A man getting into politics needs a wife who can meet all kinds. A man needs a woman knows how to loosen her corsets and sit easy."

Mrs. Halloran's voice was going on in the hall, a steady dry rattle like old newspapers blowing on a park bench. "I told you before it's no good coming to me with your troubles now. I warned you in time but you wouldn't listen. . . . I told you just how it would be, I tried my best. . . . No, you couldn't listen, you always knew better than your mother. . . . So now all you've got to do is stand by your married vows and make the best of it. . . . Now listen to me, if you want himself to do right you have to do right first. The woman has to do right first, and then if the man won't do right in turn it's no fault of hers. You do right whether he does wrong or no, just because he does wrong is no excuse for you."

"Ah, will you hear that?" Mr. Halloran asked the areaway in an awed voice. "There's a holy terror of a saint for you."

". . . the woman has to do right first, I'm telling you," said Mrs. Halloran into the telephone, "and then if he's a devil in spite of it, why she has to do right without any help from him." Her voice rose so the neighbors could get an earful if they wanted. "I know you from old, you're just like your father. You must be doing something wrong yourself or you wouldn't be in this fix. You're doing wrong this minute, calling over the telephone when you ought to be getting your work done. I've got an iron on, working over the dirty nightgowns of a kind of woman I wouldn't soil my foot on if I'd had a man to take care of me. So now you do up your housework and dress yourself and take a walk in the fresh air. . . ."

"A little fresh air never hurt anybody," commented Mr. Halloran loudly through the open window. "It's the gas gets a man down."

"Now listen to me, Maggie, that's not the way to talk over the public wires. Now you stop that crying and go and do your duty and don't be worrying me any more. And stop saying you're going to leave your husband, because where will you go, for one thing? Do you want to walk the streets or set up a laundry in your kitchen? You can't come back here, you'll stay with your husband where you belong. Don't be a fool, Maggie. You've got your living, and that's more than many a woman better than you has got. Yes, your father's all right. No, he's just sitting here, the same. God knows what's to become of us. But you know how he is, little he cares. . . . Now remember this, Maggie, if anything goes wrong with your married life it's your own fault and you needn't come here for sympathy. . . . I can't waste any more time on it. Goodby."

Mr. Halloran, his ears standing up for fear of missing a word, thought how Gerald J. McCorkery had gone straight on up the ladder with Rosie; and for every step the McCorkerys took upward, he, Michael Halloran, had taken a step downward with Lacey Mahaffy. They had started as greenhorns with the same chances at the same time and the same friends, but McCorkery had seized all his opportunities as they came, getting in steadily with the Big Shots in ward politics, one good thing leading to another. Rosie had known how to back him up and push him onward. The McCorkerys for years had invited him and Lacey to come over to the house and be sociable with the crowd, but Lacey would not.

"You can't run with that fast set and drink and stay out nights and hold your job," said Lacey, "and you should know better than to ask your wife to associate with that woman." Mr. Halloran had got into the habit of dropping around by himself, now and again, for McCorkery still liked him, was still willing to give him a foothold in the right places, still asked him for favors at election time. There was always a good lively crowd at the McCorkerys, wherever they were; for they moved ever so often to a better place, with more furniture. Rosie helped hand around the drinks, taking a few herself with a good word for everybody. The player piano or the victrola would be going full blast, with everybody dancing, all looking like ready money and a bright future. He would get home late these evenings, back to the same little cold-water walk-up flat, because Lacey would not spend a dollar for show. It must all go into savings against old age, she said. He would be full of good food and drink, and find Lacey, in a bungalow apron, warming up the fried potatoes once more, cross and bitterly silent, hanging her head and frowning at the smell of liquor on his breath. "You might at least eat the potatoes when I've fried them and waited all this time," she would say. "Ah, eat them yourself, they're none of mine," he would snarl in his disappointment with her, and with the life she was leading him.

He had believed with all his heart for years that he would one day be manager of one of the G. and I. chain grocery stores he worked for, and when that hope gave out there was still his pension when they retired him. But two years before it was due they fired him, on account of the depression, they said. Overnight he was on the sidewalk, with no place to go with the news but home. "Jesus," said Mr. Halloran, still remembering that day after nearly seven years of idleness.

The depression hadn't touched McCorkery. He went on and on up the ladder, giving beefsteaks and beanfests and beer parties for the boys in Billy's Place, standing in with the right men and never missing a trick. At last the Gerald J. McCorkery Club chartered a whole boat for a big excursion up the river. It was a great day, with Lacey sitting at home sulking. After election Rosie had her picture in the papers, smiling at McCorkery; not fat exactly, just a fine figure of a woman with flowers pinned on her spotted fur coat, her teeth as good as ever. Oh, God, there was a girl for any man's money. Mr. Halloran saw out of his eye-corner the bony stooped back of Lacey Mahaffy, standing on one foot to rest the other like a tired old horse, leaning on her hands waiting for the iron to heat.

"That was Maggie, with her woes," she said.

"I hope you gave her some good advice," said Mr. Halloran. "I hope you told her to take up her hat and walk out on him."

Mrs. Halloran suspended the iron over a pair of pink satin panties. "I told her to do right and leave wrong-doing to the men," she said, in her voice like a phonograph record running down. "I told her to bear with the trouble God sends as her mother did before her."

Mr. Halloran gave a loud groan and knocked out his pipe on the chair arm. "You would ruin the world, woman, if you could, with your wicked soul, treating a new-married girl as if she had no home and no parents to come to. But she's no daughter of mine if she sits there peeling potatoes, letting a man run over her. No daughter of mine and I'll tell her so if she—"

"You know well she's your daughter, so hold your tongue," said Mrs. Halloran, "and if she heeded you she'd be walking the streets this minute. I brought her up an honest girl, and an honest woman she's going to be or I'll take her over my knee as I did when she was little. So there you are, Halloran."

Mr. Halloran leaned far back in his chair and felt along the shelf above his head until his fingers touched a half-dollar he had noticed there. His hand closed over it, he got up instantly and looked about for his hat.

"Keep your daughter, Lacey Mahaffy," he said, "she's none of mine but the fruits of your long sinning with the Holy Ghost. And now I'm off for a little round and a couple of beers to keep my mind from dissolving entirely."

"You can't have that dollar you just now sneaked off the shelf," said Mrs. Halloran. "So you think I'm blind besides? Put it back where you found it. That's for our daily bread."

"I'm sick of bread daily," said Mr. Halloran, "I need beer. It was not a dollar, but a half-dollar as you know well."

"Whatever it was," said Mrs. Halloran, "it stands instead of a dollar to me. So just drop it."

"You've got tomorrow's potatoes sewed up in your pocket this minute, and God knows what sums in that black box wherever you hide it, besides the life savings," said Mr. Halloran. "I earned this half-dollar on relief, and it's going to be spent properly. And I'll not be back for supper, so you'll save on that, too. So long, Lacey Mahaffy, I'm off."

"If you never come back, it will be all the same," said Mrs. Halloran, not looking up.

"If I came back with a pocket full of money, you'd be glad to see me," said Mr. Halloran.

"It would want to be a great sum," said Mrs. Halloran.

Mr. Halloran shut the door behind him with a fine slam.

He strolled out into the clear fall weather, a late afternoon sun warming his neck and brightening the old red-brick, high-stooped houses of Perry Street. He would go after all these years to Billy's Place, he might find some luck there. He took his time, though, speaking to the neighbors as he went. "Good afternoon, Mr. Halloran." "Good afternoon to you, Missis Caffery." . . . "It's fine weather for the time of year, Mr. Gogarty." "It is indeed, Mr. Halloran." Mr. Halloran thrived on these civilities, he loved to flourish his hat and give a hearty good day like a man who has nothing on his mind. Ah, there was the young man from the G. and I. store around the corner. He knew what kind of job Mr. Halloran once held there. "Good day, Mr. Halloran." "Good day to you, Mr. McInerny, how's business holding up with you?" "Good for the times, Mr. Halloran, that's the best I can say." "Things are not getting any better, Mr. McInerny." "It's the truth we are all hanging on by the teeth now, Mr. Halloran."

Soothed by this acknowledgment of man's common misfortune Mr. Halloran greeted the young cop at the corner. The cop, with his quick eyesight, was snatching a read from a newspaper on the stand across the sidewalk. "How do you do, Young O'Fallon," asked Mr. Halloran, "is your business lively these days?"

"Quiet as the tomb itself on this block," said Young O'Fallon. "But that's a sad thing about Connolly, now." His eyes motioned toward the newspaper.

"Is he dead?" asked Mr. Halloran; "I haven't been out until now, I didn't see the papers."

"Ah, not yet," said Young O'Fallon, "but the G-men are after him, it looks they'll get him surely this time."

"Connolly in bad with the G-men? Holy Jesus," said Mr. Halloran, "who will they go after next? The meddlers."

"It's that numbers racket," said the cop. "What's the harm, I'd like to know? A man must get his money from somewhere when he's in politics. They oughta give him a chance."

"Connolly's a great fellow, God bless him, I hope he gives them the slip," said Mr. Halloran, "I hope he goes right through their hands like a greased pig."

"He's smart," said the cop. "That Connolly's a smooth one. He'll come out of it."

Ah, will he though? Mr. Halloran asked himself. Who is safe if Connolly goes under? Wait till I give Lacey Mahaffy the news about Connolly, I'll like seeing her face the first time in twenty years. Lacey kept saying, "A man is a downright fool must be a crook to get rich. Plenty of the best people get rich and do no harm by it. Look at the Connollys now, good practical Catholics with nine children and more to come if God sends them, and Mass every day, and they're rolling in wealth richer than your McCorkerys with all their wickedness." So there you are, Lacey Mahaffy, wrong again, and welcome to your pious Connollys. Still and all it was Connolly who had given Gerald McCorkery his start in the world; McCorkery had been publicity man and then campaign manager for Connolly, in the days when Connolly had Tammany in the palm of his hand and the sky was the limit. And McCorkery had begun at the beginning, God knows. He was running a little basement place first, rent almost nothing, where the boys of the Connolly Club and the Little Tammany Association, just the mere fringe of the district, you might say, could drop in for quiet evenings for a game and a drink along with the talk. Nothing low, nothing but what was customary, with the house taking a cut on the winnings and a fine profit on the liquor, and holding the crowd together. Many was the big plan hatched there came out well for everybody. For everybody but myself, and why was that? And when McCorkery says to me, "You can take over now and run the place for the McCorkery Club," ah, there was my chance and Lacey Mahaffy wouldn't hear of it, and with Maggie coming on just then it wouldn't do to excite her.

Mr. Halloran went on, following his feet that knew the way to Billy's Place, head down, not speaking to passersby any more, but talking it out with himself again, again. What a track to go over seeing clearly one by one the crossroads ʼwhere he might have taken a different turn that would have changed all his fortunes; but no, he had gone the other way and now it was too late. She wouldn't say a thing but "It's not right and you know it, Halloran," so what could a man do in all? Ah, you could have gone on with your rightful affairs like any other man, Halloran, it's not the woman's place to decide such things; she'd have come round once she saw the money, or a good whack on the backsides would have put her in her place. Never had mortal woman needed a good walloping worse than Lacey Mahaffy, but he could never find it in his heart to give it to her for her own good. That was just another of your many mistakes, Halloran. But there was always the life-long job with the G. and I. and peace in the house more or less. Many a man envied me in those days I remember, and I was resting easy on the savings and knowing with that and the pension I could finish out my life with some little business of my own. "What came of that?" Mr. Halloran inquired in a low voice, looking around him. Nobody answered. You know well what came of it, Halloran. You were fired out like a delivery boy, two years before your time was out. Why did you sit there watching the trick being played on others before you, knowing well it could happen to you and never quite believing what you saw with your own eyes? G. and I. gave me my start, when I was green in this country, and they were my own kind or I thought so. Well, it's done now. Yes, it's done now, but there was all the years you could have cashed in on the numbers game with the best of them, helping collect the protection money and taking your cut. You could have had a fortune by now in Lacey's name, safe in the bank. It was good quiet profit and none the wiser. But they're wiser now, Halloran, don't forget; still it's a lump of grief and disappointment to swallow all the same. The game's up with Connolly, **maybe;** Lacey Mahaffy had said, "Numbers is just another way of stealing from the poor, and you weren't born to be a thief like that McCorkery." Ah, God, no, Halloran, you were born to rot on relief and maybe that's honest enough for her. That Lacey— A fortune in her name would have been no good to me whatever. She's got all the savings tied up, such as they are, she'll pinch and she'll starve, she'll wash dirty clothes first, she won't give up a penny to live on. She has stood in my way, McCorkery, like a skeleton rattling its bones, and you were right about her, she has been my ruin. "Ah, it's not too late yet, Halloran," said McCorkery, appearing plain as day inside Mr. Halloran's head with the same old face and way with him. "Never say die, Halloran. Elections are coming on again, it's a busy time for all, there's work to be done and you're the very man I'm looking for. Why didn't you come to me sooner, you know I never forget an old friend. You don't deserve your ill fortune,

Halloran," McCorkery told him; "I said so to others and I say it now to your face, never did man deserve more of the world than you, Halloran, but the truth is, there's not always enough good luck to go round; but it's your turn now, and I've got a job for you up to your abilities at last. For a man like you, there's nothing to it at all, you can toss it off with one hand tied, Halloran, and good money in it. Organization work, just among your own neighbors, where you're known and respected for a man of your word and an old friend of Gerald McCorkery. Now look, Halloran," said Gerald McCorkery, tipping him the wink, "do I need to say more? It's voters in large numbers we're after, Halloran, and you're to bring them in, alive or dead. Keep your eye on the situation at all times and get in touch with me when necessary. And name your figure in the way of money. And come up to the house sometimes, Halloran, why don't you? Rosie has asked me a hundred times, 'Whatever went with Halloran, the life of the party?' That's the way you stand with Rosie, Halloran. We're in a two-story flat now with green velvet curtains and carpets you can sink to your shoe-tops in, and there's no reason at all why you shouldn't have the same kind of place if you want it. With your gifts, you were never meant to be a poor man."

Ah, but Lacey Mahaffy wouldn't have it, maybe. "Then get yourself another sort of woman, Halloran, you're a good man still, find yourself a woman like Rosie to snuggle down with at night." Yes, but McCorkery, you forget that Lacey Mahaffy had legs and hair and eyes and a complexion fit for a chorus girl. But would she do anything with them? Never. Would you believe there was a woman wouldn't take off all her clothes at once even to bathe herself? What a hateful thing she was with her evil mind thinking everything was a sin, and never giving a man a chance to show himself a man in any way. But she's faded away now, her mean soul shows out all over her, she's ugly as sin itself now, Mc-Corkery. "It's what I told you would happen," said McCorkery, "but now with the job and the money you can go your ways and let Lacey Mahaffy go hers." I'll do it, McCorkery. "And forget about Connolly. Just remember I'm my own man and always was. Connolly's finished, but I'm not. Stronger than ever, Halloran, with Connolly out of the way. I saw this coming long ever ago, Hallo-ran, I got clear of it. They don't catch McCorkery with his pants down, Halloran. And I almost forgot . . . Here's something for the running expenses to start. Take this for the present, and there's more to come. . . ."

Mr. Halloran stopped short, a familiar smell floated under his nose: the warm beer-and-beefsteak smell of Billy's Place, sawdust and onions, like any other bar maybe, but with something of its own besides. The talk within him stopped also as if a hand had been laid on his mind. He drew his fist out of his pocket almost expecting to find green money in it. The half dollar was in his palm. "I'll stay while it lasts and hope McCorkery will come in."

The moment he stepped inside his eye lighted on McCorkery standing at the bar pouring his own drink from the bottle before him. Billy was mopping the bar before him idly, and his eye, swimming toward Halloran, looked like an oyster in its own juice. McCorkery saw him too. "Well, blow me down," he said, in a voice that had almost lost its old County Mayo ring, "if it ain't my old sidekick from the G. and I. Step right up, Halloran," he said, his poker-face as good as ever, no man ever saw Gerald McCorkery surprised at anything. "Step up and name your choice."

Mr. Halloran glowed suddenly with the warmth around the heart he always had at the sight of McCorkery, he couldn't put a name on it, but there was something about the man. Ah, it was Gerald all right, the same, who never forgot a friend and never seemed to care whether a man was rich or poor, with his face of granite and his eyes like blue agates in his head, a rock of a man surely. There he was, saying "Step right up," as if they had parted only yesterday; portly and solid in his expensive-looking clothes, as always; his hat a darker gray than his suit, with a devil-may-care roll to the brim, but nothing sporting, mind you. All first-rate, well made, and the right thing for him, more power to him. Mr. Halloran said, "Ah, McCorkery, you're the one man on this round earth I hoped to see today, but I says to myself, maybe he doesn't come round to Billy's Place so much nowadays."

"And why not?" asked McCorkery, "I've been coming around to Billy's Place for twenty-five years now, it's still headquarters for the old guard of the McCorkery Club, Halloran." He took in Mr. Halloran from head to foot in a flash of a glance and turned toward the bottle.

"I was going to have a beer," said Mr. Halloran, "but the smell of that whiskey changes my mind for me." McCorkery poured a second glass, they lifted the drinks with an identical crook of the elbow, a flick of the wrist at each other.

"Here's to crime," said McCorkery, and "Here's looking at you," said Mr. Halloran, merrily. Ah, to hell with it, he was back where he belonged, in good company. He put his foot on the rail and snapped down his whiskey, and no sooner was his glass on the bar than McCorkery was filling it again. "Just time for a few quick ones," he said, "before the boys get here." Mr. Halloran downed that one, too, before he noticed that McCorkery hadn't filled his own glass. "I'm ahead of you," said McCorkery, "I'll skip this one."

There was a short pause, a silence fell around them that seemed to ooze like a fog from somewhere deep in McCorkery, it was suddenly as if he had not really been there at all, or hadn't uttered a word. Then he said outright: "Well, Halloran, let's have it. What's on your mind?" And he poured two more drinks. That was McCorkery all over, reading your thoughts and coming straight to the point.

Mr. Halloran closed his hand round his glass and peered into the little pool of whiskey. "Maybe we could sit down," he said, feeling weak-kneed all at once. McCorkery took the bottle and moved over to the nearest table. He sat facing the door, his look straying there now and then, but he had a set, listening face as if he was ready to hear anything.

"You know what I've had at home all these years," began Mr. Halloran, solemnly, and paused.

"Oh, God, yes," said McCorkery with simple good-fellowship. "How is herself these days?"

"Worse than ever," said Mr. Halloran, "but that's not it."

"What is it, then, Halloran?" asked McCorkery, pouring drinks. "You know well you can speak out your mind to me. Is it a loan?"

"No," said Mr. Halloran. "It's a job."

"Now that's a different matter," said McCorkery. "What kind of a job?"

Mr. Halloran, his head sunk between his shoulders, saw McCorkery wave a hand and nod at half a dozen men who came in and ranged themselves along the bar. "Some of the boys," said Mc-Corkery. "Go on." His face was tougher, and quieter, as if the drink gave him a firm hold on himself. Mr. Halloran said what he had planned to say, had said already on the way down, and it still sounded reasonable and right to him. McCorkery waited until he had finished, and got up, putting a hand on Mr. Halloran's shoulder. "Stay where you are, and help yourself," he said, giving the bottle a little push, "and anything else you want, Halloran, order it on me. I'll be back in a few minutes, and you know I'll help you out if I can."

Halloran understood everything but it was through a soft warm fog, and he hardly noticed when McCorkery passed him again with the men, all in that creepy quiet way like footpads on a dark street. They went into the back room, the door opened on a bright light and closed again, and Mr. Halloran reached for the bottle to help himself wait until McCorkery should come again bringing the good word. He felt comfortable and easy as if he hadn't a bone or muscle in him, but his elbow slipped off the table once or twice and he upset his drink on his sleeve. Ah, McCorkery, is it the whole family you're taking on with the jobs? For my Maggie's husband is in now with the Little Tammany Association. "There's a bright lad will go far and I've got my eye on him, Halloran," said the friendly voice of McCorkery in his mind, and the brown face, softer than he remembered it, came up clearly behind his closed eyes.

"Ah, well, it's like myself beginning all over again in him," said Mr. Halloran, aloud, "besides my own job that I might have had all this time if I'd just come to see you sooner."

"True for you," said McCorkery in a merry County Mayo voice, inside Mr. Halloran's head, "and now let's drink to the gay future for old times' sake and be damned to Lacey Mahaffy." Mr. Halloran reached for the bottle but it skipped sideways, rolled out of reach like a creature, and exploded at his feet. When he stood up the chair fell backward from under him. He leaned on the table and it folded up under his hands like cardboard.

"Wait now, take it easy," said McCorkery, and there he was, real enough, holding Mr. Halloran braced on the one side, motioning with his hand to the boys in the back room, who came out quietly and took hold of Mr. Halloran, some of them, on the other side. Their faces were all Irish, but not an Irishman Mr. Halloran knew in the lot, and he did not like any face he saw. "Let me be," he said with dignity, "I came here to see Gerald J. McCorkery, a

401

friend of mine from old times, and let not a thug among you lay a finger upon me."

"Come on, Big Shot," said one of the younger men, in a voice like a file grating, "come on now, it's time to go."

"That's a fine low lot you've picked to run with, McCorkery," said Mr. Halloran, bracing his heels against the slow weight they put upon him toward the door, "I wouldn't trust one of them far as I could throw him by the tail."

"All right, all right, Halloran," said McCorkery. "Come on with me. Lay off him, Finnegan." He was leaning over Mr. Halloran and pressing something into his right hand. It was money, a neat little roll of it, good smooth thick money, no other feel like it in the world, you couldn't mistake it. Ah, he'd have an argument to show Lacey Mahaffy would knock her off her feet. Honest money with a job to back it up. "You'll stand by your given word, Mc-Corkery, as ever?" he asked, peering into the rock-colored face above him, his feet weaving a dance under him, his heart ready to break with gratitude.

"Ah, sure, sure," said McCorkery in a loud hearty voice with a kind of curse in it. "Crisakes, get on with him, do." Mr. Halloran found himself eased into a taxicab at the curb, with McCorkery speaking to the driver and giving him money. "So long, Big Shot," said one of the thug faces, and the taxicab door thumped to. Mr. Halloran bobbed about on the seat for a while, trying to think. He leaned forward and spoke to the driver. "Take me to my friend Gerald J. McCorkery's house," he said, "I've got important business. Don't pay any attention to what he said. Take me to his house."

"Yeah?" said the driver, without turning his head. "Well, here's where you get out, see? Right here." He reached back and opened the door. And sure enough, Mr. Halloran was standing on the sidewalk in front of the flat in Perry Street, alone except for the rows of garbage cans, the taxicab hooting its way around the corner, and a cop coming toward him, plainly to be seen under the street light.

"You should cast your vote for McCorkery, the poor man's friend," Mr. Halloran told the cop, "McCorkery's the man who will get us all off the spot. Stands by his old friends like a maniac. Got a wife named Rosie. Vote for McCorkery," said Mr. Halloran, working hard at his job, "and you'll be Chief of the Force when Halloran says the word."

"To hell with McCorkery, that stooge," said the cop, his mouth square and sour with the things he said and the things he saw and did every night on that beat. "There you are drunk again, Halloran, shame to you, with Lacey Mahaffy working her heart out over the washboard to buy your beer."

"It wasn't beer and she didn't buy it, mind you," said Mr. Halloran, "and what do you know about Lacey Mahaffy?"

"I knew her from old when I used to run errands for St. Veronica's Altar Society," said the cop, "and she was a great one, even then. Nothing good enough."

"It's the same today," said Mr. Halloran, almost sober for a moment.

"Well, go on up now and stay up till you're fit to be seen," said the cop, censoriously.

"You're Johnny Maginnis," said Mr. Halloran, "I know you well."

"You should know me by now," said the cop.

Mr. Halloran worked his way upstairs partly on his hands and knees, but once at his own door he stood up, gave a great blow on the panel with his fist, turned the knob and surged in like a wave after the door itself, holding out the money toward Mrs. Halloran, who had finished ironing and was at her mending.

She got up very slowly, her bony hand over her mouth, her eyes starting out at what she saw. "Ah, did you steal it?" she asked. "Did you kill somebody for that?" the words grated up from her throat in a dark whisper. Mr. Halloran glared back at her in fear.

"Suffering Saints, Lacey Mahaffy," he shouted until the whole houseful could hear him, "haven't ye any mind at all that you can't see your husband has had a turn of fortune and a job and times are changed from tonight? Stealing, is it? That's for your great friends the Connollys with their religion. Connolly steals, but Halloran is an honest man with a job in the McCorkery Club, and money in pocket."

"McCorkery, is it?" said Mrs. Halloran, loudly too. "Ah, so there's the whole family, young and old, wicked and innocent, taking their bread from McCorkery, at last. Well, it's no bread of mine, I'll earn my own as I have, you can keep your dirty money to yourself, Halloran, mind you I mean it."

"Great God, woman," moaned Mr. Halloran, and he tottered from the door to the table, to the ironing board, and stood there, ready to weep with rage, "haven't you a soul even that you won't come along with your husband when he's riding to riches and glory on the Tiger's back itself, with everything for the taking and no questions asked?"

"Yes, I have a soul," cried Mrs. Halloran, clenching her fists, her hair flying. "Surely I have a soul and I'll save it yet in spite of you. . . ."

She was standing there before him in a kind of faded gingham winding sheet, with her dead hands upraised, her dead eyes blind but fixed upon him, her voice coming up hollow from the deep tomb, her throat thick with grave damp. The ghost of Lacey Mahaffy was threatening him, it came nearer, growing taller as it came, the face changing to a demon's face with a fixed glassy grin. "It's all that drink on an empty stomach," said the ghost, in a hoarse growl. Mr. Halloran fetched a yell of horror right out of his very boots, and seized the flatiron from the board. "Ah, God damn you, Lacey Mahaffy, you devil, keep away, keep away," he howled, but she advanced on air, grinning and growling. He raised the flatiron and hurled it without aiming, and the specter, whoever it was, whatever it was, sank and was gone. He did not look, but broke out of the room and was back on the sidewalk before he knew he had meant to go there. Maginnis came up at once. "Hey there now, Halloran," he said, "I mean business this time. You get back upstairs or I'll run you in. Come along now, I'll help you get there this time, and that's the last of it. On relief the way you are, and drinking your head off."

Mr. Halloran suddenly felt calm, collected; he would take Maginnis up and show him just what had happened. "I'm not on relief any more, and if you want any trouble, just call on my friend, McCorkery. He'll tell you who I am."

"McCorkery can't tell me anything about you I don't know already," said Maginnis. "Stand up there now." For Halloran wanted to go up again on his hands and knees.

"Let a man be," said Mr. Halloran, trying to sit on the cop's feet. "I killed Lacey Mahaffy at last, you'll be pleased to hear," he said, looking up into the cop's face. "It was high time and past. But I did not steal the money."

"Well, ain't that just too bad," said the cop, hauling him up under the arms. "Chees, why'n't you make a good job while you had the chance? Stand up now. Ah, hell with it, stand up or I'll sock you one."

Mr. Halloran said, "Well, you don't believe it so wait and see."

At that moment they both glanced upward and saw Mrs. Halloran coming downstairs. She was holding to the rail, and even in the speckled hall-light they could see a great lumpy clout of flesh standing out on her forehead, all colors. She stopped, and seemed not at all surprised.

"So there you are, Officer Maginnis," she said. "Bring him up."

"That's a fine welt you've got over your eye this time, Mrs. Halloran," commented Officer Maginnis, politely.

"I fell and hit my head on the ironing board," said Mrs. Halloran. "It comes of overwork and worry, day and night. A dead faint, Officer Maginnis. Watch your big feet there, you thriving, natural fool," she added to Mr. Halloran. "He's got a job now, you mightn't believe it, Officer Maginnis, but it's true. Bring him on up, and thank you."

She went ahead of them, opened the door, and led the way to the bedroom through the kitchen, turned back the covers, and Officer Maginnis dumped Mr. Halloran among the quilts and pillows. Mr. Halloran rolled over with a deep groan and shut his eyes.

"Many thanks to you, Officer Maginnis," said Mrs. Halloran.

"Don't mention it, Mrs. Halloran," said Officer Maginnis.

When the door was shut and locked, Mrs. Halloran went and dipped a large bath towel under the kitchen tap. She wrung it out and tied several good hard knots in one end and tried it out with a whack on the edge of the table. She walked in and stood over the bed and brought the knotted towel down in Mr. Halloran's face with all her might. He stirred and muttered, ill at ease. "That's for the flatiron, Halloran," she told him, in a cautious voice as if she were talking to herself, and whack, down came the towel again. "That's for the half-dollar," she said, and whack, "that's for your drunkenness—" Her arm swung around regularly, ending with a heavy thud on the face that was beginning to squirm, gasp, lift itself from the pillow and fall back again, in a puzzled kind of torment. "For your sock feet," Mrs. Halloran told him, whack, "and your laziness, and this is for missing Mass and"—here she swung half a dozen times—"that is for your daughter and your part in her. . . ."

She stood back breathless, the lump on her forehead burning in its furious colors. When Mr. Halloran attempted to rise, shielding his head with his arms, she gave him a push and he fell back again. "Stay there and don't give me a word," said Mrs. Halloran. He pulled the pillow over his face and subsided again, this time for good.

Mrs. Halloran moved about very deliberately. She tied the wet towel around her head, the knotted end hanging over her shoulder. Her hand ran into her apron pocket and came out again with the money. There was a five-dollar bill with three one-dollar bills rolled in it, and the half-dollar she had thought spent long since. "A poor start, but something," she said, and opened the cupboard door with a long key. Reaching in, she pulled a loosely fitted board out of the wall, and removed a black-painted metal box. She unlocked this, took out one five-cent piece from a welter of notes and coins. She then placed the new money in the box, locked it, put it away, replaced the board, shut the cupboard door and locked that. She went out to the telephone, dropped the nickel in the slot, asked for a number, and waited.

"Is that you, Maggie? Well, are things any better with you now? I'm glad to hear it. It's late to be calling, but there's news about your father. No, no, nothing of that kind, he's got a job. I said a *job*. Yes, at last, after all my urging him onward. . . . I've got him bedded down to sleep it off so he'll be ready for work tomorrow. . . . Yes, it's political work, toward the election time, with Gerald McCorkery. But that's no harm, getting votes and all, he'll be in the open air and it doesn't mean I'll have to associate with low people, now or ever. It's clean enough work, with good pay; if it's not just what I prayed for, still it beats nothing, Maggie. After all my trying . . . it's like a miracle. You see what can be done with patience and doing your duty, Maggie. Now mind you do as well by your own husband."

Holiday

At that time I was too young for some of the troubles I was
having, and I had not yet learned what to do with them. It no
longer can matter what kind of troubles they were, or what finally
became of them. It seemed to me then there was nothing to do but
run away from them, though all my tradition, background, and
training had taught me unanswerably that no one except a coward
ever runs away from anything. What nonsense! They should have
taught me the difference between courage and foolhardiness, instead of leaving me to find it out for myself. I learned finally that if
I still had the sense I was born with, I would take off like a deer at
the first warning of certain dangers. But this story I am about to
tell you happened before this great truth impressed itself upon me
—that we do not run from the troubles and dangers that are truly
ours, and it is better to learn what they are earlier than later, and if
we don't run from the others, we are fools.

I confided to my friend Louise, a former schoolmate about my
own age, not my troubles but my little problem: I wanted to go
somewhere for a spring holiday, by myself, to the country, and it
should be very simple and nice and, of course, not expensive, and
she was not to tell anyone where I had gone; but if she liked, I
would send her word now and then, if anything interesting was
happening. She said she loved getting letters but hated answering
them; and she knew the very place for me, and she would not tell
anybody anything. Louise had then—she has it still—something
near to genius for making improbable persons, places, and situations sound attractive. She told amusing stories that did not turn

grim on you until a little while later, when by chance you saw and heard for yourself. So with this story. Everything was just as Louise had said, if you like, and everything was, at the same time, quite different.

"I know the very place," said Louise, "a family of real old-fashioned German peasants, in the deep blackland Texas farm country, a household in real patriarchal style—the kind of thing you'd hate to live with but is very nice to visit. Old father, God Almighty himself, with whiskers and all; Old mother, matriarch in men's shoes; endless daughters and sons and sons-in-law and fat babies falling about the place; and fat puppies—my favourite was a darling little black thing named Kuno—cows, calves, and sheep and lambs and goats and turkeys and guineas roaming up and down the shallow green hills, ducks and geese on the ponds. I was there in the summer when the peaches and watermelons were in——"

"This is the end of March," I said, doubtfully.

"Spring comes early there," said Louise. "I'll write to the Müllers about you, you just get ready to go."

"Just where is this paradise?"

"Not far from the Louisiana line," said Louise. "I'll ask them to give you my attic—oh, that was a sweet place! It's a big room, with the roof sloping to the floor on each side, and the roof leaks a little when it rains, so the shingles are all stained in beautiful streaks, all black and grey and mossy green, and in one corner there used to be a stack of dime novels, *The Duchess,* Ouida, Mrs. E.D.E.N. Southworth, Ella Wheeler Wilcox's poems—one summer they had a lady boarder who was a great reader, and she went off and left her library. I loved it! And everybody was so healthy and good-hearted, and the weather was perfect. . . . How long do you want to stay?"

I hadn't thought of this, so I said at random, "About a month."

A few days later I found myself tossed off like an express package from a dirty little crawling train onto the sodden platform of a country station, where the stationmaster emerged and locked up the waiting room before the train had got round the bend. As he clumped by me he shifted his wad of tobacco to his cheek and asked, "Where you goin'?"

"To the Müller farm," I said, standing beside my small trunk and suitcase with the bitter wind cutting through my thin coat.

"Anybody meet you?" he asked, not pausing.

"They *said* so."

"All right," he said, and got into his little ragged buckboard with a sway-backed horse and drove away.

I turned my trunk on its side and sat on it facing the wind and the desolate mud-colored shapeless scene and began making up my first letter to Louise. First I was going to tell her that unless she was to be a novelist, there was no excuse for her having so much imagination. In daily life, I was going to tell her, there are also such useful things as the plain facts that should be stuck to, through thick and thin. Anything else led to confusion like this. I was beginning to enjoy my letter to Louise when a sturdy boy about twelve years old crossed the platform. As he neared me, he took off his rough cap and bunched it in his thick hand, dirt-stained at the knuckles. His round cheeks, his round nose, his round chin were a cool, healthy red. In the globe of his face, as neatly circular as if drawn in bright crayon, his narrow, long, tip-tilted eyes, clear as pale-blue water, seemed out of place, as if two incompatible strains had collided in making him. They were beautiful eyes, and the rest of the face was not to be taken seriously. A blue woollen blouse buttoned up to his chin ended abruptly at his waist as if he would outgrow it in another half hour, and his blue drill breeches flapped about his ankles. His old clodhopper shoes were several sizes too big for him. Altogether, it was plain he was not the first one to wear his clothes. He was a cheerful, detached, self-possessed apparition against the tumbled brown earth and ragged dark sky, and I smiled at him as well as I could with a face that felt like wet clay.

He smiled back slightly without meeting my eye, motioning for me to take up my suitcase. He swung my trunk to his head and tottered across the uneven platform, down the steps slippery with mud where I expected to see him crushed beneath his burden like an ant under a stone. He heaved the trunk into the back of his wagon with a fine smash, took my suitcase and tossed it after, then climbed up over one front wheel while I scrambled my way up over the other.

The pony, shaggy as a wintering bear, eased himself into a grudging trot, while the boy, bowed over with his cap pulled down over his ears and eyebrows, held the reins slack and fell into a brown study. I studied the harness, a real mystery. It met and clung in all sorts of unexpected places; it parted company in what appeared to be strategic seats of jointure. It was mended sketchily in risky places with bits of hairy rope. Other seemingly unimportant parts were bound together irrevocably with wire. The bridle was too long for the pony's stocky head, so he had shaken the bit out of his mouth at the start, apparently, and went his own way at his own pace.

Our vehicle was an exhausted specimen of something called a spring wagon, who knows why? There were no springs, and the shallow enclosed platform at the back, suitable for carrying various plunder, was worn away until it barely reached midway of the back wheels, one side of it steadily scraping the iron tire. The wheels themselves spun not dully around and around in the way of common wheels, but elliptically, being loosened at the hubs, so that we proceeded with a drunken, hilarious swagger, like the rolling motion of a small boat on a choppy sea.

The soaked brown fields fell away on either side of the lane, all rough with winter-worn stubble ready to sink and become earth again. The scanty leafless woods ran along an edge of the field nearby. There was nothing beautiful in those woods now except the promise of spring, for I detested bleakness, but it gave me pleasure to think that beyond this there might be something else beautiful in its own being, a river shaped and contained by its banks, or a field stripped down to its true meaning, ploughed and ready for the seed. The road turned abruptly and was almost hidden for a moment, and we were going through the woods. Closer sight of the crooked branches assured me that spring was beginning, if sparely, reluctantly: the leaves were budding in tiny cones of watery green besprinkling all the new shoots; a thin sedate rain began again to fall, not so opaque as a fog, but a mist that merely deepened overhead, and lowered, until the clouds became rain in one swathing, delicate grey.

As we emerged from the woods, the boy roused himself and pointed forward, in silence. We were approaching the farm along the skirts of a fine peach orchard, now faintly colored with young bud, but there was nothing to disguise the gaunt and aching ugliness of the farmhouse itself. In this Texas valley, so gently modulated with small crests and shallows, "rolling country" as the farmers say, the house was set on the peak of the barest rise of ground, as if the most infertile spot had been thriftily chosen for building a shelter. It stood there staring and naked, an intruding stranger, strange even beside the barns ranged generously along the back, low-eaved and weathered to the color of stone.

The narrow windows and the steeply sloping roof oppressed me; I wished to turn away and go back. I had come a long way to be so disappointed, I thought, and yet I must go on, for there could be nothing here for me more painful than what I had left. But as we drew near the house, now hardly visible except for the yellow lamplight in the back, perhaps in the kitchen, my feelings changed again toward warmth and tenderness, or perhaps just an apprehension that I could feel so, maybe, again.

The wagon drew up before the porch, and I started climbing down. No sooner had my foot touched ground than an enormous black dog of the detestable German shepherd breed leaped silently at me, and as silently I covered my face with my arms and leaped back. "Kuno, down!" shouted the boy, lunging at him. The front door flew open and a young girl with yellow hair ran down the steps and seized the ugly beast by the scruff. "He does not mean anything," she said seriously in English. "He is only a dog."

Just Louise's darling little puppy Kuno, I thought, a year or so older. Kuno whined, apologized by bowing and scraping one front paw on the ground, and the girl holding his scruff said, shyly and proudly, "I teach him that. He has always such bad manners, but I teach him!"

I had arrived, it seemed, at the moment when the evening chores were about to begin. The entire Müller household streamed out of the door, each man and woman going about the affairs of the moment. The young girl walked with me up the porch and said, "This is my brother Hans," and a young man paused to shake hands and passed by. "This is my brother Fritz," she said, and Fritz took my hand and dropped it as he went. "My sister Annetje," said the young girl, and a quiet young woman with a baby draped loosely like a scarf over her shoulder smiled and held out her hand. Hand after hand went by, their palms variously younger or older, broad or small, male or female, but all thick hard decent peasant hands, warm and strong. And in every face I saw again the pale, tilted eyes, on every head that taffy-colored

hair, as though they might all be brothers and sisters, though Annetje's husband and still another daughter's husband had gone by
after greeting me. In the wide hall with a door at front and back,
full of cloudy light and the smell of soap, the old mother, also on
her way out, stopped to offer her hand. She was a tall strong-look-
ing woman wearing a three-cornered black wool shawl on her
head, her skirts looped up over a brown flannel petticoat. Not from
her did the young ones get those water-clear eyes. Hers were black
and shrewd and searching, a band of hair showed black streaked
with grey, her seamed dry face was brown as seasoned bark, and
she walked in her rubber boots with the stride of a man. She shook
my hand briefly and said in German English that I was welcome,
smiling and showing her blackened teeth.

"This is my girl Hatsy," she told me, "and she will show you to
your room." Hatsy took my hand as if I were a child needing a
guide. I followed her up a flight of steps steep as a ladder, and
there we were, in Louise's attic room, with the sloping roof. Yes,
the shingles were stained all the colors she had said. There were
the dime novels heaped in the corner. For once, Louise had got it
straight, and it was homely and familiar, as if I had seen it before.
"My mother says we could give you a better place on the downstairs," said Hatsy, in her soft blurred English, "but *she* said in her
letter you would like it so." I told her indeed I did like it so. She
went down the steep stairs then, and her brother came up as if he
were climbing a tree, with the trunk on his head and the suitcase in
his right hand, and I could not see what kept the trunk from crashing back to the bottom, as he used the left hand to climb with. I
wished to offer help but feared to insult him, having noted well the
tremendous ease and style with which he had hurled the luggage
around before, a strong man doing his turn before a weakling audience. He put his burden down and straightened up, wriggling his
shoulders and panting only a little. I thanked him and he pushed
his cap back and pulled it forward again, which I took for some
sort of polite response, and clattered out hugely. Looking out of
my window a few minutes later, I saw him setting off across the
fields carrying a lighted lantern and a large steel trap.

I began changing my first letter to Louise. "I'm going to like it
here. I don't quite know why, but it's going to be all right. Maybe I
can tell you later——"

The sound of the German speech in the household below was part of the pleasantness, for they were not talking to me and did not expect me to answer. All the German I understood then was contained in five small deadly sentimental songs of Heine's, learned by heart; and this was a very different tongue, Low German corrupted by three generations in a foreign country. A dozen miles away, where Texas and Louisiana melted together in a rotting swamp whose sluggish under-tow of decay nourished the roots of pine and cedar, a colony of French emigrants had lived out two hundred years of exile, not wholly incorruptible, but mystically faithful to the marrow of their bones, obstinately speaking their old French by then as strange to the French as it was to the English. I had known many of these families during a certain long summer happily remembered, and here again, listening to another language nobody could understand except those of this small farming community, I knew that I was again in a house of perpetual exile. These were solid, practical, hard-bitten, land-holding German peasants, who struck their mattocks into the earth deep and held fast wherever they were, because to them life and the land were one indivisible thing; but never in any wise did they confuse nationality with habitation.

I liked the thick warm voices, and it was good not to have to understand what they were saying. I loved that silence which means freedom from the constant pressure of other minds and other opinions and other feelings, that freedom to fold up in quiet and go back to my own center, to find out again, for it is always a rediscovery, what kind of creature it is that rules me finally, makes all the decisions no matter who thinks they make them, even I; who little by little takes everything away except the one thing I cannot live without, and who will one day say, "Now I am all you have left—take me." I paused there a good while listening to this muted unknown language which was silence with music in it; I could be moved and touched but not troubled by it, as by the crying of frogs or the wind in the trees.

The catalpa tree at my window would, I noticed, when it came into leaf, shut off my view of the barns and the fields beyond. When in bloom the branches would almost reach through the window. But now they were a thin screen through which the calves, splotchy red and white, moved prettily against the weathered darkness of the sheds. The brown fields would soon be green again; the sheep washed by the rains and become clean grey. All the beauty of the landscape now was in the harmony of the valley rolling fluently away to the wood's edge. It was an inland country, with the forlorn look of all unloved things; winter in this part of the south is a moribund coma, not the northern death sleep with the sure promise of resurrection. But in my south, my loved and never-forgotten country, after her long sickness, with only a slight stirring, an opening of the eyes between one breath and the next, between night and day, the earth revives and bursts into the plenty of spring with fruit and flowers together, spring and summer at once under the hot shimmering blue sky.

The freshening wind promised another light sedate rain to come at evening. The voices below stairs dispersed, rose again, separately calling from the yards and barns. The old woman strode down the path toward the cow sheds, Hatsy running behind her. The woman wore her wooden yoke, with the milking pails covered and closed with iron hasps, slung easily across her shoulders, but her daughter carried two tin milking pails on her arm. When they pushed back the bars of cedar which opened onto the fields, the cows came through lowing and crowding, and the calves scampered each to his own dam with reaching, opened mouths. Then there was the battle of separating the hungry children from their mothers when they had taken their scanty share. The old woman slapped their little haunches with her open palm, Hatsy dragged at their halters, her feet slipping wide in the mud, the cows bellowed and brandished their horns, the calves bawled like rebellious babies. Hatsy's long yellow braids whisked around her shoulders, her laughter was a shrill streak of gaiety above the angry cow voices and the raucous shouting of the old woman.

From the kitchen porch below came the sound of splashing water, the creaking of the pump handle, and the stamping boots of men. I sat in the window watching the darkness come on slowly, while all the lamps were being lighted. My own small lamp had a handle on the oil bowl, like a cup's. There was also a lantern with a frosted chimney hanging by a nail on the wall. A voice called to me from the foot of my stairs and I looked down into the face of a dark-skinned, flaxen-haired young woman, far advanced in pregnancy, and carrying a prosperous year-old boy on her hip, one arm

clutching him to her, the other raised above her head so that her
lantern shone upon their heads. "The supper is now ready," she
said, and waited for me to come down before turning away.

In the large square room the whole family was gathering at a
long table covered with a red checkered cotton cloth, with heaped-
up platters of steaming food at either end. A crippled and badly
deformed servant girl was setting down pitchers of milk. Her face
was so bowed over it was almost hidden, and her whole body was
maimed in some painful, mysterious way, probably congenital, I
supposed, though she seemed wiry and tough. Her knotted hands
shook continually, her wagging head kept pace with her restless
elbows. She ran unsteadily around the table scattering plates, dodging whoever stood in her way; no one moved aside for her, or
spoke to her, or even glanced after her when she vanished into the
kitchen.

The men then moved forward to their chairs. Father Müller
took his patriarch's place at the head of the table, Mother Müller
looming behind him like a dark boulder. The younger men ranged
themselves about on one side, the married ones with their wives
standing back of their chairs to serve them, for three generations in
this country had not made them self-conscious or disturbed their
ancient customs. The two sons-in-law and three sons rolled down
their shirt sleeves before beginning to eat. Their faces were polished with recent scrubbing and their open collars were damp.

Mother Müller pointed to me, then waved her hand at her household, telling off their names rapidly. I was a stranger and a guest,
so was seated on the men's side of the table, and Hatsy, whose real
name turned out to be Huldah, the maiden of the family, was
seated on the children's side of the board, attending to them and
keeping them in order. These infants ranged from two years to ten,
five in number—not counting the one still straddling his mother's
hip behind his father's chair—divided between the two married
daughters. The children ravened and gorged and reached their
hands into the sugar bowl to sprinkle sugar on everything they ate,
solemnly elated over their food and paying no attention to Hatsy,
who struggled with them only a little less energetically than she did
with the calves, and ate almost nothing. She was about seventeen
years old, pale-lipped and too thin, and her sleek fine butter-yellow
hair, streaked light and dark, real German peasant hair, gave her

an air of fragility. But she shared the big-boned structure and the enormous energy and animal force that was like a bodily presence itself in the room; and seeing Father Müller's pale-grey deep-set choleric eyes and high cheekbones, it was easy to trace the family resemblance around the table: it was plain that poor Mother Müller had never had a child of her own—black-eyed, black-haired South Germany people. True, she had borne them, but that was all; they belonged to their father. Even the tawny Gretchen, expecting another baby, obviously the pet of the family, with the sly smiling manner of a spoiled child, who wore the contented air of a lazy, healthy young animal, seeming always about to yawn, had hair like pulled taffy and those slanted clear eyes. She stood now easing the weight of her little boy on her husband's chair back, reaching with her left arm over his shoulder to refill his plate from time to time.

Annetje, the eldest daughter, carried her newly born baby over her shoulder, where he drooled comfortably down her back, while she spooned things from platters and bowls for her husband. Whenever their eyes met, they smiled with a gentle, reserved warmth in their eyes, the smile of long and sure friendship.

Father Müller did not in the least believe in his children's marrying and leaving home. Marry, yes, of course; but must that take a son or daughter from him? He always could provide work and a place in the household for his daughters' husbands, and in time he would do the same for his sons' wives. A new room had lately been built on, to the northeast, Annetje explained to me, leaning above her husband's head and talking across the table, for Hatsy to live in when she should be married. Hatsy turned very beautifully pink and ducked her head almost into her plate, then looked up boldly and said, "Jah, jah, I am marrit now soon!" Everybody laughed except Mother Müller, who said in German that girls at home never knew when they were well off—no, they must go bringing in husbands. This remark did not seem to hurt anybody's feelings, and Gretchen said it was nice that I was going to be here for the wedding. This reminded Annetje of something, and she spoke in English to the table at large, saying that the Lutheran pastor had advised her to attend church oftener and put her young ones in Sunday school, so that God would give her a blessing with her fifth child. I counted around again, and sure enough, with

Gretchen's unborn, there were eight children at that table under the age of ten; somebody was going to need a blessing in all that crowd, no doubt. Father Müller delivered a short speech to his daughter in German, then turned to me and said, "What I say iss, it iss all craziness to go to church and pay a preacher goot money to talk his nonsense. Say rather that he pay me to come and lissen, then I vill go!" His eyes glared with sudden fierceness above his square speckled grey and yellow beard that sprouted directly out from the high cheekbones. "He thinks, so, that my time maybe costs nothing? That iss goot! Let him pay me!"

Mother Müller snorted and shuffled her feet. "Ach, you talk, you talk. Now you vill make the pastor goot and mad if he hears. Vot ve do, if he vill not chrissen the babies?"

"You give him goot money, he vill chrissen," shouted Father Müller. "You vait und see!"

"Ah sure, dot iss so," agreed Mother Müller. "Only do not let him hear!"

There was a gust of excited talk in German, with much rapping of knife handles on the table. I gave up trying to understand, but watched their faces. It sounded like a pitched battle, but they were agreeing about something. They were united in their tribal scepticisms, as in everything else. I got a powerful impression that they were all, even the sons-in-law, one human being divided into several separate appearances. The crippled servant girl brought in more food and gathered up plates and went away in her limping run, and she seemed to me the only individual in the house. Even I felt divided into many fragments, having left or lost a part of myself in every place I had travelled, in every life mine had touched, above all, in every death of someone near to me that had carried into the grave some part of my living cells. But the servant, she was whole, and belonged nowhere.

I settled easily enough into the marginal life of the household ways and habits. Day began early at the Müllers', and we ate breakfast by yellow lamplight, with the grey damp winds blowing with spring softness through the open windows. The men swallowed their last cups of steaming coffee standing, with their hats on, and went out to harness the horses to the ploughs at sunrise. Annetje, with her fat baby slung over her shoulder, could sweep a room or make a bed with one hand, all finished before the day was well begun; and she spent the rest of the day outdoors, caring for the chickens and the pigs. Now and then she came in with a shallow boxful of newly hatched chickens, abject dabs of wet fluff, and put them on a table in her bedroom where she might tend them carefully on their first day. Mother Müller strode about hugely, giving orders right and left, while Father Müller, smoothing his whiskers and lighting his pipe, drove away to town with Mother Müller calling out after him final directions and instructions about household needs. He never spoke a word to her and appeared not to be listening, but he always returned in a few hours with every commission and errand performed exactly. After I had made my own bed and set my attic in order, there was nothing at all for me to do, and I walked out of this enthusiastic bustle into the lane, feeling extremely useless. But the repose, the almost mystical inertia of their minds in the midst of this muscular life, communicated itself to me little by little, and I absorbed it gratefully in silence and felt all the hidden knotted painful places in my own mind beginning to loosen. It was easier to breathe, and I might even weep, if I pleased. In a very few days I no longer felt like weeping.

One morning I saw Hatsy spading up the kitchen garden plot, and my offer to help, to spread the seeds and cover them, was accepted. We worked at this for several hours each morning, until the warmth of the sun and the stooping posture induced in me a comfortable vertigo. I forgot to count the days, they were one like the other except as the colors of the air changed, deepening and warming to keep step with the advancing season, and the earth grew firmer underfoot with the swelling tangle of crowding roots.

The children, so hungry and noisy at the table, were peaceable little folk who played silent engrossed games in the front yard. They were always kneading mud into loaves and pies and carrying their battered dolls and cotton rag animals through the operations of domestic life. They fed them, put them to bed; they got them up and fed them again, set them to their chores making more mud loaves; or they would harness themselves to their carts and gallop away to a great shady chestnut tree on the opposite side of the house. Here the tree became the *Turnverein,* and they themselves were again human beings, solemnly ambling about in a dance and going through the motions of drinking beer. Miraculously changed once more into horses, they harnessed themselves and galloped home. They came at call to be fed and put to sleep with the docility of their own toys or animal playmates. Their mothers handled them with instinctive, constant gentleness; they never seemed to be troubled by them. They were as devoted and caretaking as a cat with her kittens.

Sometimes I took Annetje's next to youngest child, a baby of two years, in her little wagon, and we would go down through the orchard, where the branches were beginning to sprout in cones of watery green, and into the lane for a short distance. I would turn again into a smaller lane, smoother because less travelled, and we would go slowly between the aisle of mulberry trees where the fruit was beginning to hang and curl like green furry worms. The baby would sit in a compact mound of flannel and calico, her pale-blue eyes tilted and shining under her cap, her two lower teeth showing in a rapt smile. Sometimes several of the other children would follow along quietly. When I turned, they all turned without question, and we would proceed back to the house as sedately as we had set out.

The narrow lane, I discovered, led to the river, and it became my favorite walk. Almost every day I went along the edge of the naked wood, passionately occupied with looking for signs of spring. The changes there were so subtle and gradual I found one day that branches of willows and sprays of blackberry vine alike were covered with fine points of green; the color had changed overnight, or so it seemed, and I knew that tomorrow the whole valley and wood and edge of the river would be quick and feathery with golden green blowing in the winds.

And it was so. On that day I did not leave the river until after dark and came home through the marsh with the owls and night jars crying over my head, calling in a strange and broken chorus in the woods until the farthest answering cry was a ghostly echo. When I went through the orchard the trees were all abloom with fireflies. I stopped and looked at it for a long time, then walked slowly, amazed, for I had never seen anything that was more beautiful to me. The trees were freshly budded out with pale bloom, the branches were immobile in the thin darkness, but the flower clusters shivered in a soundless dance of delicately woven light, whirling as airily as leaves in a breeze, as rhythmically as water in a fountain. Every tree was budded out with this living, pulsing fire as fragile and cool as bubbles. When I opened the gate their light shone on my hands like fox fire. When I looked back, the shimmer of golden light was there, it was no dream.

Hatsy was on her knees in the dining room, washing the floor with heavy dark rags. She always did this work at night, so the men with their heavy boots would not be tracking it up again and it would be immaculate in the morning. She turned her young face to me in a stupor of fatigue. "Ottilie! Ottilie!" she called, loudly, and before I could speak, she said, "Ottilie will give you supper. It is waiting, all ready." I tried to tell her that I was not hungry, but she wished to reassure me. "Look, we all must eat. Now or then, it's no trouble." She sat back on her heels, and raising her head, looked over the window sill at the orchard. She smiled and paused for a moment and said happily, "Now it is come spring. Every spring we have that." She bent again over the great pail of water with her mops.

The crippled servant came in, stumbling perilously on the slippery floor, and set a dish before me, lentils with sausage and red chopped cabbage. It was hot and savory and I was truly grateful, for I found I was hungry, after all. I looked at her—so her name was Ottilie?—and said, "Thank you." "She can't talk," said Hatsy, simply stating a fact that need not be emphasized. The blurred, dark face was neither young nor old, but crumpled into criss cross wrinkles, irrelevant either to age or suffering; simply wrinkles, patternless blackened seams as if the perishable flesh had been wrung in a hard cruel fist. Yet in that mutilated face I saw high cheekbones, slanted water-blue eyes, the pupils very large and strained with the anxiety of one peering into a darkness full of danger. She jarred heavily against the table as she turned, her bowed back trembling with the perpetual working of her withered arms, and ran away in aimless, driven haste.

Hatsy sat on her heels again for a moment, tossed her braids back over her shoulder and said, "That is Ottilie. She is not sick now. She is only like that since she was sick when she was a baby. But she can work so well as I can. She cooks. But she cannot talk so you can understand." She went up on her knees, bowed over, and began to scrub again, with new energy. She was really a network of thin taut ligaments and long muscles elastic as woven steel. She would always work too hard, and be tired all her life, and never know that this was anything but perfectly natural; everybody worked all the time, because there was always more work waiting when they had finished what they were doing then. I ate my supper and took my plate to the kitchen and set it on the table. Ottilie was sitting in a kitchen chair with her feet in the open oven, her arms folded and her head waggling a little. She did not see or hear me.

At home, Hatsy wore an old brown corduroy dress and galoshes without stockings. Her skirts were short enough to show her thin legs, slightly crooked below the knees, as if she had walked too early. "Hatsy, she's a good, quick girl," said Mother Müller, to whom praising anybody or anything did not come easily. On Saturdays, Hatsy took a voluminous bath in a big tub in the closet back of the kitchen, where also were stored the extra chamber pots, slop jars, and water jugs. She then unplaited her yellow hair and bound up the crinkled floss with a wreath of pink cotton rosebuds, put on her pale-blue China silk dress, and went to the *Turnverein* to dance and drink a seidel of dark-brown beer with her suitor, who resembled her brothers enough to be her brother, though I think nobody ever noticed this except myself, and I said nothing because it would have been the remark of a stranger and hopeless outsider. On Sundays, the entire family went to the *Turnverein* after copious washings, getting into starched dresses and shirts, and getting the baskets of food stored in the wagons. The servant, Ottilie, would rush out to see them off, standing with both shaking arms folded over her forehead, shading her troubled eyes to watch them to the turn of the lane. Her muteness seemed nearly absolute; she had no coherent language of signs. Yet three times a day she spread that enormous table with solid food, freshly baked bread, huge platters of vegetables, immoderate roasts of meat, extravagant tarts, strudels, pies—enough for twenty people. If neighbors came in for an afternoon on some holiday, Ottilie would stumble into the big north room, the parlor, with its golden oak melodeon, a harsh-green Brussels carpet, Nottingham lace curtains, crocheted lace antimacassars on the chair backs, to serve them coffee with cream and sugar and thick slices of yellow cake.

Mother Müller sat but seldom in her parlor, and always with

an air of formal unease, her knotted big fingers cramped in a cluster. But Father Müller often sat there in the evenings, where no one ventured to follow him unless commanded; he sometimes played chess with his elder son-in-law, who had learned a good while ago that Father Müller was a good player who abhorred an easy victory, and he dared not do less than put up the best fight he was able, but even so, if Father Müller felt himself winning too often, he would roar, "No, you are not trying! You are not doing your best. Now we stop this nonsense!" and son-in-law would find himself dismissed in temporary disgrace.

Most evenings, however, Father Müller sat by himself and read *Das Kapital.* He would settle deeply into the red plush base rocker and spread the volume upon a low table before him. It was an early edition in blotty black German type, stained and ragged in its leather cover, the pages falling apart, a very bible. He knew whole chapters almost by heart, and added nothing to, took nothing from, the canonical, once-delivered text. I cannot say at that time of my life I had never heard of *Das Kapital,* but I had certainly never known anyone who had read it, though if anyone mentioned it, it was always with profound disapproval. It was not a book one had to read in order to reject it. And here was this respectable old farmer who accepted its dogma as a religion—that is to say, its legendary inapplicable precepts were just, right, proper, one must believe in them, of course, but life, everyday living, was another and unrelated thing. Father Müller was the richest man in his community; almost every neighboring farmer rented land from him, and some of them worked it on the share system. He explained this to me one evening after he had given up trying to teach me chess. He was not surprised that I could not learn, at least not in one lesson, and he was not surprised either that I knew nothing about *Das Kapital.* He explained his own arrangements to me thus: "These men, they cannot buy their land. The land must be bought, for Kapital owns it, and Kapital will not give back to the worker the land that is his. Well, somehow, I can always buy land. Why? I do not know. I only know that with my first land here I made good crops to buy more land, and so I rent it cheap, more than anybody else I rent it cheap, I lend money so my neighbors do not fall into the hands of the bank, and so I am not

Kapital. Someday these workers, they can buy land from me, for less than they can get it anywhere else. Well, that is what I can do, that is all." He turned over a page, and his angry grey eyes looked out at me under his shaggy brows. "I buy my land with my hard work, all my life, and I rent it cheap to my neighbors, and then they say they will not elect my son-in-law, my Annetje's husband, to be sheriff because I am atheist. So then I say, all right, but next year you pay more for your land or more shares of your crops. If I am atheist I will act like one. So, my Annetje's husband is sheriff, that is all."

He had put a stubby forefinger on a line to mark his place, and now he sank himself into his book, and I left quietly without saying good night.

The *Turnverein* was an octagonal pavilion set in a cleared space in a patch of woods belonging to Father Müller. The German colony came here to sit about in the cool shade, while a small brass band played cloppity country dances. The girls danced with energy and direction, their starched petticoats rustling like dry leaves. The boys were more awkward, but willing; they clutched their partners' waists and left crumpled sweaty spots where they clutched. Here Mother Müller took her ease after a hard week. Her gaunt limbs would relax, her knees spread squarely apart, and she would gossip over her beer with the women of her own generation. They would cast an occasional caretaking glance at the children playing nearby, allowing the younger mothers freedom to dance or sit in peace with their own friends.

On the other side of the pavilion, Father Müller would sit with the sober grandfathers, their long curved pipes wagging on their chests as they discussed local politics with profound gravity, their hard peasant fatalism tempered only a little by a shrewd worldly distrust of all officeholders not personally known to them, all political plans except their own immediate ones. When Father Müller talked, they listened respectfully, with faith in him as a strong man, head of his own house and his community. They nodded slowly whenever he took his pipe from his mouth and gestured, holding it by the bowl as if it were a stone he was getting ready to throw. On our way back from the *Turnverein* one evening, Mother Müller said to me, "Well, now, by the grace of Gott it is all settled between Hatsy and her man. It is next Sunday by this time they will be marrit."

All the folk who usually went to the *Turnverein* on Sundays came instead to the Müller house for the wedding. They brought useful presents, mostly bed linen, pillow covers, a white counterpane, with a few ornaments for the bridal chamber—a home-braided round rug in many colors, a brass-bottomed lamp with a round pink chimney decorated with red roses, a stone china washbowl and pitcher also covered with red roses; and the bridegroom's gift to the bride was a necklace, a double string of red coral twigs. Just before the short ceremony began, he slipped the necklace over her head with trembling hands. She smiled up at him shakily and helped him disentangle her short veil from the coral, then they joined hands and turned their faces to the pastor, not letting go until time for the exchange of rings—the widest, thickest, reddest gold bands to be found, no doubt—and at that moment they both stopped smiling and turned a little pale. The groom recovered first, and bent over—he was considerably taller than she—and kissed her on the forehead. His eyes were a deep blue, and his hair not really Müller taffy color, but a light chestnut; a good-looking, gentle-tempered boy, I decided, and he looked at Hatsy as if he liked what he saw. They knelt and clasped hands again for the final prayer, then stood together and exchanged the bridal kiss, a very chaste reserved one, still not on the lips. Then everybody came to shake hands and the men all kissed the bride and the women all kissed the groom. Some of the women whispered in Hatsy's ear, and all burst out laughing except Hatsy, who turned red from her forehead to her throat. She whispered in turn to her husband, who nodded in agreement. She then tried to slip away quietly, but the watchful young girls were after her, and shortly we saw her running through the blossoming orchard, holding up her white ruffled skirts, with all the girls in pursuit, shrieking and calling like excited hunters, for the first to overtake and touch her would be the next bride. They returned, breathless, dragging the lucky one with them, and held her against her ecstatic resistance, while all the young boys kissed her.

The guests stayed on for a huge supper, and Ottilie came in, wearing a fresh blue apron, sweat beaded in the wrinkles of her forehead and around her formless mouth, and passed the food around the table. The men ate first and then Hatsy came in with the women for the first time, still wearing her square little veil of white cotton net bound on her hair with peach blossoms shattered in the bride's race. After supper, one of the girls played waltzes and polkas on the melodeon, and everyone danced. The bride-groom drew gallons of beer from a keg set up in the hall, and at midnight everybody went away, warmly emotional and happy. I went down to the kitchen for a pitcher of hot water. The servant was still setting things to rights, hobbling between table and cup-board. Her face was a brown smudge of anxiety, her eyes were wide and dazed. Her uncertain hands rattled among the pans, but nothing could make her seem real, or in any way connected with the life around her. Yet when I set my pitcher on the stove, she lifted the heavy kettle and poured the scalding water into it with-out spilling a drop.

The clear honey green of the early morning sky was a mirror of the bright earth. At the edge of the woods there had sprung a reticent blooming of small white and pale-colored flowers. The peach trees were now each a separate nosegay of shell rose and white. I left the house, meaning to take the short path across to the lane of mulberries. The women were deep in the house, the men were away to the fields, the animals were turned into the pastures, and only Ottilie was visible, sitting on the steps of the back porch peeling potatoes. She gazed in my direction with eyes that fell short of me, and seemed to focus on a point midway between us, and gave no sign. Then she dropped her knife and rose, her mouth opened and closed several times, she strained toward me, motion-ing with her right hand. I went to her, her hands came out and clutched my sleeve, and for a moment I feared to hear her voice. There was no sound from her, but she drew me along after her, full of some mysterious purpose of her own. She opened the door of a dingy bitter-smelling room, windowless, which opened off the kitchen, beside the closet where Hatsy took her baths. A lumpy narrow cot and chest of drawers supporting a blistered looking-glass almost filled the space. Ottilie's lips moved, struggling for speech, as she pulled and tumbled over a heap of rubbish in the top drawer. She took out a photograph and put it in my hands. It was in the old style, faded to a dirty yellow, mounted on cardboard elaborately clipped and gilded at the edges.

I saw a girl child about five years old, a pretty smiling German baby, looking curiously like a slightly elder sister of Annetje's two-year-old, wearing a frilled frock and a prodigious curl of blonde hair, called a roach, on the crown of her head. The strong legs, round as sausages, were encased in long white ribbed stockings, and the square firm feet were laced into old-fashioned soft-soled black boots. Ottilie peered over the picture, twisted her neck, and looked up into my face. I saw the slanted water-blue eyes and the high cheekbones of the Müllers again, mutilated, almost destroyed, but unmistakable. This child was what she had been, and she was without doubt the elder sister of Annetje and Gretchen and Hatsy; in urgent pantomime she insisted that this was so—she patted the picture and her own face, and strove terribly to speak. She pointed to the name written carefully on the back, Ottilie, and touched her mouth with her bent knuckles. Her head wagged in her perpetual nod; her shaking hand seemed to flap the photograph at me in a roguish humor. The bit of cardboard connected her at once somehow to the world of human beings I knew; for an instant some filament lighter than cobweb spun itself out between that living center in her and in me, a filament from some center that held us all bound to our unescapable common source, so that her life and mine were kin, even a part of each other, and the painfulness and strangeness of her vanished. She knew well that she had been Ottilie, with those steady legs and watching eyes, and she was Ottilie still within herself. For a moment, being alive, she knew she suffered, for she stood and shook with silent crying, smearing away her tears with the open palm of her hand. Even while her cheeks were wet, her face changed. Her eyes cleared and fixed themselves upon that point in space which seemed for her to contain her unaccountable and terrible troubles. She turned her head as if she had heard a voice and disappeared in her staggering run into the kitchen, leaving the drawer open and the photograph face downward on the chest.

At midday meal she came hurrying and splashing coffee on the white floor, restored to her own secret existence of perpetual amazement, and again I had been a stranger to her like all the rest but she was no stranger to me, and could not be again.

The youngest brother came in, holding up an opossum he had

caught in his trap. He swung the furry body from side to side, his eyes fairly narrowed with pride as he showed us the mangled creature. "No, it is cruel, even for the wild animals," said gentle Annetje to me, "but boys love to kill, they love to hurt things. I am always afraid he will trap poor Kuno." I thought privately that Kuno, a wolfish, ungracious beast, might well prove a match for any trap. Annetje was full of silent, tender solicitudes. The kittens, the puppies, the chicks, the lambs and calves were her special care. She was the only one of the women who caressed the weanling calves when she set the pans of milk before them. Her child seemed as much a part of her as if it were not yet born. Still, she seemed to have forgotten that Ottilie was her sister. So had all the others. I remembered how Hatsy had spoken her name but had not said she was her sister. Their silence about her was, I realized, exactly that—simple forgetfulness. She moved among them as invisible to their imaginations as a ghost. Ottilie their sister was something painful that had happened long ago and now was past and done for; they could not live with that memory or its visible reminder—they forgot her in pure self-defense. But I could not forget her. She drifted into my mind like a bit of weed carried in a current and caught there, floating but fixed, refusing to be carried away. I reasoned it out. The Müllers, what else could they have done with Ottilie? By a physical accident in her childhood she had been stripped of everything but her mere existence. It was not a society or a class that pampered its invalids and the unfit. So long as one lived, one did one's share. This was her place, in this family she had been born and must die; did she suffer? No one asked, no one looked to see. Suffering went with life, suffering and labor. While one lived one worked, that was all, and without complaints, for no one had time to listen, and everybody had his own troubles. So, what else could they have done with Ottilie? As for me, I could do nothing but promise myself that I would forget her, too; and to remember her for the rest of my life.

Sitting at the long table, I would watch Ottilie clattering about in her tormented haste, bringing in that endless food that represented all her life's labors. My mind would follow her into the kitchen where I could see her peering into the great simmering kettles, the crowded oven, her whole body a mere machine of torture. Straight up to the surface of my mind the thought would

come urgently, clearly, as if driving time toward the desired event:
Let it be now, let it be *now*. Not even tomorrow, no, today. Let
her sit down quietly in her rickety chair by the stove and fold those
arms, and let us find her there like that, with her head fallen forward on her knees. She will rest then. I would wait, hoping she
might not come again, ever again, through that door I gazed at
with wincing eyes, as if I might see something unendurable enter
through it. Then she would come, and it was only Ottilie, after all,
in the bosom of her family, and one of its most useful and competent members; and they with a deep right instinct had learned to
live with her disaster on its own terms, and hers; they had accepted
and then made use of what was for them only one more painful
event in a world full of troubles, many of them much worse than
this. So, a step at a time, I followed the Müllers as nearly as I
could in their acceptance of Ottilie, and the use they made of her
life, for in some way that I could not quite explain to myself, I
found great virtue and courage in their steadiness and refusal to
feel sorry for anybody, least of all for themselves.

Gretchen bore her child, a son, conveniently between the hours
of supper and bedtime, one evening of friendly and domestic-
sounding rain. The next day brought neighboring women from
miles around, and the child was bandied about among them as if
he were a new kind of medicine ball. Sedate and shy at dances,
emotional at weddings, they were ribald and jocose at births. Over
coffee and beer the talk grew broad, the hearty gutturals were
swallowed in the belly of laughter; those honest hard-working
wives and mothers saw life for a few hours as a hearty low joke,
and it did them good. The baby bawled and suckled like a young
calf, and the men of the family came in for a look and added their
joyful improprieties.

Cloudy weather drove them home earlier than they had meant
to go. The whole sky was lined with smoky black and grey vapor
hanging in ragged wisps like soot in a chimney. The edges of the
woods turned dull purple as the horizon reddened slowly, then
faded, and all across the sky ran a deep shuddering mumble of
thunder. All the Müllers hurried about getting into rubber boots
and oilcloth overalls, shouting to each other, making their plan of
action. The youngest boy came over the ridge of the hill with Kuno

helping him to drive the sheep down into the fold. Kuno was barking, the sheep were baaing and bleating, the horses freed from the ploughs were excited; they whinnied and trotted at the lengths of their halters, their ears laid back. The cows were bawling in distress and the calves cried back to them. All the men went out among the animals to round them up and quiet them and get them enclosed safely. Even as Mother Müller, her half-dozen petticoats looped about her thighs and tucked into her hip boots, was striding to join them in the barns, the cloud rack was split end to end by a shattering blow of lightning, and the cloudburst struck the house with the impact of a wave against a ship. The wind broke the windowpanes and the floods poured through. The roof beams strained and the walls bent inward, but the house stood to its foundations. The children were huddled into the inner bedroom with Gretchen. "Come and sit on the bed with me now," she told them calmly, "and be still." She sat up with a shawl around her, suckling the baby. Annetje came then and left her baby with Gretchen, too; and standing at the doorsteps with one arm caught over the porch rail, reached down into the furious waters which were rising to the very threshold and dragged in a half-drowned lamb. I followed her. We could not make ourselves heard above the cannonade of thunder, but together we carried the creature into the hall under the stairs, where we rubbed the drowned fleece with rags and pressed his stomach to free him from the water and finally got him sitting up with his feet tucked under him. Annetje was merry with triumph and kept saying in delight, "Alive, alive! look!"

We left him there when we heard the men shouting and beating at the kitchen door and ran to open it for them. They came in, Mother Müller among them, wearing her yoke and milk pails. She stood there with the water pouring from her skirts, the three-cornered piece of black oilcloth on her head dripping, her rubber boots wrinkled down with the weight of her petticoats stuffed into them. She and Father Müller stood near each other, looking like two gnarled lightning-struck old trees, his beard and oilcloth garments streaming, both their faces suddenly dark and old and tired, tired once for all; they would never be rested again in their lives. Father Müller suddenly roared at her, "Go get yourself dry clothes. Do you want to make yourself sick?"

"Ho," she said, taking off her milk yoke and setting the pails on the floor. "Go change yourself. I bring you dry socks." One of the boys told me she had carried a day-old calf on her back up a ladder against the inside wall of the barn and had put it safely in the hayloft behind a barricade of bales. Then she had lined up the cows in the stable, and, sitting on her milking stool in the rising water, she had milked them all. She seemed to think nothing of it.

"Hatsy!" she called, "come help with this milk!" Little pale Hatsy came flying barefoot because she had been called in the midst of taking off her wet shoes, her thick yellow and silver braids thumping on her shoulders as she ran. Her new husband followed her, rather shy of his mother-in-law.

"Let me," he said, wishing to spare his dear bride such heavy work, and started to lift the great pails. "No!" shouted Mother Müller, so the poor young man nearly jumped out of his shirt, "not you. The milk is not business for a man." He fell back and stood there with dark rivulets of mud seeping from his boots, watching Hatsy pour the milk into pans. Mother Müller started to follow her husband to attend him, but said at the door, turning back, "Where is Ottilie?", and no one knew, no one had seen her. "Find her," said Mother Müller, going. "Tell her we want supper now."

Hatsy motioned to her husband, and together they tiptoed to the door of Ottilie's room and opened it silently. The light from the kitchen showed them Ottilie, sitting by herself, folded up on the edge of the bed. Hatsy threw the door wide open for more light and called in a high penetrating voice as if to a deaf person or one at a great distance, "Ottilie! Suppertime. We are hungry!", and the young pair left the kitchen to look under the stairway to see how Annetje's lamb was getting on. Then Annetje, Hatsy, and I got brooms and began sweeping the dirty water and broken glass from the floors of the hall and dining room.

The storm lightened gradually, but the flooding rain continued. At supper there was talk about the loss of animals and their replacement. All the crops must be replanted, the season's labor was for nothing. They were all tired and wet, but they ate heartily and calmly, to strengthen themselves against all the labor of repairing and restoring which must begin early tomorrow morning.

By morning the drumming on the roof had almost ceased; from my window I looked upon a sepia-colored plain of water moving

slowly to the valley. The roofs of the barns sagged like the ridge
poles of a tent, and a number of drowned animals floated or were
caught against the fences. At breakfast Mother Müller sat groaning
over her coffee cup. "Ach," she said, "what it is to have such a
pain in the head. Here too," she thumped her chest. "All over.
Ach, Gott, I'm sick." She got up sighing hoarsely, her cheeks
flushed, calling Hatsy and Annetje to help her in the barn.

They all came back very soon, their skirts draggled to the knees,
and the two sisters were supporting their mother, who was speechless and could hardly stand. They put her to bed, where she lay
without moving, her face scarlet. Everybody was confused, no one
knew what to do. They tucked the quilts about her, and she threw
them off. They offered her coffee, cold water, beer, but she turned
her head away. The sons came in and stood beside her, and
joined the cry: *"Mutterchen, Mutti, Mutti,* what can we do? Tell
us, what do you need?" But she could not tell them. It was impossible to ride the twelve miles to town for a doctor; fences and
bridges were down, the roads were washed out. The family
crowded into the room, unnerved in panic, lost unless the sick
woman should come to herself and tell them what to do for her.
Father Müller came in and, kneeling beside her, he took hold of
her hands and spoke to her most lovingly, and when she did not
answer him he broke out crying openly in a loud voice, the great
tears rolling, "Ach, Gott, Gott. A hundert tousand tollars in the
bank"—he glared around at his family and spoke broken English
to them, as if he were a stranger to himself and had forgotten his
own language—"and tell me, tell, what goot does it do?"

This frightened them, and all at once, together, they screamed
and called and implored her in a tumult utterly beyond control.
The noise of their grief and terror filled the place. In the midst of
this, Mother Müller died.

In the midafternoon the rain passed, and the sun was a disc of
brass in a cruelly bright sky. The waters flowed thickly down to the
river, leaving the hill bald and brown, with the fences lying in a
flattened tangle, the young peach trees stripped of bloom and sagging at the roots. In the woods had occurred a violent eruption of
ripe foliage of a jungle thickness, glossy and burning, a massing of
hot peacock green with cobalt shadows.

The household was in such silence, I had to listen carefully to know that anyone lived there. Everyone, even the younger children, moved on tiptoe and spoke in whispers. All afternoon the thud of hammers and the whine of a saw went on monotonously in the barn loft. At dark, the men brought in a shiny coffin of new yellow pine with rope handles and set it in the hall. It lay there on the floor for an hour or so, where anyone passing had to step over it. Then Annetje and Hatsy, who had been washing and dressing the body, appeared in the doorway and motioned: "You may bring it in now."

Mother Müller lay in state in the parlor throughout the night, in her black silk dress with a scrap of white lace at the collar and a small lace cap on her hair. Her husband sat in the plush chair near her, looking at her face, which was very contemplative, gentle, and remote. He wept at intervals, silently, wiping his face and head with a big handkerchief. His daughters brought him coffee from time to time. He fell asleep there toward morning.

The light burned in the kitchen nearly all night, too, and the sound of Ottilie's heavy boots thumping about unsteadily was accompanied by the locust whirring of the coffee mill and the smell of baking bread. Hatsy came to my room. "There's coffee and cake," she said, "you'd better have some," and turned away crying, crumbling her slice in her hand. We stood about and ate in silence. Ottilie brought in a fresh pot of coffee, her eyes bleared and fixed, her gait as aimless-looking and hurried as ever, and when she spilled some on her own hand, she did not seem to feel it.

For a day longer they waited; then the youngest boy went to fetch the Lutheran pastor, and a few neighbors came back with them. By noon many more had arrived, spattered with mud, the horses heaving and sweating. At every greeting the family gave way and wept afresh, as naturally and openly as children. Their faces were drenched and soft with their tears; there was a comfortable relaxed look in the muscles of their faces. It was good to let go, to have something to weep for that nobody need excuse or explain. Their tears were at once a luxury and a cure of souls. They wept away the hard core of secret trouble that is in the heart of each separate man, secure in a communal grief; in sharing it, they consoled each other. For a while they would visit the grave and remember, and then life would arrange itself again in another order, yet it would be the same. Already the thoughts of the living were turning to tomorrow, when they would be at the work of rebuilding and replanting and repairing—even now, today, they would hurry back from the burial to milk the cows and feed the chickens, and they might weep again and again for several days, until their tears could heal them at last.

On that day I realized, for the first time, not death, but the terror of dying. When they took the coffin out to the little country hearse and I saw that the procession was about to form, I went to my room and lay down. Staring at the ceiling, I heard and felt the ominous order and purpose in the movements and sounds below— the creaking harness and hoofbeats and grating wheels, the muted grave voices—and it was as if my blood fainted and receded with fright, while my mind stayed wide awake to receive the awful impress. Yet when I knew they were leaving the yard, the terror began to leave me. As the sounds receded, I lay there not thinking, not feeling, in a mere drowse of relief and weariness.

Through my half-sleep I heard the howling of a dog. It seemed to be a dream, and I was troubled to awaken. I dreamed that Kuno was caught in the trap; then I thought he was really caught, it was no dream and I must wake, because there was no one but me to let him out. I came broad awake, the cry rushed upon me like a wind, and it was not the howl of a dog. I ran downstairs and looked into Gretchen's room. She was curled up around her baby, and they were both asleep. I ran to the kitchen.

Ottilie was sitting in her broken chair with her feet on the edge of the open oven, where the heat had died away. Her hands hung at her sides, the fingers crooked into the palm; her head lay back on her shoulders, and she howled with a great wrench of her body, an upward reach of the neck, without tears. At sight of me she got up and came over to me and laid her head on my breast, and her hands dangled forward a moment. Shuddering, she babbled and howled and waved her arms in a frenzy through the open window over the stripped branches of the orchard toward the lane where the procession had straightened out into formal order. I took hold of her arms where the unnaturally corded muscles clenched and strained under her coarse sleeves; I led her out to the steps and left her sitting there, her head wagging.

In the barnyard there remained only the broken-down spring

wagon and the shaggy pony that had brought me to the farm on the first day. The harness was still a mystery, but somehow I managed to join pony, harness, and wagon not too insecurely, or so I could only hope; and I pushed and hauled and tugged at Ottilie and lifted her until she was in the seat and I had the reins in hand. We careened down the road at a grudging trot, the pony jolting like a churn, the wheels spinning elliptically in a truly broad comedy swagger. I watched the jovial antics of those wheels with attention, hoping for the best. We slithered into round pits of green mud, and jogged perilously into culverts where small bridges had been. Once, in what was left of the main road, I stood up to see if I might overtake the funeral train; yes, there it was, going inchmeal up the road over the little hill, a bumbling train of black beetles crawling helter-skelter over clods.

Ottilie, now silent, was doubled upon herself, slipping loosely on the edge of the seat. I caught hold of her stout belt with my free hand, and my fingers slipped between her clothes and bare flesh, ribbed and gaunt and dry against my knuckles. My sense of her realness, her humanity, this shattered being that was a woman, was so shocking to me that a howl as doglike and despairing as her own rose in me unuttered and died again, to be a perpetual ghost. Ottilie slanted her eyes and peered at me, and I gazed back. The knotted wrinkles of her face were grotesquely changed, she gave a choked little whimper, and suddenly she laughed out, a kind of yelp but unmistakably laughter, and clapped her hands for joy, the grinning mouth and suffering eyes turned to the sky. Her head nodded and wagged with the clownish humor of our trundling lurching progress. The feel of the hot sun on her back, the bright air, the jolly senseless staggering of the wheels, the peacock green of the heavens: something of these had reached her. She was happy and gay, and she gurgled and rocked in her seat, leaning upon me and waving loosely around her as if to show me what wonders she saw.

Drawing the pony to a standstill, I studied her face for a while and pondered my ironical mistake. There was nothing I could do for Ottilie, selfishly as I wished to ease my heart of her; she was beyond my reach as well as any other human reach, and yet, had I not come nearer to her than I had to anyone else in my attempt to deny and bridge the distance between us, or rather, her distance from me? Well, we were both equally the fools of life, equally fellow fugitives from death. We had escaped for one day more at least. We would celebrate our good luck, we would have a little stolen holiday, a breath of spring air and freedom on this lovely, festive afternoon.

Ottilie fidgeted, uneasy at our stopping. I flapped the reins, the pony moved on, we turned across the shallow ditch where the small road divided from the main travelled one. I measured the sun westering gently; there would be time enough to drive to the river down the lane of mulberries and to get back to the house before the mourners returned. There would be plenty of time for Ottilie to have a fine supper ready for them. They need not even know she had been gone.

The Leaning Tower

Early one morning on his sixth day in Berlin, on the twenty-seventh of December, 1931, Charles Upton left his dull little hotel in Hedemanstrasse and escaped to the café across the street. The air of the hotel was mysteriously oppressive to him; a yellow-faced woman and an ill-tempered looking fat man were the proprietors, and they seemed to be in perpetual conspiracy of some sort before open linen closets, in a corner of the dining room, along the halls, or over the account books behind a varnished desk in the lobby. His room was dark, airless, cold, and once when he had supper there, small white worms had come squirming out of the liver sausage on his plate. It was too expensive for him, besides, and he had decided to change. The café was dull, too, but with a look of thrifty cheerfulness, and Charles had pleasant associations with it. He had spent his first Christmas Eve in Europe there, among a small company of amiable noisy people who all seemed, by their conversation, to work in the same factory. No one but the old waiter had spoken to him, but the others talked heartily among themselves in what Charles recognized already as the Berlin accent, blunt, full of a wooden kind of clucking and quacking and explosive hissing. During his voyage on a German boat, the German passengers had taken occasion to praise each his own province in the matter of speech, but not one of them said a good word for Berlin in the matter, not even the Berliners themselves. Charles, who had learned his German partly from textbooks, partly from phonograph records, a little from listening to the Germans in his native town, heard with pleasure the tough speech,

436

drank his beer slowly, the good dark beer that already had spoiled his taste for any other, and rather determinedly began to persuade himself that he had not made a mistake. Yes, Germany was the right place for him, Berlin was the city, Kuno had been right and would be glad if he could know his friend was here at last.

He had thought, fitfully, of Kuno all that Christmas Eve, instead of his parents, who wrote long letters timed to reach him at the holiday saying how gloomy they would be without him. He had sent them a cable and had meant to think of them constantly, but he had not. Again, sitting in the café in the morning, with a map of the city and a pamphlet for tourists containing a list of pensions with prices, he found himself remembering Kuno in rather sudden, unexpected pictures, even seeing himself as he was then, and these flashes of memory came against still other flashes, and back somewhere in the dark of his mind was the whole story, whatever it was. He and Kuno did not remember when they had not known each other. Their first recollection was of standing next each other in a row of children like themselves, singing, or some such nonsense—it must have been kindergarten. They had lived and had gone to school together in an old small city in Texas settled early by the Spaniards. Mexicans, Spaniards, Germans, and Americans mostly from Kentucky had mingled there more or less comfortably for several generations, and though they were all equally citizens, the Spaniards, who were mainly rich and showy, went back to visit Spain from time to time. The Germans went back to Germany and the Mexicans, who lived mostly by themselves in the old quarter, went back to Mexico when they could afford it. Only the Kentuckians stayed where they were, rarely did any of them even go back to Kentucky, and though Charles heard them talk about the place often and lovingly, it seemed farther away and less desirable than Germany, because Kuno went there with his parents.

Though Kuno's mother was said to be a Baroness in Germany, in Texas she was the wife of a prosperous merchant, a furniture dealer. The Kentuckians, who were gradually starving on the land, thought the land the only honorable means to a living, unless one entered a profession; and Charles, whose family made their living, such as it was, from a blackland farm, wondered at the pride with which Kuno would lead him past his father's shop windows to show him the latest display of fashionable, highly polished and stuffed furniture. Looking through the broad clear window into the depths of the shop, Mr. Hillentafel, Kuno's father, could be seen dimly, pencil behind his ear, in his black alpaca coat, his head inclined attentively before a customer. Charles, used to seeing his father on horseback, or standing about the barns with the Negroes, looking at the animals, or walking the fields in his big boots, or riding on the cast iron seat of a plow or harrow, felt he would have been ashamed to see his father in a store, following someone about trying to sell him something. The only time he had ever felt like fighting with Kuno was after Kuno had returned from the second visit to Germany, when they were both about eight years old. Kuno one day spoke contemptuously of farmers, calling them a name in German which Charles did not understand. "They're as good as storekeepers," Charles said in a fury. "Your papa's just a storekeeper." Kuno had shouted back, "My mother is a Baroness, and we were all born in Germany, so we would be Germans. In Germany only low-down people work on farms."

"Well, if you are German, why don't you go and live there?" Charles had shouted back, and Kuno had said very proudly, "There is a big war there, and they wanted to keep my mama and my papa and all of us there, but we had to come back." Kuno then began to explain in a mystified way how they almost hadn't got back; they had almost got locked up in a prison somewhere, but some big important people came and got them out, and in the exciting but confused tale which followed, Charles forgot his quarrel with Kuno. "It was because my mother is a Baroness," Kuno said. "That is why we got away."

But after the war, Mr. Hillentafel took his family back to Germany for a few months every two years, and Kuno's postcards, with their foreign stamps, coming from far-off places like Bremen and Wiesbaden and Mannheim and Heidelberg and Berlin, had brought the great world across the sea, the blue silent deep world of Europe, straight to Charles' door. When he returned, Kuno always had new, odd but serious-looking clothes. He brought fascinating mechanical toys; and later, neckties of strange rich material, coats with stitched pockets, and blunt-toed thick shoes of light brown leather, all made by hand, he said. Kuno would say in the little accent he always brought back and which took several weeks to wear off, "No, but if you don't go to Berlin, you miss everything. We waste time always in those horrid little places, Mannheim and so on, we have to visit with our dull relatives, of course, they are stuck to the necks there, but in Berlin . . ." and he would talk for hours about Berlin until Charles in his imagination saw it as a great shimmering city of castles towering in misty light. How had he got such an image? Kuno had said only, "The streets are polished like a table top and they are as wide as—" he would measure with his eye the street they were walking in, a very narrow crooked dirty little street in an old colonial Spanish city— "oh, five times as wide as this. And the buildings—" he would glance up, disgust in his face for the flat roofs lowering over them —"they are all of stone and marble and are carved, carved all over, with pillars and statues everywhere and staircases wider than a house, winding . . ."

"My father says," Charles said once, trying to keep abreast of all this knowledge of grandeur, "in Mexico the horses have silver bridles."

"I don't believe it," said Kuno, "and if they do, it's nonsense. Who would be so silly as to bridle a horse with silver? But in Berlin, there are marble houses carved all over with roses, loops of roses . . ."

"That sounds silly too," said Charles, but feebly, because it did not sound silly at all, any more than did the silver bridles on the horses of Mexico. Those things were what he would like, what he most longed to see, and he said, easily, "I'll go there too, some day."

Kuno played the violin, and went twice a week to a stern old German teacher who cracked him over the head with a bow when he made mistakes; and his parents forced him to practice three hours every day. Charles wanted to paint and draw, but his parents thought he wasted time at it when he could have been doing something useful, like studying, so he merely scratched around with charcoal on odd sheets of paper, or dabbled for hours in some retired spot with brushes that shed hairs in his poorly equipped paint boxes. On the fourth or fifth voyage to Germany, when Kuno was about fifteen, he died there and was buried in Wiesbaden. His parents, bringing back, beside the elder brother and sister, a new baby, the second within Charles' memory, were very silent on the subject. They were all fair, tall, lightboned, rather lifeless people, and Charles, who had no friendship with any of them but Kuno, hardly saw them or thought of them any more.

Charles, sitting in the café, trying to put his mind on the necessity for beginning a search for a cheaper room, thought, If it hadn't been for Kuno I should never have come here. I would have gone to Paris, or to Madrid. Maybe I should have gone to Mexico. That's a good place for painters. . . . This is not right. There is something wrong with the shapes, or the light, or something. . . .

His father had been to Mexico when he was young and had told Charles long stories, but Charles had never listened to him as he had to Kuno. So here he was, trying to be a painter, even believing by now that he was really going to be a good one, and he had come, as he believed, on a reasoned decision strictly his own. In his new, vague, almost shapeless misgivings, his half-acknowledged disappointment in the place—what was it?—he began to understand that he had come to Berlin because Kuno had made it seem the one desirable place to be. He hardly ever thought of Kuno any more, or had not for a long time, except simply as dead, though that went on being hard to believe; still it was just those colored postcards of Kuno's and those stories, and the way Kuno had felt then, and had made him feel, that had brought him here. Soberly facing facts, he decided that wasn't enough reason, not half enough. But still he decided also to stay, if he possibly could.

It would be four days until New Year's, and Charles began to think seriously about money. The next boat would bring him a check from his father, who had decided, in a kind of mixed despair and pride in his son's talent, to help him. Charles, keeping accounts in a book, had resolved it should all be repaid. The editor of a small art magazine was publishing a series of his drawings, and was going to pay for them. If these failed, he saw clearly that even beer for his New Year's celebration would be out of the question. Still, at one time or another, the sooner the better, there would be a boat coming from America, and it would bring him money, not much, but enough to keep him going. Meantime, he thought of his expensive camera, which a Kentucky aunt had given him, and decided instantly to pawn it. He also had his grandfather's big gold watch. Why, he was rich. This settled, the question went out of his mind, except for a faint uneasiness as to where his money had gone. In the days before Christmas he had dropped, rather carelessly, without counting, small change into the hats and outspread handkerchiefs of the men along the streets, who were making the most of their holiday licenses to beg. Some of them begged in orderly groups, singing carols familiar to him from the days when his parents took him to the German Singing Society at home: "Heilige Nacht," "O Tannenbaum," Martin Luther's "Cradle Song," in the familiar singing society voices, even, full, melodious. They had stood there with their ragged shoes sunk in the slushy snow, starving and blue-nosed, singing in their mourning voices, accepting coins with grave nods, keeping their eyes fixed on each other as they beat time softly with their hands.

Others stood alone, and these the most miserable, each man isolated in his incurable misfortune. Those blinded or otherwise mutilated in the war wore a certain band on their sleeves to prove that they had more than any others earned the right to beg, and merited special charity. Charles, with his almost empty pockets, nothing in them except the future, which he felt he owned, saw a tall young man so emaciated his teeth stood out in ridges under the mottled tight skin of his cheeks, standing at the curb with a placard around his neck which read: "I will take any work you can offer." Almost furtively, Charles slipped a mark into the limp hollowed palm, then stepped into the doorway near by, and sheltered by fir trees piled before a shop, their sweet odor in his nostrils, with cold fingers he sketched hastily the stiff figure in its abject garments, surmounted by that skull of famine.

He walked on thinking it would be a relief when the necessity for appearing to celebrate something was over, remembering with the present smell of freshly cut fir the smell of apples along the curbs of New York streets, while he was roaming about the picture galleries waiting for his boat. Men stood shivering by the fruit, or patrolled the sidewalks, saying, "Brother, can you spare a dime?" The saying had become famous, a catchword, at once. Then almost overnight the whole thing had become simply a picturesque aspect of the times, a piece of local color, a current fad. Even if the plight of the men was real, it was not going to last; the breadlines were only temporary, the newspapers insisted, and gave strange wonderful far-fetched reasons for the situation, as if it had been a phenomenon of nature, like an earthquake, or a cloudburst. Here, Charles could see, the misery was acknowledged as real and the sufferers seemed to know they had no reason for hope. There was none of the raffish manner of the apple-sellers, but just complete hopelessness and utter endurance. . . . Yet back of them the windows along Kurfürstendamm and Unter den Linden were filled with fine wools and furs and overcoats and great shining motor cars. Charles, walking and gazing, compared them with the New York windows back of the apple sellers and the beggars. They were by no means so fine, but where were the buyers? In New York the buyers streamed gaily in and out of shops, dropping dimes into extended hands. Here, a few dully dressed persons stood and stared, but when he glanced in, the shops were almost empty. The streets were full of young people, lean and tough, boys and girls alike dressed in leather jackets or a kind of uniform blue ski suit, who whizzed about the streets on bicycles without a glance at the windows. Charles saw them carrying skis on their shoulders, shouting and laughing in groups, getting away to the mountains over the weekend. He watched them enviously; maybe if he stayed on long enough he would know some of them, he would be riding a bicycle and going away for the skiing, too. It seemed unlikely, though.

He would wander on, and the thicker the crowd in which he found himself, the more alien he felt himself to be. He had watched a group of middle-aged men and women who were gathered in silence before two adjoining windows, gazing silently at displays of toy pigs and sugar pigs. These persons were all strangely of a kind, and strangely the most prevalent type. The streets were full of them—enormous waddling women with short legs and ill-humored faces, and round-headed men with great rolls of fat across the backs of their necks, who seemed to support their swollen bellies with an effort that drew their shoulders forward. Nearly all of them were leading their slender, overbred, short-legged dogs in pairs on fancy leashes. The dogs wore their winter clothes: wool sweaters, fur ruffs, and fleece-lined rubber boots. The creatures whined and complained and shivered, and their owners lifted them up tenderly to show them the pigs.

In one window there were sausages, hams, bacon, small pink chops; all pig, real pig, fresh, smoked, salted, baked, roasted, pickled, spiced, and jellied. In the other were dainty artificial pigs, almond paste pigs, pink sugar chops, chocolate sausages, tiny hams and bacons of melting cream streaked and colored to the very life. Among the tinsel and lace paper, at the back were still other kinds of pigs: plush pigs, black velvet pigs, spotted cotton pigs, metal and wooden mechanical pigs, all with frolicsome curled tails and appealing infant faces.

With their nervous dogs wailing in their arms, the people, shameless mounds of fat, stood in a trance of pig worship, gazing with eyes damp with admiration and appetite. They resembled the most unkind caricatures of themselves, but they were the very kind of people that Holbein and Dürer and Urs Graf had drawn, too: not vaguely, but positively like, their late-medieval faces full of hallucinated malice and a kind of sluggish but intense cruelty that worked its way up from their depths slowly through the layers of helpless gluttonous fat.

The thin snow continued to fall and whiten rounded shoulders and lumpy hat brims. Charles, feeling the flakes inside his collar, had walked on with intention to get away from the spectacle which struck him as revolting. He had walked on into Friedrichstrasse, where, in the early evening, the thin streetwalkers came out and moved rather swiftly in the middle of the pavement, and though they all appeared to be going somewhere, they never left each one her own certain fixed station. They seemed quite unapproachable to Charles in their black lace skirts and high gilded heels, their feathered hats and grease paint. On his first evening in Berlin a young unsmiling one had spoken to him, inviting him without enthusiasm to come with her. He had stammered a phrase which he hoped meant, "I haven't time now," fearing that she would insist. She had given him a serious, appraising glance, saw, to his shame, that the market was no good, and had turned away with an indifferent, "Well, good evening." At home, his adventures had all been with girls he knew, and the element of chance had always been present. Any given occasion might go off very well, and it might not; he felt he had learned a lot from what he described to himself as the block and tackle, balance and check, trial and error method. These reserved-looking professional women, almost as regimented as soldiers in uniform, roused in him uneasy curiosity and distrust. He hoped quite constantly he was going to meet some gay young girls, students perhaps; there seemed to be plenty of them about, but not one had given him the eye yet. He had stopped in a doorway and hastily jotted a few broad-bottomed figures, sagging faces, and dressed pigs, in his notebook. He sketched a specially haggard and frustrated looking streetwalker with a preposterous tilt to her feathered hat. He tried at first not to be seen at his occupation, but discovered soon that he need not worry, for, in fact, nobody noticed him.

These rather scattered impressions were in his mind and he was very dissatisfied with all of them as he folded up his map and pamphlet and set out walking to find a room in Berlin. In the first dozen squares he counted five more of those rather sick-looking young men with fresh wounds in their cheeks, long heavy slashes badly mended with tape and cotton, and thought again that nobody had told him to expect that.

Two days later he was still tramping the snowy streets, ringing doorbells and crawling back to the little hotel in the evenings pretty well dead on his feet. On the morning of the third day, when his search brought him finally to the third floor of a solid looking apartment house in Bambergerstrasse, he took pains to observe very attentively the face of the woman who opened the door. In such a short time he had learned a wholesome terror of landladies in that city. They were smiling foxes, famished wolves, slovenly house cats, mere tigers, hyenas, furies, harpies: and sometimes worst of all they were sodden melancholy human beings who carried the history of their disasters in their faces, who all but wept when they saw him escape, as if he carried their last hope with him. Except for four winters in a minor southern university, Charles had lived at home. He had never looked for a lodging before, and he felt guilty, as if he had been peeping through cracks and keyholes, spying upon human inadequacy, its kitchen smells and airless bedrooms, the staleness of its poverty and the stuffiness of its prosperity. He had been shown spare cubbyholes back of kitchens where the baby's wash was drying on a string while the desolate room waited for a tenant. He had been ushered into regions of gilded carving and worn plush, full of the smell of yesterday's cabbage. He had ventured into bare expanses of glass brick and chrome-steel sparsely set out with white leather couches and mirror-topped tables, where, it always turned out, he would be expected to stay for a year at least, at frightening expense. He peered into a sodden little den fit, he felt, only for the scene of a murder;

and into another where a sullen young woman was packing up, and the whole room reeked of some nasty perfume from her underwear piled upon the bed. She had given him a deliberately dirty smile, and the landlady had said something in a very brutal tone to her. But mostly, there was a stuffy tidiness, a depressing air of constant and unremitting housewifery, a kind of repellent gentility in room after room after room, varying only in the depth of feather bed and lavishness of draperies, and out of them all in turn he fled back to the street and the comparative freedom of the air.

The woman who opened the door presently, he saw, was a fairly agreeable looking person of perhaps fifty years or more—above a certain age they all looked alike to Charles—with a pinkish face, white hair and very lively light blue eyes. She gave the impression of being dressed up, she had a little high-faluting manner which seemed harmless and she was evidently very pleased to see him. He noticed that the hall was almost empty but highly polished, perhaps here was the perfect compromise between overstuffed plush and a rat trap.

The landlady showed him her best room, the only one unoccupied, she explained. He might be glad to know she had only young gentlemen in the house, three in fact, she hoped he might make a fourth. "I have here," she said with pride, "a young student from the University of Berlin, a young pianist, and a young student from Heidelberg on leave, so you see the company will not be so bad. May I ask your profession?"

"I am a kind of painter," said Charles, hopefully.

"Charming," said the landlady. "We lacked only an artist."

"I hope you will excuse my poor German," said Charles, a little overwhelmed by all the high manner.

"You will learn," said the landlady, smiling graciously as a mother, and added, "I am Viennese, which accounts perhaps for any little difference you may notice between my speech and that which you hear ordinarily in Berlin. I may say, the Viennese way of talking is not the worst in the world, if you really wish to learn German while you are here."

The room. Well, the room. He had seen it several times before in his search. It was not what he would choose if he had a choice, but it was the least tiresome example of what he recognized now as a fixed style, with its sober rich oriental carpet, the lace curtains under looped-back velvet hangings, the large round table covered with another silky oriental rug in sweet, refined colors. One corner was occupied by deep couches heaped with silk and velvet cushions, the wall above it adorned with a glass-doored cabinet filled with minute curiosities mostly in silver filigree and fine porcelain, and upon the table stood a huge lamp with an ornate pink silk shade, fluted and fringed and draped with silken tassels. The bed was massive with feather quilt and shot-silk cover, the giant wardrobe of dark polished wood was carved all out of shape.

A hell of a place, really, but he would take it. The landlady looked human, and the price was no higher than he would be asked anywhere else for such a monstrosity. She agreed at once that he would need a plain work table and a student lamp, and added, "I hope you expect to stay for six months."

"I'm sorry," said Charles, who had been waiting for this. "Only three months."

The landlady concealed her disappointment unsuccessfully in a sweet little smile. "It is usual to agree for six months," she told him.

"But I am going to another country in three months," said Charles.

"Oh, really? Where are you going?" she asked, and her whole face lighted as if the prospect of travel were her own.

"To Italy, perhaps," said Charles. "First to Rome and then to Florence. And then all over Europe," he added recklessly, feeling certain for the first time that this was really true, it was bound to happen.

"Oh, Italy," cried the landlady. "I spent the three happiest months of my life there, I have dreamed of going back."

Charles was standing near the table. On the silk rug, near the lamp, there stood a small plaster replica, about five inches high, of the Leaning Tower of Pisa. As they talked, his hand wandered towards it, he picked it up lightly by the middle with his finger tips, and the delicate plaster ribs caved in. They simply crumbled at his touch, and the fragments dropped around the weighted base as he snatched back his hand. He saw in horror that the landlady had gone very pale, her blue eyes instantly suffused.

Charles' self-possession crumbled with the tower. He stammered, "Oh, I'm so sorry," seeing that to the landlady the accident was serious and feeling himself shamefully exposed before her in his proved and demonstrated clumsiness, the aimless wandering curiosity of his mind, his bad habit of pawing things. Why couldn't he have kept his hands to himself? "Please allow me to replace it."

"It cannot be replaced," said the landlady, with a severe, stricken dignity. "It was a souvenir of the Italian journey. My husband and I brought it back as a pleasantry from our honeymoon. My husband has been dead for many years. No, the little tower is not a thing that can be replaced."

Charles, wishing to escape with his humiliation into the open air, said, "Perhaps I had better go for my luggage. I will be back in an hour."

"Yes," she said, absently, gathering up the ruins bit by bit on a sheet of paper. "My only hope is, it may be repaired."

"Do please let me pay for that, at least," said Charles. "I am so very sorry."

"It is not your fault, but mine," said the landlady, "I should never have left it here for—" She stopped short, and walked away carrying the paper in her two cupped hands. For barbarians, for outlandish crude persons who have no respect for precious things, her face and voice said all too clearly.

Charles, red and frowning, moved warily around the furniture towards the windows. A bad start, a very bad start indeed. The double panes were closed tightly, the radiator cast an even warmth through the whole room. He drew the lace curtains and saw, in the refracted pallor of the midmorning, winter light, a dozen infant-sized pottery cupids, gross, squat limbed, wanton in posture and vulgarly pink, with scarlet feet and cheeks and backsides, engaged in what appeared to be a perpetual scramble to avoid falling off the steep roof of a house across the street. Charles observed grimly their realistic toe holds among the slate, their clutching fat hands, their imbecile grins. In pouring rain, he thought, they must keep up their senseless play. In snow, their noses would be completely buried. Their behinds were natural victims to the winter winds. And to think that whoever had put them there had meant them to be oh, so whimsical and so amusing, year in, year out. He clutched his hat and overcoat with a wild impulse to slip out quietly and disappear. Maybe he wouldn't come back at all. He hadn't signed or paid anything yet. Oh, yes, but he would, though. For the land-lady appeared at once, again smiling and composed, carrying a card, a slip of paper with printing on it, pen, ink, and her receipt blanks, all on a silver tray. He did not escape without leaving on that tray a full report of himself for the benefit of the police, a signed agreement to keep the room for three months, and a month's rent in marks, instead of dollars. "What a pity you have no dollars," she said brightly, and tilted her head at him in a brave gesture of acceptance. On her left hand she wore a rather inordi-nate diamond, square and blue, obviously a very fine one, set elabo-rately at great height. He had not noticed it before.

The sallow wornout looking hotel proprietess greeted him with an almost pleasant expression when he approached her desk. He was surprised at the violent change in her face when he explained that he had found another room and would be leaving at once. Instantly she seemed ready to weep with anger and disappointment.

"But I do not understand," she told him stiffly, her lids redden-ing. "You agree to stay for a month, I give you very special rates, and now in eight days you are saying you must go. Do you find us disagreeable, perhaps? Isn't your room cared for properly? What has happened?"

"It is simply true that I must find something less expensive still," he told her, carefully. "That is all."

"But our charges here are most reasonable," she said, her dry mouth working over her long teeth. "Why will you not stay?"

"They are reasonable," he admitted, feeling cornered, and as if he were making a humiliating confession, "but I cannot afford them."

The woman opened her account book and began copying from it rapidly, her face stiff with indignation as if she had caught him snatching her purse. "That is your own business," she told him, in a low voice, "but naturally you must expect to pay by the day, in this case."

"Naturally," he agreed.

"You will find you cannot change your mind for nothing," said the woman, in a severe, lecturing tone. "Indecision is a very expen-sive luxury."

"I suppose so," said Charles, uneasily watching the notations on the sheet of paper lengthening rapidly.

She glanced up and over his shoulder, and Charles saw her face change again to a hard boldness, she raised her voice sharply and said with insolence, "You will pay your bill as I present it or I shall call the police."

Charles, who had his money in hand ready to pay what she asked, believed for an instant he had not understood properly. Turning in the direction of her glance, he saw standing a few feet away the middle-aged podgy partner. His head was like a soft block, covered with scanty gray bristles. Hands in pockets he was eyeing Charles with a peculiarly malignant smile on his wide lipless mouth. Charles, amazed at the sum written at the foot of the page, counted out the money to the last pfennig, suddenly afraid that if he gave her a round sum she would not give him back the change. She swept it away from him, together with the bill, without speaking.

"Will you please give me the receipt?" asked Charles.

She did not answer, but moved away a little, and the man approached silently and said in a voice of edged, false courtesy, "I must require you, before you go, to let me see your papers."

Charles said, "I showed them when I came here," and picked up his suitcases.

"But not to me," said the man, and his pale little eyes behind their puffy lids were piggish with malice. "Not to me, I am sorry to say, and that will be necessary before you are allowed to go, let me assure you."

He seemed struggling with some hidden excitement. His neck swelled and flushed, he closed his mouth until it was a mere slit across his face, and rocked slightly on his toes. Charles had been well prepared for the nuisance of being under constant observation, experienced travelers had told him he would feel like a criminal on parole in Europe, especially in Germany, at first, but that he would soon grow accustomed to it, and he was to be certain to hand his papers over at once to anyone who asked for them. He set his suitcases down and felt in his pockets, then remembered he had tucked the flat leather case containing his papers in one of his suitcases. Which one?

He opened the larger of the two, exposing a huddle of untidy clothing. The man and the woman leaned forward to gaze at his belongings, and the woman said, "So," in a contemptuous voice.

Charles, in outraged silence, closed the suitcase and opened the other. He handed the leather case to the man, who drew out the passports and other papers one by one with maddening slowness, regarded them with a skeptical eye, puffing his cheeks and clicking his tongue by turns. With deliberation he handed them back and said, "Very good. You may go now," with the insulting condescension of a petty official dismissing a subordinate.

They continued to look at him in a hateful silence, with their faces almost comically distorted in an effort to convey the full depths of their malice. It was as if they doubted, from his manner, that he had understood the extent to which they were insulting and cheating him, or as if, being safe in their advantage, they wished to goad him to protest so they might do him further damage. Awkwardly under their fixed stare, Charles returned his papers to the suitcase, closed it with difficulty after some trouble with the fastenings. As the door closed behind him he heard them laughing together like a pair of hyenas, with deliberate loudness, to make certain he should hear them.

He felt all at once rather too poor to afford a taxicab, so he walked, lugging his rather battered possessions, and as their weight increased and the distance stretched before him, he meditated rather shapelessly on the treatment he had just received. He was a tall, personable young man, there was nothing wrong with his looks or his intentions, though at that moment, a trifle beetle-browed, hat over eyes, he seemed sullen and rather ugly. His first furious impulse to hit the fat man in the teeth with his fist had been overcome instantly by the clear cold spot in his mind which knew that this situation was hopeless, there was no chance for any sort of reparation, he could either keep quiet and escape from the two thugs or quite simply he would be in worse trouble. His anger remained and settled, took root and became a new part of him.

His landlady opened the door for him again. He observed there seemed to be no servant about the place. After a few more formalities of greeting, restlessly he took to the street again, telling himself he needed a haircut. Consulting his map, he bore towards Kurfürstendamm. The sun had disappeared, it was colder suddenly, the snow began to fall again on the smooth dark streets gleaming in the light like polished metal. The weighty laborious city was torpid in the early darkness.

The barber shop was small and clean, wrapped in white towels, shining with mirrors and full of warm soapy steam. A weakly shaped, bloodless little man took him in hand and began to tuck cloths around his neck. He had scanty discouraged hair the color of tow, and a sickly, unpleasant breath. He wanted to cut Charles' hair long on top, clip it to the skin around the back of his head in a wide swath over the ears. His own was cut that way, the streets were full of such heads, and a photograph, clipped from a newspaper and stuck in the corner of the mirror, showed a little shouting politician, top lock on end, wide-stretched mouth adorned by a square mustache, who had, apparently, made the style popular. It required a great deal of head shaking, rather desperately assembled German, some pointing to other photographs in a barber's journal of fashion, to persuade the man to a more reasonable point of view.

The barber, sad enough at his gayest, drooped rather more as he tapered Charles' hair almost imperceptibly towards the neck; and to change the whole topic he spoke of the weather. The last day or two had been mild, even milder than anyone thought, for it had deceived the storks. The papers that morning had mentioned that storks had been seen flying over the city, certain signs of good weather and an early spring. Had the young gentleman noticed a dispatch from New York that said the trees in Central Park were putting out green buds—imagine, at this time of year.

"There is nothing in the Tiergarten at this time," said the little barber, sighing. "This is a dark place in winter. I lived in Malaga once, I worked there in a barber shop for a whole year—nearly thirteen months, in fact. The barber shops there are not like ours, they are very dirty, but there, flowers were in bloom outside, in December. There, they use real almond oil for their hair lotions— real. And they have such an extract of rosemary as you cannot find anywhere else. Olive oil the poorer people use for their hair, as well as for cookery. Olive oil, imagine, here so expensive, there they pour it out on their heads. Olive oil, they told me, inside and out, that is what makes hair grow. Well, maybe. Here, everyone wants his hair dry, and mostly," he returned to the hateful subject, "they like it close above the ears and full on top. Say it is only our poor German taste," he said sourly, and then, "In Malaga, I never wore my topcoat all winter. Ah, I hardly knew it was winter." His fingers were clammy and his front teeth looked weak, as if they had never got a proper start. "It was strange there in many ways, naturally, considering the kind of people they are, but then they did not have to worry so much about living. Sometimes, there, I put my hand in my pocket and felt my last peseta, but I was not alarmed as I would have been here. I thought that when that was gone I could get more. I should have saved something there," he said, with a guilty look, "but I did not, and here I save and save, but there is nothing." He coughed, turning his head away. "In Malaga," he said, and he was like a man talking about a homeland he had lost, "I never had a cough, though here I cough all the time."

"Flu?" asked Charles, through the towels.

"No, gas," said the little barber, modestly. "The war."

After a dismal pause, Charles said, "I noticed the other day that Malaga froze stiff too, this winter."

"Well, yes, once perhaps, but only for a few days," admitted the barber, shaking his head slowly. "Once, perhaps—"

When Charles felt carefully in his pocket for the smallest coin he could give, uneasy because he knew it was not enough, but all at once unnerved by caution, not daring to reduce his cash store by a single pfennig more than necessary, the barber held out his bluish narrow hand, glanced discreetly into the palm, smiled and said with genuine feeling, "Thank you, thank you very much." Charles nodded his head, in shame, and hurried away.

The knob turned from within and the door flew open as Charles was bending, key in hand, and the landlady fluted at him sweetly. She had been expecting him, she had wondered what was keeping him, she had happened to be in the hall and had heard his step on the stair. She believed she had him nicely settled now, and at what hour would he have his afternoon coffee? Charles said he supposed five o'clock would be all right. "So," she said, smiling and tilting her head at him with what struck Charles as a slightly too intimate, possessive gleam. Still smiling, she hurried away to the farther end of the hall and rapped sharply at a closed door.

It was opened at once, and Charles got a full glimpse of a drooping heavy-set dark young man with a big cropped head and blunt features. The landlady went straight past him, talking in a rapid authoritative tone as if she were giving orders. Charles closed his own door with some relief and looked around for his luggage. It had disappeared. He glanced into the big wardrobe and saw with a peculiar sense of invasion that his things were unpacked—he had long since lost the keys and had never got into the habit of locking things, anyway—and arranged with an orderliness that exposed all their weaknesses of quality and condition. His shoes, needing minor repairs and a coat of polish, were set in wooden supports. His other two suits, the tweed with its buttons hanging, were on silk padded frames. His meager toilet articles, his frayed hair brushes and his flabby leather cases were in array on the middle shelf. Conspicuous among them, looking somehow disreputable, was his quart bottle of brandy, a third empty, and he realized that he had in effect taken to secret drinking during his search for a room. He peered into the lumpy laundry bag hanging on a hook, and shuddered with masculine shame. Its snowy sweet-smelling whiteness concealed his socks that needed darning, his soiled shirts worn too long for economy's sake, and his stringy underwear. On the pillow of his bed, half concealing the long effeminate lace pillow ruffles, lay a pair of neatly folded clean pajamas.

Last effrontery of all, the woman had unpacked his papers and his drawing material and his cardboard folders of unfinished work. Had she looked into them? He hoped she had a good time. A great many of his sketches were not meant for publication. Everything was laid out carefully stacked with a prime regard for neatness and a symmetrical appearance. He had noticed before the strange antagonism of domesticated females for papers. They seemed to look upon papers as an enemy of order, mere dust-catching nuisances. At home he had waged perpetual silent warfare with his mother and the servants about his papers. They wanted to straighten them out, or better, hide them away in the deepest shelves of a closet. Why in God's name couldn't they let his work alone? But they could not, under their curious compulsion; and neither could this woman, that was clear. Consulting his little phrase book, he began constructing and memorizing a polite sentence beginning, "Please don't trouble yourself about my table . . ."

The table was large, though not plain, the lamp was good enough, but the straight-backed chair was a delicate affair with curved spindle legs and old mended tapestry in seat and back: a museum piece beyond doubt, Charles decided, and sat upon it experimentally. It held up. He proposed to overlook and forget the whole damned situation, put his stuff in order and get to work. First he emptied his pockets of accumulated bits of notes, sketches, receipts, scribbled addresses of restaurants, postcard reproductions of paintings he had bought at museums, and the agreement he had signed to stay in this house for three months. He noticed that the landlady's name was Rosa Reichl, written in a tall, looping, affectedly elegant hand. He could not see the end of those three months. He felt a blind resentment all the more deep because it could have no particular object, and helpless as if he had let himself be misled by bad advice. Vaguely but in the most ghastly sort of way, he felt that someone he trusted had left him in the lurch, and of course, that was nonsense, as Kuno used to say. "Nonsense" was one of Kuno's favorite words, especially just after his returns from abroad.

The voices in the next room were going on, rising and tightening somewhat with an excitement that might be anger. Charles listened carefully with no sense of eavesdropping, as always surprised that he understood German so well and spoke it so poorly.

"Herr Bussen, Herr Bussen," Frau Reichl was crying, in a flighty, impassioned voice, her light Viennese accent slightly blurred, "you treat my good chairs like this, my beautiful old chairs I have had for so long—in spite of my other troubles you must add this? How can you, when you know I shall never have chairs like these again?"

Charles, who had begun testing crayons and sharpening pencils, stopped to light a cigarette, leaning back in his own chair. He balanced on the back legs for a split second and came down with a thump, his heart seeming to turn over as the thin joints complained in a human voice.

Herr Bussen, who began by defending himself half-heartedly, gave in and took his scolding dutifully as if Frau Reichl were his mother or his conscience. Yes, he knew better, Charles heard him saying in heavy Low-German, he had been brought up properly even if she did not think so. His mother had such chairs too, he would not let it happen again. Herr Bussen's speech sounded to Charles like some ungainly English dialect, but in no language would he have been a match for Frau Reichl. Charles found himself feeling very sorry for that poor devil as he blundered on apologizing; she was to excuse him this time if she could.

"Yes, this time," rejoined Frau Reichl, exasperated to a point beyond all grace, "this time," she said sarcastically in her sweetest tones, "and how many others, past and to come?"

Herr Bussen found no answer for this. After a silent moment of triumph, Frau Reichl emerged and swished past Charles' door while he waited uneasily for her to stop before it, and knocked on the door just next his at the right.

"Jawohl!" shouted the young man inside in the drowning voice of one dredged too suddenly out of sleep. "Yes, yes, come in." Then a gay and youthful voice cleared and added, "Oh, it's you, Rosa dear. Well, I thought there must be a fire."

Rosa, is it? thought Charles, hearing their voices running on together, quick and friendly, in lowered tones, with now and again a small duet of good-humored laughter. Rosa seemed very cheerful indeed, moving about the room as she talked, crossing the hall to her own apartment and back several times. At last she said, "Now then, please tell me when you need anything. Only, no more ice. There is no more."

"Who cares?" called the young man, and Rosa laughed again. Charles began to think of her as Rosa, and a nuisance, if affairs went on at this rate all day in the house.

Daylight had failed. Charles settled himself firmly to his drawing under the lamp which was better than he expected. He began with many small anxieties. Suppose that editor changed his mind? Suppose his drawing were not published and paid for, after all? How long could his father continue to send him money? How long, and this was the real question, this was what worried him most, how long should he go on taking money from his father? Should he have come to Europe at all? A lot of good painters had never been in Europe. He tried to think of one. Well, he was here, horribly disturbed and miserable really, he might as well face it, he had got a much harder blow than he expected from the place. At least he must try to find what he came for, if it wasn't to be just a wild goose chase. He refused to listen any further to the sounds in the house, but focused his eyes upon a certain spot on the paper, remembered what he meant to do, and went to work. All his energy seemed to flow and balance in his right hand, he felt steadied and at ease, he belonged to himself and knew what he was doing. Then he forgot himself altogether. Some time later he sat back and looked at what he had done. It wouldn't do, it was absolutely all wrong.

A light rap on the door saved him. He had an excuse to stop, to turn the page over and let it cool off before he looked at it again. Hardly waiting for his word, Rosa came in. She glanced sharply first at the light and then at the table, already in disorder.

"Ah, you need light early, I see," she commented, with an uncertain smile, a deprecating tilt of the head. "As for Herr Bussen, he does not work in the evenings until after supper. And Herr Mey, the Polish gentleman, quite often plays in the dark because he wishes. Our young student from Heidelberg doesn't have anything to think about but his face at this moment, and the less light on that, the better. Ah me, it is a sight. But," she said, fondly and mysteriously, "he is young, it is his first, he will know what to expect the next time. But the wound is infected, you know, he is here for treatment. Ah, the young one," she said, tenderly, clasping her hands over her breast, "he is very brave all day, but when the dark comes, it is very hard for him. He is so young and tender," she told Charles, almost tearful in her pride and pity, "but he did well, you can see. The wound—well, it is a beauty!"

She moved about the room while she talked, straightening the chairs ever so little, giving a flick at the cushions here, a whisk at the curtains there. Standing beside Charles at the table, she even reached round him to take a light turn among his papers, setting up a small commotion by moving his ash tray and the India ink a few inches out of their places. "After all, there is no more daylight," she admitted, finally, "and if you draw, you need light, isn't it true? Now I shall bring your coffee at once," she promised, brightly, and went away with that extraordinarily busy air of hers.

No more daylight. Charles, feeling helpless, as if he were taking part in a play, and had forgotten his lines if he ever knew them, watched the street as he waited, silent under the falling snow, empty in the frosty shimmer of the corner lamps. Lights were coming on one by one in the many windows of the houses opposite.

In the past few days he had watched each morning by lamplight the feeble sun crawl later and later barely to the level of the house-tops, slide slowly around in a shallow arc and drop away in midafternoon. The long nights oppressed him with unreasonable premonitions of danger. The darkness closed over the strange city like the great fist of an enemy who had survived in full strength, a voiceless monster from a prehuman, older and colder and grimmer time of the world. "It is just because I was born in a sunny place and took the summer for granted," he told himself, but that did not explain why he could not endure with patience, even enjoy, even look upon as something new and memorable to see, unfamiliar weather in a foreign climate. Of course it was not the weather. No one paid attention to weather if he had the proper clothes for it; he remembered a teacher of his saying once that all great cities are built in uninhabitable places. He knew that people love even the worst of the climate in the place they know, and can wonder at the feelings of strangers about it. At home in Texas he had seen northern travelers turn upon the southern weather with the ferocity of exhaustion; it gave them the excuse they needed to hate everything else they hated in the place, too. It would be so easy and simple, it would put such an end to the argument to be able to say, "I can't settle down in this place because the sun doesn't rise until ten o'clock in December," but that was not his trouble here.

There were the faces. Faces with no eyes. And these no-eyes, pale, lightless, were set in faces shriveled as if they were gnawed hollow; or worse, faces sodden in fat with swollen eyelids in which the little no-eyes peered blindly as if all the food, the plates of boiled potatoes and pig's knuckles and cabbage fed to the wallowing body, had weighed it down and had done it no good. The no-eyes in the faces of the women were too ready to shed tears. Charles had not understood in the least the first thing that had happened to him in Berlin. He had bought some cheap socks in a little shop. At the hotel he saw they were too small, and had gone back at once to exchange them for a larger size. The woman who had sold them to him saw him coming in with the package in his hand, had remembered him and instantly stood transfixed, the tears welling up in her eyes. While he was trying to explain in awful embarrassment that he merely wished larger socks in place of those she had given him, the tears rolled over her cheeks and she said, "I have no larger size."

"Could you get them for me?" he asked, and she said, "Oh, yes," in such pain that Charles said awkwardly, "Don't bother, I'll keep these," and ran out, annoyed and mystified. A day or two later it was all clear to him and seemed quite natural. She needed badly to sell the stock she had. She could not afford to order just a few pairs of larger socks. She was frightened at seeing the goods she had on hand, unsold, and she had deliberately given him the socks she had already, hoping he could not, a stranger, a traveler, find his way back to complain.

Men who sold wine and fruit in tiny corners did not seem to prosper in their rich and warming commodities, they got no nourishment of their company and obviously they could not afford to enjoy them. These men were silent, usually middle-aged, deeply sullen, and if Charles asked them a question, hearing the foreign voice they would shout out their answer as if in a burst of fury, though the words were harmless. Among themselves they talked in a dead tone of disheartenment that seemed an old habit. With his limited money, he was frightened to go to any place where things were for sale. Because he was poor, he went to poor places, and felt trapped, for they could not let him go until he had bought something. They tried desperately to sell him things he did not want or need, could not use, or could not afford. It was no good trying to explain this to them. They could not hear him.

No more daylight. No more ice. No more chairs with tapestry on them and legs that broke if you leaned back in them. No more of those table rugs with their nasty sweet colors. If the corner whatnot should be knocked over, just once, there would be no more of that silly bric-a-brac and a good thing too, thought Charles, hardening his heart.

"Coffee at last," said Rosa, coming in without knocking this time, carrying a very dressed up tray. No more coffee at five o'clock, unless you were a foreigner, and—it followed naturally— rich. Charles felt he was living under false pretenses of the kind his early training had taught him to despise. "I am poorer than she is," he thought, watching Rosa arrange the fine porcelain cup with butterfly handle, and spread out thin napery. "But of course not. A boat is coming from America for me, but there is no boat for her. For nobody in this house but me is a boat coming from America, with money. I can get along here, I can leave when I like, I can always go home—"

He felt young, ignorant, awkward, he had so much to learn he hardly knew where to begin. He could always go home, but that was not the point. It was a long way home from where he stood, he could see that. No more Leaning Tower of Pisa, he remembered with guilt, when Rosa, with a last little fussy pat as if she could not quite give up her coffee table, stood back and said, "Now, if you will sit, I will pour your coffee. Pity it is we are not in Vienna," she told him, with a gay little air, "then I could give you real coffee. But this is not the worst in the world, either." Then she ran away, and the flurry of her wake did not settle until some seconds after she was gone.

The coffee was indeed as good as Charles had ever tasted, more than good enough, and he had just taken the first swallow when he heard Herr Bussen's voice in the hall. "Ha," he pronounced in his loud Low-German, "how that coffee stinks."

"Don't tell me you wouldn't like it just the same," said Rosa cruelly. "Just because you drink milk like a big baby and leave the dirty bottles under the bed. Shame on you, Herr Bussen."

They were silenced in the sound of a piano, struck firmly and softly at first, and then without pause there followed a long rippling continuous music. Charles loved music without knowing how or why, and he listened carefully. That would be the Polish student, and it seemed to Charles he was doing pretty well. He sat back in a pleasant daze, hypnotized by the steady rhythm and delighted with the running melody that he could follow easily. Rosa tapped and came in on tiptoe, finger on lip, eyebrows raised, eyes shining. She approached the table and with careful lightness gathered up the napery and silver. "Herr Mey," she whispered, and then, reverently, "Chopin—" and before Charles could think of any response, she had the tray up and had tiptoed out again.

Charles, lightly asleep, dreamed the house was burning down, silently alive and pulsing with flame in every part. With no fear or hesitation at all, he walked safely through the fiery walls and out into the wide bright street, carrying a suitcase which knocked against his knees and weighed him down, but he could not leave it because it contained all the drawings he meant to do in his whole life. He walked a safe distance and watched the dark skeleton of the house tall as a tower standing in a fountain of fire. Seeing that he was alone, he said in wonder, "They all escaped, too," when a loud and ghostly groan was uttered in his ear. He spun about and saw no one. The groan sounded again over his shoulder and woke him sharply. He found he was wallowing in the airless deeps of the feather quilt, hot and half smothered. He fought his way out and sat up to listen, turning this way and that to locate the sound.

"Ah,—ahooooooooo," sighed a voice hopelessly from the room to the right, falling and dying away in a heavily expelled breath of weariness. Without deciding to do anything, Charles found himself at the right hand door tapping with the extreme tips of his fingers.

"Well, what is it?" came a drowsed but soberly indignant voice.

"Is there anything I can do for you?" asked Charles.

"No, no," said the voice in despair. "No, thank you, no no . . ."

"I'm sorry," said Charles, thinking he had been saying this to somebody or other, or thinking it, or feeling it, all day and every day since he had been in that city. The soles of his feet were tingling on the bare floor.

"But come in, please," said the voice, changing to a shade of affability.

The young man sitting on the side of the tumbled bed was of the extreme pale blondness such as Charles had often noticed among the young people in the streets. His hair, eyebrows and eyelashes were pale taffy color, the skin taffy blond, the eyes a flat grayish blue almost expressionless except for a certain modeling of the outer lids that gave him the look of a young, intelligent fox. He had a long, narrow head, with smooth, sharply cut features of the kind Charles vaguely regarded as aristocratic. So far, a good-looking fellow, perhaps twenty-one years old; he stood up slowly and was eye level with Charles' six feet of height. There was only one thing wrong with him: the left side of his face was swollen badly, the eye was almost closed from beneath, and glued along his cheek from ear to mouth was an inch-wide strip of court plaster, the flesh at its edges stained in dirty blues and greens and purples. He was the Heidelberg student, all right. He stood cupping his hand lightly over his cheek without touching.

"Well," he said, keeping his mouth stiff and looking from under his downy light brows at Charles. "You can see for yourself. Nothing to speak of, but it gives me the devil. Like a toothache, you know. I heard myself roaring in my sleep," he said, and his eyes quietly dared Charles to doubt his word. "I woke myself up at it. When you knocked, to tell you the truth, I thought it was Rosa with an ice cap. I don't want any more ice caps. Sit down, please."

Charles said, "I've got some brandy, maybe that would do something."

The boy said, "God, yes," and sighed again in spite of himself. He moved around the room aimlessly, holding his spread hand just beside his face as if he expected his head to drop and hoped to catch it as it fell. His pale gray cotton pajamas gave him the look of being about to fade away in the yellowish light of the bed lamp.

Charles, in his old blanket robe and felt slippers, brought two glasses and the brandy bottle. As he poured, the young man watched the liquid filling the glass as if he would spring upon it, but he held his hands until the glass was offered, smelled the brim, they touched glasses and drank.

"Ah," said the young man, swallowing carefully, head back and tipped to the right. He curled up the right side of his mouth at Charles and his right eye glimmered at him gratefully. "What a relief." He added suddenly, "Hans von Gehring, at your service."

Charles spoke his own name, the other nodded, there was a pause while the glasses were filled again.

"And how do you like it, here in Berlin?" Hans asked politely, warming the brandy between his palms.

"So far, very well," said Charles; "of course, I'm not settled yet." He observed Hans' face in the hope that language was not going to get in the way of their talk. Hans seemed to understand perfectly. He nodded, and drank.

"I've walked nearly all over, and have been to a lot of museums, cafés, all the first things, of course. It is a great city. The Berliners are not proud of it, though, or pretend not to be."

"They know it's no good compared with any other city at all," said Hans, forthrightly. "I was wondering why you came here.

Why this city, of all places? You may go where you please, isn't that so?"

"I suppose so," said Charles. "Yes, that's true."

Hans said, "My father sent me here to see a doctor who is an old friend of his, but in ten days I shall be back in Heidelberg. The Polish fellow is a pianist so he came here because pianists seem to think old Schwartzkopf is the only Master. Herr Bussen, down the hall, he is Platt Deutsch to begin with and he lives in Dalmatia, so anything would perhaps be a change for the better to him. He thinks he is getting an education here and maybe he is. But look at you. A free man and you come to Berlin." He smiled on one side of his face, then shuddered bitterly. "Are you staying on, then?"

"Three months," said Charles, rather gloomily. "I don't know why I came, except that I had a good friend who was German. He used to come here with his family—that was years ago—and he would say, Go to Berlin. I always thought it was the place to be, and if you haven't seen anything else much, this looks pretty good. Of course, there is New York. I stayed there only about a week, but I liked it, I think I could live there."

"Of course, New York," said Hans, indifferently. "But here, there are Vienna, and Prague, and Munich and Budapest, and Nice and Rome and Florence, and, ah, Paris, Paris, Paris," said Hans, suddenly almost gay. Imitating a German actor imitating a Frenchman, he kissed his fingers and wiggled them lightly towards the west.

"I am going to Paris later," said Charles. "Were you ever there?"

"No, but I am going," said Hans. "My plans are all made." He got up as if his words excited him, wrapped his robe around his knees, felt his cheek tenderly and sat down again.

"I hope to stay there a year, I'm going to some atelier and get some painting done. Maybe you will be there before I leave."

"Oh, I have another year in Heidelberg," said Hans, "and my grandfather, who is old, is giving me the money, so I must stop with him for at least a few months first. But then I may go, I shall be free then for a while, perhaps for two years."

"It is strange to have everything mapped out so," said Charles. "I haven't a notion where I'll be two years from now. Something might even happen to keep me from Paris."

"Oh, it is necessary to plan everything," said Hans, soberly, "or how should we know where we were? Besides, the family has it arranged. I even know the girl I am to marry," he said, "and I know how much money she has. She is an extremely fine girl," he said, without enthusiasm. "Paris will be my own, though, my holiday. I shall do as I please."

"Well," said Charles, seriously, "I am glad to be here. All Americans want to come to Europe one time or another, you know. They think there is something here." He sat back and crossed his legs, feeling comfortable with Hans.

"There is something in Europe," said Hans, "but not in Berlin. You are wasting your time here. Go to Paris if you can." He kicked off his slippers and slid into bed, piling up his pillows and letting his head down very carefully.

"I hope you are feeling better," said Charles. "Perhaps you could sleep now."

Hans frowned slightly, retreated. "There is nothing wrong with me," he declared, "and I was asleep before. This is perfectly normal, it happens quite often."

"Well, good night," said Charles, getting up.

"Oh, no, don't go yet," said Hans, starting to sit up and thinking better of it. "I tell you—knock on Tadeusz' door and get him up, too. He sleeps too much. It's just there, next door. If you please, dear fellow. He'll like it."

A moment of complete silence followed Charles' knock, and in silence the door opened on darkness. A thin, tallish young man, his small sharp head thrust forward like a bird's, appeared in the hall. He wore a thin plum-colored silk dressing gown and his long yellowed hands were flattened one above the other over his chest, the fingers lying together. He seemed entirely awake, and his keen little dark eyes were smiling and good tempered. "What's up now?" he asked in an English accent lying over a Polish accent. "Is the damnation dueler raising hell again?"

"Not exactly," said Charles, pleased at hearing English and astonished at the speech, "but he isn't resting easy, either. We were having some brandy. I'm Charles Upton."

"Tadeusz Mey," said the Pole, sliding out and closing the door noiselessly. He spoke just above a whisper in an easy voice. "Polish in spite of the misleading name. Indiscreet grandmother married an Austrian. The rest of my family have names like Zamoisky, lucky devils."

They entered Hans' room and Tadeusz said instantly in German, "Yes, yes, you are going to have a real beauty," and leaned over to examine the wound with a knowing eye. "It's doing very well."

"It will last," said Hans. Over his face spread an expression very puzzling to Charles. It was there like a change of light, slow and deep, with no perceptible movement of eyelids or face muscles. It rose from within in the mysterious place where Hans really lived, and it was amazing arrogance, pleasure, inexpressible vanity and self-satisfaction. He lay entirely motionless and this look came, grew, faded and disappeared on the tidal movement of his true character. Charles thought, Why, if I drew him without that look I should never have him at all. Tadeusz was talking along in his low voice, amiably in a mixture of French and German. The easy use of languages was a mystery to Charles. He listened acutely, but Tadeusz, gesturing neatly with his brandy glass, did not seem to be saying anything in particular, though Hans was also listening attentively.

Charles, feeling free not to talk, was trying to see Hans in Paris, with that scar. Trying to see him in America, in a small American town like San Antonio, for example, with that scar. In Paris perhaps they would understand, but how would it look in San Antonio, Texas? The people there would think he had got into a disgraceful cutting scrape, probably with a Mexican, or that he had been in an automobile accident. They would think it a pity that such a nice fellow should be so disfigured, they would be tactful and not mention it and try to keep their eyes off it. Even in Paris, Charles imagined, those who understood would also disapprove. Hans would simply be another of those Germans with a dueling scar carefully made livid and jagged to last him a lifetime. It occurred to him that nowhere but in this one small country could Hans boast of his scar and his way of getting it. In any other place at all, it would seem strange, a misfortune, or discreditable. Listening to Tadeusz chattering along, Charles watched Hans and thought hard in a series of unsatisfactory circles, trying to get out of them. It was just a custom of the country, that was all. That was the way to look at it, of course. But Charles didn't know, had never known, very likely never would know, a friend in the world who, if he saw Hans, wouldn't ask privately afterwards, "Where did he get that scar?" Except Kuno, perhaps. But Kuno had never said a word about this. Kuno had said, that if you didn't get off the sidewalk when army officers came along, you would be pushed off, and when his mother and he were walking together, she would always step into the street and let them by. Kuno had not minded this, he had rather admired the tall officers with their greatcoats and helmets, but his mother had not liked it at all. Charles remembered this for years; it was nothing related to anything he knew in his own life, yet remained in his memory as unquestioned truth, that part of Kuno's life lived in absence and strangeness which seemed to him more real than any life they had shared.

Prize fighters got cauliflower ears, but not purposely. It was a hazard of the game. Waiters got something called kidney feet. Glass blowers blow their cheeks all out of shape, so they hang like bags. Violinists sometimes get abscesses on their jaws where they hold the violin. Soldiers now and then have their faces blown off and have to get them put back by surgery. All kinds of things happen to men in the course of their jobs, accidents or just deformities that come on so gradually they are hardly noticed until it is too late to do much about it. Dueling had been a respectable old custom almost everywhere, but there had to be a quarrel first. He had seen his great-grandfather's dueling pistols, the family pride in a velvet-lined case. But what *kind* of man would stand up in cold blood and let another man split his face to the teeth just for the hell of it? And then ever after to wear the wound with that look of self-satisfaction, with everybody knowing how he had got it? And you were supposed to admire him for that. Charles had liked Hans on sight, but there was something he wouldn't know about him if they both lived for a thousand years; it was something you were, or were not, and Charles rejected that wound, the reason why it existed, and everything that made it possible, then and there, simply because there were no conditions for acceptance in his mind.

Still he liked Hans, and wished the wound were not there. But it was there, an improbable and blood-chilling sight, as if at broad noon he should meet in Kurfürstendamm a knight in armor, or the very skeleton from the Dance of Death.

"You don't speak French?" Tadeusz asked at last, turning to Charles.

"A little," said Charles, but fearing to begin.

"You are lucky," said Tadeusz. "You have a language everyone tries to learn. So have the French. But for me, I have to learn every pest of language there is, because no one but a Pole speaks Polish."

He was a narrow, green-faced young man and in the light his eyes were liver colored. He looked bilious, somehow, and he continually twisted a scorched looking lock of hair on the crown of his head as he talked, a tight clever little smile in the corners of his mouth. "I can even speak Platt Deutsch, but Herr Bussen pretends not to understand me."

"That is the fellow our landlady was scolding today," said Charles, and felt instantly that he had been tactless.

"Today?" asked Tadeusz. "She scolds him every day for one thing or another. He's very stupid. All the Platt Deutsch are stupid beyond hope. Let Rosa take it all out of him. She won't annoy the rest of us so much. She is a terror, that woman."

"Well," said Hans fretfully, pouting under his lip, "what do you expect? This is a *pension.*"

"On the recommended list, too," said Tadeusz, amiably, smoking, holding his cigarette at the base of his third and fourth finger, lighted end towards the palm. "I don't expect anything."

"It would be all right if only she would let my papers alone," said Charles.

"You're the rich American who pays the rent for all of us," said Tadeusz, smiling. "You've got the real lace curtains and the best feather bed. But if you do anything tactless, remember, Herr Bussen will catch it."

Charles shook his head at this, thinking it was too near the truth to be funny for him, at least. He poured more brandy, and they lighted fresh cigarettes all around. The visitors sat back comfortably and Hans turned on his side. They all felt well disposed and at peace and as if they were beginning to get acquainted with each other. Three sharp little raps upon the door were followed by Rosa's voice. With sweet severity she reminded them in a set speech that it was three o'clock and others in the house might like some sleep. They glanced at each other with conspiratorial smiles.

"Rosa, dear," said Hans, putting a good deal of patient persuasion in his tone, "I was feeling frightfully and they came to sit up with me."

"You do not need anyone to sit up with you," said Rosa, briskly. "You need sleep."

Tadeusz, rising in silence, opened the door suddenly and Rosa fled with small squeaks, an apparition in dressing gown and hair net. He called after her soothingly, "We are going at once," and turned back with a monkeyish gleam in his nearsighted little eyes. "I thought that would rout her," he said, "that woman is vain as if she were twenty. You'd think we were living in a damnation jail," he went on, taking his glass again, "but all Berlin is just that. Let me tell you," he said to Charles, "I can hardly wait to get back to London. You should go there by all means. Believe me, I have seen nearly all the cities—except your fabulous New York, and those photographs made from the air terrorize me—and London is the only place for a civilized man."

Hans shook his head cautiously and repeated, "No, Paris, Paris."

"All right," said Tadeusz in English. "Okay. I learned that from one of your Americans: typical 100 per cent specimen, he told me. He was a cowboy from Arizona with a five gallon hat. He was a Holy Roller and a vegetarian and he drank a tumblerful of whiskey every morning before breakfast. He was in love with a snake charmer who also did a fan dance. When I knew him he was running a little *boîte* on the Left Bank; the walls were covered with steer's horns and lariats. When he quarreled with the snake charmer, he dragged her all around the floor by one of the lariats. She left him at once, but not before putting a venomous serpent in his bed. However, no harm was done. As he said, it was all okay by him."

Hans said, "What are you saying, please? Remember I don't know English."

Tadeusz said in German, "I was explaining where I learned to say Okay."

Hans nodded. "Ah, yes, I understand that very well, okay. That is the only English I know."

By way of proving they were still men, masters of themselves, they lingered somewhat and took their sweet time about saying good night and separating.

Charles, emerging from the bathroom in the morning, met Herr Bussen in the hall. Herr Bussen was wearing a short cotton bathrobe and carrying a rather draggled towel. His fat round face wore a grieved and bewildered look, like a child who had been so sternly treated at home it did not expect better from the rest of the world. Charles had been wakened by the sound of Rosa scolding Herr Bussen about something or other. Presently she came in with coffee and rolls and butter, looking very well combed and dressed so early in the morning, but with a light sparkle of roused temper in her eyes. She opened the curtains and turned out the light, leaving the winter day like dirty water in the room. She spun away and knocked at the bathroom door, saying in a prissy voice of authority, "It is fifteen minutes, your time is up, Herr Bussen." Returning, she stripped the bed with one gesture, creating a small breeze over Charles' head as he sat at the table. Standing close beside him she sighed suddenly: "Oh, how hard it is to have an orderly and peaceful life, a correct life of the kind I was accustomed to. And the bathroom. Always shaving soap, toothpaste and water, water on the linoleum, the mirrors themselves splashed, everything so unclean, oh, Herr Upton, I do not know why gentlemen will never wash the bathtub. And oh, the Herr Bussen. Every day his bed is full of cheese and bread crumbs, there are often tins of sardines open in the chest among his clothes, he eats walnuts and hides the shells in the closet. It is no excuse to say he is going to be a professor. And every month late, late with the rent. How does he think I shall exist if I cannot have the rent promptly?"

Charles, positively blushing all over, got up and said, "If you will wait a few minutes, I am going out and won't trouble you."

"Ah, you don't trouble me. I am going about my work, you about yours. No, it is not that." She smiled brightly upon him, her despair seemed to pass. "Let me tell you, before the war I had five servants besides a gardener and a chauffeur, my frocks came from Paris and my furniture from England; I had three diamond necklaces, Herr Upton, three—so now, is it strange that sometimes I wonder what is to become of me? I make up beds like a servant," she said, "and I wash dirty floors. . . ."

Charles, feeling cornered, got his hat and coat, stammered a sentence in German unintelligible to himself even, and rushed away, appalled at Rosa's lack of decency in her confidences, and her shameful knowledge of his own untidy bathroom habits.

He pawned his camera, expecting to get almost nothing for it, but the quiet little man in the shop took his thin nose out of a book, examined the handsome contrivance with professional approval, and gave him a hundred marks without question. Feeling unreasonably rich and cheered up, Charles rushed back to the apartment hoping to work for a while. A few steps from his own door, he saw Herr Bussen going in, clutching a small brown paper parcel—bread and liver sausage, perhaps—and without an overcoat in the wolfish cold. Charles overtook him on the stairway, for Herr Bussen was moving slowly, his shoulders bent. From the back he appeared to be a middle-aged man, but the face he turned to Charles seemed even younger than it should have been, with an underlying half-spent childhood still lingering in it. His nose was red and wet, his eyes were full of tears, his bare hand holding the parcel was cracked at the knuckles.

"Good morning," said Herr Bussen, and his lumpy face lightened, just for a moment, as if he expected something pleasant to happen. Charles slowed down, they exchanged names, and went on together in silence. Rosa opened the door for them.

"Ah," she remarked, glancing from one to the other suspiciously, "so you are acquainted already?"

"Yes," they said in one voice, and strong in solidarity, they moved past her without another word. Rosa disappeared into her own part of the house, talking to herself.

"Does she insult you every time she speaks to you?" asked Herr Bussen, with resigned patience.

"Not yet," said Charles, who was beginning to find his immunity a disadvantage. He felt he was on the wrong side, he would not if he could help it be a pet of Rosa's. Herr Bussen said, "Every day she insults me for at least half an hour, then she goes and insults Herr Mey, but in a different way, for he is very sharp and answers her in little ways she does not understand, but he really insults her in turn. She makes a house cat of Herr von Gehring because he fought a *mensur,* but it won't last, and she is polite to you because you are a foreigner and pay more rent than we do. But you wait. Your turn will come."

"Well, when it does," said Charles, easily, "I'll just get out."

"And pay your whole three months' rent or have her report you to the police?" asked Herr Bussen in wonder. "My God, you *must* be rich."

Charles shook his head, feeling that it was all pretty much no use. A look of envy so deep it was almost hatred spread over Herr Bussen's face, he paused and his eye wandered over Charles from head to foot as if he were some improbable faintly repellent creatu.e of another species. "Ah, well," he said, "seriously, I advise you to observe our curious customs, and do nothing, not the smallest thing, to attract the attention of the police. I tell you this because you are unfamiliar with the country—they are not fond of outlanders here."

"Thank you," said Charles stuffily, feeling deeply offended.

This melancholy conversation first depressed him, then it put him in a temper. He sat down in a dull but pleasant fury and began to draw hastily, without plan. Now and then he raised his elbows, drew his lungs full of air. The walls seemed to be closing in upon him, he imagined he could hear the breathing of those people in the other rooms, he smelt the iodoform on Hans' bandage, the spoiled sardines on Herr Bussen's breath, Rosa's sweetish female hysteria made him ill. He drew the people at the hotel, the woman a sick fox, the man half pig, half tiger. He drew Herr Bussen's unenlightened face, several times, growing more tender with each version. There was something about the fellow. With concentrated malice he drew Rosa, first as kitchen sloven, then as a withered old whore, finally without any clothes on. Studying these, he decided he had paid off a large installment of his irritation with her, and tore them all into minute bits. Instantly he regretted it, but there was no place to hide them from her. Then quite calmly he began to draw Hans' face from the memory of that strange expression of pride in his wound, and this absorbed him so that he grew calm, was ashamed of his anger, wondered what had got into him. They were all good people, they were in terrible trouble, jammed up together in this little flat with not enough air or space or money, not enough of anything, no place to go, nothing to do but gnaw each other. I can always go home, he told himself, but why did I come here in the first place?

The sound of Tadeusz' piano stopped him. He listened with pleasure, sitting back at ease. That fellow really could play. Charles had heard a great many famous pianists, by radio, who didn't, it seemed to him, sound so much better than that. Tadeusz knew what he was doing. He drew Tadeusz sitting over the piano, bird head, little stiff wrinkles at the corners of his mouth, fingers like bird claws. "Hell, maybe I'm a caricaturist," he thought, but he did not really worry about it. He settled down again and forgot to listen.

A scurrying about in the hall and Rosa's voice raised in a shrill whimpering got through to him slowly, he did not wake up altogether until she was beating at his door, crying aloud in real terror, "Oh, God, oh, God, Herr Upton, come and help me. Come help. Herr Bussen—" Charles opened the door. Tadeusz and Hans were already at Herr Bussen's door. Rosa's face was streaming with tears, her hair was draggled. "Herr Bussen has poisoned himself."

Charles shuddered with a mortal chill of fear. He came straight out and joined the others and they went in to Herr Bussen's room together.

Herr Bussen was kneeling beside his bed, clutching a large bedroom jar in his arms, vomiting and retching, speechless except for a gasp between convulsions. Yet he could still raise his hand in a violent waving motion, gurgling, "Go away, go away. . . ."

"Get him to the bathroom," cried Rosa, "fetch a doctor, bring water, for God's sake look out for the rug," and while Charles seized Herr Bussen under the arms to lift him up, Tadeusz came with wet towels and Hans, holding his face, ran to the telephone.

"No, no, God damn it," shouted Herr Bussen, fiercely. "No doctor, no." Freeing himself partially from Charles, he doubled up over the footboard of his bed, holding his stomach, apparently in his agony, his face a terrifying purple green, a shower of sweat pouring over his eyebrows and nose.

"Oh, why did you do it?" cried Rosa, weeping. "To poison yourself, here among your friends, how could you?"

Herr Bussen collected himself for protest. "I tell you, I did not poison myself," he shouted in a good strong baritone, "I told you,

I ate something and it poisoned me." He collapsed again over the jar, and the upheavals recommenced.

"Get him to the bathroom," cried Rosa, wringing her hands. "I know," she said, turning on Herr Bussen, indignant again. "That sausage. All those sardines. That liver paste. I warned you, but no, you would not listen. No, you knew best. How many times did I tell you . . ."

"Let me alone," cried Herr Bussen, desperately. "Leave me."

Charles and Tadeusz joined forces. "Come on," said Tadeusz, in Platt Deutsch, with a conversational tone, "come on, we'll help you."

They took hold of him around the middle so that he hung down rather like a sack, and began hauling him as well as they could. "Oh, Almighty God," groaned Herr Bussen in sincere despair, "let me alone." But they got him in the bathroom, with no more regard for his feelings than if he were already dead, closed the door and locked it. At once Charles came out again, and left the apartment at a run, without his hat. He was back in a very few minutes with a large package, purchases from a pharmacy, and again closing the bathroom door, ignoring Rosa's questions, he and Tadeusz got to work on Herr Bussen seriously.

Rosa turned on Hans, her face quite sodden by then, and still weeping, ordered him back to bed. Hans said, "No, don't trouble yourself. I am better, I am going out to the clinic now."

"You will make yourself worse," wept Rosa.

"No, you may be surprised, I shall be quite all right," said Hans, coolly, leaving.

Herr Bussen, eased, soothed, cleansed, safe in bed with an ice cap on his brow, the object of all attention from his three new friends, lay in bitter, ungrateful silence. He does not seem to be very pleased with us, thought Charles, and we did a roaring good job, too. Herr Bussen—why did they call him that? He wasn't more than twenty-four years old—seemed sunken and shame-faced, he kept his eyes closed or turned to the wall, and when Tadeusz came in with hot soup from a restaurant, he shook his head and seemed about to shed tears. Rosa was injured by the sight of the soup, also.

"You must let me prepare his food," she said to Tadeusz, "I do

not want him poisoned again." She took away the soup and
brought it again freshly hot on an elegant tray. She seemed very
subdued and Herr Bussen was melancholy and without appetite.

Charles, noticing the piles of papers on Herr Bussen's desk, saw
written upon them only endless mathematical calculations which
he could recognize but not read. Rosa fidgeted among them, trying
to straighten them out. In the hall she said to Charles, "You may
not know it, but Herr Bussen is considered, at the University, to be
a very brilliant mathematician. He promises to become a very
learned man." She spoke with pride and possessiveness. "If I am
annoyed with him at times, it is because he needs someone to
teach him good habits. He eats—ah, it is no better than offal. And
now he is ashamed because you know—you have found him out in
his misery. It is a terrible thing to be poor," she said, and the tears
seemed to come not only from her eyes but from her skin, the
tears and the sweat mingled in a stream and covered her face.
"What shall we do? What is to become of us?"

Tadeusz came out and took her by the arm. "Enough of that,
Rosa," he said, shaking her gently. "Now what happened, really?
Herr Bussen eats a sardine and makes a nuisance of himself. Go
and lie down, we will look after him and not disturb anything."

"I am very nervous," said Rosa, smiling at him gratefully.

They looked in upon Herr Bussen. He was lying with his arm
thrown over his face, quietly, as if the sleeping powders were taking effect. "Come along with me," said Tadeusz to Charles, "I
have an odd spot of brandy, too."

Hans came in with his face done up in fresh lint and court
plaster, much improved. He refused brandy and said, "Do you
suppose we ought to watch him? Do you suppose?"

"No, I don't believe it for a minute," said Tadeusz, after a small
pause. "Do you?" he asked Charles.

"I think he told the truth," said Charles.

"Good," said Hans. "Have one for me," he said, and closed his
door.

Tadeusz' narrow room was crowded with an upright piano, and
a small silent keyboard which Charles examined, touching stiffly.
"I work on that seven hours a day," said Tadeusz, spreading his
hands and turning them about, "and you'd better be grateful. Now
the damnation suicide is asleep, I shan't be able to play any more

today. We may as well get drunk," he said, showing four inches of brandy in a bottle. ˙ Seriously, I don't drink. But if I stayed too long in this place I would."

Charles said, "It's getting me down, too, and I wish I knew why. Compared to really poor people, people I have seen, here and at home, even Herr Bussen is almost rich. Compared to even well-off people, I suppose I'm almost a pauper. But I never felt poor, I never was afraid of it. I always thought that if I really wanted money more than anything else, I could get it. But here—I don't know . . . everybody seems so *crowded,* somehow, so worried, and they can't get their minds off of money for a second."

"They lost that war, please don't forget," said Tadeusz, running his fingers over the silent keyboard that gave forth an even wooden clatter. "That damages a nation's personality no end, you know. But I have no sympathy for them, none. And as for feeling crowded, ha, you would have to be a Pole to know what that means. These big fat ugly people," he said, and he crossed his knees and began torturing his scalp lock. "By God they should be Poles for a while to know what it is to be hungry."

"They aren't all ugly," said Charles. "Not by a long shot."

"Okay," said Tadeusz, indifferently and his little eyes closed. Charles thought, Well, what should I say? Am I supposed to go into an impassioned defense of the Poles? Or a denunciation of the Germans? He was thinking really of his fleece-lined coat, wondering if it would be good enough to offer to Herr Bussen and how to go about it. Could he just knock at his door and say, "Here is a coat I don't happen to need?" Or (no, this wouldn't do), "If you don't have a coat with you, why not use this one for a while?" There should be some way of doing it decently. He explained to Tadeusz and asked for advice.

"Oh, never," said Tadeusz. "You can't do that. He is very proud and he would be furious as hell. And besides," Tadeusz swung a foot, "we have to realize that a man's sufferings are his own, quite often he chooses them to some ends of his own—how do we know? We pity people too often for the wrong reasons. They may not need it or want it at all, you know. Poor Old Bussen, we are able to say, and it makes us feel better, more secure, in our own fortune. Sometimes there are worse things than cold and hunger.

Had you thought of that? Do you know him at all, his feelings, or his plan for himself? I think until you do, don't interfere."

"If we hadn't interfered today, he might be dead by now," said Charles.

"We may have made a mistake even so," said Tadeusz, calmly. "Now we must wait and see. Of course if we could give him money or food without letting him know why we did it, that would be another thing. But we can't. If you go now after all that has happened and offer him a coat, just like that, why, what can you expect? He would feel like throwing it back at you. A man might accept charity if he did not fear the contempt of the giver. But only good friends can accept or exchange favors. Otherwise it doesn't do." Tadeusz stood up and walked about quickly, bent at the waist and peering at Charles. "Dear fellow, don't mind if I say, you Americans have some very odd notions. Why all this benevolence? What do you expect to gain by it?

Charles said, "I wouldn't gain anything by it, and I would expect to lose a coat. But I don't need the coat," he said, "and so far as I am concerned that would be the end of it."

"You sound morally indignant," said Tadeusz. He paused before Charles and smiled. "Don't get mad, you hear how well I speak American? You would gain from it the pride in being able to give a coat. And Herr Bussen would be warm, but he would owe his coat to the charity of a stranger, and it might spoil his whole career. Try to understand. I know more about this than you do. If ever I come to your country I will take your advice about Americans."

"I don't believe Americans are so different from other people as all that," said Charles.

"Believe me," said Tadeusz, "you are like beings from another planet to us. Don't offer a coat to Herr Bussen. He will hate you for it."

Charles said, "I can't believe it really."

"If you set yourself up as a benefactor," said Tadeusz, "you must expect to be hated. Let me tell you something. A very rich man I know wished to give good sums of money to help young musicians. But he went to his lawyer and insisted that the gift must be anonymous; under no circumstances must the giver be known Well, the lawyer said of course it would be arranged, but it would make work, mystery, why did his client want that? And this very wise man said, 'I am superstitious and I do not want them to be able to curse me by name.' "

"Good God," said Charles, sincerely horrified.

"Ah, yes, good God," said Tadeusz, amiably.

Charles left the coat in his closet, and brought milk and oranges instead to Herr Bussen. Hans was there already, sitting beside the bed-offering Herr Bussen more soup.

The invalid accepted, and swallowed the nourishment as if it were bitter medicine. Charles thought, Yes, it's true, he isn't getting any good out of it; and he saw plainly that Herr Bussen felt himself being engulfed slowly in a debt he had no hope of paying. Charles, at the foot of the bed, had a curious scene flash through his mind: Herr Bussen, the object of charity, fleeing like a stag across the snowy waste, with Hans and Tadeusz and Rosa and he, Charles, after him in full cry, bringing him down, by the throat if necessary, to give him aid and comfort. Charles heard the deep mournful voices of his father's liver-spotted hounds.

When Rosa brought the coffee tray, one end of it was occupied by an ordinary looking black japanned metal box. She stood, without pouring the coffee, her hands on the table, and said in a low voice, "This hasn't been a very good day for anybody, I suppose. But I have on my conscience my sharpness to Herr Bussen. I have told him so, and he answered—he answered kindly," she said. "But I know that you, a stranger, and from a rich country—"

"The country may be rich," said Charles, "but most of the people in it are not—"

"Couldn't be expected to understand," Rosa went on, waving his speech away without listening. "Look, I want to show you something, then maybe you will see a little of what has happened to us. Outlanders, all the world, come here with their money—"

"I tell you I am not rich, for one," said Charles, hopelessly. She gave him a stare very much like contempt for his lying speech; she knew better. He was the worst kind of rich American, the kind who pretended to be poor. "With their money," she said, angrily, raising her voice, "and then they think we are cheap because we worry about how we shall live. You despise us because we are ruined and why are we ruined, tell me that? It is because your country deserted and betrayed us in the war, you should have helped us and you did not." Her voice dropped and became bitter and quiet.

Charles said in a matter-of-fact, reasoning tone: "All the way over on the boat, the Germans kept telling me that. The truth is, I've heard talk about that war all my life, but I hardly remember it. I have to confess I hadn't thought much about it. If I had, maybe I would never have come here."

"You didn't have to think about it," said Rosa, "but here, we have nothing else to think about." She opened the black box. It was full of paper money, thick bales of it in rubber bands, such an amount of printed money as Charles had seen only in glimpses at the elbow of a clerk behind the barred windows of a great bank. Rosa lifted one of the bundles.

"These are nothing," she said with affected airiness, "these are only a hundred thousand marks each. . . . Wait." She lifted another and flirted the edges through her fingers. "These are five hundred thousand marks each—look," she said, her voice wavering. "One million marks each, these." She dropped each bundle as she spoke upon the table beside them without glancing up. Terror and awe were in her face, as if again for just a moment, she believed in the value of this paper as she had once believed. "Did you ever see a note for five million marks? Here are a hundred of them, you will never see this again—and oh," she cried suddenly, in a frenzy of grief, clutching the treacherous stuff with both hands, "try now to buy a loaf of bread with all this, try it, try it!"

Her voice rose and she wept shamelessly without hiding her face, her arms hanging loosely, the worthless money dropping to the floor.

Charles looked about as if he expected help, rescue, to come by miracle. He backed away from her thinking only of escape, saying as well as he could, "I know it is all a horrible business—but, what can I do?"

This dull question had a remarkable effect. Rosa's tears dried almost instantly, her voice deepened a note, she spoke with intense anger. "You can do nothing," she said vehemently, "nothing, you know nothing at all, you cannot even imagine—"

Charles picked up the money from the carpet, and Rosa began placing the stiff pale colored bundles again in the box, carefully, arranging them first one way and another, stopping now and then to squeeze the end of her nose with her thin little handkerchief. "Nothing to say, nothing to be done," she repeated, giving him a resentful look as if he had failed her, a look as personal and angry as if she were a member of his family, or at least a familiar friend, or—what on earth was Rosa to him? A middle-aged stranger who had rented him a room, someone he had expected to see and speak to perhaps once a week, and here she was, swarming all over him, weeping on his neck, telling her troubles, putting the blame for the troubles of the world on him, driving him nuts, and no way that he could see of getting out of it. She closed the box and leaned her hands on the table. "When you are so poor," she said, "you are frightened of the poor and unfortunate. I was frightened of Herr Bussen—no, I almost hated him. I thought every day, 'My God, such a man will bring bad luck on us all, he will drag us all down with him.' " She spoke in a very low tone. "But today, it came to me that Herr Bussen will live through everything, he is strong, he is not really afraid. And that is a comfort to me, because I am afraid of everything."

She poured the coffee, took up the japanned box and went out.

The household settled down that night for a good sleep. What a relief, thought Charles, to put a long quiet stretch of darkness between you and the thing that happened. Suppose Old Bussen had popped off? He felt warmly towards Old Bussen, who was still breathing—snoring, in fact, in long rich groans, as if he couldn't breathe hard enough.

When Charles put his head in to look at Herr Bussen the next morning, two rawboned solemn youths with identical leather-colored forelocks were sitting with him, one on the bed, one on the spindling chair. They turned and gazed at the stranger with profound blue eyes exactly alike, and Herr Bussen, looking very well and merry, introduced them. Twin brothers, he said, school friends of his, who were at that moment on the point of fulfilling a life's ambition. On New Year's Eve they were going to open a small cabaret of their own, a snug little half-cellar with the best beer, a supper table and pretty girls who could sing and dance. Nothing big, but a good place, and Herr Bussen hoped Charles would go with him to celebrate the first evening. Charles said it sounded a fine idea to him, and thought perhaps Hans and Tadeusz would like to go, too. The brothers eyed him without a flicker of expression.

Herr Bussen sat up as if he had new life in him. "Oh, yes, we will all go together." The brothers stood up to giant heights, and one of them said, "It will not be expensive, either." As if being able to give this piece of good news was pleasant to him, he grinned broadly and reassuringly at Charles, who grinned in turn. He said to Herr Bussen, "I'm going out. Could I bring you anything?"

"Oh, no," said Herr Bussen, firmly, shaking his head with a small glitter of resentment in his eye. "Thank you, nothing at all. I'm getting up now."

At the foot of the shallow flight of steps leading to the new cabaret, a dish of food scraps had been set out for the hungry small animals. A black cat was there, eating very fast, glancing nervously over his shoulder as he swallowed. One of the twins put his head out, invited his four visitors in festively, noticed the cat and said ritually, "May it do him good." He threw open the door to disclose a small, freshly painted, well-lighted little place, full of tables covered with red checkerboard cloths, a modest bar, and at the farther end, a long table set out with cold supper. It could all be seen at a glance. There was a homemade air about the colored paper decorations, the feathery tinsel draped above the bar mirror, the rack full of steins and the small cuckoo clock.

It was hardly Charles' notion of a Berlin cabaret; he had heard about Berlin night life and expected something more sophisticated. He remarked as much to Tadeusz.

"Oh, no," said Tadeusz, "this is another kind of thing altogether. This is going to be nice-stuffy-middle-class-German full of rosy emotions and beer. You could bring your most innocent child here if you had an innocent child." He seemed pleased, and so did Hans and Herr Bussen: they walked about and praised everything the brothers had done. All of them were pleasantly excited because none of them had ever known anyone who ran a cabaret, and they enjoyed a cozy feeling of being on the inside of things for once. Almost immediately they began calling Herr Bussen by his first name. Tadeusz began it.

"Otto, dear fellow, could you give me a light?" he asked, and

Otto, who did not smoke, blushed with pleasure and felt in his pockets as if he expected to find matches.

They were the first comers. As the brothers went on about their last-minute business, rushing back and forth through the swinging door leading to the kitchen, Otto led the way to the supper table, where they helped themselves comfortably but carefully, for at close range there was an air of thrift about the food, as if the cheese and sausages had been counted and the bread weighed, perhaps. A boy in a white jacket brought them tall steins of beer; they lifted them to each other, waved them at the brothers, and drank long and deeply.

"In Munich," said Tadeusz, "I used to drink with a crowd of music students, all Germans. We drank and drank, and the man who had to leave the table first paid for all. I always paid. It was a bore, really."

"A dull custom at best," commented Hans, "and of course the kind of thing foreigners would notice and tell about, as if it were typical." His face was quietly annoyed, he looked past Tadeusz, who refused to be snubbed.

"I have already agreed with you it was a bore," he said, "and after all, only an incident of life in Munich." His tone was soothing, indulgent, a little insolent. Charles, observing, thought with some slight surprise that these fellows did not like each other, after all. And almost instantly he felt indifference tinged with dislike for them both, and an uneasy feeling that he was in the wrong company; he wished pretty thoroughly he had not come to that place with them.

One of the brothers leaned over them with his open, single-minded expression, calling their attention to newcomers. A stupidly handsome young man with a careful thatch of curls above a self-consciously god-like brow was helping an olive-skinned, yellow-haired young woman with her wraps. "A star in the moving pictures," whispered the brother, excitedly, "and that girl is his mistress and his leading lady." He dived towards his celebrities awkwardly, saw them settled and was back in a moment. "There comes Lutte, a model, one of the most beautiful girls in Berlin," he said, his voice throbbing. "She is going to dance a rumba when the time comes."

They all turned in natural curiosity and saw indeed a very beauti ful slender girl, her head shining like a silver yellow peony above her rather skimpy black dress. She smiled and waved her hand at them, they stood up and bowed, but she did not approach them as they had hoped. Leaning on the bar, she talked to the boy in the white jacket. The room filled then rather rapidly, there was a rush for the long table and the brothers, flushed with success, beamed and scurried with trays and steins. A small orchestra moved into the space beside the bar.

Almost every guest, Charles noticed, had brought a musical instrument, a violin or flute or white piano accordion, a clarinet and one man lumbered in under the burden of a violoncello in a green baize-covered case. A young woman with huge haunches and thick legs, a knot of sleek brown hair slipping upon her unpowdered neck, came in by herself, looked around with a vague smile which no one returned, and went behind the bar, where she began competently to set up trays of beer.

"There you see her," said Hans, looking at Lutte possessively, "the truest type of German beauty—tell me, have you seen anything better anywhere?"

"Oh, come now," said Tadeusz, mildly, "there aren't a half dozen like her in this town. The legs and feet, surely they aren't typical? She might have French blood, or even a little Polish," he said. "Only she is perhaps a little flat-bosomed for that."

"What you seem never to understand," said Hans, in a slightly edged voice, "is that when I say German I don't mean peasants or these fat Berliners."

"Perhaps we should always mean peasants when we speak of a race," said Tadeusz. "The nobility and the royalty are always mixed bloods, the complete mongrel, really, they have no nationality at all. Even the middle classes marry everywhere, but the peasant stays in his own region and marries his own kind, generation after generation, and creates the race, quite simply, as I see it."

"The trouble with that notion," said Hans, "is that the peasantry of almost any country looks quite like the peasantry of any other."

"Oh, superficially," said Otto. "Their heads are very different, if you will study them." He leaned forward earnestly. "No matter how it came about," he told them, "the true great old Germanic type is lean and tall and fair as gods." His forehead formed a deep wrinkle which sank to a meaty cleft between his brows. His small puffy eyes swam tenderly, the roll of fat across his collar flushed with emotion. "We are not by any means all the pig type," he said humbly, spreading his thick hands, "though I know the foreign caricaturists make us all appear so. Those were perhaps the old Wendish people, and after all, they were a single tribe, they are not of the old true great Germanic—"

"Type," finished Tadeusz, mildly rude. "Let's agree then, the Germans are all of the highest type of beauty and they have preposterously fine manners. Look at all the heel-clicking and bowing from the waist and elegant high-toned voices. And how polite and smiling a seven-foot policeman can be when he is getting ready to crack your skull open. I have seen it. No, Hans, you have a great culture here, no doubt, but I think no civilization. You will be the last race on earth to be civilized, but does it matter?"

"On the other hand," said Hans with extreme politeness, smiling, a cold gleam in his eye, "the Poles, if you like that high-cheeked, low-browed Tartar style, have also great physical beauty, and though they have contributed exactly nothing to world-culture, they are civilized in a medieval sort of way, I suppose."

"Thanks," said Tadeusz, turning towards Hans as if to show his flat cheeks and narrow high forehead. "One of my grandmothers was a Tartar, and you can see how typical I am."

"One of your grandfathers was an Austrian, too," said Otto; "I'd never think of you as a Pole. You seem to me an Austrian."

"Oh, by God, I can't have that," said Tadeusz, decidedly, and he laughed with his lips tightly closed. "No, no, I'll be a Tartar first. But I am a Pole just the same."

Charles had never seen any Poles except a few short-legged broad-faced men laying railroad ties somewhere in the South, and he would not have known they were Poles unless someone had told him, and the man called them Polacks, besides. He could make nothing of Tadeusz, but Hans and Otto both seemed persons he had known before; Texas was full of boys like Otto, and Hans reminded him of Kuno. It seemed to him that the discussion was getting nowhere, and it reminded him of quarrels during his school-days between the German boys and Mexican boys and the Kentucky boys; the Irish boys fought everybody, and Charles, who was partly Irish, remembered that he had done a good deal of fighting in which all sight of the original dispute had been lost in the simple love of violence. He said, "All the way over on the boat the Germans kept telling me I was not a typical American. How could they know? Of course I am perfectly typical."

"Oh, not at all," said Tadeusz, and this time his good humor was real. "We know all about you. Americans are all cowboys or very rich, and when they are rich they get drunk in poor countries and paste thousand-franc notes on their suitcases, or light cigarettes with them—"

"Oh, God," said Charles simply. "Who started that story?" Even American tourists went about repeating it with complacent horror, as if to prove they were not that sort of tourist.

"You know what is the trouble?" asked Tadeusz, amiably. "The Americans we know are all so filthy rich. There is nothing Europeans love and crave and covet more than wealth. If we didn't believe your country has all the money, there would be nothing wrong with you, particularly."

"We're punch drunk, anyhow," said Charles. "We don't give a damn any more."

"Europeans hate each other for everything and for nothing; they've been trying to destroy each other for two thousand years, why do you Americans expect us to like you?" asked Tadeusz.

"We don't expect it," said Charles. "Who said we did? We, naturally, like just everybody. We are sentimental. Just like the Germans. You want to be loved for yourselves alone and you are always right and you can never see why other people can't see you in the same rosy light you see yourselves. Look what a glorious people you are and yet nobody loves you. Well, that's a great pity."

Otto gazed earnestly at Charles from under his deep brows, wagged his head and said, "I do not think you really like anybody, you Americans. You are indifferent to everybody and so it is easy for you to be gay, to be careless, to seem friendly. You are really a coldhearted indifferent people. You have no troubles. You have no troubles because you do not know how to have them. Even if you get troubles, you think it is just a package meant for the people next door, delivered to you by mistake. That is what I really believe."

Charles, embittered, said, "I can't talk about whole countries because I never knew one, not even my own. I only know a few persons here and there and some I like and some I don't like and I never thought it anything but a personal matter. . . ."

Tadeusz said, "Oh, dear fellow, that is being much too modest. The whole art of self-importance is to raise your personal likes and dislikes to the plane of moral or esthetic principle, and to apply on an international scale your smallest personal experience. . . . If someone steps on your foot, you should not rest until you have raised an army to avenge you. . . . And as for us, what are we doing with our evening? At this rate I shall have indigestion. . . ."

"What about our friends the French?" asked Hans, suddenly. "Can anyone find fault with them? Their food, their wine, their dress, their manners—" he lifted his stein and drank without enjoyment, and added—"a race of monkeys."

"They have very bad manners," said Tadeusz, "and they would cut you into ribbons with a dull pair of scissors for five francs in hand. A shortsighted and selfish people, and how I love them. But not as I do the English. Take the English—"

"Take the Italians," said Charles, "all of them."

"Nothing worth mentioning since Dante," said Tadeusz. "I detest their lumpy Renaissance."

"Now that's settled," said Charles, "let's take the pigmies, or the Icelanders, or the head hunters of Borneo—"

"I love them all," cried Tadeusz, "especially the Irish. I like the Irish because they are nearly as damnation patriotic as the Poles."

"I was brought up on Irish patriotism," said Charles. "My mother's name was O'Hara, and I was supposed to be proud of it, but you have a tough time being proud if you are called Harp and Potato Mouth at school where the others are all Scotch Presbyterians or of English descent."

Tadeusz said, "What nonsense," and he began to talk pleasantly and quietly about the great ancient Celtic race, slyly too, aiming at Hans; praising their ancient culture of which traces were found in all parts of Europe. "Yes, even the Germans have been improved by it," he said. Hans and Otto shook their heads, but their anger seemed to have disappeared, their faces smoothed and their eyes met openly once more. Charles was soothed and flattered to find Irish greatness acknowledged at last by somebody other than his immediate family. He said to Tadeusz, "My father used to tell me,

'Ah, the Irish, my boy. God knows they went down early in time, but don't forget this, they had a great national culture when the British were still painting themselves blue, and the old French used to exchange scholars with them!"

Tadeusz translated this to Hans and Otto, and Hans laughed so suddenly he put his hand to his cheek with a grimace. "Be careful," said Tadeusz, looking at the wound as he always did, with an air of clinical interest, which he knew Hans liked. Charles went on to say he had never seen such a statement in any history books, which seemed very vague about the Irish until they began fighting with the British. By that time, the books said in effect, they were just a lot of wild bog-jumpers. He had felt sorry for his father, trying to wring a drop of comfort out of the myth of his splendid past, but the usual run of histories on the subject hadn't borne him out. He was pleased to think he had simply got hold of the wrong books.

"They are very like the Poles," said Tadeusz, "those Irish, living on the glory of their past, on their poetry and the jeweled Book of Kells and the great cups and crowns of ancient Ireland, the memories of victories and defeats godlike in intensity, the hope of rising again to glory: and in the meantime," he added, "always fighting quite a lot and very unsuccessfully."

Hans leaned forward and spoke with importance, as if he were a professor addressing his class: "The fate of Ireland (and of Poland, too, Tadeusz, don't forget) is an example, a most terrible example, of what can happen to a country when it divides against itself and lets the enemy in . . . the Irish, so nationalistic at this late day, are yet divided. What do they expect? They could have saved themselves in early time by uniting and attacking the enemy, instead of waiting to be attacked."

Tadeusz reminded him, "Hans, that does not always work either," but Hans ignored the little gibe.

Charles, ill-informed as he was, floundering in the quicksands of popular history, could not answer, yet the whole notion was offensive to him. "But why jump on a man unless he jumps first?"

Hans, the youthful oracle, was ready. "Why, because he always attacks when you are not looking, or when you have put down your arms for an instant. So you are punished for carelessness really, for not troubling to learn the intentions of your enemy. You are beaten, and that is the end of you, unless you can gather strength and fight again."

"The Celts aren't ended," said Tadeusz; "they exist in great numbers and are scattered all over and still have influence everywhere they touch."

"Influence?" asked Hans. "A purely oblique, feminine, worthless thing, influence. Power, pure power is what counts to a nation or a race. You must be able to tell other peoples what to do, and above all what they may not do, you must be able to enforce every order you give against no matter what opposition, and when you demand anything at all, it must be given you without question. That is the only power, and power is the only thing of any value or importance in this world."

"It doesn't last, though, any better than some other things," said Tadeusz. "It doesn't always work as well as long ruse and intelligent strategy. It goes down in the long run."

"Maybe it goes down because powerful people get tired of power," said Otto, leaning his head on his hand and looking discouraged; "maybe they wear themselves out beating other people and spying on them and ordering them about and robbing them. Maybe they exhaust themselves."

"And maybe one day they overstep themselves, or a new young power rises to put an end to them," said Tadeusz; "that happens."

"Maybe they find out it doesn't pay," said Charles.

"It always pays," said Hans; "that is the point. It pays, and nothing else does. Everything else is childish beside it. Otto, you surprise me. That is a strange point of view for you."

Otto sagged, guilty and uncomfortable. "I am not a soldier," he said. "I love study and quiet."

Hans sat very stiffly, an alienated hostile glitter in his eyes. He turned halfway to Charles and said, "We Germans were beaten in the last war, thanks partly to your great country, but we shall win in the next."

A chill ran down Charles' spine, he shrugged his shoulders. They were all a little drunk, there might be a row if they didn't pull themselves together. He did not want to quarrel with anybody, nor to fight the war over again. "We were all in short pants when that war was ended," he said. Hans answered instantly, "Ah, yes, but we will all be in uniforms for the next."

Tadeusz said, "Oh, come now, dear Hans, I never felt less bloodthirsty in my life. I only want to play the piano."

"I want to paint," said Charles.

"I want to teach mathematics," said Otto.

"Neither am I bloodthirsty," said Hans, "but I know what will happen." His cheek, under its band of court plaster, was slightly more swollen than earlier in the evening. The fingers of his left hand explored tenderly along the line of angry blue flesh. He said, in a bright impersonal tone, "Look, it is most interesting to remember one thing. We should have won that war, and we lost it in the first three days, though we did not know it, or could not believe it, for four years. What was the cause? One single delayed order, one sole failure of a body of troops to move at a given moment, on that first advance through Belgium. A delay of three days lost us that war. Well, it won't happen the next time."

"No," said Tadeusz, gently, "the next time, there will be another kind of mistake, something else quite different will go wrong, who knows how or why? It is always like that. Wars are not won by intelligence, Hans. Can't you see that? All the fine planning in the world can't insure an army against that one fellow who will, when the moment comes, delay, or give the wrong order, or be in the wrong place. Why, the other side did nothing but blunder all the way through, and yet they won, that time."

"Sea power," said Charles, "good old sea power. I bet on that. It wins in the long run."

"Carthage was a sea power, but she didn't beat Rome," said Otto.

"The next time," said Hans, with cool stubbornness, "they won't win. You'll see. The next time, there will be no mistakes on our side."

"I can wait," said Tadeusz, "I am in no hurry."

"I can wait, all right," said Charles, "and meantime, let me get the beer."

The orchestra, increased by the efforts of guests with their fiddles, flutes and the violoncello, had been making a fine din, so that the four voices had been rising gradually. "Let's give it up for the present," said Tadeusz; "it can't be settled this evening."

The actor and his mistress were gone, and Lutte remained the only beauty in the room. She was sitting with several young men and another girl at a table near by, all drinking beer heartily, laughing constantly and falling into each other's arms at intervals for embraces and smacks on the cheek, the boys kissing boys or girls alike with indiscriminate warmth. Lutte caught Charles' glance and waved her beer glass at him. He waved back and smiled excitedly. She was a knockout and he hoped quite violently to know her better. And even at that moment, like the first symptoms of some fatal sickness, there stirred in him a most awful premonition of disaster, and his thoughts, blurred with drink and strangeness and the sound of half-understood tongues and the climate of remembered wrongs and hatreds, revolved dimly around vague remembered tales of Napoleon and Genghis Khan and Attila the Hun and all the Caesars and Alexander the Great and Darius and the dim Pharaohs and lost Babylon. He felt helpless, undefended, looked at the three strange faces near him and decided not to drink any more, for he must not be drunker than they; he trusted none of them.

Otto, leaving his beer, wandered away, and one of the brothers handed him a white piano accordion as he passed. The change in Otto was miraculous. From soggy gloom his face turned to a great mask of simple enjoyment, he took up the tune the orchestra was playing and roamed among the tables, the instrument folding and unfolding in his arms, his blunt fingers flying over the keys. In a fine roaring voice he began to sing:

> *"Ich armes welsches Teufelein*
> *Ich kann nicht mehr marschieren—"*

"MARSCHIEREN!" roared every voice in the place, joyously. "Ich kann nicht mehr marschier'n."

Otto sang:

> *"Ich hab' verlor'n mein Pfeiflein*
> *Aus meinen Mantelsack—"*

" 'SACK!" yelled the chorus, "Aus meinen Mantelsack."

Hans stood up and sang in a clear light voice: "Ich hab', ich hab' gefunden, was du verloren hast—"

"HAST!" bawled the chorus, and everybody was standing now, their laughing faces innocent and pure as lambs at play, "was du verloren hast."

There was a great wave of laughter after this, and the orchestra suddenly changed to "The Peanut Vendor." Lutte, with a serious face as if she were fulfilling her duty, stood up and began to dance alone, something supposed no doubt to be a rumba, but to Charles, it seemed rather a combination of the black bottom and the hoochy-coochy such as he had seen, sneaking off furtively with other boys, in carnival sideshows during his innocent boyhood in Texas. He had danced the rumba to the tune of "The Peanut Vendor" all the way from his home town, across the Atlantic and straight into Bremen harbor, and it occurred to him that here was something he could really do. He took the gourds from the quiet little fellow who was clacking them rather feebly, and began to do his version of the rumba, shaking the gourds and cracking them together with great authority.

He could hear hands clapping in rhythm all over the room, and Lutte, abandoning her solo, began to dance with him. He handed back the gourds at once and took Lutte firmly around her warm, agitated waist, very thinly covered. She held her face back from him stiffly, smiled with a fair imitation of a cinematic *femme fatale*, and rather clumsily but with great meaning bumped her hip against him. He gathered her in, folded her up to him as close as he could, but she stiffened again and bumped him, this time full in the stomach. "What say we give up the technique and let nature take its course," said Charles, with a straight face.

"What is that?" she asked, unexpectedly in English. "I do not understand."

"Well," said Charles, kissing her on the cheek, "it speaks English too." She did not kiss back, but went limp and began to dance naturally.

"Am I as beautiful as that moving picture actress who was here this evening?" asked Lutte, wistfully.

"At least," said Charles.

"Would I do for the moving pictures in America, in your Hollywood?" she asked, leaning upon him.

"Don't bump," said Charles. "Yes, you would do fine in Hollywood."

"Do I dance well enough?" asked Lutte.

"Yes, darling, you do. You are a whizz."

"What is that?"

"Something wonderful," said Charles. "Come to me, angel."

"Do you know anybody in Hollywood?" asked Lutte, sticking firmly to her one interest.

"No, but you might," said Charles; "all Germany and Central Europe are there already; you'd be bound to run into friends. Anyway you won't be lonesome long."

Lutte put her mouth like a ripe peach to his ear and blowing warmly upon it whispered, "Take me to America with you."

"Let's go," said Charles, and seizing her more firmly he ran a few steps towards the door. She held back. "No, I am serious, I want to go to America."

"So do I," said Charles, recklessly, "so does everybody."

"That is not true," said Lutte, severely, almost stopping in her tracks. At this moment Hans cut in. Charles sat down feeling cheated. Lutte's manner changed completely. She melted towards Hans, they danced slowly and as they danced, she kissed him softly and continually and gently on his right cheek, her mouth meek and sweet, her eyes nearly closed. Over Hans' disfigured face came that same look of full-fed pride, of composed self-approval—of arrogance, that was the word. Charles felt a flicker of sharp hatred for Hans. Then it passed. "Hell," he said, aloud, yet to no one, "what of it?"

"I think so too," said Tadeusz, "I think, hell, what of it?"

"Let's have some brandy," said Charles. Otto was sitting quietly, he roused and smiled.

"What a fine evening!" he said. "We are all friends, are we not?"

"Completely," said Tadeusz, "we are all friends to you, Otto." He had grown quieter and softer in his gestures, his eyes peered vaguely between his wrinkled lids, his little tight smile was constant. "I am getting damnation drunk, and my conscience will begin hurting soon," he said, contentedly. Then the others, listening dimly, heard him telling some story about his childhood in Cracow " . in the old house where my family have lived since the twelfth century . . ." he said. "At Easter we ate only pork in contempt of the Jews, and after the long fasting of Lent naturally

we gorged ourselves shamelessly. . . . On Easter morning after
High Mass I would eat until I was perfectly round, and in pain.
Then I would lie down and cry, and when they asked me what
troubled me, I would say, out of shame, that my conscience was
hurting me. They would be very respectful and comfort me, but
sometimes I thought I saw a gleam in an eye, or just a flash of a
look on a face—not my mother's, but my sister's, perhaps—she
was a horrid, knowing little thing—and my nurse's. One day my
nurse gave me some soothing syrup and rubbed my stomach with
that insulting false sympathy and said, 'There now, your conscience feels better, doesn't it?' I went howling and told my mother
that my nurse had kicked me in the stomach. Then I upchucked
all my Easter pork, so the Jews had their revenge for once. My
nurse said, 'What a little monster it is'; then she and my mother
talked in the next room, and when they came back smiling I knew
the game was up. I never mentioned my conscience again to them.
But once after I was grown up, or nearly, I was very drunk and
came home at four in the morning, and I crawled upstairs because
it seemed unreasonable, this business of people walking about on
their hind legs all the time. The red stair carpet gave me a sense of
great security and ease, and I remember feeling that I was a kind
of prophet of good for mankind, restoring an old way of locomo-
tion which would probably revolutionize all society once I had
proved its pleasures and possibilities. The first obstacle I encoun-
tered was my mother. She stood at the head of the stairs holding a
lighted candle, waiting without a word. I waved one paw at her but
she did not respond. And when I put my head above the last step
she kicked me under the chin and almost knocked me out. She
never mentioned this incident and I could hardly believe it myself
except for my sore tongue the next day. Well, such was my up-
bringing in that old city, but I remember it dearly now, something
between a cemetery and a Lost Paradise, with an immense sound
of bells. . . ."

Otto said, "Maybe we should have some beer," and with a sad
mouth he talked a little about his own childhood. His mother had
beaten him quite hard one day, without warning, when he was
cracking walnuts and eating them. With tears he had asked her
why, and she said, "Don't ask me any questions. What is good
enough for Martin Luther is good enough for you." And later in a

child's book he had read how Luther's mother had beaten him until the blood came because he annoyed her with the sound of cracking nuts. "Until then I had thought of Luther as a great, forbidding cruel man who loved bloodshed, but after that I felt sorry for him. He was once a poor helpless child like me, beaten for nothing," Otto said, "and yet he became great." His face was full of humble apology. "That was child's nonsense, but it helped me to live," he said.

The drifting smoke and the lights and the voices and the music were all mingled and swimming together around their heads. The big young woman who had been helping at the bar came then, her knot of hair slipping still further down her neck, and seemed to be pulling chairs and tables towards the wall. Her fine haunches jiggled under her tight skirt, her great breasts were stretching and falling as she raised and lowered her arms, her heavy legs were braced far apart as she pushed at a table. The men sitting about watched her without moving or offering help. Charles observed another change in Otto. He was watching the girl intently, his mouth moistening. He seemed lost in a pleasant daze, his nose twitched, his eyes grew round and took on the calculating ferocity of a tomcat's. The girl leaned over and the hollows of her knees showed; she straightened up and the muscles of her back and shoulders writhed. Slowly, feeling Otto's gaze upon her, she began to blush. Her neck turned red, her cheeks, her forehead, the whole face stiffened and darkened as if she were resisting pain, or a surge of anger. But the corners of her soft formless mouth were smiling, and she did not raise her eyes again after her first quick glance. Quite suddenly she gave a last plunge at a chair, set it in place with a thump, and ran away, her body full of awkward, contradictory motions. Otto turned to Charles, and showered upon him the remains of his impassioned gaze at the girl.

"There is a fine armful for you," he said; "I like big strong girls." Charles nodded as if he agreed, and looked again at Lutte, still dancing with Hans and kissing him.

A wooden cuckoo about the size of a humming bird leaped from his little door above the clockface and began his warning note. Instantly everybody rose and each one embraced the person nearest him, shouting, "Happy New Year, health, good luck, happy New Year, God bless you." Glasses and steins danced aloft in half circles, spilling foam on uplifted faces. A disordered circle formed, arms interlocked, and a ragged singing began which smoothed out almost at once into a deep chorus, the fine voices swinging along together in frolicsome tunes Charles did not know. He swayed with the circle, woven into it, he opened his mouth and sang tunelessly without words. Real joy, warm and careless, swept him away; this was a place to be, these were wonderful people, he liked absolutely everybody there. The circle broke up, ran together, whirled, loosened, fell apart.

Hans came over smiling on one side of his face, Lutte beside him. They put their arms around Charles together and wished him a happy New Year. He stood there swaying with an arm around each, all jealousy gone. Lutte kissed him sweetly on the mouth, and he kissed back but like a child. Then they all saw Tadeusz leaning over Otto, who was sprawled at the little table, head pillowed on his arms.

"He's gone completely, he has deserted us," said Tadeusz. "Now we must drag him about with us wherever we go for the rest of the evening."

"We aren't going anywhere else, are we," asked Charles, "for God's sake?"

Otto was indeed gone, altogether. They got him up by the arms, and in a busy sort of scramble they found themselves on the sidewalk, with a tall policeman watching mildly, getting into a taxicab, where their feet were tangled hopelessly and they all seemed to hang at once dangerously far out of the windows. Lutte was saying, to all of them alike, "Good night, happy New Year," her face shining but sober looking.

On the staircase, Otto collapsed once for all. The three pulled him along slowly, pausing at every step. At moments the whole structure tottered, they would stagger and lose hold of each other and step on Otto, who groaned and howled, but without resentment. They would heave themselves together more firmly and start again, making wild sounds of laughter, nodding at each other as if agreed on some inexplicable but gloriously comic truth. "Let's crawl," shouted Charles to Tadeusz; "maybe it will work this time." Hans disapproved of this instantly.

"No crawling," he said, taking command at once. "Every man goes up on his own feet, except perhaps Otto." They assembled themselves once more for a last effort, and arrived at the door known to be theirs.

Rosa's door was ajar slightly, a streak of light shining into the hall. They regarded it with sobering gloom, expecting the door to fly open and Rosa to rush forth scolding. Nothing happened. They changed their tactics, and dragging Otto, they rushed her door, beating on it in tattoo and shouting recklessly, "Happy New Year, Roslein, Roslein, happy New Year."

There was a small flurry inside, the door opened a few inches more, and Rosa put out a sleek, orderly head. Her eyes were a little pink and sleepy looking, but she was smiling a gay, foxy smile. Her pensioners were most lordly drunk, she saw at a glance, none the worse for it, thank God. Hans' cheek was discolored somewhat more, but he was laughing, Charles and Tadeusz were quieter, trying to appear sober and responsible, but their eyelids drooped, they leered drolly. The three were supporting Herr Bussen between them, and Herr Bussen, hanging at random, his knees bent, had a blissful innocent confidence in his sleeping face.

"Happy New Year, you owls," said Rosa, proud of her household who knew how to celebrate an occasion. "I had champagne too, with friends, and New Year's punch. I am a little merry too," she told them, boasting. "Go to sleep now, look, this is the New Year. You must start it well tomorrow. Good night."

Charles sat on the feather bed and wriggled out of his clothes, pushing them off any old way and leaving them where they fell. As he fumbled with his pajamas, his eyes swam about in his head, seeing first one thing and then another, but none of it familiar, nothing that was his. He did notice at last that the Leaning Tower seemed to be back, sitting now safely behind the glass of the corner cabinet. By a roundabout way he brought himself across the room to the Tower. It was there, all right, and it was mended pretty obviously, it would never be the same. But for Rosa, poor old woman, he supposed it was better than nothing. It stood for something she had, or thought she had, once. Even all patched up as it was, and worthless to begin with, it meant something to her, and he was still ashamed of having broken it; it made him feel like a heel. It stood there in its bold little frailness, as if daring him to come on; how well he knew that a thumb and forefinger would smash the thin ribs, the mended spots would fall at a breath. Leaning, suspended, perpetually ready to fall but never falling quite, the venturesome little object—a mistake in the first place, a whimsical pain in the neck, really, towers shouldn't lean in the first place; a curiosity, like those cupids falling off the roof—yet had some kind of meaning in Charles' mind. Well, what? He tousled his hair and rubbed his eyes and then his whole head and yawned himself almost inside out. What had the silly little thing reminded him of before? There was an answer if he could think what it was, but this was not the time. But just the same, there was something terribly urgent at work, in him or around him, he could not tell which. There was something perishable but threatening, uneasy, hanging over his head or stirring angrily, dangerously, at his back. If he couldn't find out now what it was that troubled him so in this place, maybe he would never know. He stood there feeling his drunkenness as a pain and a weight on him, unable to think clearly but feeling what he had never known before, an infernal desolation of the spirit, the chill and the knowledge of death in him. He wrapped his arms across his chest and expelled his breath, and a cold sweat broke out all over him. He went towards the bed and fell upon it and rolled himself into a knot, being rather unpleasant with himself. "All you need is a crying jag to make it complete," he said. But he didn't feel sorry for himself, and no crying jag or any other kind of jag would ever, in this world, do anything at all for him.

Berlin 1931